A Tale of a Future Once Imagined

The

SOLAR
PATROL

J.G. Miller

For Jean, Devon, and Derek. Family forever.

There's no time like the present.

— common saying

Prelude
1902 - Hell Creek, Montana

The man rested on his haunches staring at the smoothly curved surface that protruded from the dirt. Until but a few moments earlier, it had been covered by the debris of deep time, debris that had supposedly gone undisturbed for tens of millions of years. It simply lay there, its surface blanketed by a thin veil of the ever-present Montana dust, unmoving, uncaring, unfeeling, silent, and totally at odds with the man's perception of the world. A few inches from the object, next to a partially exposed petrified vertebrae of a dinosaur, lay the man's pickaxe. The pick's steel tip was missing, broken off by the nerve shattering blow the man had struck that first revealed the thing's existence. The shock of the strike had sent a spasm of pain up the man's forearm, the remnants of which were still subsiding.

He had paused in clearing the debris from the buried object in an attempt to better organize his thoughts. The sound of his heavy breathing mixed with the hollow silence of the nearly nonexistent breeze. He realized that his mouth was now as dry as the dust in which he knelt. Driblets of sweat fell from his face, either splashing on the exposed rock or making miniature craters in the dust. And still the object refused to disappear, refused to surrender to reality, but instead insisted on holding the man as transfixed as the gaze of Medusa.

He felt his eyelids close from an involuntary blink and his eyes burned. That was enough to break the trance. With a jerk, he struggled to his feet, grabbing his canteen as he stood up. He twisted open the cap of the container and poured some of its contents down his throat, quenching his parched vocal tubes. He poured more of the welcome fluid into his cupped hand in order to splash it onto his face and eyes. The man resealed the canteen as he slowly turned, taking in the seemingly limitless desolation that surrounded him. The only sign of life was an occasional ugly green, low sprawl of dry vegetation that hardly deserved the designation. The Hell Creek Formation. A fitting name indeed, at least the "hell" part. In all directions stretched an endless monotony of dry, sunbaked umber and dull brown, broken only by twisted ravines and distant, strata striped cliffs. Nowhere to be seen was any evidence of water, let alone a creek. The only reason anyone came here was entombed in the rock that lay beneath his feet. Its age was Upper Cretaceous, that is, that time in the past near the end of the Age of Dinosaurs. And that was why he and his companions now frequented this middle of nowhere. They were dinosaur hunters. But the thing that had broken his pickaxe was neither fossil nor rock. It was utterly alien to the landscape, both in time and place.

The man's gaze locked on a similarly attired individual, a good thirty yards away, on his hands and knees, using a sharp awl to scratch at the dry crust.

The man called to his companion. "Barnum, you need to see this."

The expedition leader raised his head as if in acknowledgement, then got to his feet and hurried over. The newcomer's eyes followed the pointed finger of the first man. Kneeling on the barren slope to get a better look at the still partially buried object, Barnum sounded less than amused. "What is this? A joke?"

"No, sir. I found it when I just now hit it with my pick. Look what it did to the point."

The expedition leader briefly inspected the damaged tool, then gave his head a shake. "Okay, let's find out what we have here."

The two men began using ice picks and whisk brooms to remove the gravelly soil that blanketed the unexpected find while taking great care to avoid damaging the neighboring fossil bone. Before long, enough of the artifact was exposed to allow it to be lifted from its resting place. The expedition leader reached down and grasped the spherical relic with his hands. He hefted it, letting out a grunt as he did so.

"It's heavy—really heavy." With some effort, he managed to carefully place it on the ground.

"What do you think it is?" asked his companion.

In answer, Barnum merely gave a shrug.

Except for a dark-blue, slightly raised stripe about an inch in width that encircled it, the mystery object was a perfect metallic sphere, roughly ten inches in diameter. The expedition leader produced a large rag and used it to remove the dirt and dust that still clung to the artifact. The bright chrome-like finish of the cleaned surface gleamed in the sunlight that filled the clear Montana sky.

"What's this?" said the man who had first discovered the mysterious object. "It looks like some sort of writing."

Etched on the surface on both sides of the encircling blue stripe were a series of strange looking glyphs.

"It's no writing that I'm familiar with," said the expedition leader. "Have you ever seen anything like it?" The other man gave his head a shake.

For the next few moments, the two figures merely stared at their discovery in silence. Finally, Barnum leaned forward and began to carefully wrap the artifact in the cloth he had used to clean it. "For now, we don't tell the others about this. Okay?"

"But why?"

"Because this—whatever it is—shouldn't be here. It's like we've unwrapped an ancient Egyptian mummy and found a modern pocket watch. Until we understand more about what this thing is, I think it best we keep its existence a secret."

Part I
1995 – East Pencreek, Pennsylvania

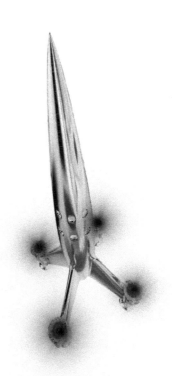

Chapter 1
The Homecoming

Diane Jones let out a contented sigh as she settled herself on the lawn chair. "Couldn't ask for a finer day," she thought, scrunching her body further into the embrace of the chair, at the same time reaching to one side to adjust the dial of a radio that rested on the small table beside her. The sound of music soon mingled with the low roar of a neighbor's lawn mower and the ringing of a distant church bell signaling nine o'clock. She continued to fidget with the radio's dial until it locked onto the local "oldies" station. "That's the ticket," Diane thought.

Satisfied with the selection, she closed her eyes and allowed her body to ooze back into the recliner as the sound of the mower faded in the distance, abandoning Diane to her thoughts.

"What a jerk to be mowing his lawn at this hour, wasting such a wonderful Sunday morning on yard work," she muttered to herself before half opening her eyes to take in the deep blue of a gorgeous cloudless sky. She then let her eyelids close again. Indeed, it was a perfect day, with only a week to go before the end of the school year.

As Diane began to mentally plan her summer vacation, her thoughts were interrupted by a low rumbling sound like that of distant thunder. The rumbling was followed by the sound of falling timber, a gust of wind, and then, except for the hum of the radio, an unnerving silence. The middle age woman jerked to a sitting position and glanced about. As there was not a cloud in the sky, she reasoned that thunder was not an explanation.

The breeze died as quickly as it had started.

Diane flicked the switch on the radio to "off." Not even the chirping of a bird broke the calm. The hairs on the back of her neck began to rise and her body gave an involuntary shudder when, as if on cue, the birds in the nearby woods resumed their songs.

Her mind searched for an explanation. Perhaps someone had fired a gun, or a car had backfired. But what about the sudden breeze? Was it a coincidence or had she just imagined it? She turned in her chair to study the woodland that bordered the far side of the street that ran in front of her home. Maybe a tree had fallen there?

The street marked the boundary between a residential neighborhood of single family homes and a forested area several acres in size, known locally as Sullivans Woods. Diane recalled hearing stories when growing up that the woods were haunted, an idea that had taken on additional credibility thirty-six years earlier when Diane was in the eighth grade. On the night of Halloween that year, three of her fellow classmates had disappeared. One story had it that the three teens had last been seen entering Sullivans Woods. The police had suspected foul play, and had issued a bulletin in an attempt to locate the kids' science teacher for questioning when he failed to show up at school the following Monday. The mystery had never been solved, nor had any credible sightings of any of the vanished people, including the missing science teacher, ever surfaced.

Diane forced a smile. "What crazy things to be reminiscing about on such a perfect day."

With a quick twist of her wrist, she turned the radio back on, sunk back into the recliner, and let the warm sunshine in combination with the music massage her thoughts.

She had grown up in East Pencreek. After attending an out-of-state college, she had returned to her hometown to marry a local boy and raise a family. To longtime residents like Diane, East Pencreek in many ways seemed frozen in time. She was a child of the fifties, which she remembered as a glorious, carefree era. Compared to the world of 1995, the 1950s were like some surreal alternate universe that now existed only as memories.

She closed her eyes and let herself drift back to that era of black and white TV with Saturday morning shows that focused on an audience of kids, shows like "Howdy Doody," "Sky King," "Roy Rogers," "Captain Midnight," and "Tom Corbett Space Cadet." It was a time when a bottle of soda cost a nickel and if you returned the empty bottle to the grocery store you received two cents—so much for the idea of recycling being something new. Back then music came on 45 RPM vinyl records that were played on "hi-fi" phonographs, and stereo sound was the latest thing. In the fifties there were telephone party lines, jukeboxes by the soda fountain in the local drug store, family doctors who made house calls, and drive-in movie theaters where, dressed in your pajamas and outfitted with your favorite pillow, blanket, and stuffed animal, you would sit in the back seat of the family car with your twit of a brother and fall asleep sometime during the second feature. And there was Elvis and Frankie and Fabian and that afternoon dance show on TV with Dick Clark who's still around and looks like he's never aged in four decades. And all those neat treats like candy cigarettes and bubble gum and those waxy soda-pop shaped bottles with the colored sugar water and Fizzies, colored tablets you dropped into a glass of water. They bubbled and fizzed, hence the name, and were supposed to make the water taste like a fruit drink but instead it tasted more like some foul, flavored medicine. And no one ever locked their doors, and even young kids would ride their bikes to a friend's house across town and no one ever worried about someone trying to do them harm. One dollar would pay for round trip bus fare to downtown, a movie ticket, popcorn, candy bar, and maybe even a comic book and you would still have change left over. Poodle skirts and teased hair and . . . It was all so long ago . . .

Diane awoke upon the realization that the radio was playing her favorite ballad, a song whose lyrics told of time's slow passing and long-ago love. Her still closed eyes began to moisten. She gave a swallow and wiped away the tears that had seeped from beneath her closed eyelids, and then as she opened—

"AHHHH!"

The sight of the young man standing next to her so startled Diane that she almost tipped over the lawn chair. Diane's sudden action in turn caused the stranger to drop the section of the Sunday newspaper he had picked up from where it had rested next to the radio.

Quickly recovering her balance, Diane barked, "Who are you?"

The stranger managed a soft smile. "Excuse me. I didn't mean to startle you."

"Well, you did," said Diane, sounding most upset.

The uninvited man appeared to be in his twenties, his handsome features accentuated by neatly combed dark hair and a clean-shaven face. Very handsome features, thought Diane, as her initial anger gave way to curiosity. And then she noticed his eyes—deep, serious, blue-grey eyes.

The young man's lips widened further into an even friendlier smile, a smile guaranteed to melt the heart of any teenage girl, or forty-nine-year-old wife and mother for that matter.

"I mean no harm. I just wanted to have a quick look at your newspaper. My apologies."

"And just what was so important that you had to come into my yard to see the paper?"

"I wanted to check the date."

"The date?"

"Yes," he said. "The year—" He broke off in midsentence. "The date—say, that's a really cool song on the . . . radio."

Something is not right here, thought Diane. A complete stranger wanders into my yard to read the date from my newspaper! He's walking around on a Sunday morning with a—backpack. Although she thought about calling for her husband who was no doubt somewhere inside the house, for a reason she couldn't explain she buried that idea and instead proceeded to continue the conversation. Perhaps it was the young man's friendly manner, not to mention—God, he was so good looking. Diane gave the stranger a dumb smile as the song on the radio ended. "Do you like the Righteous Brothers?"

"Who?"

"The Righteous Brothers," she repeated. "They did the last song."

The man's gaze passed from the woman to the radio and then back again. "Sorry, I never heard of them, but the tune did sound vaguely familiar. It was really cool."

"Cool? You think their song was cool?" Her smile broadened into one of amusement.

"Yes, cool." Another pause. "They're real space aces when it comes to music."

Diane started to laugh, but quickly stifled it. "So, you like the song, but you're telling me that you've never heard of the Righteous Brothers?"

"Yes."

"Well, you are pretty young. How about the Beatles?"

"Nope." He again flashed her that fine grin, at the same time shaking his head to further emphasize his answer.

"Michael Jackson?"

"Another singer?"

Diane let out a sigh of frustration. She was now the one shaking her head. "I give up. Do you know any pop artists?"

"Artists? I thought we were talking about singers?"

Diane leaned back on the lawn chair and let out a small laugh. "You're not from around here, are you?"

The man mimicked her laugh. "Actually, I was born right here in East Pencreek." He nodded his head in the direction of the neighboring woodland. "That's Sullivans Woods, right?"

"Yes, that's right."

"It doesn't appear to have changed much over the years."

"Those woods no doubt will always be there," said Diane. "I mean no one can build on it since it was declared a wetland."

"A what?" The stranger looked puzzled. "What's a wetland?"

"What do you mean, 'What's a wetland?' You know, a wetland—a swamp."

"Oh," was the stranger's only response, but he still seemed puzzled. He turned to look east, along the street that bordered the woods. "That the new high school?" he said, motioning towards a large building standing on a property at the start of the next block.

New high school! The question startled Diane since the school had been completed in 1965, thirty years earlier, no doubt before this young man was even born. What was going on here? The weirdness of it all made Diane press on in an effort to resolve the mystery.

"Yes, that's East Pencreek High. I teach there. Home of the Fighting Bobcats." She let out a giggle. "Did you know that when it was built, the school board decided to let the student body decide on the new mascot for the school? The name the students voted for was the Fighting Camels. Of course, that was overruled by those jerks on the school board, so instead we're the Fighting Bobcats."

That got a chuckle from the stranger. Then he glanced at the radio. "Now there's one I know. That's Elvis"

"You know Elvis, but you never heard of the Beatles?" She gave her head a shake as she studied the look of pride on the young man's face, obviously the result of having finally recognized a tune. Turning in her seat, she opened the cooler next to her chair and grabbed a can from inside.

"Would you like a beer?"

"No, thank you. I don't drink."

"Really. Somehow, I'm not surprised. You're not underage, are you?"

Her question was met with such an outburst of laughter that it almost sounded derisive. "Oh, no. Certainly not. Unless they've raised the legal drinking age since I left."

"And you are . . . ?"

"Tom," he said, a mild hesitation in his voice.

"I'm Diane."

The young man's eyes widened with a sudden recognition. "Diane Ferguson?"

Diane dropped the can of beer she was holding. "How do you know my—my maiden name?"

"If memory serves me, you grew up in this house. It was your parents' home."

"Yes, but how—?"

The stranger hesitated a moment, then ignored the question. "The Cobalts still live on Oak Lane, right?"

"Nancy and Sam?"

"Yes. They still live on Oak Lane, don't they?"

Diane noticed that as he finished asking the question, the stranger had swallowed. He stood awaiting her response with an anxious look on his face. "Yes, they do. Well, that is Nancy does. Sam just passed away. The funeral was only Friday, a week ago." The young man gave a quiet nod as if privately confirming a suspicion. "Do you know Nancy?" asked Diane, probing for more information.

"Yes. We're related, but—but, it's been some time since I've seen—," he hesitated as if searching for the right word, but simply ended the sentence with, "—her."

As she watched his reaction to the news that Nancy Cobalt still lived in town, Diane was engulfed by a feeling of melancholy, as she recalled for the second time that morning the events of so many years ago. She thought she saw the stranger's eyes begin to moisten. Diane reached for the dropped can of beer. "It was really tragic what happened to the Cobalts. Let's see it was—1959. I guess you know that their son, Tom, disappeared. They never did find out what became of him. But, of course, that was many years before you were born."

In the brief moment she had looked away to retrieve the beer, the stranger seemed to have regained his composure. The seductive smile had reappeared, but he said nothing.

"Do you know their daughter, Caroline? She and her family just left town yesterday to return home after the funeral."

"Yes. I knew Katty."

"What?" asked Diane.

"I said I know Katty."

Diane was now feeling most uncomfortable. She had known Caroline since childhood, and the only person she ever recalled who referred to Caroline as Katty was Caroline's older brother, Tom, the one who had vanished. "Of course, she lives in Virginia now," said Diane. The man didn't respond, but seemed to be looking right through Diane, as if his thoughts were in another universe. Diane was starting to feel awkward as well as uncomfortable. "What relation are you to the Cobalts?"

"Close," said the young man, still looking beyond Diane. He turned his gaze to the lawn for a moment, and then hefting his small backpack, gave Diane another grin. "Thanks for taking the time to talk. I have to be going." He turned and started walking towards the street.

"Wait," she called after him. "You never told me how you knew my name? I can't recall ever having met you."

He paused briefly. "We met a long time ago." The man gave a chuckle and smiled, as if in response to some joke that only he understood. "The Righteous Brothers, right?"

"Right," answered Diane, sounding dazed.

"Great song. I'll have to remember it."

Diane watched the young man until he was out of sight, then sprang from her lounge chair and hurried into the house. With frantic haste, she searched through the contents of a bookcase until she spied her eighth grade memory book. Pulling it off the shelf, she flipped through the pages. There, among the photos of the eighth grade class members was one of a boy whose caption read, "Thomas Cobalt." Diane studied the old photograph. She recalled how odd it had been that because the class pictures had been taken before the disappearance, his photo was still included in the yearbook—as if there had still been hope that he would turn up. In comparing the face in the photo to that of the young man, she concluded that there might indeed be a fuzzy vagueness of a resemblance. Perhaps the stranger was Tom's son? No, that made no sense. If Tom had run away from home and raised a family, and the stranger was his son, how come the young man had claimed he had once lived in East Pencreek? Besides two other classmates and a teacher had disappeared along with Tom. What had become of them?

Not only had the young man said he knew the Cobalts, but he had stated that they were related. And the way he had referred to Caroline as Katty? The man was only old enough to have known Caroline as a grown woman. Katty was a kid's nickname. And how did he know her name, and her maiden name at that? And why had he said that they had met a long time ago? Diane wrinkled her brow as she attempted to make sense of it all.

She first considered calling Caroline, then Caroline's cousin Jerry since he still lived in town. Perhaps he would be able to explain who the young man was.

Diane's thoughts were interrupted by the sound of footsteps coming up behind her. Her husband began to tenderly nibble her neck as he looked over her shoulder.

"Reminiscing about old times?" he asked.

Diane closed the book and replaced it on the shelf. "Yes. Sort of.

Actually, I think I might have just experienced an episode from the 'Twilight Zone.'"

"I don't follow."

"You remember Tom Cobalt, don't you?"

"Sure," said her husband. "He and Alex Banyon were two of my best friends, that is, until they both disappeared that one night. What about him?"

Diane hesitated, pondering whether she should say anything to her husband about the stranger. But since Brad was the local sheriff, he might jump to the wrong conclusions and . . .

"Oh, nothing. I was just thinking about what happened back in 1959, that's all." She turned and gave her husband a smile. "Well, it's back to my sunbathing. Have to practice up for summer, you know."

As Diane walked towards the front door, her husband gave her a curious look. Then his head began to throb.

It was an attractive but small home the young man stopped in front of. The yard rose about a foot above the sidewalk, the rise traversed by a pair of cement steps that fronted a walkway, which in turn led to the stairs of the front porch. The house had obviously been remodeled over the years, but it still had the original roofed front porch. On the mailbox was the name "Cobalt." The man swallowed. What should he do now? Just go up and ring the doorbell? Suppose she wasn't home, or suppose she had company? A car was parked on the side street, next to the property. Perhaps that was evidence that someone was home. Before he could reach a decision, the front door of the house opened and an elderly but still handsome woman stepped out onto the porch, accompanied by a large tabby cat. Her hair was white and she looked as if she had put on some pounds over the years, but the man had no doubt of the woman's identity.

She took a seat on a porch chair with the cat lying down next to her where it could bask in an oval of sunlight that flooded the porch deck. She was well dressed as if she was ready to attend Sunday morning church services. The woman had no sooner made herself comfortable when from beside her there came a low meow. The orange ball of fur that had been lying on the porch deck leaped to its feet, bolted down the front steps, and raced along the yard's walkway.

Recovering from her surprise, the woman called after the cat. "Tiger!"

With a single bound the cat cleared the pair of steps at the end of the walkway and landed at the foot of the stranger. The feline quickly assumed a sitting position and started meowing loudly. The man studied the verbose animal for a moment before kneeling and gently stroking the cat's head. Just as Nancy decided she should get up and retrieve her troublesome pet, the stranger raised his head and looked at her. Although a good distance separated her from the young man, she was struck by the haunting familiarity of his features. The young man straightened and started moving briskly up the front walk towards the porch, the cat strutting beside him. As Nancy peered at the approaching stranger through her bifocals, her heart skipped a beat. With an audible gasp of alarm, she stood up and started to back towards the front door. The man stepped onto the porch deck and stopped within arms' reach, towering above her.

"Mom," he said, his voice showing a noticeable tremble. He spread his hands, palms facing out, as if attempting to ease her fears. "Mom, it's me. Tom."

The woman let out a shriek, her hands flying to the sides of her face. She emphatically shook her head, her eyes revealing a mixture of terror and grief. "No!"

"I'm your son, Mom. I'm Tom."

"You can't be," she wailed, the dread now replaced with tears. "He's dead. He died long ago. You're too young. You're too late . . ."

"I'm here. I've come back. I know Dad is gone."

At the mention of her recently deceased husband, Nancy Cobalt's

13

defenses collapsed. Her face softened, and she looked at the young man with a painful longing. She started to speak but had to stop and swallow. Finally, she managed to ask, "Tommy, my little boy?"

He stepped closer, his arms still held wide. "Mom, please forgive me. I'm sorry . . ."

The woman cut off his words by folding her arms around him as best she could, resting her cheek on his chest, and gasping between sobs, "Tommy, my wonderful Tommy." All the doubts, all the yearnings, all the anguish were vanquished, replaced by a now distant bond of love that had once existed between a mother and son. The woman raised her head. After thirty-six years Nancy Cobalt looked into the eyes of a man who could not possibly be her son. Ignoring all reason, she knew in her heart that Tommy had finally come home.

Chapter 2
Reunion

Jerry Haydn was sitting between his wife and youngest son in their usual pew, third row left. As the organist began to play, signaling the start of the service, Jerry turned in his seat and scanned the rear of the sanctuary. Aunt Nan still hadn't arrived. Anne, his wife, leaned closer to him. "Tell me again what Aunt Nan said when she called this morning?"

Jerry whispered back. "She said not to pick her up, that she might not make it to the service, but would certainly meet us at the house afterwards. That someone she hadn't seen in years had stopped by, and she would bring him with her."

"And she wouldn't tell you who this old friend was?"

"No, and frankly she didn't sound normal. I mean . . . I don't know. She sounded really nervous. Kind of disturbed, maybe even excited."

"I'm worried about her," said Anne. "Maybe you should use the church office phone and give her a call?"

Before Jerry could answer, the organist started playing the opening hymn, and the minister motioned for the congregation to stand. As Jerry rose, he cast another quick glance towards the rear of the sanctuary. Still no Aunt Nan. He looked to his right and noticed that his mother-in-law, sitting next to his youngest son, Brett, was also scanning the back of the sanctuary. As Rebecca Gould turned back she caught Jerry's eye and gave him a questioning look. Jerry could only give his mother-in-law a shrug as if to say "I don't know what's keeping her?"

By the end of the service, Aunt Nan still hadn't made an appearance. Both his wife and mother-in-law were looking worried, and Jerry had to admit that he shared their concern.

While exchanging the customary handshake with Jerry at the church exit, the minister asked, "Where's your aunt today? Not ill I hope?"

"No," said Jerry. "She had some unexpected company this morning. I'm sure she'll be here next Sunday."

"That's good to hear," said the minister. "It's taking some getting used to not seeing your uncle sitting there with you, and then missing your aunt this morning . . . Well, give Nancy my best."

"Thank you, pastor. I certainly will, and a fine sermon as usual."

The reverend smiled in acknowledgment of the compliment, and then turned to greet an elderly man waiting next in line.

Jerry descended the front steps of the church to the sidewalk where his wife, mother-in-aw and youngest son awaited him. He glanced quickly about. "No, Aunt Nan, huh?"

"No," said Anne, giving her head a shake for added emphasis.

"Where's Aunt Nan?" came a voice behind Jerry. He turned to see his eldest son Kevin. "I thought she was going to join us here when we didn't pick her up."

"Don't know," answered Jerry.

Anne's mother said, "So who was this visitor she had this morning?"

"I don't know," Jerry shrugged. "All she would say was that it was someone she hadn't seen in years. I got the impression that it was some sort of long lost relative, but it beats me who it might be."

"Maybe someone from your uncle's side of the family," suggested Rebecca.

"Should we swing by her place on the way home?" said Anne.

"No," answered Jerry. "She said if she didn't make it to church, she'd meet us at home, so we'll go straight there."

When they turned the final corner onto their street, Kevin shouted, "There's her car."

"And there she is," added Anne. She had spotted the elderly woman waiting on their front porch along with a young man.

As Jerry parked the car in front of the house, he studied the two figures. His aunt had a book cradled in her arms. At her feet squatted her pet cat, Tiger, a big tawny brindled feline whom Aunt Nan and Uncle Sam had adopted when he showed up on their doorstep one morning several years ago. Beside her stood a man with a backpack slung over one shoulder.

"Who in the heck is that?" said Jerry, not to anyone in particular.

"Looks like a basketball player or something," suggested Brett. "Wonder what he's got in the backpack?"

"Duh, maybe a basketball, soup for brains," Brett's brother replied.

Mrs. Haydn gave her older son a scornful look. "Kevin, I don't want to have to tell you again about speaking to your brother that way."

"Sorry, Mom," answered Kevin. Then, as if switching on a recording, "It—won't—happen—again."

Nancy Cobalt gave the people in the van a wave. From where he sat, Jerry could see that her expression was apprehensive. Her young companion simply stood there, looking relaxed, greeting the Haydns and Anne's mother with a disarming smile. Jerry realized that they were all sitting there, staring at his aunt and the stranger. No one was moving. His mother-in-law apparently realized it too. She opened her door and began to exit the car, saying, "Well, let's find out who this mysterious young man is." That seemed to break the ice, and the four Haydns quickly followed Rebecca Gould out of the van.

Jerry led the group up the front walk but had to detour around a large tree trunk lying across the yard. The trunk blocked a section of the walkway and a good part of the rest of the lawn. It had come down during a thunderstorm, two weeks earlier, and although the limbs and branches had been disposed of, Jerry still hadn't gotten around to getting the trunk removed.

"When are we going to get rid of this thing?" asked Kevin, obviously less concerned about the identity of the stranger on the porch than the adults were.

His son's question diverted Jerry's attention momentarily from attempting to solve the riddle of the mystery man. "Maybe I'll cut it up next weekend."

"We have a Scouts overnighter next weekend. Remember Dad?"

"Oh, yeah. That's right."

"Come on, Dad. It will probably only cost you a couple hundred to get someone to cut it up and haul it away. Why not pay it and get it over with? At least that's what Mom keeps saying."

Further discussion of the fallen tree was ended by their arrival at the porch. Jerry stepped forward and gave his aunt his usual firm hug, one she returned along with a customary kiss on his cheek. Without wasting any time, Jerry said, "And who might this be?"

"Jerry, this is Tommy," said his aunt. Jerry couldn't help notice that Aunt Nan's voice quivered when she said "Tommy." He couldn't explain it, but a bad feeling seemed to come over him.

The young man stepped forward, took Jerry's offered hand in a firm grip and shook it vigorously. "Jer," the young man said, his voice cheerful. "Long time, no see."

"Huh?" was the only word that came out of Jerry's mouth. Before he could recover his surprise, he heard his aunt saying, "And Tommy, this is Jerry's wife, Anne."

The young man let go and Jerry's hand and turned to Anne, who had just finished giving Aunt Nan a hug. "My, my, what a beautiful woman you've grown into," the stranger said as he took Anne's hand to shake it.

Anne began to say, "Have we . . . ?" but was caught short as the man took a step back as if to better admire her, and then continued with, "I must say that you put a Cytherean orchid to shame. I never expected Jer to have such good taste, or judgment."

Anne graciously acknowledged the compliment, or at least she suspected it was a compliment. What exactly was a Cytherean orchid? She shot a quick glance at Jerry, who stood there, his mouth open.

"And this is obviously Brett," the stranger continued, as he stooped to shake hands with the boy who was kneeling so he could better stroke the cat's chin. As the stranger straightened, he added, "Any interest in science fiction, Brett—you know, flying saucers, death rays, bug-eyed monsters?"

Brett's eyes expanded with excitement. "Yeah!"

"Great. We'll no doubt have a lot to talk about."

Kevin gave his younger brother a shove out of the way and offered the man his hand. "Kevin Haydn," he said, impersonating an adult.

"Tom," replied the stranger, pumping the older teen's hand. Jerry couldn't help noting that he still didn't know the man's last name. He was struck by the disturbing thought that perhaps the omission had been on purpose. Although Jerry couldn't place the face, there was something oddly familiar about the stranger.

"And this is Anne's mother, Rebecca," said Aunt Nan.

"Pleased to meet you again," said the young man, causing the older woman to return his greeting with a look of surprise. "Again?" Rebecca couldn't recall having ever before met this young man. She started to say so, but the young man continued, "It's obvious from whom your daughters get their good looks."

At that Rebecca's expression turned to one of shock. Had he said "daughters?" Anne was Rebecca's only daughter, or only living daughter that is. Her eldest child, Sarah, had disappeared in 1959, along with Nancy's son. The man was obviously much too young to have ever known Sarah. Jerry immediately sensed Rebecca's confusion, and decided that the situation was starting to get out of hand. It was time that some things were cleared up. "I didn't get your last name, Tom?"

Before the young man could answer, Aunt Nan cut in. "Perhaps we should all go inside. We have a lot to talk about. Tommy's been away a long time, and . . . well, it's somewhat complicated."

"Yes, that sounds like a good idea," said Anne, moving to diffuse what was obviously becoming an awkward situation. "I should be getting dinner started, and I know Kevin at least needs to start doing some studying. Exams start tomorrow."

"Don't worry, Mom. I got it all under control," answered the teenager. "Besides, I'm dying to hear all about Tom here." He gave the newcomer a grin, that was more like a challenge, then noticed his father glaring at him, and quickly replaced the grin with a more neutral look.

"Yes, let's go inside," seconded Rebecca, studying the young man's features as if trying to recall his face.

Jerry and the visitor brought up the rear of the party. As the young man was about to enter the house, he stopped and motioned towards the immense tree trunk that lay in the front yard. "I can cut that up for you," he said.

"Thanks, but I'll get it taken care of."

"No charge," said the young man.

"No, really, I'd rather do it myself," said Jerry. As he entered the house, the nagging question of who this guy was kept repeating itself over and over in his mind.

Upon entering the Haydn living room, there came the sound of a scratching from the back door. "Brett, go let Lady in please," said Anne. The boy shot off through the kitchen and a moment later returned with a white and tan dog that resembled a small German Shepherd but was of obvious mixed breed. Brett immediately disappeared into another part of the house to do whatever it is that a nine-year-old does when he comes home from church, and the dog bounced around the

room, excitedly sniffing everyone. Jerry issued a series of stern com-
mands for the dog to sit which the dog chose to ignore. When the dog
approached the stranger, the man knelt and ruffled the fur on the top
of the dog's head.

"And what's your name, girl?" he asked, almost as if expecting the
dog to answer.

"Her name's Lady Macbeth," answered Kevin for the dog.

The man stood and gave Kevin's father a grin. "Gee, Jer, what a
dumb name for a dog."

So far it seemed that everything that the young man said rubbed
Jerry the wrong way, and the latest comment was no exception.
"Actually, my wife named her," said Jerry.

The grin vanished from the young man's face and, for the first
time, his speech showed a slight stammer, as he turned to Anne. "Yes,
well I meant to say, uh, unique—that is, Lady Macbeth, it's a unique
name for a dog."

"We call her Lady, for short," said Anne, her eyes revealing amusement at the stranger's obvious discomfort.

Anne's mother explained, "I'm afraid my daughter can have a
weird sense of humor at times. The only reason she named the poor
thing Lady Macbeth was to see the reaction on people's faces."

"Well, Lady Macbeth isn't such a bad name. After all, you could
have named her Black Cleolanthe," said the young man.

At the suggestion of Black Cleolanthe for a dog's name, the others in the room exchanged questioning looks, but no one ventured to
query the young man for additional clarification as to the identity of
Black Cleolanthe. Meanwhile Lady sniffed Tiger, who sat on the floor
and assumed the standard aloof look of a feline. Aunt Nan, still looking
uncomfortable, finally spoke.

"You're no doubt all curious to know more about Tommy. I suggest
we all sit down and we can talk about that." As she took a seat in the
living room chair that was traditionally reserved for her, she added,

"Perhaps it might be best if Kevin were excused."

"Huh?" said the boy. "No way, this is starting to sound kind of interesting."

"Go to your room and start studying for your finals," ordered his father.

"Ah, Dad. All I have tomorrow is history and trig, and they're a piece of cake."

"You sound like a good student," commented the stranger.

"Honor student," answered Jerry, before resuming the conversation with his older son, "To your room. You also have German and physics on Tuesday, and they're not so easy."

The teenager reluctantly left the room, only to find his brother kneeling behind the wall of the hallway out of sight of those in the living room. Concluding that his brother had selected an ideal location for eavesdropping on the conversation in the living room, Kevin joined him. In the meantime, everyone else had settled into a chair or couch, the young man placing his backpack on the floor next to him. Jerry thought it strange that Tiger, who usually wandered about the house exploring or just curled up on Aunt Nan's lap, squatted on the floor next to the stranger

"Okay," said Jerry, "can we now learn more about the mystery man here?"

The young man looked at Aunt Nan, still with the perpetual smile on his face. "Do you want me to do this?"

"No, I'll try," said Aunt Nan, although she looked decidedly unhappy at having volunteered. She glanced about the room making eye contact with the other three as she composed her thoughts. "I'm not sure how you are going to take this. God knows, it was difficult enough for me. As matter of fact I'm still not sure I believe it." She paused again, and then in a solemn voice said, "Rebecca, Anne, Jerry—this is Tommy."

For a reason he couldn't fathom, when his aunt again referred to the stranger as Tommy, Jerry found himself overwhelmed by panic. *Tommy! Tom! Like in cousin Tom who disappeared that night way back when I was a kid, and hadn't been seen since?* He quickly shoved the thought aside, and gave his aunt a questioning look, along with the associated hand gesture. Anne and Rebecca both looked at Jerry, and sensing that he too didn't seem to have a clue, shifted their gaze first to the young man, and then back to Nancy.

"Yes," continued Aunt Nan. "This is Tommy, my son."

Before Jerry could respond, the mystery man gave him an acknowledging nod while still radiating that seemingly glued on smile. "Long time, no see, Jer."

Jerry gave his wife an alarmed look, which Anne returned in kind.

"I know it seems impossible," said Aunt Nan, "but he really is Tommy." Her speech gave a slight quiver each time she mentioned the name. As no one else seemed about to say anything, Aunt Nan continued. "You no doubt are thinking that he's too young to be Tommy, but . . ." Her voice trailed off for a moment, before resuming. "He's finally been able to return after all these years. I know you don't believe it now, but perhaps you will after you've heard his story."

Jerry had fixed his aunt with a weak smile while she spoke. Anne looked positively horrified, while Rebecca continued to stare at the young man with a blank expression.

Jerry turned his eyes on the young man, and his body tensed. Everyone else in the room, except for the man who claimed to be Tom, waited in anticipation of what Jerry might do next. Jerry was a big man and, at forty-six years of age, was in better physical shape than most men half his age. He had served as a Marine Corps officer, which made him a man not easily intimidated, nor one who suffered fools. Anne was especially concerned about what Jerry might do if he thought that the young man, alleged to be his cousin, was in some way attempting to defraud or harm his aunt. To everyone's surprise, Jerry appeared to relax. He simply said, "So, Tom, where on earth have you been all these years?"

"Funny you should have used that expression," was the response.

"What expression?"

"Where on earth," answered the young man, wearing a grin as if he had made a joke. He then shot Aunt Nan a quick glance.

Aunt Nan at first looked puzzled, and then tried to force a smile, "Oh, I see. Yes, you would find that funny."

Returning his attention to Jerry, the man said, "Truth is, for most of the time I've been gone, I haven't been on Earth."

"What?" exploded Jerry, rising from his seat.

"I haven't been on Earth," repeated the young man calmly.

"And where in the—where have you been if you haven't been on Earth? Mars?"

"Good guess. Yes, I've spent some time on Mars."

"Neat," came a voice from the hall.

Anne jumped up and stepped quickly to the hall. "Boys! I thought I . . ."

"Oh, let them come in and hear this," suggested the young man. "They'll find out about it sooner or later."

"Don't you tell my boys what they can and can't do," barked Jerry.

"Jerry!" scolded Anne, while at the same time Aunt Nan also reprimanded him.

Jerry blinked at his wife and aunt for a moment, then abruptly sat down. The boys looked at their mother, who gave them a reluctant nod. They quickly scurried into the living room, Brett seating himself on the floor Indian style next to his great aunt, and Kevin dropping onto the couch next to his grandmother.

As the boys made themselves comfortable, the young man continued. "Like Mom said the whole thing is really pretty incredible." At the young man's use of the word "Mom" in reference to his aunt, Jerry's blood pressure took another surge upward. "If I were you," the young man continued, "I probably wouldn't be buying this either. But

24

be patient and let me tell you what happened. And then if you don't believe me, I have some proof here." He motioned toward the backpack lying at his feet.

"You said that you've been to Mars?" asked Rebecca, trying to sound nonchalant.

"That's right, not to mention other planets, moons, asteroids—even other solar systems."

"So how did you get there?"

"Well, initially I got there by traveling through time to the twenty-fourth century."

"What!" yelled Jerry, jerking forward and then thinking better of whatever it was he had intended to do, instead took a deep breath and said, "And now you've come back from the future, is that it?"

"That's right." The young man quickly glanced at Anne, Jerry, Kevin and Rebecca. From their expressions, he could tell that this wasn't going as well as he had hoped. "I know it sounds unbelievable, but bear with me. Let me start from the beginning, and I'm sure it will all make sense."

Jerry continued to give the visitor a cold stare. In what was obviously a struggle for him to keep his voice calm, he asked. "Okay, Tom or whoever you really are. I don't know what your game is . . ."

"Zero gee dodge ball."

"What?" said Jerry.

"Zero gee dodge ball," repeated the young man. "You asked me what my game was. I'm the academy champ."

When he realized that everyone was giving him uncomprehending looks, he smiled to himself and began to elaborate. "Zero gee as in zero electro—ah, you would refer to it as zero gravity . . . of course, there really isn't zero gravity, but it's like dodge ball, only played under weightless conditions. You see, the court is usually . . ."

"Tommy, I believe you're getting off the subject," said Aunt Nan.

"Oh, sorry. Well, to get back to—"

25

"Is this going to be a long story?" interrupted Jerry.

"To tell it in a convincing manner, I believe it has to be."

"Well, in that case, I suggest we first proceed with getting dinner ready. We might as well eat while we hear this incredible tale. But before we start," continued Jerry, "do you think we might get to see some of this evidence?"

"Good idea, Jer," said the young man, reaching for the backpack.

"Ah, please, don't call me Jer. The only person who ever called me that was my deceased cous . . ." Jerry stopped in midsentence. He realized that his hands were sweating.

"Sure thing, Jer—Jerry," agreed the young man, while pulling from the backpack a thing that resembled some sort of weapon, a handgun to be more precise. It had a barrel along with a handle, trigger, and trigger guard. Beyond that any similarity to a conventional firearm ceased. The section above the handle was studded with an assortment of knobs, buttons and small dials of various sizes and colors. Some parts of the "gun" appeared to be strangely translucent. From a distance it was impossible to tell if it was made of metal or plastic. The young man gripped the handle of the weapon and gazed at it proudly before twirling it around his finger, then giving it a flip into the air. The gun continued to rotate as it moved in an arc. The man sprang out of the chair and caught the gun at waist level, gave it a few more twirls about his finger, and then repeated the flip, this time spinning his body completely around before catching the weapon, still spinning, on his finger. He finally stopped its spin by gripping the handle.

"Wow, neat," said Brett, obviously impressed.

"Let's see," offered Jerry. "You say you've been to Mars so I take it that must be some sort of blaster."

"Blaster? Yes. I'm surprised you know the slang term for it. More correctly, it's a ray gun."

"A ray gun, huh. I suppose you can disintegrate things with it like little green men and monsters and such?"

"Yes, ray gun." The young man broke into a smile, as if he got the joke. "Come on Jer, you're not that much younger than I am. You remember those old Saturday morning TV shows like 'Space Cadet' and 'Space Patrol.' You know, a ray gun."

"A ray gun," repeated Jerry, closing his eyes while rubbing his temple.

"Yes. At least you're right about disintegrating things, but it can do a lot more than that."

"Do tell."

"Jer, this—"

"Jerry, if you don't mind."

"Sorry. This is not your run-of-the-mill ray gun. This is the model XR-15, the finest sidearm ever designed. This is the peacemaker, the weapon that will bring law and order to the Solar System and beyond."

Jerry looked at the other people in the room. His aunt was looking at the carpet, as if afraid to make eye contact with anyone. Anne, although trying hard not to show it, was obviously in a state of great anxiety. His mother-in-law still held that blank expression, staring at the young man with her mouth open. The boys were both enthusiastically eying the "ray gun" the young man was holding.

"Mind if I examine it?" Jerry asked.

"No, not at all, Jer. It has the safety override activated so there is no danger of it being switched into armed mode by any unauthorized personnel."

"Huh, huh," said Jerry, as he walked over and took hold of the alleged weapon. He hefted it. It was obviously well made, but surprisingly light, although it was significantly larger than a military handgun. A great piece of workmanship, he admitted to himself, whatever it was.

"And what company makes these things?"

"Trans-Solar Atomics. But, of course, you never heard of Trans-Solar. It should be obvious that the XR-15 isn't from back now."

"Back now?" queried Jerry as he began to hand the thing back to the man who claimed to be his long dead cousin.

"Can I see it?" interjected Kevin.

"I don't think you ought—," started Anne.

"It's perfectly safe," said the young man. "As I mentioned, its safety override is activated."

Jerry hesitated, then handed the whatever-it-was to his son.

"Cool," said Kevin.

"Let me look at it next," said his younger brother excitedly.

"If we may get back to my question," persisted Jerry as he resumed his seat. "You said 'back now.' What is that supposed to mean?"

"Sorry, I thought it was obvious. The XR-15 is not from now. I'm not from now. I've come from what to you is the future, although before I arrived here what is to you now the present was then for me the future. Does that converge?" Seeing only looks of puzzlement on the faces of the others, he continued.

"You see what is the future for me differs from what the future is for you, since I've been in your future while I skipped a lot of your past, although by 'your future' I don't mean that you'll actually ever be in that future, just that it's somewhere in the future from now. Or to put it another way, what to you is the future is really my past just as what is now would have been my past if I hadn't gone into the future, which although now is in my past, back then it really was in my future. Well, of course, since I'm back here now, what was the future in my past is now my present, but only because I'm here now." The young man again paused to check if anyone in the room was following him. "Well, it was tough enough for me to understand time travel without having to explain it to someone else. Maybe it's best we forget about it for now."

While the stranger was speaking, Brett had been pretending to disintegrate invisible enemies with the "ray gun" by squeezing the unmoving trigger and, in a low voice, making the appropriate sound effects. "Zap, zaaaammm, crack, zzsssshhhh."

"Brett, can you cut that out?" requested his father. "It's tough enough trying to follow any of this without you making all that noise. Give that thing back to—ah—Tom."

Brett reluctantly handed the gun back to its owner.

"So, disintegrate something with this ray gun and then I'm sure we'll all be convinced," suggested Jerry.

"That might not be such a good idea."

"Why not?"

"For one thing I'm not sure your psyche is ready for such a demonstration. Why it might do more harm than good. Consider what Mom has gone through this morning. After thirty-six years, her son, whom she thought dead all that time, shows up. Now that's quite a shock. I think it's best we go slow here. Who knows how each of you would react to seeing a ray gun in action, something you always no doubt thought was pure fantasy? How is your mind gong to accept that? You see, without giving your mind a chance to absorb what this is all about, without allowing time for your reason to gradually adjust to all this . . . well, I'm not about to take that chance. I'm afraid that for now a demonstration of the XR-15 is out of the question. It's like the old saying, 'never kiss a bilaterally inverted Polluxian Snerg Blat.'"

"Huh?" stuttered Jerry.

"If I simply gave you a demonstration of the XR-15, it might actually prove counter to what you hope would be the result. You might accept that I really came back from what is to you the future, but you would have no firm foundation on which to build that belief except a cheap demonstration. On the other hand, your mind might totally disregard the proof by failing to accept what your own eyes have seen, convincing yourself that the whole thing was a hallucination. You might even go into shock. Now where would that get us?"

Jerry placed a hand to his forehead and shook his head. Removing his hand, he said, "Why is it every time you try to clarify something, I end up more confused?"

"I'm sorry Jer. I'm not much good at explanations. I'm a man of action, not words. Out there you usually don't have time for explanations. It's either shoot first or end up deader than an Antarean mustard slime."

"A what?"

"Antarean mustard slime. It's a quasi-helical form of . . . er, never mind. Listen, Jer, let me tell my story. That's really the best way."

"Maybe we could see a tiny demonstration," suggested Anne, trying to be helpful. "Like disintegrate a bug. You know—something small."

For a moment the young man appeared to be considering Anne's proposal. "Okay, but just one," he said. Looking about the room, he continued. "See that fly on the ceiling?"

"The one by the heating vent?" asked Anne.

"Yes. I'll disintegrate that fly." Everyone turned their attention to the alleged ray gun as the man slowly raised it in the air, holding it with one hand. And then, before any of the others in the room were really expecting it, the young man squeezed the trigger. The only evidence that anything had happened was a barely audible "pop."

"There," said the young man, seeming pleased with the results. "One disintegrated fly."

The others in the room quickly turned their attention to the ceiling vent. No fly. They then instinctively looked at the carpet directly beneath the ceiling vent, Brett even getting down on hands and knees to study it more closely.

"So, where's the fly?" asked Jerry.

"I disintegrated it," said the young man, sounding proud of the demonstration's outcome.

"Oh, come off it," said Kevin. "There wasn't even a flash of light, you know, like a laser beam or something."

"Of course, not," came the guest's answer. "The ray, or 'bolt' to use the more correct technical term, is not visible to the human eye in that it is not composed of photons. However, if like me, you were fitted with a neurodic implant, you could see a flash from the muzzle of the gun, for when the bolt emerges from the combustion chamber it causes a flash of light, but not of visible wavelength."

"Yeah, right," was the teen's only retort to the man's explanation.

"Okay, Mr. Spaceman," came another challenge from Kevin's father, "how come there's no hole in the ceiling where the fly was sitting? I mean are we to believe that you disintegrated the fly, but left the ceiling untouched?"

"That's an excellent question, Jer—uh, Jerry. It shows that you are thinking. Not that your question, Kevin, wasn't also excellent. Of course, it wasn't really a question, but a comment."

"Quite stalling," said Kevin. "Answer Dad's question."

"Sorry. Unlike conventional firearms of today that use a chemical explosion to propel a solid or explosive projectile, a ray gun not only allows the intensity or strength, if you will, of the bolt to be adjusted, but also the range. The intrinsic characteristics of the bolt can be modified based on the target type and distance."

"Huh?" said Jerry and his son at the same time.

The young man smiled. "It's a lot more complicated than a gunpowder firearm. Let's see. Consider a firefight inside a spaceship. You obviously want to incapacitate your opponent, but you probably don't want any bolts breaching the hull of the ship. Of course, if it were a military type vessel, the hull would probably be made of neutronium, and . . . uh, never mind. I had best not get into that right now. Anyway, let's suppose your antagonist was human. You would set the intrinsic characteristics of the bolt to "human" at stun intensity, assuming you didn't want to kill him or disintegrate an arm or leg or something. If you missed your target and hit the hull instead, the bolt would have no effect on it. Are any of you following this?"

As the young man quickly polled the others in room, each in turn gave a negative shake of their head. "Or if the situation were more complicated, let's say your target was such that your bolt would damage or even breach the hull should you miss, you could always adjust the range of the gun so that a missed bolt would evaporate before it reached the hull. Of course, if your target was standing up against the hull, that would be a difficult shot, although I've seen such shots successfully made on more than one occasion."

"You've got to be kidding?" said Kevin.

"No, I'm not kidding. That's how the modern ray gun works."

"But," said Brett, "I never saw you making any adjustments. You just pointed the gun at the ceiling and pulled the trigger."

"Yeah, what about that?" challenged his older brother.

The young man gave the younger boy a grin. "That's an astute observation, young man."

"An a-toot—what?" asked Brett.

"An astute observation. I could have made the adjustments manually, but as is the habit of any trained patrolman, I simply made the adjustments mentally. Much faster and more reliable than doing it manually" The young man again surveyed his audience, but as all he saw were blank expressions, he continued with the explanation. "You see I have a neurodic implant."

"Yeah, neurotic is right," said Kevin.

"That's neu—rod—ic, not neurotic. As I was saying, it allows me to think the setting for the weapon and the gun immediately makes the adjustment. It has a limited range, of course, only a couple of meters. I must still manually pull the trigger to fire the weapon, so I couldn't operate a gun by remote control."

"This is insane," said Jerry. He looked at his aunt. "Aunt Nan, please, listen to me." He paused a moment as if to better organize his thoughts. "You and Uncle Sam have been as much of a mother and father to me as my own parents had been. I love you as much as I love my wife and children. I—I can't stand idly by and see this—this person con you like this." He cast a venomous glance at the young man, who

32

showed no anger at the accusation. Returning his attention to his aunt, Jerry continued. "I don't know who this man really is, or what he is after, but there can be no good come of it. I do know for certain that this man can't be Tom. There is no way under heaven or earth that he can be Tom. Tom is dead. We all have to accept that. Please, you have to see that what I'm telling you is the truth."

Although tears were running down her cheeks, Aunt Nan managed to keep her voice steady. "Please, Jerry. For my sake, please be patient. Let him tell you his story. I know it all sounds absurd, but just give him a chance."

Jerry lowered his eyes for a moment. Then he tried again. "Aunt Nan, he can't be Tom. I don't know if he's mentally unhinged, or some sort of space cadet . . ."

"Actually," interjected the young man, "I was a space cadet, but that was   "

Jerry sprang to his feet. He advanced on the young man, face red with rage, fists clenched. Anne screamed Jerry's name as she jumped up and grabbed her husband by the arm, halting his advance. At the same time the cat sitting next to the young man arched its back and gave Jerry a warning hiss. Tiger's reaction seemed to surprise everyone in the room but the young man who gave Tiger a nod of approval.

The young man held up his hands in apology. "Sorry, Jer. I wasn't thinking when I said that. I apologize. Blast me for a Martian mouse. Oops, sorry I did it again. It's difficult trying to avoid using twenty-fourth century slang. It means something like 'Boy, am I a dope!'"

Jerry turned to his aunt. "See? See what I mean? Martian mouse, Anturian something-or-other, ray guns, space cadets. Next he'll be telling us about starships."

"Now that you mention starships . . . ," the young man started to say, but then thought better of it and quickly shut his mouth.

Brett spoke up. "I'd like to hear more about Martian mice."

"Go to your room," snapped Jerry.

"Jerry," snapped Anne. "Don't snap at him. He didn't do anything."

"I don't want him anywhere near this—this—" Jerry was pointing a finger at the guest, his hand shaking, trying unsuccessfully to find an appropriate noun or adjective. Brett was looking wide-eyed, first at his father and then at the man his father was pointing at, and then back to his father.

"Jerry," said Aunt Nan, raising her voice. "Please sit down. I understand how hard this is for you, but please, please try to control yourself, especially in front of the children." She then gave her alleged son a scalding look. "And Tommy," she continued, "your flippant manner certainly isn't helping matters. Hold your tongue."

"Sorry," Jerry replied at the same time the young man said, "Sorry, Mom."

The older woman continued. "Brett, come here and sit by me. Your father is upset, and he has every reason to be, but it's not with you."

Brett squeezed into the chair beside his great aunt.

"I think it's best that Brett stay here, as it will probably help both of you BOYS," Nan continued, but her tone had turned even more stern, "to mind your manners."

Jerry returned to his chair, put his hands to his temple and massaged his forehead. Everyone else in the room tried to sit still and remain quiet until Jerry got himself back under control. "Okay," he said, at last. "Tell you what we'll do. Anne, why don't you and I go into the kitchen and start getting dinner ready? The rest of you can relax . . ." He started to laugh. The laugh was tinged with a bit of hysteria. "Relax? I can't believe I said that with Buck Rodgers sitting here in our living room." He noticed his wife looking at him like she was starting to doubt his sanity. "Then when we sit down to dinner, uh, Tom here can tell us his story. Okay? How does that sound?"

Everyone else seemed relieved that things had at least progressed to the point where Jerry seemed willing to hear the stranger out. They all voiced their agreement. But then the young man said, "Oh, by the way, Mrs. Gould. Sarah sends you her love."

At the mention of her long, lost daughter, an expression of angst appeared on Rebecca's face. "Sarah? My baby?" she said, her lips quivering with emotion. She gave a scream of anguish, then stood up and darted from the room. Anne, Jerry and Aunt Nan cast the young man angry looks, then Aunt Nan and Anne took off after Anne's mother.

"Sorry," said the young man. "I guess this wasn't the best time to bring up Sarah."

Chapter 3
Evidence

As Anne and Jerry set about preparing dinner, Anne noticed her husband on occasion eavesdropping on the conversation in the living room. Usually Aunt Nan and Anne's mother helped Anne with the Sunday meal, but Jerry had insisted the two women spend the time with the disturbing young man who claimed to be Tom Cobalt, his long-lost cousin. Earlier Anne and Aunt Nan had managed to get Rebecca calmed down after the young man's mention of Rebecca's long-lost older daughter. The two women along with the Haydn boys were now in the living room with the visitor. It was after Jerry had made a first cut into a carrot that he put down the knife and stared at the kitchen cabinet in front of him. Anne was quick to pick up on her husband's inattention to preparing the meal.

"I know it's difficult, having this young man show up with such a preposterous—"

"It's more than that. It's the man himself. I believe he might be— dangerous. I don't want him in our home and I don't want him around Aunt Nan."

"Jerry, really. How can you say such a thing? Despite his incredible story, he seems polite, and—"

Again, Jerry interrupted. "That's no boy out there!" He paused for a moment as if to collect his thoughts and then continued. "Anne, when I was in Viet Nam, I came to realize that you could tell a lot about a soldier by the way he carried himself, by the way he presented himself, by—I'm not sure I can explain it—by what you could see in his eyes. Eventually, you could sense when push came to shove who would run, who would hesitate, who would stick it out, who would … There were a few that you knew would not hesitate a moment to pull the trigger. They almost seemed to relish it." Jerry picked the knife back up and with a quick, sure blow, decapitated a carrot.

"Jerry, you can't mean to say that that young man out there . . . Come on, you can't really see something like that in someone's eyes. That's silly."

Jerry gave his wife a hard look, then again put down the knife. He walked over to the wall phone. After scanning a list of phone numbers posted on the wall, he began to enter one on the phone's keypad.

"Who are you calling?"

"Phil Bartley," replied Jerry, nonchalantly.

Anne swallowed. Phil Bartley was not only an old childhood friend of Jerry's, but also the chief of the East Pencreek Township police force.

"Phil," said Jerry, obviously getting an answer to his call. "Hope I'm not troubling you, but do you think you could come over?" There was a pause. "Right now. Actually, we'll be sitting down to dinner in about thirty minutes or so, and if you haven't eaten yet . . ." Again, Jerry paused. "Consider it a big favor to me. We have sort of a . . . let's say we have an unusual situation here. A problem if you will. Possibly a serious problem. I think your presence may prove most helpful in ensuring things don't get out of hand." As Jerry listened to the reply on the other end, he glanced at his wife, then, after seeing her look of concern, returned to studying the wall. "I really can't explain it over the phone but believe me I think it would be a great help if you came over. It would mean a lot to Anne and me." There was another brief pause. "Thanks a lot, Phil. Oh, and on your way over it might be a good idea to call in and have someone at the station do a quick scan of the wanted bulletins to see if there's anything on any fugitives that might be suspected to be in the area . . . male, mid-twenties, Caucasian, athletic build, I'd say about six feet, maybe two inches, dark hair, blue-grey eyes, clean cut with, well, no doubt most women would say he has handsome features. And that should include any escapees from the state funny farms, if you catch my drift. And, oh, be sure to pack your piece." This time Anne actually could make out Phil's voice over the phone, so loud had been his response. "Hopefully, there won't be any trouble, and I think having a police officer here might be just the ticket to ensure that." Another pause. "Really, I don't think I can explain on the phone." Pause. "Thanks a lot Phil. See you soon. Bye."

As Jerry hung up, he was startled to see his aunt's cat sitting on the kitchen floor, giving him one of those characteristic feline stares as if seeking a confession of wrong doing from Jerry. Jerry returned the kitty's stare with his best scow. Tiger appeared unimpressed.

Anne moved closer to her husband. "Jerry, what are you up to?"

"I think it would be good insurance to have Phil here. It can't do any harm. And it would certainly make me feel better."

"You're acting like you think that young man in there is some sort of psychotic killer or something. That doesn't make any sense. What would be his motive in trying to pretend he's your cousin?"

Jerry cautiously peered into the living room before answering. Apparently, the young man was describing some sort of spaceship. Brett sat on the floor gawking at the speaker with a look of hero worship. Kevin sat there with a smug expression, obviously skeptical of what he was hearing. "I have no idea what his motive would be, nor do you, but can you tell me you feel safe with that guy in our house?"

"No, not really. I mean he seems nice enough, but I know it's not smart to base your judgment of a person on . . . well, you know what I mean."

"Obviously he's not my long-deceased cousin. He's way too young. We need to find out what his real motive is in posing as Tom. It doesn't make sense. It's not like Aunt Nan has a lot of money or anything to inherit. I mean, who is this guy?"

Anne returned to preparing the meal. "Okay, we'll let him tell us his story, or whatever. Maybe that will give us some clue as to what's going on."

Jerry turned around to get back to whacking carrots and let out a yelp. The subject of their conversation was standing before him.

"By the clouds of Venus, you should have seen you jump," said the young man, sounding amused. "Uh, didn't mean to startle you, Jer. I was wondering if I might get a glass of water."

"Sure," muttered Jerry, getting a glass out of the wall cabinet.

"Who'd you call? Anyone I know?"

"Wha—," sputtered Jerry, his face turning red both from a combination of anger and embarrassment.

"Just wondering if it was someone I might know," said the young man. "Say, do you remember a Diane Ferguson? She was in my grade."

"Huh?" The question momentarily made Jerry forget the first question. "Diane Ferguson? In the same grade you were when?"

"When I disappeared."

Jerry stood there for a moment, staring at the mystery man and holding an empty glass. "Yeah, I know Diane. She married Brad Jones. Why?"

"I ran into her this morning when I arrived. Didn't recognize her at first, but I remembered her when she introduced herself. There was also a really great song playing on her radio, by the Righteous Boys, or was it the Righteous Guys?"

"Righteous Brothers?"

"Yeah, that's it. After my time though. Here, I'll take that glass. I can get the water myself."

The young man gently lifted the glass out of Jerry's hand and then proceeded to the sink as Kevin entered the kitchen.

"Here it is," said the teenager, holding out a large, hardcover book.

The young man thanked Kevin as he took the book and placed it on an open area of the counter. He opened it and began to flip through the pages with one hand while with the other he downed the glass of water.

"Here's what?" Jerry asked, having recovered his composure.

"My school yearbook from last year," responded Kevin.

"By Venus' moon," exclaimed the young man, as he dramatically brought his finger down on a picture on one of the open pages.

"Venus doesn't have a moon," said Kevin, smugly.

"It does now, uh, that is, it will." He turned to Jerry. "You wanted evidence? Here's some." He tapped the picture he had pointed to with his finger. "Take a look."

By now the others who had been in the living room had entered the kitchen. They all gathered around the one who claimed to be Tom to look at the photograph he was pointing at.

"Hey," said Kevin. "That's Mr. Rastaban, my physics teacher."

"Interesting," said the young man. There was an edge of excitement in his voice. "Physics, you say?"

"Why is it I feel as if I'm getting more ignorant with every passing moment today?" said Jerry. "Okay, please enlighten us as to why a picture of Kevin's physics teacher is evidence that you are who you say you are."

"Study the face, Jer. Does he look familiar?"

Jerry took a good look at the photograph. A distinguished looking man, clean-shaven, with dark, slick-backed hair, perhaps in his mid-thirties, peered back at him. Although he wore heavy, dark-rimmed glasses, they failed to disguise the man's aristocratic features. The figure in the picture fixed the viewer with a confident, almost arrogant, stare, and sported a wide, forced looking smile, so that one might describe it as a face that attempted to convey warmth but with a touch of the sinister added.

"Haven't a clue, other than, as Kevin says, he's a physics teacher.

I've never met the man."

"Think, Jer, think. Go back to 1959. Remember the high school guidance counselor, Mr. Serpens?"

"Yeah. What a moron," said Jerry.

"Jerry," said Anne, obviously disagreeing with her husband's assessment of their high school guidance counselor. "Mr. Serpens was a nice man. He always had a smile for everyone."

"Ain't that right," responded Jerry, "especially for cute girls like you." Anne gave her husband a warm grin. "But what does Serpens the Snake—that's what we used to call him— have to do with anything?"

Instead of answering, the young man turned to Aunt Nan. "Mom, let me see my yearbook." Aunt Nan handed the young man an old book, the one she had been holding on the porch when the Haydns had first arrived home. It was a large paperback. On its cover was the title *East Pencreek Junior High Memories–1960*.

"I had Mom bring along my old junior high yearbook from 1959, you know, the year I disappeared."

"Right," mumbled Jerry, thinking how he really wished this guy would quit addressing Aunt Nan as "Mom."

The man opened the older yearbook to a page with pictures of the junior high faculty of thirty-six years earlier and pointed to another photo. The picture was much smaller than that in Kevin's yearbook and of poorer quality. The caption under the picture read:

Mr. Serpens, Guidance

"There," said the young man, his eyes moving from one picture to the other. "Tell me they are not one and the same person. Note he doesn't even appear to have aged."

"You mean, like Dick Clark?" asked Anne.

"Wow, is Dick Clark still around?" said the young man.

"Mind if we take a look," asked Jerry.

The young man backed away to give the others an opportunity to compare the two photos. Mr. Serpens, the junior high guidance counselor from 1959 looked to be about the same age as Mr. Rastaban, Kevin's high school physics teacher. Unlike Rastaban, Serpens wasn't wearing glasses, and his hair looked a lot lighter than the science teacher's. Both Rebecca and Aunt Nan were shaking their heads.

"They could be the same person, I guess, although they certainly don't look thirty-some years apart in age," said Anne.

"There is one thing really weird about Mr. Rastaban," said Kevin.

"What's that?" asked the young man.

"He doesn't appear to have a first name, or at least no one seems to know what it is."

"Interesting," said the visitor. "Yes, it fits. What about you, Mrs. Gould? Don't you agree that they resemble each other?"

"I don't know, Tom," said Mrs. Gould. Hearing his mother-in-law address the visitor as 'Tom' caused Jerry to let out a frustrated sigh. Ignoring Jerry, Rebecca continued. "I never met either Sarah's or Anne's guidance counselor, although I sort of remember Sarah talking about him. And I certainly never met this physics teacher."

"Mom?" asked the young man, starting to sound a bit uneasy.

"I've never met either of them. I'm sorry, but I can't say."

Finally, Jerry opined, "Well, there may be some resemblance. It's not easy to say. So, what's your point? Are you trying to tell us that these two people are related?"

"More than that. They're the same person."

"Oh, come off it. You're saying that the man who was a school guidance counselor back in the fifties is now teaching science at the same school thirty-six years later?" Noticing that Jerry's voice was rising in volume as he spoke, Anne laid a hand gently on his shoulder as a reminder for him to maintain control of himself.

"That's right."

"Wow," mumbled Kevin half under his breath. "Talk about crazy."

The stranger quickly turned to address Kevin, obviously misinterpreting the substance of the boy's remark. "Oh, no. Crazy is the last thing he is," he said, pointing to the picture of Mr. Serpens, the junior high guidance counselor from 1959. "You might call him twisted, diabolical, evil, ruthless, heartless, or whatever, but I assure you he's not crazy. Besides, the man has no moral gyroscope."

"I know some of us tend to hold grudges," said Jerry, "like maybe against some school teachers that we didn't particularly like, but don't you think calling him things like twisted is going a bit too far?"

"Well, maybe he's a little crazy," said the young man. "In some ways, I guess you would say that he's as unstable as a heavy isotope."

"Unstable as a what?" said Jerry.

Ignoring Jerry's question, the young man continued. "But, you must understand. You see, he's not really a schoolteacher. That's a cover. That's what Rastaban does to blend in while he's here now, in the past."

"Please," pleaded Jerry. "Let's not get into that here, now, when, then, past, present, future thing again. I thought we were talking about Kevin's physics teacher, or was it my old guidance counselor?"

"Serpens is his real name."

"Whose real name?" said Jerry, starting to turn a redder shade again.

"Rastaban's, assuming that Rastaban really is Serpens as I suspect."

Before Jerry could reach the boiling point, Anne laid her other hand on his other shoulder. "I always thought that Serpens was a strange name," she said.

"Don't you see? It all fits. Remember the science teacher who disappeared along with Alex, Sarah and I back in 1959?"

"Sleinad Evad," muttered Aunt Nan, more to herself than to the others. "There's a name I'll never forget."

"Nor I," agreed Mrs. Gould. "I remember Sarah talking about him. And then when she disappeared, and he at the same time . . . I

43

remember his picture in the paper, and the caption, 'Have you seen this man?'"

"So, is there some connection between all these people having strange names?" asked Anne.

"Yes, there certainly is," answered the young man, "and I see it as even more evidence that Rastaban and Serpens are one and the same person. You see, Serpens must have thought it best to assume a new identity, so he chose the name Rastaban. After all, it would probably be noticed if after thirty years he hadn't appeared to age. Sort of like that guy with the painting, Dorian Gray—"

"—or Dick Clark," laughed Anne.

"Yeah, that makes sense," scoffed Kevin. "If you want to go unnoticed you choose a name like Rastaban, with no first name, and hang out with some guy named Sleinad Evad."

"I think Kevin has a good point," said Anne. "If someone needed an alias, why not take a name like Glenn Smith or Jim Miller, or something like that?"

"Sleinad Evad and Serpens no doubt agreed on Serpens' change of name beforehand in order to make it easier to locate him should contact with the Draconian Guard ever be reestablished. And why Rastaban? Rastaban is the name of the second brightest star in the constellation Draco—Beta Draconis. Being that they're both members of the high command of the Draconian Guard, not to mention both being syndroids—"

Jerry began to say, "Syn-what," then thought better of it. "Okay, okay," said Jerry, showing his impatience with the direction the conversation was starting to take. "So, our junior high guidance counselor comes back to school thirty years later and changes his name to Rasta-something and takes a job as a physics teacher. But the name's an alias and his real name's Serpens. If I thought time travel and that stuff was weird, this is even screwier. You really expect us to believe any of this?"

"Yes," came the answer, sounding somewhat on the meek side.

"So, he's not really a guidance counselor or a schoolteacher. Okay, what is his occupation?" taunted Jerry.

"Er, well, he's a—," the young man hesitated.

Aunt Nan interrupted. "Tommy, I think we should wait until dinner when we're all at ease to start explaining this. I'm not sure now is the proper time. It would probably tend to confuse things even more."

The young man looked at Jerry's aunt and smiled. "Mom, that sounds like an excellent idea. You're right, this isn't helping much." He turned to Jerry and again flashed the now familiar grin. "But I bet I got your curiosity going, huh, Jer?"

Jerry clenched his hands into fists.

"So why don't you all go back into the living room and I'll stay here and help Anne and Jerry finish getting dinner ready," said Aunt Nan.

"Okay, Mom," said the young man, but before leaving, he picked up Kevin's yearbook to take another look at the picture of Rastaban, the physics teacher at Kevin's high school. As he put down the yearbook, he turned to Jerry's oldest. "Kevin, what color clothes does your physics teacher wear?"

"Huh?" said Kevin.

"You know, his clothes. Does he wear different colors or is his wardrobe basically one color?"

"What in the blazes does the color his clothes have to do with anything?" said Jerry.

"Actually, Dad, now that I think about it, he does dress kind of strange. I mean he always wears grey suits. At least I can't recall ever seeing him wear any other color."

"Grey," said the young man, more to himself than to anyone else. "You're sure about that? Never saw him wearing any other color?"

"No, just grey—a light grey. Strange, huh?"

"No, not at all."

"Gee, after everything else that came up, why would wearing grey suits be strange?" said Jerry.

"I think that sinks the duck," said the young man, more to the kitchen wall than to anyone in particular. "Mom's right, we'd best leave you to finish getting dinner ready."

Before resuming his chores, Jerry took one more look at the two photos in the books lying open on the counter. "No, way," he muttered to himself, then picked up a large kitchen knife and used it to hack a head of lettuce in two with a single swing of the blade. At this his wife and aunt exchanged worried glances which Jerry noticed. He ignored them, and instead peered around the corner into the living room. The stranger had taken a seat and was resuming a conversation with the two boys and Rebecca.

Jerry turned to his aunt, keeping his voice low so as not to be over-heard by those in the adjoining room. "Could you try to explain why you feel convinced that this man is really Tom?"

His aunt started to busy herself with slicing a loaf of bread as she gathered her thoughts. "Call it a mother's intuition," she answered, picking her words carefully. "He's exactly what I would imagine Tommy to be like at his age. You must admit he bears a remarkable resemblance to Tommy."

"I'm not sure about that. I was only eleven when Tom disappeared. That was thirty-six years ago."

Aunt Nan continued. "And he knows things, things that only Tommy would know."

"Like what?"

"Well, when he came into the house, he looked around—he was really excited—and he recognized the rocking chair, you know the old one, the one we had when Tommy was a boy. And when he saw the painting over the mantle, he identified it as the one that Sam's brother Ray had done, but he didn't know that Ray had passed away in 1963."

"What else?" asked Jerry.

"He cried when he first saw me. Of course, I was crying too, but I can't imagine anyone faking something like that." She paused to wipe away the wetness that ran down her cheek. "It's funny. I would have thought that I would have used up all my tears by now." Anne laid a hand on one of Nan's. "He asked about Caroline, of course. He said that he probably wouldn't get a chance to see her before he had to leave. And he asked to see his old room. I didn't need to tell him which one had been his. He ran right up the stairs, taking them two at a time, like he did as a boy. And he headed straight towards his bedroom. He asked about his old friends and their families. What had become of the Banyons—you know, his friend Alex's family, and . . . Well, I told him that Mrs. Banyon passed away in '87, and her husband died in—let's see, it was three years after that, and that I didn't know where their oldest son, Alex's brother, was now."

When his aunt paused, Jerry said, "What about his age? Did he explain that?"

"Yes, and his answer seemed to make sense."

"Which was?"

"He said it would have been a lucky coincidence if he had aged thirty-six years since he had left."

"I don't understand," said Anne.

"I think I do," admitted her husband, reluctantly. "Let's suppose one could really travel through time. Tom was what? Thirteen when he disappeared. So, let's say he goes to the twenty-fourth century or whenever, and spends only two years there. Then he travels through time again and reappears here, today, nineteen ninety-five. In that case he would only be fifteen years old. See?"

"Yes," said Anne. "I see."

"Okay, so this guy was clever enough to come up with an alibi about his age," said Jerry, resuming his role as skeptic. "The explanation is obviously total baloney, but still it's an explanation. And he seems to know a lot about Tom's life. But did he ever show you any

47

physical evidence? Like did he ever disintegrate anything with that ray gun of his?"

Aunt Nan thought a moment before answering. "No, not that I can recall. You have a good point there. He never did show me anything that would prove he was definitely from the future."

"So, you admit that everything he seems to know might have been learned by talking to people who knew Tom as a kid, like his old classmates?"

"I suppose that's true . . . but, Jerry, you don't understand. You're not his mother, and I am."

"In other words, when you look into his eyes, you just know in your heart that this is Tom?"

Aunt Nan looked troubled. "I wish you hadn't brought that up," she said.

"What?"

"His eyes."

"What about his eyes?"

Aunt Nan hesitated before answering. "They're not Tommy's."

Jerry cast his wife a questioning look. Anne said, "What do you mean?"

"Tommy's eyes were brown." Aunt Nan motioned towards the living room. "His eyes are blue-grey."

"So how did he explain that?" said Jerry.

Aunt Nan lifted her hands to massage her scalp and shook her head. "He didn't. I didn't mention it. I didn't . . . I guess I couldn't bring myself to ask him about it."

"Why not?"

"I guess—I guess I was afraid to."

"Well," ventured Anne, "he could be wearing contacts. Maybe it's the style in the future to change your eye color."

"Gee, you're a big help," said Jerry, but quickly shut up when his wife shot him an angry look.

The kitchen went silent, until Jerry moved next to his aunt and placed a hand on her shoulder. "I'm sorry, Aunt Nan. You know there's nothing in the world I would want more than for you to find out that Tom was still alive, but if he were, he would be a man of my age. He would be—let's see—forty-eight years old. He certainly wouldn't look like someone in his twenties."

She reached up and patted his hand. "I guess that I should mention sometime else that bothers me."

"Yes?" said Jerry, trying to keep the tone of his voice empathetic.

"He knows all about the family. I mean he knows how old everyone is, and that Sam just died, and . . . he even knows about Carol."

"Our daughter, Carol?" said Anne. When Aunt Nan nodded, Anne continued. "You mean he knows she's in a coma, in a nursing home?"

"Yes."

Jerry seemed puzzled. "I don't understand. What bothers you about his knowing all this about us?"

"Don't you see?" said Anne. "If he just arrived from the future this morning, how would he know all this, especially about Carol?"

Aunt Nan nodded her head in agreement with her daughter-in-law, and Jerry saw the problem too. "Yeah, that is strange. Did you ask him about it?"

"No. But we haven't had much time. He only showed up this morning."

"And remember when we were introduced?" said Anne. "He kept acting like he knew us—I mean my mom and me. I was only eleven when Sarah disappeared. As I recall I might have seen Tom once, maybe twice. Except for the old photos, I wouldn't have had any idea what he looked like."

"Okay, so when we add it all up," said Jerry, "it doesn't look good for whoever that is in there."

"I know, Jerry. I know," said his aunt. "It's just that it all happened so fast. Maybe my desire for Tommy to still be alive is overwhelming my reason, but he's so like Tommy. On the one hand I know it can't be him, and but on the other hand—who else can it be?"

"But all this nonsense about spaceships and ray guns and time travel," said Jerry. "You know that can't be real. I mean, it sounds like a story some kid would fabricate, not a grown man. Really. That a future right out of the 1950s. There's is no way the future would be like that."

Aunt Nan cast her nephew a longing look before shaking her head. "There's something else you should know. Until now I didn't think it was important, but—"

"Yes," said Jerry, obviously expecting more evidence to counter the young man's claim of being his long-vanished cousin.

But surprisingly his aunt said, "It's Tiger."

"Your cat?"

"Yes. You see when he—when Tommy first appeared this morning, I was sitting on the front porch. Tiger took off. He sprinted across the front yard and stopped right at Tommy's feet. Tommy knelt down and petted Tiger, and then came up the walk to the porch, with Tiger trailing behind him."

"So?"

"He knew Tiger's name—that is, he called Tiger by name. When I asked him how he knew my cat's name, he said because it was his friend Alex's old cat, like that was obvious. But I told him that it couldn't be Alex's old cat. Cats don't live that long. He said that unlike most cats, Tiger really did have nine lives."

"Sounds to me like our mysterious stranger made a slip," said Jerry. "Somehow, he learned that Tom's boyhood friend Alex had a cat named Tiger that looked like yours but it never dawned on him that Alex's cat couldn't possibly still be alive after all these years. It's just a coincidence that both cats have the same name."

"I don't know. I suppose so. But when he was at the house, Tiger never left his side. He even kept getting up on Tommy's shoulders as Tommy moved around the house, and whenever Tommy sat, Tiger would climb onto his lap."

Jerry laughed. "Aunt Nan, we all know that Tiger is a very odd cat. I remember when you first got him you told us you kept the toilet seats up in your house because the cat used the toilet, and sure enough there he was one day using the toilet. No need for litter boxes in your house. But what is your point?"

"Tiger never behaves that way with anyone, especially total strangers. I mean, has he ever behaved like that with either of you, or the boys?"

"No, but   "

"Except for me, there's only one other person for whom Tiger ever showed that much affection towards, and that was Sam."

"Okay, I'll admit that the cat's behavior is strange, but——"

"Let me finish. Seeing Tiger sitting there, on Tommy's lap, and Tommy petting him and Tiger purring up a storm, it reminded me of those evenings when Sam would sit out on the back porch with Tiger on his lap. The two would be out there for the longest time. The way Tiger behaved with Sam and now with—him," she motioned towards the visitor in the other room, "it's so uncanny it's almost scary. It is scary. It's like that young man out there is Sam reincarnated." Aunt Nan paused a moment as she set the bread aside. "On a clear night the two of them, Sam and Tiger, would often be sitting out on the back porch looking at the stars. They would even be out there on the coldest nights of the year, studying the sky. And I would occasionally go out on the porch and ask Sam what they were doing. And Sam would say, 'Looking at the stars, and thinking.' And I would say, 'Thinking of Tommy?' and Sam would always say yes. It was all so strange. You see as more and more years passed after Tommy disappeared, we got to the point where we seldom spoke of it. I guess that's just natural. But ever since Tiger showed up, it seems that Sam would often mention Tommy. Not only did Tommy come up frequently in conversations, but I noticed a change in Sam too. It's all too horrible to have one of your children die. It was probably even harder on us than it would have normally been in that we never knew what had become of Tommy. At first, we still had hope that he would be found, but then as the weeks became months, and the months turned into years, at some point—who can say exactly when—we finally came to accept that he was dead. You can't imagine what coming to that realization is like. The thought that he's not coming back is always in the back of your mind. I could see it in Sam's eyes, and he no doubt could see it in mine. It was like when we finally accepted that Tommy was gone that part of our souls died. Fortunately, we had Caroline and a little later you. But a few years ago, I noticed a change come over Sam. Not only did we seem to talk about Tommy more, but unlike before, Sam seemed most content, perhaps even joyful when reminiscing about our son. It was as if he no longer accepted Tommy's death. It was as if he still believed our son to be alive. No, it was stronger than a belief. It was like—he *knew*—he knew that Tommy was still alive. At first, I thought that he was suffering from some sort of emotional breakdown. You know, like when one can no longer accept reality. But I said to myself that if believing that Tommy was alive made Sam happy, why try to disillusion him. So, I avoided trying to make him see reason. I now realize that the change in Sam only occurred after Tiger showed up."

"Okay, so—," but Jerry stopped in midsentence as his aunt continued

"And one night after he came in from star gazing on the back porch, Sam told me that it was really weird sitting out there with Tiger. It was almost as if the cat was talking to him, was telling him not to worry, was telling him that Tommy was okay. That everything was okay. That Tommy was out there somewhere."

"Out where?" asked Anne.

"Out there—among the stars." She paused a moment to put her hands over her eyes, then lowered them, and looked at her nephew through moistened eyes. "And that's when I remembered something

Tommy once told us. It was the summer before he disappeared. It was a cloudless, dark night, and we were all out on the back porch and Tommy was telling us about the stars. He said that his friend Alex had told him that the stars were so far away that looking at them was like looking back in time. That's what he said. That out there it was like time stood still." She paused to study Anne and Jerry's expressions. They both nodded in unison for her to continue. "And then last night I was in your old room, in Tommy's old room. I was sitting there with Tiger on my lap, staring out the open window, looking at the stars. And I had a thought. Maybe 'thought' is too weak a word. It was more of a—a vision if you will. It was one of those times that a—a vision strikes you—strikes you with such force, such clarity, that you know it must be true. Do you understand what I'm trying to say?"

"I think so," said Anne.

"I just knew that Tommy was coming home." Nan paused a moment, but when neither Anne nor Jerry said anything, she continued. "And one time this morning, when Tommy was at the house, with Tiger on his shoulders, curled around his neck, Tommy said, 'This cat really has a lot to say. Interesting stuff too.' Now you might think I've gone crazy, but when he said that, it was—well, I swear those were Sam's exact words one night when he was out there on the back porch with Tiger."

When Aunt Nan appeared to have finished, Jerry stepped to the kitchen entrance and carefully peered around the corner. There, in the living room, on the young man's lap, reclined a purring tabby.

Chapter 4
Physics Lessons

Anne was about to call the others into the dining room when her mother burst into the kitchen, chattering excitedly and followed by the two boys and the young man.

"Oh, Anne, it's a miracle," said Rebecca Gould. "To think, after all these years, that Sarah is alive." The older woman paused briefly to wipe a tear from the corner of her right eye. "Tom said that when last he saw her, she was well. That she was healthy and happy." Seeming not to notice the alarmed look on her daughter's face, she continued. "Tom said you should be proud of your sister, in that she was in the Solar Patrol!"

"The what?" said Anne.

"The Solar Patrol," repeated her mother. Then she turned to the tall, young man who had entered the room behind her, his face still affixed with that seemingly perpetual, good-natured grin. "Isn't that right, Tom?"

"Yes, that's right."

"And look," said Rebecca. "Tom even managed to bring along a couple of pictures of Sarah." She thrust two photographs at her daughter.

Anne instinctively started to reach for the photos, but pulled her hand back, as if somehow touching the pictures would precipitate some great tragedy. Jerry calmly reached over and took them from his mother-in-law. He held the photos so that Anne and his aunt could also study them.

The first photo was a close-up of a smiling girl who looked to be in her late teens. Her hair, neatly styled and shoulder length, was a light brown in color, almost blonde. The picture seemed to emphasize the girl's deep brown eyes. The eyes radiated intelligence. The girl's obvious beauty was only offset by a nose that seemed out of proportion to the rest of her facial features. Behind the girl was a wall that contained an array of instruments and assorted gadgetry, reminding Jerry of what he imagined the control room of a nuclear submarine or nuclear power plant would look like.

The second picture showed the girl standing on a neatly trimmed lawn, with a row of trees in the background. From the size and position of the shadows in the photo, it looked to have been taken around midday. The weather appeared to be warm and sunny as the girl was dressed in a very short, dark blue skirt and a grey, loose-sleeved tunic. A pair of snug fitting black boots completed the outfit. The left upper part of the tunic sported some sort of insignia, and further insignia graced the lapels of the tunic in the manner of badges denoting a military rank.

"Gee," said Jerry, switching his attention again to the first photo, "you'd think she would have been able to get a nose job in the future."

"Jerry!" three angry female voices shouted in unison.

"Ah, sorry," said Jerry. "I wasn't thinking."

Although she hadn't seen her sister in thirty-six years, Anne couldn't help but conclude that the girl in the photographs looked as she imagined how Sarah would have looked as an older teen.

Notwithstanding his slip about the nose, Jerry wasn't about to relent in his attack on the stranger's credibility. "It doesn't look like the science of photography has progressed much in three centuries. These photos could just as well have been developed at Curtain's Drug Store."

"Wow, is Curtain's Drug Store still around?" said the young man.

Jerry gritted his teeth. "As usual, you're evading the question."

"To answer the question you didn't ask, our tech group went to great trouble to ensure that these photos would be indistinguishable from photos common to the late twentieth century."

"Huh, huh," said Jerry, sounding unconvinced. "So at least you could have had the rings of Saturn in the background instead of some plain old Earth trees, or maybe the girl could be holding a Martian dog or something."

"Would that really be more convincing?" said the young man. "I doubt it. But more to the point, I can't leave anything behind that might be construed as evidence that you were actually visited by someone from the future. So naturally, these photographs were made to appear as if they had been taken in the late twentieth century."

"Leave behind?" said Jerry, sounding hopeful. "You said 'leave behind.' Does that mean you're not staying?"

"Yes, Jer, I can't stay. I must return to the twenty-fourth century, and soon. I have a limited time here to complete my mission."

"Mission, huh?" Jerry shook his head. "And what might that be?"

"I'm afraid I can't say more than that at the moment, although you'll find out soon enough."

"Mr. Man-of-mysteries," said Jerry. He again eyed the photos. "The girl in these photos looks pretty young."

"Yes, that's because they were taken some years ago."

"So how come you didn't bring along more recent photos—maybe some that were signed with a salutation, like, 'Greetings from the twenty-fourth century. Wish you were here. Love, Sarah?'"

"These photos were the only option."

"Boy, you sure are a wealth of information. But you did say that Sarah's still alive?"

"I'm not sure how best to answer that question. You see she certainly isn't alive here in the past, but at some time in—"

"Okay, okay. Let's not get into that again." Jerry studied the young man for a moment. "Whatever became of your friend Alex? You haven't mentioned him."

For a moment the question appeared to have rattled the guest's seemingly invincible air of imperturbability. When he finally answered, his tone was matter-of-fact, as if purposely trying to hide any emotion. "Alex is … fine."

Jerry had noticed the change in the man's temper so he decided to press the point, at the same time passing the photos to Aunt Nan.

"Oh, just fine? You seem reluctant to talk about Alex."

"No. He's fine."

"I don't understand," said Anne. "Can't you tell us more about Alex?"

The young man again hesitated a moment before answering, his eyes focused on the far wall of the dining room, as if searching for the right words. Then he gave Anne a smile. "It's all rather complicated, and besides it's not relevant to my mission."

But Jerry continued to press the issue. "Why are you being evasive? It's a simple question."

"The conflict is ongoing. It might be unwise to reveal to you more than you need to know. You see, we can't be certain that the past does not threaten the future. That's all I'm prepared to say."

Jerry was about to make a joke of the guest's cloak-and-dagger attitude, when Aunt Nan, who had been studying the pictures, let out a shriek, at the same time dropping the photos.

"What is it?" cried Anne.

Aunt Nan's complexion had paled. One hand was at her cheek, the other pointed to one of the photos on the floor. "It's her," she stammered.

"Who?" asked Jerry.

"I need to sit down," said Aunt Nan. Anne quickly led her to one of the chairs by the dining room table, and Rebecca fetched her friend a glass of water. Everyone else clustered about the table.

"What is it?" asked the young man, having retrieved the photos from the floor.

"I don't think I can take any more this. It's too much. First you," said Aunt Nan, "and now I see a photo of—of *her*."

"We don't understand," said Anne. "Why would pictures of Sarah upset you so?"

Aunt Nan took a swallow of water. "The girl in those pictures. I've seen her before."

"That's right," said Rebecca, trying to sound reassuring. "It's my Sarah, only she's older. It shocked me too when I first saw the pictures since I've always thought of her as a child."

"No, you don't understand," said Aunt Nan. "That's not it. I've seen her before—the person in those photos."

"We still don't understand," said Jerry.

The woman took another swig of water, and then hesitated a moment as if to both catch her breath along with her thoughts. "It was back when I was pregnant with Tommy. It was her." She reached out and took the photo from the young man and studied it again. "I'm sure of it. It was her."

"I'm sorry, but I'm not following," said Jerry. "You probably remember someone you knew back then who resembles the person in the photos."

Nancy Cobalt gave her head a vigorous shake to further emphasis her next word. "No. It was her. The more I look at these pictures, the more certain I am." Again, she paused, taking a sip of water, although her hand was visibly shaking. "It was a cold winter evening. Sam and I were out for a walk." She stopped and looked about her at the questioning faces. "I'll never forget what happened, because it was so—strange. We—Sam and I . . . until now it never made any sense. Oh, God, it still doesn't. I don't understand. What is it all about?"

Anne took a seat beside the older woman. "Please, try to explain."

Aunt Nan gave her nephew's wife a sympathetic look. "I don't think I can, dear. Now more than ever I don't understand. Like I was saying, Sam and I were taking a walk when we noticed a young woman approaching us. She was wearing a long coat and carrying a baby wrapped snugly against the cold. When she saw us, she stopped. We had to stop too as she was blocking the sidewalk. I remember it so well no doubt because it was all so bizarre. She said, 'Good evening,' or something like that. We returned the greeting. Then she stepped forward, walked right up to me, and as she did so the front of her coat fell open. The light from the corner streetlamp allowed us to see what she was wearing. At the time Sam and I thought it was some kind of uniform, you know, like majorettes in a marching band might wear. She had on tight fitting boots and a top with some kind of insignia on it and a skirt. Sam and I agreed afterwards that the skirt was scandalously short, and, of course, we found it really odd that someone would be dressed that way on such a cold night. She had long, shoulder-length hair, I remember it as blonde, and a beautiful face, except her nose was, uh—" Aunt Nan glanced at Rebecca, but when the other woman didn't appear to take offense to the reference about the nose, Nan continued. "It was her. I'll never forget that face and those clothes. The clothes she was wearing were like those in the picture, only a different color. Even in the poor light, I'm sure the top was red, not grey."

"You're telling us that my sister was there back in 1946?" asked Anne. Aunt Nan nodded. Anne looked at the young man, "And you're telling us she ended up with you in the twenty-fourth century. How do you explain this?"

"I can't," was the young man's curt reply.

"There's more," said Aunt Nan. "When the woman stopped in front of me, she leaned forward, and as she did so she smiled and then gently kissed my cheek. The whole thing was so unexpected, from a total stranger and all. I mean, Sam and I were speechless. Not only was what she did unexpected, but the way she did it. It was like we were

59

close friends, even family. Before I could react, she said—I remember her exact words—she looked me directly in the eyes, still smiling, and said, 'Your baby will be such a fine child. He'll grow up to be a great man. You will be proud of him.' Sam and I—we continued to just stand there, just staring at her. What do you say to something like that? I was only two months pregnant at the time so how did she know I was expecting? All I could think to do was to ask about her baby. She held the infant out in the light so we could see him better, and said, 'His name is Thomas, just like your child's will be.' At that Sam asked how she knew what we intended to name our baby if we had a boy? She said, 'It's written in the stars.' Then she simply gave us another smile, wished us a good evening, and moved on."

Everyone turned to look at the young man. He gave a shrug and said, "I'm sorry. I have no idea what to make of it."

"There's more," said the old woman. She looked at the cat that had positioned himself on the floor next to her chair. Tiger returned his mistress' gaze with that deep mysterious stare that only a cat can muster. "If all that wasn't odd enough, there was a cat with her. An orange tabby, if I remember right." Jerry let out a quiet moan.

"Aunt Nan?" said Anne. "You met Sarah briefly back when...er, back in 1959. Why didn't you then recall her resemblance to the woman you met that night in 1946?"

"That's a good question," said the elderly woman. "I do remember the day I first met Sarah. It was at church. I remember thinking there was a vague familiarity about her and asking Sam about it later. He shrugged it off saying that there couldn't be as this was the first time I had seen Sarah."

Further discussion was interrupted by the sound of a doorbell, followed by a bark from Lady Macbeth. "I'll get that," said Jerry. "Anne, why don't you get everyone seated."

The rest of the family and their special guest had taken their seats at the dining room table when Jerry entered the room accompanied by another man along with Lady Macbeth. The visitor appeared to be about the same age as Jerry. He was neatly dressed in a suit and tie, no doubt having also attended a church service that morning. From his overall size, it was obvious that the newcomer hadn't been as diligent as Jerry in keeping off the pounds over the years.

"You all know Phil," said Jerry in a tone of voice that seemed more relaxed than the others had been accustomed to of late. Jerry then introduced Phil to the young man who was seated between Aunt Nan and Mrs. Gould. "This is Phil Bartley, an old friend of mine." Then Jerry turned to Phil, "Phil, this is Tom."

The young man stood up and reached across the table to shake hands with Phil. "Phil Bartley?" he mumbled, half to himself. A look of recognition appeared on his face. "Ah-ah! You were Jerry's neighbor. You two always hung out together as kids. Yes, now I remember."

Phil assumed a moronic look and could only utter, "Huh?"

Jerry frowned. "Perhaps I should complete the introduction. This is Tom. Tom Cobalt. My cousin. Aunt Nan and Uncle Sam's long, lost son."

Phil, his hand still gripped in that of the young man's, turned his gaze to Jerry, his face distorted in a look of horrified puzzlement.

The young man let go of Phil's hand. "I know it's something of a shock, but it's really true. I've finally been able to return home after all these years." Then with a twinkle in his eye, he said to Jerry, "So, I bet it was Phil you called?"

"Uh, yes," confessed Jerry in a tone that sounded as if he had been caught rifling through his wife's purse.

"That also explains the extra chair," said the young man. "Joining us for dinner then Phil?" Without waiting for an answer, he resumed his seat and then continued, "That's great. I'm sure you'll find what I have to say most fascinating. I'm about to explain what really happened back in 1959." He glanced at the food adorning the table. "My, this looks delicious."

After a moment of awkward silence, Phil finally took the chair Anne offered him, while continuing to cast inquiring glances at Jerry. Before the new arrival could think of anything to say, Brett blurted out, "Tom, are you going to show Phil your gun?" That naturally resulted in another questioning look from Phil.

"I don't think we should interrupt dinner to do that," said the young man. "But, Phil, I've noticed that you're packing a piece."

"Why—yes," said Phil, a hesitant tone in his voice, obviously startled that the stranger had deduced that he was wearing a shoulder holster under his jacket. "Actually, I'm the East Pencreek Chief of Police."

"Well, congratulations! That's really neat. Who would have suspected that my cousin's old friend . . . why I remember the time you and Jerry got your behinds whipped for setting a cow cake on fire on Old Man Larson's doorstep. That's another Halloween I'll never forget." The young man looked in the direction of Kevin and Brett, who were looking at their father with surprised expressions akin to hero worship.

"By the clouds of Venus, your dad never told you that story? Well, one Halloween Phil and your father filled this paper bag with a cow cake and put it on Old Man Larson's doorstep. Old Man Larson . . . talk about an old grouch—"

"A cow cake?" asked Brett.

"You know. Cow poop. Anyway, they set the bag on fire, rang the doorbell and took off, hiding behind Larson's front hedge so they could watch the fun. Old Man Larson came out and saw the burning bag and started cussing up a storm, and what does he do but try to stomp out the fire, and the next thing you know there's manure flying everywhere!"

Aunt Nan, unable to hold back a chuckle, turned to her nephew. "I'll never forget your mother telling me about that." Phil was again giving Jerry that pleading look as if begging for some enlightenment, which Jerry, his expression again showing exasperation, failed to provide.

"Gee, Dad," said Jerry's oldest son. "You never told us that story."

"Kevin, it's not something to be proud of, and if I ever catch you doing anything like that——"

"Oh, come now, Jerry," interrupted Aunt Nan. "It's really an amusing story, and I'm sure that Kevin and Brett would never do anything of the kind."

Jerry gave his sons a look as if to say "Don't even think about it."

Having regained his self-control, the young man continued. "Really, Phil. I would have never thought that you would one day be a policeman, let alone Chief of Police." And then, as if to further confound the man, he said, "Actually, we're in the same sort of business."

"Oh?" asked Phil. "I like to think of it as a profession and not a business."

"Blast me for a Martian mouse. Good point, Phil."

"Tom, if I may interrupt," said Anne. "How did you know that Phil was carrying a gun?"

"You can tell by the way he holds his left arm that he's wearing a shoulder holster. Like I said, we're in the same business—ah, profession. It's part of my job to notice those sorts of things."

"Brett said something about a gun of yours," said Phil.

"It's in my knapsack, in the living room," answered the young man. "I'll show it to you after dinner."

"It's really neat," said Brett. "It's a real ray gun!"

"Yeah, right," responded Phil, obviously dismissing Brett's statement as the wild imagination of a nine-year old and deciding to change the subject. "So, you're Nan and Sam's boy?"

"That's right. I realize that seems farfetched. No doubt that you probably thought I was dead these last thirty-six years. Jer thinks I'm some kind of loony and that I might be dangerous. That's obviously why Jer invited you here, in case I go berserk or something." At these words, everyone else at the table looked decidedly uncomfortable. "I don't blame you, Jer. In your place, I would probably have done the same thing. So, I think I should start my story, now that we got all that out on the table so-to-speak."

Before the stranger could continue, Phil asked, "Exactly how old are you?"

"Hmm, eh," the man paused as if doing a quick mental calculation, "twenty-eight."

"Why did you pause before answering?" asked Jerry. "You had to think about how old you are?"

"Pause? I didn't pause," stated the young man.

"Yes, you did," repeated Jerry. "Phil, he paused, didn't he?"

Instead of answering his friend, Phil looked to be deep in thought. Then, he blurted out, "Ah-ah!" He pointed an accusatory finger at the man who claimed to be Jerry's cousin. "Got you! You should be forty-nine or so, not twenty-eight!" Phil began to slowly move the hand with the accusatory finger towards his shoulder holster.

"No, no, let me explain," said the young man, still smiling, holding up his hands as if to calm the applause of an admiring audience. "But first, I wouldn't reach for the gun, Phil." Phil stopped reaching, and, in what was by now becoming akin to a nervous habit, instead glanced at Jerry. Jerry started to say something, but the young man quickly continued. "I assure you that I could break your arm before you ever drew that pistol, even though I'm sitting across the table from you. Besides you've put on a few pounds over the years. Not in tip-top shape any more, are we? Spend most of your time behind a desk?"

Phil looked embarrassed as he lowered his arm. "Just going to scratch an itch," he said, and then leaned back in his seat. Jerry glared at Phil, then looked at Anne who was glaring at him in return. Jerry immediately ceased glaring.

"Getting back to the question of why I'm twenty-eight and not forty-nine. You must remember that I arrived from what is now the future by means of a time machine."

"A what?" said Phil.

"A time machine."

"Oh," said Phil. As if on cue, he again gave his friend Jerry a questioning look. Jerry ignored it.

"You make the understandable mistake of reasoning that since I've been gone thirty-six years in your time, that naturally thirty-six years must have passed in my time. To point out the error of this reasoning, suppose the time machine had returned me to, let's say, the year 1492 instead of 1995. Would I then have aged negative years?"

Kevin said, "Hey, I get it. Of course, the year of destination of the time machine doesn't have anything to do with his age. He's still whatever age he was when he left the future."

"That's right, Kevin," said the man who claimed to be a visitor from the future. "You're obviously a bright young man. No doubt you inherited your mother's smarts."

Anne blushed and Jerry gave the young man a nasty look. "Okay," challenged Jerry, figuratively picking up the gauntlet, and determined to show that he was as smart as his son and wife. "Let's assume for the moment that you are who you say you are and that you came here in a time machine." Jerry paused in his argument, as he mumbled half under his breath, "I can't believe I'm saying this." Then he continued, "What year did you say you arrived in the future?"

"2350."

"So let's say, like Tom, you were thirteen in 1959 when Tom disappeared."

"Jer, I am Tom."

"Okay, okay. You're Tom. Anyway, if you're twenty-eight now then that means that—twenty-eight minus thirteen is fifteen, you came here from the year 2365." Jerry beamed at his wife, then looked directly at the man who claimed to be his cousin. "Right?"

"Right. Very good, Jer."

"Tell Phil about spaceships," said Brett.

"Spaceships?" said Phil.

"Yeah," said Brett. "Tom travels around the universe in spaceships. He's been to other planets, even to planets in other star systems."

"Really?" Phil seemed less than convinced.

Jerry noticed his wife studying the young man. She didn't look at all happy.

"Anne?" said Jerry. His wife gave a start. "You look like you have something to say."

Anne turned to the young man, her features hardening.

"You told Brett that you've traveled to other star systems." Her tone was accusatory.

"Yes, but only three so far. Our duties usually restrict us to the Sol system."

"Yet, you say you've only been in the future for fifteen years."

"That's correct."

"Give me a moment here," said Anne. The others in the room were respectfully quiet while Anne took time to gather her thoughts before resuming.

"If I recall correctly what I was taught in my college physics classes, nothing can travel faster than the speed of light."

"That's not——," began the young man, but Anne hushed him.

"Let me finish before I lose my train of thought. So, to have been to the stars and back you must have experienced the effects of relativistic time dilation."

"Huh?" said Jerry.

"Time dilation?" said the young man.

"Yes," said Anne. "In other words, if you're only twenty-eight and you've been traveling to the stars, then a lot more than fifteen years should have passed on the Earth while you were in the future."

"Yeah," said Kevin. "Someone brought that up in Mr. Rastaban's physics class this year. It's called the twin paradox. Einstein thought it up."

"I'm not following you," said the young man.

"Einstein, in his theory of relativity, said that nothing can travel faster than light, and that time slowed down for objects that traveled at speeds approaching that of light." Anne leaned forward, gazing intently at the young man. "Yet you seem to be totally unfamiliar with those facts."

"Oh, now I remember," said the young man, laughing. "The twin paradox. Alex told me about that when we were kids. I assure you, it's all rubbish. A year's a year. The flow of time is constant. It doesn't speed up or slow down."

"Oh, yeah," said Kevin. "You should sit through Mrs. Frank's English class some time. Talk about time slowing down."

"You expect us to believe that Einstein was wrong?" said Anne.

"What can I say," said the young man. "My being twenty-eight and having only spent fifteen years in the future should prove that."

"It doesn't prove anything of the sort," said Jerry, "except that you're an imposter."

"Listen. Clocks slow down, including biological clocks and things like radioactive decay, when moving at great speed through the local jam, but in deep space where we exceed light speeds the jam is so diluted that the effect is insignificant."

"Jam," snapped Jerry. "What the heck is that?"

"Sorry. The technical term is—"

Anne interrupted. "I don't follow. You said that clocks slow down. Isn't that what Einstein said?"

"No," said the young man. "Clocks slow down because of the inertial resistance of the local jam. Einstein said that clocks moving at great speed relative to an observer appear to slow down because the flow of time itself was changing, but only relative to the observer."

"Huh?" said Jerry. "So, do clocks slow down or not?"

"That's the point," said the young man. "They do, but Einstein said they don't. Instead he maintained that it's time itself that dilates or stretches, and that, get this, how much time dilated depended on who was observing it. Trust me. Time is not a thing. It can't dilate."

"Funny," said Kevin. "Mr. Rastaban doesn't seem to think much of Einstein's theory either."

The young man gave Anne a smug look.

"Listen, I'm just a police officer," said Phil. "I don't follow any of this science fiction stuff. But tell me this. So where is this spaceship you're taking all these trips in?"

"Sorry, Phil. That's classified information. You don't have the need to know. Nothing personal, of course."

"But you're saying that in this spaceship you can not only travel through outer space but back in time?"

"We can, of course, travel through space in the spaceship. That's why it's called a spaceship, Phil. But we can't travel back in time in a spaceship unless we use it in conjunction with a time machine."

"Okay, so where's this time machine?"

"Back in the twenty-fourth century." The young man's answer solicited another loud groan from Jerry.

"Hey," said Kevin, "I remember reading something about how it might be possible to go back in time using black holes. Is that how you did it?"

"Black what?" said the young man.

"You know, a black hole," repeated the teen.

"What's a black hole?"

"What do you mean 'what's a black hole?'" said Jerry.

"Well, if you're going to press the point, I would say it was a hole in the ground so deep that you couldn't see the bottom so it would appear black." The young man again flashed Jerry a proud smile. "But I don't see what that has to do with—"

"Anne, would you mind explaining to him what a black hole is?"

"I'll try," said Anne, letting out a sigh. "Let's see. Okay, according to Einstein's general theory of relativity, gravity is caused by mass bending space."

"Give me a break," said the guest of honor.

"Shut up and let her finish," ordered Jerry.

"Thank you, dear. Anyway, if something were massive enough, like a star several times larger than the sun, once the star burned up its fuel, it would collapse under its own gravity making the curvature of space in its vicinity so great that essentially space would curve in on itself and the star would disappear from our universe. The only thing left would be a black hole. A black hole is a singularity, that is, it's so small that it really doesn't have any size at all, but its gravitational pull is so great that even light can't escape it. That's where the name black hole comes from. Anything getting too close to it would be pulled apart by the tidal forces of its gravity and disappear into the hole. There would be no escape. There's a lot more to it than that, but I think those are the essentials."

"That sounds right, Mom," encouraged her oldest son.

"Gee, Mom, you're really smart," beamed her youngest son, Brett.

"Thanks," said Anne, looking as if she was about break out in a blush.

"Okay, wise guy," came Jerry's challenge. "You say you're from the future and have never heard of black holes. Yet everyone in this room except you has heard of them." Jerry and the young man queried in turn Aunt Nan, Rebecca Gould and Phil. Each of them in turn gave an affirmative nod. "So, explain that?"

"Sorry, Jer, but I've never heard of black holes. And if I may be blunt, I must say that the whole idea of mass bending or curving space and stars disappearing into nothing and so on is probably the silliest thing I've ever heard—with the possible exception of the twin paradox and time dilation or whatever it was called. Space is not a thing. It's nothing. How can nothing bend, let alone create gravity? That idea is as nutty as time dilating."

"See, that proves it," yelled Jerry, jumping up from his seat. "You're a fraud. How can anyone from the future say they never heard of black holes?" He turned to his friend. "Phil, I think I've proved my case."

Phil gave an enthusiastic nod of agreement, at the same time moving his right hand towards the opening in his jacket. With a speed that seemed to approach that of light, the man seated across the table from the policeman snatched up the fork beside his plate and brought it, pointy-end first, down on Phil's left hand where it rested on the table. Phil let out a shriek, more of surprise than pain, and instinctively grabbed at the fork with the hand he had been intending to use to reach inside his jacket and retrieve his firearm. Without missing a beat, the young man shot from his chair and, with a swiftness that took away the breath of the others in the room, with his left hand reached across the table and inside of Phil's jacket and deftly lifted the gun from Phil's holster.

"Now, now, Phil, dinner and guns don't mix," said the young man, holding a fork in one hand and a policeman's revolver in the other. The others in the room sat frozen, as if in shock. After returning the fork to its original location next to his plate, the young man opened the pistol's magazine and swiftly emptied the weapon of its ammunition, the bullets thumping onto the table. He next spun the pistol about his finger. "Not great balance, then again without the bullets . . ." He tossed the still tumbling weapon into the air and, doing a quick full turn, caught the gun on its descent. He again began twirling the gun about his index finger.

"Wow," said Brett.

"Wow," seconded Kevin, sharing his brother's look of disbelief.

"Tom Cobalt!" Aunt Nan exploded. "Young man, you apologize to Phil this minute!"

The young man stopped spinning the gun, gave the older woman a sheepish look, then turned to the policeman. "Phil, I apologize," he said as he laid the empty weapon on the table by the side of Phil's plate. "Everyone, I apologize. It's something I do instinctively when I see someone about to pull a weapon on me."

"You stab their hand with a fork?" said Brett.

"Gee, you make it sound like it's some sort of everyday occurrence in your life, not that it would surprise me," said Jerry.

"Jerry, Tommy apologized," said Aunt Nan. "And personally, I feel better knowing that we don't have a loaded gun in the house."

"What about your ray gun?" asked Brett. "Isn't that loaded?"

"Charged would be a more correct term." said the young man.

"Okay, okay, that's all over with," said Jerry, taking a deep breath. "Maybe we should get on with the meal before everything gets cold."

Phil, still rubbing the back of his hand where it had been stabbed with the fork, said, "After what just happened, we're just going to pretend like it didn't happen and have dinner?"

Jerry's response to Phil's question was a quick shrug.

"Good idea," offered Anne, trying to sound upbeat. "Tom, would you like a clean fork?"

"That's kind of you to offer, but I don't think Phil has cooties or anything. This one will do fine."

"But you all must admit, that not knowing what black holes are proves that 'Tom' here isn't from the future," said Jerry, seating himself with a huff.

"I'm not so sure," said Mrs. Gould.

"What do you mean?" asked her daughter.

"Actually, as Jerry pointed out, who here hasn't heard of black holes. The fact that Tommy says he hasn't in one sense lends credence to his story."

"Oh, come on Grandma," said Kevin. "If black holes exist today, they must surely still exist in the future. Dad's right."

"Has anyone ever seen one of these black holes?" asked the young man.

"No, of course not," answered the boy. "That's why they're called black holes. You can't see them."

"If you can't see them, how do you know they exist?" The young

71

man grinned at the cleverness of the argument.

"It's true that no one has ever seen one," said Anne, "but I understand scientists have good reason for believing that they exist since they're necessary to explain a lot of really strange things that astronomers observe. I believe they think there's even a giant black hole at the center of our galaxy, the Milky Way."

That produced a laugh from the young man. "And people used to believe in black magic, and now they believe in black holes. Obviously, the whole idea is another wacko theory that has long been discredited by the twenty-fourth century. And I can assure you that such a thing does not exist at the center of the Milky Way."

"I suppose next you'll be telling us that there was no Big Bang," said Jerry. "Oh, wait I suppose you never heard of that either?

"Actually, I have heard of the Big Bang theory," said the young man. "I remember Alex telling me about it when we were kids. Total rubbish, I assure you. It's difficult from the viewpoint of four centuries from now to believe that some scientists could even dream up such preposterous ideas. Tell me, Kevin. Was there any discussion in your physics class this year about black holes or the Big Bang theory?"

Kevin hesitated before he answered, not looking all that happy. "Yeah."

"Did Mr. Rastaban offer any opinion on the subject?"

"Uh, yeah."

"And what was that?"

"He seemed—uh—well, skeptical about them."

"Skeptical as in that they were rubbish?"

Kevin cast glances at both his parents before answering. "You might put it that way."

"So, in the twenty-fourth century where do they think the universe came from?" asked Mrs. Gould.

"I can't answer that kind of question. If I did, then the word might get out and someone here in the past might come up with the idea before its time and then where would we be?"

"Okay, whoever you are, if you're from the future tell us who's going to win this year's World Series?" Phil looked pleased with himself, as if his question showed that his smarts were on par with everyone else's in the room.

"Oh, come on Phil," said Jerry, sounding irritated. "What kind of dumb question is that? At this point in the season he could say any team and we wouldn't know if he were lying."

"At least we would eventually know whether he was telling the truth." The policeman turned to the young man. "So, answer the question."

"I don't know," said the young man, "and why would I? If I asked you who won the 1929 pennant races would you know?"

"Well, uh—," Phil said, "—but, if you were from the future, you could look it up or something, couldn't you?"

"Yes, I could, but why would I? So you could use some future knowledge to win some money betting?" At the young man's last remark, Phil huffed, looking insulted.

"We really should start dinner," interjected Anne, trying to cut off the discussion before things turned ugly.

"Wait, I have a question," said Brett. "People live longer now than they did in the past. Is that also true in the future?"

"I take it you mean to ask if a person's average life expectancy in the twenty-fourth century is greater than that of a person in this century?"

"Yeah."

"That's an excellent question. It is. Not only that, but people age more slowly where I came from."

"Why's that?" asked Brett.

"Modern medicine," said the young man.

"Modern medicine?" said Phil, still massaging the back of his hand.

"By modern, I mean the twenty-fourth century, not the twentieth.

You see, as already your life expectancy is greater than Americans of the nineteenth century, not only is the life expectancy of the average citizen of the twenty-fourth century greater still, but we've also slowed down the aging process. Actually, in the twenty-fourth century, it's difficult to estimate the age of most adults. People in their fifties transported to the twentieth century could pass for being in their thirties or even late-twenties. Believe me, life's a lot different from back now."

"Huh?" said Phil. "Back now?"

"Never mind, Phil," cautioned Jerry. "Please, let's not get into that future-past-present thing again."

"So, what is your life expectancy?" asked Anne.

"In my profession it's difficult to say."

"What's that supposed to mean?" asked Phil.

"I mean that many of my colleagues have given up their lives in the line of duty. So far I've beaten the odds, but let me assure you, I have no thought of resigning."

Phil said, "Yeah, sure. And I suppose those other two kids who disappeared with you were eaten by some bug-eyed alien creature, which is why they can't be here with us?"

"The correct term, Phil, is B.E.M."

"B.E.M.?" said Phil. "Okay, Flash Gordon, please tell us ignorant primitives from East Pencreek what a B.E.M. is?"

"A B.E.M. is a Bug-Eyed Monster. That's the official designation. Not to be confused with an A.T.M..or a C.S.M."

"An A.T.M.?" said Jerry. "Why would one confuse a bug-eyed monster with an automated teller machine?"

"Huh?" The young man gave Jerry a blank stare. "What's an automated teller machine?"

"Never mind!" growled Jerry. As soon as he had said it, he looked at his wife, then instantly vanquished his rising anger. He took a deep breath, forcing himself to sound calm. "Please do tell us. What's an

A.T.M. and a whatever-else-it-was-you-said?"

"A.T.M. stands for Asymmetrically Tentacled Metapod, not to be confused with the S.T.M. or Symmetrically Ten—"

"We can guess," moaned Jerry.

The young man ignored the interruption. "—and C.S.M. is the common term for a Carnivorous Sauropodian Megaduolichenspam. One should, of course, never confuse one of those for a Herbivorous Sauropodian Megaduolichenspam."

"God forgive that anyone should confuse the two," said Jerry.

The young man turned to Brett. "Many would say that of the two the A.T.M. is the most to be feared as they slowly suck your brains out through your nose, but then if you were an airhead you wouldn't have anything of substance to lose." The young man stopped to grin at his joke. Everyone else at the table, with the exception of Phil and Jerry, were also grinning.

"Boy, it's great to be back," said the young man.

Anne cleared her throat. "Dinner really is starting to get cold. Let's say the blessing so we may start eating, and then perhaps Tom will tell us all that's happened to him these past few years."

"Yes, great idea, Anne," seconded Jerry, sounding relieved. "Brett, please say the blessing."

Brett didn't at first hear his father as he was staring at the stranger, a big smile on his face. The man in return gave him a friendly wink, as if the boy and he were fellow conspirators.

"Brett! The blessing please," repeated his father.

"Oh, sure Dad." Brett clasped his hands together, closed his eyes and lowered his head. "Dear Father, we thank you for all the good food we have, for our home and family, for our health, and especially for the really neat person who's visiting us from the future. Amen." Brett quickly opened his eyes and glanced at the young man. The handsome youth gave the boy a second wink and a thumbs-up. Jerry dealt his son a disapproving look. Aunt Nan was quick to cut off any further confrontation by asking the young man to please start his story.

In reply, the young man gathered his hands together under his chin, obviously considering where best to commence his tale. "Perhaps," he said, "we had best begin right here in East Pencreek, at the start of the new school year in 1959, for it was then that I first encountered Sleinad Evad."

First Interlude

1903 – Wardenclyffe, New York

At the entrance to the building, the visitor stopped and turned to take another look at the tower. The sight of the monolith was in itself worth the trip from the city to this out of the way place on Long Island. The tower's wooden grid work, which rose close to 200 feet above the ground, was impressive in its own right, but the fifty-five ton steel sphere under construction at the top of the tower was bizarre beyond anything the visitor had imagined. The man gave his head a shake as if to reassure himself that what he saw was real, then opened the door and entered the laboratory. Inside he found himself in a large room with a number of tables and shelves heaped with exotic equipment. The setting was so different from what he was accustomed to at the museum, it was almost as if he had stepped into another universe.

"Dr. Osborn?" The question interrupted the visitor's thoughts. He turned to greet the speaker.

"No. Dr. Osborn sends his regrets. Because of pressing business at the museum, he was unable to get away. He sent me in his place." The man introduced himself and then said, "Mr. Tesla, I presume."

"Yes," nodded the tall man, his voice betraying a tinge of foreign accent.

The visitor was impressed by his host's appearance. Nikola Tesla, all six feet five inches of him, looked the part of a mad genius. The man's thin, mustached face displayed an inquisitive expression, while his dark eyes blazed with such deep intellect that the visitor could well imagine that only a handful of other men in the world possessed its equal. Tesla stood there, hands clasped behind his back, straight and tall, the obvious lord and master of this most extraordinary of places.

"In his letter Dr. Osborn said he was a paleontologist—a studier of fossils."

"Yes," answered the visitor, "that's correct."

"His letter was not specific on the purpose of this meeting? I assure you that I can't imagine how I can be of any assistance to a paleontologist."

"It's—complicated."

"I suppose it has something to do with the box you're carrying."

"Yes," said the visitor. "Uh, is there someplace I can put it?"

"Certainly. My apologies." The engineer motioned the visitor to a nearby stool next to a table whose top was cluttered with an assortment of electrical gadgetry. With some effort, the visitor placed the wooden box on the table. Whatever it held was obviously heavy.

Instead of seating himself, the man opened the box and took out a thin manuscript, placing it on the table next to the box. Then, using both hands, he lifted from the box an object about ten inches in size, covered with a white cloth. He placed it on the table next to the manuscript and proceeded to unfold the cloth. Tesla had started to seat himself on a second stool, but as the spherical object that had been wrapped in the cloth was revealed, he stood back up. For a moment he stared at the thing. Then, ever so gently, he placed a hand on its hard, metallic surface. "What, may I ask, is it?"

"That's the reason for this visit. We were hoping you could answer that question."

The inventor slowly turned the object over, taking in its every detail.

"What can this possibly have to do with the study of the remains of extinct beasts?"

"Before I get to that, I was instructed to inform you that only a few men have been privileged to see this—thing." The man took a deep breath before continuing. "Dr. Osborn would like to keep its existence in strictest confidence and hopes that you will consent to take responsibility for it."

"You're leaving it in my care?"

"Yes, if you'll accept it. The museum doesn't want it, or in any way wishes to be associated with it."

"But—why?"

"If you'll indulge me for a minute I believe that will become clear when I describe to you the circumstances under which it was discovered."

"Certainly. Take your time. I'm fascinated."

The visitor hesitated a moment, obviously collecting his thoughts. "Several months ago we were on a dig—uh, that is, we were hunting for fossils in the Hell Creek formation."

"Hell Creek formation?"

"Yes. That's an area of exposed rock near Hell Creek in eastern Montana. It's of late Cretaceous age."

"Cretaceous? I'm not familiar with that term."

"It's the scientific term for a specific expanse of time in geological history. It's the final period of the age of the dinosaurs. That age is divided in three periods, the Triassic, the oldest, the Jurassic, and finally the Cretaceous, the youngest. Each of the periods lasted millions of years. We have no idea how long really, although it's possible that dinosaurs inhabited the earth anywhere from fifty to perhaps a hundred million years or more before becoming extinct. The Cretaceous is the youngest of the three periods. The fossils found in the Hell Creek formation are thought to be from near the end of that period of time, but please understand that the Hell Creek fossils are still believed to be millions of years old."

"Yes, I understand."

"Well, there's the problem. I said 'believed to be millions of years old.' That's what the prevailing scientific theories would have us believe. And when I say millions of years old, I mean millions of years before man or anything resembling man ever evolved."

"Evolved?" said the engineer. "We're speaking of Charles Darwin's theory of natural selection, yes?"

"Correct. And that is the problem that this—this thing presents. It was found in the ground, in the rock matrix to be more precise, that held an incomplete dinosaur fossil. It was encased in the rock directly below the fossil. Such a discovery contradicts the whole basis not only of the theory of evolution but of the science of geology. It just should not be."

Tesla gave a laugh. "The answer's obvious. It's a hoax. Someone's played a trick on you."

"No sir. The idea that it's a hoax doesn't work, for several reasons. First, I was a witness to its discovery. It was found in the same rocky matrix that held a dinosaur fossil. The obvious conclusion is that it had been buried about the same time as the fossil.

When we first saw the exposed fossil bone, the ground showed no sign of having been previously disturbed. I would have certainly noticed if it had been.

Also, how could anyone have known where we intended to dig? The Hell Creek formation covers a vast area, all of it desolate and fairly isolated from human habitation. It was only that morning that we had decided to search the location where this was found."

"All excellent arguments against it being a hoax," said Tesla.

"There's more. Although the circumstances under which it was discovered only add to the mystery, the object itself is proof against a hoax. Should this thing have been found lying on a sidewalk on Broadway, it would still be a riddle. You see, the thing is apparently indestructible."

"What?"

"It was found as a result of being struck with a pickaxe. The blow broke off the pick's point. Since then we've hit it with hammers, axes, you name it—it shows not even a scratch. Nor will diamond or any saw or edged or pointed instrument cut it or the heat of a furnace melt it. We've dropped it from a great height onto a steel spike. Not even a dent. It appears now as it did when it was first found."

"Fascinating," said the inventor. "Utterly fascinating." Tesla learned forward to study the object more closely. "And these inscriptions?"

"No idea. We've used the resources of the museum as well as several university and municipal libraries and have found no writing or any other system of symbols that match them—at least, closely and consistently enough to identify their origin."

"But why the secrecy about it?"

The visitor appeared to be embarrassed about having to answer the inventor's question. "Mr. Tesla, the existence of this object and the circumstances of its discovery overthrow the foundations of modern science. I'm speaking not only of the theory of natural selection, but the belief that the earth is incredibly old and that millions of years passed and untold thousands of species evolved and became extinct before humans arrived on earth. If word of this gets out to the public, my associates and I no doubt will be accused of being liars and charlatans or, perhaps even worse, should we be believed, the careers of many of our most esteemed men of science will be ruined. They'll be made to look like fools for having supported such notions that the earth is millions of years old and that life evolved." The man paused and gave Tesla a look that begged for understanding and empathy.

The inventor shook his head as if to plead forgiveness for what he was about to say. "Still, my young man, science is the search for truth. We must follow that truth wherever it may lead and regardless of whether we like the consequences."

"Please understand that we are not trying to cover up the truth.

It's just that—before we reveal to the world what we have found, we would like to know what exactly this thing is—what its function is, its purpose, and better yet, how it came to be where it was."

Tesla nodded. "I think I understand, but why me?"

"Sir, several of the people at the museum believe you to be the greatest genius alive. This thing may be some sort of device—a machine or whatever. If anyone can figure out the why of this thing, it is you."

Tesla picked up the artifact in both hands and hefted it, then placed it back on the table. "I see. Well, they may be correct in thinking that this is some sort of machine, although it is alien to anything in my experience." He paused in his speech for a moment to further study the extraordinary object that rested on the table before him. "You may tell your associates that I accept the task, but I shall return it to them if I've made no progress by—say, the end of the year."

"My associates hope that you will keep it as long as it takes you to solve its mystery. As I said before, they are glad to be rid of it. I suspect that many of them would like it to disappear and the whole thing forgotten."

"You say it appears to be indestructible?"

"Yes."

"Does it conduct electricity? Has it been subjected to a high potential difference?"

"No sir. We don't have any expertise in that area nor, as you do, the machines to perform such tests. That's another good reason to have someone like you examine it."

"But why not go public with its existence but omit the details of its discovery? After all, you could say it was found during a fossil hunting expedition. Is it really necessary to provide the details of its discovery that prove embarrassing to the present scientific orthodoxy?"

"That idea was discussed and rejected. We are scientists. To withhold information as to the conditions under which this thing was found would be dishonest."

Tesla raised an eyebrow. "And is withholding the existence of this artifact from the rest of the scientific community not equally dishonest?"

"In a way I suppose you are right, but we don't want to permanently keep its existence a secret. We wish to do so only until such time that we have a better understanding, or at least a plausible conjecture, as to what this thing might be. We hope thereby to preclude any damage to the reputation of science that premature news of its existence might engender."

The engineer began to again run his fingers over the inscriptions on the surface of the object. "Be honest with me, young man. Did Dr. Osborn really have more pressing duties that prevented him from coming here today?"

The visitor swallowed. "I really can't say for sure. All I know is that he instructed me to come in his place. Please, Mr. Tesla, try to put yourself in the position of those at the museum."

"I'm sorry but I can't do that. In the interest of science—of truth—it would seem that the odds of understanding this thing would be greatly increased should it be made available to the world scientific community rather than one man."

"You're not changing your mind about taking custody of it, are you?"

The tall man didn't respond at first. He merely stroked the surface of the ball shaped object on the table for a few moments before answering. "No, I will not reject the trust that these gentlemen have placed in me. As I said before, I shall attempt to unlock its secrets, but only through the end of the year, at which time I shall return it to the museum along with a report of my findings."

"Thank you, Mr. Tesla. I know that you'll have the undying gratitude of Dr. Osborn and my other associates for accepting this challenge."

"And this document?" asked Tesla, placing a hand on the manuscript that the visitor had first removed from the box.

"That's a report of its discovery along with a description of the results of the tests the museum performed. As I mentioned before, the results were all negative."

"Yes, thank you. One never knows. It might prove most helpful."

"Do you have any idea what it might be?"

Tesla smiled. "No, but I do have a hypothesis that possibly explains, although not its function, as least the existence of this incredible object and, at the same time, leaves your scientific theories intact."

"Really?" The man was unable to disguise the tone of hope in his voice.

"What do you think of the possibility that there may be intelligent life on other planets, even advanced civilizations?"

"Huh?" the visitor stammered. "You mean like in that book by— what was his name—Wells, H. G. Wells, about an invasion of the earth by Martians?"

"I'm not familiar with that book, but I suppose so? Anyway, a possible explanation is that this was created by an advanced civilization from another planet and left behind when they visited the earth at the end of the Cretaceous." The inventor's smile grew wide.

"But . . . I can't tell my associates that. The idea is preposterous!"

"I would say not. As matter of fact, it is possible that I actually received a communication from another planet four years ago at my Colorado Springs laboratory."

The visitor stared at the engineer, obviously having serious doubts about the wisdom of the museum's plan to leave the strange artifact with the world-famous inventor. "What evidence do you have for such a crazy notion that we've been visited by beings from another planet?"

Tesla looked at the heavy, spherical artifact resting on the table. "This."

PART II
1959 – East Pencreek, Pennsylvania

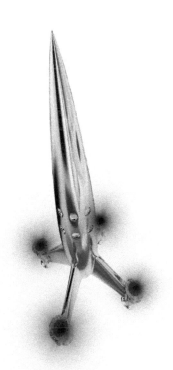

Chapter 1
The Final Days of Summer Vacation

The boy held the small, plastic figure close to his face so he could study its detail. The miniature depicted a young man dressed in a futuristic uniform. The toy figure stood with hands on hips, feet planted in an at-ease stance, looking straight ahead with a confident smile. The boy returned the figure's smile. It had been plucked from the contents of a fair-sized but shallow, open box, which lay on a table before the teen. Inside the box were more figures along with toy rockets and other out-of-this-world stuff. Several of the tiny spacemen were dressed in space suits whose collars could be fitted with clear, hard plastic space helmets of a matching scale. Others were clothed similarly to the figure the boy was holding, their outfits consisting of boots with trousers stuffed into their tops and long-sleeved shirts with large triangular shaped collars. Many of the figures wore sturdy belts to which were attached various odd-looking devices. Some were women dressed in short skirts and long-sleeved tunics. The male figures were all clean-shaven with neatly-combed, short-cropped hair. The females had carefully styled shoulder length hair. There were also figures of alien beings cast in a variety of mutations on the basic humanoid form. Many of the figures, both human and non-human, had holsters attached to their belts and several carried weapons of exotic design.

The boy returned the figure he was holding to the box and picked out another, this one dressed in a snug fitting spacesuit. The figure's torso was offset by a pair of straps, which ran from the wide belt to the shoulders and crossed at the center of the chest, giving the appearance of a large X. The head was encased in an ovoid helmet highlighted by earphone and goggle-like protrusions at the locations of the ears and eyes respectively. Twin holsters hung from the belt. The spaceman's arms were crossed over his chest in an arrogant manner.

As the boy studied the two-inch tall plastic sculpture, his thoughts turned to the many adventures he and his friends, Alex, Brad, and Wayne, had acted out with this set over the years. It had been one of their favorite pastimes. The memory gave the boy pause to wonder how much longer they would enjoy such activities as they were about to enter the eighth grade. They were at that stage in their lives where they had one foot firmly planted in childhood while the other had boldly stepped into the adult world.

"Tom." It was his mother calling. "Alex and Wayne are here."

The boy looked up to see his friends rushing down the basement stairs, followed by a large tan tabby cat, who in turn was closely trailed by a mid-sized black, long-haired dog with orange patches of fur about its face and paws. Upon reaching the third to last step, Alex launched himself into the air, landing on the floor with both feet together. Wayne followed suit, landing behind Alex. The cat came to a stop immediately behind the boys. The dog in turn stopped behind the cat and began to frantically sniff the feline. The boys each raised an arm in a clenched fist salute and announced, "Hail Ragnar."

Tom put down the toy figure, swiveled on his stool, stood and gave a similar salute. "Hail Einar, hail Ivar," he said.

Acknowledging the return of their salutes, the boys approached the table. Alex waved a white piece of paper. "Did you get your class schedule yet? Mine came this morning." Alex was shorter than either of the other boys although his skinny frame made him appear tall. Glasses rested on his larger than average nose and his teeth were ensnared by a debilitating apparatus that was inflicted upon many twentieth century American youths. Braces!

"I haven't checked the mail yet," Tom answered, as he absent-mindedly picked up a toy ray gun from the table and began to twirl it around his finger. "But if you got yours, I bet mine will come today." Tom then flipped the spinning toy gun into the air and doing a half twist with his body caught it behind his back. "Let's check, it might be here by now." Placing the gun on the table, he began to scold the dog who had begun to whine at the cat, as if upset that the cat was ignoring him. "Basil, shush! Leave Tiger alone." Turning to the other boy, Tom said, "Did you get your letter yet?"

"Heck, no," said Wayne, "we're probably the last mail stop in the state." From his appearance, Wayne Franklin could no doubt have been a nominee for the All-American thirteen-year-old boy. He would have been the number one heartthrob of most of the girls in his class if it hadn't been for the fact that Tom was also in his class, not that such concerns had yet crossed either boy's mind.

Alex picked up the toy pistol and attempted to duplicate his friend's recent stunt by tossing it in the air and then doing a half turn and catching it behind his back. Wayne snatched the gun on its way back down as its trajectory would have landed it on the dog's head instead of where Alex had intended.

"How do you do that?" asked Alex, turning back around after he realized that he had failed again to duplicate his friend's behind-the-back catch.

"Practice," said Tom. "Not to mention exceptional coordination, quick reflexes, and, less we forget, superior intelligence."

"Are you kidding? I can't believe I'm hearing this from a kid who almost flunked science last year because he couldn't remember the difference between a gymnosperm and an angiosperm."

"Hey, I still ended up with a B, and besides, what's in a name? That which we call an angiosperm by any other name would smell as sweet." The other boys rolled their eyes at their friend's attempt at 'intellectual' humor. Basil whined again at the cat. Tom growled, "Basil, I said stop that whining. Come on, let's see if the mail's here."

The boys rushed up the stairs followed by the two animals, then through the kitchen, into the living room and out the front door of the house, almost colliding with Tom's father who was climbing the steps of the front porch. "Excuse us, Dad," said Tom.

"Hello, Mr. Ko," said Alex, greeting his friend's father. "Hi, Mr. Cobalt," yelped Wayne.

Mr. Cobalt jumped out of their way, at the same time giving his son's friends a nod of greeting.

Tom reached the mailbox first and quickly emptied it of its contents, shifting through several envelopes until Alex yelled, "There, that's it!" Ripping open the envelope and unfolding the enclosed letter, Tom compared his class schedule with Alex's.

"Neat," whooped Alex. "We're in all the same classes again!"

"Yeah," said Tom. "I was worried that my grades weren't good enough to keep me in the 'A' section."

"Me, too," said Alex.

"Well, thanks for being concerned about my grades," grinned Tom.

"Not your grades, moron. I meant I was worried about *my* grades."

"Oh, sure!" said Wayne. "Like they're going to kick Alex Einstein out of the 'A' class."

"Hey, it ain't so easy with some courses, like Coach Heartburn's class last year. I mean what a total ignoramus," said Alex, referring to their seventh grade history teacher whose actual name was Heathburn. "I would have gotten a C or worse that first quarter if we hadn't caught on that you had to practically memorize the book to answer his stupid test questions."

"That's because he's a total nincompoop," said Tom, obviously in agreement with his friend's critique of the school's junior high football coach. "He pretends to teach by keeping one chapter ahead of the class. Remember that question about where the Pilgrims landed, the one that just about everyone in the class got wrong?"

"Yeah, he wouldn't accept Plymouth Rock or Massachusetts Bay for an answer," said Alex. "The only thing he would accept was Cape Cod because that's what it said in the book."

"Personally," observed Wayne, "I think the man may have taken one too many blows to the head when he was younger."

From behind them came the voice of Tom's father. "Now I'm sure that Coach Heartburn—er—," Mr. Cobalt paused and slapped his forehead with his hand, before resuming. "—Heathburn is a most qualified teacher."

"Oh, come on Dad. He has an I.Q. of a decimal two. The only reason they hired him was because the Junior High football team hasn't had a winning season since the Paleocene."

"The Paleo-what?" asked Mr. Cobalt, sounding befuddled.

"Paleocene. It's the first epoch of the Cenozoic era."

"Oh," was all his father could think to say, having forgotten completely what the conversation had been about."

"Shoot!" cried Alex.

"What?" said Tom.

"I just noticed we have Evad for Science."

"Double shoot," said Tom and Wayne.

"So?" said Mr. Cobalt. "Is that a problem?"

The three boys gave Tom's father a look like he was born yesterday.

"Dad! No disrespect meant, but sometimes you act like you were born yesterday. Everyone says that Evad is the worst teacher in the state."

"Yeah, that's for sure," said Alex. "There was a rumor at the end of last year that Mrs. Parkinson was going to retire, but why did they have to give eighth grade science to Evad?"

"So, who's this Mister or is it Misses Evad?" asked the father, innocently.

"It's an it," enlightened Tom, "I doubt if it's human."

Tom's father looked at Alex, hoping for further enlightenment.

"Not only that," said Tom's friend. "Do you know what his first name is?" And then, without giving Tom's father a chance to guess, he said, "Sleinad. Sleinad Evad. What kind of name is that?"

"Mr. Cobalt, you have to admit that no normal person has a first name like Sleinad," said Wayne.

"Okay, so his name is—unusual," said the father. "Gee, I wonder how Sleinad is spelled? Anyway, you shouldn't judge a person just because his name sounds stran—uh, unusual."

"My brother, Daryl, had him for physics last year," said Alex, as he pulled a yo-yo from his pocket and began to absent-mindedly make it climb up and down on the string. "He barely got out of the class alive."

"Hmm," said Mr. Cobalt. "As I recall your brother graduated and is now majoring in chemistry in college. It doesn't appear that he suffered too much harm by having had this Evad person as a science teacher."

Alex glanced at his friends, hoping for support.

"Believe me, Dad, the man's reputation is well deserved. If you took a vote of the students in our school on the teacher everyone wants to avoid, Evad would be the unanimous choice."

"Heck," added Wayne, "even the kids over at Central Penn would vote for Evad, and they're even in a different township. For that matter, it wouldn't surprise me if kids in the next state were having nightmares about him."

"If having this teacher worries you so much, maybe you three should go to the guidance counselor and get your schedules changed."

"Great idea, Dad."

"Yeah," said Alex. "It's worth a try. Evad can't be teaching all the eighth grade science classes because he must still have his senior high physics classes to teach."

"Only we better get to Mr. Serpens' office early," said Tom, "as everyone assigned to Evad's class will probably be there asking for a change of schedule."

"Gee, I was hoping to be in the same section again as you guys," said Wayne, "but not if I have to put up with Evad."

"Your grades were better than mine last year," said Tom, "so if I'm in the A section, you should be too."

"By the way, Alex," said Mr. Cobalt, changing the subject, "have you met your new neighbors yet?"

"Ah, yeah," said Alex, not sounding too happy about what he suspected might be coming.

"There are two girls in the family, is that right?"

"Yeah, I think so."

"I understand the oldest will also be starting the eighth grade this year."

"I dunno. She might be." Alex started inching towards the house in an effort to end the conversation, but Tom's father was relentless in keeping the subject focused on Alex's new neighbors.

"I met the Goulds yesterday. Sarah seems like a bright girl. Pretty too. Don't you think so?" Mr. Cobalt was smiling as he said it.

"Pretty?" said Alex. "Gee whiz, Mr. Ko, is that all you adults ever think about? Sex?"

Tom's father first stammered but quickly recovered. "Very funny, Alex. Now admit it. Don't you think she's cute?"

The other two boys were looking intently at Alex, smirks on their faces. Since playing both disinterested and ignorant hadn't worked, Alex switched tactics. "She has a big nose."

Tom gave a snicker at his friend's remark, but seeing his father's smile instantly vanish, the boy quickly stifled a follow-up snicker. Although Wayne had managed to partly stifle his snicker, his reaction had not gone unnoticed by Tom's father. While formulating a reply, Tom's dad studied the thin, boney features of Alex's face, but thought better of making any comparison to the boy's own nose.

"It's obvious that you three need some additional grooming in the fine art of learning to be gentlemen. As fate would have it, Alex, your father and I have already taken a step in that direction. We've arranged for you and Tom to stop by the Gould's house next Tuesday and escort Sarah to school."

"What!" said Tom, the snicker long forgotten and his features instantly distorted into one of panic. "But we always walk to school with Brad and Wayne, and I—I don't even know this girl."

"You heard me. You can call Brad and tell him that the plans have been changed. Of course," he turned to Wayne, "you and Brad are welcome to join Tom and Alex as escorts."

Wayne looked less than happy with Mr. Cobalt's suggestion.

"But, Mr. Ko, why us?" sputtered Alex. "It's not like she's our friend or anything."

"That's precisely the point, Alex. Sarah's new here. Since her sister is still in elementary school, she normally wouldn't know anyone at your school, but this way she'll start off knowing at least two of her fellow students. It will make the adjustment to a new school easier for her. Besides you're all Scouts. Isn't this the kind of things Scouts are supposed to do?"

The minds of the boys appeared to be working in sync. Was this the kind of things that Boy Scouts were supposed to do? No. Of course not. What a dumb statement. Scouting was about camping and hiking and getting filthy dirty and handling knives and axes and capsizing canoes and making fires and playing capture-the-flag in the woods in the middle of the night and cool stuff like that. All three boys opened their mouths at the same time to start to make those points, but upon seeing the expression on Mr. Cobalt's face, they thought better of it. "Besides," continued Mr. Cobalt, "I think there should be some consequence for that crack you made about Sarah's—uh, appearance."

"Hey, I didn't say anything about her nose," said Tom. "I've never even seen her."

"Don't think I didn't catch that snicker of yours. Besides, whatever you said or thought isn't the issue. Walking her to school is. It's the decent thing to do. It's another step in growing up."

"Well, at least we only have to do it the first day," said Alex. "We don't have to walk her home, do we?"

"Actually, your father and I offered to have you two walk her both to and from school, and not only for the first day of school, but every day."

"What!" exploded the Tom and Alex. Wayne gave out a hoot.

"Dad!"

"Mr. Ko!"

"How could you?"

"What a bummer!"

"Man, it's like we're being punished or something."

"I can't believe that my own father would agree to this."

"I originally only intended for you to do it the first day of school. It was your dad, Alex, who extended the offer for the whole school year, or at least until Sarah makes some new friends, and she and her parents decide that you can be off the hook."

"Hey," said Wayne, "if it makes you feel better I'll still join you, and I'll bet Brad will too as without us, he'll have to walk to school alone."

"Thanks," said Tom. "Misery loves company."

"You might change your mind," said Alex, "after you see Big Nose."

"Alex! That's the last time I want to hear words like that from you. I don't want to have to tell your parents what I just heard. Her name is Sarah, Sarah Gould, and she's a really nice girl." Mr. Cobalt turned on his son. "And Tom, if I hear anything out of you like I heard from Alex, you're going to get a taste of what sorry really means."

Tom wasn't sure what the expression "get a taste of what sorry really means" really meant, so he said, "You can count on me, Dad."

Alex said, "Sorry, Mr. Ko."

"Good. I'm glad that that's settled, and we all understand each other."

Tom was about to protest again but decided that was a bad idea as a troubling thought hit him. "Dad, did you say this girl was smart?"

"Yes. Apparently, Sarah is an excellent student."

"Uh, oh. That means she might be in the A section with us."

The only one who looked pleased at that possibility was Mr. Cobalt. Alex slapped his hands over his glasses and gave his head a shake. Lowering his hands, he said, "Gee, that would mean that what's-her-name would probably have Evad for science too. That's even more reason to switch science classes."

"Alex, her name is Sarah," said Tom's father. "A simple name like that shouldn't be so difficult for one of your intelligence to remember."

"Oh no, Dad," said Tom. "You don't understand. Alex isn't really bright. He's just the smartest of all the dumb kids in America." The three boys exchanged grins, as they resumed walking towards the house, followed by a cat and a dog.

Chapter 2
Sarah Rebecca Gould

On the day after Labor Day, 1959, neither Alex Banyon nor Tom Cobalt looked forward to the start of the new school year. Granted they didn't believe that Mr. Evad, their new science teacher, would turn out to be even half the monster he had been depicted. Prior experience had taught them that older students relished exaggerating the hazards to be faced in the upper grades, as they in turn similarly enjoyed embellishing stories about many of their former teachers for the ears of their younger siblings and friends. What actually weighed most heavy on the minds of the two boys that morning was a certain young member of the female sex by the name of Sarah Gould.

Promptly at 7:30 a.m., Tom knocked on the back door of the Banyon home. Mrs. Banyon greeted Tom as she opened the door. From behind his mother, Alex emerged dutifully attired for a new school year. He wore a white, starched, collared shirt, trousers and sneakers, and carried a notebook along with a brown bag that contained his lunch. His blond, ruffled hair wasn't slicked back, the way Tom's was. For once, the lenses of his glasses were free of smudges.

"Hello, Tom," said Alex's mother, sounding cheerful as always.

A meow caused the three to look down upon a large tabby cat with light tan, almost orange, fur sitting on its haunches and staring up at the humans.

"Hi, Tiger," said Tom. "Want to go to school with us?"

"No, no," laughed Mrs. Banyon. "Tiger has to stay here and guard the house. You boys have a good time at school today, and don't forget to pick up Sarah. She should be waiting for you. And be sure to be nice to her and treat her like a friend. Remember, she's new here and doesn't know anyone. Oh, and, Alex, did you get some change for milk?"

As the two friends made their way down the walk of the backyard, Alex responded to his Mom's instructions and queries with, "Yeah, Mom. Sure, Mom. Uh-huh. Don't worry, Mom."

After his mother closed the back door, Alex said, "Can you believe we have to do this?"

"I can believe you have to do it, after all she's your neighbor, but why my parents insist that I have to share in this upcoming torture is beyond me."

"Gee, thanks for the loyalty. Whatever happened to 'All for one and one for all?'"

"Working on the wilderness survival merit badge together is one thing," said Tom, "but walking a girl to school is going beyond the call to duty. Is her nose really that big?"

"You'll be able to judge for yourself soon enough."

Sarah's house was directly across the street from where Alex lived so the boys first walked through the side and front yards of the Banyon property before crossing the street. Once on the other side, their pace began to slow as they narrowed the distance to the foreboding looking front door of the Gould home. Alex couldn't help thinking of Zeno's paradox. Would it be possible for them to somehow pace themselves so that they would never reach their destination? Nevertheless, before he seemed to realize it, they were stepping upon the front stoop of the girl's home. The boys exchanged glances. They both swallowed. Alex assumed the responsibility of reaching for the doorbell. Before he could press it, the door opened as if by magic. A kindly looking woman wearing glasses, her dark hair drawn back in a bun, held open the door and said, "Hello, Alex, and you must be Tom?"

"Yes ma'am," said Tom, remembering his manners, and fearing that he might slip up and his parents get a bad report.

The woman stood to the side, still holding open the door. "Won't you come in? Sarah should be down in a minute."

Both boys thought to themselves, "Great! Just like a woman to be late." But barely had they thought the thought when a girl came bounding down the stairs. Upon spying the two boys standing in the hallway next to her mother, she pulled to a quick stop, the expression on her face rapidly changing from one of nonchalance to one of alarm and then panic.

"Sarah," said the woman, "this is Tom Cobalt, and of course, you already know Alex." Then turning to Tom, she said, "This is my daughter, Sarah."

Unlike most people meeting Sarah Gould for the first time, Tom's immediate attention was not drawn to Sarah's most notorious feature, that is, her nose, but oddly enough to her eyes. For a reason he could not fathom, he felt a sudden mild thump in his chest, as if his heart had skipped a beat. Nor was it the abject fear and terror that those eyes conveyed that captured the boy's interest. It was that they were the deepest, most gorgeous eyes he had ever beheld in his life, that, and the fact that the girl was staring at him as intently as he was staring at her. Upon realizing that she was staring, Sarah diverted her gaze to the floor and muttered a barely audible "Hi." Tom returned the brief greeting, and then tried to study the girl's nose without appearing to be too obvious about it. Well, he wouldn't have called it "big," but then again "petite" certainly would never be used to describe it, but it was nowhere near the rival of that of Cyrano de Bergerac's, which was what Alex had led him to expect.

Whereas Tom was on the tall side for his age, Sarah was on the short side of the norm for girls in the eighth grade. She had long, straight, light brown hair, almost blonde, and a pale complexion, the latter no doubt in part due to the raging anxiety that was coursing through every cubic centimeter of her body. When she raised her head, her slightly open mouth revealed to Tom that, like Alex, she wore braces.

Sarah's mom handed her daughter a notebook and a purse. "There's money for your lunch in there," said Mrs. Gould, indicating the purse. "Say goodbye to your father and sister before you leave."

Sarah turned and yelled in the direction of a doorway that led to the kitchen. "Bye, Dad. Bye, Anne."

In answer came the voice of a girl, followed by that of a man. "One minute, honey." A tall, balding man in a suit and tie emerged from the doorway, wiping his mouth with a napkin. He gave his daughter an affectionate hug. "Have a great first day at school, honey." Then he shook hands with the boys. "You must be Alex and Tom. I'm Sarah's father. It's awfully nice to let our Sarah walk to school with you." Both boys mumbled something that sort of sounded like, "glad-to-meet-you-we-better-get-going-or-we'll-be-late," but at least to Mr. Gould they seemed polite, which was much more important to him than any exhibition of clear diction.

As if on cue, the boys turned to leave, with Sarah following behind them, while her parents went through the same sort of goodbye salutations that Alex's mom had used. Sarah occasionally glanced back at her parents and nodded.

When the three teens had reached the sidewalk, Mr. Gould turned to his wife. "Do you think this was such a good idea?"

"I'm sure it will work out for the best," said Mrs. Gould. "At least this way Sarah will already know someone at her new school. Better yet I believe she and the boys will be in the same classes."

"Perhaps you're right. But remember what happened at Sarah's last school."

"I know," said the wife, sounding less than happy. "Sarah just has a hard time making friends. But I understand that Alex Banyon is also a good student. Maybe likes will attract. Besides, they both seem to be polite, well-mannered boys. I can't imagine them making fun of our Sarah."

"So how come she's walking behind them, instead of beside them?"

"Give it time. Give it time," said the mother, trying to sound hopeful.

During the walk from the Gould home to the nearby highway, the boys appeared to be totally oblivious of the girl who tagged along behind them. Upon reaching the street corner, the three halted to wait for the stoplight to change so they could cross. Without warning, Alex jerked around. "You're Jewish, aren't you?"

The suddenness of the question caused the girl to jump, almost as if she had received a physical blow. Tom and the girl stared at Alex, Tom appearing embarrassed by Alex's question, whereas the girl at first seemed shocked that someone had spoken to her. "What makes you think I'm Jewish?"

"Your name, Gould. Isn't that Jewish?"

The girl glared at the boy, not answering.

"Not to mention your first name, Sarah."

"Does it make a difference if I'm Jewish? I mean, your name is Alexander. Does that make you Greek?"

The look of surprise on his friend's face caused Tom to chuckle. "Actually, his parents did name him after Alexander the Great because of his blond, curly hair."

"They did not!" said Alex, eying his friend as if Tom had driven an assassin's dagger into his back. He hated to be called Alexander. "Besides, I was a baby when they named me, and in case you don't know it, babies are bald." Having thoroughly demolished his friend's statement, he turned his attention back to the girl. "So, are you Jewish, or is there a problem with the question?"

"I don't see where my religion is any of your business," said Sarah. "That's a really ignorant attitude."

Tom decided it was time to intercede. "Listen, Alex doesn't mean anything by the question. He gets weird once in a while, like sometimes asking even total strangers dumb questions. If it makes you feel any better, he's supposed to be a Catholic, although I think Alex's an atheist or the anti-Christ or something like that, but don't let his parents know."

"Agnostic," corrected Alex.

"Atheist, agnostic, I can never keep them straight," confessed the other boy.

"Atheist literally means 'without God,'" said the girl. "Usually it denotes a person who has a strong belief that there is no God. Agnostic is a term coined by the philosopher Bertrand Russell, and it literally means 'without knowledge.' So, when Alex says he's an agnostic, he means that he's ignorant of whether there is a God."

"Hey Alex, I think that's the second time she's called you an ignoramus."

"Now look what you did," said Alex, giving the girl an angry look. "You made us miss the light." He turned and sprinted across the highway, followed by Tom, with Sarah being left behind.

Reaching the far sidewalk, the boys stopped. "What was that all about?" said Tom.

"Practicing my detective skills. You know how I look up to Sherlock Holmes. I was trying to confirm my hunch that she's Jewish. It's not like I have something against Jewish people or anything."

"Sure, I know that. It just seems like an odd way to open a conversation. And how is asking her blunt out honing your detective skills?"

"Well, you notice that she never answered the question."

"So, you think she's Jewish?"

"Yeah."

"And she's ashamed of it or something?"

"Yeah."

"So?"

"So what?"

"I don't know," said Tom, confused as to what Alex was trying to accomplish, and thinking it better to drop the subject as Sarah was now crossing the highway.

"Hurry up," Alex shouted at the girl. "You're going to make us late for school."

As Sarah reached the curb, Tom spied two boys coming down the sidewalk on their side of the street. "There they are," he said, giving the approaching boys a wave. "You're late as usual," laughed Tom.

"Blame it on Wayne's mom," said Brad.

As the newcomers joined them, Tom said, "Brad, Wayne, this is Sarah."

"I'm most delighted to meet you," said the girl.

"Uh-huh," said Brad, the shortest and stoutest of the four boys. His straight, dark hair, cavernous brown eyes, and prominent eyebrows seem to add additional menace to the less than friendly look he cast at Sarah.

"Likewise," muttered Brad's companion, Wayne, trying to sound nonchalant, yet his eyes failed to hide the interest with which they studied the girl. Sarah noticed and gave the lanky boy a faint trace of a smile which, for the briefest of moments, he appeared to return.

"Hey," said Brad, "is it true we're all in Evad's science class?"

"Yeah," answered Tom, as the group started to head down the side street in the direction of the school, Tom walking beside Brad, Alex walking with Wayne, and Sarah trailing behind. "Alex and I are going to see Mr. Serpens and try to get our schedules changed."

"Lotsa luck," snickered Brad.

While the conversation between Tom and Brad continued as to how Alex and Tom hoped to avoid having the dreaded Mr. Evad as their science teacher, Wayne took a quick glance behind him at Sarah, who seemed to be intently studying the cracks in the sidewalk as she walked. The boy caught Alex's eye and made a quick motion with his head to indicate the girl, followed by a gesture of his finger pointing at his nose. Alex's response was to frantically shake his head from side to side, and at the same time silently form the word "no" with his mouth so as to make Wayne understand that the subject of Sarah Gould's nose was definitely off limits. Unbeknown to them, Sarah had noticed the exchange and had correctly interpreted its meaning. She resumed studying the cracks in the sidewalk, her eyes starting to moisten. She kept her thoughts to herself during the remainder of the walk to school

When the boys dropped her off at the school office to get her class schedule, Alex said, "Meet us back here at the end of school."

Sarah answered with an almost inaudible, "Okay."

With the morning homeroom ritual completed, the students of eighth grade section A were waiting for the bell to sound signifying the start of the first period. There came a knock at the door. Mrs. Montague, the homeroom teacher opened the door and in walked Sarah, handing Mrs. Montague a piece of paper. As Tom, Brad and Wayne exchanged glances, Alex emitted a low moan. When Mrs. Montague finished reading the note, she addressed the students.

"Class, this is a new student, Sarah Gould. She just moved here from New York."

"What did I tell you?" whispered Alex to Tom. "A lot of Jewish people live in New York City."

"She said New York," whispered Tom, "not New York City, and, besides . . ." Tom gave a frustrated sigh, and shook his head. "Oh, forget it."

"I can't believe she's in our section. That means we'll probably be stuck with her in every class."

"Courage, Einar. Remember there's always gym class."

The first class of the day was American History, taught by Miss Odavsky. The class went through the usual first day of school routine of roll taking, seat assignments, text book distribution, and so forth. With some time remaining before the end of period bell, Miss

Odavsky decided to start the first lesson.

"If you will turn to page twelve in your textbook, you will see a picture of Leif Ericson, a Viking." The students turned to the indicated page to view a picture of a bearded man wearing a conical helmet with two horns attached. The teacher continued her lesson, her face beaming. "I'm sure many of you thought that Christopher Columbus was the first one to discover America, but as you'll learn in this class, scholars now think that the Vikings did several centuries before Columbus."

"Excuse me," rang out a voice. All eyes turned to the owner of the voice. It was Sarah.

"Yes, young lady," said Miss Odavsky.

"Well, first off, it's incorrect to say that Leif Ericson was the first one to discover America, as obviously America had been discovered thousands of years earlier by the Indians."

"Ah, that's true. I guess I should have said the first European . . ."

"I'd also like to point out that the picture is inaccurate. Viking helmets didn't have horns," the girl continued. Miss Odavsky features took a downturn as she quickly consulted her seating chart.

"Sarah, if we have a comment, we raise our hand and wait to be recognized. We just don't speak out."

"I'm sorry, but I thought I should point out that the picture is wrong. The Vikings didn't have horns on their helmets."

"Well, Sarah, I don't know where you got that idea from, but everyone knows that Viking helmets had horns. And I might remind you that this textbook is written by a committee of expert historians and has been approved by the State Board of Education. I think they know more about history than you do."

"But—, " Sarah started to counter. Miss Ordavsky cut her off with a lecture on the authority of teachers and the ignorance of students.

While Miss Odavsky was "correcting" the errant student, Tom leaned towards Alex. "Hey, Einar," he whispered. "Isn't Sarah right? Viking didn't have horns, did they?"

"Yeah, that's right," said Alex. "And neither did their helmets." Alex snickered at his own joke. "Remember the movie, *The Vikings?*" Alex continued, referring to a recent movie from which the boys had borrowed the names of Einar and Ragnar. "They got it right."

"That's what I thought. So why don't you tell Miss Odavsky that Sarah's right?"

"Are you kidding? Remember old Heartburn last year? Teachers take a dim view of students who have a habit of pointing out to them that they're ignoramuses."

"And I might remind some other students in this class," said Miss Odavsky, fixing Tom and Alex with her eye, "that carrying on a personal conversation while someone else has the floor is unacceptable."

"Sorry ma'am," replied Alex, apologetically.

"It won't happen again," added Tom, trying to imitate the facial expression of a scolded hound dog.

Miss Odavsky gave the two a smile. Such polite boys, she thought, as she noted their names on her seating chart.

In the third period mathematics class, Sarah corrected the teacher's pronunciation of the name of one of the authors of the textbook. Like the history teacher, the math teacher also noted Sarah's name on her seating chart. During the next period, Sarah broke her previous record by attempting to correct the English teacher, Mr. Davies, within five minutes of the start of the class. Mr. Davies acknowledged the correction and thanked Sarah for bringing it to his attention. His attitude towards Sarah was less accommodating by the close of the class by which time Sarah had interrupted the lesson four more times, twice by correcting other students and twice more by correcting him. With the final interruption, Mr. Davies proceeded to give Sarah a personal lecture, similar to that delivered by Miss Odavsky, as to the role and place of the student in a classroom in relation to that of the teacher. Tom and Alex joined many of their classmates in shaking their heads in disbelief as to what was happening.

Lunch found Tom and Alex targeting a cafeteria table where Wayne was seated. As they approached the table, Wayne looked up and asked, "What's up guys?" Without waiting for an answer, he continued, "Wow wasn't Miss Know-it-all a pain in the neck this morning?"

Tom took a seat next to Wayne, emptying the contents from his lunch bag. "What did we do to deserve this?"

"No doubt," said Wayne, "it's all over the school by now. And to think you have to walk her to and from school on top of that?"

"It's not like we have much choice in the matter."

"Yeah," chimed in Alex. "Stupid parents and their bright ideas."

Alex opened his lunch bag as Brad sat down with his lunch tray. "Can you believe Miss Schnozzola this morning?"

Alex ignored the question. Tom asked the newcomer, "You want to trade your Jello for half my Cracker Jacks?"

"Okay," agreed Brad. "Can't tell what flavor it is anyway."

"Looks like snail barf flavor to me," said Wayne, giving the quivering bowl of gelatin a disgusted look. He elbowed Tom to get his attention. "Isn't that Banana Beak over there?" He motioned in the direction of an empty table at which Sarah was seating herself with her lunch tray.

"Sure is," said Tom. For some reason the terms the other boys were using to refer to Sarah made him uncomfortable.

Sarah unfolded a paper napkin on her lap and proceeded to glance about the cafeteria. When she spotted the four boys all staring at her, she quickly looked down at her tray and fumbled her fork when she tried to pick it up. She recovered the fork and proceeded to pick at her food.

"Well, you mush almit dat da name zoots her," said Brad, spraying some pieces of pasta out of his mouth while talking.

"Oh, I don't know," said Wayne, grinning. "If you ignore the nose, she's kind of cute. Nice body. What do you think, Tom?" He let out a snicker.

"I think you're a moron," was the answer.

"Listen, if you two want to volunteer to take our places in walking her to school," said Alex, "I'm sure something can be arranged."

"That's okay," said Brad. "We all have our crosses to bear."

"Say, do you think she looks Jewish?" asked Alex.

"Huh?" said Wayne.

"For some reason, Alex is determined to prove that she's Jewish," explained Tom. "Don't ask me why? Just that Alex probably can't stand having one of his theories proved wrong."

"Doesn't look Jewish to me," answered Wayne. "Then again, what exactly does a Jew look like? I mean, Ian's Jewish, isn't he and he doesn't look any different from anyone else. And so's Cynthia. But could you tell by looking at them?" The others pondered Wayne's point for a moment, before Wayne continued. "Hmm, that gives me an idea." With that, the boy swung around on his stool, and tapped a girl sitting at the neighboring table on her shoulder. "Hey, Cynth. See that girl sitting over there by herself?"

Cynthia Cohen, who had been in the same classes with the four boys that morning, looked over to where Sarah sat. "You mean Miss High-and-mighty-know-it-all?"

"Yeah. Does she look Jewish to you?"

"No, she looks like a jerk, same as you."

"Ouch! Say, would you do us a favor and go over and ask her? We have sort of a bet going on here."

"Go over and ask her yourself. She looks like your type of woman." At that, the other girls sharing the table with Cynthia giggled, and the other three boys all gave Wayne a smirk. But Wayne was not easily deterred.

"If you do it, we'll give you Brad's boiled broccoli."

"Yuck! You're dumber than you look."

"Give you Brad's dessert."

"Hey!" protested Brad. "Who said you could give away my cake?"

"Shut-up, Brad. We're doing serious negotiating here."

Cynthia turned and studied the cake. It actually looked appetizing, even if it was from the school cafeteria. "Okay, but first the cake."

"Deal," said Wayne, snatching up the plate with Brad's cake before the latter could stop him.

Cynthia took the plate and sat it down before the girl sitting next to her. "Guard it while I'm gone and we'll split it four ways when I get back." The other girls at the table all nodded in agreement as Cynthia got up and walked over to where Sarah sat. Everyone at the other two tables turned to watch. Cynthia sat down next to the new girl. Sarah, who had been focusing on her meal, gave a jerk of surprise when she sensed someone taking the stool next to her. Cynthia said something to the new girl who in turned simply gave her visitor a blank expression. Cynthia smiled, stood up and returned to her table. As she did so, Sarah, appearing bewildered, followed Cynthia with her eyes. She was greeted with the spectacle of two tables of students staring at her. Her look of bewilderment turned to one of alarm. She glanced to the left and right. It now seemed to her that everyone in the cafeteria was staring at her. For a moment Sarah sat as if petrified. She picked up her books, stood up, and left the cafeteria as fast as she could without breaking into a run. Upon reaching the safety of the hallway, she fumbled in her purse in search of a tissue with which to wipe her eyes.

"Hey, she left her tray on the table," observed Brad. "That's against the rules. Mr. Johnson isn't going to like that."

Cynthia sat back down.

"Well," asked Wayne. "What did she say?"

Cynthia turned around. "What else do you have to offer?"

"Hey, you—you two timing wench," said Wayne.

"Two timing wench?" said the girl. "Wench? My what a big vocabulary we have these days."

"How about half a box of Cracker Jacks?" offered Tom, holding out the box.

The girl took the offering. "She didn't say anything. Just gave me a dumb look. But I don't think she's Jewish."

"Why not?" asked Tom.

"As I said, when I asked her, she just gave me a dumb look."

"Ah, that doesn't prove anything," said Alex. "She was probably in shock from seeing your ugly face."

"What!" Cynthia jerked the box of candy at Alex, showering him with Cracker Jacks.

"Food fight," yelled Brad and Wayne in unison, and the cafeteria instantly erupted in a chaos of shouts, laughter, and flying food.

"Is telling us about what happened the first day of school really necessary?" asked Jerry, sounding irritated.

"Yes, I think so, Jer," was the guest's reply. "Just bear with me."

"I would have been ashamed if I were you," said Mrs. Gould. "I can't believe you treated Sarah so badly."

"I'm sorry, Mrs. Gould," said the young man. "I'm certainly not proud of the way I treated Sarah, but that's the way it was. Please remember that we were kids then." Then he turned back to Jerry. "Say, whatever happened to Wayne Franklin?"

"I don't know. I didn't really know the boy."

"I'll ask Brad," said Anne. "He'd probably know."

"That right," said the young man, "Brad's now the county sheriff."

Jerry sat up. "How did you know Brad was the sheriff?"

The young man's expression froze for a moment. "Uh, Mom mentioned it."

Jerry gave his aunt a questioning look. Aunt Nan glanced at the man who claimed to be her son, then at her nephew. Even without the slight shake of her head, which she tried to hide from the others at the table, Jerry could read the answer in his aunt's eyes. She didn't remember telling the young man that Brad was a sheriff.

Chapter 3
Sleinad Evad

Tom noted how different the atmosphere in this classroom was from that of his other classes. Normally there was a lot of chatter among the students while awaiting the arrival of the teacher. Instead, the ominous silence in the room reminded Tom of a morgue. Except for Sarah, who remained blissfully ignorant, the students all shared a common dread of their new science instructor, for the man's reputation preceded him like odor does a skunk. The sudden ringing of the late bell caused some of the students to jump. As if on cue, the door opened and into the room strode Sleinad Evad.

Seeing the man in the flesh did nothing to lessen their foreboding. The look of him was lean and hungry, as if his skin had shrunk over the underlying skull. The irises of the eyes that gripped the class with their stare were a striking grey-blue. His head, the top of which easily towered six feet above the floor, was capped by slicked-back hair so dark it might have been dyed with black ink. Above each eye was an equally dark eyebrow looking as if it had been painted on the underlying skin. Although many of the fairer skinned students in the classroom displayed varying degrees of tans acquired over the summer vacation, the teacher's skin was as pale as that of a henchman of Death. The suit he wore and its matching tie were of such a dark blue color as to appear black. To Tom he was the personification of Charon, the ferryman of

Hades, the grim specter who carried the dead across the River Styx.

The teacher stopped behind the lab table that also served as a desk and deposited his briefcase in a drawer hidden from the view of the students. He studied the face of each student in a manner reminiscent of a vulture surveying a field littered with dead and dying critters, candidates for its next meal. When his eyes came to rest upon Tom, they lingered there for what seemed to the boy a far longer time than he had used to scrutinize the other students. Tom gave an involuntary swallow. He could have sworn the hairs on the back of his neck were stiffening. "Why is he staring at me?" thought Tom. "I haven't done anything. He doesn't even know who I am."

What made the situation even more eerie to the boy was the realization that, as he looked into those sunken, sinister eyes, he couldn't recall them ever blinking. Before Evad broke eye contact, Tom could have sworn he saw the man cast him a hint of a smile. If such was the case, the smile immediately vanished as Evad's attention shifted to the next student.

Tom thought of Sarah. He turned to look at the new girl sitting in the back of the room. After her behavior in the earlier classes, no one seemed anxious to sit next to her, so Sarah naturally took up residence in the last row of each new classroom. He caught the girl's eye. "Don't be a fool, Sarah," thought Tom. "Keep your mouth shut. This is one really mean hombre. You don't want to cross him." Sarah gave Tom a perplexed look and forced a smile. Tom turned back around and again caught the man who reminded him more of a mortician than a teacher looking directly at him.

When the dark being finally took his seat on a stool behind the lab table, there was a sound of exhaling throughout the classroom, as if every student had been holding his breath for the past couple of minutes. Evad flipped open the attendance book in front of him and, with his left hand, picked up a pen. Looking up, he addressed the class.

"This is Introduction to Physical Science." His voice clearly enunciated every syllable as it resonated about the room with a deep baritone. "If any of you happen to be in the wrong class, leave now." Although the fondest wish of each student was to do just that, no one moved. "As I call your name, answer with 'present.' Anderson, Patricia."

"Here," came the reply from a student sitting in the second row.

The man stood and quickly walked around the lab table, stopping in front of Patricia Anderson's desk. Patricia gave Evad a look of sheer terror. The teacher leaned forward, his face close to the girl's. "Miss Anderson, I said answer with 'present.'"

"Yes, sir," said the student, her voice quivering.

"Then do it," he said. The volume of his voice had not risen, but somehow his comment sounded like a shout.

"Yes, si—i—r—r. Present."

Evad returned to his stool. He looked straight ahead as he checked off Patricia Anderson's name in his roll book. "Banyon, Alexander."

"Present," said Alex. Evad looked at Alex, and then made another checkmark in the roll book.

"Carlisle, Sharon."

"Present." Tom noticed that Evad was no longer looking at the attendance book, either to read the next name or to make sure the checkmark was positioned in the correct spot. It was as if he had the class roster memorized.

"Cobalt, Thomas."

"Ah—" Tom's mouth was dry. "Pr—present," he managed to squeak out in a hoarse whisper. Evad had again locked that awful stare on him. Tom again swallowed as he returned the stare. "Why is he looking at me?" thought Tom. "He didn't do this with the other students." Tom's right knee began to shake. He reached a hand down to steady it. Evad's stare was like that of a mythical serpent, holding its prey in some sort of diabolical, hypnotic trance. Out of the corner of his eye Tom noted that some of the other students wore puzzled expressions as they shifted their attention from him to the teacher and back again. Obviously, he wasn't imagining things. Again, Evad's mouth formed a faint trace of a smile.

"Thomas Cobalt," said Evad. Then, as if he was thinking out load, "Tom Cobalt. Interesting." For the first time since he had started taking attendance, the teacher glanced down at the open book on his desk, and with a flourish entered another checkmark. Tom looked at Alex. His friend could only answer with a shrug of his shoulders.

"Cohen, Cynthia," came the voice from the front of room. As the roll call resumed, Tom experienced another involuntary shiver.

Next to Evad's seeming fixation with Tom, the strangest thing about the class was that Sarah never made a comment. Tom concluded that either Evad had made no mistakes, or that even Sarah was too intimidated by the man to dare say anything.

As they exited the classroom, Alex turned to Tom. "What was up between you and Mr. Chuckles in there?"

"I don't know, and I think I don't want to know," answered Tom. "Why pick on me? It's not like I have an older brother who once had him for a course. From all the things your brother, Daryl, said about Evad, you'd think he would be on your case, not mine."

"It's too bad you-know-who didn't do her usual 'I'm so smart and you're all such morons' act in there," said Brad. "She could have taken some of the heat off you."

As in response to a premonition, Tom glanced behind him and saw Sarah entering the hall from the classroom only a few feet away.

"Ssh," Tom cautioned his friends. "Here she comes."

Alex lowered his voice. "Maybe it's best she knows what we think of her. I say the sooner the better. Then her parents can recruit a new pair of babysitters for her."

When the girl caught up with them, Tom said, "We're going to our lockers so we'll meet you at the same door where we came in this morning." Outside of the incident with Cynthia Cohen in the cafeteria during lunch, it was the first time another student had spoken to Sarah since she had arrived at school that morning.

"Okay," said the girl, seeming at a loss for words.

When Tom and Alex reached the rendezvous point, Sarah alone was waiting for them as Brad and Wayne were still at a meeting with the band director. As the three stood by the school exit, no one said anything. Alex, as was his custom whenever he had some time to kill, pulled a yo-yo out of his pocket and began to run through his repertoire of yo-yo tricks. After some minutes had passed, Alex and Tom began to exchange glances, and then a series of discreet hand signals, as each tried to convince the other it was *his* duty to start a conversation with the girl. During this period of silence, but one of increasingly more desperate hand signal communications, Sarah was content to engage in a detailed examination of the pattern of the floor tile. It was finally Alex who threw in the towel and accepted the duty of trying to act civil to the member of the opposite sex with the larger than average nose standing nearby. "So how was your first day at East Pencreek?"

The girl looked first at Alex, then at Tom, and then back at Alex before answering. "It was . . ." She paused, and then took a brief glance at the floor tile before continuing, "Listen, I know that I can get on people's nerves by asking—uh, so many questions and things, but it's just—just the way I am." She lifted her head and looked at Tom. "I'm sorry. It's just that I'm the curious type."

Alex's jaw dropped. He started to say something, but then snapped his mouth shut and gave Tom a pleading look as if begging him to please take up the gauntlet. Tom gave his friend a nod signifying his acceptance of the challenge. "Sarah, you didn't ask any questions. Instead you were always telling people that they were wrong. I mean, you kept finding fault with everybody, the teachers, the students . . . Why, when we were changing classes between second and third periods, you even told Mr. Hobson, the janitor, that he was using the wrong kind of brass polish."

Alex gave his friend a thumbs-up look as if to say, "Way to go, pal. That's telling her!"

At first, Sarah was speechless. She stared at the taller boy as if in shock.

"Of course, I did," she finally said. "What do you expect me to do? Don't you think people should be told when they make mistakes? I mean, this is a school. Isn't truth important? Tell me one thing I said that was wrong."

"Sarah!" Alex almost growled at the girl. "No one likes a know-it-all."

"I'd rather be right than liked. Don't you think you should stand up for truth? Or maybe it's that you're jealous. Maybe you can't stand it that a girl is smarter than you."

Alex rolled his eyes. Then he shot back. "Okay, Miss Know-it-all. If you're so darn smart, then answer this. In a non-leap year how many months have twenty-eight days?"

"That's easy," said the girl. "Just one, February."

"No, they all do," laughed Alex. Tom nodded, smiling.

"That's not fair," wailed the girl.

"Okay, try this one," said Alex. "What's the nearest star to the Earth?"

"That's easy. It's Alpha Centauri," said the girl, smugly.

Alex flashed a victorious grin, the sight of which seemed to crumble the girl's confidence in her answer. "Well, I mean it's the Alpha Centauri system, which is composed of three stars. The actual star in the system that is nearest Earth is thought to be Proxima Centauri." When she saw that her further clarification of the answer failed to pierce Alex's look of triumph, she gave the other boy a pleading look, as if asking Tom to explain where she had gone wrong.

"Actually," said Tom, "I always thought the nearest star to the Earth was the sun."

"That's not fair," whined the girl again. "That was a trick question." Both boys reacted with a triumphant snicker to which Sarah arched her eyebrows and cast them a menacing look, then turned and stomped out of the building. She stopped just beyond the doorway, and, with a sigh, let her body slump against the wall so that she was out of sight of the boys. She gave her head a remorseful shake, obviously upset at being fooled by such questions.

Sarah had no sooner disappeared when Brad and Wayne rounded the corner of the hallway. In a loud voice that was clearly audible to the out-of-sight girl, Brad said, "Hi, guys. Where's Banana Beak?"

Alex and Tom cringed. Tom started to point to the doorway with one hand while motioning the two newcomers to silence with the other, but the damage had been done. Sarah stepped into the doorway, placing herself in plain sight of the boys. She gave them the most savage look of loathing she could manage, as least the most savage one she could muster considering that her eyes were quickly filling with tears, and then turned, and broke into a run.

For several seconds the boys stood there and watched her hurry out of the school yard. Finally, Brad said, "Looks like old times again, huh?"

"Sure looks that way," said Tom, nodding his head in agreement. He noted that Brad and Wayne were smiling, but the expression on Alex's face was anything but happy.

Sarah Gould sat on the couch in her living room, huddled in her mother's arms. Among a number of pauses for some frantic sobbing, she had finally managed to complete the story of her first day of school.

"I want to go home," she wailed to her mother. "I hate this place. Why can't we go back to Albany?"

"This is our home now," her mother tried to reason. "I'm sorry, Sarah, but we have to make the best of it."

117

"Everyone here hates me," sniffled the girl. "I don't have any friends."

"You have to give it time," said her mother. "I know how tough it seems now, but things will get better."

"No, they won't. They all hate me. They make fun of me. Everyone in the cafeteria was laughing at me. No one sits with me. They all make fun of my nose. They think I'm ugly. And they're all jealous of me because I'm so smart."

Mrs. Gould gave her daughter another hug. Of course, this was not the first time she had gone through this scene with her daughter. Sarah's experiences during the two years they had lived in Albany were, for the most part, like a continual rerun of her first day at East Pencreek High, although Sarah was obviously trying to convince herself that things really had been different in New York. She had made one friend while there, and certainty one friend was better than none. "Well," thought Mrs. Gould, "I might as well cut to the chase, and get the rest of the story while we're at it."

"How were your new teachers?"

Sarah looked up. The image of her mother's face was blurred by the tears. "Most of the teachers here are as ignorant as those at my last school," she sniffed as she reached for another tissue. "None of them seem to appreciate it when I pointed out mistakes they made."

Her mother sighed. "Sarah, we've talked about this before. You're a bright person. You're only thirteen, and you're probably better read and know more than most adults, even some with a college education, but you have to realize that most people don't like to be corrected, especially in front of others."

"I'm sorry, Mom. It's just hard for me to sit there and listen to some of the dumb things they say without speaking up."

"I know dear. But I think if you try to correct other people less, that some of the problems . . . You might find it easier to make friends. It's bad enough that you're having a tough time getting along with your fellow students. You don't need to have the teachers disliking you too."

"So, what am I supposed to do? Act dumb? And even if I did, then all I would be to them is a dumb person with a big nose instead of a smart person with a big nose."

Mrs. Gould gave another sigh. "I understand, dear. I'm not saying you have to act dumb. Just try to put yourself in the other person's shoes and maybe things will make more sense to you."

"I'm sorry, Mom. Please don't make me go back there." Sarah gave another sniffle and sat up. "And I definitely don't want those boys walking me to school. I hate them."

"Please don't use the word 'hate.' You know I don't approve of that word."

"Sorry Mom. I thoroughly detest them then." Sniffle.

"I understand. I'll call their parents tonight and tell them that."

"You're going to tell the parents that I thoroughly detest their sons?"

"No, silly," laughed Mrs. Gould. "I'm going to tell them that the boys won't be expected to walk you to school." She gave her daughter another hug, and in response Sarah wrapped her arms around her mother's waist. They sat there for some time without saying anything, just emitting more sniffles. Then Mrs. Gould decided to try another tack.

"Sarah, I don't know if there's a heaven or hell. I'm inclined to believe that God certainly made a heaven for the faithful, but I can't imagine Him making a hell."

Mrs. Gould's daughter lifted her head. "Why not?"

"Because I think God is all-loving. How could an all-loving, all-for-giving God ever allow anyone to suffer for eternity?" Sarah returned her head to the crook of her mother's arm. "I think that the only place one can find hell is here on Earth. I know that bad things can happen to good people, things that are certainly beyond their control. I certainly don't understand why such things should happen. That's probably only for God to know."

"You mean like what happened to Job in the Bible?" asked the girl.

"Yes, something like that. Job certainly did nothing to deserve all the ills that befell him. But there are other people who have only themselves to blame for some of the bad things that happen to them."

"Like someone who doesn't want to work so he steals and when he gets caught goes to jail?"

"That's a good example. What I'm getting at is that some people make their own hell."

Sarah sat up. "I understand, but I don't see what this has to do with people being mean to me."

Mrs. Gould paused while a moment. "It's not only bad people who can make their world a hell. Good people can do it too." When her daughter didn't show any sign of understanding, her mother took a deep breath. "Sarah, it's hard for me to say this, but I think that you may be to blame for much of what happens to you."

Sarah's lower lip began to quiver. "What are you saying? It's not my fault that I'm ugly."

"Sarah, I'm not talking about your appearance, and you're not ugly. I agree that it's not your fault that some of the other students make fun of your appearance. What I'm talking about is your behavior at school, your habit of correcting other people. Didn't you hear anything I said earlier?"

"Yes." Mrs. Gould's daughter put her face in her hands and slowly moved her head from side to side. "Yes, I did," she said, her voice muffled by her hands. "I'm sorry." The girl dropped her hands and again looked at her mother. "It's just that I find it hard to be quiet when someone says something that I know to be wrong."

Mrs. Gould began to rub her daughter's back. "Sarah you are incredibly bright. You are probably the most intelligent person I've ever known, and I'm proud that you're my daughter. But being intelligent doesn't necessarily make one wise."

Sarah came up for air and fixed her mother with her moist eyes. "So how do I get wisdom?"

"I'm afraid that's something that usually comes only with time."

Sarah gave another sniffle, and then forced a weak smile. "Well, maybe I can use my intelligence to figure out a way to travel through time. Then I might get wisdom."

Her mother returned the girl's smile, and then continued to gently massage her back as Sarah again rested her head in the curve of her mother's arm. "Did you meet anyone at school whom you think you might get to like?"

Sarah hesitated before answering, as if taking a moment to carefully consider the question. "Actually, there was, but 'like' isn't the right word. Respect. There was one person there whom I definitely respect."

"And who is that, dear?"

"The science teacher, Mr. Evad. He seemed really intelligent. And he made all the students respect him, especially that awful Tom Cobalt."

Mrs. Gould shook her head. "That's not exactly what I had in mind, dear."

That evening Mrs. Gould called Mrs. Banyon. She said that Sarah had a good first day at East Pencreek High, and was appreciative of having Alex walk her to school. She also said that she understood how it might be uncomfortable for the boys to have to walk to school with a girl, and that since Sarah had adjusted so well, that Alex could be relieved of his escort duty. She sincerely thanked Mrs. Banyon for letting Alex help Sarah through her first day in a strange new school. She then called Mrs. Cobalt and repeated what she had told Alex's mom. She carefully avoided giving either mother cause for suspicion.

"Oh, how I remember that week," said Mrs. Gould. Anne handed her mother a tissue for the tears. "My poor Sarah. If only I could have done something more

to help her."

"Just where is all this heading?" asked Jerry, picking up a dinner roll. "It's starting to sound like a bad soap opera. When do we get to the little green men and flying saucers?"

"I assure you, Jer, it's all relevant," said the young man who claimed to be Jerry's long, lost cousin. "It's really best that I touch on certain details. After all, nothing kills a good mystery like skipping most of the story and jumping to the last page to find out who did it."

"I think we should let Tom tell it as he thinks best," said Anne. "Actually, I'm finding it interesting, although I feel for Sarah. We moved here the summer before I started sixth grade, and I can certainly relate to some of the things she must have gone through."

"Come on now," said Jerry. "You didn't have people making fun of your nose."

"Really, honey. I don't think that's the point."

"Dad, Mom," interjected Brett. "Can't we get back to the story?"

"Yes, let's," agreed Anne, giving her husband a sour look.

But before the storyteller could resume his tale, the East Pencreek Chief of Police piped up. "I take it that these three kids, Tom, Alex and Sarah, were the three that disappeared that night back in '59?"

"That's an excellent guess," said the young man. "Phil, I can see why you're now the Chief of Police. Yes, Alex and Sarah were two of the others that disappeared that night."

"When you say 'two of the others,'" asked Anne, "you mean there were more?"

"The teacher, Evad," said Jerry. "He was also never seen again after that night."

"And one other," added the young man.

"Huh?" said Aunt Nan. "I don't recall any mention of another."

"No, there was one more—five altogether. But I'm getting ahead of myself."

Chapter 4
Trials and Tribulations at East Pencreek High

As Florence Sanders exited the office of Mr. Serpens, the new junior high guidance counselor, the school secretary gave Tom a nod. "You may go in now," she said. "Just introduce yourself and get to the point."

Tom, who had been waiting on the bench in the hall with Alex, stood up and entered the office, carefully closing the door behind him. At the desk sat a man who appeared to be fairly young, like Miss Achinson, the previous guidance counselor, who had unexpectedly and tragically passed away a few days after the end of the previous school year at the age of thirty. Even seated, one could see that he was tall of stature with a trim build. Dressed in a light grey suit, he was studying some papers as Tom entered. Without looking up, he said, "Please take a seat."

Tom did as he was instructed. He cleared his throat, and began to say, "I'm Tom—," just as Mr. Serpens raised his head. As the man's eyes fell upon the boy, the pleasant smile of greeting Mr. Serpens had been wearing immediately vanished to be replaced by an expression of— shock? The abrupt change that had come over the counselor so startled Tom that his voice died in mid-sentence.

For what must have been several seconds, the two sat there with their mouths slightly open, staring at each other, the only sound in the room being that of the ticking of a clock on Mr. Serpens' filing cabinet. Then just as abruptly, the man's welcoming grin returned, as he finished Tom's sentence for him. "—Cobalt."

"Yes," said Tom, thinking he must now appear to be totally dumbfounded to the student advisor.

"And how may I help you, Tom?" said Mr. Serpens, still fixing the boy with a friendly smile along with an aura of cheerfulness that conveyed an eagerness to hear the boy's every concern and problem.

"It's seventh period science," said Tom. "I was wondering if I could rearrange my schedule to switch to the other physical science class? Oh, yeah, and, uh—actually, Alex Banyon is outside waiting to see you with the same request, so if you switch me, could you switch him too, so we have the same schedule?"

Mr. Serpens leaned back in his chair and gracefully brought the fingertips of his hands together. He looked to be in his early to mid-thirties, with a boyish charm about his features. Tom could almost liken him to a fellow student, only older.

"An interesting request, Tom. Most interesting, especially considering that you're the sixth person from Mr. Evad's seventh period science class to make that request today. That's not counting the two parents who called me at home last night to ask that their child be switched."

In a display of the famous Cobalt fortitude, Tom continued. "Well, in my case I think I might have a better reason than the others."

"Oh?" Mr. Serpens sat upright. "Let me take a guess? You think that, for some reason, Mr. Evad has singled you out from your classmates, that, let's say, he has taken a personal dislike to you. Is that it?"

"Huh?" The guidance counselor's shrewd insight caught Tom off guard. But yet again the legendary Cobalt fortitude came to the forefront. "Well, yeah, now that you mention it, that's it exactly."

If anything, Tom's answer made Mr. Serpens' perpetual grin grow even wider. After a brief pause, as if to let the smile bore deeper into the boy, the man rambled on.

"Believe me Tom, Mr. Evad has that effect on many of his new students. It's unfortunate, but for whatever reason, it takes a while for his students to come to realize that it's not personal. Usually by the end of the first marking period, their attitude about Mr. Evad has done a complete about face. By that I mean it changes from of one of anxiety to one of great respect, if not, indeed, if I may be so bold to suggest, one of outright worship." Mr. Serpens leaned back in his chair, resuming his former posture.

"Talk about cow dung," Tom thought to himself. "How does he know all this? He's new here, and yet he acts like he's been dealing with Evad's students for years."

Tom decided to turn his determination up a notch. "I'm not sure how I can convince you of this, but I honestly believe that Mr. Evad really has some sort of personal vendetta against me."

"Vendetta," Mr. Serpens broke in. "That's an interesting word to use, Tom. I always liked that word, especially how it seems to roll off one's tongue."

"What the heck is he talking about?" Tom mused. "He's a complete wacko."

"Anyway, I'm serious when I say that it's more than my imagination. Ask any of the other students in the class. They'll back me up on this. Ask Alex, he's right outside."

"Tom," said the counselor. And then, sounding like a stuck record, he continued. "Tom, Tom, Tom. Things aren't always as they seem …" Serpens paused a moment, rather for effect or to collect his thoughts wasn't clear. Then he got back into stride. "… although I'll grant that in your case, you might be right. Mr. Evad may actually have singled you out from the other students. If so, he no doubt has good reason for it." The man sat up in the chair again, and leaned forward, placing his elbows on the desk. "Tom. Would it surprise you if I told you that Mr.

Evad is probably the finest teacher at East Pencreek High?" Without waiting for the boy's answer, he continued. "Why it wouldn't surprise me if he's the finest teacher in the state. You probably don't realize it but Mr. Evad has a Ph.D. in physics."

"He has a what?" Tom didn't know what a Ph.D. was.

"Ph.D. It stands for Doctor of Philosophy. It's the highest academic degree one can obtain. Mr. Evad—actually, Dr. Evad to be more correct—could no doubt be teaching in any one of the finest universities in the land; yet, East Pencreek has been most fortunate in that he prefers to teach here at our school."

Tom was about to attempt to derail the direction the discussion had taken with, "What does this have to do with Evad harassing me?" but thought better of it. Instead he said, "Why would someone who could teach college want to teach at East Pencreek?"

For a second Mr. Serpens' grin disappeared, the boy's question seemingly having caught him off his guard, but just as quickly his former demeanor reasserted itself. "Dr. Evad has won several teaching awards. I'm certain that every year he receives numerous offers to teach at other schools, even colleges, and not only in Pennsylvania, but in other states as well. Yet, he remains here. The man is incredibly dedicated to both his students and East Pencreek. I realize that this may be difficult for you to accept having had but a single class with him, but please remember that things aren't always as they seem. Just give it time."

"I'm sorry, Mr. Serpens," persisted the eighth grader, "but I really feel it would be best for everyone if I were switched to another science class."

Mr. Serpens, still wearing that reassuring grin, stood his ground. "Tom, believe me, it would be a disservice to you if I transferred you." Tom started to object again, but Mr. Serpens, held up a hand, silencing him. "Hear me out, please. Tom, you're a bright young man. I'm going to tell you something that by rights I shouldn't. As matter of fact, I could get into trouble telling you this, so I must first ask you to promise me that what I'm about to reveal to you will be kept between the two of us, that you won't tell another soul. Not even your parents. Not even your best friend. It will be our little secret."

As the boy felt somewhat flattered to be taken into Mr. Serpens' confidence, he eagerly nodded his head in agreement at the same time saying, "You have my word on it." The boy felt certain that Mr. Serpens was about to spill some deep, dark secret about Evad.

"I have your promise then that what I'm about to tell you will be kept in strictest confidence, just between the two of us?"

"Cross my heart and swear to die."

"Good," said Mr. Serpens. "Tom, you have the second—hmm, actually, I guess that now it's the third highest IQ in the eighth grade."

Tom's reaction was to stare at the counselor, dumbstruck. He hadn't a clue as to where this was heading.

"Yet it troubles me to say this to you. Your grades are not what they should be considering your ability. What I'm trying to say, Tom, is that you don't apply yourself to your studies. You don't work up to your potential."

"Well, Mr. Serpens, it's just that I don't have any interest in some of the subjects I have to take. I mean, I don't see why they're important."

"Tom, let's take a minute here and lay all the laundry on the table. Nice and neatly stacked and folded, so to speak." Tom couldn't help wishing that in trying to make things more clear, Mr. Serpens would stop going off on some seemingly unrelated tangent that made things less clear. "You have a mild case of dyslexia. No doubt the previous counselor informed you of this handicap. It impairs your ability to read. Tom, I suspect you're using this handicap as a crutch—as an excuse not to try harder. Yet many men and women, throughout history, have excelled with far greater handicaps than you have. Why, I believe that General George Patton was dyslexic, and look at what he accomplished."

"Yeah, he was good at killing Nazis, but actually, Mr. Serpens, I don't think that's it. I think I'm just bored in some of my classes."

"No, Tom. Believe me. I'm a professional. I understand the real reason for your below expectation performance. It's that you don't feel challenged. Therefore, Dr. Evad is just the kind of teacher you need. He will challenge you to rise above yourself. He will force you to perform on a level equal to your ability, if not to actually exceed it."

"How can I exceed my ability?" thought Tom.

"Tom, a class from Dr. Evad is the perfect tonic for what ails you. And considering the gifted teacher that Dr. Evad is, it does not surprise me in the least to learn that his treatment of you is different from his treatment of other students. Tom, you are in the hands of a master pedagogue."

"A peda—what?"

"Pedagogue, Tom. It's another word for teacher."

"Oh. It's just that it sounded like you were calling him some sort of pervert or something."

"Yes—hmm. Now, where was I? Oh, yes. Mr. Evad is a teacher whose talent is far superior to any you will probably ever encounter again in your life. I have no doubt that Dr. Evad studies the file of each and every one of his students. In your case he has probably concluded that his treatment of you is the best antidote for what ails you. I guarantee that by the end of this school year, you will find yourself a changed young man, a young man who has found the motivation and desire to consistently perform up to his full potential. You'll look back on your experience with Dr. Evad as a turning point in your life. You'll no doubt view Dr. Evad as not only the finest teacher you ever had, but perhaps even as a surrogate parent."

"A what kind of parent?" asked the confused boy. If he didn't know better, he could have sworn that Mr. Serpens called Evad a pervert again.

"Surrogate. But never mind. That's neither here nor there."

"What's not here nor there?"

Ignoring Tom's last question, Mr. Serpens pressed onward. "Remember, things aren't always as they seem."

After being subjected to such a speech, Tom was almost speechless, but not quite. As was noted earlier, being a boy of great fortitude, he still hadn't given up, but unfortunately, at the moment, he couldn't think of another tact to use, so to play for time, he asked, "You said Mister—uh—Dr. Evad has a doctoral degree. Where did he get it?"

"University of Bucharest, if I'm not mistaken."

"Bucharest?" said Tom. "Isn't that in Romania?" As he finished speaking, it occurred to the boy that perhaps he had been wrong about the geography class he had last year which, at the time, he assured himself was perfectly useless.

"Yes, that's correct."

Tom's mind started racing. "Romania? Transylvania was in Romania. Count Dracula, the vampire, was supposedly from Transylvania. Apparently, the story of Count Dracula had some connection with a medieval Transylvanian ruler called Vlad the Impaler, after the habit Vlad had of ordering his enemies to be impaled on sharpened stakes, kind of like human shish kebab. Is it a coincidence that the name Evad has a similar ring to Vlad? Besides, if there was a role that seemed to fit Evad to a tee, it was that of a vampire. He not only looks the part but seems to be acting it. Does the man not convey the image of a cruel, cold, heartless, and totally ruthless being? But the theory's not perfect as vampires supposedly never come out in the daytime since sunlight's fatal to them. Well, so much for that idea. It's obvious that, though his skin's pale, Evad definitely has no fear of sunlight."

The boy's racing thoughts were interrupted by Mr. Serpens' voice. "Was there anything else on your mind, Tom?"

"Uh . . ." He hadn't thought of any new arguments to get out of Evad's class so it was back to stalling until he came up with a better ploy. "Yes, I think I just thought of an easy way to cure my handicap."

"An easy cure for dyslexia? Really? I'd like to hear your idea."

"Well, last year in English class we learned that there are forty different sounds in the English language."

"Yes, I believe that's right."

"That's what my teacher, Mrs. Sherman, said. Now there's a great teacher."

"Yes, Mrs. Sherman is definitely a fine teacher, but please, let's hear your idea."

"As you know there are only twenty-six letters in the alphabet. To get all forty sounds some letters are assigned more than one sound, or sometimes we even combine two letters together for certain sounds."

"Like the letter 'a' has more than one sound, and the combinations 's-h' and 't-h' have separate sounds. Yes, I think I'm beginning to see where you're going with this, but do continue."

"So why don't we add more letters to the alphabet so that each letter stands for just one sound, and all the possible different sounds are covered? In other words we have an alphabet of forty letters. I think the term for that is a phonetic alphabet. Anyway, wouldn't that make it a lot easier for people to learn to read and spell?"

"An excellent idea, Tom." Mr. Serpens' eternal smile, if possible, appeared to grow even wider, and his eyes gleamed with delight. "Only problem is that your idea is a couple centuries ahead of its time." The man glanced at the clock on his desk and then back at the boy. "See Tom, that's what I mean by using your full potential. Was there anything else?"

Tom took the hint, decided to finally accept defeat, and stood. He started to turn towards the door but hesitated. "Mr. Serpens, you said that my idea was a couple centuries ahead of its time. I don't understand what you meant by that."

Again the guidance counselor gave the boy that wonderful grin, seeming to show more teeth than Tom thought was biologically possible. "I didn't mean for it to sound like I had some actual knowledge of the future. What I meant was that I think your idea has great merit, and that no doubt someday society will adopt it."

"Oh," said Tom, sounding disappointed. "Yes, of course. Well, thank you for seeing me." Mr. Serpens gave the boy a friendly nod as if to say, "You're welcome."

As the boy opened the office door to leave, Mr. Serpens added cheerfully, "Remember, Tom, things aren't always as they seem."

Closing the door behind him, Tom caught the eye of his friend Alex, still sitting on the bench in the main school office corridor outside of Serpens' office.

"Don't waste your time. Mr. Serpens seems to think that Evad is East Pencreek's answer to *Our Miss Brooks*," said Tom, referring to the lead character of a popular TV show about a school teacher.

As Tom concluded his detailed account of the events in Serpens' office, Alex said, "Interesting, especially the part about Evad being a Romanian. Watson, I think the game is afoot."

"How come I'm always Watson and you're always Holmes?" asked Tom.

"I'm the one with the superior intellect," said Alex.

"Okay, then how come the game is always a 'foot' and never a 'hand?'"

"I'll hand it to you that that's a good question, but let's get back to Evad the Impaler being from Romania."

"Actually, Mr. Serpens said that Evad got his degree in Romania. He didn't say he was born there. Besides, I didn't notice that Evad has any kind of accent."

"True," agreed the boy genius, "but you have to admit the coincidence is intriguing."

"What coincidence?"

"Evad, Romania. Vlad, Evad. It's obvious. It all fits. Evad's a vampire."

"Oh, come on now."

"Anyway, if he has a doctorate in physics, why isn't he teaching at a college or doing scientific research? You know, physics type stuff. Of all places, why does he insist on hanging out in East Pencreek, cesspool of the Middle Atlantic states?"

"Beats me."

"But it hasn't beaten me yet. That's why you're Watson and I'm Holmes."

"Well, Einar, remember, things aren't always as they seem."

"Huh? What's that supposed to mean?"

"I don't know. Mr. Serpens, must have said it ten times while I was in there. I mean, he tried to make it sound like having Evad for a teacher was going to be more fun than snakes on a gorgon."

"Speaking of gorgons, there's Miss Know-it-all heading to gym class. Well, at least this is one class where we won't have to put up with her."

"Are you sure that's what Sarah's mom said when she called last night?" Tom was lacing up his street shoes in the boys' locker room.

"Yep," answered Alex. "And my mom said that Sarah's mom said to thank us for taking her to school and that everything was okay and that she was going to call your parents next."

"Strange, my mom said the same thing. It doesn't make sense. I mean I can imagine what kind of stories she might have told her parents about us, especially when she overheard Brad referring to her as Banana Beak."

"Yeah, well who can understand girls?"

"Hey, I thought you were a genius?"

"Even genius has its limits."

Further speculation between the two boys about what the new girl might be up to was interrupted by Mr. Heathburn, the gym instructor.

"Tom, would you step into my office for a minute. I'd like to have a word with you."

"Sure, Coach." Tom followed the big man into the office that ad-joined the locker room.

"Tom," said the coach as he took the seat behind his desk. "I've watched you in gym class all last year. You have outstanding athletic ability and on top of that you're big for your age."

"Thank you, sir," said Tom, clueless as to where the discussion was headed.

"Frankly, son, I'm really surprised that you haven't gone out for the Team." The way Coach Heathburn emphasized the word "team" made it sound like it should be capitalized.

"Team, sir? What team is that?"

"Why the Football Team, of course!" said the coach, the crescendo of his response revealing both frustration and surprise. "What other Team is there?"

"Oh, yes, of course, the football team," said Tom, trying to sound apologetic, and being careful not to stress the words 'football' and 'team' so they didn't sound like they were capitalized.

"Yes, son, the Team. Why we had a shot at the district champion-ship last year, as you no doubt remember. And with a fine athlete like you as part of the Team . . . Who knows? I think this year we could even be looking at state."

"Well, gee, thanks for the vote of confidence, Coach, but I don't think I'm interested in going out for football."

"Not interested? I can't believe what I'm hearing. Listen, Tom, I'm surprised, no, flabbergasted that you don't see the big picture here. Son, with your ability, you could be our starting quarterback. I re-member how well you played that position last year in gym class, in the touch football games. Why Bernie Gordon, our present quarter-back, doesn't have half the arm that you do. Besides, who's the big man on campus?" Tom was about to tell the coach that he didn't know what the term 'big man on campus' meant, when the coach answered his own question. "Why the quarterback, son. Everyone looks up to the starting quarterback. He's the most popular boy in school, and you know what that means. Think about all the attention you'll be getting from some of those sweet little fillies around here." At the mention of fillies, Tom immediately pictured some horses grazing in a farm pasture. "I know I certainly didn't mind all those fillies fawning over me that when I was your age." The gym teacher gave the boy a knowing wink, but the only reaction from the teen was a look of puzzlement.

"I'm sorry, Coach. I'm not following you. How did we get from football to horses?"

"Horses?" Now it was the coach's turn to look puzzled. "What do horses have to do with anything?"

"But Coach, you were just saying that when you were my age, you liked horses—or maybe it was the other way around."

"I said no such thing," roared the coach. "We were talking about football. You do like to play football, don't you, son?"

"Sure, I like to play football. Why about every weekend this time of year a few of us usually get a game up in the vacant lot behind Snyder's gas station. But I can't go out for the team. I don't think I could make all the practices."

"Can't make the practices! Why not?"

"Well, Monday evening is my Scout troop meeting, and Tuesday after school I have piano lessons, and Wednesday evening I'm taking a Bible study class at church, and I need time to do my homework, and—"

"Piano lessons! What kind of a boy prefers piano lessons to football?"

"Gee, Coach, it's not that I—"

"You a mommy's boy?" said the coach, almost spitting out the words as if to emphasize his contempt for Tom. "Is that it? A sissy? Your mommy wants you to take piano lessons, huh?"

"Well, actually, it was my father's idea," said Tom. "Besides, I like playing the piano, and Mrs. Johnson is a great teacher—"

At that Coach Heathburn's face turned a noticeable shade of red, almost as if he were suffering from heartburn. "I know what you are. You're yellow! That's it. You're chicken."

A bell sounded. "Sorry, Coach, but that's the late bell. I have to go as I'm already late for my next class." With that, Tom started walking towards the locker room exit, but as he reached it he paused and turned. "Eh, Coach, don't worry. I won't tell anybody about you and the horses."

"What?" said the coach, looking baffled by the boy's comment. Then he recovered and shouted after the departing student, "I know your father! I'm going to call him tonight and tell him what a yellow-belly sissy his son is! That his son let down both his school and his classmates. Then we'll see whether or not—" The remainder of the coach's tirade was cut short by the closing door.

"What was that all about?" asked Alex, who had obviously overheard some of the coach's parting rant from where he was waiting in the hall playing with his yo-yo.

"Coach Heartburn wanted me to go out for football."

"Why? Doesn't he already have a football?" Both boys laughed uproariously at Alex's joke as they walked to their next class.

Almost as surprising as Sarah's apparent failure to tattletale on the boys' treatment of her the previous day was her newly found habit of keeping her mouth shut in class. Granted she almost always raised her hand whenever a teacher would ask the class a question, and always answered the question correctly when called upon, but never once did she make an attempt to interject any additional comments or correct either a teacher or a fellow student. The math teacher seemed especially conscious of Sarah's presence, no doubt remembering the events of the previous day, and seemed to many of the students to be somewhat jumpy, as if she were expecting any minute to be called to task for some mortal failing by the female with the prominent nose sitting in the back of her classroom. The nervous state she was in became even more evident as she made several errors while writing problems on the blackboard. Each time she did so, Tom cast a glance towards the back row of desks where Sarah sat alone as if in quarantine, and each time Tom observed the young girl staring at the top of her desk and wringing her hands as if struggling to keep herself from reverting to her former behavior. The third time he turned around, he found the girl looking at him. Tom jerked about so as to face towards the front of the classroom and Sarah, her eyes wide with a mixture of surprise and alarm, just as quickly dropped her head and shifted her attention again to the top of her desk.

Lunch period found everyone at the same tables they had occupied the day before. Sarah again ate alone, never once looking up to confirm her suspicion that many of the other students were watching her every move. When she finished eating, she opened one of her textbooks and began to do some homework.

"Weird," said Brad. "Really weird."

"Are you referring to someone besides Wayne?" asked Tom, since Wayne, for a reason that no one ever understood, had a habit of always stirring his milk with his finger before drinking it.

"Yeah. I'm talking about Big Nose over there."

"Actually, I think her name is Sarah. Sarah Gould," said Tom.

"Hey, do I detect some affection from Tom Cobalt towards this person? Maybe her name will be Sarah Cobalt someday," chuckled Brad.

"Yeah, right, and maybe someday someone will find your brain where you left it."

Alex, who had been spending the better part of the lunch period working some sort of problem on a piece of paper, finally spoke up. "Children, children. Let us not bicker over yon wench."

Brad gave up trying to needle Tom and instead decided to pester Cynthia who was again sitting at the neighboring table. Turning in his chair, he poked the girl on her shoulder. "Hey, Cyn. Did Miss Banana Beak make you look like a moron again today?"

Cynthia didn't bother turning around. "Stuff it up your nose, twit."

Further verbal banter between the two was interrupted by Alex exclaiming, "That's it! I got it!"

"Got what?" said the other three boys in unison.

"I figured it out. Evad's name. I broke the code!"

"Huh?" said the other three.

"Evad's name. Sleinad Evad. Say it backwards."

"Evad Slcinad," said Wayne, after licking the milk from his finger.

"No, no! I mean spell Sleinad Evad backwards."

"You do it," Wayne suggested to Tom. "I can't even spell it forwards."

Tom took a stab at the challenge, although he had to write it down to ensure that he did it correctly. "D-A-N-I-E-L-S D-A-V-E. Daniels Dave." he said uncertainly, then reversed the word order. "Dave Daniels."

"See!" said Alex in a tone that sounded like he had just made a discovery that would win him the Nobel Prize in physics.

"I don't see," said Brad. "Wayne, do you see?"

"See what? Hey, get your finger out of my milk!" said Wayne, as Brad began to stir Wayne's milk with his finger.

Removing his finger, Brad turned to Tom. "What about you, Tom?"

"Are you saying that Sleinad Evad's name is really Dave Daniels and for some reason he changed to a new name by spelling the old one backwards?"

"Yes! That's precisely it," said Alex, unable to contain his excitement.

"So why change his name?" said Tom.

"I'm not sure. He could be a fugitive from the law. Romania's a communist country. Maybe he had to flee the country and he's using an alias to escape assassination by the Commie Secret Police."

"Wouldn't using a name like John Smith make more sense than spelling his real name backwards?" suggested Wayne.

Tom shook his head. "Dave Daniels doesn't sound Romanian to me."

"It means something," said Alex, with his usual persistence. "It can't just be a coincidence."

"It must be a curse to be as smart as you," commented Brad.

"Let's see," said Tom, using a pencil to quickly scribble some letters on his flattened paper lunch bag. "What's Brad Jones spelled backward? Darb Senoj." That got a laugh from everyone.

"And Tom Cobalt," added Alex, also scribbling some letters next to those of Tom's, "is Mot Tlaboc." More laughter.

"And my name would be—," there was a brief pause as Wayne did some deciphering with a pencil on his napkin, "—would be Enyaw Nilknarf." The accompanying laughter was even louder this time.

"Nilknarf, that's great," said Brad, wiping away some of the tears of merriment that had flooded his eyes. He swung around on his stool and tapped Cynthia Cohen on the shoulder. "Hey, Cyn. Say hello to Enyaw Nilknarf."

"Stuff it in your ear," was the girl's disinterested reply.

Alex was obviously the next target of their newfound game. "Xela Noynab. Xela? That sounds like a girl's name," said Wayne.

"Let's see. What would Sarah Gould be backwards?" asked Tom.

"Gib Eson," said Brad.

"Huh?" Tom gave Brad a questioning look. Then he got it. "Oh, I get it."

Further speculation was interrupted by the sound of a bell announcing the end of the lunch period. "Okay, okay," said Alex, as he stuffed his trash into his lunch bag and gathered up his books. "Make fun of it if you will, but I'm calling my Uncle Don this evening. He's a physics professor. I'll see if he ever heard of a physicist named Sleinad Evad or Dave Daniels."

On their way out of the cafeteria, the boys passed the table at which Sarah had been sitting. Tom happened to glance at a piece of paper the girl had left on the table. He stopped and grabbed Wayne's arm.

"Ouch," yelled Wayne, at the same time giving his friend a nasty look.

Tom ignored the protest. "Look." He pointed at the piece of paper.

The three other boys leaned forward to get a better view of the notebook page. On it was written

Sleinad Evad

and below that was

Daniels Dave

"Jeepers," said Alex, sounding impressed.

"Talk about coincidence," said Wayne.

Alex picked up the paper and let out a low whistle.

"I don't think she could have heard us from way over here," suggested Tom.

"I think you're right about that," agreed Alex, as he continued to stare at the writing. "Almost scary, ain't it?" Then he carefully folded the paper in half and placed it in his notebook.

As he was to be his custom at the beginning of every class, Evad entered the room just as the bell rang signaling the start of the period. Without looking at the students, he walked behind the teacher's lab table at the front of the room and deposited his briefcase in one of the table's drawers. Then he quickly scanned the class, as if mentally taking the class roll. The students all returned his gaze, each fearing that to do otherwise would be interpreted as a sign of inattention. The man's attire and demeanor appeared unchanged from that of the day before.

"Clear your desks except for a pencil and piece of 8 ½ inch by 11-inch lined notebook paper. Today's quiz will cover chapter three of the textbook." The announcement was met by gasps of disbelief from the class. A number of hands shot up, vying for Evad's attention. Evad looked at Bonnie Trent. "Yes, Miss Trent, you have a question?" Tom realized that Evad hadn't even consulted the class seating chart before calling on Bonnie. As matter of fact, Tom couldn't remember Evad having even taken out a seating chart. The only explanation seemed to be that the teacher had memorized the class roster, and already knew every student by sight.

Bonnie Trent swallowed, lowered her hand and said in a voice that betrayed a slight quiver, "We haven't covered chapter three yet."

"That's a comment, not a question," was the response from the teacher. "I suspect what you really intended to say was to ask something along the lines of why have a quiz on material we haven't covered yet? Was that your intention?"

"Yes," Bonnie gulped in a manner that seemed to plead, 'please, don't hit me.'

"Yesterday I handed out the lesson plan for the entire year. We will stick to that plan with the exception of snow days or other unforeseen changes to the schedule. Yesterday's homework assignment was to have read chapter three in your textbook. The material in the textbook is clearly presented. If you had read it carefully, you should have had no difficulty comprehending it. To determine if you did what you were assigned to do, we are having a quiz on that material."

Alex bravely raised his hand. The dark instructor acknowledged the boy. "Yes, Mr. Banyon."

"Isn't it customary to start with chapter one, then cover chapter two before getting to chapter three?"

"Good question, Mr. Banyon." Alex smiled with pride at having received a positive sounding acknowledgment from the dark lord. "You might notice that like some of your other textbooks, this one was written by a committee. There hasn't been a committee in the history of the world that ever produced a quality text. Your textbook for the most part is trash. Unfortunately, the textbook is not selected by the teacher but by the school board, an elected committee of ignoramuses as far as the sciences are concerned." At the last remark, Bobby Lewis looked indignant as his father was on the school board.

"The first two chapters contain total rubbish about what science is all about and a bunch of wishy-washy tripe about the nature of the universe. Only beginning with chapter three do we encounter any material of substance, the atomic theory of matter. Be assured that in this class I will not waste your time, nor will I permit you to waste mine. Since I will not waste your time, there is no need to write down the questions. Number your paper from one to twenty. Question number one . . ."

Like most of the students in the class, Tom didn't have a clue as to what the answers to several of the questions were. After Evad collected the papers, he began to lecture the class while at the same time correcting the papers. It took him less than ten minutes to correct all twenty-six quizzes. During that time, he never paused in his presentation. When he had finished correcting the last quiz, he passed them back to their owners, all the while continuing to elaborate on the development of the atomic theory of matter. Many of the students let out barely audible moans when they saw their scores. When Evad reached Tom, he slapped the quiz face down on the desk as was his custom so that other students could not see the grade and interrupted his dissertation on the nature of the atom with, "Nice try, Mr. Cobalt. Next time do the assignment."

After Evad had passed on to his next victim, Tom carefully lifted the top of the page until he could make out the number thirty written in red and enclosed by a circle of the same color. "Thirty out of a hundred!" Tom mumbled to himself. He looked over at Alex who had also received his quiz, and showed Alex the grade, while grinning sheepishly. Alex returned his grin and flashed his score, an impressive eight-five. Probably highest in the class thought Tom. Then as if reading each other's thoughts, the two boys simultaneously turned in their seats to look at Sarah. To their surprise they found her staring at them with a dead pan expression on her face. Then her face broke into a less than gracious grin as she held up her quiz paper so that the boys could read the grade at its top. The three red integers thus displayed formed the number one hundred. Sarah stuck out her tongue and returned the quiz face down to her desk, as Tom and Alex exchanged glances and shook their heads in disgust.

Tom was passing his mother the butter during the evening meal, when his father broached a new topic of conversation. "Coach Heartburn, er ..." Sam Cobalt paused, then gave his wife a smile, before clearing his throat and continuing with his statement. "Coach Heathburn called me at work this afternoon."

"Oh?" said Tom, having a good idea as to the subject of the phone call.

"He said he was most disappointed that you didn't go out for football this year."

"Oh?" said Tom, repeating his prior statement.

"He also said that you got smart with him. Is that true?"

"Wall gagh Dlad . . ."

"Don't talk with your mouth full," said Tom's mother.

Tom took a couple of chews and then swallowed. "Sorry, Mom. Gosh, Dad, I mean it must be tough for most people to talk to Coach Heartburn and not sound smart in comparison." His sister let out a giggle.

"Tom, you know what I mean." At the strict tone of her father's voice, Caroline immediately focused her attention back to her dinner. "Now what exactly happened between you and the coach this afternoon?"

"Well, he said he was surprised that I didn't go out for football—or 'The Team,' as he calls it, like it's the only thing in the universe that matters. Anyway, I told him that there were other things that I preferred to do with my time, and then . . . Frankly Dad, I wasn't disrespectful, well, at least not until he started treating me disrespectfully."

"I see," said Mr. Cobalt. "Can you give me an example of how he was disrespectful to you?"

Tom chewed on a green bean while he thought about his answer. "Well, first he made it sound like I was some sort of fool for not wanting to be the school quarterback. He said that I'd be real popular and I'd have girls hanging all over me and stuff like that." Another giggle erupted from Tom's sister.

"Quarterback, huh?" For a moment it seemed to Tom that he saw a glint of pride in his father's eyes. "He may not be so dumb there. My guess is that you'd do a better job than Bernie Gordon is going to do at quarterback, and you probably would have the girls hanging all over you."

"Sam!" said Nancy Cobalt, shooting her husband a far from kindly look.

Mr. Cobalt gave his wife a grin, and then turned again to his son. "Go on."

"When I told him that I had other things I'd rather do with my time, he started calling me a coward and a yellow-belly and stuff like that."

"He was just trying to goad you into doing what he wanted you to do."

"Listen, Dad. I certainly like playing football, but Coach Heartburn—er, Heathburn is such a—well, some of the boys I know on the team tell me what a jerk he is as a coach. And I can believe them considering how he behaves in gym class sometimes. I don't think I'd care to have him as a coach." Tom paused to see what his father's response would be.

"No point in doing something you don't like doing if you don't have to do it."

"Do you think I'm a coward for not wanting to go out for football?"

"No, of course not," said his father. "I think your standing up to Heathburn took a lot more guts than playing football. And after what you told me, I wouldn't give my permission for you to play football under that imbecile." Mrs. Cobalt and Caroline both nodded in agreement with Tom's father, but Tom's expression was still troubled.

"He also said that by not playing I was letting down my school and my classmates. Do you think that's true?"

"Tom, you don't owe your school anything. And you don't owe your classmates anything either, at least as a group. It's the citizens who make that school possible through the taxes we pay, and that includes the salaries of the people who work there, including Coach Heartburn—er, Heathburn. We're the customers, Tom, not that the government gives us much choice in the matter. People like Heathburn are paid to serve us. If he gives you any more trouble, let me know."

"Okay, Dad." Tom began to reach for his dessert, but hesitated. "Dad, exactly what did you tell the Coach on the phone?"

"I told him . . ." Tom's father gave his wife an embarrassed look. "I, er, told him in a—er, roundabout way that the decision was yours to make, and that I supported whatever you decided."

Mrs. Cobalt looked at her son, her eyes twinkling. "Actually, your father can't really repeat what he said because, as you know, we frown upon using foul language in this house."

Tom gave his father a big grin. "Thanks, Dad." As he returned to his dessert, his mother changed the topic of conversation.

"It was very nice of you and Alex to walk Sarah Gould to school yesterday. Sarah's mother said it made Sarah's first day at a new school a lot easier."

At his mom's words, Tom froze, and then returned his fork with a skewered piece of pie to the plate. His conscience was starting to do flip flops in his mind, and he knew he looked like someone who had the word "Guilt" smacked on his forehead with a giant ink stamp.

His parents exchanged puzzled looks before his father spoke up. "Is something the matter?"

"Er—well—yes. You see, I don't think Mrs. Gould told you the whole story about what happened yesterday."

"Oh?" was his father's only response, although the way he said it reminded the boy of a tough, grizzled policeman giving a suspect the third degree, with a rubber hose, brass knuckles and similar implements useful in convincing one to spill his guts.

"Yeah. You see we didn't walk Sarah home from school."

"And why not?" said his father.

"Well, for one thing as we were leaving school she got mad at us, and just stormed off."

"And why did she get mad at you?"

"One reason might be because we were having a—discussion and she didn't like the way it was going."

"She got mad over a discussion?"

"Well, that and the fact that she heard Brad make a comment about her—you know—her looks."

"What's wrong with her looks?" asked Caroline, innocently.

Tom gave his parents a pleading look hoping one of them would answer his sister's question but saw from their expressions that neither was about to rescue him. "She's rather, I guess, sensitive about them."

"Why? Is she ugly?"

"No, not really."

"Is she pretty then?"

Tom gave his head a quick shake. "How would I know?"

"Yes, she's pretty," said Mrs. Cobalt, whose answer didn't carry much credibility with Tom as it seemed to him that it was some sort unwritten code of conduct that mothers always referred to any girls

145

whose age approximated that of their sons as being pretty.

"I don't understand," said Caroline, not understanding.

"I think she's sensitive about her nose," Tom said. "She thinks it's too big or something."

"Why would she think that?" asked Caroline, showing no sign of losing any momentum in her seemingly never-ending interrogation of her brother.

"Er, probably because it really is a little on the bi—that is, it's a little larger than your everyday ordinary nose."

"Sarah Gould?" Tom's sister said half to herself. "I think she has a sister. There was a new girl at our school yesterday. She's in my class. She doesn't have a big nose."

"So. what did Brad say?" asked Tom's mother.

"He made a comment about how big her nose was."

Tom's mother looked agape. "Brad told her she had a big nose to her face?"

"No, Brad wouldn't do something like that. Well, maybe he would, but he didn't. She was around the corner, out of sight, when he said it. She happened to overhear him."

"Wow, what exactly did he say?" asked Caroline, now looking really, really interested.

"Never mind nosey," was Tom's answer.

"Okay, so she got mad because of what Brad said and stormed off," said Mr. Cobalt. "No doubt she told her parents about it." He paused to exchange glances with his wife, before continuing. "I think you should call her up and make it clear that you didn't have anything to do with what Brad said."

"Dad!" said Tom, aghast at his father's suggestion. "I can't do that. You don't understand. This girl is really weird. I mean really weird. It's like she's from Mars or something."

"You're right. I don't understand, and no doubt Sarah doesn't either. So, I think you need to put things right here."

"Listen, when I say weird, I don't just mean weird. She's super-weird, you know, like not only strange but—but—obnoxious to boot. She insults everybody, even the teachers. She acts like a know-it-all, like she thinks she's Albert Einstein and everyone else is a downright moron."

"Really, Thomas." It seemed to be his mother's turn to let him have it, and the fact that she used his proper first name was definitely a bad sign. "Your father and I both met Sarah the other day, and she seemed like a polite young lady, if a little shy."

"That may be true, Mom, but at school she was like Jekyll turning into Hyde. She's in all of the same classes with Alex and me, so we get a full dose of her. Even the teachers can't stand her. She kept interrupting some of them and telling them they were wrong and stuff. If you don't believe me ask Alex."

"Okay, so she's smart," replied Mrs. Cobalt. "So is Alex, and you don't find him obnoxious."

"Yeah, but Alex doesn't go around advertising it. I'm telling you, you have no idea what a pain-in-the-neck this girl is. Well, okay, I admit she seemed to have sort of mellowed out today compared to yesterday. Maybe the formula wore off or something. You know what? I bet her parents grilled her until she finally admitted what a total freak act she put on in school yesterday, and they really let her have it, and that's why she almost acted normal today. Why I wouldn't be surprised if some of the teachers, or even the principal, called them last night. And her parents felt bad about saddling Alex and me with the Creature from the Black Lagoon daughter of theirs and that's why they let us off the hook." Tom paused to see how well his theory played out with his parents.

"Nice try," said his father, "but I'm not buying it. Try to remember it was her first day in a strange new school. She was probably trying extra hard to impress her teachers and her fellow students and show everyone that she isn't a dummy. No doubt, she came off a little too strong."

"A little too strong? Listen, Dad. It's not exactly smart when you have a nose like that and you're in a new school to call attention to yourself by insulting everyone."

"Wow, how big is her nose?" asked Caroline again.

Mr. Cobalt shook his head. "Okay, end of discussion about how Sarah acted in school yesterday. That's neither here nor there. What we're going to talk about is what you're going to do here and now." At those words, Tom gave an involuntary flinch. He knew that he wasn't going to like what his father was about to suggest. "You're going to call Sarah as soon as dinner is over, and you're going to apologize to her—"

"But Dad, I didn't—"

"You're going to apologize to her for Brad's comments and ensure her that you did nothing to encourage them."

"But why should I apologize for something that Brad . . . ?"

"And then, you're going to ask to speak to one of her parents. And you're going to explain to them what happened yesterday, and also ensure them that you had nothing to do with it. Then you are going to again offer your services to escort their daughter to school."

"But Dad, I didn't make the offer to walk her to school in the first place, you did, and—"

"No ands, ifs or buts. That is what you are going to do."

Tom's response to his father's order was to let his face crash onto the table.

"Sam," said his mother. "Maybe we should give this some more thought. After all, Tom is right in that he wasn't at fault for what Brad said. He certainly has no control over his friend's behavior. And they're only teens. You know how boys and girls are at this age. Besides, Sarah's mother said everything went well yesterday. Maybe Sarah was uncomfortable walking to school with the boys and found the incident with Brad a convenient way to get out of the arrangement."

Tom could see his father pondering his mother's argument. Maybe there was hope yet. Unfortunately, just then his sister had to open her

148

big mouth. "Is her nose really that big?"

Without thinking, Tom replied, "Yeah, it's pretty big."

"On second thought," said his mother, "You will do exactly what your father said."

"Hello, this is Tom Cobalt. Is this the Gould residence?" Tom gave his parents standing behind the sofa across from him a quick glance, before turning back to the phone. "May I speak to Sarah please? What? Oh, er, well—huh? In half an hour? Okay, I'll call back then." The boy had a strange look on his face as he returned the phone to its cradle.

"Was Sarah not home?" asked his mother.

"No, she was home." The boy was now staring into space as if the gears of his mind were turning at supersonic speed. He then gave his parents a look that seemed to border between disbelief and awe. "Her mother said she was taking a bath."

At their son's answer, Nancy and Sam Cobalt exchanged a knowing glance, then his father suggested "Okay, so try again later."

"Yeah. Sure," said Tom, still looking like his thoughts were elsewhere, which they indeed were, for never before in his life had he ever considered the possibility that girls took baths. For a moment he tried to picture Sarah Gould taking a bath, and as he did so he felt really weird. It was a kind of weirdness that was totally new to him.

Sarah's mom rapped on the bathroom door. "Sarah?" When her daughter acknowledged her from the other side of the door, Mrs. Gould continued. "There was a phone call for you. I asked them to call back in a half hour."

"A phone call, for me?" The voice showed a slight alarm. "Who was it?"

"Tom Cobalt."

"What? Wha—what did you tell him?"

"I told him you were taking a bath and to call back in a half hour."

"You told him I was taking a bath!" Sarah sounded hysterical. "Why did you tell him I was taking a bath?"

"Because you are, that's why," said her mother.

"Well—what did he want?"

"He didn't say."

"And you told him I was taking a bath?"

"Yes, what's wrong with that?"

For a moment there was no reply. Then Sarah said, "When he calls back, could you tell him that I can't come to the phone?"

"Why would I tell him that?"

"Please. I really don't want to talk to him."

"Why not? I know you said something about Tom being an awful person, but I wasn't clear about what he had done that was so awful."

"Oh, please." The words were now intermingled with sobs. "I don't want to talk to him."

"Sarah, you will talk to him when he calls back. It would be rude not to. So, you finish up and make sure you're downstairs in plenty of time to receive his call."

"Okay," came a mournful sob from the other side of the bathroom door, followed by a dull thud that could have been the sound of a head hitting a wall.

"Hello," said the voice over the phone's speaker, sounding almost bereft of life.

"Er, hi, Sarah, this is Tom Cobalt."

"Hello." The speaker, if anything, seemed even closer to expiring than before.

"Er, about yesterday, after school. Listen, I didn't have anything to do with what Brad said, and you left in such a hurry that we—well, I mean, we didn't have a chance to—er, anyway I wanted to apologize for what Brad said." Tom took a hard swallow and waited for a reply. When none was forthcoming for several seconds, he said, "Hello? You there?"

150

"That's okay. I accept your apology. Thank you for calling."

Tom could have sworn that he heard a sniffle at the end of the last sentence. She had sounded awfully tired. Maybe that bath was a little too relaxing. "Oh, and I'm sorry I caught you in the bath when I called the first time." "Jumping Jehoshaphat," Tom thought, "I can't believe I said that." At the other end of the line Sarah's complexion took on a reddish tint. "Eh, can I talk to one of your parents?"

Without answering, Sarah turned to the hallway where her mother and father stood. She put her hand over the phone's mouthpiece and said, "He says he wants to talk to one of you."

"I'll take it," said her father, stepping into the room. Receiving the phone from his daughter, he said, "Hello, Tom, this is Sarah's father."

"Hello, Mr. Gould," said Tom, feeling a great relief that he no longer had to converse with a member of the opposite sex. "I wanted you to know that Alex and I had nothing to do with what Brad said about Sarah yesterday. I swear we didn't put him up to it, and I apologized to Sarah for what happened."

"Thank you, Tom. I appreciate that and I'm sure Sarah does too, but what exactly was it that—did you say his name was Brad—what exactly was it that he said?"

"Er—well—I'd rather not go into that. I just wanted to make sure that you knew that we didn't say it."

Mr. Gould smiled to himself, then turned to see his wife standing in the hallway with her arm around Sarah's shoulder, while Sarah hugged her mother with both arms. "I think I can guess, and again I appreciate your call."

"Oh, there's one more thing. If you want, we can—well, I mean I can—I can't speak for Alex—but I can walk Sarah to school if you want."

"Thank you for the offer, Tom. I'll tell you what. Let me have a chance to discuss your offer with my wife and Sarah, and I'll get back to you on that. Okay?"

151

"Okay, Mr. Gould. Well, good-bye." As Tom put down the receiver, he let out an audible sigh. Thank goodness that was over and done with. Now all that was left was for the Goulds to decide that they didn't want him to walk their daughter to school. Yet as he finished that thought, he found himself reflecting, almost subconsciously, that perhaps walking Sarah to school wouldn't be such a bad thing after all.

As he returned the receiver to its cradle, Mr. Gould turned to his wife and daughter. His wife raised her eyebrows as if to ask "Well?" while Sarah seemed to tighten her hold around her mother's waist as if she was a shield against any possible bad news.

"The boy apologized for what happened yesterday at the end of school and wanted us to know that he had nothing to do with it. Apparently one of his friends had said something rude about Sarah. Is that true, Sarah?"

"Yes," was the meek reply.

Mr. Gould walked closer and put his hand on Sarah's shoulder. "I think that was a nice gesture for Tom to call, don't you?"

"I suppose so," said the girl, giving her father a soulful look, and looking like she was about to collapse.

"It also was probably a hard thing for him to do. I think it took a lot of courage on his part."

"I bet his parents made him do it," said the girl.

Her father gave a laugh. "No doubt they did, but I think it still took courage on his part. Oh, and by the way, he offered to walk you to school again, if we thought that would be a good idea."

"No," came the horrified reply. "Please, no! You didn't say he could, did you?"

"I said we'd think about it."

"Please, no. I don't want to walk to school with him. He and his friends, they're like the Four Horsemen."

"The Four Horsemen?" Sarah's father sounded perplexed. "Why

would you compare them to the Notre Dame football players?"

"Not those four horsemen!" Sarah gave her father a look of disbelief. "The Four Horsemen of the Apocalypse."

"Oh, yes, of course." Mr. Gould exchanged glances with his wife. "Don't you think that's a little extreme comparing them to slaughter, pestilence, death, and—eh—whatever the last one is?" When Sarah didn't answer, he continued. "Let's give it a couple of days and see how things go. Then we'll give him our answer."

"Let me get this straight," said Jerry Haydn, sounding incredulous, "Sleinad Evad's real name was Dave Daniels and he got a doctorate in physics from the University of Belgrade?"

"Bucharest," said the young man.

Kevin let his eyes do a roll, and said, "Somehow little green men and ray guns are sounding more believable."

"Actually, the green men are about our size," said the young man.

Chapter 5
Neutronium

Sarah Gould successfully resisted any transformation back into Miss Hyde until the following Monday when the Sarah of the first day of school resurfaced with a vengeance. In history class Miss Odavsky made a casual comment about the United States being the first democracy since ancient Athens. She hadn't even completed the second syllable of the word "Athens" when Sarah's hand shot up.

"Yes, Sarah," stated Miss Odavsky, attempting to sound friendly.

When running in "correction mode," Sarah never bothered opening the attack with a superficial warning cut such as prefacing her comment with something like "I believe you might be mistaken." Instead Sarah went directly for the jugular. "The United States is not a democracy. It's a republic."

Either Miss Odavsky had forgotten the episode on the first day of school or she was willing to give the girl a second chance. "I'm afraid I don't see the difference, dear."

"The Constitution sets up the federal government as a republic, not a democracy. It also guarantees a republican form of government to the states."

"Well, Sarah, that might be true but I still don't see the difference. You always hear our leaders talking about our great democracy. Remember President Woodrow Wilson trying to make the world safe for democracy? Don't we have democratic elections in this country?"

"We might have democratic elections," continued the girl stubbornly, "but that's different from the type of government. You see—"

"Sarah, I'm afraid there's no point in discussing this further. As your teacher I'm telling you that our government is a democracy. Should you put down any other answer in a test I will mark it wrong. Now class, where were we?" There were a few giggles in the classroom. Sarah glared at her hecklers, then went back to taking notes.

Tom whispered to Alex. "Let me guess. Republic right, democracy wrong?"

Alex nodded.

In English class Sarah compounded the sin of always being right with that of being bluntly candid. Emily Flowers had finished reading her essay to the class on what she liked best about her school when the teacher, Mr. Davies, asked the other students for comments. When no one volunteered, Mr. Davies committed the all-time, number one blunder of calling on Sarah. "Sarah, is there any comment you'd like to make about Emily's essay?" Tom noted that Emily gave an involuntary cringe when Mr. Davies addressed Sarah.

"It stunk. I would give it a D." Obviously Sarah was starting to crack under the strain of ostracism by the other students.

"Sarah Gould, I think that was an awfully rude thing to say." said Mr. Davies. "I believe you owe Emily an apology."

"Why? You asked for my opinion and I gave it. I have nothing personal against Emily. Apologizing won't change the fact that her essay stinks. It definitely needs more work."

"Sarah, are you refusing to apologize?"

"Yes."

"Sarah, you apologize right now or you'll be going to the office, and a note will be going home to your parents."

Sarah's eyes were beginning to redden when she stood up and

slammed her notebook closed. "You asked me what I thought. If you don't want an honest answer, then don't ask me! What do you want me to do, lie?"

If Sarah was flustered, it was contagious. Mr. Davies stammered, sputtered, spit, and then finally managed to get out, "You go to the office this minute—and I'm sending a note home to your parents about your unacceptable behavior at school!"

Sarah tried to grab her stuff but kept dropping things like books, papers, pencils, purse—picking up what she had just dropped and in the process dropping something else, all to the accompaniment of giggles and snickers from many of her fellow students. After what must have seemed like an eternity to the girl, she finally got everything together and hurried from the room, her vision now blurred by tears.

As the door closed behind her the room erupted in a chorus of chatter, causing Mr. Davies to switch from a state of flustered to a state of mild hysteria. Tom poked Wayne who was sitting in the seat in front of him on the shoulder. "Who said 'honesty is the best policy?'"

Wayne turned in his seat. "Probably one of Sarah's ancestors."

"Students, please," shouted Mr. Davies. After several more attempts, the beleaguered teacher finally managed to restore order. "Now class, please hand in your essays from yesterday and then take out a pencil and paper. You may use the remaining class time to start work on tomorrow's writing assignment. The theme of your new essay is 'How I would run the country if I was president.'"

Wayne put up his hand.

Mr. Davies hastily consulted his seating chart and then said, "Yes, Wayne."

"What country are you referring to?"

"Why America, the United States, of course."

"Okay, just checking."

Alex immediately raised his hand.

"Yes—uh, Alex."

"Shouldn't that be, 'if I *were* president?'"

"Huh? What do you mean?"

"Well, you said the theme is 'How I would run the country if I was president.' I think that's incorrect. Shouldn't it be 'How I would run the country if I were president.'"

"I don't see what difference it makes—*was, were*. Just write the essay."

"I think it makes a lot of difference, considering this *is* English class."

"Don't you get smart with me, Mr.—uh—Banyon or you'll be joining Miss—Miss—Gould at the office."

Brad raised his hand.

After giving a sigh and again consulting his seating chart, Mr. Davies said, "Yes, Brad."

"By president do you mean like president of General Motors or president of the PTA or—"

"I mean President of the United States," said the teacher, his voice now raised to a shout. "Good God, what's wrong with you people? Can't you understand a simple essay question? Now, no more questions. Get to work!"

The last outburst was followed by the sounds of the scratching of pencils on paper. After a few minutes of casting threatening glances about the classroom, Mr. Davies finally took a seat behind his desk. He had been seated but a minute when Tom's hand shot up.

"Yes, Tom."

"Mr. Davies. How do you spell quagmire?"

"Quag-what?" came the startled reply.

"Quagmire. You know, like in muskeg."

"Muskeg? What in—what does that have to do with being president?"

"I'd rather not say as I don't want any of the other students using my idea."

"Okay, so just use musk—use that other word that you said it means."

"If I thought that muskeg was a better choice, I would have used it. Quagmire is really better, much better. So how do you spell it?"

"Look it up in the dictionary, Tom. That's why we have dictionaries."

"How can I look it up if I don't have any idea how to spell it?"

"Don't get smart with me young man."

"In other words, you don't know how it's spelled either."

Mr. Davies leaped to his feet, his face turning red and his voice squeaking. "I've had enough of this smart-alecky back talk. You go to the office right this minute . . ." Mr. Davies started sputtering, spit flying out of his mouth and showering the students in the first row of desks. "And you better believe I'm sending a note home to your parents."

Tom calmly put away his pencil and paper and gathered his books together, then stood and walked to the doorway where he stopped. "Mr. Davies, I bet you don't even know what quagmire means."

"Yes, I do," screamed the teacher. "It means musk—, musk-something. See I'm not as dumb as you think I look. Uh, that is . . ."

"Like I said, you have no idea what a quagmire is." With that Tom exited the classroom.

Mr. Davies stood with his mouth open, unable to think of a suitable retort as he watched Tom disappear. Then before he could resume his seat, he noticed that Brad had his hand raised. A quick glance at the seating chart and he said, "Yes, Brad." Somehow, he just knew he was going to regret acknowledging another question.

"Mr. Davies how to you spell pterodactyl?"

"Pterodactyl? Pterodactyl! What in blazes does a pterodactyl . . . ?"

Sarah was wiping away a stray tear when she felt the presence of someone taking the seat next to her on the "punishment" bench outside of the assistant principal's office. "Tom? What are you doing here?"

"Things were sort of turning into a quagmire in Mr. Davies' class, so I decided to come here."

"Oh," said Sarah, not having any idea what Tom was talking about.

For a couple of minutes, they both sat there staring straight ahead with Sarah letting out an occasional sniffle but trying to do so in a way that Tom wouldn't notice. Finally, Tom spoke up.

"You know, being right can sometimes be tough."

"What do you mean?"

"Well, I guess I mean that it can take real guts to speak up and tell the truth, even though you know that it won't be appreciated—or something like that, I think."

"Are you talking about me—about what happened in English class?"

"Yeah, of course."

"You think I have guts?"

"Yeah. Standing your ground like that in the face of authority— that takes courage." Tom turned to face the girl, who was staring at him and looking like she was suffering from mild shock. "Don't get me wrong," he continued. "It wasn't the smartest thing to do, but it took guts."

Sarah continued to stare at Tom, her expression being akin to that of a young lady transfixed by the hypnotic spell. For a few moments both teens were silent. Finally, Sarah switched her gaze to its customary target, the floor, and muttered, "Did you get the homework assignment?"

"Yeah. We have to write another essay, this time on what you would do if you were president or something like that."

"President of what?" asked Sarah.

As the students were leaving English class, Emily Flowers turned to Diane Ferguson who was exiting the room with her.

"And to think, I was about to try to make friends with her today.

You know, sit with her at lunch."

Diane gave Emily an affirmative nod.

Wayne who was walking a couple of feet in front of the girls motioned to Alex, keeping his voice low, "Yeah, right." He stopped and turned around. "You know what, Emily? I wouldn't have given your paper a D. I would have given it a B."

"Really," said Emily, giving the boy a big smile.

"Yeah, I believe in being kind to dumb animals."

The boys didn't see Tom or Sarah again until lunch. As always, Sarah sat at the same table, alone.

"Hey, Alex," said Tom, or at least that is what Alex thought he said, since Tom was talking with his mouth full of food. "Did you ever ask your uncle about Evad?"

"Yeah, I called him and he said he never heard of a physicist by the name of Sleinad Evad, or Dave Daniels for that matter. But he said there were thousands of physicists in the world and unless Evad had made some important discovery or published a lot of scientific papers, there's no reason he should have heard of him. And how many scientific papers does a high school physics teacher publish?"

"Just wondering."

With the ringing of the seventh period bell, Evad strode into the room and went through the ritual to which the class had by now become accustomed. Without looking at the students, he stopped behind the teacher's lab table at the front of the room and deposited his briefcase in a drawer. Then he gave the class a quick scan. "I see that Mr. Lowenson is not with us today." He flipped open his attendance book and made a mark in it. Closing the book, the man, wearing as was his habit a suit of such dark blue that it could have been easily mistaken for black, positioned himself on the high stool that stood behind the lab table. "Mr. Lowenson should consider himself lucky. I had originally planned to give a quiz today, but since we will miss class tomorrow due to the assembly program, we shall press on with our discussion of atoms. Sometime—" The man paused. Then in a voice intended more for himself than the class, he whispered a single word, "Time." As he did so, his eyes focused directly on Tom.

It was the same look that Tom remembered from the first day of school. To the boy it seemed as if those cold, grey-blue eyes were trying to probe into his mind. Without having to look about him, he guessed correctly that all his classmates were also studying him, trying to decide what it was about Tom that so seemed to captivate the Grim Reaper. As holding eye contact with Evad was becoming unbearable, Tom glanced at Alex and, as expected, his friend returned the acknowledgment with a quick shrug of the shoulders, signaling that he had no idea what was going on.

When Tom shifted his gaze back to the teacher, he was surprised to hear the man say, "Mr. Piers. What is the name for the negatively charged particles in an atom?" whereupon Evad turned his attention to the surprised Bobby Piers.

"Electrons," came the answer.

"Miss Featherson, what two subatomic particles compose the nuclei of atoms?"

"Uh, neutrons and protons?"

"Are you telling me or asking me?"

"Uh, telling you, I guess—sir."

Evad slowly moved his head from side to side with a droll but weary look on his face.

"Miss Flowers."

Emily Flowers jumped a couple of inches out of her seat, let out a barely audible shriek and dropped her pencil on the floor. She ignored the pencil as she tried to focus her attention on the question.

"What is the name for matter that is composed solely of neutrons?"

A look of horror appeared on the girl's face and a look of bafflement appeared on the faces of the rest of the students. "I'm afraid I don't know, sir."

"Mr. Banyon."

Alex blinked his eyes, startled to hear his name called. "I don't know."

"Anyone? Does anyone know the name for matter that is composed solely of neutrons?" No one volunteered an answer. "Neutronium!" Evad boomed, as if the answer were obvious. "Neutronium," he repeated. "Neutrons are bound together in neutronium, the state of which depends on the strength of the local gummion field." His explanation was met by blank expressions on the faces of the students.

Alex raised his hand. Evad ignored him and called on Sarah who had also raised her hand. "Miss Gould."

"How do you spell that, sir?"

"Spell what?"

"Gummion?"

"G-U-M-M-I—" Evad stopped. For a moment he didn't move, then he jerked his head to one side to stare at the calendar on the wall. Its heading read:

SEPTEMBER 1959

"Something's wrong," thought Tom. "He's unsure of himself. He's made a mistake."

Evad turned back to the class. Alex still had his hand up. And then Evad did something that no student had expected. He smiled. It was neither a threatening nor sarcastic nor cynical type of smile, but a friendly, normal type of smile. He looked at Alex who still had his hand up. "It's a joke, Mr. Banyon. Neutronium and gummions are a joke." Alex lowered his hand.

The grim reaper turned on Tom, baring his teeth in the process.

"Mr. Cobalt." Tom could have sworn that the man hissed his name like some humanoid serpent. "Tell me. If you discovered some new, exotic elementary particle, what would you name it?"

"Huh? What's an erotic elementary particle?"

"Not erotic," growled the teacher. "Exotic, you imbecile, as in unique, unusual. Protons, neutrons, and electrons are elementary particles. Didn't you read the assignment?"

"Uh, yea—yes. I did read the assignment. It's just that first word kind of threw me."

"Not that I'm surprised. So, do you have an answer, Mr. Cobalt?"

"I can't remember the question."

Wayne, sitting two rows to the right of Tom, had swiveled around in his seat to get a better view of the action. Wayne snickered.

The undertaker's head jerked, his eyes locking on Wayne.

"Yes, Mr. Franklin. You have an answer?"

The suddenness of the teacher's move caused Wayne to snap to attention.

"Uh, well, uh . . ."

"You sounded like you had something to contribute to the conversation," sneered Evad.

"Ah," said Wayne, stalling for time. "You asked Tom that if he discovered some new elementary particle what he would name it."

"That's correct. And now I'm asking you."

"Are you asking me what I think Tom would name it or what I would name it?"

Evad swiftly moved next to where Wayne was seated and placed his right hand on the top cross piece of the back of Wayne's chair. He began to squeeze the wood and as he did so, the boy could have sworn that he heard the fibers begin to crack.

"Don't try me, Mr. Franklin."

The boy swallowed. "I'm sorry sir, I don't have an answer."

"No, I thought not." Evad lifted his hand from the chair. Wayne turned to stare at the top cross piece, now imprinted with an imbedded relief of Evad's fingers.

"Quark," came a female voice from the last row of seats.

Evad again spun around. "Yes, Miss Gould? You have something to say?"

"Quark," said Sarah. "I would call it a quark."

To Tom's surprise, the teacher's smile returned.

"Interesting," he said. "How do you spell that?"

Sarah at first stammered. "I'm—not sure. Q-U-A-R-K, I guess. Quark."

"And where did you find such a word?" inquired Evad, his smile growing even wider.

"I just made it up. I thought that a new particle should be given a name that's—you know, different. A name that doesn't really mean anything to anyone."

"Interesting," said Evad. "Most interesting." The man seemed immensely pleased with the girl's answer.

For everyone in the class, with the possible exception of Sarah Gould, no bell ending a period was more welcome than that that ended the seventh period science class. When Evad said, "You're excused," the students quickly gathered their things and hustled themselves to the exit, as if each dreaded being the last to leave. Today, the last three out the door were Alex, Tom and Sarah, in that order. As Alex reached the doorway, Evad casually stepped from behind the lab table. His right hand shot out, grabbing a fistful of Tom's hair. The move was so sudden and unexpected that Tom failed to stop in time to prevent a few of the hairs actually being pulled out of his scalp.

"Ow," he squawked as his head was pulled back and he came to a stop. Sarah almost collided with him, but stopped in the nick of time, looking shocked at the teacher's action.

"I assure you, Mr. Cobalt, there are no owls in here," said the Grim Reaper, as if he were making a joke. "This is physical science, not zoology."

"Did you want something, sir?" asked Tom as he rubbed the spot on his scalp that was now populated by several fewer hairs.

"Yes, Mr. Cobalt," came the answer. "I'll overlook your behavior in class today, but from now on I expect you to take this course more seriously. Is that understood?"

"Eh, yes sir," said Tom, not having a clue as to what behavior Evad was referring to.

"You're excused." With that Evad returned to the lab table and the three teens hurried off, Tom still rubbing his scalp.

"Joke, my buttocks!" said Alex when they were safely out of earshot of Evad. "He messed up. He made a mistake. Mr. Almighty Infallible Doctor of Philosophy messed up."

"What are you talking about?" said Tom. "And what was that about my misbehaving in class? Did you think I misbehaved in class?"

"Forget the behavior thing. Just accept reality. Evad has it in for you and there's nothing you can do about it. I'm talking about the neutronium thing. When he mentioned neutronium, he made a mistake of some kind."

"I'm not so sure. Maybe it really was a joke," said Tom. "He's just not very good at making jokes, that's all. Lack of practice is my guess."

Sarah was tailing along behind the two boys, attempting to stay far enough away so as not to be noticed but at the same time close enough to hear what they were saying. She failed in her first objective when Alex abruptly stopped causing Sarah to almost bump into him. "Have you ever heard of neutronium?" Alex said to the friendless girl, more in the tone of a command than a question.

All she could think to do to respond was to nod no.

Alex turned around again and resumed walking. "See. Sarah hasn't heard of neutronium and I haven't heard of neutronium."

"So?" challenged his friend. "What's your point?"

"Neutronium. He said neutronium. No, there's more than meets the eye here. He almost acted like he said something he shouldn't have. And then he looked at the wall, or—at the calendar on the wall. The mystery deepens, Watson."

"You're telling me that you think Evad knows some kind of scientific secret or something and he goofed up and let the cat out of the bag?" Alex didn't answer, as he was obviously totally focused on his thoughts. "Let's say that this—neutronium really exists," Tom continued. "Then what was all that about gummy-somethings or whatever?"

Instead of answering, Alex again spun around. "How did you figure out that Sleinad Evad was Dave Daniels spelled backwards?" He almost spate the words at Sarah, as if to insinuate that in doing so she had violated some unwritten code of conduct.

Sarah had stopped so abruptly to avoid bumping into the boys that a couple of her books slipped out of her arms. As she stooped to pick them up, she started to mutter, "Well, I, er, I thought—, that is, I—how did you know?"

"That's what I thought. Dumb luck," said Alex, again turning around and continuing to walk down the hall. Tom, who had knelt to help Sarah with her books, had to run to catch up with his friend.

"I'll call my uncle tonight and ask him about neutronium. He'll know for sure whether Evad's spilled the beans or is just crazy. He'll know."

Reaching their lockers, the boys packed what they needed for homework that evening. When they left school, Sarah was nowhere to be seen.

Sarah's mother read the two notes, one from Mr. Davies and one from the school's assistant principal. Sarah sat beside her on the coach, her hands folded on her lap, staring at the floor. When Mrs. Gould had finished the notes, she gave her daughter a tender but pained look. Her voice was gentle but pleading. "Sarah, we've talked about this before.

You have to be sensitive of the feelings of others. Sometimes it's best not to say anything, or if you have to say something, sometimes a little white lie is better than the truth."

"I know, Mom." The girl's voice was barely above a whisper. Her mom reached over, put her hand on her daughter's, and gave it an affectionate squeeze. "Sometimes it's just hard to remember," the girl continued. Sarah lifted her head so she could make eye contact with her mother. "Are you going to tell Daddy?"

"He should know. Yes, I intended to, but if you don't want me to, I won't."

"No, you should." Both women were silent for a moment, before Sarah continued. "I just don't look forward to getting the same lecture twice in the same day, once from you and then again from Daddy."

Her mother smiled and again squeezed the girl's hand. "Have you made any friends yet at school?"

"No." It was the answer her mom had expected.

"Well, now that we're unpacked and settled, we'll start looking around for a new church. Maybe there you'll find some people your age you'll like."

"Mom, it's not about me liking them. It's about them liking me. And I know why they don't like me. It's because of my nose and the fact that I can't keep my big mouth shut."

"Sarah, there's nothing wrong with your nose."

"It's big. Everyone says so. They call me Big Nose here like they did back in Albany. Of course, they call me other things too."

"You're a kind and generous person." Mrs. Gould fumbled for her next words. "You're also pretty. You have beautiful hair, and eyes, and—"

"And a big nose!"

Mrs. Gould didn't complete her sentence. She gave her daughter another sympathetic look, and then said, "Give it time and soon enough things will be better. You'll make some friends who'll like you just the way you are. Time heals everything."

"I'm not smart! I'm stupid. If I were smart I'd keep my mouth shut. And I'm not cute, I have a big nose. Why did I have to be born with such a big nose?"

"I don't know what else to say, dear. But time heals all. It really does. You have to give it time."

Sarah directed her gaze at the far wall, but her eyes were not focused on it. "Time," she said. "Why did he look at the calendar?"

"Huh? Who are you talking about?"

"Mom, can you take me to the library tonight?"

"Er, yes, I guess so." Mrs. Gould was startled at the sudden change in Sarah's disposition. "School work?"

"No. I wanted to see if I could find anything about neutronium."

"About what?"

"Never mind. It's not important." She turned to her mom, and forced a small smile, her vision still blurred by the recent tears. "Just something I'm interested in."

"Okay," said Mrs. Gould. "Well, I guess I should start getting dinner ready." As she stood up she continued. "Oh, by the way. You remember how you said you were having trouble seeing the blackboard from the back of the classroom. I made a four o'clock appointment tomorrow to have your eyesight checked."

"Eye exam," cried Sarah, alarm in her voice. "No, not glasses. Not glasses on top of everything else!"

That evening Mr. Gould called the Cobalts and, after thanking them, politely rejected the offer for Tom to walk Sarah to school.

"I don't get it," said Jerry, leaning back on his chair, "I mean about the neutronium thing. If Evad was making a joke, what's the big deal?"

"We didn't know about neutronium back then," explained the young man, "because in 1959 neutronium hadn't been discovered."

"I never heard of neutronium," said Phil Bartley.

Ignoring Phil, Jerry continued. "If no one knew about neutronium in 1959 then how did this Evad guy know about it?"

"Gee, Dad, that's easy," said Brett. "It's because he's from the future."

Jerry let out a moan.

Chapter 6
The Bearing of Arms

A loud crack echoed across the field. "Another bull's eye," yelled a boy, peering through the eyepiece of a spotting scope.

"I'm certainly impressed," said a casually dressed man to his companion who was wearing the uniform of a scoutmaster. "He's as good as you said he was."

The sound of another shot was again followed by a yell. "Bull's eye."

"I take it you've never met Tom's father, Sam Cobalt?" said the scoutmaster.

Crack! "Bull's eye."

"He was a marine. May be the reason Tom's such a marksman."

"Has he ever shot anything other than a twenty-two?"

Crack! "And another bull's eye."

"Oh, yes," said the scoutmaster. "We have a couple different caliber hunting rifles for the boys to use. I've also seen Tom use a revolver as well as a shotgun–shooting skeet. It makes no difference. He's just as accurate with whatever he's shooting. Even bow and arrow. I made sure I was there . . ."

Crack! "Bull's eye. Well, I think it was a bull's eye," said the boy at the spotting scope. "Heck, Tom, the center of the target looks like one big hole."

"Okay, Tom, that's enough," called the scoutmaster. "Wayne, you're up. Where was I? Oh, yes. I made sure I was there to see him test for the archery merit badge. He said it was the first time he ever used a bow. After learning the fundamentals and going through a few practice shots, he started putting them in the center circle like he had used a bow for years. The kid's a natural. I wouldn't be surprised seeing him win a national competition someday."

"Incredible," said the other man, who then called to Tom. "Tom, come here a second, please."

"Yes, Mr. Seasons," the boy answered.

"Don says you're the best marksman he's ever seen. Did your father teach you to shoot?"

"No, sir."

"Well, who taught you?"

"Uh, Don did," said Tom, giving the scoutmaster a nod. "He taught us about gun safety and how to load and fire and stuff like that."

"That's true, Tom," said the scoutmaster. The air was again ruptured by the sound of a shot, followed by the familiar yell of 'bull's eye' as Wayne started his series. "But I didn't teach you to shoot. That you learned on your own."

"Interesting," said the other man as he stooped down and opened a gun case that was lying on the ground. "Do you know what kind of rifle this is?" he said, lifting a deadly looking firearm from the case.

"Sure." said the boy. "It's an M-1, the gun that won the Second World War. We have one at home."

"Oh, so you've shot one."

"No, sir."

The answer seemed to surprise Mr. Seasons. "Doesn't your father take you shooting, or hunting?"

"No, sir. My father doesn't hunt. I think he might have when he was a kid, but he told me that since being in a war, if he ever hears another gunshot it will be too soon."

"I see," Mr. Seasons gave the scoutmaster a knowing look. "I can appreciate that." Then he turned his attention back to the boy. "Would you like to shoot the M-1?"

"Sure," Tom nodded eagerly.

"You don't think your father would mind?"

"Oh, no sir. As matter of fact, he's glad that I'm a scout and learning about firearms. He told me that it should be the duty of every citizen to know how to shoot. He told me that if the Minutemen hadn't known how to shoot, we'd have Queen Elizabeth's picture on our coins."

"Wow! That's an M-1, isn't it?" came a voice from behind the men.

"Yes, Alex," said the scoutmaster. "You know Mr. Seasons, don't you—Barry's dad?"

"Yeah. Hello Mr. Seasons. Is that yours?" Alex pointed at the M-1.

"Yes," said Mr. Seasons. He held the rifle out to Alex. "Want to heft it?"

"Sure," said the grateful boy, accepting the weapon from the scout father. "Can we shoot it?"

"Sure, right after Tom."

"Oh, right. Give Annie Oakley first crack so that the rest of us will look like we're half blind."

"I'll tell you what," suggested Mr. Seasons, taking back the firearm. "It will take me a couple of minutes to attach the sight and get it checked out. Why don't you and Tom see if any of the other boys want to try it. Then you can draw straws to see who shoots first."

"Okay," agreed Alex. "Come on Tom."

As the two boys started walking towards a group of seated scouts, Alex said, "I almost forgot to tell you. I asked my uncle about neutronium. Guess what he said?"

"He laughed."

"Yep! He said there's no such thing, that you can't have matter composed only of neutrons."

"Any reason why not?"

"Well, for one thing neutrons outside the atomic nucleus decay into protons, electrons and something called an antineutrino."

"Decay?" said Tom. "You mean like in radioactive decay?"

"Yes. I believe my uncle said the half-life of a neutron is fifteen minutes."

"Half-life," mused Tom. "If I remember what that is, that means that if neutronium actually existed it would be radioactive and that in fifteen minutes half of it would disappear."

"Yep."

"And then after the next fifteen minutes, half of what was left would also disappear and so on until there was nothing left."

"Boy, for a moron, you're pretty good at remembering what I've taught you."

"Yeah, well, this stuff is interesting. I mean, how come we never learn interesting stuff like this in school?"

"If they taught us interesting stuff, no one would ever want to leave, right? So, by boring us half to death, they give us incentive to keep passing so that eventually we'll graduate and get out of there and do something useful with our lives."

"You know," said Tom, "that's one of the stupidest ideas I've ever heard. Then again, considering some of the classes we've had to sit through, I think you might be on to something."

The boys' conversation was interrupted by a yell. "What are you two doing standing there?" said the scoutmaster. "Get the other boys. We're about ready to demonstrate the M-1."

"Sorry," yelled back Tom. "We were discussing nuclear physics."

The scoutmaster gave his head a shake, as the two teens resumed walking.

"Okay," said Tom. "I'm not sure I understand why neutronium can't exist but you at least convinced me of one thing."

"What's that?"

"That Evad was just making a joke."

"I can't see that man ever seeing humor in anything," said Alex.

"How about watching another human being writhe in agony?" said Tom.

"Well, now that you mention it, he might find that amusing. He certainly expends enough energy torturing his students."

Chapter 7
Life at East Pencreek High

Life at East Pencreek High School struggled on in the days that followed. Tom continued to suspect that Evad was giving him the evil eye. Hardly a science class went by without the pedagogue from purgatory singling out Tom for one reason or another, usually followed by the man making a belittling remark about the boy. Even though Tom's mastery of the course material, with the exception of Alex, Sarah and Wayne, excelled that of his classmates, it was always Tom whom Evad seemed to select as the target for his ridicule and criticism. Taking the quizzes and tests became nightmare experiences for Tom, for whenever he happened to look up from his paper, there was the ubiquitous undertaker fixing him with a cold stare that reminded the boy of some primeval carnivore eyeing its next meal. The boy found Evad's special attention that seemed directed only at him unnerving. As a result, he often erred on questions that, in more normal circumstances, he would have had no problem answering correctly.

His experience with the first test was typical. As Evad passed out the exams, he gave the students dire warnings as to how he would ruin their lives should any of them even dare contemplate cheating. He completed his harangue with the statement, "Remember, Mr. Cobalt. I have my eye on you."

"Huh? Why me?" Tom asked himself. By the time Tom ceased

dwelling on Evad's comment and regained his composure so he could focus on the test, a good ten minutes had elapsed. The resulting grade of a D was mostly due to his running out of time, a direct result of those lost minutes.

The day after the test, Tom managed to get another appointment with Mr. Serpens, the Junior High guidance counselor. Despite Tom's best efforts to describe Evad's discriminatory treatment of him and how it was affecting his performance in science class, Serpens' responses were as cheerful and condescending and unhelpful as they had been during the boy's first visit.

"I'm certain much of this is just your thirteen-year-old imagination running a little wild. Remember what we discussed in our earlier meeting about how having Mr. Evad as a teacher will ultimately be for your betterment? It's exactly the medicine you need to make you work up to your potential. Give it more time and I'm sure you'll begin to see the truth in what I'm saying. And please remember Tom," said the tall, debonair man, whose grey eyes seemed to match perfectly the color of the suit he wore, "things aren't always as they seem." By the end of the meeting, the boy's feelings towards the Junior High guidance counselor had progressed from contempt to pure loathing. Tom began to imagine that Serpens and Evad were co-conspirators in some sort of dastardly scheme to destroy him.

As Tom exited Serpens' office, his face almost collided with a yo-yo. Alex had been attempting an around-the-world while waiting in the hall. "Well, how did it go?"

"How did Custer make out at the Little Big Horn?" said Tom, as if the answer hadn't been obvious from the expression on his face. He then began to mimic someone banging his head against a wall. "Only eight months until summer vacation, that is, if Evad doesn't kill me first."

The other new factor in Tom's life that school year, Sarah Gould, at least seemed to be proving less of an annoyance of late. Tom, along with the rest of the students at East Pencreek High, continued to keep their distance from the girl. Sarah ate alone in the cafeteria at lunch time, walked to and from school alone, and sat in the back of each class alone. Her hope of making some new friends was long forgotten. Several school mornings she told her mother that she was too sick to go to school and pleaded with Mrs. Gould to let her stay home. At first Mrs. Gould relented, although she suspected that Sarah wasn't physically ill. The mother reasoned that perhaps an occasional break from the stress of school would do Sarah some good. However, after the third absence, Mrs. Gould insisted that Sarah return to classes. She suggested to her daughter that she could again ask Tom and Alex to escort her to and from school, but Sarah only said that would make things worse and her mother was forced to admit that maybe her daughter was right.

At school Sarah continued to struggle against the compulsion to correct the errors of others, both students and teachers. Her greatest challenge was tolerating Miss Odavsky, the history teacher, as Sarah knew far more about American history than did Miss Odavsky. The girl's struggle to keep this fact suppressed seemed to her on par with the Twelve Labors of Hercules. But what went on in history class paled in comparison to what happened that fateful Monday in English class when Sarah was forced to reveal a secret that soon earned her a second nickname from many of her fellow students to rival the ever popular Big Nose. As the teacher started to write a sentence on the blackboard, Sarah, sitting at her desk, hesitantly reached into her purse and pulled out a small case. She studied her fellow students in an attempt to ensure that no one was watching, and then opened the case and took out the pair of dark-rimmed eyeglasses. She put them on and began to copy down the sentence from the blackboard. The question of how long it would take for someone to notice the optical aids now balanced on her nose was immediately answered when the teacher, Mr. Davies, said, "Well, Sarah, I see you now have glasses. They look nice on you." Immediately all eyes in the room turned and stared at the girl, followed by snickers from several of the students. To the nickname Big Nose would no doubt now be added Four Eyes or some other similar term of derision. Sarah quickly lowered her gaze, but then, as if drawn by some irresistible urge, she raised her head and looked at Alex. The boy in turn was looking right at her through the lenses of his own glasses, but with no expression of jest or derision. Instead, the girl thought she saw a look of empathy.

At the end of each school day Sarah was careful to position herself at a strategic point within the building where she could watch the main exit. She never left for home until she first saw the quartet of Tom, Alex, Wayne and Brad leave. Avoiding the boys on the way to school in the morning was more of a problem. On occasion she found herself exiting her house just as Tom and Alex were leaving the latter's home directly across the street. Then she would have to hurry in an attempt to get far enough ahead of them so they wouldn't catch up with her, or pretend to have forgotten something so as to return to her house to give them time to gain a sufficient lead. The day after the new glasses fiasco turned out to be one such occasion when she had no sooner entered the street in front of her home then the two boys appeared from behind Alex's house. They were only a few paces behind her and with their longer strides were steadily closing the gap. Worse yet, the other two of the foursome, Brad and Wayne, would no doubt be waiting for their friends at the highway not far ahead. In a panic, Sarah turned left at the next intersection. "I'll cut over one block and take a parallel route to school," she thought. "It won't be that far out of my way."

"I wonder where she's going," Alex asked Tom, having noticed the girl's detour.

"Maybe she hasn't adjusted to her new glasses yet," suggested the taller boy, "and is meandering off blindly."

Alex stopped, which in turn caused Tom to stop. The two stood there and watched the girl proceed down the wrong street, Tom all the time wondering what was going through his friend's mind. Finally, Alex said, "Maybe we should follow her?"

"Huh? Why? She surely knows the way to school. I think she's trying to avoid us."

"Yeah, you're probably right."

"Not that that isn't something that we shouldn't be thankful for."

"Wow," said Alex, sounding impressed. "A triple negative."

"Huh?"

"You said 'Not that that isn't something that we shouldn't be thankful for.' You used the word 'not' three times in one sentence, not to mention the triple 'that' thrown in for good measure. Frankly I don't know if you mean we should be thankful or not."

"Didn't you just use a double negative?" observed Tom. "But then that's not neither here nor there. If we follow her, we'll miss Wayne and Brad."

"Yeah. Good point." With that, the two boys resumed taking the more direct route to school.

Having successfully navigated the detour, Sarah was approaching the school yard when she noticed three older youths leaning against a bike rack at the edge of the school property. The one in the middle looked to be bigger and older than the other two, and by his demeanor, was no doubt the acknowledged leader of the trio. Although Sarah had never met him, she rightly deduced that the boy in the middle was Jack Paine. He was the type whose reputation preceded him. Paine's last name was aptly chosen since he spent a good deal of his time and energy inflicting pain on the younger students. Jack was seventeen years old, but still in the ninth grade, at least on those days when he decided to show up for school. He was the kind of student who was not particularly keen on academics. The tough wore a white t-shirt, a black leather jacket, a two-day growth of beard, a four-day amassment of body odor, and a look that said to one and all that he was king of the world—well, at least of the schoolyard— and if others knew what was good for them, they had better not dispute the fact. Jack and his two friends, who were similarly attired, had their hair slicked back in classic "greaser" fashion. Smoke drifted from the cigarettes they held.

Sarah realized her present course would carry her directly in front of the three. At first she considered detouring around them, but it had rained the night before and the ground on both sides of the sidewalk had changed to mud. Besides, changing her course would look like an obvious attempt to avoid them, and might lead to worse consequences than simply continuing on her present course and acting like they didn't exist. Fixing her eyes firmly on the walkway, Sarah took a deep swallow, and continued on down the sidewalk. As she was passing the three, she heard one of them say, "Hey, look at the beak on her." There was laughter. Then the boy called after her, "Hey, honey, want to join me for a smoke?"

She kept walking, attempting to do a fair impression of a deaf person. She was almost convinced that she had avoided an incident when something hit her on the back of the head. The blow caused the girl to drop the books she was carrying as she pitched forward onto the sidewalk. As her left knee hit the hard concrete of the walkway, she let out a yelp of pain, at the same time bruising the palm of her right hand in attempting to break her fall.

"Strike!" yelled a triumphant Jack, admiring the damage done by his well aimed mud ball.

"Did you see that?" cried Alex, for he and his friends happened to be entering the schoolyard not far from where Sarah had fallen.

"Wow, good shot," observed Wayne, obviously impressed by Jack's skill with mud balls.

"Aw, a blind man could have hit her from that distance," said Brad.

Displaying a reaction to the incident obviously at odds with that of

Brad and Wayne, Alex started toward the girl. Tom grabbed the right sleeve of Alex's jacket, stopping his friend's progress. "Are you nuts? That's Jack Paine!"

"Yeah, and that moron just hit an unarmed girl," said Alex. With that, he pulled his sleeve from the other boy's grasp and stomped off towards Sarah, who was now lying on her side, holding her injured knee with both hands and sounding like she was about to enter the realm of hyperventilation.

Tom watched his friend for a moment, and then shaking his head as if trying to convince himself to reconsider what he felt certain was a bad idea, took off after the blond kid. Brad and Wayne both looked at the other two as if they had been struck with madness and stoically stood their ground.

The three hoodlums were still laughing at the unfortunate girl's plight when Alex reached Sarah and knelt down beside her. He held out a hand and said, "Are you okay?"

Sarah gave him a startled look, having until then been focusing only on the pain in her knee and hand. "No," she bawled at him in a tone that seemed to say, "What a dumb question!"

Seeing Alex, Jack's smile immediately twisted into an even more evil version of itself. He flicked the cigarette he held to one side and balled his hands into fists. But as he started to take a step towards Alex and Sarah, one of his companions pointed towards the school entrance. "Hey, that looks like Coach Heartburn."

"We better scram," said the other boy. Jack gave a reluctant nod, and the three hoodlums began walking away, Jack nonchalantly pulling out another cigarette from the pack in his jacket pocket and lighting it.

Meanwhile Alex was toiling about Sarah like some crazed mother hen. "Well, I was only trying to help, I mean—here let me get your books and we should probably take you to the school nurse, although I'm not sure she's in yet." All the while Sarah was rocking from side to side, still holding her knee and sobbing.

181

"Wow, it looked like you hit hard," said Tom. "I hope nothing's broken."

Sarah made a sound sort of between a hiccup and a cough as she jerked her head up to see Tom, and then amazingly stopped sniveling. She carefully rolled over on her stomach and started making motions as if to stand up. The two boys took that as a cue and, with the girl positioned between them, each grabbed one of Sarah's arms and pulled her to her feet.

"Let go of me!" she screamed.

Letting go, Tom said, "We're just trying to help."

"It's all your fault," she sniveled again, now adding irrational to hysterical.

"What did we do?" asked Alex, stooping down to pick up the neat stack of books he had assembled, and offering them to the girl.

"Hey, Alex," said Tom, as if getting a brilliant idea. "This might be a great chance to practice first aid. You know, since we're testing for the merit badge at the next troop meeting."

"What!" screamed Sarah. "Leave me alone," spit the girl, while attempting to grab her books from Alex. However, when her hand with the bleeding bruise came into contact with the books, she gave out a yelp and again dropped them. At that she sat back down on the walk, a motion that caused her to bend her injured knee, sending another spasm up pain up her leg. She sat here and sobbed, her hair having fallen over her glasses which didn't matter as she wasn't looking at anything in particular.

The two boys stood there dumb founded as to what to do next, when a voice from behind them said, "What's happened here?"

"Hello, Mrs. Jenkins," said Alex, addressing the approaching teacher. "Jack Paine hit Sarah with a mud ball or something, and she fell down. We were helping her."

Mrs. Jenkins knelt next to the battered girl. "You poor dear. Here, we'll get you to the nurse and call your parents," she said, gently taking the girl's arm and helping her up. "Would you boys get her books and purse?" Alex and Tom gave Mrs. Jenkins a nod, and then proceeded to gather together Sarah's belongings. Sarah limped towards the school building with Mrs. Jenkins' arm around her waist for support.

In all the commotion, no one had noticed a tawny brindled cat sitting on the other side of the street that bordered the school yard. Having concluded that the incident was over, the cat lazily rose to its feet, and then proceeded to saunter down the street in the direction taken by Jack Paine and his fellow thugs.

Sarah didn't attend classes that day or the next. Rumor had it that there had been a long discussion between her parents and the school principal about the incident. Starting the following morning a teacher was posted at each corner of the school yard both before the start of and at the end of the school day. Rumor also had it that Jack Paine had been expelled from school for anywhere from one week to the start of the next century. It was a difficult rumor to confirm for, on one hand, Jack was more likely to be truant than to attend classes and, on the other hand, he had a habit of showing up even when expelled, for he found it difficult to bully anyone when all his potential victims were at school and he wasn't.

It was Friday when Sarah finally returned to class. She was still favoring her left knee. Although a few of her classmates, especially those who had had a run in with the infamous Jack Paine, started to look upon the girl with more sympathy, others seemed to view the girl's recent ordeal as some sort of well-deserved divine punishment. Tom and Alex had expected a phone call from Sarah's parents again requesting them to escort their daughter to school. To their relief, no such call had come.

Brad and Wayne had finished lunch early that day and had left the cafeteria to dress out for gym class. That left Alex and Tom at their lunch table. The taller boy had taken the first bite out of his desert, a chocolate cupcake that, by some miracle, had survived the morning in the boy's lunch bag without being squashed into a shape more resembling that of a cookie, when it occurred to him that Alex, sitting across the table, was unusually quiet. Looking up he noticed his friend intently staring across the cafeteria at Sarah. As was customary, the girl was sitting at her private table, alone. Tom stopped in mid bite. Alex sat there as if mesmerized by the girl with the larger than average nose, seemingly oblivious to all else, not an easy feat considering the state of pandemonium that was going on all about him in the high school cafeteria. The girl appeared to be studying one of her textbooks and had not noticed Alex staring at her. As Tom studied his best friend studying Sarah, he had a thought. "Maybe Alex is starting to like Sarah." For a reason he couldn't fathom, he found the idea troubling.

"Why are you staring at Sarah?"

"Huh?" came the answer, as if the blond-haired boy had been shaken from a daydream.

"I said why are you staring at Sarah?"

Without breaking his trance, Alex answered, "You know, the more I look at her . . . there's something strangely familiar about her face."

"Yeah, her nose. So what?"

"No, I mean there's something—peculiar about her."

Tom gave a soft chuckle. "Peculiar as in odd? I'll say."

"No, not like that. I mean, there's something—sort of familiar about her."

"Yeah, her nose. It reminds you of your nose. There is a resemblance, you know?"

"No, I'm not kidding. It's been bothering me. I can't seem to put my finger on it."

"Well, you better stop staring at her," said Tom, "or the next thing you know people will start saying you have a crush on her or something."

Alex jerked his head around, giving his friend a panicked look. "Oh my gosh, you're right! What was I doing?" He then looked back towards Sarah's table. Tom saw his friend take a hard swallow, and without thinking Tom turned in his seat to follow the direction of his friend's gaze. Sarah Gould was looking at them. She couldn't have heard them, not with all the noise in the cafeteria. For a moment the girl appeared to be trying to reach some sort of decision, then she broke eye contact and began to gather up her things.

Tom spun back around in his seat. "What was that all about?" he asked Alex, trying to keep his voice low.

"Don't look now, but she's heading this way."

"What?"

"Don't turn around, you moron. Let me handle this."

Tom noticed that the girls seated at the table behind Alex had shifted their attention to Alex and Tom, as if intent on not missing a detail of what was about to happen. Included in the flock of females was Cynthia Cohen, still a member in top standing of the I-loathe-Sarah-Gould fan club. That definitely was not good. Then he heard a voice behind him say, "Alex, Tom." Tom watched his friend nod a greeting, and then he rotated on his seat to confront Sarah Rebecca Gould. She stood there in all her glory—glasses, braces, long, straight, light brown, almost blonde hair, a pink dress, and a bandage on her left knee.

The girl clumsily cleared her throat before continuing. "I wanted to apologize for the way I behaved Tuesday morning. I realize now that you were only trying to help and—well, I wanted to thank you for coming to my—uh, helping me." A chorus of feminine giggles erupted from the neighboring table.

Tom waited for Alex to say something, after all his last words were, "Let me handle this," but his friend just sat there, mute. Worse, he was getting that transfixed look on his face again.

Just as the silence was starting to be embarrassing, Tom heard himself blurt out, "That's okay." Well, that sunk the duck. No sense in not shoving his foot even further down his throat. "I mean you probably shouldn't apologize, that is, we were trying to help but we probably didn't do a very good a job of it—at all—that is." More giggles. Now several other tables had gone silent.

"Well, uh, thank you again," said Sarah, starting to make a motion as to leave.

"Sarah," said Tom's audible voice, while at the same time the voice inside of him was asking himself just what in tar nation was he doing? She had started to leave. Now she had stopped.

Tom's voice continued as if on autopilot, while his mind inwardly screamed for him to shut up. "You need to watch out for that Jack Paine character. He's a real mean one." No sense going this alone. "Isn't that right Alex?"

"Huh?" was all Alex got out, his trance-like state seemingly impeding his thought processes.

"I'll try to be more careful," said Sarah.

"Eh, if you want, I could, I mean, we could walk you to school." The giggles from the table behind them were replaced by a number of audible gasps. Had their ears deceived them? Did the best looking, most popular boy in the East Pencreek High eighth grade just offer to escort Banana Beak to school?

The reaction of the peanut gallery had not escaped Sarah's attention. She broke out in a blush that noticeably contrasted with the pink of her dress. "That's very nice of you to offer, but my parents spoke with the principal and he promised that everything would be okay from now on."

The alarm signaling the end of the seventh and eighth grade lunch period sounded. The notion that they had been saved by the bell occurred to both Sarah and Tom.

"That's good to know," said Tom. "Well, we had better get on to gym class."

"Okay. Bye Tom. Bye Alex."

"Bye," quipped the two boys. As Tom turned and stood to pick up his books, he noticed the girls at the next table were all staring at him with both their eyes and mouths wide open.

The last period classes for the day had been cancelled for a special assembly, to the obvious relief of everyone, with the possible exception of Sarah, in Evad's science class. On the way to the assembly Sarah decided to visit the girls' washroom. As fate would have it, the obvious choice was the one next to Miss Odavsky's classroom. The girl entered the washroom and placed her books and purse on a shelf. Three of her classmates were engaged in some mindless conversation by the sinks. After Sarah entered and shut the door to one of the stalls, the trio of girls exchanged knowing looks. A couple of minutes later Sarah heard the others leave the restroom. Emerging from the stall, she was startled to see that a message had been scribbled on the washroom mirror. It appeared to have been written with red lipstick. It read

Ms. Odavksy has an I.Q. of a decimil 2

Next to the message was a poorly drawn stick figure, no doubt intended to be a rendition of a low I.Q. Miss Odavsky. As Sarah was wondering why the girls would have done such an awful thing, the door to the restroom flew open and in walked the subject of the mirror message. Acting as if she had already been informed of what to expect, Miss Odavsky stopped and studied the mirror for a moment before turning to Sarah.

"Well, Miss Gould. No doubt you thought you would get away with this despicable prank."

"Me?" said Sarah, momentarily taken off guard by the accusation. "I didn't do that."

"What do you take me for, a total moron?" said the teacher.

Sarah was tempted to answer, "Not a total moron, more like an eighty or ninety percent moron." Instead she said, "It must have been one of those girls who were just in here. Besides I wouldn't have misspelled 'decimal' or your name, and I can certainly draw better than that, and I don't have any lipstick."

"Oh, no," said the teacher. Without any hesitation Miss Odavsky stepped over to the shelf where Sarah's purse lay. To Sarah's horror, she noticed that the purse's flap was unfastened and open. The teacher deftly reached inside the purse and pulled out a lipstick container.

"That's not mine!" said Sarah. "One of those girls must have put it there."

Miss Odavsky crossed over to the mirror, flipped the cover off the tube of lipstick and drew a line of red next to the word "Ms." The match in color was perfect. Before Sarah could offer another word in her defense, the teacher grabbed the girl by her right ear and led her screaming and protesting out of the washroom and down the hall towards the office. On the way to the office, the teacher and her prisoner passed what no doubt seemed to Sarah as half the student body, including two boys who had stopped to get a better view of the spectacle.

"I wonder what that's all about?" said Alex.

"History was first period this morning," said Tom. "You know, Sarah hasn't opened her big mouth in class much lately. Maybe she was having withdrawal symptoms and couldn't resist visiting Miss Odavsky's room and letting her have one."

"Sounds like a plausible hypothesis, Watson," said Alex.

"Or then again, maybe Miss Odavsky was having withdrawal symptoms and decided to let Sarah have it for old time's sake," was Tom's second guess.

"Watson, sometimes you amaze me."

"How was your day at school, dear," called Mrs. Gould from the kitchen when she heard Sarah enter the house.

"Oh, the usual," came the less than enthusiastic reply. "You know, one step forward and two back." The girl entered the kitchen and held out a note for her mother. Mrs. Gould put down the plate she was drying and noticed that her daughter's eyes were once again red and moist. The mother took the paper and opened it. While she read the note from Mr. Elkins, the Assistant Principal, Sarah took a seat at the kitchen table.

"Sarah, you didn't write something about one of your teachers on the rest room mirror, did you?"

"No, of course not, Mom. I was framed." The girl leaned forward and covered her face with her hands.

"Did you tell Mr. Elkins that?"

"Yes, of course."

"And what did he say?"

Sarah put down her hands. "He didn't believe me. And then he paddled me."

"He what!"

"He made me lean over his desk, and then he took that big paddle he has hanging on his wall, the one with the holes in it, and he hit me with it." As she said it, she looked directly at the mother with her reddened eyes.

Mrs. Gould quickly took a seat next to her daughter. "I don't believe it. That's horrible. He paddled— but you're a girl."

"He said I was only the third girl he's ever had to paddle in his fifteen years at the school. Not only that, I lost my purse. I must have left it in the washroom."

Mrs. Gould laid a hand on her daughter's shoulder. "This is an outrage. Wait until your father hears about this."

"Mom!" exclaimed the girl. "I wish you wouldn't tell Daddy. Where's Anne? I don't want her to know either."

"Your sister's over at the Cobalt's."

"What? What's she doing there?"

"Tom's sister, Caroline, invited her over. They've become good friends. But why don't you want me to tell your father?"

"You're the only one who knows. I don't want anyone else to know, not even Daddy. I'm afraid it will get out—that the other students at the school will find out what happened. It was so—humiliating."

Sarah words evaporated into sobs. Mrs. Gould encircled her daughter in her arms as she knelt beside her. "I still think we need to tell your father. It's not right that you've been paddled, not only because you did nothing wrong, but also because you're a girl. I never heard of such a thing."

"Please, don't," came a whimper. "I don't want Daddy to know. I don't think I could stand it if he knew I was paddled."

"Well, I'll think about it, but I won't promise anything." Mrs. Gould began to rock her daughter gently in her arms. "Is there anything else you want to tell me?"

The girl took a deep swallow before answering. "I thanked Tom and Alex for trying to help me the other day, like Daddy asked me to."

"I'm glad you remembered to do that. They're nice boys."

"Yes," said Sarah. "Especially Tom. He even offered to walk me to school again."

That seemed to surprise her mother even more than the news that her daughter had been paddled. "He did?"

"Yes."

"Well, what did you say?"

"I thanked him, but said I was okay walking by myself."

"I see," said Mrs. Gould, not really sure she saw. "I must say that you've had a really tough week, but at least it's good to know there's at least one person at school who likes you."

At her mother's words, Sarah sat up straight and cast her mother a hopeful look. "You think he might really like me?"

"Well, yes. I mean in a chivalrous sort of way. Tom seems like the type of person who would always stand up for what was right. You know, like defend the weak and . . ."

The look of hope vanished from Sarah's face. "And ugly," she said.

"Hey, Tom. Guess what?"

"What?" came Tom's voice over the phone.

"Old Man Elkins paddled Sarah today."

"You're kidding!" Tom screeched into the receiver so loud that his father looked up from across the living room where he was sitting reading the newspaper. "He hit a girl!"

"Sure did. Wayne called and told me all about it. Apparently, Elkins really let her have it, not just once, but several times. They say Sarah could hardly walk afterwards."

"No kidding. He hit her seven times? Wow! Hey, how the heck did Wayne find out about it?"

"Who knows, but I wouldn't put it past that creep Elkins to do something like that."

"Yeah, neither would I. So, what did she do that he hit her?" By now Tom's mother had also caught a part of the conversation. Both his parents were eavesdropping with rapt attention.

"Apparently she wrote something really nasty about Miss Odavsky on the girls' room wall, and Miss Odavsky caught her not only writing it, but caught her smoking too."

"Oh, come on. Sarah doesn't smoke?"

"Yeah, I don't buy that part," said Alex.

"And I also don't buy Sarah writing nasty things about Miss Odavsky. I mean, I know she can't stand the woman and all that, but I can't see her writing nasty things about Miss Odavsky in the girls' room."

"Yeah, I don't buy that part either. Besides, I think that even if she did it, Sarah's not dumb enough to get caught."

"Sounds like a set up to me."

"You know, Watson, lately you're really starting to amaze me," said the boy genius. "That was my guess too."

"Oh, sure it was, now that I already mentioned it."

"Anyway, I wonder what's going to happen at school on Monday. I mean by then everyone will know about it."

"Yeah, poor Sarah," said Tom. "Even she doesn't deserve this."

"I agree. I almost wish we could do something about it."

"Like what?"

Alex paused before answering. "Like finding out who really wrote it, and paying them back, and maybe even giving Elkins a taste of his own medicine."

"It wouldn't surprise me if Cynthia Cohen had something to do with it. She really despises Sarah."

"So do most of the other girls in our class, Einstein, not to mention most of the boys. For all we know, a boy could have snuck into the girls' room and done it."

"Yeah, you're right." Then Tom had another thought. "Maybe I should call Sarah and make sure she's okay or something. You know—maybe tell her we don't believe she did it?"

"Are you nuts? Forget what I said earlier about you amazing me. Now you're amazing me in the opposite direction. How would you feel if you just got your butt whipped for something you didn't do, and then someone calls you up and tells you they know about what happened?"

"Er, yeah, I see your point. Okay, we'll forget that idea."

"Good. Anyway, I'll see you tomorrow morning around ten, right?"

"Yeah, around ten. Okay, thanks for the news. Bye." As Tom hung up the receiver, his thoughts turned to the assistant principal, Mr. Elkins. He had always believed Mr. Elkins to be a jerk, but now he downright hated the man.

Having finished tuning the radio on the nightstand next to his bed, Tom propped a pillow against the bed board and leaned back. He reached over and picked up the book that lay next to the radio, resting it on his stomach so he could more comfortably study its pages. It was his favorite book. His grandmother had given it to him on his last birthday. His grandmother was cool. What other grandmother would give her grandson a book about a subject that most adults had once considered pure nonsense? He stared at the front of the book's dust jacket. The title read *The Conquest of Space*. Below the title was a picture of a powerful looking rocketship resting upright on its tail fins in what appeared to be a crater on the moon. Figures in spacesuits were performing various tasks about the rocket. A crescent Earth hung in the black sky of space above the crater's mountain walls. Below the picture were the words, "A preview of the greatest adventure awaiting mankind with text and pictures based on the latest scientific research." The cover credited the book's paintings to an artist named Chesley Bonestell and the text to one Willy Ley. The name Willy Ley was familiar to the boy. He was no doubt the same man who had been the technical advisor for one of Tom's favorite TV shows, *Tom Corbett Space Cadet*. People, well, adults that is, had laughed and made fun of the show when it was still on the air, as well as another one, set even farther in the future, *Space Patrol*. The term "space cadet" had even become a popular phrase used to describe someone who was sort of an airhead. Then two years ago the Russkies had launched Sputnik, and now no one was laughing. Space flight no longer seemed so far fetched as both the Americans and the Soviets were racing to be the first to actually put a man into orbit.

Tom flipped opened the book to a random page. Some of the ideas presented in the book had at first been difficult for Tom to understand, but fortunately he had already loaned the book to Alex. Alex, of course, had devoured it in a single evening and then explained it all to Tom. He flipped through a few more pages to a set of pictures. Some of Bonestell's paintings figuratively took the boy's breath away. The one he stopped at showed a reddish Mars as seen from the surface of its nearest moon Deimos. A polar ice cap was clearly visible on the planet along with greenish areas and the famous canals. Better yet, the artist had added three men in spacesuits floating above a rock outcropping of the moon. Because Deimos was only a few miles in size, its gravity was so weak that a strong jump was enough to launch a man into orbit about the moon. The boy found it all so incredibly fascinating. Imagine what it must feel like to be one of those spacemen floating under a pull of gravity so weak as to be almost non-existent. Better yet, to be able to look down on the planet of the war god and see the canals of Mars, the mysterious canals that might actually be evidence of the last valiant attempt of a dying or extinct civilization to survive the doomsday of the ever-encroaching desert. Someday, thought the boy, someday I'll be there. I'll stand on the edge of a Martian canal.

The boy noticed that a new song had started playing on the radio. It was an Elvis hit, *Can't Help Falling in Love*. For a moment, the image of a Martian canal in the boy's mind was replaced by that of a thirteen-year old girl with braces and glasses and a larger than average nose, features that all weighed on the unattractive side of the ledger. But those wonderful brown eyes staring at him through the glasses and … Tom gave his head an emphatic shake. "Huh?" Tom mused. "Women! God forbid they ever put women on spaceships. What were those guys who wrote the scripts for *Space Patrol* thinking?"

The girl flipped to the next page as she settled back onto her pillow. The book's open pages displayed a painting of the planet Saturn. *The Conquest of Space* was Sarah's favorite book. Reading it was almost like reading a fantasy novel. It was a book in which for a moment she could lose herself and forget about her horrible experiences at school. Unlike a book of fiction, this book seemed to her like some magical prophecy of the future.

Before her was a painting of the planet Saturn as viewed from the surface of one of its nearer moons, Mimas. The picture showed the great gas giant filling most of the sky, its edge on ring casting a black band of a shadow across the smooth sphere of the planet's outer atmosphere. The barren, inhospitable surface of the moon showed no life except for several tiny figures dwarfed in the shadow of a rugged rocky cliff. "Spacemen!" Sarah thought. "Would men some day travel to such distant worlds and see such astonishing sights?" The question caused the girl to shiver. The girl reflected upon the imagination the artist must have had to create such a fantastic landscape with such a view. Yet it was an imagination steeped on hard fact, on a reality that actually existed somewhere out there in the cold void of deep space. Oh, to be able to travel to the planets, and perhaps even to the stars!

The girl remembered a television series she had watched when she was younger called *Space Patrol*. Although kind of silly, with ray guns and evil bad guys, and the usual handsome hero . . . Well, maybe that part wasn't so silly. At least most of the characters appeared to be smart, except for the goofy space cadet. But the best thing about the program was that it had two women characters who were members of the Space Patrol. They piloted spaceships, performed scientific research, and shared dangers with the men. Maybe the real problem with her life and, for that matter, the twentieth century was that there was no Space Patrol, no spaceships, and no adventures to be had in the company of other intelligent, bold and daring men and women. Sarah gently ran her hand over the picture. If only, some day . . . to travel to the stars.

A yawn reminded her that it was getting late. She carefully closed the book and laid it on the small table beside her bed. Then she turned on the radio next to where she had placed the book and adjusted the volume to a faint whisper. As she turned out the nightlight Elvis' words about falling in love gently caressed her thoughts. The girl gave a contented sigh and closed her eyes.

Alex Banyon bounced onto his mattress, awakening the cat lying there. "Hi, Tiger," he said, and gave the big kitty a scruff behind the ears.

The tawny feline bared his teeth with a yawn, and then repositioned himself closer to the boy. Alex clicked on the radio and the words of Elvis Presley met his ears. "Wise men say . . ." "Yuck," said the boy, scrunching up his nose and adjusting the tuning dial. The welcoming, deep, sonorous chords of massed strings filled the room. "Beethoven," he said with a yelp of triumph. "That's more like it, huh Tiger?" The cat lifted his head, eyes half shut, and gave the boy a positive nod, then shifted back into sleep mode.

"Let us turn to page 145 in our hymnal and stand, as we sing "Praise to the Lord, the Almighty." At the pastor's request, the congregation rose as one. Notes thundered from the pipes of the organ as the organist worked the keys and peddles, and then after a brief introduction, the hall was filled with the sound of voices.

Praise to the Lord, the Almighty, the King of creation!

Tom stood at the end of the pew, next to the inner aisle. He shared a hymnal with his mother, while his father and sister, standing on the other side of his mother, shared a second hymnal. The singing was Tom's favorite part of the service, the sermons his least favorite as he usually found those boring. As the congregation reached the end of the first verse, the minister said, "Let us have the ladies do the second verse. Ladies only, please."

Tom dutifully shut up, and listened as his mom and sister, along with the other females in the sanctuary, continued with the words of the hymn.

Praise to the Lord! Over all things He gloriously reigneth.

The boy reached up and carefully loosened his tie a notch. That was another negative about church, having to dress up. As he did so he let his gaze leisurely sweep the pews to his right. There was cousin Jerry and his aunt and uncle in the front row of the set of pews against the far wall. Jerry was engaged in a giant yawn and making no effort to hide it. Jerry could be a real jerk sometimes. Actually, it seemed like most of the time now that Tom thought about it. And a couple of rows behind Jerry was . . . Sarah! The girl was looking at him.

As soon as their eyes met, Sarah's seemed to grow in size, the illusion no doubt aided by the glasses she wore. She quickly lowered her gaze to the hymnal she was holding. Tom felt his lower jaw go slack, and then he did the same thing. "What's she doing here, and why was she staring at me?" Tom asked himself. It suddenly seemed warm inside the church. He hesitantly cast another glance in the direction of the girl. She was looking at him again! As if having exhaustively rehearsed their actions, both teens immediately looked down at their hymnals. "She was staring at me again!" thought Tom. "What is going on? Why is she here? "The boy vaguely heard the minister saying something about "the gentlemen now."

"Tom." He heard his mother's concerned whisper, and at the same time felt a gentle poke of his left arm. He gave his mother a startled look. She in turn motioned towards the hymnal with a nod of her head.

Ponder anew what the Almighty can do,
Who with His love doth befriend thee.

The end of the third verse again brought forth the cheerful words of the pastor. "Now let us all join together for the last verse."

In his mind, Tom was holding a conversation with himself. "I'm not looking over there again. There's no way I'm going to look over there. I can't believe this. You'd think I would at least get the weekend off. Don't' tell me she's going to be going to my church now. Oh my gosh, what if Jerry should find out that we know each other? Worse, what if Jerry finds out we know each other, meets Sarah, and then says something about her nose? Why couldn't she be Jewish? Whatever you do, don't look up." Of course, telling oneself not to look up is a sure invitation to look up. Tom gave his head a slight tilt, as best he could without being overly obvious, and tried to view the far pews out of the corner of his right eye. Sarah was still looking at her hymnal. That was a relief.

The boy straightened up as the congregation sang the Amen. As he began to sit down he gave another quick glance in Sarah's direction. Of course, he found the girl taking a quick glance in his direction. "God, why me?" thought the boy.

Tom had managed to shake the minister's hand and exit the church without having run into the girl or any of her family. Now if only his parents wouldn't tarry on the sidewalk in front of the church as they did every Sunday, weather permitting. Of course, once his parents reached the sidewalk at the foot of the front steps of the church they tarried. "Maybe I can sort of make my way to the car and when they're done they can meet me there," the boy was thinking, when he heard his little sister yell, "Anne, over here." "Anne?" thought Tom. "Isn't that Sarah's sister's name?" He immediately heard a voice answer, "Hi, Caroline," followed by an exchange of giggles.

"Steve, Rebecca," he heard his father say, "so nice to see you here." That was followed by a flurry of exchanged pleasantries between the adult Goulds and Cobalts. Before Tom knew it, there was Sarah standing before him. For what seemed like an eternity, the two teens stood there, absently listening to their parents and siblings ramble on, trying not to make eye contact, yet trying not to appear too obvious that they were trying not to make eye contact. It was the one with the more prominent nose who finally broke the ice.

"Hi," said Sarah.

"Hi," said Tom. "Uh, what did you think of the sermon?"

"It was very good," said the girl, giving Tom a suspicious look. "I especially liked the joke he told about Sodom and Gomorrah."

"Huh?" said Tom, sounding surprised. "The minister made a joke about Sodom and Gomorrah?"

Sarah grinned. "No, of course not. I just wanted to see if you were paying attention. I bet you can't even tell me what the sermon was about?"

"Sure, I can." There was a brief pause before Tom continued. "It was, uh—it was about God and Jesus and the Bible and stuff, like it is every Sunday."

"That's what I thought. You weren't paying attention. Shame on you. You're going to hell." But she didn't look at all serious when she said it. Instead she was still grinning at him, her head slightly bent, looking up at him with those deep brown eyes bordered by those gorgeous long eyelashes. Tom, without giving it a second thought, instinctively returned her grin.

"I guess this means you're not Jewish?"

"My father is, so maybe that makes me half Jewish," laughed the girl. "You won't tell Alex, will you? He seems to have some sort of weird fixation about whether I'm Jewish or not, and I'd rather let him stew a while longer not knowing."

"No, I won't tell Alex. By the way, how's your knee?" The girl's one knee was covered by an adhesive bandage.

Before the girl could answer, her father interrupted. "By the way, Tom, I didn't get a chance to thank you for coming to Sarah's rescue the other day."

"Eh, it was nothing." Tom could feel his complexion taking on a reddish hue. "And I didn't rescue her or anything."

"I think it was swell what you did. And it took courage. If Alex and you hadn't showed up, who knows what those other boys might have done next." Then he turned to Tom's father. "Sam, you have a fine boy there."

"Thank you, Steve," said Tom's father with obvious pride.

"It's good to know there are students like Tom at school who will look out for someone like Sarah." The color of Sarah's complexion was now quickly changing to a shade close to Tom's as both teens were fervently wishing that their fathers would either shut up or change the subject.

"I know it must be tough for Sarah starting a new school and all and trying to make new friends," said Mr. Cobalt, in a manner akin to a torturer throwing salt on a freshly opened wound. "I hope that incident in the girls' rest room got straightened out."

"Oh nooooo!," thought the girl. "If Tom's father knows about it, then surely the whole school does!"

"Unfortunately, not yet," said her father, "but I'm going to call Elkins, the assistant principal, tomorrow morning and demand both an explanation and an apology for paddling Sarah."

"So, it's really true about Sarah being paddled," said Tom's father. (Sarah groaned to herself.) "Tom got paddled by Elkins last year for running in the halls, but of course he's a boy, and that's different. But paddling a girl, especially a good student like Sarah . . . I certainly don't blame you for being outraged."

"Regardless of what Elkins has to say," continued Mr. Gould, "I'm then calling the School Superintendent and asking him to explain what kind of school he's running here."

"A couple of the school board members are friends of mine," said Mr. Cobalt. "I'll give them a call this afternoon and let them know what kind of jerk the assistant principal is."

"I certainly appreciate that, and I know Sarah does too. Isn't that right, honey?"

"Huh?" was the girl's immediate reaction, as if she had been shaken out of some horrid nightmare. "I'm not sure, Daddy. I just wish they'd leave me alone, that's all."

"Don't worry, Sarah. We'll see to it that it doesn't happen again," said her father. "Well, I guess we had better let these good people go. It's good to see you, Sam," Mr. Gould said, shaking Mr. Cobalt's hand,

and then giving Tom a nod, "and you too, Tom."

"Sure," replied Tom. He looked at Sarah, who gave him a weak smile. "Well, er, see you in class, I guess," said the boy.

"Yeah, see you in class," said Sarah, who then turned and followed her family towards their car.

When Tom did an about face, he almost collided with his cousin, Jerry.

"So, who's your girlfriend?"

"Just someone in some of my classes at school, and she's not my girlfriend."

"You two seemed awfully friendly just now."

Tom first instinct, to tell Jerry that he was a jerk, was replaced by a brainstorm. "Actually, she's Alex's girlfriend."

"No kidding." Jerry smiled. "Of course, that figures. She looks way too smart for you."

"How come I don't remember that incident?" said Jerry. "And what does this have to do with anything?"

Before answering, the guest took a swallow of water from his glass. "To answer your first question, why would you remember something that happened—," the young man paused to do a quick calculation in his head, "—thirty-six years ago, especially something that seemed to be of no consequence to you at the time? To answer your second question, I could have skipped over a lot of the details, except that I'm sure Anne and Mrs. Gould would like to hear more about what happened to Sarah back then, especially as it will help them to understand why Sarah disappeared."

"Oh, come now," said Jerry, with a snort. "So far you haven't said anything to convince me that you really are Tom and that this picture here is my wife's long dead sister." As soon as he had said it he regretted it for he caught his mother-in-law's expression. "Sorry, Mom. I didn't mean it to come out that way."

Anne reached over and gave the back of her husband's hand a gentle pat. "Jerry, why don't we let Tom continue?"

Chapter 8
The Countdown Starts

It might be said that the string of events which would lead to the disappearance of the three teens all started in Tuesday's history class, the week of Halloween. Miss Odavsky was lecturing the students on why the United States Constitution was necessary.

"Everyone realized that the Articles of Confederation wasn't working and that the country needed a stronger central government."

Sarah thrust her hand in the air.

Miss Odavsky gave a sigh, and then acknowledged Sarah, hoping that the girl just wanted to use the hall pass to visit the rest room.

"I beg to differ. First off people like Patrick Henry and Richard Henry Lee—"

"Sarah Gould," interrupted the teacher. It's always a bad sign when teachers, like parents, use your full name. In this case Miss Odavsky would have used Sarah's full name had she known it. "Are you about to tell me that what I said was wrong?"

Sarah decided to change her approach. Perhaps she could get her point across by asking questions. "Actually, I'm not sure what you meant when you said that the Articles of the Confederation weren't working. Why weren't they working?"

Sarah switch of tactics caught the teacher momentarily off guard. Miss Odavsky paused a moment to think, an exercise with which she was not all that familiar.

"Well, for instance, the seaboard states could tax goods coming into their ports from overseas. That would be unfair to the landlocked states when they tried to buy those goods."

"That doesn't make any sense. At the time there were no landlocked states," corrected Sarah.

"Are you telling this class that what I said was wrong?"

Sarah broke eye contact with Miss Odavsky and instead studied the top of her desk before answering. "Yes, Ma'am. What you said wasn't entirely accurate."

"Sarah, Sarah. Everyone back then agreed that the Articles of Confederation were a failure." Miss Odavsky was doing a good impression of a parent scolding a small child. "They couldn't have a real country without a stronger government."

Upon hearing the patronizing tone in the teacher's voice, Sarah's backbone stiffened. "Darn it," thought Sarah. "Miss Odavsky's a blithering idiot. She isn't fit to teach dead people how to lie still." Sarah looked up. Miss Odavsky was out of focus since the girl had taken off her glasses. "Ma'am, if I can tell you what I know. I read a book on Patrick Henry—"

"Sarah, you seem to be forgetting that I have a degree in secondary education, with a major in history, and that I am licensed to teach in this state and have done so for six years, and that you are only a child and are here to learn from me. I don't care what you think you read. You have to believe me when I say that everyone knows that what I said was the truth. And I might warn you that any other answer on a test will be marked wrong. Now I think we've wasted enough time on this subject."

"But—"

"Uh, oh," thought Tom, seeing the veins on Miss Odavsky's forehead start to swell. "Lift off."

"Sarah Gould!" Along with her veins, the volume of the teacher's voice was also swelling. "I'll hear no more of it. I think you owe me and your fellow students an apology for what just happened."

Sarah sat there, certain that there was no way she was going to apologize to anyone, least of all to Miss Odavsky, when as far as she could see she hadn't done anything wrong. When no apology was forthcoming, Miss Odavsky said, "Very well, Sarah. You are excused. Go to the office and wait for me. I'll be along after class. Your parents will once again be getting a note from me about your behavior." Then casting a sardonic look at the girl, she added, "And I wouldn't be surprised that when Mr. Elkins hears about your behavior, he may decide to administer additional punishment, just like the other day."

Sarah's lower lip trembled. She carefully picked up her glasses and put them on, then slammed her books and notebooks together and gathered them in her arms along with her purse. As she stood up, she could hear the usual chorus of snickers and whispers from some of her classmates. She started to walk up the aisle towards the classroom door, being careful not to make eye contact with anyone. As she exited the room, Miss Odavsky closed the door behind her and then turned to address the class. That's when Alex stood up. Without waiting to be recognized, he said, "Miss Odavsky, I don't know what Sarah was going to say, but I do know that you obviously don't know lentils about history."

Miss Odavsky's initial response to Alex's outburst was to stammer incoherently. What had gotten into Alex Banyon? Alex was her star pupil. He got straight As. He never disagreed with anything she said. He never caused trouble. Before she could gather a coherent sentence together, Alex continued. "It's you who owes Sarah an apology for being such a poor excuse for a teacher." For a moment the only sounds in the room were those of Miss Odavsky stammering and the students in the class sucking in their breath, all the students, that is, except Tom and Alex. Tom was whispering to Alex, "Sit down you fool. What do you think you're doing?"

Miss Odavsky finally managed to blurt out, "Alex Banyon!" Uh, oh. There was that full name thing again. "Whatever are you going on about? I have nothing to apologize for!"

"How about the fact that you're a blithering idiot?" said Alex, the tone of his voice calm and reasoned, as if he were pointing out the most obvious of facts.

"Alex Banyon!" screamed Miss Odavsky. Then she sputtered and stuttered and sprayed a couple unfortunate students who were sitting in the first row with some spit as she attempted to complete the sentence. "Go to the office! Now!"

Still showing remarkable coolness under fire, and with the hint of a smile on his face, Alex picked up his books and headed for the exit. When he arrived at the door, he turned and surveyed the class. While the rest of the students sat there dumbstruck, Tom, Brad, and Wayne all raised a clenched fist. "Hail, Einar," they shouted.

Alex smiled, returned the salute and exited the classroom.

Arriving at the school office waiting area, Alex took the only available seat on the bench next to Sarah. The girl didn't seem to notice him as she was busy studying the pattern of the floor tiling and, having removed her glasses, dabbing her eyes with a tissue. Alex quietly listened to the girl's soft sobs, until the office clerk, who sat behind the counter across from the two students, happened to glance up from her paperwork and recognized Alex. The clerk knew Alex, and also knew he was an A student who was never in trouble. "Alex," she said in an uncertain tone of voice, "why are you here?" At that, Sarah realized with a start who was sitting next to her.

"Miss Odavsky sent me here. Same offense as Sarah."

Both Sarah and the clerk gave Alex a stunned look, then the clerk nodded and returned to her paperwork, still seeming slightly dazed by the revelation.

"What did you do?" asked a confused Sarah, ending the question with a sniffle.

Alex looked at Sarah as if he were about to perform a confession. "I couldn't stand it any longer. I told Miss Odavsky in so many words that she's a disgrace to her profession." He grinned.

Sarah at first stared at him, mouth hanging open. Then she got a grip on herself, closed her mouth, put her glasses back on, clasped her hands together on her lap and directed her attention straight ahead. They sat there like that for several minutes, neither one looking at the other nor saying anything until a teacher entered the office. It was Mr. Roseman, Alex's favorite teacher from the previous year. When he spied Alex sitting on the "discipline" bench, his expression also turned to one of surprise.

"Alex, what are you doing here?"

"Miss Odavsky sent me here. We had a disagreement about something that happened in history."

"Hmm," said Mr. Roseman. "Well, I wouldn't worry too much about that. After all, Miss Odavsky's a blathering idiot!"

"So, what happened?" asked Wayne, hardly able to control his excitement. "How many swats did you get?"

Wayne and Brad were all ears. Tom had already heard about Alex's experience with Mr. Elkins, the assistant principal, and therefore seemed more interested in examining what Wayne and Brad had on their lunch trays than in Alex's discourse on what had happened in Mr. Elkin's office.

"Three," was the answer. "He gave me three good ones with the big paddle, you know the one with all the holes so it stings more."

"Wow!" said Brad, obviously impressed. "The maximum!" Alex's status among his peers had risen to the highest level possible. Here was a boy who had both called a teacher a blithering idiot and had received the maximum three swats with a paddle by Mr. Elkins, and all within the span of an hour.

"See, didn't I tell you?" taunted Wayne to Brad. Then he turned to Alex. "I knew by the way you walked when you came in here that Elkins must have hit you at least three times with the 'big sucker.'"

"Is that all that happened?" asked Brad.

"No, I have to write an apology to Miss Odavsky, and, of course, I have a note for my parents to sign. And I also have to write an apology to Mr. Elkins."

"How about your pie for my cookies?" said Tom.

Wayne ignored both Tom and his offer. "Did it hurt? The most I ever got was two swats from Mr. Foye."

"Not as much as having to write an apology to Miss Odavsky will."

"I bet the only reason you got the maximum was that Elkins was trying to impress Odavsky. You know he's sweet on her, don't you?" said Brad.

"Come on," said Tom, disbelievingly. "What makes you say that?"

"Come on, yourself. Everybody knows it. Just look at them in the hall, making googly eyes at each other."

"I think I'm going to be sick," said Tom. "Okay, how about my cookies and a nickel for your pie?"

Wayne picked up his pie and took a big bite out it. Having had a chance to judge the quality of his dessert, he looked at his friend and said, "Deal."

"Not after you already took a bite out of it, you chowder-head!"

"What did he say to you?" asked Brad.

"He gave me a long lecture about respecting my elders, and how Miss Odavsky was one of the school's finest teachers . . ."

"Yeah, right!" said Tom. At least it kind of sounded like that was what he was trying to say because Tom had a mouth full of sandwich.

". . . and how I was a spoiled brat in that just because I get good grades didn't mean I was better or smarter than everyone else, and that if I were his son, I would never have been raised to be such a smart aleck, and on and on. It was all I could do to stay awake."

207

"How can he say Miss Odavsky is one of the school's finest teach-ers?" asked Wayne. "Did he ever sit through one of her classes?"

"Of course not," said Tom, before Alex could answer. "They always say that. It's in their contract or something. A teacher could be a homi-cidal maniac, and they would still say he's the greatest thing to educa-tion since the invention of corporal punishment."

"What does punishing corporals have to do with anything?" asked Brad.

Alex cut in before Tom could answer Brad's question. "Actually, he probably said it because he graduated with honors from the Miss Odavsky School of Incompetence."

"What about Miss Know-it-all?" asked Wayne.

"Her name's Sarah," said Tom, looking less than pleased with Wayne.

Wayne ignored Tom's remark. "How many swats do you think he gave her?"

"I don't think Elkins is going to be paddling any more girls," sug-gested Tom. "At church on Sunday, Sarah's dad said he was going to call Elkins yesterday and give him a piece of his mind."

"Well, either he didn't call or Elkins wasn't impressed because he hit her twice," said Alex. "I could hear it because I was right outside his office. He called her in right after me, and I could hear him hit her. Twice. You could also tell when she came out."

"Wow!" said the other three in unison.

"He also said some nasty things to her like calling her Miss Prissy Pants and telling her she was pretty dumb for someone supposedly so smart, and that he was going to show her who was running this school. That's when he let her have it."

Another "Wow" was the repeat response. At that Tom turned and looked in the direction of Sarah's private lunch table, to find Sarah looking back at him. Tom's sudden move had obviously surprised her as she quickly looked down at her meal, hoping to make it seem as if she hadn't been watching him. To Tom it appeared that she had looked none too happy, and understandably so. It must have been obvious to her that she was the topic of conversation.

"I bet she screamed her head off when he hit her," said Brad, sounding a bit too gleeful for the comfort of the others.

"No, actually, she didn't," said Alex. "Yeah, I was kind of surprised by that too. When she came out, you could tell she had obviously been crying, but she kept looking at the floor, picked up her books and left. Didn't say a thing. Other than two swats instead of three, I gather her punishment is the same as mine, having to write apologies and all."

"Hey, you and Sarah should get together and write the apologies. You know—two identical apologies. See if anyone notices," suggested Brad.

"You know, Brad, sometimes you surprise me," said Wayne, looking at his friend seemingly with a new respect. "You're not nearly as big of an imbecile as everyone says you are?"

"Who says I'm an imbecile?"

"Interesting you put it that way, Wayne," interrupted Alex, looking thoughtful. "If everyone in the world really knew what everyone keeps saying everyone knows, there wouldn't be any need to say it, would there?"

"Funny, that's what started this whole thing," said Tom. "Miss Odavsky said that *everyone knows* that the Articles of Confederation weren't working and that the country needed a stronger central government. Obviously, you and Sarah didn't know that, so doesn't that prove that everyone didn't know that, which therefore disproves her point?"

"Very good reasoning, Watson," said Alex. "Of course, you forget that Miss Odavsky graduated with honors from the Mr. Elkins School of Stupidity."

Brad rolled his eyes towards the ceiling. "How come listening to you two 'reason' always seems to give me a headache?"

After that the boys concentrated more on replenishing their energy stores than on conversation until Wayne looked at the wall clock.

"Hey, look at the time, buddy," he said to Brad. "We'd better get going if we're going to talk to Heartburn before gym class."

"Good point," agreed Brad. "I can't believe that dumb class is all the way at the other end of school. Brad and Wayne quickly gathered up their books and trash. "See you two later," they said, as they hurried away from the table.

"Yeah, see 'ya," mumbled the other two, who had resumed eating, trying to finish desert in the five minutes left before the bell rang ending the lunch period.

As he munched on a cookie, Alex started to stack his books together when he stopped and pulled out a blue, loose leaf notebook from the bottom of the pile. "Hey, Tom, this isn't mine." He flipped it open and read the name inside the front cover. "It's Sarah's. I must have picked it up by mistake when we left the office." At that the two boys turned in their seat to see if Sarah was still there, but she had already left the cafeteria.

"I guess she must have left early for gym class," said Tom. "After what happened this morning, I'm surprised she's still here." Then turning around, he exclaimed, "Hey, what do you think you're doing. That's Sarah's notebook."

"Shut up, Ragnar," said Alex, paging through the notebook. "I'm seeing if there's any incriminating evidence in here. And don't worry. I'll give it back to her after gym class, assuming she's fool enough to stick out the rest of the school day."

"What do you mean by incriminating evidence?"

"You know. Slanderous statements about teachers or other students, deep dark secrets we can blackmail her with, or . . ."

"Well, you shouldn't be reading it without her permission. Besides, what do you care?"

"I don't. I'm just curious about what kind of notes she takes, that's all," said the blond-haired boy, turning another page. "Say, did Sarah and I miss anything in history after we got kicked out of class?"

"Are you kidding? Miss Odavsky went on and on about how humiliated she was, and how we have to respect our elders, especially blockheads like her, and what awful kids you and Sarah are, and how you should be expelled, and deserve a slow death, and should have your tongues cut out and stuff like that."

Alex had been only half listening as he continued to read Sarah's notes. He flipped over another page, and then let out an "Oh-my-gosh!"

"Huh! What? Did you discover that she's smarter than you?"

"By the beard of Zeus! This is—unbelievable."

"What?"

Alex cast his friend a look of sympathy as he closed the notebook, but he left a finger inside to mark the page. "No, it's too horrible. It's best you don't know."

"What? What!" cried the taller boy, his voice rising with excitement. "Tell me or I'll—"

"Okay, if you insist, but don't say I didn't warn you." With a sickening grin, Alex flipped open the notebook to the page of interest. A look of anxiety appeared on Tom's face as his friend read the shocking words written in the page's margin.

"Tom. Tom. Tom. Tom," he said. "Hmm. Not much in the way of development. Oh, wait. Here's one. Thomas." Then he continued, "Tom, Tom, Tom. It has a nice rhythm to it, don't you think?"

"It can't be. She can't mean me," said the dark-haired boy, the rising fear beginning to turn his stomach inside out.

"Oh, no? Let's see, there's Tom Ross and Tom Jacobson. No, I doubt she knows either of those Toms very well, because they're not in any of our classes. I'm afraid, old friend, that she must be referring to none other than you know who."

"No, it can't be. It just can't be. It's probably some old boyfriend of hers, back in wherever it was she came from."

Alex looked up from his reading, giving a less then convincing effort of looking sympathetic. "Come on Tom. Face reality. Try to imagine for one moment Sarah Gould with a boyfriend."

"Yeah, I see what you mean," said the other boy with increasing dejection and loss of hope. He began to scan the row of lockers lining the far wall as if he were contemplating smashing his head against them. Alex flipped to the next page, at which his eyes went wide.

"Uh, oh. That sinks the duck. Do you really want to hear this?"

"What?" cried Tom, turning his attention back to the ominous notebook. With a look as if he was being marched to the guillotine, he said, trying to sound heroic, "Okay, let me have it."

"Let's see," said Alex, trying unsuccessfully to suppress a snicker of amusement. "Tom, Tom, Tom. Okay, hold on, here it comes. Mrs. Thomas Cobalt."

"Noooooooo!" The scream of agony attracted the attention of most of the remaining students in the cafeteria."

"It gets worse. Mrs. Sarah Cobalt. Then it's back to Tom, Tom, Tom."

"With the possible exception of one or two or you, you're all ignoramuses." Evad was returning to his seventh period students their graded tests along with his usual words of encouragement. "You might as well end your miserable lives right now as none of you appear headed for even mediocrity let alone greatness."

Alex's hand shot up causing Sleinad Evad to roll his eyes. "Yes, Mr. Banyon."

"What makes a man great?"

"This is science, not philosophy, Mr. Banyon. That question is off the subject."

"You just assured us that none of us were headed for greatness. I would consider that an empty statement, unless you can offer up a definition of whatever you think it is we have no chance to achieve."

Tom along with the rest of the class marveled at Alex's gall, yet for a reason he couldn't explain, the boy expected Evad not to react as most teachers might, that is, simply using their authority as a crutch and seeking to punish Alex, but instead to take up the boy's challenge. Tom turned out to be right, as Evad stopped what he was doing and confronted the blond-haired student.

"Very well, Mr. Banyon. *Greatness* is one of those ill-defined concepts like *evil* or *greed* . . ." Tom noted that most people might have used positive examples like *good* as opposed to *evil*, but not Evad. ". . .that can mean different things to different people, so perhaps an example would serve our purpose best. Give me the name of someone you think was a great man? Let's restrict ourselves to the twentieth century."

"President Franklin Roosevelt," answered Alex, without any hesitation.

Evad gave out a derisive laugh. "You consider a man who was an intellectual midget and whose imbecilic policies prolonged an economic depression an additional fourteen years great?"

"Well, eh, I thought he ended the Great Depression," said Alex.

"By any rational measure, it ended only after he was dead and many of his policies repealed."

"But he won World War II." Alex wasn't about to give up easily.

"He got the United States involved in a war in which it had no business and from which it had nothing to gain, and on top of that he unnecessarily prolonged it because he subscribed to the foolish idea of unconditional surrender."

"But . . ."

"This isn't history class, Mr. Banyon."

"Albert Einstein." Wayne hadn't even bothered to raise his hand.

"Einstein? Hah!" Evad almost shouted the exclamatory. "A man who set science back a hundred years because he convinced his peers that abstract mathematical equations were reality. Or do you really believe that space, empty nothingness, can cause gravity by bending?" The teacher had actually leaned in close to Wayne when he cast his taunt. As Wayne had no idea what Evad was talking about, the boy simply gave his head a negative shake.

Sarah raised her hand.

"Yes, Miss Gould. You're probably the forlorn hope to convince me that there's at least one person in this class with a glimmer of a mind."

"Eleanor Roosevelt," said the girl, sounding confident. Her confidence was dashed by another guffaw from the teacher.

"She was a spoiled twit."

When there appeared to be no more takers, Alex again spoke up. "So, give us an example of a great man, Mr. Evad."

"Other than myself," the man gave the boy a smirk, "the greatest man of the twentieth century was no doubt Nikola Tesla."

Evad's statement was met by silence and quizzical stares.

Sarah raised her hand again but didn't wait to be acknowledged. "Who is Nikola Tesla?"

"I might have guessed that not one of you has heard of the man, a sorry statement on a system that is euphemistically referred to as public *education*."

The teacher walked over to stand by the wall light switch. "Among many other marvels, Tesla gave you this." He gave it two quick flicks, turning the ceiling lights off and then back on.

"He invented the light switch?" said Brad.

"No, you moron!" said Evad.

"I thought Edison invented the light bulb," said Tom.

"Not the light bulb, you imbecile," roared Evad. "Alternating current, not to mention radio, the Tesla . . ."

"I thought Marconi invented radio," said Wayne.

Evad shook his head. "I take back what I said earlier about there possibly being one or two exceptions in this class. You're all ignoramuses. You have the collective mentality of a school of guppies."

The end of the school day found Wayne, Alex and Tom waiting for Brad outside the building's main entrance. "Uh, oh. Is that who I think it is over there?" said Alex, motioning with his head towards some older boys sitting on the school lawn.

The subject of Alex's question was Jack Paine, the terror of East Pencreek High, along with his two accomplices in bullying. The three of them were smoking cigarettes, a violation of the rules for minors on school property. As always, Jack was wearing his signature white t-shirt and matching black leather jacket. The three appeared to be taking their usual interest in the students leaving the school. From the facial expressions they were making, it appeared obvious that whatever they were saying about their fellow classmates was far from complimentary.

"Yeah, it's Paine all right," said Wayne. "And let's not try to draw attention to the fact."

"That's for sure," said Tom. "I thought he got expelled last week. What's he doing back?"

"What he always does," said Wayne. "Hanging out and looking for trouble."

Jack and his buddies sat with their backs resting against a chain link fence that ran parallel to a cinder and gravel walkway. Students whose projected route took them past the three delinquents and who happened to notice them in time either changed direction if they were not close enough to Jack and his buddies to appear too obvious in doing so, or averted their eyes and hoped that Jack Paine wouldn't take any special interest in them that day.

"Hey guys, thanks for waiting." The three turned to greet Brad coming through the doorway. Not far behind Brad, but unnoticed by the boys, walked Sarah. When she spied the boys, she carefully walked behind them and headed down the path that led past Jack and his cohorts. Obviously, she was unaware of Jack Paine's presence for he was the one person she would have sought to avoid at all cost.

"Uh-oh," said Wayne, noticing Sarah. "Look where Sarah's heading." The other three followed his stare. Seeing Sarah's route, Alex and

Tom, without saying a word, immediately started walking after the girl. "Hey, where are you going?" called Wayne after his two friends.

Sarah was strolling along in her customary stance with her books and purse clutched tightly to her chest, and her eyes studying the ground in front of her, being careful not to look to either side so as to avoid any eye contact with another human being. What happened next was to set off a chain of events that would ultimately result in decisive consequences four centuries in the future. Jack nonchalantly stuck out a foot and tripped the girl, taking her completely by surprise. Sarah let out a shriek as her purse and books went flying from her grasp. She hit the path hard, badly skinning one of her knees and both hands as she tried to break her fall. Her face also hit the gravel, knocking her glasses off and bruising her chin.

"Hey, watch where you're going," laughed Jack.

"I don't think she could," said the thug to his right. "Her nose was in the way."

Sarah sat up, wincing with pain. Blood was already seeping out of the cut on her knee. The bruises on her hands were also turning red. At the sound of Sarah's cry, everyone nearby had stopped to look at the girl—everyone that is except Alex. At the moment Jack tripped Sarah, Alex dropped his books and broke into a run. Pulling up in front of the oversized bully, Alex clenched his hands into fists. He fairly spat the words at Jack. "What did you do that for, you jerk?"

Jack jumped to his feet and before Alex could react, the older boy grabbed the eighth grader by the wrist. As if he were playing with a rag doll, he wrenched Alex's arm behind his back. Alex yelped with pain as Jack's grip on his arm forced him into a defenseless position.

"Get on your knees and lick my sneakers, maggot," commanded Jack, a sneer on his face. For good measure, he pulled Alex's wrist up higher forcing the boy to immediately drop to his knees. Jack's next words were cut short by a fist seemingly coming out of nowhere and colliding with his jaw. The sound of the blow echoed across the school yard. The greaser's head snapped back, the cigarette butt flying from his mouth. Jack released Alex's wrist as his body crashed to the ground.

For a moment Jack Paine sat there, a look of shock and surprise write on his face. Being knocked to the ground was a completely new experience for him, along with the pain that was flashing in his jaw. But he quickly regained his senses and looked up to identify his assailant. Tom stood there in a classic boxing stance, both his hands formed into fists, positioned so as to protect his face while at the same time being poised for another strike. Jack, being stupid in other things besides academics, and with the little judgment he possessed having already been cast to the winds by his mounting rage, struggled to his feet. The bigger and older boy was still confident in his ability to rectify the recent setback, after all he had four years and a good forty pounds on his opponent. "Why you——," was all he got out before a second, even stronger blow from Tom, landed square on his nose. The collision of fist with face was accompanied by the sound of cartilage breaking. It could have all been in the imaginations of the witnesses, as the sound of breaking cartilage is what one would expect from a blow that seemed to bend and then flatten the nose of its recipient. The hoodlum crashed to the turf in imitation of a huge sack of potatoes having been dropped from a great height. Paine let out a scream of pain. Blood was spurting from his nose even before his head touched the grass. Tom yelled, "Ouch," and grabbed the hand he had used to break Paine's nose.

From behind Tom came an adult's voice. "What's going on here!" Mr. Elkins, the assistant principal, the same Mr. Elkins who had disciplined Sarah and Alex that morning, was forcing a path through the crowd of students that had quickly gathered to watch the fight. He had arrived in time to see Tom land the decisive blow. Before him writhing on the ground lay a vanquished Jack Paine, holding his bloodied nose with both hands and crying, "He bwoke my nose! He bwoke my nose!"

To one side was Alex, massaging his sore arm as he got to his feet.

Further down the path sat Sarah, a look of shock on her face, having witnessed Alex's doomed rescue attempt and Tom's subsequent triumph over the forces of evil. Then there was Tom, glaring his defiance at his prostrate opponent while rubbing the knuckles of the hand he had used to break Jack's nose. The assistant principal's first action was to grab Tom by his collar.

"Well, I might have known," said Elkins, ignoring Tom for the moment and turning his attention to Sarah and Alex. "My two smart alecks causing even more trouble. Miss Gould and Mr. Banyon, you will report to my office first thing in the morning." Sarah started to protest, but Elkins immediately cut her off with a shout. "Not one word out of you, you brat."

Sarah screamed back at the man, "I hate you and this accursed school of yours. May you all rot in Tartarus." Then she turned her back on Elkins, and began to retrieve her possessions, ignoring both the administrator and the hurts from her still bleeding bruises.

Elkins' only response to Sarah's defiance was to blink his eyes in surprise. He had no idea what she was talking about. Then he turned to Jack, who still lay on the ground, squirming about in obvious pain. "Son, you might want to see a doctor about that." Tom couldn't believe it. Elkins acted as if he were ignorant of both Jack's identity and his reputation. Perhaps the man was even afraid of Paine?

"And as for you, I know who you are," Elkins said to Tom. "You're Tom Cobalt. Not only a smart aleck, but someone who likes to start fights. Your behavior disgusts me, hitting a defenseless boy. Why that poor boy hadn't even gotten to his feet when you attacked him." With those words, Elkins gave Tom a shove in the direction of the school building.

Wayne stepped in front of Mr. Elkins, blocking the route of the administrator. "Mr. Elkins. Tom didn't—"

"Out of my way, son, or you'll be joining Cobalt for some disciplining."

"But—"

Elkins poked Wayne in the chest with his finger. "Didn't you hear me, son? What do you take me for—an idiot?" Elkins failed to notice Brad standing behind him, energetically nodding his agreement with Elkins assertion that he was an idiot. "Now out of my way," he shouted.

Wayne hesitated before reluctantly moving to the side, and Elkins proceeded to shove Tom towards the school building.

When Tom emerged from the school about thirty minutes later he found his three friends waiting for him.

"How many?" said Brad.

Tom didn't have to ask Brad to elaborate.

"Two," answered Tom, smiling.

"Two!" said Wayne in obvious disbelief. "He gave Alex three just for calling Odavsky a blithering idiot."

"Of course," said Alex, defending his punishment. "Fights happen every day, but how often does a student critique a teacher with such eloquence?" Then he asked Tom, "Did he give you a note for your parents to sign?"

"Yep! That's three notes going home from three different students. Probably some sort of record for East Pencreek. And by the way, thanks for waiting for me."

"We figured it might be a good idea," said Brad. "Jack might be waiting somewhere to ambush you."

"Yeah, but I don't think he'll take on four of us," said Wayne.

"I doubt he'll be waiting for me this afternoon. He's probably at the doctor's getting that ugly snout of his fixed. But thanks just the same."

As the boys started walking home, Alex piped up. "Jack would never start a fight if he didn't think he had the odds stacked in his favor. That kind of slug only preys on the weak and defenseless."

"I doubt if he'd even want to try Tom alone after what Tom did to him," added Brad.

"Right," said Alex. "But he's just the kind of snake to take his humiliation out on Sarah. You know, see her as a scapegoat for what happened today."

"Why would he think Sarah looks like a goat?" said Brad.

Alex ignored Brad. "Tom, I was thinking . . ."

As she attended to the yet another cut on her daughter's knee, Mrs. Gould's thoughts were racing in a riot of emotion. What was happening to her daughter's life? She had not only come home with a note from the assistant principal that accused Sarah, among other charges, of being disrespectful to a teacher and making up historical facts, but the same hooligan had again attacked her after school, a situation that the school administration had sworn would never again happen. Then, according to her daughter, Alex and Tom had again come to her aid. Yet the assistant principal accused her of causing a fight and she was to report to him in the morning.

"Sarah, I'm still somewhat confused about all this."

"Ouch!" Sarah jumped as her mom applied another dab of antiseptic to one of the girl's bruises.

"Could we start again with what happened in history class?"

"Mom, please, not now. I don't want to talk about it anymore," sobbed Sarah.

"Well, can we at least talk about the boy who tripped you? Do you know him?"

"No, I don't know him, but he's the same bully who hit me with the rock. I don't even think he's a student. He looks like he's twenty or thirty years old, and some sort of criminal."

"And you say Tom beat him up?"

Sarah gave her mom a frustrated look. "Don't you believe me?"

"Of course, I do. It's just if he's that old, I don't understand why he would be on school property."

"I don't know. All I know is that he's the big bully around here, and that Tom beat the snot out of him and I'm glad he did it. I just wish that Mr. Elkins hadn't arrived to stop Tom from beating even more snot out of him."

"Sarah Gould! That's an awful thing to say. You should never wish bad things on someone."

"Mom! He tripped me! I was minding my own business and he tripped me. I don't even know him. I have cuts on my knee and my hands and my chin and I almost broke my glasses and my dress is probably ruined. Do you think the blood will wash out?"

Mrs. Gould finished putting the bandage on Sarah's knee. "Go up to your room and change and I'll wash your dress. Your father will be home soon. Then we'll talk more about what happened."

Sarah got up from the chair and started to leave the kitchen, favoring the knee with the cut as she walked. She stopped and turned to face her mom, her eyes focused on the floor. "Oh, I almost forgot. I have to write an apology to Miss Odavsky, and also Mr. Elkins."

"I understand," said her mom.

Sarah looked up. "But I didn't do anything wrong! I didn't make up facts. Miss Odavsky doesn't know what she's talking about."

"That's not the point, Sarah . . ."

"Then what is the point? Is it right that students are taught things that aren't true?"

Mrs. Gould's answer to Sarah's question was interrupted by the front door bell. Sarah's younger sister, who was supposed to be upstairs in her room so as not to be able to hear the conversation between Sarah and her mother, shouted from the top of the stairs where she had been eavesdropping, "Can I answer it?"

Mrs. Gould gave out an audible sigh. "Yes, Anne. Please do." She got up and followed Sarah into the hallway.

Anne opened the front door. There stood Alex and Tom. Alex

started to ask, "Is your mom home?" when he noticed Sarah standing in the hallway, her chin, hands and knee covered with bandages.

When Mr. Gould arrived home, he was surprised to find his wife and two daughters sitting at the kitchen table with the Tom and Alex. Both of the boys were focused on devouring some milk and cookies, Tom doing so with his left hand as his right was lying on the table under an ice pack. Then he noticed the bandage on his daughter's chin. Before he could say anything, his wife cut in. "Stephen, you better pull up a chair and join us. You're not going to believe what all happened at school today. Alex, I hope you won't mind starting from the beginning again for my husband's sake. I'll be glad to give both of your parents a call if you think they might be worried about why you're late getting home."

"So you see," said Alex, "Miss Odavsky's really is a blithering idiot. In my opinion she's not qualified to teach history."

"Heck," said Tom. "I don't think she's qualified to . . ." He stopped when he saw the looks on the faces of Sarah's parents. "Uh, never mind."

"Anyway, that's the whole story," finished Alex, but then as an afterthought he added, "Ah, Sarah, please don't take this the wrong way, but for your own good you have to learn to keep your mouth shut."

Sarah nodded and said, "I'll try."

Sarah's parents exchanged glances before Mr. Gould addressed the boys. "Sarah's mother and I would like to thank you for what you did for Sarah today. I guess you know she hasn't made any real friends at school yet. I'm not saying that calling Miss Odavsky a . . . blithering idiot was it?" Alex nodded. ". . . was the right thing to do, but I must say I appreciate your taking my daughter's side. Misery loves company and I'm sure Sarah feels better knowing that she isn't the only one who, uh, has trouble respecting Miss Odavsky. And I think it was very gallant of both of you to stand up to that bully."

"Well, that's another thing," said Tom. "Jack Paine's a real mean one. I wouldn't be surprised if he somehow doesn't blame Sarah for what happened today, so, uh, we, uh . . ."

Alex finished for his friend. "What Tom's trying to say is that we think it would be best if Tom and I—and our friends Brad and Wayne—walked Sarah to school. With the four of us with her, you wouldn't have to worry about Jack trying anything."

Mr. Gould smiled. "Seeing that the school administration didn't do a very good job of keeping this Jack Paine in line, I think that's a wonderful idea. What do you think, dear?"

Mrs. Gould also agreed, then concerned that she didn't know what Sarah thought of the idea, turned to her daughter. "Is that okay with you, Sarah?"

Sarah looked directly at Tom. "Yes, I'd like that." Alex also glanced in Tom's direction. He could have sworn that his friend was blushing.

"I would think you would want to get a doctor to look at that hand of yours," said Mr. Gould to Tom.

"I think it will be okay. Just bruised or something."

As the boys stood up to leave, Alex turned to Sarah. "Hey, you know, Brad had a neat idea. He suggested that you and I should get together and write identical apologies to see if either Odavsky or Elkins notices. What do you think?"

Sarah smiled and nodded, "Okay."

"Great. Suppose I come over about seven and we can write them."

"That Jack Paine's a bad egg," said Tom's father, as he dished a second helping of mashed potatoes onto his plate. Naturally, the topic of conversation at the Cobalt dinner table that evening was that day's events at school, just as it was at the dinner table of the Banyon's and the Gould's and several other families in town. "I know his father. The man spends too much time drinking, if you ask me. I don't think anyone knows what's become of the kid's mother. He hasn't had one as long as I can recall."

"You don't think he'll try to get back at Tom, do you?" asked Mrs. Cobalt, the concern showing in her voice.

"If he's the traditional bully, he'll avoid Tom like the plague. Most bullies are cowards. But I don't know about Jack. From all I've heard, he's a really mean cuss." Mr. Cobalt noticed that the look of concern on his wife's face had deepened. "Don't want to alarm you, dear, but one can never tell about these things." Then he looked at his son and smiled. "Tom can take care of himself if anyone can. Right, son?"

"I'll give it my best shot," said Tom with some difficulty as he had a mouth full of green beans.

"Tom. Don't talk with your mouth full and don't stuff your mouth so full to begin with," said Mrs. Cobalt for what must have been the hundredth time.

"I wouldn't worry," said Mr. Cobalt, turning back to his wife. "There's not much chance of anything happening while they're at school, and they'll be walking to and from school as a group. It's only the last couple of blocks after Tom drops Alex and Sarah off that he's alone, and I can't recall ever seeing Jack Paine around here. Which reminds me. I'm not signing the note from that jackass of an assistant principal."

"Sam!" cried Tom's mom, obviously shocked at her husband's language.

"No, let me finish. We're not signing that note. Instead, I'm going to school tomorrow morning. I've got a few things to tell Elkins." The volume of Mr. Cobalt's voice was rising. "For one thing, I'm informing the superintendent and the school board that he allowed that hoodlum to assault students on the school grounds. And the punk had already been expelled on top of everything else. And then he has the nerve to blame my son for the incident, and not only that, to paddle him! And I'm calling the Banyons and the Goulds and advising them that their kids don't go in and see Elkins in the morning. I'll be there in their place."

Tom and his sister sat there with large grins on their faces. They loved it when their dad got all spun up over some injustice. Mrs. Cobalt wasn't smiling but was trying to calm her husband. "I feel the same way as you do, dear, but we shouldn't be calling a teacher a, uh, beast of burden in front of the children. After all, they need to respect the position, if not the person."

"Yeah, and Elkins is going to learn to respect us and our children."

"Are you going to hit him, Dad?" asked Caroline, as if hoping for an affirmative answer.

"No, Caroline," said Mr. Cobalt. "Grownups don't hit each other. I'm just going to explain the facts of life to him."

"You mean he doesn't know about the birds and bees?" said Caroline, astonished.

Tom laughed. Mrs. Cobalt quickly explained, "No, dear, Daddy doesn't mean those facts of life."

"Well, anyway," continued Mr. Cobalt, attempting not to laugh at his daughter's expense, "I'm proud of what you did today, son. Not only for taking care of Jack, but for again offering to walk Sarah to school."

"Uh, actually, that was Alex's idea."

"Really," said his parents, together.

Caroline snickered. "Sounds to me like Alex might have a crush on Sarah."

"Shut up," growled Tom to his sister.

"Okay," nodded Mr. Cobalt. "But how did you get Wayne and Brad to go along with it?"

"I'm not sure, but I think part of it might be that they don't want to miss out on seeing any of the havoc Sarah causes."

Mrs. Cobalt gave Tom a scolding look. "I'm not sure that was a nice thing to say about Sarah."

"It's true, Mom. It's like the girl took a special course in how to find trouble."

"She seems like a nice girl. After all, she and her family go to our church now, and I've never heard of her causing any sort of disturbance there."

"Yeah, well, Jerry goes to our church too, remember?"

"And what, pray tell, do you find annoying about your cousin?"

"Never mind, Mom. Forget I said anything."

"I'll tell you what's wrong with Jerry," said Caroline. "He's always—"

"Caroline! Let's not get off on a discussion of your cousin tonight," ordered Mrs. Cobalt, nipping the topic in the bud.

Mr. Cobalt gave his family a smile as he leaned back in his chair, obviously finished with the meal. "Yes, son, I'm proud of you. Alex, too. Don't worry about Mr. Elkins. Like I said, I'll take care of him in the morning." He winked at Tom. "Semper fidelis."

"Semper fidelis," said Tom, returning his father's wink. "Semper fidelis," thought Tom, the motto of the United State Marine Corps. It was Latin and meant 'always faithful.' That was one thing he would always be to his family and friends. Faithful.

Mrs. Gould closed the door to Sarah's bedroom after saying goodnight to her daughter. She stood for a moment, alone with her thoughts, then made her way downstairs. Her husband met her at the foot of the stairs wearing a knowing grin. "That was Sam Cobalt on the phone. He said that Sarah shouldn't report to Mr. Elkins tomorrow morning—that he was going to handle everything. It certainly was some day."

In reply, Mrs. Gould threw herself into her husband's arms. Between the tears and the sobs, she managed to say, "It's going to be okay. Sarah's going to be okay."

"I suppose it would be asking too much if Sarah would make some friends that were girls, instead of all boys," teased Mr. Gould as he hugged his wife.

"It's going to be okay," repeated Mrs. Gould, almost in a whisper.

Chapter 9
The Briefcase

When early the next morning four boys arrived at the Gould home to pick up Sarah, they were greeted at the door by Sarah's parents. Brad and Wayne had to endure being introduced to Sarah's parents and her sister, Anne. This was followed by Mr. and Mrs. Gould repeatedly thanking the boys for escorting their daughter to school, thus making all five teens feel ill at ease. Sarah's only contribution to the conversation was to give her escorts a curt "hi" that was returned with an equally curt "hi" from each of the boys. Tom finally managed to get all of them out of the house with a "Well, we better be off," as Mr. Gould was shaking his left hand for the second time. Sarah's father was careful to avoid shaking the hand Tom had used to break Paine's nose. As the boys exited the house, Sarah's parents gave her a hug and her mother kissed her on the cheek. She hurried off to catch up with the others who had stopped halfway down the front walk to wait for her.

Sarah said she was sorry about all the fuss her parents had made.

"That's okay," said Alex.

She then asked Tom how his hand was.

"It will be okay."

After that, they walked on in silence, no one being able to think of anything more to say until Wayne spoke up.

"So, Alex, did you write an apology?"

"Sure did." As Alex said it, he gave Sarah a knowing wink unseen by Wayne.

"Well then, at least you didn't listen to Brad's moronic idea."

"Hey, that idea wasn't moronic," said Brad.

Wayne scrunched up his nose at his friend. "Sure it was, and I can prove it."

"Huh?" said Brad. "How?"

"Let's ask Sarah what she thinks of your dumb idea." Wayne turned to the girl. "Brad suggested that you and Alex should have gotten together and written identical apology notes. Now isn't that a dumb idea?"

Sarah could hardly suppress a smile as she answered. "No, not at all. I think it was a clever idea. That's just what Alex and I did."

Brad's bearing seemed to soar. "See, gnat brain. Sarah says I'm clever."

Wayne scoffed. "She may not think it was such a great idea if Elkins or Odavsky catch on. Then she'll think you and your idea are both screwballs."

By the time the group reached the schoolyard, the score on insults was Wayne seven and Brad six. Brad was trying to think of a way to even the score, when Alex interrupted the contest.

"Hey, Tom, isn't that your dad's car?" Alex pointed to a '58 Chevy parked on the street next to the school.

"Yeah. Dad said he wanted to be early enough to make sure he had Elkin's undivided attention." The other boys laughed.

"Undivided attention," said Wayne, "like in, 'Hey, look at me while I punch your ugly face in.'"

When the five eighth graders entered the school, the other students in the hall stopped whatever they were doing and turned to stare at them. By now every student at East Pencreek High, from the lowliest seventh grader to the loftiest senior, had heard of yesterday's episode with Jack Paine. There were even senior boys impressed by the fact that an eighth grader had broken Jack's nose, as the juvenile thug's past history had shown no respect for a student's age, only his size. Yet Tom and his friends were so engrossed by Wayne's conjectures of what Mr. Cobalt might be saying, or better yet, doing to Mr. Elkins, that none of them noticed the stares they were receiving or the mummer of conversation that erupted behind them as soon as they had passed.

Entering the school office, they stopped outside Mr. Elkins' door. The muffled sound of Mr. Cobalt's voice was easily recognizable. The tone was far from friendly. It reminded Tom of a marine drill sergeant making life a living hell for a new recruit. For a good minute the five hung on every word and made no comment except for an occasional snicker. During that time it was as if Mr. Cobalt had never taken a breath. Not a single word of response was heard from Mr. Elkins. Sarah's complexion was starting to redden from hearing some of the highly colorful adjectives and nouns Mr. Cobalt was using in reference to both Mr. Elkins and his actions of the preceding day. On occasion Mr. Cobalt even introduced the listeners to some new vocabulary, although from the context in which the unfamiliar words were used, the teenagers could make a confident guess as to their meaning. When the early warning bell sounded, the students reluctantly hurried off to their homeroom, the sounds of Mr. Cobalt's tirade against the assistant principal fading in the distance.

Wayne pointed to one of the offerings on the lunch counter and said to the server, "I'll have some of that brown stuff."

"You mean the meatloaf," was the indignant reply.

"That's meatloaf? On second thought forget it. Give me some of those things that look like peas."

"They are peas!" said the cafeteria worker, sounding even more indignant than before as she dropped a spoonful of the green things on the boy's plate.

"I told you they were peas," said Brad, who was in line in front of Wayne.

"I guess you won't be sitting with your friends today," came a voice from behind Wayne.

"Huh?" said Wayne, turning his head to look at Cynthia Cohen. "Why not?"

"Because Little Miss Snotty Pants is sitting with them."

Wayne looked over to the table where he always ate lunch as he placed a dessert on his tray. There sat Sarah with Tom and Alex. "So?"

"You're not telling me you're going to sit with Miss Know-it-all?"

"Sarah meets all the requirements for a girl being allowed to sit at our table."

Wayne's response momentarily left Cynthia speechless, but she quickly recovered. "And what are these high-and-mighty requirements?"

"She has to be smart and pretty instead of dumb and ugly like you."

Cynthia let out a shriek. Enraged, she picked up a plum and threw it, aiming at the back of Wayne's head. With incredible premonition, Wayne suavely ducked in time for the purple projectile to soar harmlessly over his noggin. It collided with the back of Mr. Johnson's head. Being a ripe plum, the sound of the impact was more of a "splat" than a "bop." Mr. Johnson, the cafeteria monitor, spun around, his hand feeling the back of his head and neck where the plum had landed. "Who threw that?"

The look of horror on Cynthia's face and the fact that her throwing arm was still extended were enough for Mr. Johnson to confidently convict her of the charge. Nevertheless, to make doubly sure that he had no doubt as to whom the culprit was, both Brad and Wayne were pointing at Cynthia.

"Alright Miss, we'll have to spend some of our lunch period today having a little chat with Mr. Elkins."

"But he called me stupid and ugly," wailed Cynthia, pointing at Wayne.

"I certainly have to agree with the stupid part," said Mr. Johnson, picking up a napkin from Wayne's tray and wiping off some of the overripe plum still clinging to the nape of his neck.

"Mr. Johnson," said Brad. "Mr. Elkins isn't here. He left early today."

"Huh?" said Mr. Johnson.

"Yeah. Apparently, he had an unpleasant experience this morning and went home ill."

"In that case," said the cafeteria monitor, turning back to Cynthia, "I'll guess we'll have to go see Mrs. Morrison, the principal."

"What was that all about?" asked Tom as Brad and Wayne took their seats at the table.

"Cynthia was just having one of her fits," said Wayne.

"Yeah," said Brad. "I think she's jealous of Sarah."

"Why would she be jealous of me?" asked a baffled Sarah.

"Because you got invited to eat lunch with the four coolest guys at East Pencreek High, and she wasn't," said Wayne. "Hey, Tom, I'll give you my plum for your pretzels."

"That's a good trade," added Brad. "The plum's nice and ripe."

Sleinad Evad acknowledged Alex, who had his hand raised. Evad appeared to hold all students in disdain, but there were two types of students whom he seemed to especially despise—the dumb ones and the smart ones. "Yes, Mr. Banyon."

"I was wondering, Mr. Evad. Do you think time travel is possible?"

"That's off the subject, Mr. Banyon."

"I realize that." Alex stood his ground as was his nature. When Alex deemed a goal worthy, the boy's level of persistence in obtaining it rose to such heights that not even one of Evad's stature seemed able to deter him from his course. "It's just that there's no one else I know who could answer such a question—you being so knowledgeable and all about physics."

The deadpan look on the face of the walking horror changed to a menacing grimace. "Don't try flattery with me, Mr. Banyon. You will rue the day if you ever attempt it again."

"Yes, sir," replied Alex, finally looking cowered.

"Besides, I happen to know that your uncle is a professor of physics. Why don't you ask him?"

"I did, and he laughed. He said that anyone who believed in time travel was a fool, like people who believe in things like fairies or flying saucers."

The grimace disappeared, as the corners of the teacher's mouth rose, taking the form of a grin that Evad usually reserved for a bout of sarcasm. "He did, did he? Did he give any reason for rejecting the possibility of time travel?"

A hopeful look returned to Alex's face. "He said it violated the concept of simultu— similtany—simul—"

"Simultaneity?"

"Yeah, that sounds right. He also said something about it being illogical. That if travel backward in time were possible, what would happen if you went back in time before you were born and killed your father?"

The smile on Evad's face broadened. For once it lacked menace. "Did he happen to mention the principle of temporal immutability?"

"Er, no." The class was silent, all eyes focused on the teacher. Was Evad actually going to reveal some profound piece of evidence or argument that time travel might be possible?

Instead the clone of an undertaker paused as if struck by a troubling thought. He turned and looked at the calendar on the wall, as he did the day he mentioned neutronium. For a moment he again appeared to be hypnotized by the calendar.

"Uh, oh," whispered Tom. "I think we just had another neutronium moment." He gave a low chuckle of amusement.

Evad swung around, his eyes targeting Tom. He had no doubt

heard Tom's remark, but instead of laying into the boy, he addressed the entire class. "For homework tonight read the remaining sections of chapter nine and answer questions eight through twelve at the end of the chapter in that miserable piece of pulp the school board has selected for a science text." He always referred to the text book in such disrespectful terms. "And Mr. Cobalt," the grin had returned, "you will stay after class so we can discuss further that remark you made." Tom lowered his head and emitted a barely audible moan. Then the bell rang. It was another uncanny talent of Evad that he always seemed to know when the period was about to end although he wore no watch and Tom couldn't recall the man ever looking at the clock on the front wall of the classroom.

"Sorry, Tom," mumbled Alex as he rose to leave. "I'll try to think of something to get you out of this."

"That's okay," replied Tom, keeping his voice low, while remaining seated. "It was my stupid fault."

Sarah stopped on her way out of the room beside Tom's desk. "Tom, what happened?" she asked, also keeping her voice low.

"Alex will tell you", whispered Tom. "Don't worry. If I can handle Jack Paine, I can handle Evad."

"Miss Gould. I don't remember asking you to stay."

"Sorry, Mr. Evad." Sarah hurried from the classroom leaving the boy alone with his nemesis.

The man took his time in walking up to the desk in front of Tom's, then seated himself on the desk, facing the student with his feet resting comfortably on the chair seat. The position seemed to make him even more menacing than usual. He appeared to tower over the teenager, reminding the boy of a vulture peering down on its next meal. For some time Evad said not a word as he studied the boy with those penetrating, dark eyes. Tom didn't attempt to return the stare. Instead he looked at the top of his desk. Evad began to crack his knuckles, one at a time. Tom twiddled his thumbs in response. Then realizing that Evad might interpret that as impudence, he stopped.

Finally, the teacher spoke up. "I heard about your fight with that Paine character yesterday? That was either very courageous of you or very stupid. Then again sometimes they're one in the same. So, tell me, Mr. Cobalt. Did you enjoy it?"

Tom lifted his eyes. He found no mockery in Evad's expression. It was back to the neutral, emotionless stare that his students were usually accustomed to. "Well, I was mad—and afraid. Both at the same time, I guess."

"Did you enjoy it?"

So puzzled was Tom by the repeat of the odd question, that it was a moment before he answered. "No."

"Not at all?" It seemed to the boy that he detected a faint shadow of amusement in Evad's voice.

"Well, maybe a little. I mean, I was happy that I won."

"If you had had the chance, would you have terminated him?"

The boy thought to himself, "What the heck does he mean by 'terminate him?'"

"Sir? I'm not sure I understand the question, or for that matter, what the fight has to do with anything."

"I was impressed. I was impressed not only by the fact that you took on a boy who was obviously much bigger and stronger than you, but I was even more impressed by the fact that you won." His eyes seemed to grow larger. "Mr. Cobalt, there is no substitute for victory."

"Yes, sir."

"Mr. Cobalt. Are you adopted?"

"What!" puzzled the boy. "Where is this conversation going? What does being adopted have to do with anything?"

Seeing the look of confusion on Tom's face along with his hesitancy to answer, the teacher continued. "Believe me, Mr. Cobalt, I can tell whenever anyone lies to me. Answer the question. Are you adopted?"

"No."

"Are you sure?"

"Yes. I mean, I'm thirteen years old. I think my parents would have told me by now if I were adopted. Besides, everyone is always telling me how I have my mom's eyes. I'm kind of big for my age. My dad's six foot-two." Tom paused. "I don't know what else to say to convince you that I'm not adopted." Tom was picking up his courage. "What does that question have to do with anything?"

"Things aren't always as they seem."

"Huh?" thought Tom. "What does he mean by that, and isn't that what Mr. Serpens keeps saying?"

The teacher stepped down from his seat on the desk. Standing, he again studied the boy for a moment, then turned and walked to the front of the classroom, stopping behind the lab table which served as his desk. Turning again to face the boy, he said, "I understand you're an excellent marksman."

"Well, I don't know about that. I've earned the merit badges in—"

"You're too modest. Coach Heartburn—"At the slip of the tongue, Evad paused. The look on the boy's face was torn between amusement and shock. "Coach Heathburn tells me that you're the finest athlete he's ever seen. Normally I don't put much stock in anything that fool says, but the man does seem to have some aptitude for recognizing athletic talent."

Tom continued to sit there, puzzled, and not saying anything unless asked a direct question. For a number of seconds Evad was again silent. He simply stared at the boy, making Tom more and more uncomfortable with each passing moment. Then with a movement so sudden and unexpected that it surprised Tom, Evad reached behind the lab table. Tom could hear the sound of a drawer being opened. The next thing the boy knew, the man had placed his briefcase on top of the table, his left hand coming to rest on it. He again fixed the boy with his eyes, and this time Tom felt like the man's gaze was attempting to bore into his very soul.

"Do you believe time travel is possible?"

"My gosh!" Tom told himself. "First we talk about yesterday's fight, then whether I'm adopted, and now we're suddenly on time travel."

The boy turned the palms of his hands up, as if to gesture that he hadn't given the topic much thought. "I dunno. I guess I never gave it much thought."

"Never?" The way Evad said it, it sounded like an accusation, like he was accusing Tom of lying. "Never?" he repeated, this time louder. The man's left hand began to squeeze the top of the briefcase, at the same time his head began to show a barely noticeable twitch, as if the man were undergoing some sort of inner struggle, as if he were being gripped by some grave indecision. "Never?" he rasped for the third time.

Before Tom could answer there was the sound of a buzzer and a yellow light bulb on the wall next to the door flickered on and off three times. It was the school's means of alerting a teacher that he should report to the school office, typically because he had an urgent phone call. Evad looked as if he had been rudely awakened from some deep meditation. He turned his head to stare at the now unlit light bulb, then lifted the briefcase before lowering it out of sight behind the table. There was the sound of a drawer closing. "Wait here," was all he said as he swiftly exited the room, leaving the door open behind him.

Tom remained seated but a second. Then as if struck by a divine inspiration, he jumped out of his chair and hurried to the doorway. He glanced both up and down the hallway. It was empty. No one was in sight. It would take Evad a couple of minutes at least to get to the office, answer the phone and return. Tom turned to look at the teacher's lab table. The drawer in which Evad always deposited his briefcase when entering the classroom was ajar. The boy's curiosity was suddenly akin to that of a cat. Without wasting any more time, Tom crossed the room to the table. He couldn't explain what made him do it. Why would there be anything special about what Evad carried in his briefcase? Yet the man was so strange, so different, Tom sometimes imagined him to be other than human. It seemed to the boy that he had to take advantage of the opportunity. He had to know if there was some clue to the man lying within that drawer. He again glanced at the door and listened. No sound of footsteps. He took a deep breath and pulled open the drawer. There was a squeak as wood slid over wood. It wasn't loud but to Tom it sounded as if an alarm had been sounded, blaring loud enough to be heard clear up in the school office.

There sat the briefcase, looking as if it hid some fatal secret. When the boy spied a lock on the clasp, he felt an immediate downing of his hopes. It there was some deep secret residing inside that satchel, surely one as methodical as Evad would not have left it unlocked so that any Tom, Dick or Harry (or perhaps Tom, Alex, or Wayne would have been more appropriate) could open it and peer inside. But why stop now? He pushed the latch on the leather clasp of the briefcase. It moved. It was unlocked!

Gripping the two sides of the briefcase, the boy pulled. The briefcase opened. Tom leaned over and peered inside and as he did so he emitted an audible sigh of disappointment. Inside was a box, a wooden box. The box was of a size that filled much of the available space within the briefcase. He had gone this far, why stop now? Ignoring the sweat that was forming on his brow and on the palms of his hands, he hesitated nary a moment, but reached in and pulled out the box, sitting it on top of the lab table. The box was scaled approximately to the shape of a book, the narrower sides being bisected by a thin, shallow indentation. As more evidence that the top of the box functioned as a lid, on the side that faced Tom were a pair of hinges. Tom gave the box a half turn so as to view the other side. His optimism of discovering the contents of the mysterious container were immediately dashed for that side of the box displayed a cleverly designed combination lock that was imbedded in the wood. "Rats!" He again glanced at the door and listened for the sound of approaching footsteps but heard none. To make doubly sure, he hurried to the doorway and quickly glanced up and down the hall. No one was in sight.

Returning to the mystery box, he studied the lock. There were three tumblers, each displaying a single number. The combination was presently set to "one-two-three." There were a thousand possible combinations, if one included "zero-zero-zero." There was no way he could even try a fraction of those thousand combinations before Evad returned. Tom carefully surveyed the problem. The lock's design was unlike that of any lock Tom had ever seen. There was no latch present, just a piece of metal that held the three tumblers, the rim of each tumbler displaying a single digit. The suspicion dawned on the boy that perhaps this was something that had been personalized for Evad. If so, perhaps the owner could reset the combination to one of his choosing. If he were Evad what would he select for a combination? "Bah!" It was still impossible. He didn't have any idea what combination Evad would select, even assuming such an option had been exercised instead of the combination having been set to some random number by the lock's manufacturer. Best to return the box to the briefcase and close the drawer before curiosity killed the Tom cat.

As he reached for the box, he stopped. He was struck by an inspiration—a diabolical inspiration it seemed. A smile crossed his face. Instead of picking up the box, he spun the first and second tumblers until the combination read "six-six-three." His hand began to shake as he advanced the third tumbler to a third six. As the six clicked into place, an even louder click was emitted from the lock and the lid of the box popped up. Tom gave a nod of satisfaction as he stared at the number "six-six-six." It was the number of the beast from the Book of Revelation. Of course, it only made sense that Sleinad Evad, obviously some spawn of Beelzebub himself, would pick such a number to guard a great secret, and Tom, eighth grader Tom Cobalt, had guessed it. Alex would be proud of him.

Tom lifted the lid. What greeted his eyes was a rectangular shaped grey material that was sized to exactly fit the inside of the box. He touched it. It felt spongy but was made of a material of which Tom was unfamiliar. Its purpose, no doubt, was that of packing; that is, to either protect any objects that lay within, or perhaps to keep such an object from rattling should the box be shaken. The strange piece of material had an incision running from top to bottom, about a quarter the distance from one edge, that split it into two sections. The boy grabbed the smaller of the two sections and lifted it. Five shiny grey cylinders lay within, each resting in its own compartment. The ends of each cylinder were rounded, like that of the front end of a pistol bullet. He picked up one of the odd-looking cylinders and examined it. The object was surprisingly light, with a smooth surface that exhibited no breaks. It felt warm to the touch. "Strange," thought the boy.

Time must be getting short. The boy returned the bizarre cylinder to its cradle, which was made out of the same material as the cover but included a depression that matched the shape of the cylinder so that when the object was inserted correctly, it was snuggly protected. Tom replaced the small cover and then reached to the left and removed the larger one. What lay beneath caused the boy emit a gasp. The object was too large in size for a man to easily conceal it on his person without arousing suspicion. It was cradled in another block of the grey, spongy material. Without hesitation Tom reached down and, using his uninjured hand and not the one he had used to smash Jack's nose, grasped the object almost as if by instinct. He lifted it and held it before him. Although Tom had never seen a real one before, he had no doubt as to what it was. A ray gun!

Chapter 10
The Incident in the Hall

As Tom held the weapon before him, he studied its every detail. It was obviously made to function as a pistol in that, like most handguns, it had a handle, trigger guard, and trigger. It was about a foot in length. There was a single barrel of a dull, metallic blue color. Beyond that there was no similarity to any firearm Tom was familiar with. The end of the barrel had no opening from which a bullet could emerge, but was encircled by a triple set of rings, at which point the barrel's appearance changed from opaque to translucent. Tom failed to locate any means by which one could insert either individual bullets or an ammunition clip. The area of the weapon above the grip and forward to approximately the midpoint of the barrel contained various buttons, knobs, and gauges, perhaps a dozen in all. The gadgets that looked like gauges were covered with strange symbols. Nowhere on the gun did a symbol recognizable as either a letter or number appear. Strangest of all, the material of which it was made had the look of plastic but the feel of metal.

Tom hefted the piece in his left hand. It was surprisingly light. And then he did something he would never have done with a "real" gun. He began to twirl it around his finger, in the manner of a cinema cowboy. With a small laugh, he tossed the still spinning weapon into the air and, doing a quick about face, attempted to catch the gun behind his back. Remembering at the last moment that his right hand was still recovering from its recent collision with Jack Paine's nose, he nevertheless successfully managed to catch the weapon with his other hand. His face assumed a triumphant grin which just as quickly disappeared, as he thought to himself, "What am I doing? What if Evad walks in? If it's a real ray gun, what if it accidentally discharges?" Tom's eyes widened in alarm. Without another thought, the boy returned the gun to its cradle, slapped the cover on top, and closed the lid of the box with a click. He gave each of the tumblers a spin, shoved the box back into the briefcase, pushed the latch on the briefcase to lock it, and with a slam, closed the table drawer. The sound of the drawer closing made him jump. He glanced behind him to make sure that Evad wasn't entering the room, and then bolted for his desk.

He had not been sitting for more than a few seconds when he heard footsteps coming down the hall. The teacher entered the room scowling. For a moment, Tom pondered asking about the phone call, perhaps putting forth an inquisitive statement like, "Bad news?" but then thought better of the idea.

Evad stopped behind the lab table and in rapid succession looked at Tom, then at the drawer that contained the briefcase, and then back at Tom. The eighth grader swallowed. Evad's scowl deepened. He opened the drawer. Tom distinctly heard the sound of the briefcase being opened, and then he remembered that he had just spun the tumblers on the wooden box's lock. He had not reset the combination to one-two-three—that is, to the setting as he had found it. Evad was staring at the combination. It read "four-five-six." The teacher closed the briefcase, then the drawer and returned his gaze to the student, scowling even more deeply than before. This time, Tom swallowed so hard that he emitted an audible "gulp."

The teacher's scowl was replaced by an evil grin. Actually, on anyone else it might have appeared to be a friendly grin, but any attempt by Evad to smile by definition appeared evil. "Where were we?" he

241

asked, pleasantly enough. "Ah, yes. Time travel." Before the Lord of Darkness could continue, a girl's scream erupted from the adjoining hall. His grin replaced by a scowl, Evad quickly turned and left the classroom at a brisk walk. As soon as he disappeared through the doorway, Tom jumped up from his desk and sprinted after him.

On entering the hall, the boy skidded to a stop. Evad was standing only a few paces in front of him. About twenty feet further down the hall stood Jack Paine, along with Sarah and one of Jack's goons. Jack's accomplice was holding Sarah around her waist. He had a hand clamped over her mouth, stifling her attempts to utter a second scream. All three were looking at Evad, Sarah with an expression of relief, and the goon with a look of alarm that indicated he was none too happy that a teacher had appeared, especially one as intimidating as Evad. By contrast, Jack Paine looked as if he welcomed the teacher's arrival for he glowered with pure malevolence. The bandages that formed a crisscross pattern on the punk's busted nose and the one blackened eye did nothing to soften his appearance. But when Jack spotted Tom, his features turned psychotic.

"You!" He fairly spat the word at Tom, at the same time indicating the boy with the finger of an outstretched hand. "I have something for you." Jack reached into a back pocket of his blue jeans and pulled out what appeared to the handle of a knife, or perhaps a razor. As he advanced towards Tom, he cast a quick glance at Evad. "And you, Teach—if you know what's good for you, you'll mind your own business." Tom had to admit Paine's obvious lack of dread of Evad showed either remarkable courage, or more likely, an abysmally deep level of utter stupidity. Then there was a click, and a nasty looking blade sprang from the handle. Okay, reasoned Tom, maybe it was neither courage nor stupidity, but a reasonable assessment of the situation that explained Paine's boldness.

Evad calmly took a step forward, purposely placing himself between the juvenile delinquent and his intended victim. Jack's accomplice relaxed his grip on Sarah, transfixed by the developing drama. For a moment, the relaxed manner by which Evad placed himself in harm's way along with the fact that although Jack was of respectable bulk, the teacher could still look down on him, seemed to give the teen thug pause. But Jack quickly recovered his former purpose, as he yelled, "Get out of the way!"

First Evad's expression changed to one of contempt, and then he gave Jack a wink that sent the youth into a frenzy as a fuse ignites a bomb. Jack pulled back his arm holding the switchblade and, with a quick lunge forward, he thrust the blade straight at Evad. Sarah let out a muffled scream, Tom and the other boy a yell, and all three of them gave an involuntary flinch as they expected to see the blade bury itself in Evad's body. Instead, with a speed like that of a striking snake, Evad's left arm shot up and deflected the thrust of the blade just as it looked to be entering his abdomen. At the same time, he gripped the wrist of Jack's knife wielding arm with his right hand and gave a quick twist. There was a sharp snap of yielding ligament and bone, followed by a hideous scream of Paine—eh, pain. Jack dropped first the knife and then his body to the floor, holding his injured wrist with his good hand, and continuing to utter horrible howls of rage.

For a moment no one moved as they watching the writhing delinquent thrash about on the floor of the hallway. Then, to Tom's surprise, Jack jumped to his feet, swiftly turned, and sprinted down the hall almost knocking over Alex, Wayne and Brad, who had appeared at a run around the far corner of the hallway.

Evad resumed walking towards Sarah and Jack's accomplice. Too late, Paine's fellow thug released his hostage and turned, attempting to duplicate Jack's exit. As he took his first step, Evad grabbed the teen by the collar of his shirt with one hand and by his right arm with the other. Apparently with little effort, he lifted the thug clear off his feet and then slammed the boy's body against a row of lockers. Evad released his hold, and let the scoundrel collapse to the floor, unconscious.

Tom's three friends had stopped only a few feet from Evad and the pile of hoodlum. They all looked at Tom as Alex blurted out, "What happened?"

Tom didn't reply. He was watching Evad walk calmly back to where the knife lay. The boys looked at Sarah, who was breathing hard, chest heaving, and obviously in no condition to comment. As the teacher stooped to retrieve the blade, Tom said, "Mr. Evad, are you okay?"

The teacher retracted the blade of the weapon and put it in his coat pocket. "Yes, Mr. Cobalt, I'm fine, although I'm skeptical if that's the answer you most wished to hear."

"Wow, I thought he might have stabbed you—" Tom noticed a growing red stain on the front of the teacher's white shirt where the suit jacket hung open, just above the belt. Sarah and the other boys saw it too. Sarah, appearing to have finally recovered her breath, opened her mouth as if to give out another scream, but instead simply resumed her labored breathing.

Evad looked down to see what they were staring at. At first upon seeing the blood, he paused as if trying to decide exactly what was happening. He laid a hand on the red stain and then turned it over as if to confirm that it was indeed his blood that coated his fingers. Amazingly, he still appeared to be the only one unperturbed by the sight. "A mere scratch, I assure you," he said. He calmly returned his hand to cover the wound. "Now you students get on home. I'll call the police." With that he walked over to where Jack's unconscious cohort lay, took hold of the thug's collar, and began to unceremoniously drag the boy's body down the hall. Except for the sound of Sarah's breathing, the five teens remained mute. When Evad reached the turn in the hallway, he glanced back and said, "Might I remind you that this is no excuse for not having your assignments turned in tomorrow."

On the way home, the boys naturally chatted excitedly about what had happened. Sarah, looking understandably pale, didn't contribute to the conversation, but had at least stopped shaking and was no longer taking in deep gulps of air.

"When Sarah and I passed the office, I noticed there was no one behind the counter," said Alex, "so I went in and pushed the pager button for Evad's classroom."

"Clever," said Wayne, giving Alex a worshiping look.

"So that was why Evad thought he had a phone call," said Tom. "I would have liked to have seen his face when he got there."

"Sarah and I peeked around the corner so we could see what was happening in the office," said Alex. "We saw Miss Clark enter the office right after Evad did. Not long afterwards, we heard Evad and Miss Clark arguing about whether or not someone had pushed the pager button." Alex gave out a chuckle. "Miss Clark even told Evad that he must have been imagining things. Isn't that right, Sarah?"

Sarah made her first contribution to the conversation with a simple nod of her head.

"Anyway, Evad was heading back to the classroom when you two showed up."

Alex gave Brad and Wayne a nod. "We were wondering how long Evad was going to keep you," he said, turning back to Tom, "when Sarah suggested that she go back to the classroom, pretending she had forgotten something, and try to find out what was going on. The three of us stayed far enough behind so Evad wouldn't spot us and that's when we heard Sarah scream, and then Paine yelling.

"I still can't believe that Evad pulled some sort of judo move on Paine," said Brad.

"I've never seen anything like it," said Tom, "even in the movies. I'm surprised that Paine actually managed to stab him."

"I'll tell you this," said Wayne, "If I had a knife stuck in my gut, I sure wouldn't still be standing."

"Well, one good thing came out of this," said Brad. "We won't have Jack Paine to worry about. No doubt, the police already have a warrant out for him. Attacking someone with a knife ain't exactly a misdemeanor, even in this township."

"So, what went on between you and Evad in the room?" asked Alex, changing the subject.

"It was weird, really weird," said Tom, "but not nearly as weird as what I found after he left to visit the office."

"What?"

Tom stopped, as did everyone else. He looked to be about to say something, but instead shook his head and started walking again. Everyone else immediately fell in behind him.

"On second thought, you'd never believe it. Forget I said anything."

"What do you mean forget it?" said Wayne. "Like get us all worked up and then drop it. Come on, out with it. What did you find?"

The other two boys joined Wayne in badgering Tom, until he gave in. "Okay, but don't say I didn't warn you. You're not going to believe it."

"Yeah, yeah," said Alex. "Come on, out with it."

"Well, when Evad left the room I got up and looked in his briefcase."

"You didn't?" cried Alex. Everyone stopped again, including Sarah.

"What did you find?" asked Wayne.

"A box. A wooden box."

"Yeah, and . . . ?"

"The box had a combination lock on it."

"Huh?" said Brad. "You mean like the ones on our lockers?"

"No. It was strange. It had three separate tumblers. Anyway, I opened the box."

"You're saying the box wasn't locked?" said Alex.

"Yes, it was, but I figured out the combination."

"You figured out the combination?" said Wayne, sounding dubious.

"Yeah."

"Okay, what was it, Mr. Superbrain?"

"Six-six-six."

"The number of Satan," said Sarah, half under her breath.

"Yeah, right," said Alex. "Why not one-two-three?"

"Well, actually——," started Tom, but then he thought better of it and stopped.

"So, anyway, you opened the box," said Alex, "and found . . . ?"

"A, uh——" Tom's thoughts began to haunt him. His friends would think he was nuts if he told them he found a ray gun. Even Sarah, who probably was a little nuts herself, would think he was nuts. Three pairs of male eyes began to bore in on him, turning increasingly demanding, while a pair of female eyes gave him a perplexed stare. "A gun."

Wayne gave a whistle. Brad said, "You're kidding. A real gun?"

"I think so."

"What do you mean, 'you think so?'" asked Alex. "Was it a real gun or not? I mean, if anyone can tell the difference, you should be able to."

"Well, I'm not sure."

Trying to be helpful, Wayne asked, "What kind of gun was it?"

Tom swallowed and looked back and forth among his friends before answering. He closed his eyes, took a deep breath, opened his eyes and said, "A ray gun."

The stunned silence on the part of Tom's listeners was finally broken by an uproarious burst of laughter from Alex and Brad. Wayne smiled and Sarah continued to give Tom a wild-eyed stare.

"I told you, you wouldn't believe it.'"

As Alex and Brad struggled to control their smirks, Wayne said, "Let's summarize what we have here. A teacher who dresses like an undertaker, whom everyone hates and most fear, whose name pronounced backwards is 'Dave Daniels,' who gets stabbed by a knife and acts like it was nothing, who knocks out a punk without even working up a sweat, carries a ray gun to school in his briefcase." The teenagers all exchanged looks. "On second thought, it doesn't sound all that crazy."

"Come on, Wayne," said Brad. "Tom's playing a joke on us. He never even looked in the briefcase." But by the changing expressions on

Alex and Wayne's faces, those two no longer appeared so certain that it was a joke.

"What kind of mad house did you send me too?"

Sarah's mom hugged her daughter closer as they sat on the living room couch.

"First everyone hates me and makes fun of me, and I even get in trouble with the teachers, half of whom are morons. Then this overgrown hoodlum, who should have been locked away years ago, trips me and a fight breaks out and I get in even more trouble. Then when I finally make some friends, I get grabbed by two hoodlums, and this same horrible boy stabs the only real teacher in the school, and most of that happened in the last two days."

"Now, now, dear," said Mrs. Gould, trying, if possible, to hug her daughter even tighter. "You're safe now."

"I know, I know!" sobbed Sarah, breaking her mother's hold and getting to her feet. "But I can't take any more of these awful things happening to me. I don't want to go back to that horrible school."

"I understand," said Mrs. Gould. "But are you sure that boy stabbed your science teacher? I mean, when someone gets stabbed by a knife, they usually don't stand there and then go on like nothing happened."

"Call Tom. He'll tell you that's exactly what happened. I don't want to ever go back to that school from hell. The place is a living nightmare. Why Tom says he even found a ray gun in Mr. Evad's briefcase."

"A ray what?"

"A ray . . ." Sarah stopped in mid-sentence, realizing that she had possibly destroyed Tom's credibility as a witness. "Never mind. I just don't want to go back to that horrible place."

Mrs. Gould's was looking at her oldest daughter with a growing sense of desperation. She was starting to think she had better arrange for her daughter an appointment with a psychiatrist. As if psychic, the girl seemed to sense what her mother was thinking, and her expression turned to one of even greater panic when the doorbell rang.

"Mrs. Gould?" inquired the township police officer who was standing on the front porch when Sarah's mom opened the door. He continued when she nodded. "If your daughter is home, I would like to speak with her. She no doubt told you about the events she witnessed at school today."

"I'm not sure this is the best time. She's terribly upset. Please realize that this is the second day in a row that she's been physically attacked at that school."

"I know that, Mrs. Gould, but it's probably best that I get her account of what happened while it's fresh in her mind." Mrs. Gould gave a sigh and, wishing her husband was home to help her shoulder the burden, allowed the officer to enter.

The officer was writing in his notepad as he took down Sarah's testimony. "And what happened after Paine stabbed Mr. Evad?"

Sarah hesitated before answering. She was starting to tremble as she relived the event in her mind. Her mom laid a hand on Sarah's arm in an attempt to calm her.

"Mr. Evad had grabbed his arm and I think he broke his wrist or something."

"He made Paine let go of the knife?"

"Yes."

"And?"

"And Jack Paine was lying on the floor screaming, and then he got up and ran away, and the other boy let go of me and tried to run after him, but Mr. Evad grabbed him and smashed him into the lockers. I guess he knocked him out. And then I saw that Mr. Evad was bleeding, but he didn't seem at all fazed by it."

Mrs. Gould shifted her attention to the policeman, a look of pleading in her eyes. "Officer, my daughter has been under a lot of stress lately. Surely, she might have imagined . . ."

"No, it's alright," said the lawman, holding up his hand. "Actually, your daughter's recollection seems to jive perfectly with that of the Cobalt boy. I had stopped at the Cobalt home before coming here."

"But you don't think that—?" Sarah's mother tried to continue.

"I think that both children's accounts may be accurate. I've also talked with Mr. Evad. He says that Jack Paine did indeed stab him, but it was hardly more than a scratch as the knife had been deflected by his belt. He said it looked a lot worse than it was."

"Oh," replied Mrs. Gould, sounding immensely relieved. Then she turned to her daughter. "I'm sorry I sounded like I doubted you dear." Sarah, looking exhausted, only managed to give her mother a nod.

"I think that's enough for now," said the officer. "We have a warrant out for Paine's arrest. I'm sure it won't be long before he joins his friend behind bars." The officer stood up. "Thank you for taking the time to talk to me, Sarah." The girl failed to acknowledge the officer. She was staring at the carpet.

Mrs. Gould saw the officer to the door. As he was saying goodbye, the woman asked, "By the way, Tom Cobalt didn't mention anything about Mr. Evad keeping some kind of gun in his briefcase, did he?"

"A gun? No, he didn't say anything about a gun. Does Sarah know something about a gun?"

"Er, no. It's not important," answered Mrs. Gould, smiling. "I must have misunderstood. Good day, officer."

"Dad, I'm telling you that from all that blood, it wasn't just a scratch. I know what I saw. He was as close to me as I am to you right now."

"Oh, I believe you know what you saw," said Mr. Cobalt. "From what you say, Evad is a large man, and obviously can handle himself in a tough situation. Still I don't think there's any way that he could have done what he did if he had been seriously hurt." Sam Cobalt looked at

Mr. Gould who was seated across from Tom and his mother.

"I'll have to agree with your father, Tom," said Mr. Gould. "Please, understand, I'm not doubting you. Sarah told the same story." He studied the pipe he held before continuing. "My wife and I are concerned about Sarah. She's had a rough time adjusting to her new school—especially after these last two days." He smiled at Tom. "Then again, I suspect that you too have found the last two days somewhat trying." Tom gave a good-natured nod of agreement. "I want to again thank you for coming to Sarah's aid yesterday, and for befriending her when she really needed a friend."

Tom shifted his gaze to the floor and mumbled something unintelligible to the others. Then he looked up. "Well, actually it was Alex who tried to stop Paine the other day. I kind of got involved after that."

"I understand," said Sarah's father. "But there's one more thing I need to ask you?" He hesitated as if to first better form the question in his mind. "Sarah said you told her that you found some sort of—strange gun in Mr. Evad's briefcase."

Tom failed to disguise a look of alarm. "What kind of gun?"

"Well, you know, Sarah wasn't quite clear about that. My wife thought she said a ray gun." He grinned at the Cobalts, who, except for Tom, returned the grin. "Anyway, neither my wife nor I could get Sarah to say any more about it, which is why I'm asking you."

Tom forced a smile. "Oh, that." For the first time he could remember, Tom lied in front of his parents. "That was a little joke of mine." He glanced about the room nervously. "I told everyone that I found a ray gun in Evad's briefcase. You know, after all that happened, I thought we all could use a laugh. I guess Sarah was so upset that she didn't get the joke."

Mr. Gould and Tom's mother gave the boy an appreciative nod, but Sam Cobalt gave his son a curious look, as if he suspected that Tom had not told the truth.

The fugitive picked up his pace, not only in the expectation that the added exertion would help ward off the night chill and perhaps take his mind off the continuing throbbing pain in his injured wrist, but also because he was nearing his destination, the home of the remaining member of his gang. His other accomplice was no doubt behind bars after the botched episode that had occurred at the high school that afternoon. His remaining friend's place seemed to the renegade his only hope for a chance to rest, get some grub, and then figure out what to do next. After all, the police had no doubt staked out his own home where his old man lived. Of course, there was a good chance that the police were already waiting for him where he was now headed since several students had probably told them who his associates were, if not some of the students, then that moron, Mr. Serpens. The guidance counselor had had him in his office only a few days earlier, asking him all sorts of inane questions including who his friends were.

The sidewalk on which the delinquent was hurrying ran along the side of a building. On the other side of the street bordering the sidewalk was a high chain-link fence marking the boundary of an elementary school playground.

As the young man was nearing the street corner at the end of the building, a figure stepped out the shadows onto the sidewalk. The man's hands were thrust into the pockets of the trench coat he wore, his features obscured by the darkness cast by a streetlight at the intersection.

The fugitive jerked to a halt. "Bud, is that you?" he asked, hoping against hope it was the friend he sought.

The man's answer was simply a wicked laugh that caused the boy's body to quiver as if he had been struck by a sudden chill.

"Who are you?"

"I am your destiny, Mr. Paine," said the stranger.

"Huh?" Jack Paine decided he had heard enough. He did a quick about face and set off in the direction from which he had come, breaking into a run. He managed but a dozen steps when he again stuttered to a stop. A second figure shrouded by the evening's darkness and similarly attired to the first was standing on the sidewalk at the far end of the block, effectively blocking Jack's proposed avenue of escape. The new stranger began to move towards him, at the same time Jack could hear the steps of the first stranger approaching from behind him. He took a quick glance across the street to confirm that the barrier presented by the school fence ended any chance of flight in that direction. The only option was the alley that opened off to his left.

Jack had no clue as to the identity of the two men who continued to close in on him, except that they were obviously not the police. He decided he didn't want to stick around to discover what their intentions were. Grabbing his injured wrist with his good hand, the teen hoodlum again broke into a run.

Reaching the entrance to the alley, Jack made a swift turn and disappeared into its shadows. His breathing became labored, as Jack was not used to exercise, other than that afforded by abusing his smaller and weaker victims. Not far ahead he could make out the alley's exit, framed by the illumination of the nearest streetlight. He had covered perhaps half of the distance to the exit when a black form materialized before him. So sudden was the apparition's appearance that Jack almost collided with it as he skidded to a halt.

"Out of my way, moron," raged the delinquent.

For answer, an arm shot out and a giant hand, or at least in the brief moment of life Jack had left, he imaged it to be a hand, closed about his neck.

The boy gasped for air. "What . . ."

As the figure leaned in closer, its features were briefly illuminated by a sliver of light emanating from a second story window of one of the neighboring buildings. Jack's last emotion was that of profound fear, for never had he imagined anything as totally horrifying as that which now held him in a death grip.

There was the sound of shattering bone, and Jack Paine was no more.

Chapter 11
The Final Days

"Tom, I've been asked to have a chit-chat with all the students who were involved in yesterday's incident," said Mr. Serpens displaying his usual cheerfulness and wearing his usual light-grey suit.

"Yes, I know. You already talked with Alex." Tom couldn't help feeling nervous, sitting there in the chair in the guidance counselor's office. What if Alex had mentioned the ray gun? He didn't have to worry about Sarah, as she hadn't come to school today.

"Tom, first off, I want to assure you that you have no need to worry about Jack Paine. Even though the police haven't apprehended him yet, it's only a matter of time before he's behind bars." If anything, Mr. Serpens' usually wide grin had managed to spread even wider. "Also, you'll be glad to know that the injury Mr. Evad suffered was just a scratch. Fortunately, his belt got in the way of Paine's knife thrust."

Tom gave the man a disbelieving look.

Mr. Serpens gave a laugh, misinterpreting Tom's expression. "So, we're still not crazy about Mr. Evad, are we?"

"No, I'm not, but that's not the point. I saw the blood stain on his shirt. There's no way it could have been a scratch."

"Tom." Why did Mr. Serpens have to start practically every sentence with his name? "People often—imagine things when in a stressful situation. One's memory can exaggerate actual events, especially if

254

they find the memory of those events troubling."

"I didn't imagine it. That's exactly what I saw and that's what I told the police."

"Yes, I know. But there remains the fact that Mr. Evad is walking around today as if nothing had happened. Paine couldn't have stabbed Mr. Evad—at least, as seriously as you remember it."

"I know that things don't seem to make sense. But Sarah and Alex and Wayne and Brad saw the blood too."

"Tom, consider your feelings towards Mr. Evad. It's possible that because of your—ah, animosity towards him, that you imagined that Paine seriously stabbed him—sort of wishful thinking on your part."

"What? That's ridiculous. I may not like Mr. Evad, but I certainly never wished anyone to stab him."

Mr. Serpens shifted in his chair, leaning forward and looked directly into Tom's eyes, the smile being replaced by a look of concern. "Besides thinking he has it in for you, is there anything else that troubles you about Mr. Evad?"

Tom didn't reply at first, taking some time to try to gauge exactly what Mr. Serpens was asking. "No, I don't think so."

"I think you're being dishonest with me, Tom, and if you sincerely believe that, I think you're being dishonest with yourself too."

Tom loathed people who talked like that, who used psychological gibberish. It was dishonest, and . . . well, yes, he was being dishonest, but he had a good reason to be and that reason was none of Mr. Serpens' business. Tom decided to meet the man halfway. "Well, he's a little strange. Occasionally he says things that make no sense whatsoever, but I'm not really troubled by it. It's sort of funny, if you know what I mean."

"I see."

Tom translated that response to mean that Mr. Serpens didn't see. Not only didn't he see, he disagreed with Tom's answer and still thought Tom was being dishonest which, of course, Tom was.

The lean, young counselor leaned back in his chair and briefly studied the ceiling. Without looking at Tom he said, "I heard that yesterday, right before the Jack Paine incident, you found something interesting in Mr. Evad's briefcase."

It was a statement, not a question. Nevertheless, Tom said, "Who told you that?"

The counselor's eyes again fell on the boy. "Sorry, Tom, that's confidential. All my conversations with students are confidential. So, what was it you found?"

It couldn't have been Alex, thought Tom. Alex would never tell Mr. Serpens anything like that. Then again, Mr. Serpens had probably called all their parents this morning to inform them what the school was doing about yesterday's incident. He could have heard it from a parent. His own mom could have told Mr. Serpens. That line about conversations with the students could be a red herring. He wouldn't put it past Mr. Serpens to be clever like that.

"I didn't mean to look in Mr. Evad's briefcase. It was sort of like an accident."

"Tom, we both know that looking into the briefcase was the wrong thing to do, but I'm not going to tell anyone about that. I give you my word I won't even tell Mr. Evad. My concern is about you and how you're handling all of this. You and a couple of your friends have had a rough two days. Tom, I assure you that anything you say to me will be held in the strictest confidence, but I can't help you unless you're completely open with me and tell me the truth."

Help him? Tom didn't need any help. It seemed to Tom that the best thing that Mr. Serpens could do to help him would be to dismiss him. "I don't think I need any help. I'm handling everything fine. Really, I am."

"Tom." The friendly smile had returned. Tom was really beginning to detest that smile. "What did you find in the briefcase?"

At this point, Tom decided that lying would only complicate things.

Nevertheless, he hesitated a moment before answering. "A weapon."

"I see. What sort of weapon?"

"A gun."

"I see. Exactly what type of gun was it?"

"I don't know. It was just a gun."

"Tom, I think you do know. Would you please describe the gun?"

"It was—strange. I've never seen one like it before."

"I see. Would you call it a pistol?"

"Yeah, I guess. It was shaped sort of like a pistol."

"I see." No, you don't see, thought Tom. Why didn't Mr. Serpens drop the subject and let him leave?

"Would you say it was some sort of revolver?"

"No."

"I see. What kind of pistol would you say it most closely resembled?"

"Well—I know you'll think this is crazy—but it kind of looked like a—a—a ray gun . . ." Tom's voice trailed off at the end of the sentence.

Mr. Serpens was silent for a moment. Then he continued. At least, for once, he didn't begin a sentence with "Tom" or "I see." "A ray gun, you say? Would that then make Mr. Evad some sort of alien?" Mr. Serpens accentuated his statement with a smile

Tom was far from smiling as he answered. "I didn't say it was a ray gun. I said it looked like a ray gun."

"I understand, Tom." There was another brief pause.

"Tom, do you like science fiction? You know what I mean by science fiction don't you? Stories written by people like Robert Heinlein, Isaac Asimov—people like that."

"Sure, doesn't everyone?"

"When you were younger did you watch TV shows like *Space Cadet* and *Space Patrol?*"

"Sure. Didn't everyone, that is, everyone who had a TV set?"

"I see." Mr. Serpens briefly massaged his chin with his hand before continuing. "What's your favorite movie?"

Tom was now at a complete loss as to guessing what Serpens might be up to. "*Bedtime for Bonzo,*" he answered, attempting to suppress a smirk.

From the puzzled look on his face, it appeared that the guidance counselor had never heard of "*Bedtime for Bonzo.*" Then he noted the boy's hint of a smile. "Don't be coy with me," said the man. "Seriously, your favorite movie, please."

"*Forbidden Planet,*" Tom said, figuratively throwing in the towel.

"Interesting. Very interesting." There was another brief pause during which Mr. Serpens seemed to be collecting his thoughts. "Tom, remember earlier when I said about how one's imagination can be a powerful thing? That sometimes, especially when we find ourselves in a stressful situation, our mind can—"

"But I saw the gun before Jack Paine showed up. I wasn't under any stress then."

"Well, that's possibly true, but you obviously feel some tension when you're around Mr. Evad, and he had asked you to stay after class, had he not?"

"Yes, but—"

"And it was only the day before that you had that run-in with Jack Paine. Surely that was still fresh in your mind?"

"Well, yeah, but—"

"Tom, I never said that I didn't believe you. I never said that I thought you imagined things when you said you saw a ray gun in Mr. Evad's briefcase."

"I didn't say it was a ray gun. I said it looked—"

"I'm asking you to think about what we discussed here. Think about it carefully. I suspect you might see things differently tomorrow after you've had a good night's rest."

"I slept fine ..." Tom gave up. What was the use? Nobody believed he saw a ray gun. He wished he had never mentioned it. He'd probably spend the rest of his school days having people look at him like they did Sarah, like he was some kind of loony.

Mr. Serpens continued. "Remember what I told you in the past? Things aren't always as they seem."

"Yes, I remember. Funny. Mr. Evad said the same thing."

"What did Mr. Evad say?"

"Things aren't always as they seem."

"Did he now? How interesting." Mr. Serpens leaned back in the chair. "I think we've accomplished a lot today. Please remember that I'm here to help. That's my job."

Tom took the hint and stood up. As the boy was about to grasp the door knob to leave the office, Mr. Serpens said, "Tom, I seriously doubt that the future will be about ray guns and robots and spaceships. Part of growing up is accepting that our childhood fantasies are just that, fantasies. Have a good day, Tom."

"You too, Mr. Serpens." Tom didn't bother to look at the guidance counselor as he spoke his farewell and left the room.

For several moments after Tom had left, Mr. Serpens sat as if frozen, his eyes staring at the closed door. If any of the students had seen him then, they would have been startled at the sudden transformation in the man's countenance. His seemingly ever present, good-natured smile had been replaced by a frown, a most serious frown. When the man finally moved, his first action was to pull a key from his left pants pocket. With a swift motion, he slid the wheeled chair on which he sat across the floor of the office, stopping in front of a filing cabinet. Quickly he used the key to unlock the cabinet's drawers. Except for the bottom drawer, the cabinet contained confidential student records. It was the bottom drawer that the guidance counselor pulled open. Inside rested a rectangular wooden box. If Tom had been there, he would have thought the box to be identical to the one he had found in Evad's briefcase, not only because of its shape and size, but also because of the presence of a combination lock with three tumblers. Mr. Serpens reached down, grasped the box, and lifted it out of the drawer, placing it on his lap. For a moment he studied the lock's combination. It read one-two-three. A few deft flicks of his index finger changed it to read six-six-six. There was a faint click. Mr. Serpens lifted the lid of the box. As he stared at the object that lay inside, his familiar smile reappeared.

"Can we talk about something besides ray guns?" said Tom, trying to keep his voice low so that the occupants of the neighboring lunch tables wouldn't hear him.

"Hey, I'm just saying that the more I think about it, the more I'm starting to believe that it might really have been a ray gun that you saw." Alex tried to sound sympathetic. Brad and Wayne exchanged glances. Brad made circles around his right ear with his finger. Wayne shrugged in reply to Brad's assertion that one or both of their friends weren't playing with a full deck.

Tom picked up his carton of milk but sat it back down without taking a sip. "You didn't tell Mr. Serpens about the briefcase when you saw him this morning, did you?"

"No way," said Alex. "You know, I'm beginning to think that maybe Mr. Serpens isn't playing with a full deck. I mean, he's a really nice guy and all, especially for an adult, but what's with his playing shrink every time you're in there? I thought his job was supposed to be advising you on what courses to take."

"I'm with you there," said Tom.

"Well, I have to see him right after lunch," moaned Brad.

"Hey, I like Mr. Serpens," said Wayne. Then, focusing on a more important topic, he said, "Are you going to eat that apple?"

"Nah, you can have it," said Alex. "No, listen. It all fits. What if the Grim Reaper is from the future?"

"Oh, no," said Brad, putting a palm to his forehead. "Here we go again. I feel a headache coming on."

"No, really. I mean that would explain some things like making references to scientific theories that don't exist."

"Huh?" asked Brad, looking confused as usual.

"That's nutty," said Tom. "Like future scientists are going to name something a gummion."

"It would explain the ray gun, though," said Wayne. He gave Brad a wink.

"Can we please stop bringing up ray guns?" said Tom.

"Fine by me," agreed Brad, who popped a Fizzy into a glass of water. The wafer immediately started to violently foam, causing the water to bubble as if it were some evil witch's brew.

"How can you drink that?" said Wayne. "It tastes worse than castor oil."

"Do you have any more?" asked Alex.

"Yeah." Brad reached into a trouser pocket and pulled out two foil covered Fizzies. "Do you want grape or lime?"

"Lime."

"Yuck," said Wayne as he watched Alex open a foil and plop a large green tablet into his glass of water. Like the water in Brad's glass, it began to violently fizz and bubble. The water turned a pale green. "It looks like panther piss and tastes as bad."

"How would you know what panther piss tastes like?" said Brad.

Wayne ignored the question. "Hey, with Sarah not here we can go back to talking about guy things."

"Yeah, that's right," agreed Brad.

"What exactly is a guy thing?" asked Tom.

"You know. Guy things, like cars and sports and—"

"Girls?" suggested Brad.

"Yuck," said Alex, having taken a sip of his lime-flavored water.

"See, I told you it tastes like panther piss."

"Not yuck to the Fizzy, I mean like yuck as in girls as a topic of conversation."

Wayne looked from Brad to Tom, a knowing grin on his face. "And just what is Sarah?"

"She's not a real girl," said Alex. "She's too smart to be a real girl." At that they all laughed. Tom felt relieved that the conversation had at last steered away from ray guns.

"Okay, I found it. Take a look."

Alex straightened and moved to his left, carefully stepping around his cat Tiger and Tom's dog Basil Ratbone, who lay side by side on the lawn next to Alex's telescope. Tom stepped up to the scope and placed his right eye over the lens of the eyepiece, shielding his left eye with his hand. The conditions that evening were ideal for stargazing, especially considering that the moon wasn't out.

"Wow," said Tom. "The Pleiades are really cool."

"It's an open cluster. That means that all the brighter stars you see are actually held together in a group by their mutual gravitational attraction. The stars in the cluster that you can see with the naked eye were known to the ancient Greeks as the seven daughters of Atlas, or simply the 'Seven Sisters.'"

Tom raised his head and studied the cluster without the aid of the telescope. After a moment, he said, "I only count six."

"Boy, I wish I had your eyesight." Alex absently adjusted his glasses as he studied the group of stars. "Even with my glasses I can't be certain how many are up there."

"If they're called the Seven Sisters," asked Tom, "why is it I only see six? It seems like a pretty clear night to me."

"Good point. I believe that typically no one can see more than six with the naked eye."

"So why then did the ancients call them the Seven Sisters?"

"Maybe one blew up since ancient times."

"You're kidding."

"Nope. Stars do blow up. But it's more likely that one of them faded in the last couple of thousand years."

"Wow," said Tom, again. "You usually don't think of stars changing in just a few thousand years."

Tom's dog let out a low bark, jumped up and took off for the hedge at the edge of the yard.

"Basil, shut up, you dumb mutt," yelled Tom. "It's just a dumb rabbit or something."

A human scream came from behind the bush.

"That scream sounds familiar," said Alex.

"On second thought, sounds like a rabbit named Sarah," said Tom. He and Alex broke into a run in the direction of the commotion.

As they rounded the hedge, the boys found Tom's dog standing on its hind legs, its front paws effectively pinning a figure against the tall shrubbery. Basil's captive was futilely attempting to push the dog away. Even in the dim glare from the distant street light, it was obvious to the boys that it was Sarah.

"Sit," yelled Tom in a commanding voice. The dog immediately sat, whimpered, and gave his master a look of disappointment.

"Methinks your faithful hound hath caught a spy. What say you, Ragnar? What do we do with this irksome wench?"

Sarah was making motions as if to brush off some dirt that Basil had deposited on her skirt, although in the dark she couldn't really be sure there was any to brush off. "What did you call me?" she said, obviously upset at the use of the word 'wench.'

"A wench," said Alex. "A spying wench."

"I wasn't spying. I was out for a walk when your beast attacked me."

"You were spying," said Alex, sounding confident in the truth of his assertion. "Note that where thou standeth is a good ten royal feet from yonder path. What say you, ruthless Ragnar, is a fit punishment for this lowly wench, who speaketh with a forked tongue?"

"If her hair was braided we could lock her in the 'wheel' and try to cut her braids with throwing axes, like Einar did in the Vikings movie."

"You two have lost your marbles," said the girl. "I hope your mutt hasn't ruined my skirt."

"Skirt, smirt. To the wheel of adultery with her, Ragnar." Without further ado, the boys grabbed Sarah's arms and pulled her backwards into Alex's backyard.

"Wheel of what?" yelped Sarah. "What are you doing? Let go of me or I'll scream."

"You already screamed, when Basil caught you," said Tom, "and we were the only ones to respond to your cries for help."

"Basil? You named your dog Basil?" said the girl.

"Basil Ratbone is his full name," said Alex.

"Basil Rathbone? You named the dog after the actor?"

"Not Rathbone," corrected the taller boy. "Rat-bone. Not long after we got him as a puppy he caught and killed a rat." That information elicited a "yuck" from the girl. "So, Dad added the Ratbone to his name as kind of a joke."

Having arrived at the telescope, the boys promptly let go of Sarah's arms, causing the girl to let out another shriek as her bottom hit the damp earth. "Behold the wheel of adultery, faithless wench," said the boy genius, gesturing towards the astronomical instrument. Tiger, who during the whole incident had never moved from his spot on the grass, let out a loud meow as if to accentuate his master's words.

"Oh, it's your cute kitty," said Sarah, still on the ground. She reached out a hand to stroke the cat's cheek while ignoring the wheel of adultery.

"He's not a kitty, and he's not cute," said Alex. "He's a dangerous and highly rare, miniature, short-fanged, saber-tooth tiger, *Smilodon midgetus.*"

"No, he's a cute kitty," repeated the girl. She got to her feet at the same time gently picking up the cat and rubbing its head. Tiger responded to the attention with a series of purrs.

"I'm warning you, wench. Put that beast down before he tears you to ribbons."

Sarah ignored Alex's command, and continued to pet the feline. "What were you looking at?"

"The Seven Sisters," said Alex.

"Oh, the Pleiades. Can I see? I've never looked through a telescope before."

Tom gave a shrug as he said, "So why doesn't it surprise me that she knows that the Seven Sisters are the Pleiades?"

The other two ignored his comment, as Alex showed Sarah the telescope's eyepiece.

"What a strange looking telescope," said the wench. "Why is the eyepiece near the top and on the side?"

"Ah-ah," said Tom. "It looks like we've finally found a weakness in the wench's armor. There's actually something she doesn't know."

"It's a reflector, not a refractor," said Alex.

"Oh, you mean like the kind Newton invented?"

Tom moaned. "I take back what I said."

"That's right," said Alex. "It uses a mirror, here at the bottom, to collect the light instead of a large objective lens. From there the light is bounced off a diagonal mirror near the top of the tube and focused at the eyepiece. Give me a minute to get the Pleiades into view again." The boy stooped and looked into the eyepiece and then slowly adjusted the scope's alignment. "I can't afford a clock drive. If I had one of those, the telescope would track an object automatically once I got it calibrated."

Sarah nodded as if it all made sense. Then she shocked the boys by saying, "I really don't know much about astronomy. Where are the Pleiades?" Tom pointed them out to Sarah as Alex finished adjusting the telescope.

"How far away are they?"

"Roughly four hundred light years," said Alex.

"I don't understand. What do years have to do with how far they are?"

Alex straightened up and exchanged surprised glances with his friend. "Whoa, you really don't know much about astronomy?"

"I'm sorry," said Sarah in a tone that sounded like an apology.

"Hey, there's nothing to be sorry about," said Tom. "Everything I know about astronomy, Alex taught me."

Alex started to explain. "Four hundred light years means that it takes the light from the Pleiades four hundred years to reach us."

"But——," Sarah paused as she did some quick calculations in her head. "That's impossible. Light travels at 186,000 miles per second. In four hundred years it would travel . . . gosh, I can't even begin to guess how far that would be."

"That's right," smiled Alex. "The universe is so vast that it makes no sense in trying to measure distances in miles or even billions of miles, so astronomers use the time it takes light to travel between places as a measure of distance."

"One night Alex showed me the Andromeda galaxy. It's the farthest thing one can see with the naked eye. Take a guess how long it takes light to reach us from Andromeda."

"I don't know. Ten thousand years?"

"Two million," said Tom, with a knowing smirk on his face.

"Two million! That means that light left there before there were humans."

"That's right."

Alex returned to his scope. "Okay, Sarah. Look through here and try not to close the other eye when you look. It's best to keep both eyes open."

Sarah put down the cat and then removed her glasses as she had seen Alex do when he looked through the telescope's eyepiece. The night was so dark that Sarah had difficulty lining her eye up with the ocular. "I can't see anything."

"Here, I'll help you," offered Tom. He leaned close to Sarah in an attempt to see where exactly the girl was looking. "Move your eye a little towards me," he suggested. As she did so her hair brushed Tom's face. At the same instance he felt her warm breath on his skin and his nostrils were struck by a sweet scent that seemed to advertise the girl's closeness. Tom gave an involuntary jerk as if he had been pricked by a thorn.

Sarah covered her one eye with her hand and placed the other over the eyepiece. "Oh-my-gosh. It's beautiful!"

Tom reached down and gave the right ascension knob a small twist, moving the telescope slightly to counteract the effect of the earth's rotation and bring more of the cluster back into Sarah's field of view. The girl emitted a gasp. "It's like dozens of glistening jewels floating on a dark sea."

"Sounds like Homer," said Tom.

"It looks like they're slowly moving."

"That's actually the effect of the earth's rotation you're seeing," said Tom. "Here, let me take a quick look and I'll adjust the scope again to get them back into the center of the field."

Sarah raised her head, and Tom leaned over the eyepiece. As he adjusted the scope, he again felt the girl's warm breath, now on the back of his neck. For a moment he thought his heart had skipped a beat.

"Do you think we'll ever go there?" asked Sarah, again peering into the eyepiece.

"Where, the Pleiades?" said Tom.

"Yes. You know, the stars?"

When Tom didn't answer, Alex cut in. "Do you?"

"Yes," answered the girl, without hesitation. Sarah was still studying the view in the eyepiece. "I know it sounds crazy, especially when you think how far away they are." She raised her head and looked at Alex. "I mean, most people thought Jules Verne was crazy for imagining people traveling to the moon, and until tonight I never thought about how impossibly far away the stars really are. But I think someday we will travel there. Do you think I'm crazy for believing that?"

"No. I'm with you," said Alex.

"Wouldn't you love to be able to travel to the stars?"

"Sure," said the fair-haired boy.

"Do you think there is other life out there?"

"I wouldn't be surprised."

"What about you, Tom?"

"I'm with you all the way. Hey, I can not only imagine there being starships someday and alien life forms, but maybe even alien civilizations."

"It's too bad we'll probably never live to see it," said Sarah.

"Who knows?" said Alex. "After all, we now have satellites and we're planning to shoot men into space and then on to the moon. Surely at the rate things are happening, we'll be on Mars within our lifetimes."

For several moments the three stood there looking up as the great sphere of the heavens continuing its slow eternal movement above them. Sarah broke the silence.

"Tom, did you really find a ray gun in Mr. Evad's briefcase?"

"Where in heck did that question come from? Look, I'm not sure what I saw. After all, what does a ray gun look like? Halloween's coming up. Maybe Evad's going to a Halloween party as a spaceman or something. Maybe it's part of his costume."

"Hey, I never heard that theory before," said Alex.

"It just occurred to me. All I can say is that it sure looked like a ray gun. Better than any toy ray gun I've ever seen. If that's what it is, then Evad doesn't spare any expense in his costumes."

"Well, that sounds plausible," agreed Sarah. "It's about the only idea that does."

"I don't know." Alex rubbed his chin. "I can't imagine Evad going to a costume party. And if he did he could just go as an undertaker and spare himself any extra expense."

"Not to change the subject again," said Tom, "but how come you weren't in school today?"

"My parents are making me stay home until the police catch Jack Paine."

Alex chuckled. "Well, you don't have to worry about old Jack any more. Didn't you hear the news? The Harrisburg police found him last night. Apparently, he stole a car and crashed it. He's deader than a doornail."

"He's dead?" said Sarah.

"That's what my dad said he heard."

"I'll have to admit that it sounds like a fitting end for that jerk," said Tom, "but it seems strange that if Evad broke his wrist, that he could drive a car."

"Maybe Evad didn't break his wrist," said Alex, "or maybe that's why he crashed, trying to drive with a broken wrist."

"It's getting late and I'd best be getting home," said Sarah. "Thank you for letting me look through your telescope, and I'll be sure to tell my parents about what happened to Jack Paine."

"So, I guess you'll be going to school tomorrow," said Alex. "In that case we'll pick you up."

"Thanks, I'd like that."

"Yeah, don't forget that there's still another one of Jack's goons not accounted for," Tom said, "so we can't be too careful. And that reminds me I should be going to."

"That's right, you get up much earlier than us normal people," said Alex. "Hey, Sarah, guess what Tom does every morning?"

The girl looked at Tom, and since the boy appeared to be embarrassed by the subject, she decided it was best not to hazard a guess. Nevertheless, Alex continued. "He gets up every morning and runs about ten miles in the dark."

"You run ten miles every morning? Even in the winter?"

"Well, not when the weather's bad, and it's not ten miles. At best maybe three or four."

"Why?"

"That way he can be ready in case World War III breaks out," laughed Alex.

"Huh?" said Sarah.

"Ah, well, actually, I think I should keep in shape. It's—well, my father was a marine, and—I don't know—I just started doing it last year and I kind of like it.'

"Isn't that one of the craziest things you ever heard?" said Alex.

"No, I don't think it's crazy at all," said the girl. "I think it's wonderful. I mean we should all try to keep ourselves healthy and . . . three or four miles . . . I could never imagine myself running that far."

"Eh, yeah, well, er—come on Basil, we have to get home."

The dog sprang to its feet, gave a spirited bark, and started off towards the Cobalt home, followed by his master.

As Sarah and the two boys left Sarah's house the next morning, Tom mentioned that they were taking a detour to Wayne's house.

"Why?" asked the girl.

"Wayne has to take his shadow box project for Miss Odavsky's class to school, so we have to give him a hand, like carry his books and stuff."

"Oh," said Sarah. "I haven't been assigned my project yet. Have you?"

"If we're lucky, maybe between having to put up with you and Alex, she'll have a nervous breakdown or something before she gets around to the rest of us."

Alex laughed, but Sarah looked alarmed. "That's an awful thing to wish on someone," said the girl. "Even Miss Odavsky."

"I was kidding," said Tom.

"It sounds like a good plan to me," said Alex. "Come on Sarah, I don't believe you wouldn't be pleased to have a part in driving Miss Odavsky bonkers."

"Well, maybe a little," smiled the girl, who then gave a nervous glance at her wristwatch. "Are you sure we won't be late?"

"No, we should have plenty of time," said Tom as he grabbed the girl's wrist to get a closer look at her watch. "I don't believe it." Tom halted. "A Minnie Mouse watch?"

"Yes, what's wrong with that?"

"You're in the eighth grade and you're still wearing a Minnie Mouse watch?" said Alex, shaking his head.

"Well, it still fits and it runs fine so why should my parents waste money in buying me a new watch?"

"Good point," said Tom. "Actually, I guess I'd still be wearing my Space Cadet watch if it still fit."

"See," said the girl. "Besides, you're not even wearing a watch. How do you know what time it is?"

"I ask Alex," laughed Tom. Alex held up his wrist to reveal a wristwatch. "Okay, sorry I brought it up. It's just that—well, things like wearing a Minnie Mouse watch help make you a—target, if you know what I mean."

"Yes, I suppose so," said Sarah as the three resumed walking. "I have to confess that my parents did mention that I might get a new watch for Christmas."

"One can only hope," said Alex.

A stiff, damp breeze seemed to add to the gloom of the gray, overcast morning. Arriving at Wayne's house, Sarah stopped to stare at the dark woods at the end of block on which Wayne lived. Tom noticed that Sarah's attention seemed to be riveted to the foreboding growth of trees.

"That's Sullivans Woods," said the boy. "Some people believe it's haunted."

"Why?" asked the girl, trying to disguise the feeling of dread she felt.

"Don't know. We often played army and stuff in there. It's a cool place, except for the bog in the center."

"Yeah," agreed Alex. "Wayne, Brad, Tom and I even slept there overnight a few times. Didn't see any ghosts or walking dead or anything."

"All I know is that no one goes near the place during Halloween," said Tom.

"Yeah, that might be pressing your luck, if you know what I mean?"

At that Tom stepped onto the small slab porch of Wayne's house and rang the doorbell. The front door opened revealing an attractive woman who looked to be in her mid twenties, the length of the brown hair that flowed down her back almost to her waist reinforcing the impression of youth.

"Hi, boys," she said, displaying a warm smile. "Come on in. Wayne and Brad are in the basement."

Tom and Alex stepped into the living room, both mumbling something that sounded like, "Good morning, Mrs. Franklin," followed by Sarah, who entered looking uncertain.

"And you must be Sarah," the woman said in a friendly tone.

"Yes, ma'am," said Sarah, startled at how young the woman looked, especially if she was, as Sarah suspected, Wayne's mother.

"I'm Wayne's mother." Mrs. Franklin turned and cast the two boys a stern, but obviously teasing look. "And being boys, I didn't expect them to introduce us."

"I'm happy to meet you," said Sarah.

"You can all go down to the basement if you wish," said the woman.

"Wait until you see Wayne's basement," said Alex. "It's like some secret laboratory. Wayne's dad is an inventor and has all sorts of neat stuff down there."

Sarah started to follow the boys towards the basement stairs when she noticed a baby grand piano in the adjoining living room. Trying to sound sociable, she turned to Wayne's mother.

"What a beautiful piano. Do you play?"

"No. Unfortunately I've never learned how. Wayne's father is the musician in the family. Perhaps when there's more time, you'll have the opportunity to hear him play. He's quite talented."

"Yes, I would like that," said Sarah, and then she resumed following the boys down the basement stairs.

When she reached the bottom step, she stopped and looked about in amazement. Several tables filled the room, each of which held an assortment of gadgets, instruments, tools, electronic parts, and similar equipment. The floor was a maze of electric cords and cables. In one corner stood Brad and Wayne studying the contents of a large cardboard box that no doubt housed Wayne's history project.

"What did we tell you?" said Alex.

"My gosh," said the girl, "it's like some mad scientist's laboratory."

"I'll consider that a compliment," came a voice from the top of the stairs. Sarah looked up to see a man whose uncombed red curly hair, along with a mustache and goatee, fit perfectly with what the girl imagined a mad scientist would look like.

"Hi, Mr. Franklin," said Alex. "What are you working on now?"

As the man bounded lightly down the stairs, he ignored the question. "Aren't you going to introduce me to your friend?"

"That's Sarah," said Wayne from across the room. "She's a girl."

"I'm so sorry," said Sarah. "I didn't mean what I said about a mad scientist."

"No need to apologize. I said I considered it a compliment. It's nice to meet you at last."

As the man's eyes locked on to hers, Sarah found herself unable to move, as if she were held in some hypnotic trance, not only by the intensity of his stare, but also by the appearance of the scars on his face, one of which curved from above his left eye to the front of the neighboring ear, and the other, as if to balance the first, from his right cheek downward, disappearing beneath the hair of his beard. Besides his distinctive features, Sarah sensed there to be an odd familiarity about the man that she could not put her finger on. For a long moment both man and girl simply stood there.

"Ah, Sarah, do you mind," said Wayne, who was standing behind her, holding his project. "You're blocking the stairs."

"Oh, sorry." The girl and Mr. Franklin stepped to the side to allow the boys to pass. Sarah then followed them up the stairs, stopping at the top. She looked back at Mr. Franklin, still standing at the bottom of the stairway. "It was—n-nice meeting you," she stammered.

"Likewise," said the man who gave her a grin, and then he began to ascend the steps. He followed the teens to the front door where his wife gave Wayne a peck on the top of his head to Wayne's obvious embarrassment. As the group of eighth graders made their way down the front walk to the street, Sarah cast a quick glance behind her. Wayne's parents were standing in the doorway watching them.

Instead of closing the front door against the morning chill, Mrs. Franklin turned to her husband and laid a hand on his shoulder. "It was something of a shock to see her again after all these years."

The man didn't answer except to give his wife a knowing smile and a nod of his head.

The woman put her arms around her husband's neck, raised herself on tiptoes, gave him a tender kiss, and then whispered in his ear, "And so it begins."

"So how did you get that hickey?" asked Tom as he opened his lunch bag.

"I don't know," said Brad, absent-mindedly rubbing the slightly swollen looking lump on the back of his neck. "Maybe a mosquito bite or something."

"In October?" said Tom.

"Hey, I said I didn't know. So anyway, what are you guys doing for Halloween?"

"I think we're too old for trick-or-treating," said Wayne from across the lunch table.

"At least the treating part," said Tom. "But one is never too old for tricking. Remember what my cousin Jerry did last year?"

"My dad would kill me if I set a bag of cow poop on fire on someone's doorstep," said Alex.

"Cow poop?" said Sarah, not really wanting to hear more. The thought of eating lunch now seemed less than appetizing to the girl.

"My cousin Jerry's an idiot," said Tom, as if that explained the whole thing. "Fortunately for us, he's in sixth grade, so we won't have to put up with him until next year, although if you're unlucky you might run into him at church. If you do, ignore anything he says as it's a lie."

"You can't mean that?" said Sarah. "I'm sure he's a nice boy."

"No, no, no," said Alex. "You don't know Jerry. He's a jerk. Isn't he, Brad?"

"He sure is, almost as big a jerk as Wayne here."

"Hey, that was uncalled for. Just for that, I'm not trading you my cupcake for your apple."

"Oh, yeah, like you were going to," challenged Brad.

"Say, Sarah, what do you have for lunch?" asked Wayne.

"I'm not sure," said the girl as she opened her metal lunch box and lifted out a small thermos bottle. It wasn't clear whether the care she used in retrieving the thermos from her lunch box was due to habit or in deference to the adhesive bandages that graced the lower palm of each hand, still protecting the bruises she had suffered three days before as a result of the Jack Paine incident. Unscrewing the lid of the thermos, Sarah peered inside. "Broccoli and lentil soup. Doesn't it smell delicious?"

"Yuck!" yelped Brad. "It looks like someone's throw up."

"Oh, that's so gross," said the girl, the proud look disappearing from her face.

"What the heck is a lentil?" said Wayne, scrunching up his nose.

"It's a leguminous plant," enlightened the girl.

"A leg-you-mint-must-what?" asked Tom.

"Did you make that in the chem lab or something?" said Alex.

"No . . . oh, you boys are so ignorant. It tastes really good."

"Hey, speaking of the chem lab, how come the Grim Reaper's been spending so much time in there?" said Wayne to no one in particular.

"Well, why shouldn't he?" said Alex. "He also teaches chemistry and physics."

"I don't mean just for the chemistry classes. You know Bobby Mason? His dad's one of the school janitors. He says his dad is always complaining about Evad spending so much time in the chemistry lab. He's in there working on something almost every evening after school. He even comes in on weekends. Anyway, Bobby says that his dad says it's a real nuisance trying to get the room cleaned while working around Evad."

"Wow, that's dedication," said Tom. "I know the guy is nuts, but that's kind of like a math teacher going home and solving math problems for the fun of it. I mean, how much weirder could you get?"

"But I like doing math problems," said Sarah, looking hurt by Tom's remark.

"Yeah, but that's different," said Tom. "You don't do extra problems for the fun of it, do you?"

"Well, actually . . . ," began the girl, her expression changing from hurt to embarrassed.

"That seems suspicious to me," interrupted Alex, saving Sarah from having to explain. "Does Bobby's dad have any idea what Evad is up to?"

"Of course not," answered Wayne. "He's a janitor. He wouldn't know which end of a test tube was open?"

"Yeah, like you would," laughed Brad.

"Stuff it in your apple," said Wayne.

Tom was nodding his head in agreement. "It seems suspicious to me too. I'd sure like to take a look around that lab."

"If you get a chance, take me with you," said Alex. "Whatever's he's doing in there, he's up to no good. I'll bet on it."

"Oh, this is ridiculous," said Sarah, having finally swallowed her first spoonful of delicious broccoli and lentil soup. She tried to hide the look of disgust on her face. "You two are paranoid."

"Better paranoid than sorry," said Tom.

"But you have no business in there," said the girl. "If a teacher or someone found you in there snooping around, you could get in trouble."

"Trouble's my middle name," said Tom.

"I thought it was Jefferson," said Brad.

"You know," said Wayne, "sometimes I think we were all born in the wrong century."

"Talk about changing the subject," said Alex.

Brad looked confused. "Since when were we talking about changing the subject? I thought we were talking about Tom sneaking into the chem lab."

Tom ignored both Alex and Brad. "What do you mean?"

"Well," said Wayne, "remember that test we all took last year and then we had to go and see Mr. Trot to talk about what it all meant?"

"You mean the aptitude test?" asked Alex.

"Yeah, that's it. The one that was supposed to tell you something about what you should be when you grow up."

"Yeah, I remember it," said Tom. "So?"

"So, what did Trot say the test said you should be?"

"Uh, an accountant or something, I think."

"Alex?"

"I believe it was either a machinist or engineer, although I'm not sure if it meant engineer like in the guy who drives a locomotive or the other kind."

"Brad?"

"Heck, I don't remember."

277

"Figures," said Wayne. "Trot told me the test said I should be a teacher. What boring jobs. That's my point. We were all born in the wrong century. There's no adventure anymore."

"I don't see anything wrong with those jobs," said Sarah. "Someone has to do them."

"That's because you're a girl. You're probably going to grow up to be a housewife and mother or something."

"And you're all going to no doubt be fathers and have families and have jobs like those. So even if we lived in a different time, I don't see where it would make any difference."

"But it would," said Wayne. "Here's Tom scheming to break into the chem lab to get the goods on Evad."

"Actually," said Tom, "I didn't say break in, I just—"

"There's no way Tom was born to be an accountant or I'm going to be a teacher. That's absurd."

"Okay," said Sarah. "What kind of things do you think we were born to do?"

Wayne took a moment to ponder the girl's question before answering.

"Now Brad—he belongs in the Old West. He'd make a good sheriff."

"Cool," said Brad.

"And Alex, he'd be a general."

Sarah looked startled. "Why do you think Alex would be a general?"

"Because he always beats everyone in *Tactics II*." Seeing the girl's puzzled expression, he continued. "It's a board game about a war between two make-believe countries. You get to move around military units like infantry and armor divisions, and Alex always wins."

"And you think an aptitude test is absurd," said Sarah, rolling her eyes. "Okay, what about me?"

"You would be a damsel in distress."

"What? Why?"

"Because you're always getting in trouble." The other boys snickered.

"Okay, if I were a damsel in distress, who would be the chivalrous knight that would rescue me?" Sarah looked at Tom. Tom gave Wayne a look that said, "Don't you dare!"

"Not Tom. He ain't no knight in shining armor, that's for sure. Like me, he'd be a pirate."

"Pirate?" Sarah looked horrified. "Why would you be pirates?"

"Because we have no respect for authority."

"This is really strange," said Alex, having again checked the time on the classroom wall clock. "Imagine, Evad being late for class." He sent his yo-yo back towards the floor on the first leg of another round trip.

"Maybe he'll give himself detention," suggested Tom, sounding hopeful. The two boys turned in their seats so they could converse with Sarah.

"Well, we know he's here," said the girl, "since we saw him in the chemistry lab on the way to class."

"Yeah," said Tom. "All alone in the lab, chuckling to himself with that evil grin of his and wringing his hands. I bet if the door hadn't been closed, we would have heard him mutter, 'It's alive!'" Tom glanced across the room to Wayne, who gave Tom a knowing nod.

"You better put that yo-yo away," Sarah suggested to Alex. "It might not sit well with Mr. Evad if he sees you playing with it."

"Nothing sits well with Evad," retorted the blond boy.

"Sarah's right, Alex. I'd put it away if I were you. Just sit there and enjoy the moment. Science class without Evad."

"Yeah, I guess you're right," agreed Alex.

As Alex was pocketing the yo-yo, the Grim Reaper came flying through the doorway. With one hand he rapidly closed the door while with the other he untied the knot of the lab apron he was wearing. Not only was being late uncharacteristic of Evad, but so was entering the room not immaculately dressed in his suit coat, apparently having left it behind in the chemistry lab. His subsequent actions were equally as uncharacteristic of the man. He skipped taking attendance. Instead he tossed the apron onto the top of lab table as he walked across the front of the room to the window, where he stood for a moment, arms crossed in front of this chest, staring at the scene outside. Then he turned and fixed his eyes on Tom for a moment, but instead of the cold, penetrating stare that he usually gave the boy, he gave Tom a quizzical look that only served to puzzle the boy more. Then, he further startled everyone by changing over to a smile.

"Now, where were we?" he asked.

Chapter 12
The Conversation

"How much longer do you think she'll be?" said Alex as he started a new maneuver with his yo-yo.

"Anywhere from another minute to the next ice age," replied Tom. "After all, she's a woman." The taller boy was leaning against the inside wall next to the school entrance, intently studying his friend's performance with the yo-yo. "Cool, I've never seen that one before. What's it called?"

"Splitting-the-atom."

"Do it again."

"Okay, I'll try, but I'm kind of rusty on it." Alex tossed out the yo-yo and repeated the trick flawlessly. "Boy, wouldn't you like to eavesdrop on the conversation between Sarah and Mr. Serpens?"

"Yeah. They're probably driving each other nuts. Then again, they're both already a little zany so . . . Can one crazy person make another crazy person even crazier?"

"How would I know?" said Alex. "Do I look crazy?"

Tom decided to switch to a different topic. "So, any new guesses as to why Evad's been spending so much time in the chem lab?"

"Nope, but I plan to sneak in there some time when there's no one else around and do some investigating. Do you—ouch!" Alex grabbed his forehead where it had been bonked by the yo-yo.

"Cool. That was even neater than splitting-the-atom," said Tom. "What do you call that?"

"How about the klutz?"

"Can you do it again?"

"Here," said Alex, holding out the yo-yo to his friend. "With your natural born talent, you're bound to get it right on the first try."

"No thanks. I wouldn't think of attempting something like the klutz with my limited experience."

"Hmm, I think I thought of a plan."

"How so?"

"Well, at the end of school someday, I'll hang out in one of the boys' rest rooms, and later, after everyone has left the school, I'll go to the chem lab and open one of the windows. It's on the first floor, so you could be waiting outside and get in that way. And then we'll see if we can figure out what Evad's been up to."

Tom listened with a skeptical scowl. "Wait a minute. I think the janitors clean the johns right after school. They'd find you hiding there and make you leave."

"Okay, we'll just have to find a better hiding place. How about behind the bleachers in the gym?"

"Besides," added Tom, still sounding skeptical, "I know for a fact that they clean all the classrooms every night, and when they're done I think they lock them too, so unless you could sneak into the chem lab between the time they cleaned it and the time they locked it, it still wouldn't work."

"Boy, some days you can be a real killjoy. Okay, Ragnar, here's plan B. At the end of school one of us sneaks into the chem lab before they get around to cleaning it and locking the door and makes sure one of the windows is unlocked. And then, late at night, we return to the school, and get into the chem lab through the unlocked window."

"And how late do you think might be late enough to be sure no one else is around?"

"Around elevenish."

"Is elevenish a word?"

"Of course, it is. I just used it. Anyway, is Ragnar in or not?"

"And what if we get caught? I mean we could get charged with breaking and entering. That's pretty serious."

"We'd say we forgot something in the chem lab and as we just happened to be passing by, thought we'd try the window and—?"

"At eleven o'clock at night? Are you daft? Face it, it's a dumb idea. Besides, suppose I get caught sneaking out of the house at eleven at night? What would I tell my parents? Gee, Dad, remember that madman I have for science? Well, he's obviously been up to something really bad in the chem lab, and I thought I'd break into the school tonight and find out what kind of evil stuff he's been working on."

"Okay, you made your point," said Alex. "But you could always make up a story, couldn't you?"

"Lie? That would be lying."

"Yeah, I guess you're right." Alex went back to splitting-the-atom.

"What kind of story did you have in mind?"

"You could tell them you were sneaking out for a romantic rendezvous with Sarah."

"What? What kind of crazy idea is that?"

"Well, if you told them ahead of time about what Sarah wrote in her notebook, you'd have the perfect alibi. They'd certainly believe you."

"What Sarah wrote . . . ? Why I'd have to have peanuts for brains to tell them about that." Tom paused, a look of anxiety crossing his face. "You didn't tell anybody about her notebook, did you?"

"Of course not. Cross my heart and swear to die, and I think the phrase you were looking for was a brain the size of a peanut. I'm not sure what exactly peanuts for brains means."

"Shush," shushed Tom, hearing footsteps approaching from the neighboring hallway. "Someone's coming." A moment later Sarah rounded the corner and uttered a small shriek as she nearly collided with Tom.

"Tom, what are you doing here?"

"Er, we thought we'd wait for you as—er—you know, we're suppose to—er—make sure you get home safely."

The girl gave the two boys a big smile. "Why that's so sweet of you."

"It was Tom's idea," enlightened Alex.

"No, it wasn't," hissed Tom between clenched teeth at his friend, attempting to keep his voice low so Sarah didn't hear.

"Besides," chuckled Alex, "someone has to look out for you since you seem to attract trouble like a skunk attracts stink."

"That's an awful metaphor," said the girl, wrinkling up her nose. "Skunks don't attract stink."

"Okay," said Alex, "point well taken, but that's neither here nor there. So, what did Mr. Serpens want, if I'm not prying?"

"Well, he said he was concerned—oh-my-gosh, I don't have my purse. I must have left it on the bench outside of Mr. Serpens' office. Could you wait another minute while I run back and get it?"

"Sure, go ahead," said Alex. "It will give me more time to work on my yo-yo repertoire."

"I'll try to be quick. I'm so sorry." Sarah set down her books and then disappeared around the corner, followed by the sound of rapidly retreating footsteps.

Alex resumed his yo-yo practice. "Why do girls have purses?"

"Good question," said Tom. For a brief moment he reflected on the matter, and then said, "Why don't they just put pockets in the dresses?"

"Too much stuff for pockets I guess."

As the minutes passed, Alex proceeded to work his way through his catalog of yo-yo tricks. The two boys discussed other odd things about the female of the species, especially young teenage ones, and particularly one who wore glasses and had braces, long straight, light brown—almost blonde—hair, brown eyes and a larger than average nose.

Much to Tom's chagrin, Alex was starting to speculate on why teenage girls wrote the names of boys they had a crush on over and over again in their notebooks, when a cat rounded the corner of the hallway and sprinted past the two boys, heading towards the exit.

"Hey, that looked like your cat," said Tom.

"It sure did," said Alex.

"What would Tiger be doing in school?"

Further speculation on Tiger's possible educational endeavors was interrupted by the sound of rapidly approaching footsteps coming from the direction that the cat had appeared. As Sarah rounded the corner, she came to a sudden stop, gasping for breath. Her features were pale and her eyes wide with alarm.

"Sarah, what's wrong?" said Tom.

The girl opened her mouth to talk, but nothing came out but more gasps for air. Tom laid his hand on her shoulder. "Take it easy. Tell us what's wrong?"

Sarah forced herself to swallow and attempted to slow her rate of breathing. She glanced behind her as if to ensure herself that they were alone. "Outside," she gasped. "I can't tell you in here."

As the three quickly gathered up their books, Tom noticed that Sarah at least had her purse. They hurried out through the double doors of the school's main entrance, Sarah leading the way. Instead of heading across the school yard, she turned to the right and walked several paces along the wall until she came to a place of concealment created by a line of large bushes that grew along the building. It was a place where certain students liked to hang out after school and sneak a cigarette, for the foliage did a reasonable job of hiding anyone from the view of others in the schoolyard. Upon reaching the spot she had selected, Sarah abruptly sat down, resting her back against the school wall. Tom noted that such behavior was unusual for a girl, especially for one of Sarah's obsessive fastidiousness. Surprisingly, the girl seemed oblivious to the fact that sitting on the ground might soil her dress. She quickly pulled her jacket more tightly around her in a futile attempt to stop herself from shivering. As the boys settled on the ground opposite of her, with their backs to a large bush, it seemed to them that the cause of Sarah's shivering wasn't the cool October air.

"Okay," said Alex. "You going to tell us what's going on?"

The girl took several more deep breaths, as if trying to relax herself. Still breathing heavy, she finally managed to blurt out, "You're not going to believe me."

That made Tom and Alex exchange glances. Then Tom gave the girl a smile and said, "If it's about ray guns, you're right, we won't believe you."

That caused Sarah to emit a cry that sounded almost hysterical. Then she gave her head a shake and returned Tom's look, her eyes appearing as if they were about to tear up. "I—it was all so confusing. I'm—I'm—"

Alex tried to sound sympathetic. "Start at the beginning. That usually works."

"Okay." She took yet another deep breath. "When I got to office, I spotted my purse on the bench. Mr. Serpens' door was cracked open. I could hear Mr. Serpens talking to someone." She again paused and glanced at both boys as if to signify that it should mean something, but they both shrugged. "Well, I was quiet as I didn't want to disturb Mr. Serpens, and then I heard him say something—something really strange so I—I know I shouldn't have, but I stayed behind the door where I couldn't be seen, and I listened to the conversation." She gave the boys a look of embarrassment.

Tom gave her a big grin and said, "Good girl."

"Way to go," said Alex.

That caused Sarah to emit an almost hysterical laugh, followed by a sniffle.

"Well, what did you hear?" asked Tom.

"It was all so strange at first, and then so frightening. I'm not sure if I can remember it all."

"Give it your best shot," said Alex, hanging on her every word.

"Okay. Well, what got my attention was I heard Mr. Serpens say, 'It can't be! It's impossible!' And then I recognized the voice of the other person in the room. It was Mr. Evad."

"Wow," said the boys, echoing each other.

"Mr. Evad said that it would seem so—since they found that the DNA was identical."

"The DNA? What's a DNA?" said Alex.

"I don't know. But I'm certain he said DNA, as they used that word several more times. Anyway, Evad said he was certain of his results. That he had done one more test this afternoon and it also came up negative."

"What came up negative?" asked Alex.

"I don't know, but it might have had something to do with clones."

"What's a clone?" asked Alex.

"I don't know."

"Will you shut up," interrupted Tom, "and let her talk. Go on Sarah."

"Well, he said the results were negative. And then he said, I think these were his exact words, he said, 'His DNA is identical but he's definitely not a clone.' "

"Huh?" said Tom.

"Shhh," hushed Alex. "Obviously none of us have any idea what they were talking about. Go on, Sarah, you're doing great."

"Then Mr. Serpens said that that left only two possibilities. That either Tom and the Commander were identical twins or they were one and the same person, but how could either be possible?"

"Who's the Commander?" asked Tom.

"I don't know," whined Sarah.

"Tom?" said Alex. "Was he talking about our Tom?"

"I think so," said Sarah.

"Do you know anybody called the Commander?" asked Alex.

"No," said Tom. "Now will you shut up and let Sarah continue?"

"Go on Sarah," said Alex.

"Okay, so Mr. Evad agreed with Mr. Serpens that whatever it was they were talking about was impossible, that Tom and the Commander had to be the same person, but they couldn't be. And then he said, Mr. Evad that is, he said that if only they could have known earlier, but the lab equipment was so primitive, and that he wasn't a molecular biologist." She paused, saw Alex looking like he was about to ask another question, and preempted him. "No, I have no idea what a molecular biologist is. I know what a biologist is and what molecules are, but I never heard of a molecular biologist. At least, that's what I think he said he wasn't. Anyway, then Mr. Serpens started talking about Tom and the Commander again. He said that he had to admit that every time he sees Tom, he's struck by the eerie, he actually used the word eerie, he was struck by the eerie resemblance between Tom and the Commander, and that ever since Evad found their DNA to be the same, he knew it was more than coincidence."

"Okay," said Alex. "Sounds like whatever this DNA thing is, both Tom and this Commander guy, whoever that is, have the same DNA, and that means they're the same person."

"Yes," said Sarah. "That's what I'm thinking too. But then Mr. Serpens went on. He said that it didn't matter. That if Mr. Evad's calculations were correct, the tunnel would open any day now, if not tonight, and they'd be out of here."

"They're leaving?" said Tom, looking cheerful. "That's great. Good riddance. But what did he mean by some tunnel opening?"

Sarah ignored Tom's question and continued. "But then Mr. Evad said that he was changing the plan. That Mr. Serpens was staying here. Mr. Serpens didn't sound pleased when he heard that."

"Hey, so what?" chirped Tom. "Who cares about Serpens? But Evad's still leaving, right?"

"Apparently. Like I said, Mr. Serpens didn't seem too pleased with Mr. Evad changing the plan. He said something about being stuck here in this—I think the word he used sounded something like cytherian. That's another strange word I never heard before. He said—I think he said something about 'being stuck here in this cytherian swamp of a time.' I'm not sure about that. And then he asked Mr. Evad why he had to stay here. And, I'm certain about this, when he asked Mr. Evad that, he called him Maximum Leader."

"Huh?" said both boys at the same time.

"Maximum Leader. He called Mr. Evad Maximum Leader."

"Hmm," said Alex. "I believe that was one of Stalin's titles."

"Stalin?" said Tom, more as an exclamation than a question.

"Yes, Joseph Stalin, the ruthless, communist dictator of the Soviet Union," said the other boy.

"I know who Stalin was, you moron, but why would Serpens call Evad Maximum Leader? Hey, Evad's from Romania, right, and Romania's a communist country? That's it. They're both commie spies."

"No, I don't think so," said Sarah.

"No, Tom may be right. That makes sense."

"No, it doesn't," said Sarah, raising her voice. "Will you both shut up and stop interrupting. There's a lot more you have to know."

"Sorry," was the dual response.

"When Mr. Serpens called Mr. Evad Maximum Leader, Mr. Evad got angry. He said, "Admiral, don't use that title.""

"Evad called Serpens an admiral?" said Tom. "Why would he—?"

"Will you please shut up and let me finish," growled the girl. "How many times do I have to tell you, I don't have any idea what it was all about?"

"Sorry. Go on, please," said Tom.

"Mr. Serpens asked Mr. Evad why he had to stay here, and Mr.

Evad said it was because of Tom."

"Tom?" said Alex at the same instance that Tom said, "Me?" Both boys immediately shut up as Sarah glared at them.

"As I was saying, he said it was because of Tom. He told Mr. Serpens that there was something about Tom that bothered him, and it bothered him now more than ever since he now knew that Tom wasn't a clone. He said he had an instinct for those sorts of things. And then Mr. Serpens said, 'Surely you don't think there's some connection between the boy and Quadrant Five? Why we're talking centuries.'"

"Quadrant Five?" said Tom, more to himself than to the others. "What could that be?"

Sarah continued. "Mr. Evad told Mr. Serpens that his staying here might better serve the—the cause, and Mr. Serpens asked him how. And—oh, it's all so awful." The girl paused, and gave Tom a look of anguish, as her body started to shake again. The boys remained quiet, allowing Sarah to regain a grip on herself.

"Mr. Evad said—" She gave a sniffle and her lower lip quivered. "He told Mr. Serpens that his calculations predicted the next tunnel wouldn't be until 1995. And then he said—I believe these were his exact words—he said, 'If you don't hear from me by then, your orders are to kill him.'"

"Kill him?" said Alex. "Who?"

"That's what Mr. Serpens asked. Who? And Mr. Evad said, 'Cobalt.'"

"What?" said both boys.

"He told Mr. Serpens to kill Tom. And then he said, 'Better yet, why take chances? Kill them all, the entire family.'"

At that the three lapsed into silence, the quiet being broken only by an occasional rustle of the bushes from the light October breeze or another sniffle from Sarah. Tom appeared to be studying the wall behind Sarah, and Sarah and Alex appeared to be studying Tom. Finally, Tom gave his best friend a grin and said, "Boy, Evad really does have it in for me."

At that Sarah wailed, "Tom, I'm not kidding. He told Mr. Serpens to kill you. And Mr. Serpens' response was to ask why he shouldn't kill you and your family now. He said if he did it now he wouldn't have to stay behind. And not only that, apparently it wasn't staying here in East Pencreek that upset him so. He complained about having to stay behind here in this—this miserable century."

That caused the boys to again exchange glances. "And what did Evad say to that?" asked Alex.

"Give me a moment." Sarah was obviously trying to remember what Evad had said next. "He said that he didn't want Mr. Serpens to do it now, because he was unsure how dangerous it would be to attempt to change the future. Yes, that was it. Evad said that he was confident that when he returned he would be able to avenge their defeat at Quadrant Five."

"Quadrant Five again," said Tom. "Sounds like they might have been talking about a battle or something, although that sounds like a strange name for a battle."

"He said that if they were victorious, that there was no need to try to change the past. But if they lost, and if for some reason he couldn't contact Mr. Serpens, that they might as well take a chance. He used the term 'toss the dice.'"

After another brief silence, Alex said, "Anything else?"

"Yes. Mr. Serpens told Mr. Evad that he now understood the reason for his staying behind, and that Mr. Evad could depend on him to carry out his orders. Then he told Mr. Evad he was concerned about the ... something he called ... I think what he said was 'the Darwinian.'"

"Darwinian?" said Alex. "Darwin. Like in Charles Darwin, the biologist?"

"I think so," said Sarah. "That's what it sounded like to me."

"Do either of you know what a Darwinian is?" asked Tom.

"No," was the simultaneous response.

"I was afraid of that."

"Anyway—let me think for a moment. Mr. Serpens sounded like he was concerned about this Darwinian. He said something about them often being—unpredictable and violent. And he said that this one would be more so, considering whose brain it had feasted on."

"Feasted on a brain?" said Tom. "Yuck."

"Then Mr. Evad told Mr. Serpens that everything should be okay since they had implanted the…, the…, I think he said 'mindbender'--right after it had hatched, but before it had eaten."

"Implanted? Like they put a plant in it?" asked Tom.

"Hatched?" said Alex.

"How should I know what they were talking about? Yes, I believe he said 'hatched,' and I think the other word was mindbender, or at least that's what it sort of sounded like. Anyway, at that point I got really scared, and I was afraid they might see me so I snuck away and came here as fast as I could."

Sarah looked from one boy to the other and was startled to see them both smile.

"Wow, Sarah, you're a regular Jack Hawkins hiding in the cracker barrel," said Alex.

"I think you mean apple barrel," corrected Tom.

"I thought it was a cracker barrel."

"What are you two arguing about?" shrieked Sarah. "Don't you see how serious this is?"

Tom's smile widened. "You really had us going there. I never would have expected it of you."

"What! You think I'm making all this up? But it's true," Sarah said. "Every word of it is true."

"Yeah, just like Tom's story about the ray gun was true."

"Hey, wait a minute. I wasn't making that up. I really did find a ray gun in Evad's briefcase."

Sarah let out a loud scream. "I'm not making this up. I wouldn't make up such a horrible story, about someone going to kill Tom." Her outburst not only caught the boys by surprise, but also Sarah's respiratory system. She started to take in rapid gulps of air.

"Okay, okay," said Tom. "Take it easy. We believe you. You weren't pulling our leg."

The girl took a couple of more deep breaths and then seemed to relax. "No, you don't Tom," she said sadly, "but you have to, you just have to. I would never lie to you. Never. Cross my heart and swear to die."

Tom turned to Alex, but the other boy simply gave his shoulders a shrug to show that he had nothing to offer.

"Anything else you can remember?" said Tom.

"No—yes. But it's really not related."

"You never know," said Alex. "Sherlock Holmes would never overlook any piece of information, no matter how insignificant it might seem."

"Well, as I was leaving the office, trying to sneak away without being heard, a cat ran past me."

"It didn't happen to look like Alex's cat, Tiger, did it?" asked Tom.

"Yes," said the surprised girl. "What . . . ?"

But Tom cut Sarah short as he was obviously looking at something in the school yard beyond Alex. He whispered, "Look," at the same time pointing in the direction of the school entrance. When Sarah and Alex turned to look they beheld Evad and Serpens standing on the walkway having obviously just descended the steps of the school entrance. Neither of the men appeared to be aware of the three teens lurking behind the nearby shrubbery.

"It's not like you'll be going this alone," said Evad. "You have both the Darwinian and our new agent provocateur to assist you, not to mention the other two in reserve."

"But it will take a couple of more days until the Darwinian's transformation is complete. And the agent provocateur—he's but a kid. Perhaps we should have saved the final mindbender for a more promising host?"

Evad gave his cohort a cold stare before he responded. "Admiral, I'm beginning to have my doubts about assigning you this mission."

"Maximum Leader, I assure you that your trust in me will not be misplaced," said Serpens.

"Then we'll consider the issue closed. We rendezvous tonight at 2230 hours."

"Yes, sir."

Serpens started to move on, when Evad called out, "Wait."

The guidance counselor stopped and turned.

"I just recalled something. When I entered your office, there was a girl's purse on the bench in the hall."

"It was probably Miss Gould's. I was meeting with her right before you arrived."

"I don't recall it being there when we left just now."

"So?"

Evad looked off into the distance, hands stuffed into the pockets of his trench coat, no doubt forming a response.

"You think she may have come back to get it and perhaps overheard some of our conversation?" asked Serpens.

"Yes, it's possible. We should really be more conscious about keeping our sensors activated."

"But then we risk draining the power supplies."

Evad turned to face his companion.

"I believe you should have another meeting with Miss Gould Monday morning. Find out if she knows or suspects anything. Get deep into her mind."

"How deep?"

"Terminally deep, if that's what it takes."

Serpens nodded, and the two men proceeded to move on, each heading off in a different direction.

"Well, I'll be," said Tom.

Sarah nodded her head vigorously as if to say, "I told you so."

"You weren't making it up," said Alex.

Sarah again gave a nod, but less vigorously this time.

"Now I'm even more confused. Did Evad not just say something about an agent pro-something-or-other being a kid? What were they talking about?"

"And he mentioned a Darwinian and he used that word 'mind-bender' again. What does it all mean?" said Sarah.

When neither of the boys offered any ideas, she continued. "And what he said about me, about Mr. Serpens getting into my . . . We need to tell somebody. We should tell our parents. They may know what to do?"

"Sarah, our parents would never believe us," said Alex. "They'd either think we were pulling their leg or had gone nutso or something. Why until a few seconds ago we didn't believe you."

But Sarah was adamant. "I know my parents. They would believe me. They would never think I was crazy."

"I don't see why," said Alex. "I think you're crazy."

Sarah gave Alex a hard look at the same time Tom hit him on the shoulder with a book.

"Hey, I was trying to ease the tension."

"How can you make jokes at a time like this?" asked the girl.

"No, Alex is right. You have to be realistic, Sarah. Not only does the whole thing sound preposterous, it doesn't make any sense. I mean all those things like Maximum Leader, and the Commander, and Quadrant Five, whatever in the heck that is, tunnels opening up, and DNA, and clones, and talking about 1995 and the 20th century like they're from some other time. It all sounds like some sort of bad science fiction story."

"Actually, it sounds like a pretty good science fiction story when you think about it," said Alex.

Ignoring his friend's remark, Tom continued, "Especially the part about killing me. Heck, what did I ever do to Evad? We're talking about a school science teacher telling the school guidance counselor not only to knock off a student, well maybe two students considering what they said about Sarah, but his entire family as well."

"I guess you're right, but we have to do something?"

"I know what I'm going to do," said Alex.

"What?" asked the girl.

"You said they mentioned something about a tunnel that might be opening tonight, and apparently Evad's leaving by this tunnel, right?"

"Yes, if I remembered it right."

"I know where Evad lives. Tonight, I'll pretend to go to bed early, then I'll sneak out of the house and go over to Evad's place and spy on him. If he leaves to find some tunnel, I'll follow him and learn what the whole thing's about."

"What if he gets in his car and drives off?" asked the girl.

"Evad doesn't own a car. Isn't that right Tom?"

"Yeah, I think so. At least, he apparently always walks to and from school."

"Okay," said Sarah. "What if Mr. Serpens picks him up and takes him somewhere?"

"Hmm, you have a point there," admitted Alex. "Serpens probably has a car. Well, that's a chance we'll have to take. Who's with me? Ragnar? Sarah?"

Sarah gave Alex a horrified look that effectively answered for her. Tom thought a moment and then said, "Remember what we were talking about earlier, about what if I get caught sneaking out of the house?"

"Oh, right," said Alex. "Well, like I said, you just mention Sarah's notebook and—" He stopped.

"What does my notebook . . . ?" She leaped to her feet. "You didn't! You looked in my notebook?" As she said it, her lower lip began to tremble, and she cast Tom a quick glance.

"I'm sorry, Sarah", interjected Alex. "It was an accident. It was my fault. Tom had nothing to do with it."

"How can you look in someone's notebook accidentally?"

"Hey, I said I'm sorry. Besides, there's nothing to be ashamed of. Why, probably every flighty girl in the eighth grade has a crush on Tom."

Sarah did an imitation of a statue, staring at Alex, with her mouth hanging open. Tom put one hand to his forehead, and slowly shook it from side to side as he looked at the ground and muttered, "Alex, how can anyone as smart as you be so dumb?"

The other boy straightened up and placed a hand on Sarah's shoulder. "Listen, Sarah. Forget the notebook. There are more important things to be thinking about like figuring out what Evad and Serpens are up to."

The girl again looked at Tom, who gave her a nod, as if almost begging her to please drop the subject of the notebook. "Okay. Yes, you're right."

"From what I remember, you said Serpens wasn't supposed to kill me until 1995. So, what's to worry about? We have almost forty years to come up with something. And Sarah just stays away from Serpens."

"Yeah, assuming that they were really talking about 1995, which doesn't make any sense whatsoever, just like everything else Sarah heard makes no sense."

"Good," said Tom, now joining the other two in standing up. "So, we all go home and think about it, and try to find out what exactly things like clones and DNAs are."

"Maybe so, but I'm still intending to sneak out and see what Evad's up to tonight, even if none of my *brave* comrades-in-arms have the guts to join me."

"Alex, I don't dare do something like that," said Sarah. "What if my parents found out?"

"You just make up a story like—ouch!" Alex grabbed his shin where Tom had kicked it. "On second thought," he said to Sarah, who seemed perplexed as to why Tom had kicked his best friend in the shin,

"No one's expecting you to do it, you being a girl and all."

"Just what do you mean by that?"

"Don't take it the wrong way," said Tom. "He's just saying, uh—exactly what are you saying, Alex?"

"Never mind. Listen, I'm going to go back in the school and see if the chem lab is still open. Tom, why don't you take Sarah home?"

"Why don't we all go back in and see if the chem lab's open," suggested the girl. "Three heads are better than one."

"Listen, your mom's probably already worried that you're not home yet, and the next thing you know she'll be calling the school or the police, and do you want them finding you snooping around the chem lab after school?"

"No, I guess not."

"Good, then it's settled. I do the snooping and Tom walks you home."

"Hey, wait—," began Tom, but Alex cut him off.

"After all that's happened this week, I think Sarah's mom would feel a lot better if she knew that one of us walked Sarah home, rather than Sarah came home alone."

"So why don't you take Sarah home and I snoop around in the lab?"

"Because you're an ignoramus when it comes to chemistry, that's why."

"Okay, touché. I can't argue with that."

"Listen, it's okay. I'll walk myself home. After all, Jack Paine's not around any more." Although it was her proposal, Sarah didn't seem too happy about having made it.

"No, Alex's right," said Tom. "I'll walk you home. It will not only make your mom feel better, but at least one of Jack's friends is still around, so you can't be too careful." At that, Sarah's mood seemed to improve.

"Good!" said Alex. "I'll call you later about how I made out in the chem. lab."

Sarah noticed that Alex hadn't bothered looking at her when he said he'd call. "What about me? Aren't you going to tell me what you find out?"

"Sure," said Alex. "You're part of this conspiracy too, whether you like it or not. After all, if you hadn't been so nosey we would never have known about Evad's dastardly plan." The boy had no sooner said it, then he realized from the girl's hurt expression that the use of the word 'nosey' was a poor choice, on two accounts. "Uh, I didn't mean to say nosey, I meant . . . Sorry."

"That's okay, but I wasn't being nosey. I just happened to overhear them."

"Are you still planning to snoop on Evad later?" asked Tom.

"Of course, and I'll call you two again tomorrow morning to let you know if I find out anything."

"I'll be at services in the morning, but I should be home by eleven."

"Services?" said Tom. "Tomorrow's Saturday."

"You know—the synagogue."

"You're Jewish?" said Alex. "See, Tom, I told you she was Jewish."

"You're half right," said Sarah. "My father's Jewish and my mom's a Christian. They decided that they would raise my sister and me in both faiths. When we become adults, we can decide which we want to be."

Alex laughed. "That helps explain why you seem so confused all the time."

"I am not!" growled Sarah.

"What happens if you decide to become an atheist?" asked Alex.

"That's no more about to happen than you deciding to be likeable."

"Knock if off, you two," said Tom. As the other two knocked it off, Tom decided to change the subject while Alex and Sarah were still talking to each other. "Listen, Sarah, we'd better get going. As Alex said your mom's probably starting to get worried by now."

As Tom walked Sarah home, he realized that without Alex around he felt uncomfortable in the girl's presence. If he could have read the girl's mind he would have been surprised to discover that she was feeling the same way. Neither teen had anything to say to the other until Tom noticed that Sarah's knee was still graced by an adhesive bandage.

"I take it that bandage is for the cut you got when Paine tripped you?"

"Yes." The girl held out one of her hands so that Tom could see its palm, "and this one," and then, after shifting her books to the other hand, the other palm, "and this one too."

"Wow, it must have hurt a lot."

"Not at first, but they were really hurting by the time I got home. My mother was upset that I didn't go to the school nurse. She was also upset that Mr. Elkins seemed more concerned about what you did to Jack Paine than about what happened to me."

"Yeah, Elkins is a real jerk."

"I'm just lucky that you and Alex were around."

Tom felt like he was starting to blush. "Well, you're lucky it wasn't any worse."

"Oh, my chin got cut too, but I took the bandage off yesterday. See." Sarah stopped and lifted her chin. In the fading daylight, Tom had to lean close to the girl to get a better look at the bruise. As he did so his gaze shifted from her chin to her liquid, enchanting, brown eyes—eyes that stared at him through the lenses of her glasses.

For what seemed to the boy like the longest of moments, they stood there, their faces so close together that their nostrils could absorb each other's scent. Each gave an involuntary swallow, and then Tom stammered, "Uh, yes, you're lucky it wasn't worse." The boy awkwardly straightened up.

Sarah instinctively took a step forward, her eyes still locked on Tom, and promptly fell off the edge of the curb.

"You sure you're okay?" asked Tom. "You're still limping."

"I'll be fine, really," said Sarah, limping.

"Boy, for a girl, you really get banged up a lot."

When Sarah didn't immediately respond, Tom thought that he may have said the wrong thing. Girls were weird in that they often took things the wrong way. Then again, he didn't have much experience talking to girls other than his sister, and Katty, being his sister, didn't really count. He cast a quick peek at Sarah. She was looking straight ahead but seemed to be deep in thought. As they had at last reached the front walk to Sarah's home, there was no point in continuing to worry about whether he said the right thing or not.

"Then we're agreed that you're not going to say anything to your parents about what you overheard?"

"Yes," said Sarah, stopping before her front steps. "I think you're right that they'd never believe me, and even if they did, what could they do?"

"Okay, then we'll see you later."

"Er, Tom." Uh, oh, thought the boy. There was something about the tone of her voice, along with the fact that she was staring at the pavement instead of making eye contact that set off alarm bells in the boy's mind. "About what I had written in my notebook . . . I was—well, I guess I was—that is, I sometimes do silly things like that."

"Geez--what do I say now?" thought the boy. "She's obviously really embarrassed about the notebook thing. I should say something."

"I hope you understand that it was Alex who snooped in your notebook, not me. I would never have—"

"I know. I wanted you to understand that it—well, I wasn't serious about what I had written."

Well, that hadn't helped. The boy kept trying to think of something appropriate to say. Then, as was often his wont when flustered, he spoke before he weighed exactly what it was that he was going to say.

"Actually, I'm sorry to hear that. I felt . . . Well I guess I was flattered that you might have—er, that is . . ."

"Really?" Sarah wasn't studying the ground any more but looking

301

directly at him with an expectant expression.

"Yeah. Well, I better get going."

"Okay, please call me and let me know if Alex finds anything."

"Good night." Tom's mind was in turmoil. He had really blown that one.

"Good night, Tom," she answered, then turned and opened her front door.

"Sarah, is that you?" asked Mrs. Gould. When she received no answer, Sarah's mother glanced into the front foyer to see her daughter heading toward the stairway to the second floor. Mrs. Gould wasn't sure what surprised her the most, the fact that Sarah had left the front door standing wide open, the fact that she was walking with a slight limp, or Sarah's expression, somewhere between blissful and dazed.

"Sarah, are you limping?"

Sarah stopped and gave her head a slight shake as if she were awakening from some hypnotic spell. "Huh? Uh, no."

"Yes, you were, and please close the front door. Is something wrong?"

"No," said Sarah, turning around to close the door. Then as she turned back to face her mother, she looked startled and said, "Yes! No, I mean no!"

"Did something happen again at school today?"

"Yes, uh, no. Nothing. I guess I'm just tired from everything that happened this week. I think I would like to go upstairs and lie down a bit before dinner."

"Okay," said her mother, sounding like concerned mothers everywhere. "But I'm concerned about that limp."

"It's wonderful, I mean it's okay," said Sarah, limping up the stairs.

"And how was your day?" asked Mr. Gould, noting that Sarah hadn't spoken at the dinner table. When Sarah seemed not to have heard her father but continued instead to subconsciously stir her soup with a spoon, Mr. Gould repeated the question, louder.

"Huh, what?" Sarah looked up. "Oh, it was fine, father."

"Anything interesting happen?"

"Yes—er, no."

Sarah's father exchanged glances with his wife who in turn gave her husband a look as if to say, "I told you so." Sarah's younger sister, Anne, was busy devouring the mashed potatoes on her plate, oblivious to her sister seemingly being in another universe, and her parents' concern about that possibility. Before Mr. Gould could continue the conversation, the phone rang.

"I'll get it," said Sarah, dropping the spoon in her soup as she jumped up from the table. She rushed into the living room where the telephone gave a second ring.

"See," said Mrs. Gould. "Have you ever known Sarah to rush to answer the phone before?"

"Hello," said Sarah into the mouthpiece, sounding winded.

"Sarah?" came the voice over the receiver, then the owner of the voice, having assured himself that his guess was correct, continued, "It's Alex."

"Oh," said Sarah, sounding less than enthusiastic.

"Hey, listen, how many times do I have to apologize about the notebook?"

"Oh, no, it's okay." Sarah attempted to change the tone of her voice. "I'm glad you called. Did you get into the lab? Find anything?"

"Yeah, I got into the lab. Must have searched the place for the better part of a half hour, but if Evad left any clues there as to what he's up to, I certainly couldn't find them. Anyway, we're switching to plan B which is to stake out Evad's place tonight. I already called Tom, but he's still chickening out, so what about you? In or out?"

"No, I couldn't possibly do that, and you shouldn't either."

"Come on, where's your sense of adventure?"

"What will you tell your parents if they catch you sneaking out?"

"I'll tell them I was sneaking out to see you."

"What! They'd never believe that."

"Yes, they would, especially if I told them you had my name written all over your notebook."

"Alex Banyon, you wouldn't. That would be a perfectly horrid thing to do."

"Sarah, I'm teasing. Anyway, I'll give you a call tomorrow morning and let you know how things turn out."

"Okay. Oh, Alex?"

"Yes."

"I looked in the dictionary for DNA and couldn't find anything, but I did find a definition of clone."

"Cool. Is it spelled c-l-o-n-e or k-l-o-n-e?"

"It's spelled c-l-o-n-e. I couldn't find anything under the other spelling."

"Neat. So, what's a clone?"

The girl pulled out a piece of paper from a skirt pocket and read from it. "A clone is a group of plants all of whose members are directly descended from a single individual, as by grafting or budding."

"Huh? What the heck does that have to do with Tom?"

"I know it doesn't make sense. I remember Evad saying that Tom's DNA and the Commander's DNA were the same, and somehow that was like they were the same person, but that he had proved in the chem lab that they were not clones. Or I think that's what he said. I'm not so sure anymore."

"Okay, so Tom's not a plant. I could have saved Evad a lot of time and told him that."

"Don't get silly. The word clone must have another meaning to Evad, one that's not in the dictionary. But I also remember him saying something about having the same DNA was like being identical twins?"

"Yes, but didn't you say he said that wasn't possible either?"

"Yes, I think so" agreed Sarah. "So, there is a mystery about Tom and this Commander fellow apparently being identical, but Evad doesn't understand it because it doesn't seem possible that it could be."

"And we don't understand it because we have no idea what in the blazes Evad is talking about. All the more reason you should go with me tonight to spy on that crummy creep."

"Alex, I told you I can't."

"Yeah, yeah. Anyway, I'll call you tomorrow after you get home from the synagogue. Goodnight."

"Goodnight—oh, Alex."

"Yeah."

There was a brief pause as the girl collected her thoughts. "You're a good friend of Tom's—probably his best friend, right?"

"Yeah, I guess so."

"Well, do you know if he has a—, I mean, if he likes—, uh, what I'm trying to ask is—"

Alex gave out a sigh. "Come on, Sarah, spit it out. I haven't got all night."

"Don't rush me." Sarah tried to sound calm. "Listen. First you have to promise you won't tell Tom."

"Won't tell Tom, what?"

"What I'm about to ask."

"I take it you want to ask something about Tom. Suppose I don't know the answer? In that case can I ask Tom your question so I can get the answer, in which case why don't you just ask him yourself?"

"No!"

"No, what?"

"No, I can't ask him myself, and no, you can't ask him the question either."

"Okay, so what's the question?"

"You have to promise not to tell Tom, or anyone else for that matter."

"If I promise, will you join me tonight?"

"No! Oh, forget it."

Alex chuckled. "Let me take a wild guess, and if I'm right I promise not to tell a living soul, cross my heart and hope to die. Is the question 'Does Tom have a girlfriend?'"

The pregnant pause at the other end of the line was followed by a meek, "Yes."

"Come on, Sarah, does Tom look dumb enough to have a girlfriend?"

"No, I mean yes, I—what kind of dumb question is that?" Sarah could imagine Alex grinning on the other end of the line. "Alex Banyon, you are the rudest, most despic—"

"Now, now. You wouldn't want me to renege on my promise and tell Tom?"

A shout of alarm erupted over the line. "You wouldn't! You promised."

"Sarah, relax. I'm teasing."

Sarah sank into the seat, in obvious relief, then happened to glance up. Her parents and sister, who were still sitting at the dining table in the next room, were giving her quizzical looks. She quickly turned her back to them and nuzzled the mouthpiece with her hand to dampen the sound of her voice.

"But now that you bring it up," continued the boy, "I have noticed Tom hanging around a certain someone lately." Alex could have sworn he heard a sniffle on the other end of the line, but when Sarah failed to respond, he said, "Don't you want to know who it is?"

The image of Lynn Reynolds immediately popped into Sarah's mind. Lynn was easily the most attractive girl in the eighth grade and without a doubt the biggest flirt. "I guess I already know," she said softly. "Lynn Reynolds, right?"

"That airhead?" laughed the boy. "No, this girl is so weird that she's the last person you'd ever expect Tom to show any interest in."

"I give up," said Sarah, now sounding like she wanted to end the conversation. "Who?"

"Like I said. She's a real weirdo. Name's Sarah Gould."

"What! Alex Banyon, that the meanest thing you've ever done."

"I'm not joking, Sarah. Boy, for a smart person, you sure can be dumb at times."

"You're serious? You think Tom really, you know, might actually like me?"

"Hey, don't start reading too much into it. I'm just saying he never seemed to like hanging around with any girl until you showed up. You must admit that you're not like most girls in that you're kind of strange and are always getting in trouble, and it's getting late, so I'll call you tomorrow."

"Okay. Goodnight."

"Goodnight."

"Oh, Alex?"

"Yeah."

"Be careful tonight, okay?"

"Gee, Sarah, you're starting to sound like my mother."

Chapter 13
The Pod

Most residents of East Pencreek referred to it as Sullivans Woods, although no one seemed to know the origin of the name, or if the correct spelling included an apostrophe—that is, Sullivan's Woods as opposed to Sullivans Woods. After a good rain, the woodland often contained pools of standing water that discouraged both human visitors and human development. Stories about the place being haunted, told to many a local youngster, usually by an older sibling or even a mischievous uncle, were no doubt only a means of discouraging exploration of the area by said youngsters. Those who failed to heed such stories often returned from the wetlands carrying additional, unintended weight through the accumulation of a sizable amount of an exceedingly moist form of earth, also known as mud. Ignoring all warnings, Alex and Tom, usually in the company of Brad and Wayne, had on occasion visited the forbidden woodland for the purpose of playing "war" in a setting seemingly more realistic than one of their backyards, or camping out under a full moon. Alex, Tom and Brad along with their newfound co-conspirator, Sarah Gould, and Alex's faithful though seemingly disinterested cat, Tiger, now stood across the street from the dark habitat of trees and brush.

"It was right about there," said Alex, pointing to a spot where the tree line began across the road, "that Evad and Serpens went in."

"And you didn't follow them?" asked Sarah.

"Do I look stupid?" said Alex, starting to roll his eyes, but immediately ceasing when Sarah assumed a hurt look. "Listen, Sarah. It was dark, and I didn't have a flashlight. You've never been in those woods. Half of it is swamp. There's probably even quicksand in there. Why just last year the Byerly kid went in there and was never heard from again. Isn't that right, Brad?"

"Huh?" said Brad, sounding a tad uncertain. "Richard Byerly? I thought he moved away."

"Whatever. Same difference. Anyway, even if I had a flashlight, shining one around in there would have probably tipped off the goon squad that someone was following them. Plus, I didn't have loyal Tiger here to lead the way and check for quicksand."

"Oh, come off it. You don't really expect me to believe that there's quicksand in there?" said Sarah.

Before Alex could come up with a witty retort, Tom decided to steer the conversation back to firmer ground. "Okay, let's recap. Last night you were hiding across the street from Evad's apartment, and about ten-thirty you saw Evad and Serpens leave the building, and Evad had a large duffle bag slung over his shoulder?"

"Right," said Alex. "And it appeared to be full and kind of heavy."

"You followed them here and saw them disappear into the woods?"

"Roger."

"Who's Roger?" asked Sarah. The three boys gave Sarah annoyed looks.

"It means 'yes,'" explained Tom, "like in Roger, Wilco, and out."

"Oh."

"Where were we? Then you saw them disappear into the woods and you waited about a half hour, and since nothing else happened, you went home?"

"Roger."

Tom studied the trees across the road for a second, before

continuing. "Sounds like our next move is to see what's in them thar woods." He stepped into the street, followed by Brad, Alex and the kitty. They had only gone a few paces before they stopped and looked back, except for the cat who continued to the tree line where he stopped and began to inspect the scent of the nearby weeds. Sarah was still standing on the shoulder of the road, looking uncertain.

"Well, are you coming or not?" asked Tom.

"What if they're still in there?"

"They're not in there."

"How do you know?"

The boy let out a sigh. "Because after Alex called me this morning and told me what happened, I called Evad and then Serpens, and they both answered their phones."

"You what?" exclaimed the girl and Alex at the same instant.

"I called them to see whether they were still in town."

"But what did you say when they answered?" asked the girl, if anything now looking even more startled.

"Nothing. I just hung up. Are you coming along or not?"

"Okay," she said, sounding more reluctant than assured as she hurried across the road. "But it doesn't make any sense. I remember Mr. Evad saying something about leaving by a tunnel, but he's still here. Do you think there's a tunnel somewhere in there?"

"I don't know about a tunnel," replied the dark-haired boy, stopping a couple of paces into the brush, "but there's a path." Tom pointed to a spot a few feet ahead where a recently worn path appeared between the closely spaced trees.

"Ah ha," exclaimed Alex. "The plot thickens, Watson."

"If your Holmes, and I'm Watson, who are Sarah and Brad?" asked Tom.

"Brad is Inspector Lestrade and Sarah's our loyal bloodhound," said Alex. "Go ahead Fido, lead the way."

"What! Was that intended to be some kind of wisecrack about my nose?" Sarah's voice grew shrill as she stooped and picked up a stout section of broken tree branch that lay by her feet. She shook it threateningly at Alex.

"Uh, no, Sarah." Alex stammered. "Honest. It kind of popped into my head. Hey, you wouldn't hit a guy wearing glasses, would you?"

"Come on you two, knock it off," ordered Tom. He started walking down the path. "You better hold on to that stick, Sarah. You never know, it might come in handy." His suggestion didn't seem to reassure the girl.

"So how come Wayne isn't here?" said Sarah.

"When I called Wayne this morning," said Tom, "he told me that he and his parents were about to leave town for the weekend. They were going to spend the night in Philly—something about his father's work."

Brad piped up. "I find that awful strange. I've never known Wayne's family to go anywhere."

"I bet he made the mistake of spilling the beans to his parents, and they benched him, and he didn't want to own up . . ." Alex stopped to point at a spot in the trail in front of Tom. "Hey, look. Two pairs of footprints. So far, so good."

"Yeah," said Tom. "Looks like we're on the right path." He resumed walking, with Sarah directly behind him, then Bard. Alex and Tiger were now bringing up the rear. Tom stepped over an exposed root that lay across the path. He started to turn to warn the others of the hazard. "Watch out—" Sarah tripped over the root, emitted a high squeal, and pitched forward into Tom, catching him off balance. As they were falling the boy instinctively grabbed Sarah in an embrace. They crashed to the ground, Tom landing on his back with Sarah on top of him. Sarah's glasses had slid forward becoming wedged in the angle formed by their noses. For what to each seemed like a small eternity, they lay there breathing heavily, the girl's hair having cascaded over the boy's face, each staring into the other's pupils through Sarah's glasses, and both thinking what wonderful brown eyes the other had. Finally, Tom gave a hard swallow and, in a half whisper, asked, "Are you okay?"

"Yes," gulped the girl. "Sorry."

"Hey, you two," said Alex. "You can smooch later. We got work to do." As if to emphasize his master's words, Tiger let out an impatient meow.

Sarah made a move to stand, but as she applied weight to her right foot, it slipped on the underlying slick ground, and back down she went, giving out another squeal as she again landed heavily on Tom. Alex and Brad reached down, grabbed her arms, and pulled her to her feet. Sarah thanked the two, straightened her glasses and began to brush the dirt from her skirt as Tom stood and did likewise to the back his trousers. Seeing how both their complexions had turned a shade towards the red end of the spectrum, Alex gave his head a shake.

"Okay, can we get on with it now?"

"Sure," grunted Tom. He resumed moving down the path. Alex again brought up the rear, but first he stopped and picked up the "club" that Sarah had dropped.

They had gone perhaps a hundred yards when Tom abruptly came to a stop. Sarah, who had been more intent on studying the foliage that bordered the path instead of where she was going, bumped into Tom. She muttered a 'sorry' and then peered around the boy to discover the reason for the halt. "Oh-my-gosh!" she gasped.

Brad, who had pulled up beside the other two also let out an exclamation. "Well I'll be . . ."

Where the path ended a few feet in front of them was a small, circular clearing. In the center of the clearing stood a wooden platform approximately eight feet square, and three feet high. At first the teens stood their ground and exchanged glances, each hoping one of the others could offer some explanation. Showing no interest in ascertaining the reason for it all, a furry, orange-tan shape moved with unconcern into the clearing. Tiger headed directly towards the wooden platform and with a quick jump mounted the structure. The four teens cautiously followed, circling about the periphery of the area from which the trees and larger brush had been removed. Tom took a closer look at some of the freshly cut tree stumps that littered the clearing. The tops of the stumps were all nearly level with the ground. The centers looked as if they had been scooped out in that some held puddles of recent rain water. "Strange," muttered the boy, stooping to give one of the stumps a closer examination.

"I'll say," replied Alex. "There's no sign of fresh graves. So much for my zombie theory."

"Not that. I mean there is no way this was cut by a saw. It's almost concave, not level as one would expect if it were cut by a saw. By the look of it and the platform there, this was all done quite recently."

"You're right." Alex took a knee next to his friend. "Never seen a tree stump cut like that."

"And where's the sawdust?" said Tom. He looked at Alex who gave a hard swallow. Then he looked up at Sarah, whose complexion was growing paler.

"Don't say things like that, Tom. You're starting to scare me."

"Me too," agreed Brad.

Tom got to his feet. "And there's no sign of any tree trunks or branches having hit the ground after they were felled. Or even signs that they were dragged away."

Sarah eyes searched the surrounding woods. "And where are all the trees that were cut down? I don't see any in the woods."

"It's as if they were disintegrated," said Brad.

"You mean like—by a ray gun?" Sarah felt a shiver run through her body as she asked the question.

"Exactly," said Tom. "Just as if they were disintegrated by a ray gun. Let's see, whom do we know who has a ray gun?"

Alex swept the clearing with his eyes. "Okay, we have a good theory

313

as to how it was done. But why?" He walked over to the wooden platform on which Tiger had settled himself, the cat seemingly bored by the discussion. The boy struck a thinking pose, resting his right elbow in the palm of his left hand, his chin in his right hand. He studied the platform. "Odd."

"What's odd?" asked Tom.

"What isn't?" seconded Brad.

"The boards in this platform," said Alex.

"What about them?" Tom walked over to stand next to Alex, followed by Sarah and Brad.

"Look at them. They're different widths, and the edges aren't exactly straight. I don't think they were cut in any sawmill."

"You're right, Holmes," said Tom. "By golly what incredible powers of observation you have."

"Big deal," said Brad. "A blind man would have noticed that close up."

Tom ran his hand over the top surface of the structure. "I bet they were simply carved out of some of the missing trees. Many of the trees here are maple, and so are these boards."

"Yes, that makes sense," said Alex. "Whatever they used to cut down the trees could no doubt also have shaped these boards from some of the trunks."

"Well, at least they used nails to build the thing," noticed the girl. "But we still don't know what it's for, and there really isn't any proof that Mr. Serpens and Mr. Evad had anything to do with building this."

Alex gave a quick laugh. "I think it's pretty obvious who's behind it all. Remember Occam's razor."

"Occam?" asked Brad. "Who in the heck is Occam, and what does his razor have to do with anything?"

Sarah started to explain. "Occam was a medieval theologian . . ."

"Oh, great," moaned Tom. "Okay, what's a theologian?"

"A philosopher who studies the nature of God," said Alex helpfully. "You know, like Saint Thomas Aquinas."

"Boy, for an agnostic, you sure know a lot about religion," said Tom. "But what does religion have to do with it?"

"Nothing," answered Sarah, before Alex could. "Occam's razor is an idea proposed by Occam. It's a cornerstone of the scientific method. It simply says that the simplest explanation for something is probably the correct one."

"Somehow, I just knew that you would know that." Tom gave his head a shake. "Okay, what were we talking about before we started talking about some guy's razor?"

"Alex was using it to argue that Serpens and Evad are obviously the ones behind this."

"No kidding," said Tom. "Boy, sometimes it's really tough being a normal person around you two eggheads."

"Don't look at me," said Sarah. "Alex brought up Occam. Anyway, we still don't have any idea what this is all for, and how it fits into Mr. Evad leaving town."

"Why I should think that would be obvious," said Tom, with a smug expression.

"Well?" said Alex.

"If I may borrow Mr. Occam's razor . . . Say, was that a straight razor or an electric he used?"

"Enough," said Alex. "Just tell us what you think this is all about."

"Notice the circular shape of this clearing. It's a landing pad for a flying saucer. He's leaving by saucer."

"Now you're being silly," said Sarah.

"No, I'm not. Listen. Evad has a ray gun. That in turn explains how they could have cut the clearing by simply disintegrating the trees, except for the ones they used to make the planks to build this." Tom patted the top of the platform catching Tiger's attention. The cat crawled closer to the boy and was rewarded by Tom giving its neck a scratch. "And if a ray gun's possible, then why not a flying saucer, or, by Occam, do you have a better idea?"

"I don't," said Alex. "And I have to admit, it all fits. I always thought Evad wasn't exactly human. He's an alien and he's waiting for a flying saucer to pick him up."

"Awfully small flying saucer," objected Brad, noting the size of the clearing.

"Well, it wouldn't necessarily have to be a flying saucer," said Tom. "Any type of spacecraft—it could be shaped more like a rocket ship, or who knows—any type of spacecraft would do."

"But what about the tunnel?" said Sarah. "I distinctly remember them talking about a tunnel."

"Hey, two out of three ain't bad," beamed Tom.

"Beats me," said Alex. "But I like the spaceship idea. Makes sense."

"No, it doesn't," said the girl. "Why go to all the trouble to land it way out here in the middle of a woods? Why not just pick Evad up at his apartment?"

"Secrecy," suggested Tom. "They obviously don't want us Earthmen to know that we're being visited by aliens. Look at all the reports of UFOs in the past few years."

"Yeah, that makes sense," said Brad. "Do you have any better ideas? I sure don't."

"No," said Sarah. "Maybe we should report this to the police."

"Are you nuts!" said the three boys as one. They looked aghast at the idea.

"You tell the police about this," said Alex, "and they'll think you're nuts."

"Yeah, Sarah," added Brad. "What are you going to say? My science teacher and the junior high guidance counselor are aliens. They've cleared a landing area for their spaceship in the middle of Sullivans Woods. They're probably up to no good, so you should arrest them, but be careful because they have a ray gun."

316

"Okay, okay. But tell me, Mr. Know-it-all. If this is a landing pad for a spaceship, what's this wooden platform for?"

"Beats me," said Brad.

"Me too," agreed Alex. "But Rome wasn't built in a day."

"I hate it when you do that," said Tom. "Okay, what does Rome have to do with anything?"

"Never mind," sighed Alex. "What's important now is deciding what to do next."

Brad gave his friend a nod. "Okay, any ideas on that, other than Sarah's really idiotic one about going to the police?"

Sarah started to whine, "It wasn't so idiotic."

"We need more information," said Alex, "and the best bet for finding some is obviously Evad's place. I think we should give Evad a visit."

"And Brad called my idea idiotic. What are you going to do? Walk up and ring his doorbell?"

"Sure, why not? We can say we have some questions about the test he scheduled for Monday. Yeah, that's it. And while we're there, who knows what we might find."

"I don't know," said the girl. "It sounds kind of risky. What if he suspects something?"

"Sarah has a point," said Tom. "I mean he'll know something's fishy when he sees me."

"That's why you're not going—just Sarah, Brad and I. You'll wait at my house until we finish our mission. Tiger will keep you company."

"What? Now wait a—"

"Alex's right," said Sarah. "Listen Tom, Alex and I are the only ones who ever ask questions in class. That's because we're the best students. Only students who don't need help ever ask questions. You should know that." The girl then turned to Brad. "For that matter, maybe it's best that you don't go with us either."

"I should feel highly insulted by that remark, but since you may have something there I'll save feeling insulted for another time."

"Okay, I guess you're right," sighed Tom.

The two teens mounted the steps onto the large roofed porch of the apartment building. Without any hesitation, Alex opened the door and entered the first floor hallway, followed by Sarah who kept nervously looking about.

"Will you stop being so jittery. If anyone sees you they'll think we're up to no good."

"But we are up to no good."

"Sssh. Keep your voice down," hissed the boy. He proceeded to scan the mailboxes on the wall inside the entrance.

"Well, don't you think whispering looks suspicious too?"

The boy ignored Sarah's remark. "Apartment 2B. Must be on the second floor." Alex then proceeded up the inside stairway followed by Sarah who, in spite of Alex's cautions, kept looking about nervously.

"2B," said Alex, keeping his voice low. "Okay, who's going to knock and start the conversation?"

"What if Mr. Serpens is in there too?"

"That might be even better. We might catch them in the middle of discussing their top secret plans to destroy the Earth."

"I guess you better knock."

"Okay." The boy took a deep breath and rapped the door that said 2B with his knuckles. At first contact, the door squeaked open a crack, causing both students to jump.

Alex looked at Sarah and as he did so, he arched his eyebrows twice and grinned. "Didn't I see this in a movie somewhere?"

"Knock again," whispered Sarah.

Alex did so, trying not to push against the door as hard as he had the first time he had knocked. Nevertheless, with a slight squeak the door swung open several more inches.

"Well, isn't this convenient." Alex pushed the door open even farther, but his effort to step into the room was halted by Sarah grabbing the sleeve of his jacket.

"You're not thinking about going in there?"

"Didn't you ever hear the saying 'opportunity knocks?'"

"Yes, and I also remember the saying 'the first dodo in is the deadest.'"

"Huh? Where did that come from?"

"My aunt says it all the time."

"It figures. Weirdness must run in your family."

"Alex, what if he's in there and he catches us in his apartment uninvited?"

"Well, what do you suggest?"

Sarah stood for a moment, obviously thinking. Then she stuck her head through the doorway and called in a loud whisper, "Mr. Evad?"

After a moment of silence, Alex stuck his head in behind Sarah's and shouted, "Mr. Evad," causing Sarah to almost jump out of her dress.

"Guess he's not here," said the boy, after stepping into what appeared to be a living room. "Okay, I'm going to search the place whether you want to or not."

"Alex, this is crazy. We could be arrested for trespassing."

The boy turned, placed his hand on the girl's shoulder, and smiled. "Be stout of heart, oh fearful wench. Do you want to live forever?"

"Alex, I can't," she whimpered. "I'm not brave like you. I've been in enough trouble already. I just can't."

"So why don't you go back down to the porch and watch the street. If you see Evad, you can warn me."

"Okay," she nodded, before having second thoughts. "Maybe we should go and get Tom. He could stand guard and then I could help you."

"One must strike while the iron is hot. The ogre who lives here could return at any time. Be a good girl and go stand guard."

The girl gave another nod and then turned to leave. "Good luck."

"Fortune favors the bold," said the boy, and then he disappeared inside the apartment.

She stood in the center of the front porch of the apartment building, continually moving her head from side to side so she could scan the street first in one direction and then the other. When the front door to the building behind her opened unexpectedly, she jerked and gave out a small yelp.

The couple who were exiting the building apologized for startling her. As the man and woman descended the front steps, Sarah overheard the woman say, "My, what a nervous Nelly."

The man gave his companion a knowing look. "I think that may have been Sarah Gould, you know, the one Jessica told us about who's in her classes."

"Oh, yes," nodded the woman. "The weird, obnoxious girl. You may be right—the glasses, the nose . . ."

Sarah's brows knitted and her eyebrows scrunched together. If the girl's eyes had been ray guns, the couple would have been transformed into smoldering cinders on the sidewalk. Without further hesitation, Sarah turned on her heels and marched back into the apartment building, up the steps, and into Evad's apartment. Alex was in a room adjoining the living room, examining a mass of papers covering the top of a desk. Sarah's sudden appearance in the doorway resulted in a shriek of surprise from Alex, and his nearly falling over the chair he had been standing behind.

"You about gave me a heart attack," he gasped. "Is Evad coming?"

"No, but I thought two of us could work faster than one."

"Well, ah . . . Don't you think one of us should stand lookout?"

"Whatever happened to all that fortune favors the bold stuff?" fumed Sarah.

"Touché. Okay, we'll go without a lookout. Try to keep your ears peeled for the sound of someone coming up the stairs. Then again,

Evad's such a skunk you could probably smell . . ."

"That better not have been the start of another nose joke," said the girl, glaring.

The only response from the boy was that of a sheepish grin that displayed a lot of teeth with braces.

"Did you find anything?" asked Sarah.

"So far just a locked room, probably to the bedroom, and all these papers here." The boy motioned to the desk beside him. The desk top was littered with what must have been a couple hundred pieces of notebook paper, all of which were filled with mathematical computations and equations. Sarah moved closer and picked up one of the pieces of paper to better examine it.

"I've had the chance to page through some books on advanced math and physics at my uncle's house. He's a physicist. I don't understand calculus and abstract algebra and such yet, but I'm familiar with some of the notation—things like integral signs and Greek letters . . ." The boy pointed to examples of each as he mentioned them. "Here's something my uncle called vector notation, but this stuff here—I have never seen anything like it."

Sarah put down the page she was holding and pointed to some notation on one of the other papers. "Look at this. It looks like a simple algebra equation. See here is where he's substituting numbers for the variables, and there's the answer, but where's the arithmetic?"

"Yes, I know. Strange, huh? Here's a simpler one. 0.0459678 divided by 1.2874593, and the answer is 0.0357042. Well, that looks about right, but I sure don't know anyone who could do that in their head, and I don't see where there's an adding machine or a slide rule around."

"I believe an idiots savant could do that in their head," said the girl.

"What's an idiots savant?"

"They are people with extraordinary arithmetic abilities. Apparently, some can even mentally multiply two numbers, each of a hundred digits."

"Wow," said Alex. "You think Evad's one of these idiot guys."

"Unfortunately, usually idiots savants are mentally less than normal in other areas. From what I've read about them, he doesn't behave like one. But if he's an alien and came here in a spaceship like you and Tom seem to believe, he probably does all the figuring with some kind of miniature calculating machine."

"Yeah, that figures." Seeing Sarah giving him a disgusted look, Alex chortled, "Oops, sorry for the pun."

"What I'm trying to say is if that's a real ray gun he has, then it wouldn't be surprising if he had some kind of calculating machine that could do all the arithmetic." The girl stepped back and swept the desk with her eyes. "But what's it all for? This can't have anything to do with his teaching science. He's obviously been really busy trying to solve some kind of complex problem, but we don't know enough about math and physics to possibly figure it out."

"Yeah, I'm with you there," said Alex. "Okay, let's try to attack this more systematically."

"How? And don't forget we probably don't have much time. He might return at any moment."

"Okay, first assume that all this has something to do with the conversation you overheard, that Evad's leaving for parts unknown, and that in turn has something to do with what we found in Sullivans Woods."

"How does that help us?"

"Oh, ye of little faith," scoffed the boy.

"I thought you were an agnostic? Why appeal to my faith?"

"Just bear with me, okay? Where was I?"

"You made an assumption."

"Yeah, right. Now he was working on solving a problem. Next we'll assume he solved it so where's the answer?" The boy pointed at a page lying somewhat in isolation from the rest. "Maybe, here."

The teens leaned closer to better examine the piece of paper. The final entries at the bottom of the page were arranged as if in a table.

.0004 Oct. 28 2204 - 0114
.0019 Oct. 29 2228 - 0104
.0285 Oct. 30 2330 - 0102
.9212 Nov. 1 0004 - 0052
.0355 Nov. 2 0058 - 0315
.0092 Nov. 2 0204 - 0544
.0033 Nov. 3 0250 - 0716
1.0

"Alex, you're a genius! Those dates must refer to now. It couldn't be just a coincidence that today is October thirty-first."

"I'm not sure about the genius part. More like dumb luck. But what do the numbers before and after the dates stand for?"

"The ones after look like military times, you know, twenty-four-hour military times." Alex shook his head to indicate that he didn't understand. "2204 means 22 hundred hours and 4 minutes. In other words, 10:04 p.m. And 0004 is 4 minutes past midnight. 0000 or 2400, they're the same, that is, midnight, and 1200 is noon. Get it?"

"Oh, neat. Let's see, the numbers following October thirtieth are separated by a dash, so would that mean a time from eleven-thirty last night and one-oh-two in the morning today?"

"I guess so. That seems to make sense."

"But today's missing," pointed out Alex. "There's no entry for October thirty-first."

"Yes, there is. You just said it. The time period after the October thirtieth entry spans both yesterday and today. See?"

"Yeah, I see. Boy, I feel stupid."

"But probably not as stupid as you look," giggled Sarah.

"Okay, I deserved that one."

"What time did you say you saw Evad and Serpens leave here last night?"

"About ten-thirty."

"That means they got to the woods about . . . ?"

"Hey! It must have been a little before eleven o'clock that I saw them going into the woods. And if this here is what we think it is, it means that something was going on in the woods between eleven-thirty and one-oh-two a.m. Holy mackerel, we're on to something here. Now if we could only figure out what the numbers to the left of the dates mean?"

Sarah gave her shoulders a shrug. They stood there, staring at the mysterious numbers, seemingly oblivious to the passage of time except for the ticking of a clock that sat on the table, until Sarah spoke up. "They could be probabilities."

"Huh?"

"See, they add up to one. He even wrote the sum below them. One-point-oh. The sum of the probabilities for an event should add up to one."

"Yeah, you might be right. Gee, you're smarter than you look."

"And you're dumber than you think."

"Okay. Maybe I deserved that one too. So. converting the numbers to percent, the one-point-oh of course converts to one hundred percent, that is, a certainty that something happens. The first number is .0004 which is only four-hundredths of a percent. Not much chance of anything going on Wednesday night."

"Nor Thursday night," said Sarah. "It was only 0.19 percent. But last night was 2.85, almost three percent."

"And tonight, well, actually it will be tomorrow morning, is a whopping ninety-two percent."

"If these are probabilities that means that whatever is going on is most likely to happen tonight between four and fifty-two minutes after midnight."

Alex straightened up. "If we're reading this right, we should find Evad and Serpens leaving for the woods tonight around eleven assuming it takes them about a half hour to get there and they target being there about a half hour early like they did last night. And that means that tonight is most likely the night of the big show."

Sarah nodded her head in agreement. "Let's leave now."

"Okay," said Alex. "I think we got what we came for." But as they exited the room on to the way to the front door, Alex hesitated.

Sarah also stopped. "Now what?"

Alex was staring at the locked bedroom door.

"Alex, let's go," said the girl, in a loud whisper.

The boy ignored her and instead reached into one of his pockets and pulled out a Boy Scout pocketknife. He lifted the can opener tool out of the knife's handle, approached the locked door, and began to fiddle with the bedroom door's lock.

"Alex, what are you doing? Let's go before Evad comes back."

There was a click and Alex triumphantly turned the door knob opening the door.

"Alex, please!" Sarah begged, but the boy was already through the open doorway into the room, after which Sarah heard a barely audible "Oh-my-gosh!"

Feeling beads of sweat forming on her forehead, Sarah entered the bedroom. Alex stood there with his back to her, his attention fixed on the large object lying on the floor beside the bed. It was split into two hollowed-out halves still attached at midpoint. Each section was a good eight feet in length and about three feet across, narrowing to points at each end. Both the inside and the outside of the pale brown halves were covered with what appeared to be a mass of sticky green spider webs. A queasy yellow liquid filled part of the bottom of one of the halves and the floor was stained with what appeared to be dried puddles of the same fluid. A musty, repugnant odor filled the room.

"What is it?" asked the frightened girl.

"A pod."

"What's a pod?"

"That's a pod. Didn't you see the movie *Invasion of the Body Snatchers?*"

"No. I don't understand."

"It's like a huge eggshell. Someone, or something, was growing inside that. Then it hatched."

"Hatched?" said the girl. "Oh-my-gosh, I remember Evad saying something to Serpens about something hatching."

"Yeah, that's right. They must have been talking about whatever came out of this thing."

"But what was it?"

"I don't know. Whatever it was, I don't think I want to meet it."

"Go long," yelled Tom. Brad took off in a sprint down the street. Tom waited for what seemed like a reasonable time factoring in the combination of Brad's present location and his speed, and then heaved a pass. The moment Tom released the ball, Brad, as if telepathic, looked back. Keeping his eye on the spiraling football to better judge its trajectory as he ran, Brad had no way of knowing that Nancy and Sandy, two neighborhood girls who each Saturday afternoon collected the money for Sandy's brother's newspaper route, were in the football's targeted landing zone. The resulting collision elicited screams from the girls and a cry of surprise from Brad, as the three figures collapsed onto the pavement and the bag of money Sandy had been holding went flying out of her hand, spilling coins and some dollar bills. In spite of everything, Brad had somehow managed to keep his focus and with a supreme effort had extended his arm, making a fantastic one hand catch of a football that had yet to hit the ground as it bounced off his head. The cushioning of his fall by the girls' bodies was no doubt a factor in allowing him to make the play.

As Brad rolled off the girls, he was met by howls of outrage. "You nincompoop! Get off, you creep!"

"Gosh, I'm sorry girls," said Brad, sounding genuinely sorry, and rubbing the spot on his head where the football had hit him. "But did you see that catch?"

"I could care less about your stupid catch," screamed Sandy, managing to stand. "Look at my dress."

Her friend Nancy sat up and began to examine a scrape on her knee. A loud meow made her glance in the direction of its owner. "Hi, Tiger," she said, smiling. Then she noticed the money strewn everywhere on the pavement. "The money!"

That sent the four teens on a mad scramble to pick up the scattered loot and return it to Sandy's money bag before either a car came by or the dollar bills were further scattered by a gust of wind. All the time Tom and Brad kept saying they were sorry and apologizing to the girls while Tiger sat on the curb, looking vaguely amused by the whole affair.

A familiar voice from behind them caused the four to pause. "Didn't your parents ever tell you morons not to play in the street?"

"Alex!" yelled Tom, as he was putting the last of the coins in Sandy's bag. "What did you find out?"

In answer Alex grinned. Sarah stood behind him.

"Yeah, what did you find out?" seconded Brad, ignoring the fee collectors.

"We're telling your parents," hissed Sandy. "Yours too, Tom."

"Get out of here," said Brad, changing his tone, "and the next time watch where you're walking." The two girls stomped off, engaged in a discussion about whose parents to call first.

"Well, any luck?" asked Tom, repeating his question.

Disappointment covered Alex's face. "Evad wasn't home."

"Shoot!" said Brad.

"So, you didn't learn anything?" asked Tom.

"I didn't say that." Alex broke into a big smile. "I just said that Evad wasn't home."

"Huh?"

"Evad left his door unlocked," said Sarah, "so Alex just walked on in and started snooping around."

"He WHAT?" exclaimed Brad.

Brad, Sarah and Tom were sitting on the top step of Alex's front porch. Alex was pacing back and forth on the walkway at the bottom of the steps, fiddling with his yo-yo while he provided the details about all that Sarah and he had discovered in Evad's apartment. Sarah sat between Brad and Tom and would on occasion add something to what was otherwise an Alex monologue. It seemed to Tom that Sarah was sitting uncomfortably close to him, almost to the point of leaning against his arm. Maybe she's cold, reasoned the boy. Tiger was curled up in Sarah's lap, letting out an occasional purr as the girl stroked the tawny hair on his back. Tom thought that strange as the cat usually sat on his lap when he was at the Banyons.

Having finished his tale, Alex paused a moment.

"Did I leave anything out?"

"I don't think so," reassured the girl, as the front door of the house opened behind them. Mrs. Banyon stuck her head out.

"Oh, you're back," said Mrs. Banyon, noticing her son. "Has the mail come?"

"Not, yet," Tom answered.

"Okay, would you let me know when it arrives?"

"Sure, Mom," said Alex, as his mother disappeared back inside and closed the door. Alex fixed Tom with his eyes. "Say, did my mom ask you where I was while we were gone?"

"Huh, huh," said Tom. "I told her you and Sarah wanted some time together alone, so——"

"You WHAT!" yelled Sarah and Alex at the same time, making Tiger jump.

Both Brad and Tom started chuckling. They stopped when they noticed the girl standing at the bottom of the steps. She bore something of a resemblance to Sarah, except for being younger, not wearing glasses, and possessing a decidedly smaller proportioned nose.

"What'cha doing?" asked Anne, Sarah's sister.

"We're doing something important," said Sarah, trying to sound important, "and it's none of your business so go home."

"Okay," said Anne, seemingly unruffled by her sister's reply, "Mom, sent me to find you. I'll tell her you're here. She said to tell you to be sure you're not late for dinner."

No one said anything until it looked like Anne was out of earshot. "So, Einar, what's the plan for tonight?" said Tom.

"Okay, instead of terrorizing trick-or-treaters tonight as usual, we'll all tell our parents we're tired and insist on going to bed early. Then we'll sneak out of the house and rendezvous at the corner hedge in my back yard at ten-thirty, not a minute later. That should give us plenty of time to get to the clearing and hide before Serpens and Evad show up. And when they do, well—we'll finally know what this is all about."

"Cool," said Brad. "Okay, I'm in."

"Me too," said Tom.

Sarah started to say something, hesitated, and then finally got out, "Me three."

"No way," said Alex. "This isn't a job for girls."

"Besides all the screaming and stuff might give us away," added Brad.

"I'll be quiet. Honest. I can be quiet."

"Hear that?" said Brad. "A quiet girl. Isn't that one of those ox-and-morons?"

"That's oxymoron, Brad," corrected the boy genius.

Tom put his hand on Sarah's head and turned it so she faced him. "Did you see *Invasion of the Body Snatchers?*"

"No. I'm not allowed to watch scary movies."

"Well, if you had, you would realize that anything that comes out of a pod is really bad—and I mean really bad like some bloodsucking piece of primordial ooze."

"Really, Tom, you're talking about a movie. We have no idea what was inside that thing."

"Come on, Sarah," said Alex. "That thing, whatever it is, hatched in Evad's bedroom. And then there was the part about eating someone's brains. If that's not enough to give you the creeps, I don't know what is."

"But you're all going. If it's so dangerous . . ."

"No girls and that's final," said Tom.

Sarah glared at Tom for a moment, then turned to Alex. Alex shrugged his shoulders. Sarah stood and hurried down the steps. She stopped at the sidewalk.

"Alex Banyon, you would have never figured out what all that stuff in Evad's apartment meant if it hadn't been for me." She then sprinted across the street to her house.

"Well, men, that leaves the three of us," said Brad. "We rendezvous here at ten-thirty, right?"

"Right," agreed Tom. "Not a minute later."

"All for one and one for all," said Alex.

"Semper fi," said Tom.

"Victory or death!" yelled Brad, raising a quenched fist in the air.

"Let's not get carried away," said Alex, looking at Brad as if he were some sort of fruitcake.

Chapter 14
Sullivans Woods

As the Jones family ate their evening meal, a pair of inhuman eyes carefully studied Brad's every move. The creature, crouched under the dinnerware cabinet, nodded in satisfaction as Brad took another gulp of milk and then placed the glass back on the dining table. The boy picked up his fork and speared a piece of ham. As he started to lift the morsel to his mouth, he yawned. The yawn appeared to startle the boy, as well as the wave of fatigue that seemed to have come out of nowhere, sweeping through his body. Thoughts raced through the boy's mind. "Why am I so tired all of a sudden? This is no time to be tired. Maybe I'm not getting enough sleep because of those nightmares I've had the last couple of nights. Maybe I should take a nap after supper? Yeah, that might be a good idea. I'll set my alarm clock just in case."

Brad forced the piece of meat into his open mouth and started to chew. As he did so he found himself yawning again.

"Sleepy?" asked his mother.

"Yeah, a little. Maybe I'll grab a quick nap after supper."

"Okay, sweetie. That might be a good idea."

Still unnoticed by the Joneses, the four-legged creature, covered in a soft, orange-tan fur, noiselessly scurried out from under the cabinet and crossed the dining room floor into the next room.

It had been a good hour since the last of the trick-or-treaters had knocked at the front door. Alex gave a yawn attracting the attention of his parents who were watching TV with him in the living room of the Banyon home.

"Tired?" asked his mother.

"Yeah," answered Alex, giving another fake yawn. "Think I'll turn in early tonight."

"Okay, dear. Give me a kiss before you go up."

Alex walked over to where his parents sat on the couch, leaned down, and, as he did every evening before retiring, kissed his mother on the cheek. As he started to straighten up, Mrs. Banyon grabbed his hand. The move was so unexpected that it surprised the boy. He was even more startled by the look in his mother's eyes that conveyed to Alex a terrible longing. Neither the boy nor his mother moved. Time momentarily seemed at a standstill, she holding onto his hand, their eyes locked on one another.

Finally, Alex broke the spell. "What?"

As he uttered the word, his mother's expression changed. "Oh, nothing," she replied.

Mr. Banyon shifted his gaze from the TV to his son, and then to his wife.

"Anything the matter?" he asked.

Mrs. Banyon gave her head a quick shake, signifying that every-thing was okay, and released her son's hand. Then she stood up and gave him a long, forceful hug. Before she released him, she said in a soft voice, "I love you, Alex. I'll always love you." Alex could have sworn that he saw tears in her eyes.

Alex hesitated a moment, then turned to his father. "Night, Dad."

"Goodnight, son," his father said, turning his attention back to the TV.

Up in his room Alex changed into his pajamas in case his mom or dad decided to look in on him. Earlier he had carefully hidden a change of clothes, his jacket, and a flashlight under his bed. He climbed onto the mattress and checked the clock that sat on the night stand. No sooner had he done so then the door to the room opened and his older brother entered.

"Don't you know how to knock?" asked Alex, attempting to disguise the uneasiness he actually felt.

"I only knock for my superiors," said his brother, Daryl. Daryl crossed the room, pulled the chair away from Alex's desk, and sat on it backwards so he faced his brother. "So where did my little, scheming brother sneak off to last night?"

"Huh?" said Alex. He put on his "innocent me" face.

"You heard me, and don't give me that 'wax in my ears' crap you give Dad and Mom whenever you wish to avoid answering a question."

"Oh, ah, last night?" Alex decided a change in tactics was in order. "And what business is that of yours?"

"Okay," said the older brother, now showing a smirk. "I'll tell Mom and Dad and let them beat it out of you."

Accepting that his bluff had been called, Alex lied. "Ah, I went out to look at the stars. You know me and astronomy." There was no way that a moron of an older brother was going to outmaneuver the boy genius of East Pencreek.

"No, you didn't. I checked. You weren't in the backyard."

Nice try, but Alex was starting to get into stride now. "I went over to Tom's. If you don't believe me you can call him."

"I recall it being pretty cloudy last night."

"So? We astronomers are eternal optimists. You never know when the cloud cover might break."

"You didn't get home until after eleven-thirty."

"So? It was Friday night. What does that matter?"

"Curfew's at eleven in this township. What do you think Mom and Dad's reaction would be if the police show up at our door late some evening with you in tow?"

"Oh, come off it. Curfew, snur-few. Our township police couldn't catch a cripple in a broken wheelchair let alone a thirteen-year-old boy." Alex flashed his older brother a victorious grin, then quickly changed his expression to a more humble one. "Okay, you're right. The next time I want to stay out late, I'll ask Mom and Dad first."

Daryl stared at his younger brother for a moment before rising and returning the chair to the desk. On his way out, he stopped when he reached the bedroom door. "Alex, you might be another Einstein or something, but even the smartest people in the world can do the dumb things. Just don't do anything stupid, okay?"

"Okay," said Alex. He offered Daryl both a smile and a thumbs-up. Daryl gave his head a shake and closed the door behind him.

Alex checked the time again. He would get dressed at about a quarter past ten and exit the house by his bedroom window. The window opened to the roof of the back porch next to which a tree grew. The tree was conveniently located to allow a daring soul a means of easy descent to the ground. Sneaking out without being seen would again be a piece-of-cake.

Although neither boy had shared his plan with the other, Tom's tactics were nearly identical to those of Alex. First there was the feigned sleepiness followed by an early retirement to bed. Tom had also hidden a change of clothing under his bed. As he donned his pajamas, he could hear his parents and younger sister getting ready for bed. It was ten o'clock. Fortunately for Tom, his parents liked to retire early. As the boy was checking the time on his bedside clock, there came a gentle knock at his door.

"Come in."

Nancy Cobalt entered. She hadn't as yet changed for the evening. Without saying a word, she crossed the room and sat on the edge of the boy's bed.

"What's up, Mom?" asked Tom, trying to keep his voice relaxed.

His mom at first didn't answer. She sat there looking at him, studying him with deep, loving eyes for what seemed to the boy like the longest of times. Tom began to feel self-conscious. As his mother's silence continued, Tom imagined that his face had the word "guilt" written on it in large, black letters. Finally, he could no longer tolerate the silence.

"Mom, is something wrong?"

In response, she gave him a faint smile. "No, Tommy. Everything is fine. I was just thinking."

"About what?"

Mrs. Cobalt took her son's hand between hers and gently rubbed it. "When you were a baby, I often worried so. I would sit for hours in your room, watching you sleep, and pray to God that nothing bad would ever happen to you." She paused. "I guess it was partly because you were our first. Goodness knows, I certainly never worried like that about Caroline when she was a baby." She looked down but continued to softly glide her hand over his. "Even when you were no longer a baby, I would often stand by your doorway when you were asleep and watch you for the longest time." Her eyes shifted back to Tom, and the smile returned. In the dim light of the room, Tom could make out streaks of moisture starting to move down her cheeks. "I would often wonder what my little Tommy would grow up to be. You're growing up so fast. How many days I wished I could slow the flow of time. But time goes on. We can't stop time, can we?"

"No, Mom." Now he could feel his own eyes starting to moisten. "We can't stop time."

"It's just that it's been a while since I have stopped by to watch you when you were sleeping. I can't explain it, but I thought I had to check on you tonight." With that, she released his hand, leaned over and gave her son a strong hug, just as Mrs. Banyon had hugged her son that evening, but Tom's mom held it even longer. Tom returned her embrace, and for a reason he couldn't explain he felt terribly sad—sadder than he had ever felt before in his entire life. At that moment he wanted to confess everything—to tell her his suspicions about Sleinad Evad, about the ray gun, and about what Alex, Brad and he were planning to do that night. "Mom . . ."

His mother released her hold. "I'm sorry, Tommy. You're growing up, and there's nothing I can do about it. It's greedy of me to want to keep you a boy forever. It's that, for some reason, I have this awful feeling tonight. The fears I had when you were a baby seemed to have come back. I can't help it. I fear that I might lose you. And when those thoughts came back—well, I had to come in to make sure everything was okay."

"Everything's okay, Mom." Tom leaned forward and again embraced his mother. "No matter what may happen, I will always be okay. I will always love you."

"I know. I know." Mrs. Cobalt paused to wipe the tears from her eyes. "Some days I fear I'm just too much of a mother for my own good. I guess all mothers are like that."

"No, mom, all mothers aren't like that. You're the best mother in the whole world."

"Thank you, Tommy." She patted his hand again, then leaned over and kissed his forehead. "I love you," she said. Then she reached into the pocket of her dress and retrieved an object which she pressed into his hand. "Here, Tommy. I want you to have this."

Tom looked at the flat, round, metallic object, about the diameter of a half dollar. A thin leather strap passed through a hole near one of its edges. In the semi-darkness of the room he couldn't make out what it was. He gave his mother a puzzled look.

"It's a Saint Christopher's medallion," replied his mother to his unasked question.

"You mean like a Catholic saint?" His mother shook her head in the affirmative. "But we're not Catholic."

"I know. It was your grandfather's. Of course, he wasn't Catholic either, but he always swore by it. He wanted you to have it. For some reason, I just remembered his wish tonight."

"What do you mean, 'he swore by it?'"

"It's supposed to protect travelers. Daddy—that is, your grandfather, believed it worked for everybody—whether you were Catholic or not."

"But, Mom, I'm not going on any trips."

"I know. I know it all sounds silly. I know you're not superstitious either. But for my sake, will you remember to carry it with you whenever you go somewhere?"

"Sure, Mom." Tom studied the medallion. "Hey, there's something inscribed on the back."

"Your grandfather's initials. I don't know why he bothered to do that."

"I think it's kind of neat. Thanks. I'll be sure to keep it with me."

His mother gave him another hug, then stood up and walked slowly to the door where she turned and gave Tom a weak smile. After she closed the door, Tom could hear her crying as she moved down the hall.

As Mrs. Gould passed the kitchen doorway on her way upstairs to check on Sarah's sister, she noticed Sarah sitting on a chair by the kitchen table staring at the wall clock.

"It was really nice of you to take Anne trick-or-treating tonight." At the sound of her mother's voice, Sarah almost fell out of the chair, as if she had been caught performing some grave misdeed.

"I'm sorry, honey," her mother apologized. "I didn't mean to startle you."

"It's okay. I was just—thinking."

"About what, might I ask?"

"Nothing," came the patented answer.

"Okay." Mrs. Gould maneuvered around the table to sit on a chair next to her daughter. "Is there anything you want to talk about?"

Sarah's expression was that of a child who had just swallowed her mom's wedding ring. She broke eye contact with her mother. "No."

The mother leaned closer to the girl and gently stroked her hair. "I understand what a stressful week it's been for you, but now that you have some friends, I think you'll find everything has changed for the better."

"Yes." Sarah was still staring at the tabletop. "I suppose so."

"You're sure there's nothing you wish to talk about?"

"Yes. I'm sure."

Mrs. Gould gave a sigh. Her conversations with Sarah of late often seemed to end in a sigh. "Well, good night." She dropped her hand to her lap then rose, giving her daughter a pained look.

Sarah jumped up and threw her arms around her mother. She started crying. "I'm sorry, Mom. I'm so sorry. I didn't mean to be such an awful daughter. I can't—" The words were cut short by more sobs.

Mrs. Gould returned Sarah's embrace. "It's okay, Sarah. There's nothing to be sorry about." She began to slowly rock her daughter in her arms. "I love you. I couldn't ask for a more wonderful daughter."

"That's not true," said Sarah. "I've caused you and Dad all sorts of grief. It's been all my fault."

"It's not your fault. You're just a child."

She released her hug and knelt before her daughter, gently wiping away the girl's tears with her fingers. Sarah lowered her head to meet her mother's gaze.

"Listen, Sarah. You're a very intelligent person. All your life you'll probably be running into people who are envious of that intelligence. Some of them may try to belittle you. Some may even try to hurt you, to make your life miserable. You'll just have to learn to ignore those people. What's important is that you do what you think is right. You will find that people who are your true friends will respect you if you stick to your principles. As for the others—well, there will always be others." Mrs. Gould hesitated a moment, before continuing.

"But, I think you should also live by the Golden Rule." She smiled. "Try to use a little tact sometimes. It will make things easier, believe me."

Sarah returned her mother's smile. Then as her mother stood, she gave her another hug.

"Okay, now I think you should be off to bed, after all it's past ten."

Sarah glanced at the clock again. It was a quarter past ten. If she was going to beat the boys to the woods she would have to leave soon. The thought that she might actually go through with it filled her mind with panic. "Mom," she said as she tightened her embrace, "just remember I love you and Dad."

"I know you love us." Mrs. Gould patted her daughter's back.

"Whatever happens, please remember that I love you." Sarah buried her head against her mom's breast.

It was something in the tone of Sarah's voice that Mrs. Gould found disturbing. Sarah had never acted this way before. "I know you love us," repeated Mrs. Gould. At that Sarah tore herself away from her mother and ran upstairs to her room.

Tom tested the flashlight. "Drats!" The batteries were weak. Well, that couldn't be helped. He didn't want to take the time rummaging through the house to find fresh batteries. Besides he might alert his parents. Hopefully, Alex and Brad would have flashlights. Replacing the flashlight on the shelf at the top of the basement stairs, Tom carefully closed the cellar door. He walked quietly across the darkened kitchen, opened the outside door and stepped onto the back porch. Just as carefully, so as not to make more noise than necessary, he closed the door to the house. As the latch clicked into place, a voice said, "Going somewhere?"

Although there was no moon, the reflected glow of the nearest streetlight was enough to allow Tom to identify his father sitting on the porch swing. The boy might have expected to find his father there on a warm summer evening, but it was the end of October, Halloween, hardly the time to relax outside on the back porch.

"Er—well—I couldn't sleep so I thought I would take a walk."

"Really?" was his dad's only immediate comment. Then the ashes in the bowl of his pipe glowed orange as his father took another puff.

"Yes, sir."

"I'm having trouble sleeping myself. Mind if I walk with you?" In the dark, Tom couldn't make out the smile on his father's face.

The boy knew he had to do some fast thinking. "No, not at all. I thought I would walk over to Alex's. It looks like a good night for observing. If I know Alex, he'll be out there with his telescope."

Tom's father changed the subject. "Your mother was crying tonight. She said she couldn't help thinking about how fast you and Kattie are growing up."

"Yeah. I know."

Mr. Cobalt leaned forward on the swing. Although it was too dark to see them, Tom knew that his father's eyes were fixed on him. "Tom, do you think that not telling someone about something important is the same as lying?"

That caused the boy to take a nervous swallow. To buy some time before answering, the boy walked to the edge of the porch and took a seat, not looking in the direction of the swing, but instead pretending to study the stars. "I suppose so."

"Is there anything you want to tell me?"

Tom bent his head low and gave it a shake from left to right. Then he turned his face in the direction of his father. "Dad, I can't. Believe me I just can't. You would never believe me."

"Does it have something to do with this science teacher of yours and what happened at school this week?"

"Yes, but if I tell you, you'll think I'm crazy. All I can say is that you'll have to trust me on this one."

For a long moment neither father nor son said anything. Both sat there and watched the stars perform their timeless magic, as if they were the keepers of time itself. Then the father spoke. "Okay, you've never violated my trust. Just answer me this. Are you in any kind of trouble?"

"No. I swear to you, I'm not in any kind of trouble."

"Is Alex in trouble?"

"Are you kidding? Alex is never in trouble, at least not real trouble."

At that his father laughed. "Anything I can do to help?"

For a brief instance Tom was almost tempted to invite his dad along, but then thought better of the idea. The presence of his father might discourage Alex or Brad from going through with the plan. "I'm afraid not. But in a couple of hours it should all be over. We'll know for sure whether Evad is . . ." Tom stopped. Had he said too much?

"From another planet?" was his father's helpful suggestion.

The boy gave a faint moan. He had really blown it.

"I thought so." Tom's dad stood up. He took a deep breath. "You better get going or you might be late meeting Alex and whomever else might be involved in this secret scheme of yours."

"Huh?" Tom also stood up. "You mean it? I can go?"

"Yes, but be careful." Mr. Cobalt gave his son a hug and patted him on the back. "From what I've heard of him, this Evad character might just be from another planet."

Tom descended the porch stairs, then broke into a jog.

"There's no moon tonight," called Mr. Cobalt. "Do you want a flashlight?"

"No," said the boy over his shoulder. "I'm sure Alex or Brad will have one. Besides," he laughed, "if a flying saucer shows up, what good will it do?"

"Goodbye, Tom," said Mr. Cobalt in a voice so low that it was more of a comment to himself than to the boy. He then asked himself, "Why did I say 'goodbye?'" He watched the shadowy figure of his son until it disappeared around the corner, headed in the direction of Alex's house. And then he uttered one more phrase, and after he had done so it dawned on him that he had no idea why he had said it. It was, "Spaceman's luck."

The girl drew the jacket more tightly around her. The night was colder than she had expected. She stopped to pull up one of her long wool stockings. Why couldn't she have had a brother? She could have borrowed a pair of his jeans. This wearing of dresses and skirts everywhere was just plain dumb. She remembered her mother's words. "Young ladies wear skirts. Young men wear pants." At the thought of her mother, an uneasiness flooded her soul. Was this a good idea? So far nothing had gone amiss. She was probably ahead of the boys, but it wouldn't do any harm to check. As she had done sporadically since leaving the house, she glanced behind her. As she did so she swore that she saw someone or something quickly duck behind a parked car halfway down the block. Was she imagining things? The streetlights, although adequately illuminating the intersections where they stood, cast little light away from the crossroads. Perhaps it had been a dog. If she turned back now, she might run into the boys and that would spoil everything. She ventured on.

A few minutes later, she stood across the street from Sullivans Woods. A less than cheerful thought entered her mind. "It's the point of no return. Gosh, that sounds so final." Again, the girl cast a glance behind her. No one was in sight, but the homes here had lots of hedges and bushes in their front yards, plenty of places for someone who wished to remain unseen to hide. On top of that, the nearest streetlight was burnt out. Sarah stood perfectly still and listened. The gentle whisper of the wind on the fallen leaves was the only sound that came to her ears. She turned and looked at the woods. Perhaps it would have appeared even spookier if the moon had been out to reveal the barren branches of the naked trees. October 31, 1959. Halloween had not more than an hour to go in East Pencreek, Pennsylvania. Sarah took in a great, deep, breath, turned on her flashlight and shined it across the road. There was the spot where she and the boys had entered the woods that afternoon. The spaces between the trunks of the trees illuminated by the weak beam of her flashlight seemed to ooze with impenetrable black gloom. For a moment, the girl's thoughts turned to her mother and father and Anne and the warm bed that awaited her back home. Then they were replaced by images of Tom and Alex, and of the great, unknown mystery that awaited possible solution in just another hour or so. Heck, what was inky darkness to a thirteen-year-old who defied peers, adults and authority in the name of truth, justice and always-being-right? Sarah silently muttered to herself, "Darn the second thoughts, full speed ahead!" A vision of Admiral Farragut crossed her mind, as she boldly stepped onto the street pavement. She jumped back with a shriek as a black cat scurried in front of her. Catching her breath, the teenager laughed at herself, "How appropriate for Halloween," she thought.

From behind a hedge but two houses away, a creature not of human form watched the girl's every move.

"It's almost eleven," said the blond-haired youth, shining the flashlight beam on his wristwatch. "Where is he?"

"Well, we sure can't go in your house and call him," said his companion, keeping his voice low. "Time's running out. I say we leave without him. If Brad catches up, he catches up."

"I agree," said Alex. "If we wait any longer we might run into Evad." The boy raised a clenched fist and whispered, "Hail Ragnar."

Tom returned the salute with a "Hail Einar," and the two were off.

The beam of her flashlight caught the wooden platform that stood in the center of the clearing. Everything looked about as she remembered it from that afternoon except spookier. She traced a circle with the beam around the edge of the clearing searching for a suitable hiding place. What if she picked the same place as the boys? Well, that would be their tough luck. There would be no way they could make her leave, and if they tried to argue with her she could point out that the longer they did so, the more likely the plan would be ruined by the arrival of Evad and Serpens.

A twig snapped from the direction of the path behind her. Sarah jumped, quickly stifled a scream and swung the light around, aiming it up the path. She had removed her glasses for fear of scratching them on a branch as she maneuvered through the woods, so it was a few seconds before she recovered them from a pocket of her jacket and put them on. Even with the glasses, she couldn't make out anything unusual, but the path was far from straight. It disappeared after a curve but a few yards from where she stood. Perhaps it was the boys and, having seen her light, they were trying to sneak up on her? She quickly switched off the beam and stood there, listening for any unusual sounds, but the only ones that greeted here were the occasional rustle of some leaves by the wind and that of her own deep breathing. With each additional breath she seemed to doubt more and more the wisdom of her decision, and could only envision one awful thing after another happening to her, alone in a dark, creepy woods at midnight on Halloween.

A nearby owl gave out its distinctive call. It startled her and, at the same time, broke the spell of impending doom that had settled over her. What creature as wise as an owl would hang around here if danger were afoot? With renewed determination Sarah turned her light back on and made her way across the clearing. Her search for a hiding place ended with a spot a good five feet from the clearing's edge. She carefully made her way through the underbrush and, settling on the ground, turned off the flashlight. The girl hugged her knees with her arms and gave an involuntary shiver. The woods slowly came alive with sounds, all sorts of sounds. She certainly wasn't alone, but the rational part of her mind told her that there was nothing to fear. The irrational side conjured up all sorts of dreadful things lurking in the darkness, studying her, and creeping closer.

"Darn it. Watch where you're going," said Alex. "You stepped on my heel again"

"Sorry. It's hard to see with you in front of me," said the taller of the two.

"Well, if you would have brought your flashlight, this would be easier. Don't walk so close."

Tom held back some. "The clearing shouldn't be too far ahead. Ouch!" Tom went crashing to the turf.

"What happened?" Alex aimed the beam of his light at his friend who lay sprawled face down on the damp, leaf-covered ground.

"I think I tripped on a root."

Not far away, Sarah held back a giggle. Another minute passed, and the clearing was illuminated by Alex's light. Sarah peered past the thin trunk of a sapling, being careful to make no sound. She was surprised to see two boys instead of the expected three. From their voices she was able to determine that Brad was the absent one. For the next minute or so the two boys stood part way into the clearing and repeated Sarah's strategy of searching for a suitable hiding place using Alex's flashlight. They finally selected a spot not twenty feet from Sarah's location.

"Okay, let's get comfortable and I'll turn off the light."

"The sooner the better," said Tom, "in case Evad isn't too far behind."

"Hail Ragnar." Alex kept his voice low as he gave his friend the clenched fist salute of a Viking.

"Hail, Einar," whispered Tom, returning the salute.

"Hail Bozo and Clarabell the Clown," thought Sarah to herself. "What a couple of morons—well, Alex maybe, but not Tom."

There was a click and the flashlight beam disappeared.

"Not a word," whispered Alex. "His hearing might be more sensitive than anything we can imagine."

"In that case he'll probably be able to hear my heart beating."

"Yeah. Well, we'll just have to hope for the best."

Tom didn't find his friend's statement too reassuring.

In all the commotion caused by the arrival of the two boys, Sarah had not sensed the presence of a shadowy form steadily but silently making its way through the woods towards the spot where she sat in wait. With seemingly supernatural ease the creature carefully placed first one of its feet and then another upon the dead leaves and twigs that littered the forest floor so as to make no sound discernable to the ears of the humans. Every possible pitfall that might have announced its presence was avoided for its vision was such that the dark landscape appeared to it as illuminated as it would have been to a human in the light of day. When the thing was finally within a foreleg's reach of the girl's back, it slowly settled on its haunches, and then sank farther into a comfortable resting position on the ground. And there it sat, silent except for a gentle breathing that seemed to blend with the sound of the breeze, the girl completely unaware of its presence. As the stars continued their steady march above the treetops, marking the relentless, never ceasing passage of time, the creature ran over in its mind what its next course of action would be. As it did so it casually examined the arsenal of weapons it was never without, as if to guarantee all was in working order. For years it had anticipated the events that would unravel in the clearing that evening. It was supremely confident that it would not fail in its mission.

There was no logical explanation why a premonition came to Sarah that something was watching her. The creature that studied the girl with a pair of malevolent eyes that could pierce through the darkness of the night had done nothing to alert Sarah to its presence. Still

Sarah had the feeling that someone or something was sitting behind her. The fact that the hairs on the nape of her neck were standing on end clinched the argument. Attempting to make as little noise as possible, Sarah slowly unclasped her arms from around her knees. As she did so her body gave a shudder. Slowly she began to twist her body, at the same time turning her head so as to be able to look behind her. Sarah stared into near total blackness. All she could make out were the dim trunks of some nearby trees. She was about to reach out a hand to feel the space where her eyes were attempting to focus when Tom's voice broke the silence.

"Any idea what time it is?"

Sarah turned back around and shifted her gaze to the spot where she calculated the boys to be.

"Not so loud, you nincompoop," came Alex's hushed voice. "Do you want to tell the whole world we're here?"

"Sorry, but, hey, you're telling me to shut up louder than I was asking you what time it was?"

"I was not louder, and—will you just shut up!"

"Okay, okay. I said I was sorry."

"Keep your voice down."

"Okay," responded Tom, in what was now a loud whisper.

The unexpected outburst from the two boys caused Sarah to forget her suspicion of being watched. Instead her anger rose as she recalled how the boys had said that this was no mission for a girl. Those two were about to blow the whole thing.

For no more than a couple of minutes the forest was again undisturbed by human voices. Then in a loud whisper, whose owner Sarah immediately identified as Alex, the girl heard, "This reminds me of that game of capture-the-flag we played during the last camping trip."

"Yeah. Remember when Benny came running back yelling that he had the flag, and it turned out to be Will's snot-rag?"

That brought a chortle from Alex, quickly joined by one from Tom.

"Too bad we didn't bring any water," said Alex.

"Why?"

"Because I have some Fizzies in my pocket."

"Cool."

"God help me," thought Sarah, "I could strangle them. And they talk about girls being chatty."

Again there was a period of quiet that was finally broken by what sounded to the girl like the call of a distant owl.

"Sounds like an owl," came Tom's whisper.

"Yeah," agreed the other boy.

Just as Sarah was having thoughts about jumping up and shouting at the boys, "Will you imbeciles shut up," there came to her ears the sound of movement from the direction of the path. Although it was a moonless night, by now her eyes had adjusted sufficiently to the blackness to make out the shapes of trees against the night sky, more so in the direction of the path, where the barren tree tops were silhouetted against the distant glow from the town's streetlights. Although a few scattered clouds graced the sky, the Milky Way was clearly visible against the cold black ink of endless space. The Pleiades rode high on the celestial sphere with Orion rising in the east and the Great Square of Pegasus positioned to the west. It was a magnificent stage for the drama that was about to unfold.

"Whoever it is isn't using a flashlight," Alex whispered.

"Shush," came the reply. "Does it surprise you that they wouldn't need one?"

The boys focused all their senses in the direction from which the sounds were emanating. Not long after, at the spot where they imagined the path to enter the clearing, a large, indistinct shape emerged from out of the blackness. As it moved closer its appearance sharpened into that of a tall human form carrying a large bag on its shoulder. The first figure was immediately followed by a second. About where one would imagine the eyes of the first apparition to be, there materialized a pair of soft, green flashes. Sarah felt her body begin to tremble. She couldn't stop herself from shaking. What had she done? Whatever had possessed her to come here tonight?

Unknown to the teens, the two newcomers were men of long military experience. If they had suspected that someone might be concealed nearby, they would have been on the alert and no doubt would have easily detected the teens. But instead, perhaps due in part to the anticipation of the events that they hoped were about to unfold, their thoughts were focused on the immediate task before them. The first figure stopped next to the raised platform where he dropped his baggage to the ground. His companion stopped a few paces behind him. As Tom focused on the second figure, he was startled again by what his mind perceived to be a pair of faint green flashes. Or was he just imagining things? The boy had little time to reflect on what was reality and what was his imagination, for from the spot where the first two men had emerged into the clearing, there appeared a third specter.

Tom felt Alex touch his sleeve. The boy could imagine his friend blowing their cover by whispering in far too loud of voice, "There's three of them."

Tom frantically shook his head as his mind seemed to explode while at the same time he silently mouthed the words, "I know!" To the taller teen's great relief, his companion remained silent.

It was too dark to be able to identify any of the three intruders, although Tom noted that the latecomer's face was a dark void with no hint of faint, green flickers. The boy now felt confident that the one who had first entered the clearing was Sleinad Evad.

That figure knelt, turning his attention to the bag that lay at his feet. A blue glow appeared from the vicinity of the bag, helping to illuminate the man enough that Tom had no doubt he was indeed the science teacher from hell. Evad started to exchange his outer garments with new attire he had drawn from the duffle bag, after which he got to his feet, the silhouette of his body being outlined by the faint glow of the town lights that filtered through the trees. Whatever it was that Evad had donned, except for a thick, doughnut shaped collar around his neck, the new clothing was most form fitting. The man reached his left hand towards the collar. There was a faint sound of clicks. The collar seemed to expand upward in a series of jerks, quickly encasing Evad's head in what appeared to be some sort of cylindrical shaped helmet. Tom noted that the helmet sported a pair of identical, blue, luminescent "eyes," matching the shape and size of a pair of glasses or goggles. Evad bent over and pulled another item from the bag. Perhaps a dozen or so tiny lights glowed from various parts of the new article. The man proceeded to fit it around his waist, in the manner of someone putting on a heavy, wide belt. He lifted two more objects from the bag, holding one in each hand. They too were each studded with several faint lights. With distinct snaps that to Tom's ears sounded like pistols being shoved into holsters, the objects disappeared from sight. Tom mouthed the words, "Ray guns." The darkness continued to obscure most of the details as to what was going on in the center of the clearing, but none of the three onlookers doubted that their most incredible suspicions were being confirmed. Neither boy would have been surprised if from out of the night sky a flying saucer suddenly appeared.

The dark apparition next glanced at its wrist as if viewing a watch or some similar device. He turned his gaze upward towards the constellation Pegasus, then again knelt. There was a sound like the closing of a zipper. Evad picked up the bag and tossed it in the direction of the second figure to have entered the clearing. With a deft move, the science teacher mounted the platform and walked to its center.

He stood there, arms folded across his chest, legs spread at shoulder width. With the exception of the soft radiance of some of the lights on his belt, and the glow of the two viewing ports that pierced the helmet he wore, he resembled an unmoving, three-dimensional shadow.

The man in whose direction Evad had tossed the bag reached

down, grasped it, and slung it over one shoulder where it hung by a strap. As Tom studied the second being he again imagined he saw a pair of faint green flashes from the vicinity of its eyes. Tom concluded that it was Serpens, but as to the third figure's identity, he had no guess.

Something seemed to snap inside the boy's brain, and then his mind was screaming, "Wake up! Wake up!" He opened his eyes to see Tom standing there, holding a ray gun aimed directly at him.

"Too late, Brad," his friend smirked, his eyes taking on a malevolent look. "You blew it. Too late, too late." He could see Tom's finger begin to squeeze the weapon's trigger. There was a flash . . .

Brad jerked awake. "What?" He sat up and glanced at the alarm clock on the nightstand next to his bed. It said five minutes past midnight. "What?" he repeated, this time even louder, a note of panic in his voice. He had overslept. How could he have overslept? The boy's mind screamed at itself in a rage. He was sure he had set the alarm. Why hadn't it gone off? He picked up the clock. The alarm hand pointed to ten o'clock. He turned the clock over. The alarm set lever indicated "Off." How could that be? He definitely remembered having set the alarm. Had it gone off and had he awoken, and then, his mind still drowsy, had he turned it off and fallen back asleep? The mission! Was it too late to complete the mission?

Brad stumbled out of bed, grabbed his jacket from the bedpost, and stuffed his arms into its sleeves. After shoving his stocking covered feet into a pair of shoes, he reached under his bed and drew out a knapsack. He threw one of the pouch's straps over his left shoulder, and then scooted over to a large wooden toy box. Throwing open the box's lid, he frantically began removing some of the larger items that lay within, until he located what he was looking for. Having only recently acquired the thing, he reflected that hiding it in the toy box was a most clever idea, as should his parents discover it, they would no doubt conclude it was one of his old toys and give it no second thoughts. Brad grabbed hold of the thing and rammed it into his knap-sack. He raced out of the bedroom, down the stairs and across the living room. Throwing the front door open, he took two long strides across the front porch, cleared all the porch steps in a single bound and sprinted across the front lawn. At the sidewalk the boy paused and gave a quick glance first to his left and then to his right. There is was, the car belonging to his next door neighbor, Old Man Brehm, parked at the curb close by. The boy hurried over to the automobile, ripped open the door, leapt into the driver's seat, lifted the floor mat, and searched the darkness with his hands. The teen knew that Old Man Brehm had a habit of leaving the ignition key under the mat. Brad's hand caressed something small and metallic. Success! Picking up the key he thrust it into the ignition slot and started the engine. With his left hand he slammed the car door shut, then pushed down on the ac-celerator with his foot. The car immediately took a lurch forward and stalled.

"Drats!"

The car's transmission was a manual. Brad had never before driven a car with a manual transmission. Then again, Brad had never before in his life driven any kind of internal combustion engine powered ve-hicle, so the fact that the car had a manual transmission instead of an automatic didn't make much difference. With some grinding of gears, and an awkward working of the clutch and gear shift, Brad finally got the car moving. He shifted into second gear more by blind instinct than being conscious of what he was doing. He smashed the accelera-tor pedal to the floor. With a squeal the car burst forward. In accor-dance with Newton's first law of motion, Brad's body was slammed back into the driver's seat. The vehicle continued to accelerate as it headed down the street. The turn Brad made at the first intersection was so wide the car actually mounted the far sidewalk before he man-aged to steer it back onto the street. A second turning maneuver at the end of the next block went better, although he almost took out a fire hydrant. Feeling more confident with each near miss, the boy shifted into third to the tune of some more grinding sounds, and then made a beeline down the street towards Sullivans Woods.

He was entering the next intersection when the form of another moving automobile appeared from the right. The two vehicles smashed into each other with the sickening sound of collapsing metal. The boy was thrown against the door on the driver's side as his car was spun in a clockwise circle by the collision before coming to a stop. With a loud thud, his head struck the door's window, and for brief moment he felt as if he would pass out. He gave his head a quick shake as he placed his hand on the spot that throbbed with pain. His hand came away covered in a liquid that was obviously blood.

He had to act fast. Lights were coming on in some of the nearby houses. He looked at the vehicle with which his had collided. It was a township police car. There was no movement inside. With an incredible presence of mind, Brad pulled the car keys from the ignition and thrust them into his pants pocket. He wiped the steering wheel and gear shift with the material from the bottom of his jacket. No doubt Mr. Brehm would be shocked when the police informed him that his car had been stolen and involved in an accident with a township police cruiser. There would be no fingerprints, however, to provide a clue as to the culprit's identity.

The boy next wiped the inside door handle. Using the jacket like a glove, he opened the door and leaped from the vehicle. His legs felt unsteady and he stumbled to the pavement. Rising to his feet he immediately wiped the outside door handle. Doing a quick survey of the two cars, Brad concluded that neither one offered a viable means of getting him to his destination. He hobbled over to the other car and peered inside. On the front seat lay a police officer, groaning.

Seemingly oblivious to the fact that he had been involved in a near fatal car wreck, Brad broke into a sprint, heading down the street in the direction of the Sullivans Woods. His breath came in great gasps as he pumped his legs and arms, ignoring the throbbing hurt in his head and the aches from various parts of his torso and left arm. The knapsack still hung from his shoulder. His pace was such that the East Pencreek High School track coach would have eagerly recruited Brad for his team. As the boy ran, he thrust his right hand into the pouch that hung from his shoulder and pulled out something that any adolescent in 1959 America would have had no problem recognizing. It was a ray gun.

As the minutes passed and the three figures in the clearing continued to remain motionless, the teens began to relax. Tom's heart no longer felt like it was going to explode from his chest, and Sarah's shakes had subsided. Alex's mouth was so dry that he was surprised when he discovered that he could still summon up some spit. The boys remained mute as each believed that to try to communicate with his friend would have assuredly revealed their presence.

The specter on the platform dropped his arms to his side and looked upwards. The gazes of the three teens instinctively followed that of the man. Directly overhead the sky appeared to take on a faint glow. The glow transformed itself into a hemispherical shape whose apex was directly above Evad and whose base touched the platform on which he stood. It continued to grow in size and brilliance, now extending to the ground beneath the platform. The closest figure, the one whom Tom suspected to be Serpens, took several steps backward towards the edge of the clearing where the path ended, until he ended up standing next to the third intruder. The second man was obviously determined on staying outside of the freakishly glowing half sphere. Tom noticed that its luminescence decreased with distance from the geometric center until it seemed to finally merge with the surrounding darkness. Both boys sensed a faint trace of a strange odor, though neither knew at the time that it was ozone, nor did they have any idea that the fabric of the time continuum in the vicinity of the clearing was starting to buckle and rend, opening a pathway to a destiny un-dreamed of. As the intensity of the glow increased, more details of the figure standing on the platform were revealed. Tom noticed two metallic looking cylinders on Evad's back that were connected to the rear of the helmet by a pair of hoses, analogous to the oxygen breath-ing system one would expect of a spacesuit. Tom shifted his gaze to the other two. Indeed, it was clear now that the one who shouldered the bag was indeed Serpens, but the features and even the dress of the third man still defied recognition.

A noticeable breeze kicked up in the clearing as if the mysterious, nebulous enclosure was sucking in the surrounding air. Evad, standing on the platform at the center of it all, raised his arms to the heavens as if offering a supplication to some unseen deity. He clenched his fists and gave a shout of triumph. "Yes! The Guard has not failed me."

His cheer of elation was joined by that of Serpens, who snapped to attention and gave a salute with his left arm held straight aloft, reminding the kids of a Nazi fanatic. "Hail, Maximum Leader." The salute was immediately followed by a noise from the direction of the street that sounded like someone or something crashing its way down the path.

Evad and his henchman exchanged surprised looks, or at least one could have imagined that Evad gave Serpens a look of surprise consid-ering that his features were hidden by the helmet. Serpens released the bag that hung from his shoulder, reached inside the opening of his trench coat and pulled out what was clearly a weapon, made an abrupt about face, and darted up the path, disappearing into the surrounding night.

Sarah sat as if paralyzed by the sight before her. Serpens had no sooner disappeared from the scene, when a shrill inhuman screech erupted directly behind the girl and something that felt like the fear-ful talons of a demon sank into the back of her neck. In reaction to the sudden pain and horrifying shriek, the girl let out an anguished scream and lurched forward onto her feet, stumbling off balance and into the clearing. While reaching behind her with one hand trying to grab whatever had attacked her, she thrust forward the other in a fruitless attempt to break her fall.

As Sarah tumbled to the ground within the unworldly sphere of light, Evad spun around to confront the source of the disturbance. With a quick, liquid motion he snapped open the left holster, drew out the weapon housed therein, and leveled it at the girl.

At the same moment, the apparition who had been stationed at the path's entrance emitted a cry of rage and sprang towards the girl. In doing so his features were finally revealed by the hemisphere's illumination. The newcomer's dress was fairly common, being comprised of a white T-shirt, open black leather jacket, blue jeans and sneakers. The ray gun it brandished in his right hand was anything but common. Yet it was the intruder's face that held the attention of the two boys, for despite the demonical expression of madness that distorted his features, he was still recognizable. It was Jack Paine.

"Holy cow," said Alex in a voice whose volume caused Tom to cringe. "It's Paine!" at which point Alex abruptly stood up. Evad in turn jerked about shifting his focus from Sarah to Jack, and then to Alex. Tom started to reach up in an attempt to grab Alex and pull him back down, but before he could do so, Alex had bolted into the clearing, yelling, "Come on, you take Jack, I'll get Sarah." Without a moment's hesitation, and obviously without taking the time to consider the absurdity of his friend's suggestion, Tom was up and on Alex's heels.

As Jack lurched towards the prone Sarah, he raised his weapon, taking aim at the girl. In the split second remaining before he could squeeze the trigger, Evad had once again spun around and the muzzle of his weapon erupted with a loud staccato zap. Jack Paine crashed to the ground. The zap from Evad's gun was immediately followed by two similar bursts of sound from the direction of the street.

Tom had taken it all in as he crossed the boundary of light. As he did so, a sensation hit him like that of a flashbulb going off inside his brain. His vision was erased, submerged by a light so bright it became darkness. At the same instance his stomach gave a nauseous wrench, and his sense of direction became completely disoriented. His muscles seemed to involuntarily go limp, causing his body to fall to the ground directly behind Alex who seemed to be experiencing similar sensations. Then the enfolding hemisphere of light vanished along with all it had enclosed.

To an outside observer it would have looked like the luminous enclosure had imploded in upon itself, the only evidence of it having been there being a rush of air and a sound reminiscent of distant thunder. What only a moment before had been the clearing containing a wooden platform and five figures was now an empty, shallow, circular depression.

The man stood in the side yard of a house across the street from Sullivans Woods, having selected his location so that the low bushes effectively shielded him from the view of those who had earlier entered the woodland. Not long after the otherworldly glow from deep in the forest had vanished, a low slung, four-legged creature emerged from the trees and crossed the street. It stopped at the man's feet and sat on its haunches. The man looked down, giving the feline a friendly nod. The cat returned the man's greeting with a low meow.

Second Interlude
1942 -- New York City

The man felt a great sadness as he surveyed the small hotel room and reflected on its occupant. "That one of the greatest men in history should be reduced to this," thought the visitor. "This is the man most responsible for the modern world. His inventions have given his fellow men luxury and prosperity undreamed of by even the most powerful kings of old, yet today he is all but forgotten." The visitor noted an old wooden box, two manuscripts, and an opened package of crackers on a small table next to an armchair. "Has he been reduced to subsisting on crackers?" That possibility transformed the visitor's emotions from sadness to anger. The sound of a toilet flushing in the adjoining bathroom interrupted the visitor's train of thought.

The appearance of the man who entered the room was that of an individual with one foot already in the grave. Although taller than most men, he now looked as if he could not have weighed more than ninety pounds. His body was so shrunken from lack of proper nourishment that his face reminded the visitor of a skull covered by skin with little flesh underneath to pad out the features. With some difficulty the old man sat down in the armchair across from the visitor.

"My good friend," said the fragile elder, breaking into a warm smile. "I have a favor to ask of you."

"Certainly," said the visitor.

Before continuing the dying man hesitated a moment, as if collecting his thoughts. "The men from the government were here yesterday."

"Yes?"

"As had already been agreed, they took with them many of my documents. No doubt they hope to find therein plans for some exotic death ray or other engine of terror that will shorten the war."

The speaker hesitated. His visitor decided not to say anything but wondered what this had to do with the favor that was to be asked of him.

"Ungrateful buffoons," mumbled the old man. "I doubt if either one of them would know the difference between an amp and an ohm." At that he gave his visitor another grin. The man sitting across from him returned the smile.

"Damn misfits. They stole from me the credit for inventing radio and gave it to that Macaroni."

"I know, sir, and his name was Marconi."

"Marconi, Macaroni, Spaghetti, was does it matter? The man was a thief. Anyway, then they come here and want all my other discoveries and again they probably won't ever give me credit for them. No doubt they'll hush them up as top secret and hide them away in a vault somewhere and people will never know about them."

"That's no doubt likely, sir."

"Did I mention how arrogant they were? They acted like they almost expected me to feed them while they were here."

The visitor nodded.

"Anyway, that's beside the point." The old man made an effort to straighten himself, and as it did so for a moment it was as if a younger, more virile man had taken possession of the fragile, thin body. He reached over and patted the wooden box that lay on the table next to his chair. "But I made sure they didn't get this?"

"What is it?" asked the visitor.

"It's a wooden box." The old man gave out a soft guffaw. "Pardon me, George, I couldn't resist the opportunity."

The visitor also chuckled.

"It's what's in the box that's important."

"And what is in the box?"

"Take a look."

The visitor hoisted himself out of his chair and walked over to the table. Lifting the box's hinged cover, he found lying within a spherical object about ten inches in diameter, cradled in a folded white cloth that covered the bottom of the wooden container.

"What is it?"

"Darn if I know?" chortled the old man. "I've been studying that thing for almost forty years and I haven't a clue. Touch it."

The visitor placed his hand on the object and immediately jerked it back. Then more cautiously, he again rested his hand on it. "It's warm," he said in astonishment.

"Yes, and it's been putting out heat like that for almost forty years. Its temperature never changes."

"Amazing."

"Now watch this," said the old man. "He reached over and switched off a floor lamp that stood by the side of the armchair where he sat. As night had fallen and the lamp was the only source of light in the hotel room, the room was plunged into darkness. "Wait a moment for your eyes to adjust."

The visitor glanced at the spot where he had last seen the mysterious object. It was glowing. "It's luminescent," he said, sounding even more astonished than he had when he had touched it.

"Yes," the old man replied as he switched the light back on. "Go ahead, lift it."

The visitor did as he was requested. After a moment's struggle, he discovered that he needed both hands to heft it comfortably. "And you have no idea what it is?"

"That's correct. But have a seat and I will tell you the story of how

360

it came into my possession."

And with that Nikola Tesla related to his visitor the events of thirty-nine years earlier at his laboratory at Wardenclyffe.

As the old man finished his narrative, the visitor asked, "And what of the inscriptions on it?"

"Again, I have no idea what their significance is. Over the years I sent copies of the inscriptions to several prominent linguists, foreign language experts, and even experts in ancient languages such as Egyptologists and Sumerologists, but all for naught."

"And the heat and glow?"

"Ah, now that's an interesting point. Neither were present when I first obtained it. But one night at Wardenclyffe, after we had initiated an exceptionally high voltage discharge, I happened to inspect it. That was the first time I noticed it being warm to the touch. And then after turning out the lights I also discovered the luminescence. I can only surmise that it was the high voltage field that caused those properties to appear. Unfortunately, it wasn't long after that I had to close the lab. As you know, I haven't had access to such facilities since. But in all those years, it was the only time that there occurred any change in the object."

The inventor continued. "I'm sorry, George, that I kept this from you, but please understand I had made a promise not to share this information or the existence of this object with anyone. I had agreed to return it to the museum at the end of the following year, but when I contacted them to do so they acted as if they had no idea what I was talking about. Although they failed to keep their word, until now I nevertheless kept mine."

"Yes, I understand and I would never have expected you to go back on your promise," said the visitor. "But why are you now showing me this?"

"Because I'm dying." Before George could protest, the old man continued. "And that brings us to the favor I have to ask of you. There is a man, an engineer at the Carnegie Institute in Pittsburgh. I've written to him about this, and he's agreed to take custody of it and try to figure out what it is."

"Why not give it to the government? They certainly have facil—"

Tesla raised his voice. "Those imbeciles. Like I said, they'd probably lock it away and that would be the end of it."

"Yes. Sorry I suggested it."

"That's okay. I should not have raised my voice to a good friend like you. Anyway, would it be possible for you to see that this gets to Pittsburgh?"

"Yes, I would be most happy to."

"Excellent. Here's his name, address and phone number." Tesla held out a slip of paper to his friend. "Again, I can't thank you enough for agreeing to do this. I would hate for such a strange and wonderful thing to be lost." He motioned towards the manuscripts that also lay on the table. "Here is the report of its discovery that the man from the museum gave me almost forty years ago, along with a summary of my own experiments with it. They are also for the professor."

The visitor stood. Using the cloth that was at the bottom of the box to wrap the artifact, he carefully placed it back inside the box along with the two manuscripts. As he did so he said, "Have you ever come up with a plausible explanation of where it came from or its purpose?"

"Only as to its origin," said the inventor. "My hypothesis seems to fit all the evidence. I came up with it on the very day I first saw it."

"And what is that?"

Tesla flashed his friend another grin. "That this thing was made by an advanced civilization from another solar system, and that they left it behind when they visited Earth towards the end of the Cretaceous period." The inventor's grin vanished. "Do you think that I'm crazy for thinking such a thing?"

George shook his head. "No, sir. If there is any man alive who is not crazy it is you. You are the greatest man it has ever been my privilege to know, and I mean that sincerely."

"Thank you, George." At that, Tesla, relaxed back into his armchair. "And as to its purpose, I could never come up with an intelligent guess." The inventor sat there for a moment, a wistful look on his face. Then he said, "You're sure you don't mind making this trip? I can't give you any money to pay your expenses or . . ."

"No, not at all. As matter of fact, if the train schedule permits, it will give me a chance to visit an old friend of mine who lives on the route between here and Pittsburgh. It's a little town in Pennsylvania. East Pencreek."

Part III
2350 – Sol System

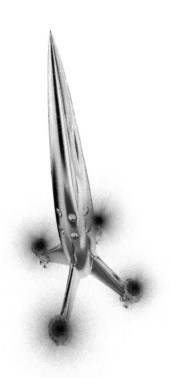

Chapter 1
Epimetheus

It was as if he had been cast into a bottomless pit. The darkness coupled with the sickening sensation of endless falling combined to scramble his senses. Although he was sure he was falling, he couldn't tell which way was up. Had he lost consciousness? Was he dreaming? What had happened to the stars? Where was the distant glimmer of the town's streetlights? Was there also no sound? He couldn't be sure, as his ears felt like they were about to pop. He tried to focus his eyes on something, but there was nothing to focus on. Everything was disconnected. The universe had gone wrong. He was nauseated and dizzy and weightless. In a panic, he closed his hands. As he did so he felt them grab something. Weeds! He must still be in the clearing of Sullivans Woods.

The burst of brilliant light was accompanied by a loud bang as if a heavy metal door had slammed shut. In actuality, the drop through the temporal tunnel had lasted barely a moment, but due to the chaos into which the boy's senses had been tossed, it had seemed significantly longer to Tom. Since the time spent in the tunnel had not been long enough by local time to significantly degrade the boy's night vision, the sudden explosion of light caused his pupils to contract while jarring his vision into focus. He squinted. They were inside some sort of metallic dome, perhaps thirty feet in diameter. The walls of the dome themselves seemed aglow, providing the bright source of illumination.

Evad was still standing on the wooden platform holding the weapon in his left hand, just as Tom had remembered before the night seemed to have collapsed upon him. He could now clearly make out the details of the metallic blue spacesuit that Evad wore. The man's feet and hands were encased in tight fitting boots and gloves. A pair of belts crossed his chest and his neck was encircled by a wide collar. The face plate that covered the front of the tall, ovoid helmet was opaque but mirror-like. A pair of holsters graced the man's instrument-studded belt. For the first time Tom noticed in the center of Evad's chest, directly below the broad collar, an insignia. It was a black silhouette of what appeared to be the fore body of a dragon. In one of its paws the beast clutched a pair of crossed lightning bolts.

Before the platform, stretched out on his stomach and face down in the dirt, was an unmoving Jack Paine with a ray gun lying not far from his outstretched hand. Tom was unable to ascertain whether the delinquent was dead or just unconscious.

A voice came from Tom's right.

"What happened?"

Like Tom, Alex was on his hands and knees and giving his head a shake as if attempting to clear his senses. Next to Alex, Sarah was kneeling, hands on her knees, staring at the boys, her eyes filled with fright. That caused Tom to glance behind him where he noticed the trunk of a small sapling whose base was barely a foot from the dome. The top of the trunk disappeared into the curved dome wall. About the sapling a number of severed branches were drifting towards the ground, falling so slowly as to seem surreal. A terrible dread swept over the boy as he realized that what he was witnessing were the upper branches of the sapling that had been cleanly sliced off where they contacted the dome. Tom glanced down at his right foot, stretched out behind him. Another couple of inches and the front of his shoe along with his toes would have also been amputated by the lethal boundary of the dome wall.

There was a second loud bang. The boy felt an invisible force slam down on him. He began to jerk involuntarily as his stomach engaged in a series of dry heaves. Alex was having a similar reaction but Sarah, or at least her digestive system, seemed to be unfazed by the sudden reappearance of weight. Fortunately, it had been several hours since the three had eaten dinner, so their stomachs contained nothing of substance to regurgitate. Although Tom realized that his weight had returned, for some unaccountable reason, he still felt strangely light. The severed limbs of the tree, which had been gently floating downward, immediately dropped to the ground.

A third bang and a curved triangular opening appeared in the dome. It was perhaps four feet wide at the base where it intersected the ground, narrowing to a point at the dome's apex. The bangs now came in a rapid staccato, spaced at a fraction of a second. With each one the opening enlarged. It was as if they were inside the dome of an astronomical observatory whose viewing window was growing in size by discrete steps for so the wall of the dome appeared to be collapsing in upon itself.

Evad seemed unfazed by it all. He ignored the three teens as he holstered his weapon and then stretched out his arms towards the ceiling of the rapidly shrinking containment. "I'm back!" The sound of his voice took on a strange echo, as if being broadcast from a loudspeaker. As soon as he had spoken, the rhythmic banging sound ceased. What had formerly been a full dome was now but a single curved triangular piece.

Tom began to frantically look around. His first impression was that it was still night, for although the surroundings were well lit by a number of lamps, a black sky appeared overhead; yet they were obviously no longer in Sullivans Woods. Instead it was as if they had been transported to the set of a Hollywood science fiction movie. The scene resembled that of a mad scientist's laboratory like he had seen in many of those Saturday matinee movies, only everything was on a more gigantic scale. Everywhere were strange contraptions and exotic machines, many of which were studded with blinking lights of different colors.

Evad's shout of triumph was followed by a cry from Sarah causing the two boys to look in her direction. She was pointing at the boys—no, she was pointing at something behind them. Her lips were moving as if trying to speak, but no sound issued from them. Alex and Tom both simultaneously jerked their heads around to see what she was staring at. Framed against the gem-like sparkle of scattered stars loomed an immense, curved shape—so enormous that it filled most of the boys' fields of vision. To Tom it seemed that if he reached out his hand he might touch it. The surface of the giant globe was covered by a series of hazy parallel bands of color tilted at an angle of about thirty degrees. For the most part, the bands were of various shades of pale yellow and brown although they became greener towards the edge of the sphere, about half of which was obviously obscured the horizon. The apparent symmetry of the bands was broken on one side of the sphere's equator by an exceptionally thick dark band divided into several smaller bands by thin bright lines, as if it was an immense shadow cast by a series of closely spaced rings that encircled the mammoth orb. From left to right the sphere steadily darkened, finally ending in a dark crescent whose edge marked the day-night terminator. But it wasn't the size and unexpectedness of the gargantuan ball that was the real mind blower. It was the thin beam of light, bright as a full moon, that ran parallel to the bands and bisected the globe. The pencil of light extended far out into space where it then appeared to curve back on itself as if it were encircling the giant object.

"What is it?" gasped Tom.

"It has to be," said Alex. Then he gave his head a shake as in disbelief. "But it can't be?"

"What?" said Tom, unable to take his eyes off the cosmic spectacle that dominated the sky.

"Saturn!" Alex took a deep breath. "It has to be Saturn. That bright streak of light must be its rings. We're seeing them edge-on. And the large dark bands are the rings' shadows. We must be on one of Saturn's moons."

Tom didn't know which he found more amazing, the incredible scene before him or his friend's ability to coolly analyze the situation in which they found themselves.

"I feel—strange," said Tom. "Like I don't weigh enough."

"Me too," said Alex. "The gravity of wherever we are is no doubt a lot less than Earth's."

Further speculation by the teens was cut short. From somewhere behind them came the sound of a host of hard-soled boots on the metallic deck. Just when Tom had thought that nothing could surprise him more than the sight of the giant, ringed planet, he found himself proved wrong. Approaching them were a dozen figures weaving their way through the maze of exotic machinery. Roughly half of the figures appeared to be human, outfitted in spacesuits similar to that worn by Evad. The suits were of a dark green color except for that of the man in the lead whose spacesuit was a dark metallic grey.

Immediately to the right of the lead figure waddled a short, squat creature that looked as if it had just crawled out of some interstellar black lagoon. Attached to the center of its circular head was a round faceplate similar in appearance to that of a diving mask worn by a Navy frogman. A short hose protruded from the bottom of the face mask and connected to a rectangular container attached to the being's chest. Two large triangular appendages, reminiscent of the ears of a cat, symmetrically adorned the top of its head. The spacesuit itself, or perhaps it the creature's actual skin, was of a scaly texture. The suit's appendages ended in webbed feet and hands, or perhaps boots and gloves respectively. Whatever it was, the fact that it hadn't unlatched its faceplate no doubt meant that the present atmosphere was hostile to its physiology.

The four beings bringing up the rear of the group were the real shockers. They were tall, perhaps a good seven feet or more in height, even considering their gangly build and the fact that they walked slightly crouched. They wore no spacesuits nor helmets, but were dressed in tight fitting tunics and trunks. Their torsos were roughly triangular, wide at the shoulders and narrowing to the waist. Each wore a wide belt from which hung a holster that housed a sidearm. Their oversized heads were more square than oval, and were flanked by equally large ears that resembled small wings. The ears appeared to be flexible, their owner no doubt being able to willfully control them as they would occasionally bend forward or change shape. The head's remaining features were equally alien, for although in number and position the facial features were similar to those of humans, in form and size there was little similarity. The large eyes bulged from the face as if someone had tried to force two lemons into cavities too small to properly house them. Even the dark pupils of the eyes, the size of large olives, appeared to protrude from the rest of the pale, yellow eyeballs. Each eye in turn rested above a prominent cheekbone that formed the boundary of a wide, curved mouth that seemed set in a perpetual grin. By comparison, the forehead and chin were relatively diminished in size, except for a heavy eyebrow type groove that ran above each eye. The top of the head was adorned by a pair of blunt knobs as if the creature had decided to start growing horns. Perhaps the most bizarre feature of all was its nose, resembling in every way, except in color, a large carrot. Tom had the odd thought that if the creature ever told a lie, its nose would start to grow in size like Pinocchio's. Overall the creature's appearance, excepting its sickly grey skin, struck the boy as a badly formed caricature of some giant, grotesque cartoon mouse, especially considering the fact that a long whip-like tail whose tip just reached the ground emerged from the seat of the creature's trunks. Each of the alien monstrosities carried a deadly looking weapon approximating the size and shape of a large rifle.

Upon viewing the approaching entourage, Sarah stumbled to her feet. Although she experienced some difficulty in keeping her balance in the reduced gravity, she nevertheless managed to scurry behind Tom.

"Wha . . . what are they?"

Tom didn't answer. As he rose to his feet, he felt a sudden discomfort in his right arm due to the force of Sarah's two-handed grip on it.

Jack Paine, oblivious to all that was transpiring, continued to lie unmoving on the piece of earth where the blast from Evad's ray gun had planted him.

The group of newcomers came to a halt at the edge of the circular piece of turf that was all that remained of Sullivans Woods. The lead figure took a single step forward and with one of his gloved hands touched something on his chest. With a faint whoosh, his helmet immediately collapsed from the top down as if it were composed of flexible fabric, the headwear ending in a roll about the neck like some exotic Elizabethan collar. The face revealed was that of a man of about thirty with finely chiseled features but with a hard look. The other humans followed suit, revealing the features of six more men, a tough looking lot.

The leader thrust out his left arm in a Nazi-like salute. "Hail Sleinad Evad!" he roared. "Hail Maximum Leader!" Immediately, the others imitated the salute, although a couple of the non-human creatures in the rear, apparently confused, threw out their right arms. The cry of "Hail Sleinad Evad, hail Maximum Leader," rang throughout the chamber. As the echo from the salute died out, Evad took a confident step in the direction of his admirers and, as the other humans had done, retracted his helmet.

"I have returned!" he shouted. He formed his left hand into a fist to emphasize his next words. "From this moment on the Guard resumes its march towards total victory."

That brought another couplet of hails from the tough looking assembly and a whine from Sarah. "Who are they?" She applied even more pressure on Tom's arm. "Where are we?"

To their surprise, Evad turned to face the teens. "Epimetheus, if my calculations are correct." He sounded confident. Then he addressed the one who had led the salutes. "Am I correct, proconsul?"

"Correct as always, Maximum Leader."

Alex muttered in a low voice, "Teacher's pet, no doubt."

"I take it the base's security has been nullified?" asked Evad.

"Yes, sir," said the man whom Evad had addressed as proconsul. "And these?" He motioned towards the teens.

"Stowaways," said Evad. The answer seemed to startle the proconsul. He took a step towards the teens, drawing from his holster a weapon that looked to be a close twin to the one Evad had used. His arm straightened and Tom found himself staring directly into weapon's barrel.

Just as Tom was thinking that he was about to die, the man dropped the ray gun to his side. "Smoke and rockets," he muttered, failing to hide the surprise in his voice.

That brought a low guffaw from Evad as he deftly dismounted the wooden platform and stepped beside the other man. "Allow me to introduce you. Proconsul Sokar, this is Tomas Jefferson Cobalt."

The dark grey attired figure turned his head towards Evad. "But— . I don't understand, Maximum Leader. Cobalt is dead."

"Dead?" exclaimed Evad. "Are you sure?"

"Yes, Maximum Leader. Killed at Quadrant Five. Commander Cobalt boarded your flagship and died in the resulting detonation."

"I must say, that's excellent news, not that it does anything to clear up this mystery."

"So, should I dispatch him or not?" asked the man whom Evad had called Sokar, and who again aimed his weapon at Tom.

"No," commanded Evad, holding up a hand to further emphasize the order. "One can never be certain of his destination until he plots a trajectory."

Sokar turned to the squat, aquatic-looking being standing next to him, "Are you recording this?"

"Yes, proconsul," was the reply from the webbed alien, its voice sounding as if it were speaking in an echo chamber. "Maximum Leader's words have been recorded for prosperity."

Alex rolled his eyes, "I feel like I have to puke again."

Tom ignored his friend's comment. "Where did he say we were? Epi—Epi-me-ist?"

"If that's Saturn then we're on one of its moons, one that I've never heard of," guessed Alex. "It must be a very small moon, but it seems like there's more gravity here than a small moon would have."

Evad, who had obviously been listening to the boys' conversation, emitted a chuckle as he turned to address the teens. "A most astute observation, as one would expect from my best student." Sarah gave Evad a sharp look. "But if you look up, you will find the explanation for the enhanced gravity about a hundred eighty meters above your head."

The three students looked up. Barely visible against the backdrop of deep space and balanced on a tall, cylindrical pole, was a dull grey, saucer-shaped object. Tom judged to be about five meters in diameter. It seemed to hover above them, encased in a faint, bluish glow. As the boy studied the strange object, he noticed that parts of the surrounding sky would momentarily appear to shimmer with the same blue ghostly glow. The curved shapes thus produced gave the boy the impression that he was inside of some sort of immense, transparent dome.

Apparently done with his explanation, Evad turned back to his lieutenant. "Proconsul, what is the situation?"

In a response that reminded Tom of a bad impersonation of an overzealous Nazi sycophant from some World War II film, the man snapped to attention.

"A Class Five Cetian Infiltrator awaits your Excellency." Sokar gestured to his left. Tom looked in that direction and there, the view of the object partly obscured by some of the machinery, was a—

"Oh my gosh," said Tom. "It's a—"

"—flying saucer," said Alex, finishing Tom's sentence.

The strangeness of his surroundings prevented Tom from making an accurate guess as to the vehicle's size. The only thing he was certain of was that he was looking at a real flying saucer. It had the classic saucer shape with a diameter roughly four times its height. Its perfectly smooth surface displayed no detail but gleamed with a uniform silver sheen. The vehicle was resting on a platform of sorts—a landing pad was Tom's guess.

"Class Five, you say?" said Evad. "My, some things have changed since I left."

"Excuse me, Maximum Leader," said Sokar, "but considering the proximity of the patrol base on Iapetus not to mention Huygens city on Titan, perhaps we should hasten to raise ship."

"Do you have reason to suspect that they may know we're here?"

"No, Maximum Leader."

"Then indulge me. Allow me to savor the moment—the heady thought that my return has taken place right under their nosecones and yet they know not of it. Continue with your report."

Evad's lieutenant started rattling off a stream of jargon. For all the sense that Tom could make of it, the man might as well have been speaking Bulgarian.

Tom's attempt to eavesdrop further was interrupted when Sarah gave his arm another squeeze. "Tom, I want to go home."

"No kidding," said Tom. "What I can't understand is if that's Saturn out there, how did we get here?"

"A matter transmitter is my guess," said Alex. When both his friends responded with blank stares, he continued. "You know, like in that movie we saw last year, *The Fly*. You step into a machine in one place and it sort of disassembles all your atoms into, well, eh, say pure information, and it then instantaneously shoots it across space, and you get reassembled in another machine somewhere else. I guess that was the 'tunnel' that Evad referred to."

"Yeah, that seems to make sense," said Tom.

"No, it doesn't," said Sarah.

"Okay, then you explain it?" challenged the boy genius.

"I can't, and I don't care how we got here. All I want to do is go home."

Alex gave his head a shake, and then ignored the girl as he turned to study further his surroundings. "I wonder what all this stuff is for? Hey, look at that."

He pointed to a metallic humanoid form that stood in front of a large assemblage of gadgetry only a few paces from the teens. Over six feet in height, the figure's head resembled a rugby ball stood on end. A thin, transverse crest, that reminded Tom of the crest on an ancient Roman centurion's helmet, ran across the top of the head, and a horizontal, oblong faceplate occupied the area where one would expect eyes. The only other features on the head were a couple of truncated cylinders, one of each side of the head, located about where a human's ears would be. The upper body was roughly triangular in shape as was the pelvic area, the two parts being connected by a cylindrical waist of smaller diameter whose purpose seemed to be to allow the two body halves to turn independently of each other. The arms and legs appeared unusually thin considering the robust size of the body, but at each joint, shoulder, knee, elbow, ankle and wrist, the arm or leg part was encased in a thicker jacket. Large hands and feet, or perhaps gloves and boots would be a more fitting description, completed the body. Across its chest the metallic being held an intimidating looking weapon, reminiscent of a mutated Browning automatic rifle, not much different than that yielded by the grotesque mouse aliens. No doubt some sort of powerful ray gun guessed Tom. Dead center on the metallic man's chest, directly above where the weapon was positioned, was a small circular red object that reminded the boy of some sort of pushbutton. Whatever the robot-like thing was, it seemed obvious that it was a fixture of the base, and not part of the pack of humans and aliens that had so enthusiastically greeted Evad.

"Golly, it must be some sort of robot," said Tom. "Do you suppose it's guarding something?"

"I don't know and I don't care," whimpered Sarah, still holding onto the sleeve of Tom's jacket but loosening her grip on his arm. "Can't we just go home?"

"Get a grip on yourself, Sarah," said Alex. "How do you suppose we do that? If that's Saturn then we're at least—780 million miles from home, and that's taking the shortcut."

"How do you do that?" asked Tom.

"Do what?"

"You know. Figure out we're 780 million miles from Earth? You always seem able to come up with such incredible facts, just like that."

"It's quite simple, Watson. See the Earth is roughly 92 million miles from the sun, a distance which astronomers call an astronomical unit. It's easier to remember planetary distances in astronomical units than miles, so since Saturn—"

"Stop it!" Sarah's sharp command not only got the boys attention, but also that of a couple of the members of Evad's entourage. Sarah's voice had not only changed to a high, pitched squeal, but also included a heavy dose of hysteria. "What's wrong with you two? We're who knows how many millions of miles from home, with all these horrible—whatever they are, and people and all, and we don't know what's going to happen to us and, and . . ." The girl's words were cut off by a staccato of sobs, and the force of her grip that had shifted back to Tom's arm noticeably tightened.

"Er, sorry," muttered Alex. "But I was just answering Tom's question."

"Look, Sarah. Alex is right. Since we seem to be stuck here, we might as well try to make the best of it."

"I'm sorry." The girl gave another sniffle, released her grip on Tom, and removed her glasses. She wiped some of the tears from her eyes with the sleeve of her jacket. Replacing her glasses, she realized that she needed to blow her nose. She unconsciously grabbed the tail of Tom's jacket and used it to blow her nose. Tom was about to say something but thought better of it when he saw Alex shake his head. Sarah motioned towards the curved triangular object that was all that remained of the dome in which they had arrived. "Couldn't we go back the way we came?"

"Yeah, I guess we could," nodded the taller boy, "assuming we could convince Evad to allow it."

"Well, would you please ask him?"

"Me? Don't you remember? He hates me. Besides aren't you curious? Don't you want to stick around some and find out what this is all about?"

"Noooo! Please, Tom. I'm scared." She gave the group assembled next to Evad, and especially the one called Sokar, a nervous glance.

"Hey, Tom. Look at this." Alex had wandered over to the robot. The blond-haired teen was staring intently at the red, button-like object in the center of the robot's torso.

"Hey, you!" yelled one of men. "Don't touch that! Get away from that guardian!"

"Who, me?" said Alex.

"Yes, you, spaceslug!"

Alex took a step back. "No need to yell. I was just looking."

The man turned and said something to one of the horrid looking creatures with the huge head and ears standing next to him. The creature nodded and began to move towards the teens.

Sarah let out a barely audible squeak and quickly positioned herself behind Tom, resuming her grip on the boy's arm. To the boy, it felt like she was applying a tourniquet. "It's coming over here," she squealed.

"It's probably just curious," said Tom. "Maybe it never saw a girl before. Try to stay calm."

"I can't," moaned Sarah.

Alex boldly stepped between his friends and the creature. As he started to open his mouth to speak the odor hit him. "Yuck," he squawked, and cringed backward, squeezing his nostrils shut with his fingers. Immediately the other two teens caught a whiff of the alien's aroma. To Tom it stank of aged, moldy cheese.

"Double yuck," said Tom, imitating his friend by grabbing his nose in an attempt to block the pungent odor. "Something needs a bath."

Ignoring the boys, the creature continued its advance, its large, protruding eyes fixed on Sarah. She released her hold on Tom, took a step backwards, and tripped over the raised edge of the low circular enclosure that contained the patch of Sullivans Woods. With a thud she landed on her side, at the same time letting out a yelp of pain. Before Tom could react, the grotesque brute had reached out its enormous hand that held the weapon and used it to shove the boy aside, at the same time extending its other maw towards Sarah.

"Leave her alone, you overgrown rodent," yelled Alex. He picked up a hefty piece of broken branch from the ground, a remnant of Sullivans Woods, and made a threatening gesture with it. The over-grown rodent ignored Alex and continued its advance on the girl.

Alex swung his makeshift club at the monstrosity's head and in doing so unintentionally demonstrated the excellence of the alien's peripheral vision. Never taking its eyes off the girl, it caught hold of the branch with its free hand, stopping Alex's swing. The creature squeezed its hand shut on the club, and the thick branch snapped in half, as if it were but a piece of thin balsa wood.

Sarah attempted to struggle to her feet, but before she could steady herself the giant's hand shot forward and closed about her arm, effec-tively preventing any flight. Scream followed scream as the mouse-like monstrosity pulled the struggling girl towards it, its large mouth taking on an even more wicked-looking grin. It dropped the weapon it held freeing its other hand to close about the girl's neck.

From seemingly out of nowhere shot a closed fist that landed squarely on the creature's face below its left eye. By a lucky accident, Tom's fist had fortuitously connected with one of the few vulnerable areas of the alien's anatomy. With a screech of rage the freakish fiend released its hold on the girl, its head having been thrust backward with such force that it lost its balance, crashing to the deck on its back. At the same time Tom started dancing around, holding the hand he had used to strike the alien, the same one he had injured earlier that week when he had used it to break Jack Paine's nose. He was yelling, "Ouch, ouch, ouch."

The giant, its face still wreathed with that eternal devilish grin, began to get to its feet. Tom gave its head a hard kick. This time the big-eared varmint let out an ever louder howl of rage, as its body again crashed to the pavement.

"Stop it," commanded Evad.

"Hey, that thing started it," said Alex, pointing at the now horizontal, overgrown rat from hell.

"I think I might have broken something," said Tom, still nursing the hand he had struck the alien with but being somewhat impeded in examining it as a sobbing Sarah was now clinging to him from behind, her arms wrapped tightly around his waist.

The tough looking man who had warned Alex to keep away from the robot spoke up. "Maximum Leader. I ordered the Mickey to make sure those kids didn't fool with the guardian. The skinny one there looked like he might be going to activate it."

"Get over here," growled Evad. The two boys sheepishly began to shuffle over to where Evad stood, Tom's movement being hampered by Sarah who was still clinging tightly to him. The thing that the tough looking spaceman had referred to as a Mickey was slowly getting to its feet.

"What shall we do with them?" asked Sokar. Before Evad could answer there came the excited voice of a man who stood behind the proconsul.

"Maximum Leader, we have a contact. Unidentified ship on intercept trajectory and closing. At its present acceleration, it will reach the engagement threshold in approximately eight-point-four minutes."

"Have you a signature?" asked Evad.

"It's registering now. It's a patrol starcruiser!"

"Pluto's freeze. Of all the blasted luck."

"No doubt, from Iapetus Base," said Sokar.

Evad spun around. "Astrogator. Assuming maximum gee acceleration, how long after liftoff until we can activate the stasis field?"

The man who had been addressed as the astrogator answered, "Eighteen minutes with a ninety-five-ninety-five safety margin. It's the close proximity of Saturn—"

"I'm familiar with the physics, you Triborian twit," said Evad. "Give me an estimate for a fifty-fifty margin." At that the other men look startled, many of their faces showing obvious concern if not downright alarm at whatever it was Evad was proposing.

"A fifty-fifty? But your Excellency—"

Evad's voice filled with anger. "I'm awaiting an answer."

"Yes sir," replied the man who then cast a quick glance at a gadget on his wrist. "Twelve-point-two minutes."

Evad turned to his companion. "Still not good enough. We need to buy time." Then, to no one in particular, he said, "Communications. Put me in contact with the starcruiser. Place the receiver point here." He pointed to a spot on the pavement about ten feet in front of him. "Make sure the projection can't see the machine." From Evad's gesture, Tom guessed by the "machine" he was referring to what remained of the dome that had transported them from Earth to Epimetheus. Evad barked, "Inform the *Fornax* to prepare for liftoff and to go to general quarters." He then pointed towards the triangular piece into which the dome had collapsed and said to Sokar, "After we lift off, we'll blast it to atoms—destroy the evidence."

A new voice appeared, Tom being unable to pinpoint its origin.

"This is the Solar Patrol starcruiser *Antares*." There was a faint flash of blue light over the spot on the floor where Evad had indicated that the "receiver point" should be. Then as if by magic there appeared a man standing on the very spot. The apparition wore a close-fitting grey uniform with blue trim, and on his left chest was prominently displayed an insignia of a sleek vertical spaceship eclipsing a ringed planet. About his waist was a belt with a pair of holsters, one of which held a ray gun. The other, the one on his left side, housed a different sort of pistol with its handle facing backwards, no doubt to allow its owner to draw it with his right hand.

The spaceman stood facing Evad, his feet about shoulder width apart, hands on his hips. The man's striking features immediately reminded Tom of some classical Greek statue come to life. His hair was dark and short cropped and his face was adorned with the most noble looking of noses and brown, intelligent eyes whose contours Tom thought resembled those of an oriental. He was clean shaven and his chin looked like it could have been carved from granite. It was as if the features of a Tarzan and a medieval Japanese samurai had been pooled into a single individual. The man's appearance screamed confidence, strength, dignity, courage, and integrity.

"Captain Rex Krater commanding the Solar Patrol starcruiser—" The man abruptly stopped when his eyes fell upon Sleinad Evad.

"Greetings, Captain Krater," said Evad. As he spoke his lips curled into a triumphant smile.

For a moment the newcomer looked surprised, but he quickly regained his composure. "A trick no doubt. Whoever you are, you impersonate a dead man."

"No, captain, I assure you it is I. No doubt your underlings have already run a voice analysis among other diagnostics on my image, and they are reporting to you that all the results do indeed confirm that I am—me. My, it seems so long since we last had a chat."

While Evad was speaking, the captain had been looking off to the side, although at what Tom couldn't tell. The man again made eye contact with Evad. "Okay, assuming that you really are that scum-sucking, slug-like spawn of a brainless Omicronian Trog-Turbler known as Sleinad Evad, by the authority of the Solar Patrol, I order you and your crew to surrender."

"Surely you jest," said Evad.

"In a few minutes, we'll see who is jesting."

To Tom it seemed that there was an unnatural pause of a couple of seconds before each time the 'captain' had spoken.

"Captain, before I terminate this communication I have someone here you will no doubt find most interesting."

The captain gave a sigh. "Yes?"

"Bring him here," said Evad, pointing at Tom.

One of the men grabbed Tom by the collar of his jacket while a second man pulled Sarah off him. The first man shoved the boy towards Evad who grabbed him by the arm and turned him to face the eerie ghostlike projection of the man who had materialized out of nowhere.

The image of Captain Krater looked directly at the boy. A shocked look of recognition dawned on the captain's features.

"Ah, hah!" said Evad. "He looks familiar no doubt." Then he turned to Tom. "Tell him your name?"

"Huh? Er, Tom," said Tom.

Evad slapped Tom on the side of his head. "You're full name, imbecile."

"Tom Cobalt."

"Give him your full name," repeated Evad.

Tom swallowed. "Thomas Jefferson Cobalt. What's going on?"

"I assure you that just as I am not a clone, neither is the boy. He's geneophysically identical to the Commander."

"I don't understand," said the captain, obviously perplexed at what was transpiring before him.

"Neither do I," said Evad. "And although I would dearly like to keep the boy with me to discover the answer to this mystery, I have better uses for him. We'll be lifting off momentarily. The boy, along with a couple of his friends, stays here. We're destroying the electro-gen upon launch. That should put you on the horns of a dilemma. Pursue me or save three lives." Evad then barked, "End transmission." The three-dimensional image of the captain vanished.

Evad turned to face the cluster of mouse-like aliens.

"You two," he said, "fetch that to the ship." He pointed at Paine's prostrate body. "And you two," he indicated the other two grotesque figures, "Purge the area. Everyone else to the ship, double time." At that Evad, along with his remaining followers, took off at a fast clip in the direction of the flying saucer.

Sarah gulped. "Purge the area?" She looked at Tom. "What does that mean?"

Chapter 2
Firefight

"Purge the area?" Tom repeated Sarah's question. "I don't like the sound of that. Start backing up but try not to look scared." At Tom's suggestion, Sarah and Alex began to back away from the mouse-like aliens. Alex gave the creatures a grin along with a nonchalant wave of his hand. As always, Sarah looked scared.

Two of the aliens gathered up Paine's body as if it were but that of a child and began to move off in the direction of the saucer. The other two each used their free hand to draw a ray gun looking weapon from their holster and began to advance on the teens.

"Get behind me," said Tom. Sarah jumped behind Tom, once again hugging him around the waist. Then to Alex, Tom said, "Toss me your yo-yo."

"Huh?"

"Hurry. The yo-yo."

Alex tossed Tom the yo-yo, almost missing his target as he failed to allow for the lesser gravity.

Tom snatch the yo-yo out of the air and tried to turn, but not with great success due to Sarah's impersonation of a backpack. He saw the alien on his right raise its ray gun and take aim at Alex.

"Let go," yelled Tom. He tried to get Sarah to release her grip so he could attempt to do something to stop the giant mutant mouse from turning his best friend into a burnt cinder.

"I don't want to die," sobbed the girl, not releasing her hold on Tom.

Before the alien could pull the trigger, Tom managed to jerk around and with a prayer and all his might threw the yo-yo in the direction of the lifeless metallic man. The flying wooden toy scored a direct hit on the red button-like object at the center of the robot's chest, then rebounded in a graceful arc, and, as if by some preordained plan, ended up in Alex's hand.

There was moment of stunned silence from the alien creatures as Alex subconsciously shoved the yo-yo back into his pants pocket and gave Tom a puzzled look. The silence was broken by a blare of alarms. "Arang! Arang! Arang!" The guardian's arms jerked upward. It leveled the muzzle of its weapon directly at Alex. A loud crack broke the monotonous dirge of the alarms and the robot exploded, parts flying in all directions. Some hit Alex. The boy collapsed to the deck.

Tom stared at the leveled ray gun in the hand of the alien who had been aiming at Alex. It was the obvious origin of the bolt that had destroyed the guardian. No doubt the alien had considered the guardian a higher priority target than Alex and had adjusted its aim accordingly.

Tom twisted around intending to get to Alex's side. His sudden move caused Sarah to release her grip. As she caught her balance she found herself staring into the muzzle of the second alien's weapon. Her scream of "Tom!" caused the boy to look back. There was a loud zap from somewhere off too his left. The alien's head gave a jerk and from its left side a glob of purple slime exploded, spraying its companion. The alien's body twisted as it fell. As it did so the head turned to follow the abnormally slow collapsing body. Tom saw that a large hole, perhaps the diameter of a tennis ball, had been drilled clean through its head.

The other mouse-like creature turned to view its fallen partner and came face to face with a second robot, identical to the first both in appearance and armament.

The new robot got off a second shot, hitting the surviving alien in its left arm, which went limp, causing it to drop the ray rifle. Unfortunately for the guardian, the alien was holding its pistol in its right hand. Hit by the return fire, the guardian stiffened, then toppled forward in slow motion to crash to the deck.

While this exchange of fire was taking place, Tom was desperately searching for a weapon. He spied the first guardian's ray rifle next to the smoldering hulk of its former owner. The boy threw himself on the floor, managing to snatch up the weapon as he slid across the smooth surface of the deck. As he did so he felt a spasm of pain shoot up his arm, a result of the damage he had done to his hand when he had struck one of the mutant mice. Ignoring the pain and coming to a stop, he flipped over on his back, dragging the gun with him. Both the boy and the muzzle of the weapon he held now faced the surviving alien. As he lifted the gun, he almost dropped it as the throbbing hurt again flashed up his arm. His whole body seemed to shake as he attempted to aim the space rifle at the mouse-like monstrosity that was now directing its attention back to Sarah. Tom had never used a ray weapon before, yet his reflexes responded to it as if he had practiced with one for years. An old oriental saying that his father had taught him touched his mind. "The bearing of weapons changeth the mind of the bearer." The boy no longer felt helpless. Instead confidence and courage seemed to surge through his body. With a grunt, he leveled the gun at the grinning mouse from hell just as the thing was attempting to get off a shot at Sarah. He squeezed the trigger. The rifle emitted a loud zap. The weapon's recoil surprised the boy, not only because he had not expected any, but because the force of impact was so great that, at first, he thought it had broken his shoulder. The alien froze. A large hole appeared in its chest right about where the heart would be had the creature been human. Tom immediately squeezed off three more shots, each squeeze of the trigger slamming the weapon's stock against his aching shoulder. Three more holes appeared, forming a neat diamond shape on the chest of his antagonist. The fiend dropped its weapon and collapsed to the deck.

The sounds of explosions mingled with the zaps of ray guns were now coming from the direction of the flying saucer. Showers of sparks that erupted from some of the futuristic looking machines were followed by billows of smoke.

Tom dropped the rifle and scurried over to kneel next to the unmoving Alex. As the boy was lying on his side, Tom grabbed Alex's shoulder and gently rolled him over onto his back. "Alex——," he started to say. Alex's eyes were closed, and the left side of his face was covered by an ugly bruise.

"Is he . . . ?" Sarah's voice from behind Tom choked off in mid sentence as she caught sight of the boy's appearance.

Tom pressed an ear to Alex's chest. "He's still breathing——"

"Tom!" Sarah screamed.

Tom jerked his head up and looked in the direction of the flying saucer. Emerging from behind a row of exotic machines were the remaining two giant mice beings, one with the limp body of Jack Paine draped over its shoulder.

Tom jumped to his feet, grabbed the barrel of the rifle with his bad hand and Sarah's wrist with his good hand and yelled, "Move!" The pain in his hand almost caused him to lose his grip on the weapon.

"I don't want to die," sobbed Sarah as she stumbled after Tom, still trying to adjust to the lesser gravity. He pulled her towards a nearby row of machinery similar to that from behind which the aliens had appeared. Just before he reached the shelter provided by the equipment he glanced in the direction of the approaching mutant mice. Both had dropped their rifles and drawn their ray pistols, the one who had been carrying Paine having also dropped the unconscious delinquent's body.

Once behind the row of equipment, the boy dived to the deck dragging Sarah with him. He turned as he fell so that he landed on his back with Sarah falling on top of him. She immediately wrapped her arms around him reminding the boy of a spider grabbing its prey. As she did so there came a rapid series of ray gun bursts which were immediately followed by a number of holes being punched through the machinery that screened the two teens from view of their antagonists. Sarah gave out a shriek as one of the bolts nipped off a piece of the collar of her jacket.

"We're going to die," said Sarah, clinging to Tom so tightly that the boy was finding breathing less than easy.

"Sarah, let go. I can't shoot them with you holding onto me."

More zaps and more holes appeared, but further down the line of equipment from where the two teens lay.

Sarah gave the boy a startled look, her lower lip shaking, and then relaxed her grip. Tom slid out from under her and turned over on his stomach. He crawled along the row of strange contraptions until he found an opening through which he could observe the two aliens, now only a few steps away. Behind him Sarah lay on the floor, sobbing, her hands covering her face.

Tom shifted the gun around so it pointed through the opening. He had to act fast before the aliens were outside of the restricted line of vision allowed by the opportune firing hole. The boy sized up the situation. "If they get on this side of the machinery I probably don't stand a chance," he reasoned. "I wonder how many shots I have left?"

Not wasting another second by attempting to aim, he instinctively pointed the weapon towards the feet of the two grotesque beings, tensed his body, and squeezed off several bursts, a searing burn inflaming his right wrist and shoulder with each squeeze. The second bolt shattered the trailing creature's foot causing it to stumble forward and fall onto its comrade's back, thereby knocking the lead alien to the deck. It landed directly before the opening through which the boy had fired. As the evil grinning fiend raised its head, it found itself looking into the muzzle of Tom's rifle. Before the being could swing its hand around to bring its ray gun to bear, the boy blew a hole clean through its skull, a purple fluid flying out the back of its head and more oozing from the entry wound where the head came to rest on the floor. The fact that the deceased alien's body now blocked the boy's view of its comrade didn't deter Tom a moment, as he kept squeezing off bolts one after the other, sweeping the muzzle of his gun from left to right as much as the size of the opening permitted until the body before him resembled a giant piece of Swiss cheese lying in a rapidly expanding puddle of deep purple muck.

The boy scrambled to his feet, ignoring the searing pain in his wrist and shoulder. Sarah, sensing that Tom had stood up, raised her face from her hands. "Is it over?"

"I think so but stay put until I check." Sarah put her face back into her hands.

The teen hefted his rifle as best he could and cautiously worked his way past Sarah to the end of the line of equipment. As he did so, he gasped for breath, his heart seeming to pound faster than he had imagined possible. He peered around the end machine with the muzzle of his rifle pointed before him. There on the floor lay two alien corpses in a pool of purple ooze, both bodies punctured with holes. Not only was purple slime oozing from the perforated bodies but also that horrible odor.

"It's okay," he said. "I think they're either stunned or dead."

Sarah put her hands down and slowly stood up turning to look at the boy. Then she sprinted to him. Grabbing Tom in a bear hug, she almost knocked him to the floor.

As he attempted to maintain his balance an awful thought occurred to the boy. "Sarah, didn't Evad say something about destroying the machine that brought us here?"

"I...I think so," sniffled the girl. "Why?"

Tom looked over to where Alex lay near the circle of dirt from Sullivans Woods. "We have to move Alex."

"But that might hurt him more, even kill him," said Sarah.

Tom noted that the sounds of battle from the direction of the saucer had ceased. Instead a high-pitched whirling sound was coming from the saucer, its outer rim spinning at a tremendous rate.

"Hurry," said Tom dropping the rifle. The two teens rushed over to where their companion lay. "Grab an arm," said the boy. Tom grabbed one of Alex's wrists with his good hand and Sarah grabbed the other. They began to drag the blond-haired boy over the smooth pavement. "This way," said Tom, indicating the direction they had just come from. Although Sarah was using both her hands to pull Alex compared to Tom's one and Alex's body weighed significantly less than what it would be on Earth, Tom kept getting ahead of the girl causing Alex's body to swerve and twist from one side to the other as it was dragged across the floor. The pitch of the saucer was getting higher.

"How far?" gasped the girl.

"As far as we can."

They had just turned a corner so that a large weird-looking gizmo blocked their view of the collapsed dome when the saucer lifted. Both teens stopped and turned to watch the spaceship rapidly accelerate upward. Flashes of light erupted from it and there was an explosion behind them. Flying debris caught both teens in the back knocking them to the ground. Tom remembered hearing a scream from the girl that was quickly choked. He rolled over on his back, grimacing with pain. He looked upward at the strange object that seemed to float high above them, that he recalled Evad saying it had something to do with the gravity. It exploded.

Tom lay still for several moments, breathing deeply. Then, with some difficulty, he managed to sit up. Sarah was lying face down next to him, one arm thrown out beside her head, the other at her side. Some ugly red spots were forming on the back of her jacket. He reached over and turned the girl onto her back. "Sarah?" he said. There was no answer. Her eyes were closed and her mouth was slightly open.

A growing spot of red was staining the left side of her torn blouse near her waist. He didn't know what to do. He had taken first aid as a scout, but his training hadn't prepared him for this. He straightened up, although still on his knees. "Help, is anyone here?" He shouted it again, this time louder. There was no answer.

He sat back down and looked over at Alex. The boy, although unconscious, appeared to be breathing. Tom leaned over and placed his ear against the girl's chest. She was breathing, but it was a shallow breath. With some difficulty because of his injured hand, Tom managed to take off his jacket. He folded it a couple of times and then pressed it against the wound, tucking some of it around the girl's injured side and under her. He placed his good hand on top of the jacket and applied pressure. "How do you stop a wound in the abdomen from bleeding?" he asked himself. It was the only thing he could think of to do.

As he sat there keeping his hand pressed on the makeshift bandage, he had the odd sensation that he was getting lighter. He looked up remembering that he had seen the contraption that had hovered above them disintegrate. He began to reason. "Hadn't Evad said something about it providing the gravity? That must be it. The artificial gravity is getting weaker. It will keep decreasing until the only gravity left is that of the moon's natural attraction. But moons don't have atmospheres. That means that as the gravity diminishes, the air will slowly disappear. That's bad, very bad. But how to be sure that was what was happening?" The boy almost smiled to himself. "Not that it mattered." He looked about. A scrap of metal lay at his feet. He picked it up and held it a couple of feet off the ground with his bad hand as he was still using his good one to attempt to stem Sarah's bleeding. He released it. It clanked to the floor almost immediately.

Tom looked about, studying his surroundings. He didn't have any idea what all this stuff was for. He looked up at the sky. Saturn still dominated the heavens.

Now he could swear he was getting lighter. Was it his imagination, or was the air also growing thinner? He again picked up the piece of metal and let it drop. It seemed to the boy that it took longer this time to hit the floor. He continued to drop the object at what he estimated to be about one minute intervals. The fifth time he dropped it, it definitely appeared to take longer to fall. He now knew it was true. Like a capacitor discharging, the strength of the artificial gravity field was decaying and as it did so the air was vanishing into space.

Chapter 3
Iapetus Base

Tom studied the girl lying next to him. Her life spark appeared to be gradually dimming. "Is she still alive?" he asked himself. "What about Alex?" For some reason, he didn't want to know. He felt alone, more alone than he had ever felt in his entire life. He stared at the magnificent ringed planet that towered above the horizon and thought, "That's a view to die for." He forced a grin at his morbid sense of humor and took a deep gulp of air. It tasted fine—well, that is, he was sure it would have tasted fine if air had any taste. He wondered how much time had passed.

Since he didn't wear a wristwatch, he leaned over the girl's body and looked at the Minnie Mouse wristwatch that Sarah wore. The watch face stared back at him. He tapped it, then put his ear next to it. "Drats!" he muttered to himself. "It must be broken." He straightened and began to study one of the strange contraptions behind which they had sought shelter. On one part of the machine appeared several lines of red illuminated characters. Some were numerals whose values were rapidly changing, others were letters, and still others were symbols that were foreign to the boy. The letters and strange symbols were grouped as if they were words, many of which looked almost familiar except for the alien characters. The realization of the truth struck him. "My gosh. It's a phonetic alphabet. It has to be." For a brief instance the elation he felt at his discovery pushed from his mind his recent depression, but the joy lasted but a second and then it was gone. "How much air . . . ?"

It was hopeless and the boy knew it. He was going to die here on some moon whose name he couldn't even remember, let alone pronounce. When the last oxygen dissipated into space he was going to die along with Sarah and Alex, assuming they weren't already dead, or perhaps before the lack of air killed him his lungs or body would explode due to the reduced air pressure. There was no one to rescue them and, even if someone knew where they were, why should they care and, even if they cared, how could they possibly get to them in time?

The boy relaxed his thoughts and focused on his body. It seemed as if he could hear every breath he took. He told himself that he was going to die. Was dying really that awful? Maybe the worst thing about it was that no one would know what had happened to him. Not his mom, his dad, his sister—no one. Why had he ever been so foolish as to go into Sullivans Woods tonight? Why? Here he was untold millions of miles from home—from Earth. He watched the stars as they slowly marched across the blackness of space, then another glance at Saturn's magnificent rings. He asked himself, "Where was Earth—where was home? It's somewhere out there in that endless void, no doubt appearing as a star noticeably brighter than the others." If would be some comfort if he knew it when he saw it. It would be the last time he would ever see his home.

Tom returned his gaze to Sarah, his good hand still pressing his jacket against the wound on her side. The jacket was saturated with blood. "I might have at least stopped the bleeding, but is she turning blue or am I just imagining that? Is she still breathing?" He found that he didn't want to know, and even if he did know, what good would it do? Being careful not to move the hand that held the fabric against the girl's wound, the boy carefully lay back on the floor. He closed his eyes.

"Is it getting harder to breathe?" he asked himself. His chest heaved, attempting to fill his lungs with air. Yes, it seemed so or again perhaps it was his imagination. He used the sleeve of his shirt to wipe away some of the beads of sweat that had formed on his forehead. "Odd. I'm sweating yet the air feels colder?" He could swear he could hear his heart beating, straining, gasping for oxygen—for life. And then there was music—the great swelling strains of a symphony orchestra. He must be hallucinating. The music was majestic, stately, music that only the master of all composers could write. It was Beethoven's Eroica symphony—the "heroic." "There is always hope," he thought. The music—it seemed to lift his spirits from the depths of despair. He opened his eyes. Stars. Endless stars. He closed them again. Along with the music, images from the past began to bombard his mind. He reasoned that he was viewing his life passing before him. He forced a smile. It all seemed so—weird. Agony. His lungs were in agony. "I guess I should say a prayer. Mom would certainly want me to do that."

"The Lord is my shepherd; I shall not want ..."

As he ran through the prayer in his mind, he forced his eyes open again. He wasn't certain if what he saw moving majestically across his field of view was real or a hallucination brought on by oxygen deprivation. It was a spaceship, only not the flying saucer type of spaceship that Evad had departed in. This one resembled more the proverbial rocket ship. It gleamed like a finely polished piece of sterling silver and appeared to Tom how he always imagined a spaceship should look— smooth and streamlined, its nose tapered to a fine point. The stern of the ship was also tapered but less dramatically than the bow. Instead of coming to a point, the stern was truncated by what were no doubt the nozzles of its main engines. Three sleek, angled tail fins were equally spaced about the rear hull, each capped by a double ended tube that ran parallel to the axis of the ship's main body. Midway along the vehicle's fuselage were a pair of swept-back wings, no doubt for use in maneuvering through a planetary atmosphere. The hull of the ship was

397

unmarked and smooth, apparently uncluttered by the presence of any kind of window, porthole or door. The only exception besides the tail fins and wings were several long, menacing tube-like objects that projected from near the nose of the craft and pointed forward. Some kind of deadly space artillery or missile launchers was Tom's hunch.

As the ship started to drift from his field of view, Tom felt his eyelids closing. Before he lost consciousness, two thoughts occurred to him. One was the memory of Sarah falling on him as he lay on his back in Sullivans Woods, her long hair cascading over his face and those gorgeous brown eyes of hers staring into his. The other was that he could have sworn he felt something bump against him.

"What!" Tom gave a jerk as if a high voltage electric current had been sent through his body, his eyes flicked open, he looked straight up, and— "Ahhhhhh!"

He found himself staring at a creature more horrible and more bizarre than any he had ever imagined, including those in his recent nightmare about somehow ending up on a moon of Saturn that didn't exist. If the boy had been asked to write down his first impression of the monstrosity that hovered over him, it would have been that it was a werewolf, but a werewolf whose transformation from man to beast had gone terribly awry. Unlike the creatures from the Saturday matinees, this thing had fangs instead of teeth, fangs so large that there was no room for the upper set to be housed inside the mouth. Instead they protruded outside and over the lower jaw. Though the beast's head was covered with long, brown hair, the snout was hairless and covered with scales, reminding Tom more of an alligator than a wolf. Four eyes held the boy transfixed, bloodshot eyes, with slits for pupils not unlike those of a viper. The ears were long and tapered to sharp points, held stiffly aloft. And a single horn rose from the crown of the head, curving forward, an additional weapon of lethal portend. To add to the terror of the scene, gobs of saliva dripped from the lower jaw, and a disgusting pale green, mucous-like substance ran from each nostril at the front of the snout. The freakish apparition was made even more threatening by the scene behind it, that of a graveyard at night, the trees barren of any leaves, and not one, but two moons hanging in the sky, before which swift clouds were blown by an unseen wind.

The thing opened its ominous maw, but instead of a bloodcurdling roar, the wolf-gator said in articulate English, with a distinctive American twang, "I can't believe we missed Halloween, and me with the coolest costume ever." The voice sounded like Alex's, except a little muffled, like he was speaking from inside a mask.

As Tom sat upright in bed, the only thing that popped into his mind to say was, "Alex?"

"No, it's Vlad the Impaler," came the sarcastic reply. "Here we could have gone trick-or-treating, looking so horrid that we could have scared the piss out of Beelzebub himself, but no, you had to go spying on Evad."

"I thought that was your idea?"

"Listen Einar," continued the werewolf, or whatever it was supposed to be, who sounded like Alex in the most fabulous of Halloween costumes, "that seems like so long ago that I can't even remember."

"Actually," corrected Tom, "You're Einar. I'm Ragnar. Not only that, but you're not real because you can't buy costumes that cool, and you surely didn't make it. Besides my bedroom is not a graveyard, and you're the one who is always telling me that if something doesn't make sense, it's probably nonsense. So, get lost and let me go back to sleep. Besides I kind of liked the other dream better."

"Which one was that?" inquired Alex, the big, bad werewolf, just as one of those yucky gobs of green slime fell from the front of his snout.

"The one where you and I and Sarah—"

"You mean Miss Schnozzola?"

"I wish you wouldn't call her that."

399

"Why? Don't tell me you think she's cute?"

"Come off it, Alex. If you would stop kidding around for a minute, you know as well as I do that if you look beyond her nose, she's really pretty attract—that is, she's not really all that—"

"Ah ha! I knew it. You like her." The boy beast broke into a sing song. "Tom likes Sarah. Tom likes Sarah."

"I don't like her, you moron. I'm just saying it's not right to make fun of somebody because of the way they look. Besides who are you to howl? Look at the size of your proboscis."

"Yeah, but mine is one-hundred percent functional. Every ounce has a purpose."

"I thought you said it was a costume."

"Uh—it is. But if it were real, it would be functional. Now, where was I? Oh, yeah. Tom likes—"

"I don't like her."

"Then you won't mind if she marries me?"

Tom's hands formed into fists. He swung his legs over the side of the bed, and leaned forward, his face but inches from that of the creature. But then he relaxed, and the grimace on his face was replaced by a grin. "Nice try, snot puke. That's the same tactic my mom tried to use in the previous dream."

"Still think this is a dream, huh?" was the werewolf's response.

"Yeah," came the confident answer.

"Okay, you just said 'proboscis.'"

"I, did?"

"Yes, you did. Don't deny it. You said, 'Look at the size of your proboscis.'"

"Why would I have said that? I don't even know what pro—pro-basket means."

"Not probasket. Proboscis. That's my point. If this were a dream, would you be using words that you don't know?"

"What? That makes no sense at all," said Tom, feeling confused.

"Okay, Mr. Einstein. What is my pro—pro-boss-kiss?"

"Not your proboscis. My proboscis."

"I thought you said 'your proboscis?'" inquired Tom.

"No, you said 'your proboscis,' which means my proboscis."

Tom shook his head in an attempt to clear it. As he did so he glanced up at the sky. "Two moons!" he shouted triumphantly. "Two moons in the sky! Proboscis, snarf kiss. That proves it. This is a dream."

"Not so fast," came the quick counter thrust. "What makes you think you're on Earth? One of those moons happens to be Epimetheus."

Tom's look of triumph expanded into a smile. "Ah, the first dream. The one with you, me and, what did you call her, Miss Schnozzola, on a moon of Saturn."

"Wait until I tell Sarah what you called her. Miss Schnozzola. Shame on you."

"I didn't call her that, you did!"

"See, you wouldn't be so sensitive about the matter if you didn't like her. Admit it."

"You keep trying to change the subject."

"Which was?"

"That this is a dream. That you're not real."

"Of course, I'm real. You don't really believe you could dream all this, do you?"

"If I could dream up all that stuff about aliens and flying saucers and stuff, I could certainly dream this up."

"But all that was real too. Remember, I just said one of those moons is Epimetheus."

The boy reflected on what Alex the Disgusting Thing said. "No, it can't be. Both of these moons look like the Moon—Earth's moon. I don't think Epimetheus was round."

"Very good, Tom." The wolf beast gave the boy a big, toothy smile, so toothy as matter of fact that he resembled more the Big Bad Wolf of the fairy tale than the horrid creature Tom had first encountered.

"Go away, Alex, or whoever you are, and let me wake up back home," Tom said as he fell back into his bed.

"One more thing, Tom, before I disappear."

"Yeah, what is it?"

"If they ever make these dreams of yours into a movie, do you think this is one of the dreams they'll cut because including it will make the movie too long?"

"Probably," mumbled the boy, as his vision grew hazy.

Before Alex the Boy Canine vanished along with the graveyard, he sneezed, sending disgusting green boogers everywhere.

What felt like a soft, but moist, hand massaged the boy's forehead. It felt good.

"Mom?" Tom said, without opening his eyes. There was no reply. The gentle pressure on his forehead continued, slowly gliding back and forth, just below his scalp. He was obviously lying on his back, his arms extended beside him. His body seemed weirdly light, sort of like he was floating but at the same time not.

"Sooner or later I'll have to really wake up," thought Tom. "It might as well be sooner." He opened his eyes. Directly above him extended a bluish translucent tube an inch or so in diameter, which was most likely attached to whatever was massaging his head. He focused his eyes upwards. The tube extended through the surface of a transparent sphere that appeared to be either suspended from or was floating directly below the ceiling. The boy judged the sphere to be about two feet in diameter and filled with a clear liquid, probably water was Tom's guess. Within the sphere and filling a sizeable part of its volume floated what looked to be a cross between a jellyfish and a giant amoeba. It continually changed shape. The tube which had first caught Tom's attention was attached to the strange creature, that is, assuming the thing was alive, and protruded through an opening in the sphere. It was as if the thing had extended a long tentacle to enable it to touch the boy.

Despite the strangeness of the scene, Tom was surprised that he didn't feel startled. Instead he felt as if he were mildly drugged. He yawned, and then said in an amazingly calm tone of voice, "Let me guess. You're some kind of alien?"

No voice answered his question, at least none which was detected by the boy's sense of hearing. Instead it was as if the answer formed within the boy's mind, in the vicinity of his forehead to be more exact. "From your perspective, I believe the answer would be yes. Of course, from my viewpoint, you're the alien"

Tom ignored the discourse on the proper use of the word *alien*. "Where am I?"

"In the infirmary of Iapetus Base."

"Okay, dream number one is back."

"You are not dreaming."

Tom focused his vision on the shapeless blob floating in the spherical aquarium which hung directly above him. As he did so he involuntarily flexed his brow as if trying to see what was at the end of the tentacle where it touched his forehead. "Are you the shapeless blob floating above me?"

"Yes."

"What are you?"

"I am a Panthergenian."

"No, kidding. I'm an American teenager. Are you going to suck out my brains or something?"

"No. I will not harm you. I am here to help you. I've alerted the *Antares'* medical officer that you are conscious. He'll be here shortly to examine you."

"Antares? That's a star."

"Yes, but in this case, it's a starcruiser."

"Starcruiser, huh. That sounds kind of neat. And the doctor from this starcruiser is coming to see me? What's his name? Doc?"

"His name is Lieutenant Maser. Normally a base physician would be attending you, but because of the special circumstances surrounding your rescue, access to you is restricted to members of the crew of the *Antares*. I am the exception."

The boy didn't understand much of what the alien was telling him but thought better of asking it a bunch of questions. Instead, he looked past the Panthergenian hovering above him, focusing his eyes on the ceiling. The room brightened causing Tom to momentarily squint his eyes. The entire ceiling seemed to diffuse light, almost as if it were a window and daylight was pouring in from the outside. Tom looked to his left. There, on a platform that reminded Tom of a hospital's operating table, lay Alex, on his back with his arms crossed over his chest. The boy's body appeared to be partially sunk into the top of the table it was lying upon as if the tabletop was in some ways similar to a soft mattress. Except for the absence of his jacket, Alex was still dressed as he had been on Halloween night. A thin tube was attached to the side of his head, directly in front of the earlobe. The boy appeared to be in a deep sleep.

"How long have I been asleep?" asked Tom. The boy was finding it strangely humorous that he was holding a conversation with some sort of giant, intelligent amoeba.

"Sixteen hours. Both your body and your mind had undergone severe shock and stress, not to mention some physical damage. All the damage has been successfully repaired. You should shortly feel both wide awake and refreshed."

"Is Alex okay?"

"The other boy? Yes, he's fine. He should shortly be recovering from sedation."

The teen rotated his head to look to the other side. There rested Sarah on a platform identical to the one on which Alex lay. She too was unconscious. Several cables were attached to various parts of her head. With the exception of her jacket, she was dressed as she had been the evening before, although her garments in places were torn and soiled with dried blood. Like Alex, her glasses were missing.

"What about Sarah?"

"You mean the girl? She is still undergoing treatment. She suffered several external lacerations, internal injuries, and, of course, severe mental trauma. Fortunately, a cyber medic got to her in time to save her life. Although she should also be recovering consciousness soon, it will no doubt be several more hours before she is at optimum health."

A swishing sound came from somewhere behind him, causing Tom to again swivel his head. The hatch in the bulkhead behind Alex had disappeared and a man dressed in some sort of uniform was stepping through the open hatchway, followed by a grey tabby cat. Like cats everywhere, the feline wore an expression that seemed to say that he was lord of all he surveyed. As soon as the cat cleared the hatchway, the hatch swiftly reappeared from the top of the opening and dropped back into place with another swishing sound. The man's dress consisted of a grey, long-sleeved jumper, and loose fitting, grey trousers with front pockets, tucked into the top of a pair of black boots. Both shirt and trousers were trimmed in blue. The ends of the sleeves ended in what looked like black wrist guards. A large triangular collar crowned the top of the jumper, the apex of the triangle ending about midway down the chest. Next to the collar, about where the man's heart would be appeared an emblem on the jumper, that of a spaceship eclipsing a ringed planet. The wardrobe was completed by a thick belt upon which were fastened a host of gadgets and pouches. A closed holster hung from the right side of the belt.

The man offered the boy a friendly smile, no doubt in the tradition of physicians throughout the history of the profession. "Well, my boy, how are we feeling?"

With little effort Tom sat up although he almost lost his balance due to his attempt to over adjust to the strange lack of weight his body was experiencing. Equally odd was the fact that the shape of the table on which he sat changed to conform to the change in his posture. It was soft, yet firm so as to be most comfortable. "Okay." And then he added the qualifier, "I guess, except that I still feel—light."

"Light? Oh, that's because we're at Iapetus Base. Landed about two hours ago."

"Iapetus Base? The last I remember I was on some moon of Saturn's. Where in the heck am I now?"

"Iapetus is another moon in the Saturn system, although significantly farther from the planet than Epimetheus. Hmm, I'm surprised you don't know that. Anyway, like the base on Epimetheus, the gravity at Iapetus Base is artificially generated to equal a third of Earth's. Without the electrogen, you would feel even lighter."

"I think that made sense," said Tom.

"You're obviously not used to dealing with low gravity environments," smiled the man. He then motioned towards the floating alien. "I see you've met Auxfeed."

"Auxfeed?"

"Yes." The medical officer motioned towards the airborne shapeless blob of jelly in the fluid filled sphere above the boy. "The Panthergenian." When the boy gave him a blank stare, the man continued. "Do you mean to say you've never met a Panthergenian before?"

"Met one, I don't even know what that thing is other than some sort of giant, talking amoeba."

The man gave a short chuckle. "Giant amoeba. That's a good one. Did you like that answer, Auxfeed?"

The boy rolled his eyes. "That wasn't a serious answer. I was being sarcastic."

The ship medical officer appeared to be a little taken aback as he cleared his throat. "Of course. Sarcasm. Yes, well—" The man hesitated a second, searching for his next words. "It's just that I wasn't prepared for some levity on your part, especially considering what you must have been through recently." At that, the grey tabby jumped up on Tom's bed, seated itself next to the boy and fixed him with a hard stare. The boy reached down and slid his hand down the cat's back, getting a familiar purr for an answer.

"So exactly what is Auxfeed then?"

"You really don't know?" The doctor gave the boy a look that seemed a combination of surprise and suspicion. "He's a Panthergenian, a highly advanced life form from the Taurus Eight system. They're aquatic, although the chemical composition of their seas differs from Earth's, neither fresh water nor salt. For some reason, still not understood, at least by us, they have an uncanny ability to perform psychotherapy on humans. They can sooth trouble minds, even to the point of curing some forms of human insanity. It's almost as if they evolved with that end in mind."

"Can they read minds?" asked Tom, staring at the alien

"As far as we know, not to the extent that they could transcribe what you were actually thinking. But they can often get the general drift of it, just from what your emotions are telling them."

Tom moved his head to make eye contact with the medical officer. "What makes you think it's a 'he?'"

"Actually, 'they' would be a fairer description. Auxfeed is more akin to a colony of individuals than a single organism, yet a colony that acts with a single mind. It's really not easy to explain it on such short notice. But to answer your question," the lieutenant was looking at the boy now with even more suspicion than before, "it just seems more 'human' to think of Auxfeed as a 'he' or even a 'she' than an 'it.' Besides, when Panthergenians speak to us, they of course speak English, and it is their preference to refer to one another as 'he.'"

"So where am I, how did I get here, and who are you again?"

"You are in the Iapetus Base infirmary. We brought you here in the Solar Patrol starcruiser *Antares*, Captain Rex Krater commanding. I am the *Antares'* medical officer, Lieutenant Maser, although most people call me Doc."

"Yes, I know that. That's what that thing said." Tom limply motioned with his left hand toward the hovering creature.

At Tom's words, the Panthergenian turned a bright yellow and withdrew its tentacle from contact with Tom's forehead. The moment the tentacle was removed, Tom's state of bliss evaporated.

"Auxfeed doesn't like to be called a 'thing.' I believe you owe him an apology." The lieutenant's tone sounded gruff.

"I'm sorry." The boy looked at the Panthergenian. "I apologize. It's just that I've never seen anything—anybody like you before."

For some reason Tom then recalled having severely injured the hand he had used to strike the Mickie. He looked at it and then flexed the fingers. Other than seeming a little stiff, it appeared to be as good as new. "My hand . . ."

"Yes, you fractured one of the bones."

"But it's healed."

"Yes, of course," said the lieutenant, sounding as if there was nothing amazing about the fact.

"Oh," said Tom. He flexed his hand again. "So, we're on a base on the moon—Iapetus, is that right?"

"Yes."

"When I was on that base on Epi—Epi—whatever, I could see the stars. Here I'm in a room with no windows."

"The base on Epimetheus was an abandoned industrial base. Iapetus Base is a Solar Patrol base. Most of it is underground although there is a domed section above us, next to the landing area."

"I see," said Tom, not sure that he saw. "And what exactly is a starcruiser?"

For an awkward moment, the medical officer stood there, giving the boy an odd stare. Then he took Tom by the arm and helped him off the table.

"Come with me. It's time for your interrogation."

"Interrogation?" Tom didn't like the sound of that.

"Debriefing, if you will."

The compartment's hatch slid open and a robot entered. Although shorter, there were many similarities between the appearance of this new robot and the guardian robots Tom had seen on Epimetheus. The robot featured a metallic blue 'skin,' and, like a guardian, its limbs were basically elongated cylinders encased by enlarged flexible joints that made up its shoulders, elbows, hips and knees. The feet displayed no individual toes and along with the hands, looked larger than those on a human of comparable height. Like a guardian, the torso was split into two parts, the top being a broad chest that narrowed towards the waist and the bottom a wide pelvic section to which the hips were connected. The upper and lower torso sections rotated independently of each other. In contrast to the relatively featureless body design of a guardian, a variety of knobs, buttons and electronic looking gizmos were displayed on its chest. The head was the shape of an upright egg that rested on a broad collar. It lacked a mouth and nose but had two protruding cylinders that housed orange lights for eyes. In lieu of ears, a short cylinder protruded each side of the head. A cable projecting from each 'ear' bent upwards to connect with its opposite partner at the top of the head. Although it appeared to be designed to emulate human locomotion, it instead glided across the deck as if it were on roller skates.

"It's a robot," stammered the boy.

"Yes," said the doctor, as if the appearance of a robot was the most common of everyday sights. "Are you going to tell me that you've never seen a robot before?"

"There were a couple back on that moon, but those were the only ones I've seen before this one."

Again, the doctor gave the boy a suspicious look.

"This is Dave. He'll be on duty here in our absence." Without any further introduction, the lieutenant exited through the open hatchway with Tom awkwardly attempting to follow him. The hatchway swiftly closed behind the boy as he cleared it. Tom found himself in curved hallway. The lieutenant led Tom about thirty feet down the hallway to a hatch in the wall similar to the one they had exited. The hatch opened. The lieutenant motioned for Tom to pass through the opening, then followed him into a room similar in size to the infirmary. Like the infirmary, the room contained no windows, the only exit being the hatchway through which they had entered. Behind a long, gracefully curved table before the far wall were seated four men dressed in uniforms similar to that worn by the lieutenant. On the table were a number of items that the boy recognized as the contents of what had been in his pants pockets along with, no doubt, those of Alex's and Alex and Sarah's wristwatches. Besides the chairs on which the men were seated, there were also two empty futuristic looking chairs, one behind the table to the far left and the other immediately in front of Tom, facing the table. Another man stood to Tom's right, beside the hatchway. Although his uniform was similar in style to those of the others in the room, its color differed in being a dark blue with red trim. The man was a giant, with bulging muscles and a hard-cut countenance that boded ill for anyone foolish enough to cross him. As Tom stepped into the room, the big man grabbed him by the neck of his shirt, pushed him forward, and thrust him into the solitary chair. The 'guard' then resumed his position by the now closed hatchway as the lieutenant took the remaining empty chair behind the table.

Tom recognized the man seated at the center of the table as the one whose apparition had materialized on the moon. It was with relief that he noted that the man gave him a smile.

"Good day, young man," he said. "My name is Rex Krater. I am captain of the starcruiser *Antares*."

"Starcruis—?" Tom began to say, but immediately shut up as the captain began to introduce the other men in the room.

"This is Major Sargon, my executive officer—" He motioned to the man on his immediate right. The sound of Sargon's name seemed

410

to fit his appearance. A dark, handsome man, by the cold look he gave Tom, he didn't seem any happier to see the boy than had the giant, gruff man who had forced Tom to have a seat. "—and next to him is Lieutenant Maser, the ship medical officer whom you have already met." The captain turned to his other side. "Ensign Chandrasekhar, the ship's astrogator—" The astrogator gave the boy a slight nod, but if there was no hostility in the gesture, neither was there any sign of friendliness. "—and Lieutenant Tanner, our chief engineer." The engineering officer also displayed no emotion, nor did he make any gesture towards the boy when introduced. "The mean looking cuss you met when you entered this compartment is Sergeant Rhino, commander of the ship's marine detachment. I now convene this officers' review. Please state your full name."

"Er, Thomas Jefferson Cobalt."

"Your place and date of birth?"

"East Pencreek, Pennsylvania." The boy's answer was met by blank stares from the men behind the table.

"Where exactly is East Pencreek, Pennsylvania?" said the captain.

"Pennsylvania. It's a state in the United States—the United States of America."

The stares of the officers changed from blank to incredulous.

"What's the matter?" said Tom. "You look like I said I was from Mars of something."

"What's odd about being from Mars?" asked Ensign Chandrasekhar. "I'm a Martian."

"Huh? I thought Martians would be little green men or something."

The captain gave the boy a scowl and then turned to the doctor. "You confirmed that he has no neurodic implant?"

"Yes," said Lieutenant Maser.

For several moments the room was silent, no one saying anything, but on occasion one of the men would turn to make eye contact with another as if they were holding a conversation. Tom kept shifting his gaze from one member of the panel to another. "I don't understand—" he began, but when the officers all ignored him he shut up. At one point he turned and looked at the sergeant standing by the hatchway. The sergeant was watching him with an intensity that reminded the boy of a crocodile eyeing its next prey. He quickly turned his attention back to the men at the table when it dawned on him that they were having a conversation among themselves—a conversation that required no speech. Although he couldn't hear what they were saying to one another, Tom had no doubt as to what the topic was.

He almost jumped out of his seat when the captain spoke. "Age?"

"Thirteen."

"Standard years, I presume?"

"What?"

"Never mind. Date of birth?"

"August 15, 1946."

"You expect us to believe that?" said the one called Sargon. "First you tell us you were born in the United States of America and now this. Let's cut the tubes here. Are you not an agent of the Draconian Guard?"

"The Draconian what?"

"You know very well what the Draconian Guard is. Don't play dumb with us. Answer the question. Are you not a member of the Draconian Guard?"

"Listen, I never heard of—this Drapo, whatever."

"Answer the question, yes or no."

"Yes."

"Ah-hah, so you admit you're a guardsman?"

"No, I'm not."

"But you just said you were."

"No, I didn't. I just answered the question which was whether I was not a member of whatever it is I'm not a member of."

"He's obviously a Draconian agent," said Sargon, sounding positive.

"Let's toast him, or better yet space him."

The captain held up his hand. "Major." That ended the major's suggestions of various means of Tom's demise. The captain studied the boy for a moment before again speaking. "What is today's date?"

"October—no wait, by now it would be November first. Why?"

"And the year?"

"The year? 1959, of course."

"I can't believe the insolence of this—," started Sargon, but again a gesture from the captain cut him off.

The captain gave Tom what the boy thought was an empathetic look. "Son, the year is 2350."

Tom shot back, panic starting to creep into his voice. "No, it's not. It's 1959." When the captain didn't respond, Tom continued. "You're kidding me. This is some kind of a joke, right?"

"It's not a joke."

Tom glanced about the room trying to collect his thoughts. Much of what he had experienced since leaving Sullivans Woods all pointed to a technology far in advance of what had existed in the twentieth century. If the year really was 2350 that could only mean that he arrived here in a time machine!

Lieutenant Tanner, the one Tom remembered to be an engineering officer, spoke up. "You claim your name is Thomas Cobalt, correct?"

The boy was starting to get a little miffed at the questions. "Yeah, that's my name." He didn't like the attitude of these people. "Don't wear it out."

"What?" said the lieutenant.

"I said that's my name, don't wear it out."

The lieutenant looked at the captain, who shrugged his shoulders in reply. The lieutenant forged on. "Any relation to 'the Commander.'"

"Who?"

"The Commander. Commander Thomas Cobalt of the Solar Patrol. Do you claim any relation?"

413

"Listen, I'm the only Tom Cobalt I know. My father is Sam Cobalt and my mother is Nancy Cobalt. As far as I know, I don't have any Cobalt kin by the name of Tom, living or dead and buried."

"If as you claim you were really born in the twentieth century, explain how you came to be here," said the captain.

"Gee, that's kind of a long story, but the short answer is—I'm not sure."

"Just give us the essentials," instructed the captain.

Tom did his best to relate the events of the past few days or, if what these men were asserting was true, events that had occurred almost four centuries in the past.

During the telling of his story, the men made no comment, that is, until he got to the part where he mentioned the conversation that Sarah had overheard between Sleinad Evad and Mr. Serpens, the school guidance counselor. The mention of Mr. Serpens' name seemed to cause a stir among the seated officers.

"Serpens, you say?" said the captain. "How do you spell that."

"Darn if I know," said Tom. "S-E-R-P-E, or maybe it's an A, N-S. You know, Serpens, kind of like some sort of slimy snake."

"Snakes aren't slimy," said Lieutenant Tanner, the engineering office.

"Well, yeah, I know that," said the boy, "but Serpens sure was."

The captain seemed to give a nod of agreement with Tom's assertion about Mr. Serpens. He asked the boy to continue. For a while Tom's narrative seemed to elicit little response from the panel, until he got to the part about Alex and Sarah finding the pod in Evad's apartment. Tom sensed an increase in interest from the men as they exchanged glances with one another.

"Of course, I wasn't there. I'm just telling you what Alex and Sarah said they saw."

Tom continued with his description of the events that had taken place in Sullivans Woods which to the boy had occurred only the previous evening. "I could swear," said Tom, "hey, I know it sounds hokey, but it looked like their eyes, you know, Evad's and Serpens', were glowing."

"Glowing?" asked the captain.

"Yeah, kind of—green. Not bright, just sort of a faint green glow. You would probably only notice it in the dark."

The four other officers all gave Major Sargon a quick glance. The major in turn, continued to fix the boy with a hostile stare, but one that seemed now to have transitioned from dislike to total malevolence.

There were no further interruptions until Tom was describing how he killed the last of the mouse-like aliens on Epimethcus. Major Sargon, the executive officer gave the boy a scowl.

"You expect us to believe that you killed three Mickies?"

"Er, what's a Mickie?"

"The alien creatures you claimed to have shot and killed with a guardian's rifle, as if you didn't know."

"Yes. Was there something I did that was wrong? I mean I didn't mean to kill them, it's just that I'm not sure what else I could have done."

Instead of getting an answer to his question, the one known as Ensign Chandrasekhar said, "You realize that time travel is impossible?"

"Why would it be?" asked Tom.

"For many reasons. For instance, if it were possible, why aren't we overrun with visitors from the future?"

"Gee, I don't know. Maybe they wouldn't have any interest in coming here from the future—sort of like I have no interest in going to visit my Great Aunt Mildred in New Jersey." At that, Lieutenant Tanner let out a chuckle, and the captain forced a smile. "Listen, I can't answer that question. I'm just a kid. I've only made it to the eighth grade so far. But I do remember that one day in class Alex asked Evad if time travel was possible."

"And what did Evad say?" asked the captain.

"You see Alex's uncle is a physics professor, and he told Alex that time travel was impossible due to the principle of—well, I can't remember what it was he said now. Anyway, when Alex asked Evad, he turned around and asked Alex if his uncle had mentioned the principle of—of temporal immu—temporal immu—"

"Temporal immutability?" said Major Sargon.

"Yeah, that sounds right."

The men behind the table began exchanging looks, and as before Tom reasoned that they were again engaged in some sort of secret conversation among themselves, a conversation he obviously couldn't hear. When the silent discussion had ended, the captain looked at Tom and motioned towards the objects on the table. "Would you identify these items."

"Sure," said Tom, leaning forward. "Obviously you took them out of my pockets, and it looks like Alex's also. Let's see. There's two quarters, two nickels, some pennies, four Fizzies, three pieces of Double Bubble bubblegum, Alex's yo-yo, our Boy Scout pocketknives, my snot rag—"

"What was that last thing?" said Lieutenant Tanner.

"My snot rag. You know, a handkerchief. My mom makes me carry one."

"And what again are these things?" asked the doctor, pointing at the Fizzies.

"They're Fizzies," responded the boy. "You take one out and put it in a glass of water, and it fizzes and you get a fruit drink. Three are cherry flavored and one lime. They're Alex's. He likes Fizzies. I don't. I think they taste like panther piss."

"Panther piss?" repeated Ensign Chandrasekhar. "You mean panther urine?"

"Yeah. Of course, that's just an expression. I really don't know what panther piss tastes like." Tom gave the men behind the table a sheepish grin, but they said nothing, just stared at him. "I mean I never tasted any."

"Unbelievable," was the doctor's response.

"If you get me a glass of water, I'll show you," offered the boy. "Or take it out of the wrapper and taste it. You'll see."

"No, I don't think that will be necessary," said the doctor.

"Anyway, this is my grandfather's St. Christopher's medal and Alex—"

"What's the purpose of the medal?" asked Major Sargon.

"I believe it's supposed to protect travelers who wear it."

"You believe it has magical properties?" sneered the major.

"Not really. My mom gave it to me—last night." The boy paused and then forced a swallow. "St. Christopher was a Catholic saint, and we're not Catholic, but it was my grandfather's, and he wasn't Catholic either, but I guess my mom thought . . ." Tom's voice trailed off.

"Please continue," said the captain.

"Sure thing. Let's see, there's Alex's wristwatch and Sarah's Minnie Mouse watch."

Ensign Chandrasekhar picked up Sarah's watch to examine it more closely. "Is the picture that of a Minnie Mouse?"

"Yes."

The ensign gave his head a shake and placed the watch back on the table.

"And those are Alex's glasses and those are Sarah's."

"And their function is—?" asked the major.

Before Tom could answer, the doctor broke in. "Lenses to correct less than optimal vision. They were quite common back in the twentieth century. In period photographs you'll often see people of the time wearing such things. In attending to the injuries of the other two teens, I took the liberty of correcting their vision."

"What happened to your 'glasses?'" asked the Captain.

"My vision's good—twenty-twenty. I don't need to wear glasses," said Tom.

"What can you tell us about this?" said the captain. Jack Paine, or at least a life size projection of his body, materialized before Tom, causing the boy to sit up with a start. The juvenile delinquent was horizontal, face up, eyes closed with his wrists crossed over his chest. His body seemed to hover in midair.

"That's Jack Paine. He's the one I told you about, a really bad character. We thought he was dead, you know, killed in a car wreck—well, at least that's what they said in the news. Then the next thing we know he's there in Sullivans Woods last night. He even had a ray gun. Like I told you, he looked like he was going to shoot Sarah when Evad shot him." Tom couldn't think of anything else to tell them about Jack, so he asked, "Is he dead?"

"No," said the captain.

Tom took another glance at Paine's face and then said, "Something's wrong."

"What do you mean?" asked the captain.

Tom took a moment to study the face more closely. "I thought he was Jack Paine, but somehow he looks different. Now I'm not so sure this is Jack. I mean, it's not like I was a buddy of his or anything. Like any sane person, I tried to avoid him like the plague. But now I not so sure it's really Jack."

"Interesting," said the captain. "You're telling us have no idea what it is?"

"What it is? Don't you mean who it is?" said Tom.

"No, I mean what it is. It's not human."

"How would I know what it is then?"

There was a brief pause before the captain spoke. "Since there are no further questions, Sergeant, you may escort the—Tom—back to the infirmary."

"Yes, sir," said the human tank guarding the door, as he snapped to attention.

"Wait a minute," blurted out Tom. "I have a few questions." But Tom's comment was ignored as the marine sergeant took hold of the back of the boy's shirt collar, lifted him to his feet, and gave him a shove towards the compartment's exit.

Chapter 4
Examination Results

It was but a few paces from the compartment where the interrogation had been held to the base infirmary. When Tom reached the infirmary's hatch it popped open as if it had sensed the boy's presence. The gruff marine sergeant gave the boy a not so gentle shove causing Tom to stumble into the room. As the hatch dropped swiftly back into place, Tom was greeted by a welcome face. Alex was conscious and sitting on the table on which Tom had last seen him lying. He looked as if he had been having a friendly chat with the robot, Dave. Across the room the alien Auxfeed hovered over a still unconscious Sarah. The floating airbag had its main tentacle attached to the girl's forehead as it had previously done with Tom. The tubes that had been attached to Sarah were now gone.

Spying Tom, Alex gave his friend a clenched fist salute. "Hail Ragnar." Considering all that Alex had recently gone through, he seemed amazingly calm and none the worse for wear. Tom guessed that his friend had been given some sort of drug to relax him.

"Hail Einar." Tom returned the salute.

"Who was that with you?" said the blond-haired boy.

"His name's Sergeant Rhinoceros or something like that."

"Mean looking cuss," observed Alex.

"You got that right."

"Wow, isn't this all really weird?" said Alex. "Look, it's another robot—" He pointed at Dave. "—and another kind of alien." Alex motioned towards Auxfeed.

"Yes, I know," said Tom, carefully shuffling his feet in an effort to effectively adjust for the lower gravity. He took a seat on the table next to his friend while at the same time giving the unconscious Sarah an anxious glance.

"I've been briefing Mister Banyon on the situation," said the robot. "He seems to be handling it all quite well. Then again that is no doubt in part due to the injection that Lieutenant Maser gave him."

"Yeah. To think we're at some kind of space base on the moon Iapetus. Eh, where were you and who was that guy again?"

"That guy's a marine. I think his name is Sergeant Rhino—"

"Yes, that is correct," said the robot.

"—and I was being interrogated by a bunch of officers."

"Interrogated?" Alex was starting to sound more in tune with the reality of their situation. "Why?"

"Best as I can guess there seems to be some sort of problem with us being here."

"Were they human?"

"Well, they appeared to be human. And they speak English, although it sounds a little strange, just like when Dave here speaks."

"So where are they from—I mean, they're obviously not from Earth as no one on Earth has this kind of futuristic stuff."

"They are all humans," said the metal man, "although not all were born on Earth so technically they're not all Terrans."

"Huh, huh," said Alex. "That was clear as mud."

"But mud is opaque," said the robot.

"Say, Alex, do you realize that your braces are gone?"

"Huh?" said the other boy. He opened his mouth and felt his teeth.

"And your glasses?"

Alex looked about the room, his excitement growing.

"By golly, you're right. I can see fine. Boy, this is really great. I guess these guys you met must have done it."

"Probably the doc."

Alex got back on topic. "You were saying that there seems to be a problem with us being here? I mean Dave says we were brought here in a spaceship. If that's true, can't they take us home?"

Tom gave a sigh. "Alex, according to the people I talked to it's not 1959. The year is 2350."

"A.D.?"

"Yes, A.D."

Alex became quiet. Tom decided it was best not to try to elaborate but instead let his friend digest this latest information. For a few moments Alex studied the deck while he oscillated his feet back and forth. Finally, he looked up. "This is a dream, right?"

"I don't think so," said Tom. "Can we be sharing the same dream?"

"I don't think so," said Alex, who still didn't sound convinced that he wasn't having a dream.

"Maybe this will help." Tom landed a quick, hard punch on his friend's shoulder.

"Ouch!" The blow seemed to have had the intended effect of knocking the uncertainty out of Alex. "You're not kidding. We're on the moon Iapetus and it's really the future."

"Apparently."

Again, Alex was silent for several seconds, sitting there as before deep in thought, except now he had a dejected look about him and was absently rubbing the spot on his shoulder where his friend had punched him. Then he perked up again, turned to Tom, flashed him a forced grin and said, "I feel like I don't weigh as much as I should, kind of like I did back on Epimetheus. Is it me, or do you feel light too?"

"I'm light too. Apparently, they have one those artificial gravity gizmos here like they did back at that other place, Epi-something-or-other."

"Epimetheus."

"How do you do that?"

"Do what?"

"Remember things like the name of that place we never heard of before?"

"All the moons and planets are named after characters from Greek and Roman mythology, so the name's familiar to me, but I can't recall who exactly Epimetheus was. We're really on Iapetus, huh?"

"That's what they say, not that it surprises me that you've actually heard of this place."

"Cool!" said Alex.

"I'm sorry," said the robot. "The atmosphere in the base's common spaces is kept at a temperature of twenty-two degrees Celsius, but if you're uncomfortable, we can easily raise the temperature in this compartment."

Both boys laughed. "No," corrected Alex. "What I really meant was neat."

Dave gave the boy an uncomprehending blink, that is to say, the lights on his head, positioned at the location where one would expect eyes, flickered. The robot then did a quick visual scan of the infirmary. "Yes, we try to keep things neat. After all this is a Solar Patrol base."

"Okay, that's one more strike against thinking that I'm dreaming," said Alex. Then as if finally satisfied that he really was in the twenty-fourth century, Alex turned to Dave. "Who are you guys, and what happens now?"

"We're the Solar Patrol."

"I should have guessed," said Alex. "From that sergeant's uniform, he looked like he was in some sort of 'patrol.'"

"Excuse me," said the robot, "but I must take my leave. Should you require any assistance, just ask."

"Hey, wait a minute," said Tom. "Ask who? And what about Sarah? Is she going to be okay?"

"Just ask," said the robot. "And as for Sarah, Lieutenant Maser told me that it will be fine and that it should be regaining consciousness momentarily." With that the hatch swished open, the robot exited the room, and the hatch again dropped back into place.

"Why did he refer to Sarah as an 'it?'" asked Alex.

"I don't know," answered Tom. "Maybe it's not very smart for a robot or maybe there are no women in the future."

Both boys stared at the unmoving girl.

"Boy, that's one scary thought," said Alex. "Sarah Gould, the last woman in the universe. You know, she doesn't look so good."

"Yeah, I know." Tom hopped to the deck and, after hesitating a moment due to the unaccustomed slowness of his fall which seemed to take a fraction of a section longer than normal, shuffled over to stand next to the girl. Sarah's skin appeared awfully sickly to him. It seemed to have a grey tinge to it.

Alex decided that it might be best to change the subject. "Well, it's just you, me, Sarah, the cat, and some kind of alien thing."

"Yeah," said Tom, noticing for the first time the grey cat perched on an empty table, staring intently at him.

"So, what all did they ask you?"

"They wanted to know who I was, where I came from, stuff like that. They seemed really shocked when they learned we were from the twentieth century." Tom returned to his seat next to Alex. "How do you suppose we got here, in the future I mean?"

"I think that's obvious. We were transported here by some sort of time machine."

"Yeah, I guess that makes sense."

"So. they—these patrol guys—didn't expect us, huh?"

"Apparently not." Tom was surprised that in the few seconds since he had examined her up close, Sarah's complexion seemed have turned a healthy pink. "I also got the feeling they weren't too happy to see us."

"What all happened after I got knocked out?"

Tom began to relate to Alex all he could remember of what had taken place since Alex lost consciousness on the moon Epimetheus. As Tom told of his recent adventures it was not only Alex who listened to the boy's story. Besides the grey feline that seemed to focus on Tom's every word, unseen eyes watched the two boys and unseen ears listened to Tom's tale.

Rex Krater, the captain of the Solar Patrol starcruiser *Antares*, along with his executive officer, Major Sargon, sat facing the bulkhead that separated the compartment they were in from the base infirmary. It was as if the bulkhead didn't exist for they could watch the boys' every move and hear their conversation as easily as if they were in the same room.

In a low voice, so as not to interfere with their eavesdropping and not because of any fear of being overheard by the boys, Major Sargon was continuing to make his case to the captain.

"We have no definitive proof that it was really Sleinad Evad. By the moons of Jupiter, assuming that he somehow survived the Battle of Quadrant Five, what was he up to on Epimetheus? He certainly didn't arrive there by way of any time machine."

"I'm not so sure that Sleinad Evad isn't back from the dead," said the captain. He leaned forward in his seat, his eyes focusing on Tom. "Besides you appear to be ignoring the physical evidence from the Epimetheus site that seems to collaborate the boy's story."

"Such as——?" asked the executive officer.

"The terrestrial soil found on the soles of their shoes and the molecular traces of terrestrial flora and fauna detected in the vicinity where the boy indicated the time machine had been located."

"It's obviously all part of some devious plan of the Guard. They would have thought of all that. I think all three of them, including the——," he hesitated, as if the word was distasteful to him, "——girl, are Draconian agents. They've been prepared to be passed off as innocent children. As to why, I haven't any answer to that, especially as to why they should have been given such an absurd cover story as being from the twentieth century. And then there's the fourth one, whatever kind of life form that thing might be. That kid would have us believe it's another human from the twentieth century. The whole thing smells worse than an Epsilian Slag Belcher. And it certainly smells of Sleinad Evad. And to think, if that really was Evad, we had him in our grasp and let him escape."

At the major's last comment, the captain straightened and then swiveled his chair to face his subordinate. "You no doubt disagree with my decision to break off the pursuit in order to rescue the children?"

The captain's retort seemed to have taken the major by surprise. He hadn't really intended to breach the subject in so open a manner. "Sir, I didn't mean—" He stiffened. "Yes, sir. I believe it was the wrong decision."

"Major, if I had to do it over again, I would give the same order."

"But sir, if that was really Evad whom we allowed to escape, who knows how many more lives will have to be spent until this is finally ended. Put that against the life of three teens and one whatever it is and—on top of that I still maintain they're all Draconian agents."

"The Solar Patrol is sworn to preserve and protect life," said the captain. "It is my conviction that that duty takes priority over the taking of life, even if it might be argued that such an action may, in the long run, result in the loss of even more lives."

"Sir, I didn't mean any disrespect in bringing this up."

"Yes major, I realize that. I expect you to voice your objections— at least in private. Besides, I must admit that in other circumstances I might indeed have taken your recommended course of action. But—," the captain again fixed his gaze on the taller boy in the next room. "— there's something special about this boy. He certainly seems to be the Commander resurrected from the dead."

"What do we tell the crew?"

"You mean what story do we make up to explain to them why a

boy we've rescued on Epimetheus bears a striking resemblance to the Commander, including even having the same name?"

"Yes."

"If I had a good story to make up that would appear to explain it all I would, but I don't. Any suggestions, major?"

"No, sir."

"Then we inform the crew that all information relating to the Epimetheus incident is classified, including the existence of the three children we rescued. Although that certainly won't end any speculation on their part as to what it's all about, it will at least stop news of what happened from spreading beyond the crew of the *Antares*."

"Captain, perhaps it would be wise if we had the boy—the one who resembles the Commander—change his name. At least, that would tend to draw less attention to him."

"It's probably too late for that," said the captain. "Considering the number of crew members that were in the control room and witnessed my exchange with Evad, no doubt the entire crew now knows about the boy. To come out with a new name for him at this point would no doubt be seen for what it is."

The compartment hatch opened. Lieutenant Maser, the ship medical officer, entered the room.

"The final medical report?" asked the captain.

"Yes sir." The ship physician handed the captain a thin rectangular piece of plastic about the size of a piece of twentieth century typewriter paper.

The captain began to study the 'document.' "What are your conclusions?"

"All data is consistent with the three children being human teenagers. Best guess at their biological ages would be thirteen terrestrial years for all three. The examinations revealed nothing artificial or non-human about them, with one exception?" Before continuing, the ship physician gave his two companions a grin. "I'll bet Lunar that they weren't born thirteen years ago?"

"Ah-ah," said Major Sargon. "I thought so!"

"Oh," quipped the captain. "Then how old are they?"

"Biologically, thirteen terrestrial years."

"But you just said they weren't born thirteen years ago," retorted the executive officer. "Then how could they be thirteen years of age?"

"Because, with one exception, the evidence points to their being born four centuries ago. As I said, there's nothing artificial about them. That's what so unusual. There are no bionic enhancements, no genetic interweaves, no neural taps, no vision modification, well apart from the ones I recently performed, no neurodic implants, nothing. Take the girl for instance. The only thing unnatural about her body is that three of her teeth have had holes drilled in them and the holes filled with a metallic substance. Also, her tonsils have been surgically removed."

"That makes no sense," said Sargon.

"Tooth decay?" asked the captain.

"Exactly. Until a couple of centuries ago, tooth infection was quite common in humans. In the twentieth-century, and on into the twenty-first, the infection was typically removed by a surgical drill, no doubt along with some of the surrounding dentine and enamel matrix."

"Destroyed by drilling," said the captain. He looked at his exec. "You have to admit that that's certainly primitive."

Sargon snorted.

"The resulting cavity—actually a common term for the infection or decay as it was often referred to back then was 'cavity'—say, that's an interesting play on words—"

"Please continue," said the captain.

"Yes sir. Anyway, the cavity or hole was then filled with a metallic or ceramic substance, like that found in the girl's teeth. Also, the tonsils were sometimes removed during that period in history as a preventive medical procedure. The dark-haired boy has also had his tonsils removed and both boys have some repaired dental decay similar

428

to that of the girl."

"I don't find it at all surprising," said Sargon. "All of this would have been done by the guard to promote the deception that these children are from the twentieth century and to disguise the fact that they are Draconian agents."

"But why such an elaborate ruse?" questioned the captain. "What's the point of trying to convince us that Evad survived the Battle of Quadrant Five by escaping through time to the twentieth century? Then he shows up three years later on Epimetheus." When neither of the other officers ventured to offer a comment, the captain continued. "It doesn't converge."

"But I'll tell you what does," said the physician. He addressed the executive officer. "Major, apply Ockham's razor to the problem—you know, the simplest explanation is the most likely. What is the simplest explanation that fits all the evidence?"

"I give up, Doc. What in your opinion is the simplest explanation?"

"That those three children were transported here from 1959 in a time machine. If that's true, then it is most likely that Evad did not perish three years ago but is alive and was on that guard ship that launched from Epimetheus."

The captain swiveled in his seat. "You said there was an exception found during your examination."

"Before I go into that, it might be best that I go over some other findings first."

"Go on."

"First, the DNA of the boy and the Commander are identical."

"Okay," said the captain. "Doesn't that put the lie to the theory that they time traveled here from the twentieth century? The boy's a clone".

"No, captain, he's not a clone. The clone tests were negative. To be doubly sure, I had Dave check the results, and then Dr. Purnell, the head of the base lab here. She agreed that the DNA was not cloned."

"I trust that Dr. Purnell was not aware of whose DNA it was?" said the captain. "I suspect that everything that has to do with this incident will end up being placed under the highest security classification."

"I did not identify the DNA's donor. I put a security lock on the data with instructions to erase it after the test was complete. The only test performed by Dr. Purnell was the clone test. She is aware that the test and its results are confidential."

Sargon groaned. "Okay, the boy's not a clone. Where does that leave us?"

"Based on our present knowledge of molecular biology, he's either the Commander himself or his monozygotic twin."

"Monozy-what?" said the captain.

"Monozygotic twin—that's the technical term for an identical twin."

"Doc, I knew the Commander as well as any man in the patrol," said the captain. "I can't recall him ever mentioning having had a sibling, let alone a twin. And that theory still doesn't account for the age difference between the two. For that matter, assuming that the boy really is from the twentieth century, then how can identical twins have been born four centuries apart?"

"Suppose they were both born in the twentieth century," said he lieutenant, "and placed in suspended animation, but reanimated at different times, say years apart?"

"Okay, I'll grant you that works, but only if the Commander had an identical twin, and like I said, there's no evidence for that, let alone for his being born four centuries ago."

It was Sargon's turn. "Doc, from what I recall of biology, if somehow the Commander and this boy were identical twins, although their DNA would be identical, certain other biological characteristics would differ. Is that true?"

"Yes, Major. Although monozy—ah, identical twins have the same genotype, or DNA, because they were formed from a single fertilized egg that split, yet they have different phenotypes, meaning that the same DNA expresses itself in certain physical characteristics that actually differ. For example, fingerprints, physical appearance, retinal scans, psythrutic imprints, and so on. That's because of the interplay between the fetus' genes and the environment in the mother's uterus during its growth. Strange as it may seem, while a DNA test can't distinguish between identical twins, something as simple as fingerprints can. Then again, if they were both raised in identical artificial wombs . . ."

"Well, what about the boy's fingerprints? Do they match those of the Commander?" asked the captain.

"Captain, there are no records of the Commander's fingerprints or any other of his phenotypic characteristics on file either in the base's database or the *Antares'*. The only records we have of the Commander are photographs, his service record, and his DNA scan."

"What? But those characteristics are on file for all patrolmen," said the captain.

"I know," said the doctor. "All I can tell you is what the data search turned up for the Commander. Zilch."

"Well, no matter," said Sargon. "Patrol HQ will have the Commander's complete records, although I'll admit that it's strange that they're missing from both the ship and base databases."

"I believe we pretty well disintegrated that point," said the captain. "Let's move on. What's next?"

"The girl has scratches on the back of her neck. One of the scratches had imbedded in it a piece of sheath from a cyber-cat claw."

"Neutronium's?" asked Sargon.

"No. I ran a check on the DNA. It's not from any of the patrol's cyber-cats."

"But the Draconian Guard doesn't employ cyber-cats, at least as far as we know," said the captain.

"You're telling us that we can't identify the cyber-cat?" asked Sargon.

431

"That's correct. Perhaps HQ can when they receive the data."

"Okay, next."

"And now we come to the exception I mentioned earlier. It appears that one of the teens has had a physical modification performed on him with technology that was not available in the twentieth century."

"Ah, hah!" said Sargon. "The Cobalt kid."

"Sorry, Major. As far as I can discover, he and the girl are clean. It's the other boy, Alex Banyon."

"What is the modification?" said the captain.

"As you know most human babies have a genetic scan done while still in the womb. Should any genetic irregularities appear, for instance the possibility of a genetic disease, the problem is typically fixed at the time of the scan."

"I thought that it's not possible to determine if such a procedure was performed," said the captain.

"Untrue. The procedure almost invariably leaves a signature in the host's DNA identifiable by a prelim scan. Physicians typically refer to such a signature as a tag."

Sargon let out a whistle. "And this other kid's DNA has such a tag?"

"Possibly."

"What do you mean possibly?" Sargon said.

"In rare circumstances, we're talking less than one in about ten thousand, a tag can occur naturally."

"Physically, what exactly is this tag?" asked the captain.

"Physically, it doesn't exist," said the lieutenant. "The term 'tag' refers to the occurrence of groups of unusual sequences in the DNA. It's essentially a statistical result that implies that the natural genetic sequences have been artificially tampered with."

"I see," said Captain Krater. "Can we tell to what degree the DNA was modified?"

"To a limited extent. I don't believe we can say with any real certainty exactly what changes were made. Then again genetic engineering is not my field. Perhaps the academy specialists will be able to do more with the data."

The executive officer spoke up. "Besides curing some genetic defect, might there be other reasons for performing such a modification?"

"Good question. Perhaps to enhance some physical attribute like—I don't know—say the subject's strength. Or it might be done to disguise the subject's true identity."

"You mean change his physical appearance?" said the captain.

"Yes, certainly, or even his lineage."

"What about the one called Tom?" asked Sargon. "Could his DNA have been modified to be identical to that of the Commander's?"

"Not likely," said the lieutenant. "At least, I don't believe we have the capability of doing such a thing. An attempt to perfectly duplicate another's DNA would most likely fail, perhaps even killing the subject. Besides, the Cobalt boy possesses no tag."

"But didn't you say that was a one in ten thousand chance that a tag wouldn't show up?" asked the captain.

"I said there was a one in ten thousand chance that what appeared to be an artificially induced tag was in effect natural. That refers to the occurrence of a false positive, or is it a false negative? By the moon of Venus, I always get confused which is which. Anyway, the one in ten thousand refers to the occurrence of a natural sequence that happens to mimic the appearance of an artificial modification. As I recall, it's not possible to make an artificial modification that does not result in a tag."

"One in ten thousand," said the executive officer, unable to disguise his sarcasm. "That's pretty definite proof that the Banyon kid is not from the twentieth century."

"I agree that the Banyon boy having this tag in his DNA does seem to demolish the other boy's story," said the captain.

"Definitely," said Sargon. "They're both, no doubt, Draconian agents. As such they've been extensively conditioned to avoid negative readings by truth probes. That's why we had no positive results when we subjected the Cobalt boy to them during the interrogation."

"But what would be the purpose of constructing such an elaborate ruse?" said the physician.

"To infiltrate the Patrol," said Sargon.

The physician laughed. "Major, we'll no doubt turn those children over to the care of some civilian authorities and they'll end up in an orphanage. So how will their being enemy agents then benefit the Guard?"

"Very well, I'll concede that point, but they're surely not from the twentieth century, so why do they pretend to be?"

"I believe that Ockham may disagree with you on that point?" said the ship physician. "As a doctor I would have to say that, at least for the girl and one of the boys, the evidence from my examinations supports that they were not born in this century, at least in any human community that we're familiar with. On top of that, I've been wrestling with a suspicion that their arrival here in our century was no accident."

"Funny you should say that," said the captain.

"Sir?"

"That their arrival here was no accident."

"I don't understand."

"I'm starting to wonder if our arrival at Epimetheus was an accident."

"How so?" said the major.

"As we were about to set out from Iapetus Base, we received a last minute change of orders from patrol HQ to proceed to Epimetheus and check the condition of the abandoned base there. Why?"

"That's easy," said Sargon. "When the guardsmen landed there, the first thing they did was shut down the base security system. Then, assuming for that sake of argument that this fantasy about time travel is true, they would need time to assemble the time machine. Of course, a ship in distress can always override the security system at an abandoned base and land there in safety simply by sending out a distress beacon. As they wished to cloak their presence, the guard ship didn't issue a distress beacon. Although the base's active security functions had been disabled, it would have still issued a message to patrol HQ that the system had been breached. When HQ received the message, considering we had the shortest transit time to Epimetheus of any patrol ship, they ordered us to investigate."

"Seems like an airtight hypothesis to me," said the captain.

"Thank you, sir" said Sargon.

"Especially the part about the reason the guard was on Epimetheus was to construct a time machine."

Sargon's jaw dropped. "Well, actually, that was . . ."

"So why then were they on Epimetheus?" asked Maser.

"Okay, I have no idea why they were there, but it certainly wasn't to build any time machine."

"Let's move on," grinned the captain.

"Next up is the alien life form, the thing that the boy Tom referred to as Jack Paine," said the lieutenant. "Darn if I know what it is. It certainly isn't human. For that matter, it doesn't match any alien life form in our database. But it does seem to be engaged in some sort of ongoing metamorphosis, and it had a mindbender implant. I, of course, deactivated the mindbender."

"That would be consistent with the Cobalt boy's testimony," said the captain. "When we showed it to him during the interrogation, he said that although it resembled this Jack Paine space slug, on closer inspection it certainly wasn't Paine."

"He also mentioned a news report that Jack Paine was dead," said Sargon.

"Sir, my guess is that there may be some link between this creature and the boy's story that his two friends found some sort of large pod in Evad's dwelling," said Maser.

"Yes, that seems to fit," said the captain.

"Only if the boy is telling the truth," said Sargon. "But if we may return to this alien, what exactly did you mean when you said it was engaged in some sort of ongoing metamorphosis?"

"The structure of its DNA appears to be slowly changing."

"What?" said the captain. "How is that possible?"

Maser spread the palms of his hands. "I have no idea. All I know is that every time I do a DNA scan on it, the results differ slightly from the previous results. That's another one for the academy science team to look into."

"And from the boy's description of the hatched pod his friends discovered," said the captain, "except for its size, it seems to resemble those things that the Commander discovered on the *Hydrus*."

"Yes, not a pleasant thought," said Maser.

"So where do we go from here?" asked Sargon.

"We'll interrogate the girl next," said the captain.

"Yes," said Sargon, "she'll no doubt be easy to break."

"Major, might I remind you, the purpose of the interrogation is not to break the subject."

"Yes, sir," said the major.

"Hopefully the result of the remaining interrogations will provide us with some additional clues as to what this thing might be and whether the Cobalt boy was telling the truth," said Captain Krater.

"Here's a question," said Sargon. "How did Evad happen to have access to the Commander's DNA profile back in 1959?"

"Recall that at one time Evad had open access to all the patrol's personnel files," said the captain. "No doubt he took the opportunity to copy them into his neurodic memory."

"Okay, that converges," said Sargon. "In his place, I would have done the same."

"Captain, that wraps up my report. How do you want the results of the examinations classified?"

"We don't classify them."

"What?" said Maser. "If this gets out—"

"Throttle your rockets, Doc. I'm not finished. Not only do we not classify them, we create a new report that contains nothing that would raise a suspicion that these children might be from the twentieth century, or anything else unusual for that matter, including mention of the alien. Modify the results so that they still look genuine but so there's nothing strange about them like the similarity between the DNAs of the boy and the Commander."

"Sir," said Sargon. "Shouldn't we at least alert HQ about the real results? I mean—"

"No. Classify the fake report as confidential and forward that to Patrol headquarters. I will review it before you transmit it. Make one copy of the original. We'll keep that in the ship's vault. The other I will forward as personal correspondence to the commander-in-chief. Oh, and all communications dealing with this subject, both incoming and outgoing, are to be routed through the *Antares* and not the base."

"But sir," said Sargon, "why?"

"As you know, on the way here I filed a preliminary report of the incident on Epimetheus to HQ. Not long after we landed, I received a personal correspondence from the commander-in-chief with those instructions. That's also why none of the base personnel have been briefed on what happened on Epimetheus, and why this part of the base is off limits to all but *Antares* personnel. Needless to say, Major Manning, the base commander, isn't too happy with the situation."

"A personal correspondence from the C.I.C.?" said Sargon, "and it wasn't classified."

"No, just as my next communication to him won't be."

"You don't think that guard agents have infiltrated the Patrol?" asked Maser.

"Yesterday I wouldn't have, but after what I've seen today, with this report and with Sleinad Evad apparently having returned from the dead, I hazard that I wouldn't be surprised that there might be a spy among us. That's my guess as to why critical communications concerning this matter with the C.I.C. are not being classified. No doubt the C.I.C. is hoping that the lack of a security classification will preclude any spy from thinking such communications are anything other than personal correspondence and, therefore, not worth the trouble of intercepting.

I realize that in doing this we—and by we, I mean both the C.I.C. and I—are breaking regulations. Then again, the Commander always said that he never met a regulation that didn't deserve to be broken. By the clouds of Venus, he certainly violated enough of them in his day. I even had a hand in aiding him in breaking a few of them."

"Suppose something happens to us? Suppose we're all killed, including the commander-in-chief?" said the doctor. "This information would die with us. We would have betrayed our duty and our oath."

"Good point, Doc. That's why we'll store the vital data in an archive container. I'll put a guardian lock on it and send it to the base's vault. The guardian program will routinely scan the patrol records. If it ever determines that we are all dead or missing in action, it will transmit the data under the highest security clearance level to HQ and the new commander-in-chief. No doubt the C.I.C. is taking similar precautions."

"I still believe it would be better to transmit a classified copy to HQ," said Maser. "Surely, patrol HQ wouldn't be infiltrated by Draconian agents."

"Can we be sure of that? Besides, I'm guessing that the C.I.C. believes that if some of those HQ ground pounders got a hold of this, they'll jump to all the wrong conclusions and foul things up."

"How so?" asked Sargon.

"Major, would you like to see those three kids in top security retention, having their minds being probed and dissected like some new exo-zoological specimen?"

The major cast the teens in the neighboring compartment a quick glance.

"Actually, that was going to be my next recommendation."

Chapter 5
Reunited

As Tom finished telling Alex of the recent events, the grey tabby cat began to rub its side against the boy's leg. Made aware of the cat's presence, Tom in turn let his hand gently glide down the smooth fur of the animal's back.

"You'll never guess what the cat's name is?" said Alex.

"Alex,"

"What?" said Alex.

"Huh?" said Tom.

"You said Alex," said Alex. "What?"

"What? What do you mean what? I was just answering your question."

"Huh?" said Alex, duplicating his friend's earlier response.

"You know, about the cat's name."

"Yeah, so what do you think the cat's name is?"

"Alex."

"WHAT?"

"No, I mean I think the cat's name is *Alex*," said the exasperated taller boy.

"Oh," said Alex. "No, it's not Alex."

"So is it *What?*"

"No, it's not What either. What a dumb name that would be."

"Okay, Alex, so it's not Alex and it's not What. Then what is it?"

"Neutronium," said Alex.

Tom's lower jaw took a noticeable drop. "You mean like in . . . ?"

"Exactly."

"N-e-u-t-r-o-n-i-u-m." Tom drew out the pronunciation as if he were thinking out loud.

Alex hopped down from the examination table he had been using as a seat and awkwardly began pacing the compartment for like his friend he was still adjusting to the lower gravity. "Of course, that makes sense. When Evad mentioned neutronium his mind was drifting back into the future—well, actually it was his past—but you know what I mean. There must really be something called neutronium."

"Unless he was referring to this cat here," said Tom.

"Don't be silly. Besides Neutronium's no ordinary cat."

"Looks ordinary enough to me," said Tom.

"Dave says Neutronium's a cyber-cat."

"Huh? What's a cyber-cat?"

"Apparently they've been modified somehow, sort of like an android," explained Alex. "Dave says they live as long as humans."

Alex stopped next to where Sarah lay. "Say, Tom. Remember some of those bruises and cuts Sarah had?"

"Yeah."

"Well, they're gone."

"Huh?" Tom slid to the deck and joined Alex next to where the girl lay. "Yeah, you're right. Her skin color's looking better too. I guess it must be the futuristic medicine. They can no doubt speed up the healing process."

"I wonder about that old cut she had on the knee," said Alex. "You know, the one she got when Jack the Jerk tripped her." Alex began to lift Sarah's skirt, but Tom quickly slapped his hand away.

"What are you doing, moron?"

"I'm seeing if that cut on her knee has healed."

"Suppose Sarah comes to and finds you looking under her skirt?"

"Oh, good point."

"Boy, you sure can be an idiot sometimes."

"Yeah, you're right. You look."

"What?"

Further discussion was interrupted by the sound of the infirmary hatch opening. A robot stepped into the compartment.

"Dave, is that you?" asked Tom, the boy having a hunch that if robots were mass produced in different models, say like automobiles, then there might be more than one robot of the same model at Iapetus Base and therefore, not easily told apart.

"Yes," answered Dave.

"What kind of name is Dave for a robot?" asked Alex. "Robots should have names that sound like—well, like serial numbers or something. You know, like C2D2 or 3ER5 or K9P or something, instead of just 'Dave.'"

"C2D2?" said the cybernetic machine. "By the rings of Saturn, what kind of name is that? Of course, we have real names. After all, robots have feelings too. But that's beside the point. I'm here to feed you, assuming you're hungry. I have to know if you have any food allergies or special dislikes that we should be made aware of before serving you?"

"Broccoli," Alex answered without hesitation. "And lima beans."

"Are those allergies or dislikes?" asked the robot.

"They're yucko!"

"Yucko? Is that standard English?"

"It's standard American," said Alex, "like in super yucky."

"Dislikes then but no allergies, not that it matters, as lima beans are not on the standard base menu."

The ovoid orange lights which appeared to be the machine's equivalent of human eyes shifted to Tom. "Pork chops and pizza with anchovies. Both yucko, just for the record." Then as an afterthought, "And anything with peanuts like peanut butter, peanut pie, peanut brittle.

But no allergies. At least none I'm aware of."

"No artiodactyl cuts, Italian fish, nuts or allergies," noted Dave to himself. He did an about face, the hatch swished opened, and Dave exited the compartment.

"That seemed to go well," said Tom as the hatch closed behind the robot. "You know, I liked that last name you suggested, K9P. If I had a dog robot, I'd name him that."

"K9P?" Alex gave his friend a puzzled look. "Why K9P for a dog robot?"

Tom answered with a grin.

"Oh, I get it," laughed the other boy, smacking his forehead. "K9P. Dog piss."

As both boys chortled over Tom's joke, the hatch swished open again and in stepped another robot, this one a different model. It still had a humanoid form but appeared to be both thinner and lighter. Each of its metallic hands held a tray filled with various items, including a bowl with something that resembled soup, a cup holding a pale green liquid, eating utensils, standard spoon, fork and knife made of some kind of plastic-like material, and an assortment of colorful items that were no doubt different foods.

"Allow me to introduce myself, my name is Benedict and mess is served." He offered each boy a tray which they accepted. Then, like his predecessor, Benedict did an about face and left the compartment.

Both youths stood there, holding the trays and studying the contents. About the only recognizable item was something which looked like a bread roll. Except for the soup and drink, the other items resembled mush of different colors.

"Boy, mess is right," said Alex.

"You know," said Tom, "I sort of thought that in the future you'd take a pill and that would be the whole meal."

Alex stuck his finger in a reddish colored mush, then licked it. "Not bad. Tastes sort of like apple sauce."

"It's probably broccoli in disguise," suggested Tom as he took a seat next to an empty table. The cat followed him, leaped up on the table, and dutifully sat down next to the tray of food, eyeing the contents wishfully. "After all, this is the twenty-fourth century. They could no doubt disguise not only a food's appearance but also its taste."

"Well, if it's broccoli," laughed Alex, "they've converted me."

Alex continued to chatter as the two boys ravenously wolfed down whatever it was they were eating. "I can't wait to see the spaceship we came here in. I bet it's really neat."

Tom put down the spoon he had been using and stood up. He walked over to the hatch, walked right up to it, and then touched it. The hatch refused to open. Tom said, "Open sesame." Nothing happened.

"Looks like we're prisoners, huh?" said Alex.

"Yeah, looks that way." Tom resumed his seat and went back to wolfing down some more of the glop he had been served.

A minute later Tom was finishing up the last of some bluish gelatin stuff on his tray. Alex said it looked like an ogre booger, but to Tom it tasted more like a sweet potato. "I wonder what they're—"

His sentence was cut short by a loud scream that erupted behind him. Both boys turned to find Sarah awake and staring at Auxfeed. The alien was rapidly retracting the tentacle he had attached to the girl's forehead. Before either boy could utter a word, the girl pushed herself back a couple of inches on the table she was lying on, then twisted her body in the direction of the boys as if to get out of the reach of the thing that hovered above her. Unfortunately, she made the move without allowing for the unfamiliar lower gravity. As she made eye contact with Tom, she lost her balance on the table and went crashing to the deck of the compartment, a crash that was less serious than it would have been on Earth. The girl's landing was accompanied by another shriek, this one not of terror but of surprise.

As Tom arrived at her side, the girl was lying on the deck, holding her right arm in a way which signified a new injury from the fall. She was still staring at the alien creature, which had now turned a pale blue, a color that Tom was later to learn signified fright. Sarah's chest was heaving, and her lips moving, or more accurately quivering, but no sounds were coming from her mouth except that of a rasping gasp for air.

"That's Auxfeed," said Alex, trying to sound reassuring. "He won't hurt you. He's just a harmless bag of air."

Sarah looked at Alex, then at Tom.

"Didn't anyone ever tell you to look before you leap?" said Tom. He knelt down beside the girl. "Here let me look at that arm. You might have broken it."

"And calm down," ordered Alex. "You're hyperventilating again."

The girl shook her head violently from side to side. "I want to wake up!" she yelled in a voice so shrill it caused both boys to flinch. "I'm tired of this nightmare! What's wrong? I don't feel right."

"Take it easy now," cautioned Tom. "This isn't a dream. When you fall out of bed in a dream, you wake up before you hit the floor."

"Or in this case, before you hit the deck," offered his friend, trying to sound helpful.

"Where are we?"

"We're on a base on Saturn's moon Iapetus," said Alex, beaming. "Cool, huh?"

Sarah's response told them she obviously didn't think it was so cool. "I want to go home. I want Mommy and Daddy." Further words were choked off by sobs, as the girl sat there, still holding her right arm, her body shaking.

Tom reached out a hand as if to touch her shoulder in an attempt to comfort her, then thought better of the idea. "Maybe we should get the doctor or something," he suggested to Alex.

"Good idea," was the answer, as the other boy started for the hatch. He had no sooner taken a step towards it than he heard a purring sound and stopped. The grey tabby was rubbing itself against Sarah's outstretched leg. The girl looked down, sniffled, and then stroked the soft fur of the cat's back with the hand of her injured arm. "Nice kitty," she said, or at least that's what Tom thought she said, as she was trying to whimper and talk at the same time.

"Yeah, his name is Neutronium," said Tom.

"Neutronium?" said Sarah. "You're kidding?"

"No, Neutronium really is its name," said Alex. "Just like the word Evad used."

The girl tried to give a smile. "Is that a boy's name or a girl's."

"Gee, I don't know," said Alex. "Tom, take a look and see."

"And get my face scratched. No way."

"It's a boy," said Sarah, sounding confident.

"How do you know?" asked Alex.

"I just do," she said, still stroking the cat, who continued to rub himself against her leg and purr contentedly. "Woman's intuition."

"How's your arm?" said Tom.

"It's okay. I mean it's not broken or anything." Then she looked up again at Auxfeed who still hovered near the ceiling above the table but had switched back to its normal color. "What is that thing?"

"It's an alien life form," said Tom, "but it's apparently harmless and it doesn't like to be called a *thing*."

"Where are we?"

"Like Alex said, we're on a base on the moon Iapetus. It belongs to some guys who are called the Solar Patrol or something. They're humans like us, and they don't seem to be fond of Evad. One of them was a doctor and he fixed you up, apparently with the help of Auxfeed there." Tom motioned towards the hovering alien jellyfish. "You got pretty banged up in that fight. Remember?"

"I'd rather forget. So, are they going to take us home?" At that, both boys exchanged troubled glances that the girl couldn't help but notice. "What's the matter? If this is some kind of moon base and they

445

have spaceships, can't they take us back to Earth?"

"You explain it to her," said Tom.

"Well, ah—" was as far as Alex got. He knelt down beside the other two. "Sarah, maybe it would be best if the doctor was here. He could probably explain it better."

"What?" said a flustered Sarah. "What's going on? You said they were humans like us." Then she paused a moment, her features becoming alarmed. "We're being kidnapped! They're not really human, they just look like us. They're clouding our minds. It's like in this story I read. They're going to do experiments on us. Maybe use us for breeding."

Tom bent his head down and placed a hand over his eyes, then slowly nodded his head from side to side. "No, no, no," he mumbled. "It's nothing like that—or at least I don't think it is." He removed his hand and looked up. "I think they really are human. And they seem friendly and all, well, somewhat friendly except for this marine sergeant and some joker called Sargon who's a really ornery cuss."

"From what I could gather they sure have it in for Evad. We seem to have landed in the middle of some kind of interstellar war."

"Is that why they can't take us home, because right now they're at war?"

"Well, not exactly," said Tom.

"What's the problem then?" The girl gave Tom a perplexed look.

Tom looked at Alex again for help. The latter took a slow breath. "The problem Sarah is that there is no home."

"What do you mean? We just left it. It couldn't have been more than a day ago."

Alex reached out his hand and placed it gently on the girl's shoulder, giving her an empathetic look. "Sarah." He paused. "That was four centuries ago."

"What was four centuries ago?" The girl stopped stroking the cat. "I don't understand."

"Halloween. The night we left home. It was four centuries ago. We came here in some sort of time machine. The year is 2350."

"A.D.," added Tom, nodding his head, and trying to sound helpful.

"2350 . . . ?" It was a whisper.

"A.D.," said Tom again.

The three sat there in silence for several seconds, the boys waiting for the girl's reaction to the reality of their situation. Sarah looked down at the cat which had stopped rubbing himself against her leg, but instead sat on his haunches and stared at her as if to confirm the truth of the boys' statement. "Well, can't we use the time machine to go back?"

"It was destroyed," said Tom. "And I think these people here were as surprised to learn that time travel is possible as we were. I don't think they know how to send us back."

"No! No! NO!" Sarah began to beat her thighs with her fists. "It can't be. It just can't be! We're not in the future. We're not on some faraway moon. This isn't real. It isn't happening. I want to go home." Then she broke down again and started crying, holding her face in her hands.

The boys again looked at each other, as if each were saying, "Do something."

Tom spoke first. "I'm sorry, Sarah. But that's the way it is. We have to make the best of it."

"What's going to happen to us?" she sobbed and dropped her hands.

"Hey, look on the bright side," said Alex, ignoring the question. "We're in the twenty-fourth century. Think of it. This is the future. This is the world of Tom Corbett, Space Cadet. This is Space Patrol and Forbidden Planet and all those nifty Edgar Rice Burroughs and Isaac Asimov and Robert A. Heinlein tales all wrapped up into one. We're at a real moon base. We actually saw the rings of Saturn, not through a telescope, but up close. There are robots and aliens and spaceships and death rays and all that neat stuff. Why by now they've probably cured every disease in the book. And any question we have about science, about how the universe works, they probably have the answer. Think of it. It's like we've died and gone to heaven." He was beaming, his face cast in an aura of nirvana.

The girl looked up at him with red, bloodshot eyes through a tangle of long hair that had fallen over her face. She gave another sniffle, then turned to Tom and stammered, "Don't you understand? Who cares about robots and spaceships?" She started shaking again and the volume of her voice fell back to normal. "We can't go home," she said, as if pleading with Alex to try to empathize with her distress. "We've lost our families. They're all gone. They've been gone for centuries. We have no one."

Alex gave Sarah an uncomprehending look but said nothing. Tom leaned back, bracing himself against some kind of large, complicated-looking gizmo which was located conveniently behind him. "That's not completely true," he said. "We have each other."

In the adjoining compartment, Captain Krater gave his ship physician a nod. "Okay, Doc. It looks like it's time for you to get back in there." Maser stood up, returned the captain's nod, and left the compartment without further comment.

"Captain," said Sargon. "What now?"

"We'll wait to see what the commander-in-chief says."

"Did you make a recommendation to the C.I.C. about what to do with these kids?"

"Yes."

"May I ask what that recommendation was?"

Captain Krater couldn't help suppress a grin before answering his executive officer's question.

"For starters, I recommended that when the *Antares* lifts off again, the three teens be aboard."

"Aboard the *Antares*? Why? I mean, captain, the boys I can

understand, but one of them is a . . ." He stopped, as if unable to utter the word.

"A female?" offered the captain, his features still showing amusement.

"I respectfully protest," said Sargon. "The *Antares* is a patrol star-cruiser. It's not designed for females."

"Kass is a female."

"But she's not human."

"Major, I believe that learning more about these children and how they came to be here may be vital, perhaps even critical, to the successful prosecution of our war against the Draconian Guard. Unless we get orders to the contrary, they will be on board when we lift off."

"Can't we leave them here?"

"These children have undergone great stress. Assuming their stories are true, everything they have ever known or cared about has been ripped from them. The only thing remaining to them with which they are familiar is one another. I believe, and I think the doc will back me up on this, that for the next few days, or maybe even weeks, the less they are subjected to new sights and wonders, the better it will be for their adjustment. In other words, they need time to become comfortable with their new surroundings."

"The next few weeks?" said Sargon.

"Major, for your information, I've included this recommendation in my correspondence to the commander-in-chief. From Iapetus Base, I suggested we proceed to Patrol Headquarters on Terra, but that we take our time getting there. Exactly how long will depend on Doc's assessment of their progress in adjusting."

"It looks like that Alex one has already adjusted," said Sargon.

"It may be the excitement of the moment. Tomorrow his attitude might do a one-hundred-eighty degrees about face."

"But the girl. After all a teenage girl alone on a starcruiser with no female companionship. Don't you see that as a problem, especially as

449

she already seems about to go space happy on us?"

The captain could no longer suppress a smile. "That's why I also recommended that we add a woman patrolman to the crew."

Sargon gave the captain an alarmed look. "And did you also make a recommendation as to that new crew member?"

"Yes. She would transfer from the *Agincourt* after it lands at Iapetus Base. It would be Major Dale—Major Cynthia Dale. I believe you know her."

The expression on the executive officer's face resembled that of a man who had been read his death sentence.

"I'm sorry, sir, but I don't understand. The *Antares* is a starcruiser. How can you—how can we justify having these children aboard?"

"As my executive officer, I believe you deserve an explanation." The captain paused a moment as if to better organize his arguments. "Let me start by pointing out that the Commander and I went through the academy together. As cadets, we were in the same training unit. He was my closest and best friend." The man paused before continuing. "When I look at the boy Tom, it's like I'm seeing the Commander again—only younger. His mannerisms, the way he carries himself, everything about him. Now don't mistake what I'm saying. I'm not submitting to sentimentality here, to wishful thinking. I assure you I'm being coldly rational about this. The fact that this boy shows up with Sleinad Evad and he even makes the seemingly preposterous claim that he's from the twentieth century . . . Let's just say I believe, no, I'm confident that that boy holds the key to the future of the Solar Patrol and everything we stand and fight for. That boy is our destiny. As long as I have any control over the matter, I'm not about to give him up."

Major Sargon made no comment. He simply stared at the captain.

Captain Krater let out a sigh. "Well, let's be realistic about this. In a couple of hours, we should have the commander-in-chief's response. No doubt you will get your wish and we'll be ordered to turn the kids over to the base commander."

"In the meantime, captain, shouldn't we question the other two? The Cobalt boy was rather vague about what went on in Evad's cabin—"

"You mean his apartment?" said the captain.

"Yes, apartment. The Cobalt boy claimed that his two associates were there. Their recollection of events may be more enlightening, and we would have three separate accounts that we could cross check for consistency."

"That's a good point, major. If the Doc thinks the other two are up to it, we'll reassemble the officers' board."

Chapter 6
Cosmos

"Sarah, things could be a lot worse." The girl, who was sitting on one of the examination tables, didn't make eye contact with Tom. Instead, she was absently stroking the grey cat behind its ears, her eyes focused elsewhere. "I mean, we're lucky to be alive—especially you. I'm not sure there was any way a doctor from our time could have saved your life."

"Our time ..." The girl spoke in a half whisper, as she continued to stare at the deck. She raised her head, looking at Tom through eyes that were bloodshot from the recent flood of tears. "But I don't want to stay here in this time. I want to go home. I have to go home," she sniffled. "We all do. We have a math test Monday."

The boys, sitting on an examination table across from Sarah, exchanged glances. Alex began to say something, but quickly changed his mind as he decided that whatever he said would no doubt be the wrong thing. "Can't these people get us back to our own time? If Mr. Evad was able to get us here, surely they can get us back."

Before the boys could answer, the hatch opened and Lieutenant Maser entered followed by Dave. At the sight of the robot, Sarah gave a start. The lieutenant walked up to the girl and placed a small instrument against her forehead.

"Hello, I'm Lieutenant Maser, the *Antares'* ship physician. How is

452

our patient? Hmm. Yes, everything seems to be functioning normally."

"Stop it." Fists clenched, Sarah hopped down off the table and almost lost her footing, unaccustomed as she was to the strange gravity. "I'm not your patient. I didn't ask to come here. I want to go home. Don't patronize me." She swung around and pointed at the Panthergenian still hovering near the ceiling in the center of the compartment. "And get that horrible thing out of here!" Auxfeed's color switched from clear to light blue.

"That's Auxfeed. He won't harm you," said the lieutenant. "As matter of fact, Panthergenians make better nurses than humans."

"I don't want a nurse. I want to go home." Sarah's demeanor changed from rage to pleading. "Can't you send us home?"

"Have a seat," said the officer. To Sarah's surprise he placed his hands on both sides of her waist, lifted her, and set her on the examination table. He then took a step back so as to better address the three teens. "We can't send you home. We don't know how."

"But how did we get here then?" said Sarah.

"Apparently you came here in a time machine with Sleinad Evad. At present that's the hypothesis that seems to best fit the facts. If you're surprised at finding yourself in the twenty-fourth century, believe me, we're just as surprised. Until now we didn't think time travel was possible—that is, no one in the Patrol thought it was possible."

"I don't understand," said Sarah. "If you didn't think time travel was possible, then who invented the time machine that brought us here?"

"Apparently Sleinad Evad, or someone else in the Draconian Guard."

"What's the Draconian Guard, and why can't they take us home and . . . who are you?"

The lieutenant took a deep breath as he considered how to best address the girl's list of questions.

"We're the Solar Patrol. Our purpose is to maintain the peace and to protect the sovereignty and liberties of the nations, associations and confederations of the Solar Alliance from both internal and external aggression and piracy.

Presently there exists a state of war between the Solar Patrol and the Draconian Guard under the leadership of Sleinad Evad. Because of that, I don't think Evad will be too willing to turn over to us the plans for a time machine so we can transport you back to the twentieth century."

"But we're not at war with anybody. We're innocent bystanders. We're not supposed to be here." She gave the two boys a glance as if seeking their assistance in supporting her argument, but both remained silent as they studiously tried to avoid eye contact with the girl. "Can't you call Mr. Evad and ask him to send us back?"

Maser couldn't help but grin at the girl's suggestion. "We could 'call' Evad, but I doubt if getting you back to the twentieth century is anywhere on his list of things to do.

This is all new to us. Perhaps now that we have possible evidence that time travel may be feasible, we'll be able to come up with something."

As Sarah appeared to have run out of questions, Tom spoke up. "I'm sure that these people would help us if they could. After all they saved our lives. As matter of fact, I believe that in rescuing us they may have missed a chance to capture Evad."

Sarah sniffed again. She looked at the doctor. "I'm sorry. I didn't know."

"That's okay. Now getting back to seeing to your recovery, would you like some food."

"No, thank you. I'm not hungry."

"That's understandable seeing how we kept your body on injected nutrition while it was healing. I think it's best that you get some more rest. I'm going to have Dave take the boys to quarters we've arranged for them and—"

"Who's Dave?" asked the girl.

The doctor indicated the robot. "I'm sorry you haven't been introduced. Say hello, Dave."

"Hello, Dave," said Dave.

"A robot named Dave?" There was a note of disbelief in the girl's voice.

"Please, let's not get into that," said Alex.

"As I was saying," continued the lieutenant, "I'm going to give you a sedative so you can get some more rest and allow your body to complete its recovery."

"I don't want to go to sleep. I'm afraid I'll have nightmares." She cast another glance at Auxfeed. "And I don't want to be alone. Please can't the boys stay here?"

The doctor started to answer, but then hesitated as if he were listening to a voice that the others could not hear. "Very well. Perhaps that would be best. Dave, see that bunks are prepared for our three guests." The doctor did a quick scan of the infirmary and then turned back to Sarah. "I'll have Auxfeed leave since his presence makes you uncomfortable."

Dave pushed some buttons on a nearby instrument panel and three bunks emerged from the far bulkhead. Two were at the same level close to the deck and the third immediately above the one to the right. A meow echoed through the compartment.

"What about Neutronium?" asked the lieutenant.

"Oh, please, let the kitty stay," said the girl.

"Fine. If you need to use the head, it's the first hatchway to your right as you exit the compartment."

"The what?" asked Sarah.

"The john," said Tom.

"John?" The doctor gave Tom a puzzled look.

"John, rest room, toilet, commode, crapper, outhouse," said Alex, helpfully.

"Oh," said Maser, grinning. "Yes, the human hygienic and waste facility." He cleared his throat. "Dave will be in the corridor right outside the hatch. If you need anything see him."

"Hey, what about toothbrushes and toothpaste?" said Tom.

"And pajamas?" said Sarah.

"Pajamas?" The lieutenant looked puzzled.

"I believe 'pajamas' refers to clothing designed to be worn when sleeping," said Dave.

"Yeah," said Tom. "And now that you mention it I could use the head."

"Okay," said the doctor. "Dave will make sure you get the right compartment. I believe we can dispense with the other stuff—at least for tonight. You see the present sciences of nutrition and medicine are such that we don't need to regularly clean our teeth."

"Cool," said Alex as Tom exited the infirmary along with Dave and Auxfeed.

"Cool?" said the lieutenant. "We can raise the temperature—"

"No, ah, never mind."

"I would really like some pajamas to sleep in," said Sarah. "One shouldn't sleep in their clothes. They'll get wrinkled." Considering how both her blouse and skirt were soiled and torn, Alex and the lieutenant gave the girl questioning looks.

"Unfortunately, we don't have any … pajamas. Both the base and the *Antares* have the capability of manufacturing clothing, although I doubt that pajamas are included in the facility's database. But now that you mention clothes," said the doctor, "we should probably have some new ones made for you. I'll have Dave take your measurements so we can have some ready for you by the time you awake."

"Can we take a peek outside—you know, at the surface of Iapetus?" said Alex.

"I can do better than that and you won't even have to leave the infirmary," said the doctor.

The doctor's answer puzzled the boy, but before he could pursue the question further, Sarah spoke up.

"What's going to become of us?"

"I honestly don't know," said Maser.

"Hey, could we join the Solar Patrol?" asked Alex.

"You're all under age."

"No, we're not," laughed the boy. "Heck, we were all born four hundred years ago."

Shortly after Tom returned, Sarah decided she needed to use the facilities. As the girl stepped up to the infirmary exit on her way to the head the hatch popped open. Sarah let out a high-pitched scream, no doubt startled by the sight of the dinosaur standing on the other side of the open hatchway. Still screaming, Sarah turned and bolted in the direction of Tom, misjudged her step due to the lesser gravity, and crashed into an examination table.

"It's only Kass," said the doctor. "She won't hurt you."

Sarah stopped screaming and cautiously picked herself off the deck. The creature that was the cause of the commotion entered the compartment. To Tom it was nothing less than a miniature version of what he had always imagined your standard issue meat-eating dinosaur would look like in the flesh. The creature was a biped with a long tail that extended straight behind it, serving as an effective counter-balance to the front part of its body. Her head, which she held about four feet off the ground, included a large mouth that exhibited the classic Tyrannosaurus grin. The thing about her appearance that belied its prehistoric persona was the harness that encircled her body, upon which was the spaceship and ringed planet insignia of the Solar Patrol. Attached to the left side of the harness was a holster that housed a weapon whose handle had obviously been modified for use by the dinosaurian. The creature entered the room cautiously, apparently somewhat startled by Sarah's reaction. The fall

457

of the sharp talons of her feet on the deck made a series of clicking sounds. Across her extended forearms were draped a stack of blankets and pillows.

"What . . . ?" stammered the girl.

"Those are blankets and pillows for tonight," said the lieutenant. "I thought having them would allow you to sleep better."

"No, not those. The thing carrying them."

"This is Kass," said the lieutenant. "She's a *Dino sapiens* and member of the crew."

"You have dinosaurs in your crew?" said Tom. "Cool."

"Neat," said Alex. "This just keeps getting better."

"Kass, this is Sarah," said the lieutenant. "She gets one of the blankets and pillows."

As Kass extended her arms to offer the items to the girl, she opened her mouth and let out something that sounded like a forced gasp of air. Sarah was none too reassured for when Kass did so she displayed a fine set of sharp teeth obviously designed for the shredding of flesh.

"Oh, I forgot," said the doctor. "You don't have neurodic implants so you can't understand her."

Sarah tentatively reached out and took a blanket and pillow. The blanket was thin and felt like silk while the small pillow was made of a firm but very malleable material unlike anything in the girl's experience. "Thank you," Sarah said, her voice showing a noticeable tremble.

The dinosaurian nodded and then began to sniff the girl in the manner of some overgrown, mutant dog. Sarah clenched her teeth, clutched the blanket and pillow to her chest, and gave the ship physician a pleading look.

"She's just registering your scent. It's sort of like shaking hands among humans."

After sweeping its snout from the girl's head to her knees, it started to nuzzle Sarah under one of her armpits, all the time continuing to expand and contract its nostrils.

"Doctor—," Sarah began.

"It's quite alright," said Maser, trying to sound reassuring, but not at all succeeding as far as the girl was concerned.

Kass straightened and turned, repeating the procedure it had gone through with Sarah with each of the boys. When the dinosaurian stuck its snout under Alex's armpit, the boy laughed. "Hey, that tickles." Having finished delivering the bedding and gathering the requisite quantity of 'scent,' Kass exited the cabin to the accompaniment of more clicks.

"I have to leave for a few minutes. While I'm gone, Dave can measure you for uniforms."

"Uniforms?" said Alex.

"Yes," said the doctor, right before he stepped through the open hatchway. "They'll be patterned after Solar Patrol uniforms, but without any insignia. They can be easily produced on short notice. It will only take a minute to do the measurements and then Dave can escort you to the head if you wish."

As the hatch closed behind the doctor, Dave said, "Who's first?"

When neither of the boys spoke up, Sarah stepped forward. The robot simply looked her up and down and then said, "Turn to your right please."

"Huh?" said the girl. "Aren't you going to measure me?"

"I am. Please turn to your right."

"Okay," said Sarah, turning to her right.

The girl had no sooner turned then the robot said, "And now again with your back towards me."

Sarah did as she was told, at which point the robot said, "Next."

"You mean that's it?" said Sarah. "I don't understand. How could you measure me without using a measuring tape?"

"Measuring tape?"

"I mean, how could you measure me by just standing there?"

"I simply store three images of your body—front, side and rear. From those images and knowing the distance you are from me, I reconstruct a three-dimensional, virtual model that provides all the necessary data for fitting you with a uniform."

"But she has her clothes on?" said Alex. "Seems like the uniform might be a bit bulky in places."

"Naturally I ignore her clothes when taking the measurements."

"What?" said Sarah. "How can you ignore my clothes?"

"I look right through them."

"You mean you saw me naked?" The girl immediately started to cover herself with her hands as if she were nude.

"I suppose that's one way to look at it," said Dave. "What I actually monitor is the infrared radiation emitted by your body."

The boys exchanged glances and at the same time said, "Cool."

"No, it's not cool," said Sarah. "He can see right through my clothes. That's awful!"

"Why?" said Alex. "He's a robot. I doubt if it means anything to him. Besides, would you rather have him using a tape measure on you?"

Sarah considered Alex's point for a moment and then said, "Well, I guess it's okay."

Dave stood there still looking perplexed, that is, assuming he had had the capability to look perplexed.

"Okay, my turn," said Alex.

As Dave finished measuring Tom, the boy stepped closer to the robot. He leaned forward, placing his mouth near to where Dave's ear would be if he had had an ear, and whispered, "Say Dave. Would it be possible for me to see those pictures you took of Sarah?"

The robot swiveled its head to face the boy and then, in a voice that could be clearly heard throughout the cabin, said, "Yes, Tom, it is possible for you to see the images I took of Sarah."

Tom flinched as Sarah shrieked, "Tom Cobalt! Dave, you will not show those to Tom, or to anyone else for that matter!"

Tom's skin took on a redder hue. "Er—I—I meant . . . Look, Sarah. I wasn't asking to see them. I just wanted to know if it was possible. I was making a scientific inquiry."

"I'm telling the doctor about what you tried to do?" said the girl as she walked briskly to the hatch. Tom started after her.

"Listen, Sarah. I didn't mean—"

As the hatch closed behind the two teens, Alex said, "Dave. How about letting your old buddy, Alex, see those pictures?"

"Sorry, Alex, you must have misunderstood. When I said it was possible for Tom to see the pictures, I meant that it was physically possible for him to see them, not that I would allow him to see them."

Although Alex knew that he was only imagining it, he could have sworn that the robot was grinning at him.

After the commotion over being measured for uniforms had abated and everyone had had a chance to visit the head, the three teens were finally ready to turn in.

"When you're ready to go to sleep," said Maser, "ask Artemis to adjust the lighting. I'd suggest you display the *cosmos*. Most patrolmen prefer it."

"What's the cosmos and who's Artemis?" asked Alex.

"Sorry, I keep forgetting. Artemis is the base brain, like Cleo is the brain of the *Antares*."

"The base and ship have brains?" said Tom.

"Let's see. Artemis is the base computer. Does that make more sense?" The three teens nodded. "And the cosmos is—well, here I'll show you. Artemis, cosmos display please."

Three gasps erupted as the room seemed to disappear, the ceiling and walls being replaced by the heavens and the floor by the surface of a barren, dark alien landscape. It was as if they had been transported to the surface of an alien moon. The sky was a deeper black than Tom

461

had ever imagined, filled with stars. To his right, about twenty degrees above the distant horizon of the moon floated Saturn with its magnificent rings, the rings spanning a size several times the diameter of a full moon as seen from Earth. Unlike as seen from Epimetheus, the rings appeared as a wide band. Aligned with the rings, some of Saturn's larger satellites were visible. A good distance to the right of the lighted crescent side of the giant planet burned a star brighter than any other, with a noticeable disk only a tiny fraction the size of the sun as seen from the Earth. There was sufficient light given off by the stars and the muted sun to allow the teens to make out various objects in the compartment as well as each other, Neutronium, the examination tables, and the location of the hatch. Only the bulkheads, ceiling and deck seemed to have disappeared.

After the gasps of amazement from the teens had died down, the doctor said, "This is how things would appear if you were standing on the surface of Iapetus directly above us, and the base and landing pads had all vanished. The sun, that's the bright object there," the doctor pointed to a spot on the far bulkhead, "has been artificially dimmed so you can better enjoy the view. I suggest you all try to get some rest. We'll wake you at a suitable time, assuming you're still asleep." The three teens were so enthralled at the transformation of the compartment, that at first the doctor didn't think any of them had heard him. "Very well, we'll see you at reveille."

"It's beautiful," said Sarah. "Doctor?"

"Yes, Miss Gould."

"If I can't get to sleep, could you give me some kind of sleeping pill?"

"That would be no problem. If you decide you want one, ask Artemis and it will be taken care of." He paused a moment, then said, "Will there be anything else?"

"No," said the girl.

The lieutenant turned on his heels and exited the compartment.

As soon as the hatch closed, Alex yelled, "I claim top bunk."

"Drats," said Tom.

At first Tom and Sarah lay in their bunks listening to Alex expound on the various wonders of the heavens that seemed to encapsulate them. There were so many stars that it took some time for Alex to be able to identify familiar constellations. Finally, Alex ran out of steam, and for a few moments all was quiet. Then Tom heard a sniffle. His first instinct was not to say anything, but then he decided that perhaps talking would make the girl feel better.

"Listen, Sarah, I know you're upset about all this, I mean who isn't, but ..."

"That wasn't me."

"Huh?"

"Er, it was me," said Alex.

"Oh," said Tom.

"I was thinking about—you know—my parents and brother and all, and how I'll probably never see them again."

There was another sniffle, and this time it obviously wasn't Alex.

"I know," whimpered Sarah. "I was trying not to think about my mother and Daddy and Anne and . . ."

Tom wiped away a tear from the corner of one of his eyes. "Darn, I wish there was some Kleenex in here."

A female voice seemingly out of nowhere said, "I'm not familiar with the word 'Kleenex.' Please provide me an operational definition or description of what it is you wish."

"Who's there?" said Sarah.

"I think it's Artemis," said Alex.

"Yes, that is correct," said the mysterious voice.

"It's kind of like a thin paper. You use it to blow you nose and then usually throw it away," said Tom. "Does that help?"

"Yes. Is it tissue paper you wish?"

463

"Yes," said three voices in sync.

"One moment please."

"Well, you have to admit, this place has great room service," said Tom.

The hatch flew open and Dave entered. He went over to one of the examination tables and began to fiddle with something under the table, hidden from the view of the three teens. Then as he made the rounds, he proceeded to drop several pieces of tissue paper on the lap of each of the youngsters.

"Eh, thanks," said Alex.

Sarah gave out a loud honk as she used one on her nose. "What do we do with the used ones?"

"Drop them in the disposal. It's the small hatch on the bulkhead next to your bunk. If you need more, ask Artemis." Having finished his task, Dave exited the compartment.

After a few moments of sniffing and the blowing of noses, Sarah said, "Do you think these people are telling the truth about not being able to send us home?"

"Sure," said Alex. "Why would they lie? The doctor seems pretty forthright. Don't you think?"

"You can't judge a book by its cover," said the girl.

"Well, the guys that interrogated me—they seemed awfully surprised when I told them I thought it was 1959."

"I suppose you're right," said Sarah. "It's just that the only one, well the only human that is, that Alex and I have met so far is the doctor."

"Hey, I did see this other guy, the one that pushed Tom in here. He looked like one really tough, ornery dude."

"He was a marine sergeant," said Tom. "I guess that marine sergeants haven't changed much in four centuries."

"Wow, four centuries later and there are still United States marines," said Alex.

Alex's statement made Tom feel very uneasy. "Artemis," he said.

"Yes."

"Is there still a country called the United States of America?"

"No."

"That's what I was afraid of."

"What made you ask that?" said Alex.

"It's the way they talked in there—during the interrogation. They seemed surprised when I told them I was from Pennsylvania."

"No United States," said the girl. "How can that be?"

"That marine sergeant, Rhino," said Tom. "His uniform was similar to that of the others, different color but it still had that insignia with the rocket ship on it. I think the word marine just means a soldier that fights on a ship, only now they're on spaceships instead of ships that travel on water."

"Yeah, that makes sense," said Alex.

"I wonder what happened to America," said Sarah.

"Why don't we ask Artemis?" said Tom. "Artemis, what became of the United States of America?"

"I'm sorry, but I cannot answer that question."

"Can't answer?" said Alex. "Can't answer as in 'don't know' or can't answer as in 'not allowed to?'"

"The latter," said the female voice.

"Well, that killed about a thousand questions I had," said Alex.

"I'm scared," said Sarah. "I have the feeling that we're prisoners here."

"I doubt that," said Tom, trying to sound confident. "They're probably being cautious. Captain Krater—he seemed pretty upright and trustworthy to me. Sort of like the exact opposite of Evad, if you know what I mean."

"Yeah, but what about that other guy you told us about? Major Sargon." said Alex.

"Touché. Okay, so he could have been Evad's evil twin. Still I think you have to give people the benefit of the doubt, at least until you know more about them. Besides, since they're no doubt listening to everything we say, it probably doesn't matter much either way."

"You think they're listening to us?" In alarm Sarah sat up in her bunk and looked about the cabin. Neutronium, who had been sleeping on one of the examination tables, lifted his head and gave Sarah one of those mysterious, feline stares.

"Sure. I mean, we know the computer, Artemis, is, so why wouldn't they be?"

"You think they can see us too," said Sarah, clutching the blanket more closely about her neck.

"Why not?" said Tom.

"What about when we used the rest room?"

"Well, if they're gentlemen, they certainly wouldn't have spied on you in there and, so far they seem to be pretty well mannered and all."

"Except for Sergeant Rhino and that Sargon guy, at least the way you tell it," said Alex.

"Well, yeah."

Tom noticed that Sarah was still frantically looking about the cabin, as if trying to discover the location of a hidden camera.

"Sarah, there's no use worrying about it. What is, is."

"Tom, how can you be so calm about it all?"

"He's always like that," said Alex. "The word worry isn't part of his vocabulary."

"Very funny," said Tom.

"I don't believe you two. This is crazy. Don't you realize we're on a moon of Saturn four centuries in the future and we're prisoners of some people whom we don't have any idea who they are and what they plan to do with us?"

"Well, it could be worse," said Tom.

"Oh, really," said the girl. "How?"

"We could be back in Evad's class."

Alex laughed. "Good one, Ragnar."

"Hail, Einar," said Tom, giving a clenched fist salute.

"You know," said Tom, "I always wondered how a spaceman would use a toilet when weightless."

"Me too," said Alex, "and now we know, not that we needed to go through the weightless procedure since we aren't weightless here on Iapetus Base. I take it Dave filled you in on the details?"

"Yep. Of course, he didn't tell me how a girl would—you know—do her business if weightless. He didn't happen to tell you, did he?"

"Nope."

"Er, Sarah—"

"Can we please change the subject?" said Sarah. Both boys let out a snicker.

"How about that neat elevator gizmo?" said Tom.

"Yeah," said Alex. "You think it's a solid curved wall, but you just walk right through it and then, zip, you step out onto the next floor. Dave said they have the same kind of thing on the *Antares* to get from one deck to the next."

"I wonder if they have ladders in case they lose power?" said Tom.

"Of course, if we were on a spaceship and in free fall we wouldn't need ladders," said Alex.

Sarah was happy that they had changed the subject from the workings of outer space toilets.

In the neighboring compartment, Ensign Chandrasekhar asked, "Who are Ragnar and Einar?"

"No idea," said the captain.

She felt her body give an involuntary jerk. She was awake, but afraid to open her eyes to confirm whether the nightmare was true. She just had to be lying in her own bed, in her home with her parents asleep in the room across the hall and her sister in the adjoining bedroom. She swallowed and then opened her eyes. Stars. She was looking at stars. "No," she groaned. The girl sat up in her bunk and scanned her surroundings to reassure herself that she was indeed in a compartment of a moon base four centuries in the future. It hadn't been a nightmare. It was real.

Two other bunks seemed to drift in space at the foot of hers. "Tom," she whispered. "Alex." There was no response. How could they sleep? She allowed her body to collapse back onto the bunk. Stars. It was all so beautiful, so chillingly beautiful. Never had the night sky at home been filled with so many stars, so bright, so sharp, so terrifying. She was on a moon base hundreds of millions of miles from home, and four centuries from yesterday. Her parents and her sister were long dead, they're bodies long decayed—

No, don't think about that. Think of something pleasant. But I can't, not while I'm looking at the stars. I need to close my eyes. Strange. It's four centuries in the future yet some things haven't changed. The stars are still there. There are still people, and Alex and Tom are here. And I feel so light. So light.

As Sarah lay there with her eyes closed, thoughts tumbled like an avalanche upon her mind. She opened her eyes. Stars. And there to her right was the most unreal of visions—Saturn with its awe-inspiring rings.

Think of something pleasant. No, that's not working. Think of my faith. Think of God and his love for me, of how he watches over me. Yes. Perhaps the words to a hymn. What hymn?

Sarah began to imagine a church choir singing. As the words began to drift through her mind, she again closed her eyes.

Lead, Kindly Light, amid the encircling gloom;
Lead Thou me on!
The night is dark, and I am far from home . . .

She opened her eyes. *The night is dark, and I am far from home?* No, no, no. She reached up with her hand and felt the moisture forming at the corners of her eyes. *God help me, please God, help me. I need to think of a different hymn.* She stared at the perfect specks of light that punctured the black void above her. Stars. A hymn about the heavens above. How do those words go? *God of our fathers. And the next line was . . . ?*

As the girl lay there, her eyes drinking in the stars and her mind searching for the words to the hymn, she was unaware of the alien shape that had entered the cabin and drifted across the room until it hovered next to her. A tentacle reached out and ever so gently made contact with her forehead. Immediately a chorus of sound filled her mind.

God of our fathers, whose almighty hand
Leads forth in beauty all the starry band
Of shining worlds in splendor through the skies
Our grateful songs before Thy throne arise.

Sarah's eyelids closed, she lost consciousness, and her body dropped into a deep, dreamless sleep.

Chapter 7
The Spanish Inquisition

There was a plunk as the metallic object, approximating a small coin in size and shape, dropped into the bowl-like receptacle. Spaceman First Class Solomon Dakar aboard the starcruiser *Antares* picked up the message chit.

"By the moons of Pluto, it's an Alpha priority message."

"What?" came a voice over the intercom. "Say again."

"It's an Alpha priority message from Terra HQ. I've never seen a message with Alpha priority before. Top secret, for Captain Krater's eyes only."

"Well—get it to the captain pronto."

The two men were seated opposite each other at an oval table. One of the men placed the message chit in the center of a circular white disc on the table. For a split second, a thin blue beam of light from the chit targeted the man's left eye. Captain Krater then placed his right forefinger over the chit. The chit ejected a needle, so thin as to be almost invisible, into the tip of the captain's finger, sampling his blood and DNA, along with his nervous system.

"You would think that there would be a less intrusive way to do this," said Major Sargon.

There came a beep from the closed compartment hatch. "Come

in, doctor," said the captain. The captain waited for Lieutenant Maser to seat himself before continuing. "This is an Alpha priority message, ultra top secret, for my eyes only, but, at my discretion, its contents may be shared with others cleared for codeword trinity. It is direct from the commander-in-chief."

This time three beams were emitted from the message chit, each of the beams targeting the left eye of one of the men. Both the executive officer and medical officer repeated what the captain had done, each placing his right forefinger over the chit to have his identification confirmed. With the security procedure completed, the captain said, "Message transmittal, codeword trinity." Before each of the officers, at a comfortable reading distance, appeared blue text.

Codeword Trinity

To: Captain Rex Krater, Commanding Officer, Starcruiser Antares
From: Commander-in-chief, Solar Patrol
Contents: Ultra top secret, codeword trinity material

The C.I.C. accepts and approves all recommendations contained in transmission Ant T-2350-04.

At that, Major Sargon appeared to be most irritated.

All information and data contained in transmission A-105 is hereby classified ultra top secret under codeword trinity.

"I take it that refers to Doc's medical report that was transmitted to the C.I.C. by non-secure channels?" said Sargon.

"No doubt," said the captain.

Any new information or data that in any way reflects on the contents of said transmission or on the implications of the contents of that transmission is similarly so classified.

Major Cynthia Dale is approved for access to codeword trinity classified material. Major Dale is hereby reassigned from the battlecruiser Agincourt to the starcruiser Antares. The standard procedures of operation for the starcruiser Antares shall be modified, where applicable, from those for an all-male human crew complement to those for a mixed-sex human crew complement.

Both the captain and lieutenant stole glances at the major who, if anything, appeared to becoming even more irritated.

The humans Alex Forrest Banyon, Sarah Rebecca Gould and Thomas Jefferson Cobalt shall be offered the opportunity to enlist in the Solar Patrol. Upon their acceptance, they shall be inducted into the Solar Patrol with the rank of cadet apprentice. Descriptions of the rank's insignia, seniority, duties, training requirements, and responsibilities are provided as Attachment I.

The three cadet apprentices shall compose a training unit. Training shall be conducted on board the Antares under the guidelines provided in Attachment I.

Upon the transfer of Major Dale and the induction of the new cadet apprentices, the Antares shall embark on mission assignment 2350-AntM02, as assigned prior to the Epimetheus excursion.

"What?" said Sargon. "We're not transporting them to Earth?"
"No, major," said the captain.
"But sir, we could be taking those children into combat."

"That's correct, major."

Sargon clamped his lips shut and returned his attention to the text.

Captain Krater is granted full command authority over any and all Solar Patrol forces and personnel involved in any operation that, in his judgment, falls under codeword trinity jurisdiction. Should Captain Krater no longer be able to exercise command, such authority will immediately transfer to the next in line for command of the starcruiser Antares. Should the new commander not be codeword trinity privileged, that privilege shall be immediately granted to the new commander along with access to all information and data relating to codeword trinity.

"Nothing like reading your last will and testament," said the captain. The other two officers exchanged looks.

Captain Krater will acknowledge receipt and acceptance of these orders at his earliest convenience along with their verified destruction. As per standard operating procedure, these orders shall stand in full force until revoked by order of the Commander-in-chief, Solar Patrol.

The message ended with the signature and identification stamp of the commander-in-chief of the Solar Patrol followed by an additional line of text. The added text surprised those present both for its content and the fact that never before had they seen an official communication of the patrol that did not end with the sender's signature line. The final line of text read

HAIL RAGNAR HAIL EINAR

"What the . . . Who are Ragnar and Einar?" said Sargon.

"By the moons of Neptune, I have no idea." The captain was

looking as baffled as his executive officer. "For some reason though those names seem familiar?"

"I recall the two boys using them when greeting each other," said the lieutenant.

"I believe you're right," said the captain. "Like some sort of nicknames. But why would the C.I.C. end his transmission like that?"

"Could it be some random encryption code mistakenly left in the transmission—an incredible coincidence?" said the doctor.

The captain gave a shrug.

"I also find it strange that there were no instructions as to what should be done with the teens should they not care to enlist," said Sargon.

"Yes," said Maser. "Not like the C.I.C. to leave out something like that."

"Apparently should any of them fail to enlist, what to do with them is up to me," said the captain. "Any others questions before I receipt and destroy the transmission?" The other two officers shook their heads. "Very well. Artemis, lift the security blanket."

"Done, captain," came a female voice.

The captain then briefly touched his thumb to the message chit. As soon as he removed it, the chit first melted and then simply disappeared as if it had evaporated.

"Mr. Dakar, receipt the Alpha priority message."

"Yes, sir," came a reply that, like the computer's, seem to have no source of origin.

Tom was the first to awaken. As he opened his eyes he noticed the night sky quickly fade to be replaced by the compartment lighting he had previously been accustomed to. The boy stretched his body and then rolled over on his side. Peering back at him was the grey cat, perched on his haunches on one of the examination tables.

"Good morning Neutronium," said the boy.

"Meow," said Neutronium.

Alex stirred in the bunk above him.

"Hey, sleeping beauty. Wake up."

"Huh?" Alex's eyes fluttered open. "Shut up." He turned in his bunk so as to face the bulkhead, pulled the cover closer around his neck and closed his eyes. No sooner had he done so when his eyes popped back open. He flipped over to better scan the compartment.

"Wow, it wasn't a dream. We're really here, in the future."

The boy sat up, swung his legs over the side of the bunk and dropped to the deck. He began to frisk himself starting with his pants pockets.

"What are you doing?" asked Tom, who was now sitting on the edge of his bunk.

"I wonder what they did with my glasses?"

Alex stopped frisking himself and instead began glancing around the compartment. He held his hand up to his face as if he were studying it. Then he looked straight ahead.

"That's right," he smiled. "I forgot that I don't need glasses anymore."

Tom arose from his bunk. A yawn from the vicinity of the third bunk caused both boys to turn. Sarah stirred and opened her eyes to behold the boys staring at her, the taller with a concerned look on his face and the other with a toothy grin.

"Sarah," said Alex. "Where are your glasses?"

"Huh? What?" The girl rubbed her eyes.

"Your glasses? Where are they?"

"Uh, I don't know. I don't remember having them since—I don't know." She gave Alex a strange look. "Where are yours?"

"That's just it. I don't need them anymore. My vision's been fixed."

"Huh?" The girl started looking about the cabin. "My gosh. Everything seems so clear. I can see fine."

"Yep. Pretty cool, huh?" said Alex.

Sarah got out of her bunk and began to walk around the room in an awkward manner. "But how?"

"The doctor apparently did it yesterday when we were zonked out."

Neutronium gave out another meow, whether as an affirmation of Alex's statement or a plea for attention was unclear

"That's not all." Alex opened his mouth wide to display two rows of teeth. "Notice anything?"

"It looks like you still have all your teeth. So—ohmigosh! Your braces are gone!" As soon as she said it, the girl started feeling her teeth.

"Mine too!"

Before anyone could say another word, the cabin's hatch opened and in stepped Dave carrying three trays loaded with cups, eating utensils and piles of assorted colored mush.

"Breakfast," he announced.

"Wow, that's great service," said Tom.

The robot sat the first tray on the examination table next to Sarah.

"What is it?" asked the girl.

"Breakfast," repeated Dave, sounding a little surprised that the girl hadn't understood him the first time.

"My guess is boiled snake, baked bug-eyed-monster brains and colored monkey blood," said Tom.

"Yuck, that's gross," said the girl.

"Why would we serve such items for breakfast?" said the robot.

"Oh, so you serve it for lunch then?" said Alex.

"No, of course not. We never serve such items."

"They're teasing us," said Sarah.

The lights that substituted for Dave's eyes blinked. "I've never been teased before."

"But really, what is—what's on the tray?" asked Sarah.

"It's eggs, pancakes, bacon and orange juice," said Dave. "We checked some history files to try to determine typical breakfast menus in the United States of America in the mid twentieth century and this was the result."

"But it doesn't look like any of those things," said Sarah. "The liquid in the cup is purple, not orange like orange juice."

"It's not natural food except for that grown in the hydroponics locker," said Dave. "The rest of the food is manufactured in the base laboratory from our biological materials inventory. One can't expect the texture, shape or color to match the actual item."

Tom had taken a seat on the edge of Alex's bunk and was already digging into the stuff on his tray. "The brown mush is the eggs," he said. "I'd like a little more pepper on mine."

"It's in the black vial on the side of your tray. To operate, give it a gentle squeeze," said Dave.

Tom picked up the black vial next to the white, held it before his face and gave it a gentle squeeze. A cloud of green dust squirted from the vial, some of it going up his nose and causing the boy to sneeze. Sarah laughed.

"I think Dave forgot to tell you to point it at your food," said Alex.

"Yes, that's correct" said the robot. "You point the top of the vial toward the object you wish to add its contents to. The other vials are salt, butter, sugar, and maple syrup. We also have water, various teas and coffee available as beverages should you not care for orange juice."

"No, orange juice is fine," said Alex. The other two teens nodded in agreement.

"Which one should we question first?" asked Sargon.

"The girl," said the captain. "Do you concur?"

"Yes. The girl should be easier to break."

"Major, I'll remind you again that the purpose of the questioning is to gather information, not to 'break' someone."

"Yes, sir."

"Very well, assemble the other officers and then have Sergeant Rhino fetch the girl. Oh, and tell Sergeant Rhino to use his best manners."

Sarah had raised the question, "What do you think will happen to us?" for the fourth time since they had awakened when the hatch opened and the marine sergeant entered.

"You," he said, pointing at Sarah. "Come with me."

An alarmed Sarah stood up. "Me? I didn't do anything."

"I didn't say you did anything. You're being summoned by the officers' board."

"Why?"

"I don't know. Now move it before I come over there and drag you."

"Go ahead, Sarah," said Tom. "I'm sure it will be okay."

Sarah gave the taller boy a pleading look before turning to follow the sergeant through the open hatchway.

The group of officers awaiting the arrival of the girl was the same as Tom had faced the day before: Captain Krater, Major Sargon, Lieutenant Maser, Ensign Chandrasekhar, and Lieutenant Tanner. When Sarah stepped into the compartment, she was startled to see the men in the room immediately rise to their feet, all that is except for one who fixed her with a hostile glare. As the girl was to later learn, the men stood not because of any required military courtesy, but from the fact they considered themselves gentlemen, and it was only good manners for a male to stand when a member of the female sex entered a room. Captain Krater got Major Sargon's attention by clearing his throat.

Major Sargon looked about and then immediately got to his feet.

Sergeant Rhino showed less courtesy as he placed one of his great paws on the girl's shoulder and half-guided, half-pushed her towards the solitary chair in the center of the room. Upon Rhino more or less forcing Sarah onto the seat, the officers immediately resumed theirs and the marine took his position by the hatchway. Sarah hesitantly glanced behind her at the sergeant, not that she had any intention of making a run for it. Where would she go even if she could evade the marine?

Captain Krater started the proceedings by introducing the members of the board. He tried to sound pleasant and put the girl at ease, but to no avail. Sarah sat there staring at the deck, nervously balling up the hem of her skirt in her hands.

"You are Sarah Rebecca Gould?" said the captain.

Without looking up, Sarah answered in a whisper.

"Please speak up and directly address the board when you answer?" said the captain.

Sarah looked up, her lower lip trembling. "Y-e-s." As she answered she realized what she was doing to her skirt and with a flustered gesture tried to straighten it.

"Miss Gould," said the captain, "please realize that this is not some sort of trial. We're only attempting to gather some information, to get a better understanding of how you came to be here."

"Okay," said the girl, absently balling up the hem of her skirt again.

"Good." Captain Krater turned to his fellow officers. "Gentlemen, let's have your questions."

Major Sargon spoke up. "What is your relationship to Sleinad Evad?"

"Sleinad Evad?" The girl seemed confused. "I don't have any relationship with him. He's my science teacher."

"Do you not claim to have come here with him in a time machine?"

"I'm not sure how I got here or even where here is. I just want to go home," whined the girl.

"Stop whining and answer the question," growled the major.

To the surprise of all, including Sarah, she leaped to her feet and started shouting at the assembled men. "I didn't ask to come here and don't yell at me. I have my rights. You can't subject me to this Spanish Inquisition!"

"Sit down!" said the major.

Sarah sat, clutched the hem of her skirt and resumed studying the pattern of rivets in the deck. The other four officers all glared at Sargon.

"Major," said the captain, half under his breath.

The major gave the captain an uncomprehending look.

"Let us continue," groaned the captain.

"Miss Gould," said Maser. "When we earlier questioned—Tom, he said that you and the other boy, eh, Alex, had an opportunity to explore Sleinad Evad's apartment. Would you tell us—"

"I know that was wrong, that we were trespassing. I don't know why I went along with it."

"Miss Gould." The lieutenant sighed. "We're not accusing you of any wrong doing. We believe what you did took great courage."

"You do?" Sarah wasn't use to being accused of being brave.

"Yes. Now would you please describe what you found in that apartment."

When Sarah got to the discovery of the pod, it seemed to create a stir among the officers. They made her describe it in as much detail as she could recall.

"And is there anything else you can tell us about this pod?" said Ensign Chandrasekhar.

The girl knitted her brow. She was almost starting to enjoy herself. It was as if she had a captive audience that was hanging on to her every word, a situation the girl couldn't recall having ever before experienced. "I'm not sure if this has anything to do with that pod thing, but when I overheard that conversation between Mr. Evad and Mr. Serpens in Mr. Serpens' office—I didn't mean to eavesdrop, it's just that—"

"Yes, we're sure you didn't," said the captain. "Please go on."

"Well, I remember Mr. Evad saying something to Mr. Serpens about something hatching."

That caused another stir, so then Sarah was asked to again repeat everything she could remember about the conversation between Evad and Serpens.

Before she resumed her narration, the girl asked, "May I ask what was in that pod?"

"We don't know," said the captain. "That's one of the many questions we're trying to discover the answer to."

"Do you think that whatever it was, was dangerous?" The girl swallowed as she asked the question.

"Yes," said Sargon, casting the girl an evil grin. "If it was in Evad's compartment, it was no doubt your worst nightmare come alive."

Upon seeing the girl's horrified reaction to the major's statement, the captain first gave a sigh and then turned to his subordinate. "Major . . ."

"Yes, sir?" Sargon gave the captain a look of innocence.

"Never mind," said Captain Krater.

"Did you ever hear Evad mention the name Sobek," asked the captain, "perhaps in his conversation with Serpens?"

"No," said the girl.

"How about Serapis?"

"Another name?" The girl shook her head.

"Can you recall Evad ever using the titles proconsul or admiral?"

"I believe that Mr. Evad did refer to Mr. Serpens as an admiral. I thought that was kind of strange."

Lieutenant Tanner addressed the others at the table. "That seems to confirm that this guidance counselor is indeed the syndroid Serpens, especially considering the man's fondness for wearing grey." The other officers nodded their heads in agreement.

"So, if both Evad and Serpens survived the Quadrant Five

engagement, then perhaps Sobek did too." The captain looked very displeased. "Here we thought that four of the Satanic Six were dead and disintegrated but now it looks like only one may be certain." The captain turned back to the girl. "Please continue, Miss Gould." Sarah continued.

"Let's reconfirm that last," said the captain. "You say that Evad ordered Serpens to kill Tom, but not until the year 1995?"

"Yes, that's right. I remember distinctly he said 1995. And he told him to kill all of Tom's family too. And when Serpens objected and asked why he shouldn't do it then, Evad said something about being afraid of changing the future, or maybe it was about it being dangerous to change the future, I'm not sure which."

The room lapsed into a momentary silence until Lieutenant Tanner spoke up. "Tom told us that this Jack Paine character had never been apprehended by the police but had apparently died in some kind of accident. Any ideas then on how he showed up in the woods that night?"

"No," said the girl.

"Tom mentioned that he thought that Jack had a ray gun."

"Yes, I think so. It was some kind of weapon, but it was pretty dark except for that strange glow. Can someone tell me what that was all about?"

For reply, the captain displayed the palms of his hands. "That's what we're trying to discover. Any other questions?" The captain had addressed his fellow officers.

"Yes," said Major Sargon. "Can you tell us who Ragnar and Einar are?"

"Vikings."

"What?"

"They're Vikings," said Sarah confidently.

As Sargon seemed at a loss for words based on the girl's answer, the captain said, "Any other questions?" When no one spoke up, Sarah raised her hand.

"Yes, Miss Gould." The captain gave the girl a smile.

"What's going to become of us—I mean Tom, Alex and I?"

"Since you're orphans and legally under age to be considered adults, it looks like there are two choices. One is to place you in a foster home—preferably on Earth somewhere." The girl looked none too happy at that prospect. "The other is for you to enlist in the Solar Patrol." The second option seemed to startle the girl, whether out of surprise, dread or some other emotion wasn't clear.

The captain continued. "Before we end this—debriefing, we have something we wish you to take a look at." To the girl's astonishment a scene materialized before her. It was as if she was viewing a three-dimensional film, but the clarity of the scene was such that it seemed almost real. A figure dressed in a silver spacesuit faced the girl. Although the figure's features were hidden behind the helmet's reflective faceplate, from the snug fit of the spacesuit, the girl deduced that its wearer was male. The man was reaching towards the girl with one of his hands. As he straightened and took a step back, the girl noticed he held a ray gun in his other hand. The figure was standing in the center of a corridor or hallway, both sides of which were lined with shelves. The girl perked her ears in an attempt to detect some audio but concluded that the holographic film had none. With his free hand, the figure motioned toward the shelves on his left. The view zoomed in. Sarah let out a small shriek as she recognized what filled the shelves. Pods! The shelves were filled with stacks of pods. Each pod was identical to the one she had seen in Evad's apartment except for being smaller in size, perhaps only a foot in length. The shelves must have contained hundreds, perhaps thousands of them, all sealed. The girl clutched the hem of her dress with both hands, her mouth fell open, her eyes widened in terror, and her body began to shake uncontrollably.

"No need to ask the question," said the captain, studying the girl's reaction. Then he ordered, "Cut the scene." Right before the scene disappeared, the figure leaned forward allowing the girl to read the characters lettered above the helmet's faceplate.

KOBƆLT

Even after the scene with the stacks of dreaded pods had vanished, Sarah continued to tremble. She couldn't distract her thoughts from Sargon's words, ". . . no doubt your worst nightmare come alive." Her state of distress was such that she didn't notice Auxfeed drifting into a position directly above her. The Panthergenian extended his tentacle until it gently touched the girl's forehead. Sarah collapsed on her seat, unconscious.

"Sergeant, please see Miss Gould back to the infirmary," said the captain, "and bring in Mr. Banyon. Oh, and sergeant, remember. Manners."

Sergeant Rhino snapped to attention. "Yes, sir," he barked.

He walked over to the unconscious girl. With seemingly no effort he picked up Sarah, cradled her in his arms, and exited through the hatchway.

"State your full name please," said the captain.

"I plead the Fifth," said Alex.

"What do you mean?"

"As an American citizen, I plead the Fifth Amendment to the Constitution of the United States of America, that is, I cannot be forced to provide any testimony that might be used against me. I also want an attorney."

"Mr. Banyon," said the captain. "The United States of America no longer exists."

"What happened to it?" asked the fair-haired boy.

"We'll ask the questions," said Sargon, displaying his teeth as a carnivore would to intimidate its prey.

"Very well," said Alex, "then I refuse to be provoked into providing any testimony that might be used against me under my natural rights as a human being. Also, I'm not answering any questions until you explain what it was you did to Sarah."

"How did it go?" asked Tom.

"Darn if I know," said Alex having arrived back in the infirmary. He was relieved to see Sarah sitting next to Tom on one of the tables, conscious and looking none the worse for her experience.

"Wow, that Sargon guy sure is touchy," continued Alex. "I'm willing to bet there must have been a half-dozen times while I was in there that he looked like he was going to draw his ray gun and blast me to atoms."

"Well, Alex, you know how you can really get on people's nerves when you want to," said Tom.

In the control room of the *Antares*, Starman McDonald swiveled his seat so as to more easily address the compartment's only other occupant, Lieutenant Tanner, the *Antares'* chief engineer.

"Sir, may I ask you something?"

"It's about the directive regarding the three kids, right?"

"Yes, sir."

"Go ahead, but I probably don't have any answers for you. You no doubt know as much about what's going on as I do."

"Well, you were present at the interrogations . . ."

"Yes."

"And these three teens all claimed they were Americans born in the twentieth century?"

"Yes."

"Well, I mean, how by Saturn's rings is that possible?"

"I don't know how it's possible, assuming it's true. I'm not sure that anyone knows if such a thing is possible. Then again, we thought that Sleinad Evad was deader than an Antarean mustard slime but he's apparently still alive. Like I said, you know as much about it as I do."

The starman nodded. "What about the captain? Do you think he knows something that we don't?"

"I sure hope he does. Of course, if that's true and he's not telling us, then it's for a good reason."

"Yes, sir."

"Any other questions I don't have the answers to?" The engineering officer grinned.

"About these youngsters enlisting in the patrol. The minimum age for enlistment is eighteen Terran years. How old are these youngsters?"

"All three are apparently thirteen. At least that's what I heard the doc say. Because of the unique nature of this mission, the Standards for Enlistment are being amended. That's the reason for the newly created rank of cadet apprentice."

"And a cadet apprentice is one rank lower than a cadet?" asked the starman.

"That's correct."

"Suppose they don't agree to enlist, then what will happen to them? According to interplanetary law, no citizen or member of an established state, free association or constitutional confederacy can be compelled to surrender his sovereignty to any other such entity, which I believe includes the Solar Patrol."

"Yes," said the lieutenant. "But if indeed they are from the twentieth century, then the established state of which they were citizens, the United States of America, no longer exists. But it's probably a moot point. I figure that the captain is confident that they'll enlist of their own free will."

"And if they don't?"

"I believe," the lieutenant chuckled, "that the captain will have Major Sargon, perhaps with Sergeant Rhino's assistance, persuade them otherwise."

Starman McDonald again nodded his head. "One more question. Is it true that Major Cynthia Dale is being assigned to the *Antares?*"

"Yes. Major Dale is presently serving aboard the *Agincourt* which is scheduled to touch down within the hour. She'll then transfer for duty aboard the *Antares*."

"That should please Major Sargon to no end."

Both men shared a laugh. Then the starman continued. "Sir, may I speak freely?"

"Go ahead."

"Sir, I think these orders are insane. First, a thirteen-year-old girl, and now a female officer aboard a starcruiser."

"I'm inclined to agree. No doubt some Ursian Jelly Gloc at Patrol HQ thought up this lunacy."

Chapter 8
A Time Travel Primer

"Mr. Khan," said the captain, "I understand you are prepared to present the results of your investigation on the possibility of time travel."

James Khan surveyed the *Antares'* officers sitting around the circular table. "Yes, sir, but I must admit that I'm puzzled as to why I was selected for the task."

"You were selected because, according to patrol records, you possess the highest aptitude for physics of any of the available personnel, and that includes the staff of Iapetus Base. As to the relevance of your investigation," the captain paused, "that is something we hope to be better able to judge based on your report."

"With all due respect, sir, I should think that the science brains at the academy could provide you with a much more authoritative overview of the subject than I ever could."

"No doubt they are busy investigating the subject as we speak. Still I feel it's important to obtain some deeper insight on the matter while awaiting their response." The captain leaned forward. "Based on your research . . ." He then hesitated as if listening to something. "Very good. Have her report to conference room 2 Alpha." Captain Krater straightened. "Gentlemen. Major Dale is on board. I've requested that she join us."

Lieutenant Maser could not help noticing Major Sargon's reaction at hearing the news of the female officer's pending arrival.

"Sir," said Sargon, "if I may detour from the business at hand for a moment." When the captain gave his consent, the executive officer continued. "What specifically will be Major Dale's duties aboard the *Antares*?" The others in the room could not help but notice the cynical tone in which the question was stated.

"One of her duties will be to serve as a mentor to the girl."

"So now the patrol is providing babysitters?"

"I wouldn't put it that way, major, but you are certainly free to communicate with the C.I.C. and ask him if that was his intent. Without a second female crew member available, as you are the ship XO, I believe it would only be fitting that the girl would address any questions she has regarding 'female issues' to you." That brought a grin from the other men in the room, except for the major whose expression changed to one of alarm.

"Me? Why me? I would think that the ship physician would be the person to answer such questions."

"Patrol regulations," cited the captain. "Ship personnel are to address any concerns of a personal nature to the serving executive officer. That being the case, do you still object to Major Dale being part of the ship complement?" When the XO made no response, the captain continued "I thought not. As to Major Dale's other duties, her primary responsibility will be to assist you in the training of the new recruits, that is, assuming they accept the offer to join the patrol."

"Training—?" The major gave the captain a questioning stare.

"That's right. I haven't yet conveyed to you those orders. Very well, you are to be the officer in charge of the training of the new cadet apprentices. Since these new duties will demand some time from your regular ones as ship XO, you can split the executive officer responsibilities with Major Dale as you deem best. I'm giving you this assignment, major, because I feel you are the officer best qualified for this task. I have every confidence that in carrying it out you will be firm but fair."

Major Sargon quickly recovered from the shock of the announcement that he was to be the teens' training officer. "Am I to understand that I have complete freedom of action in both deciding on and administrating the training program, including the awarding of demerits and the administration of deserved punishment?"

"Yes, major, within the guidelines provided by the training standards of course."

"Sir," said Ensign Chandrasekhar. "While we're off the subject, I should like to pose a question."

"Go on, ensign."

"Should both you and Major Sargon no longer be able to exercise command of the *Antares*, would that not put Major Dale in command?"

"That is correct," said the captain. "She's a line officer."

On hearing the captain's reply, the other men about the table exchanged concerned glances with the exception of Major Sargon who now was the one with the smug expression.

At that moment, the hatchway door popped open and into the cabin stepped Major Cynthia Dale. The men in the room immediately rose to their feet. The woman major snapped to attention and gave the captain a salute.

"Major Cynthia Dale, reporting as assigned for duty aboard the starcruiser *Antares*." She was attired in the standard uniform for a woman patrolman, that is, a close-fitting tunic over a blouse with long, loose sleeves clinched at the wrists, a skirt that was scandalously short by the standards of the 1950s, tights, and lastly calf-length boots. A holster housing a ray weapon hung from her belt. The woman's looks were so stunning that she could have served as the model for a recruitment poster for the patrol, no doubt enticing many a young male to enlist for all the wrong reasons.

Captain Krater returned the salute. "Welcome aboard, major.

I believe you know Lieutenant Tanner, our chief engineer, Ensign Chandrasekhar, our astrogator, Lieutenant Maser, the ship physician—," the female officer exchanged nods with each of the men as they were introduced, "—and, of course, Major Sargon, our executive officer." The captain failed to suppress a trace of a smile as he did the last introduction. While Major Dale continued to appear pleasant, Major Sargon looked far from pleased.

"And this is Spaceman Second Class James Khan."

"My pleasure," said the major, giving the spaceman a nod.

"Likewise, major" returned the spaceman, unable to keep from staring at the woman officer.

The pleasantries completed, the captain offered Major Dale a seat as the men resumed theirs.

"I take it you have been briefed on the situation here?" said the captain.

"Yes, sir," replied the female officer. "The whole thing is—well, unbelievable is the only word that comes to mind."

"My sentiments, exactly," growled Sargon.

The captain nodded. "Mr. Khan, being the best authority on the subject available, was about to brief us on the possibility of time travel."

At the mention of his name, James Khan who was still unashamedly studying the blonde major, jerked to attention.

"Ah, yes sir."

"You were about to enlighten us about time travel, Mr. Khan."

"Yes." There was a moment's hesitation as Mr. Khan redirected his thoughts. "Of course, I can't give you a definitive answer to the question of whether time travel is possible, and there will probably be none until someone either successfully builds a time machine or we have indisputable evidence that time travel has occurred."

When no one commented, the spaceman continued.

"There are several ideas in the literature on how time travel might be accomplished. However, if we took a poll of physicists, it's most likely that the odds-on favorite among the competing models would be Apocason's principle of temporal immutability and the theoretical physics associated with it. Compared to other hypotheses, his ideas appear to contain the least number of roadblocks in permitting travel through time. I thereby based my assessment solely on Apocason's ideas."

"We're wasting our time with this discussion," said Major Sargon. "Time travel is obviously not possible due to the paradoxes it presents." He turned to address the enlisted man. "Answer me this, Mr. Khan. Suppose someone went back in time and killed his father before he was conceived?"

"Actually, Apocason addressed that very paradox," said Mr. Khan.

"And his answer was . . . ?"

"Apocason's answer was that if one travels to the past, he is prevented from performing any act that would change the future. In this case, our time traveler would not be able to kill his father, or at least do so before he was conceived."

"Isn't that convenient," scoffed Sargon.

The spaceman continued. "Hence, the name given to his principle, that is, the principle of temporal immutability.

The principle essentially states that the present has already been defined by the future, or perhaps it makes more sense to say that the present has already been defined by the past. In that case, a person could not prevent their conception by traveling to the past and killing their father before they were conceived."

"By the moon of Venus, that makes no sense," said Sargon. "I would presume that the seemingly most insignificant of actions would in some way impact the future."

"That's true," said Khan. "But that wouldn't be something the time traveler would have to worry about, since he has arrived from a future that has already been set by the past."

"What rubbish," said Sargon. "Are we discussing physics or

metaphysics?" Before anyone could offer an opinion, the major continued. "Let's explore further my example. If I were able to travel to the past, what would prevent me from killing my father if I so chose to do so?"

"In your particular case, maybe the fact that you had no father," said Lieutenant Tanner.

"That's beside the point," said the major.

"According to Apocason, some event would arise to ensure that any attempt by a time traveler to kill his father before he was conceived would somehow fail," said Khan. "His reasoning was based on the simplest way to eliminate the paradox; that is, if time travel is possible then there can be no way that any event in the past could change an already established present. Or to put it another way, the past has already been set along with its impact on the present. In other words, any time travel to the past has already happened."

"That's doubletalk," said Sargon. "Cyclical reasoning."

"It sounds to me like Apocason was saying that there's no such thing as free will," said the captain.

"I don't think he viewed it that way. If I understand the theory correctly, you could attempt to change the future all you wanted and perform any action you desired. However, the result of any such action would never turn out as planned. For example, if the time traveler tried to disintegrate his father with a ray gun, the gun would perhaps malfunction as he pulled the trigger. But I'm not a philosopher, and I believe that's where this discussion is presently headed. Let me again try to make it clear. It's nothing metaphysical—"

"Suppose I return to my present location five minutes earlier," said Sargon. "Would I meet myself?"

"I would think so," said the spaceman.

"Could I not then change the past, and in doing so, also the future?"

"Not according to Apocason. The 'you' that was five minutes earlier in your past was already there with the time traveler 'you' when the latter 'you' arrived five minutes into his past. Of course, I guess the past 'you' would probably still be there with the future 'you' when the future 'you' left for the past."

"What?" said Sargon. "This is nothing but doubletalk, assuming that I actually understood what you said . . . which, upon further reflection, I probably didn't. If that were true I could start making copies of myself over and over again."

"Theoretically yes," said Mr. Khan. "But if I may continue, there are other aspects to the problem which, I believe you'll see, make such a scenario highly unlikely if not impossible."

"Yes, let us move on," said the captain. "Obviously, we'll never know if such a paradox really exists until time travel actually becomes a reality, and even so how would we ever know if something we did in the past had changed the future, or even the present."

"For that matter." asked Major Dale, "isn't it a paradox to maintain that such a thing as a paradox can exist?"

"Good point, Major Dale," said the captain. "I see where this sort of discussion can get very confusing, so instead of spending more time on these types of questions, if there's no objections, let's move on to the physics of time travel."

"Yes, sir," said Mr. Khan, seeing that there appeared to be no objections. "First off, we'll define a time tunnel as a path that links the past with the present. Apocason's theory requires a transmitter, a time machine if you will, at one end of the time tunnel. The transmitter will be the device that provides the actual power required to transmit an object through time. At the other end of the time tunnel must be a receiver. Both of these components contain a complex device known as a temporal manifold modulator. Here arises the first major barrier to time travel. The transmitter can only open a time tunnel into its past. That precludes time travel into the future if there exists no time machine there. Is that clear?"

The captain took a mental poll of those in the room. "Not quite, but perhaps it will become clearer as we proceed."

"The receiver could be another time machine, that is, a transmitter can also act as a receiver, but only when connected to another transmitter in its future. For that matter, it could be connected to itself at some future time. The function of the receiver is to focus the signal from the transmitter. That's only possible when the receiver is in a large electro-force field. The proximity of a massive charged object such as, at a minimum, a small planet, will suffice. The transmitter, or time machine if you will, only requires sufficient power to operate and could, therefore, be located practically anywhere including deep space." The spaceman studied the faces of the officers, but as there appeared to be no questions, he resumed his presentation.

"The greater the mass to be transported, the higher the power requirement for the time machine and the more massive the charged anchor has to be on the receiver side of the time tunnel that forms."

Again Mr. Kahn paused to see if there were any questions.

"You use the term 'time tunnel,'" said Ensign Chandrasekhar. "Is the time it takes for the object to travel from one time to another dependent on the length of the tunnel?"

"By my understanding, to a time traveler the trip would seem essentially instantaneous. Think of the universe being composed of four dimensions instead of the normal three spatial dimensions, with the fourth dimension being time. Since we can't really think in four dimensions, it's probably more practical to imagine a universe of only two dimensions, that is, one spatial dimension and the time dimension. The universe is then like a flat piece of paper with space being measured say lengthwise across the paper and time being measured along the width of the paper. What a time machine does is warp the universe, that is, bend the paper, until two different points are in contact, creating a shortcut between one place and time and a different place at a different time. The length of the time tunnel, both from a space and time perspective, is zero. Of course, that's just an analogy to help you understand the theory. Apocason naturally doesn't suggest that space and time actually bend or warp."

"You mean like Albert Einstein did back in the twentieth century?" said Sargon. "I recall that he proposed that gravity was caused by the bending of space."

That got a laugh from everyone.

"What an absurd notion," said Major Dale.

"Any guess as to how much power would be required to transport, say, five people from Earth to Saturn over a span of four centuries?" asked Lieutenant Tanner.

The starman shook his head. "I'm sorry sir, but I couldn't even begin to guess, let alone calculate such a thing. You'll have to get that answer from the academy."

"You mentioned that the time machine cannot project into the future," said Major Dale, "and that there must be a receiver at the other end of the tunnel."

"Yes, major."

"Then for time travel to be possible between now and the twentieth century, a receiver must have already existed in the twentieth century," said the blonde officer.

"Ground zero, major," said Sargon. "Mr. Khan, how difficult would it be for someone to have built a receiver with twentieth century technology?"

"I would guess that that would be well neigh impossible."

"And why is that?"

"According to Apocason, there are a number of aspects to building one that would be beyond twentieth century Earth technology. For example, the receiver requires neutronium II B. Excuse me for reiterating the obvious but, as you all know, neutronium II B has a density three orders of magnitude greater than lead. The only known way to create it is to irradiate neutronium I B with n-rays such as those produced by your typical ray weapon. Since neither the means of producing n-rays nor a source of neutronium I B was available to the inhabitants of Earth in the twentieth century . . ."

Sargon flashed a look of triumph. "I guess we've killed this crazy story about those kids being from the twentieth century."

"Please continue, Mr. Khan," requested the captain.

"One thing I neglected to mention is that the possibility of opening a temporal tunnel depends on the relative values of three key parameters that Apocason assigned to space and time. They are the absolute directiveness of space, the temporal elasticity, and the zeroth interaction criterion. The values of the first two parameters vary with time, that is, each oscillates slightly about a mean value. Time travel is only possible when the values of the first two parameters are in resonance in universal space and time and the zeroth interaction criterion is fulfilled at the transmission end of the time connection. Apocason calculated that such a resonance now exists in our part of the galaxy with a lifetime of about fifteen centuries. The resonance arose in the early tenth century and will continue to sometime in the twenty-fifth century. After that, another window of opportunity won't occur in this part of the universe for several tens of thousands of years, or so claimed Apocason. That effectively addresses the issue of our time being overrun by visitors from the future."

"How convenient," said Sargon.

"Furthermore, the resonance requirement results in a minimum limit to the time interval. That also will vary with time but Apocason was never able to generate a set of conditions that permitted time travel over a period of less than about one hundred twenty years. That of course prohibits Major Sargon's scenario of traveling only five minutes into the past."

"Too convenient," snorted the executive officer.

"Which brings us to another constraint known as the momentum transfer problem. With our technology, it may well be possible to create a time machine that would allow one to travel back and forth between now and a future time at which that time machine was still in existence, assuming it was more than one hundred twenty years in the future. Again, the time travel could only be initiated from the future end of the time tunnel. Even so, the problem of momentum transfer would need to be addressed. Consider that the transmission point is traveling through space with a certain velocity relative to that of the target reception point. Unless the relative velocity difference between the two points is close to zero, the time traveler may well have a serious momentum mismatch problem at the destination end of the tunnel. It's analogous to a man jumping from a high-speed ground transport vehicle. If the speed of the vehicle relative to the ground is too great at the time of the leap, the man will contact the ground at such a high speed that he would be killed. Is that clear?"

The officers all gave Mr. Khan an affirmative nod.

Major Dale spoke up. "So Sleinad Evad would have had to somehow compute the relative velocity difference at the time of the transfer between his location on the Earth and the base on Epimetheus four centuries later to ensure that the relative velocity between the two was essentially zero?"

"He couldn't have possibly performed so precise a calculation while in the twentieth century," said Lieutenant Tanner.

"No," said Sargon, appearing to speak more to himself than to addressing the other people in the room. "But he only had to be approximate as to the time and conditions of the transfer." He looked at the captain. "Remember what the girl said about the calculations she and the Banyon boy found in Evad's compartment? The detailed accurate computation would no doubt have been done from the Epimetheus end, and they certainly had the computational resources to do it."

"Why major," said the doc, "suddenly you don't sound so skeptical."

"I'm still skeptical," said the major. "Just being objective."

"Anyway, you can see how the momentum problem further reduces the available windows of opportunity for time travel," said Khan, "especially since the receiver end has to be anchored near a large, charged mass. The charged mass and power requirements also limit the length of the time tunnel both from a temporal and spatial standpoint. The energy and charged mass requirements go up exponentially with the magnitude of the time and spatial intervals to be crossed."

"You mentioned a third necessary condition, the zeroth interaction something-or-other," said Ensign Chandrasekhar.

"Zeroth interaction criterion," said Mr. Khan.

"Yes. What exactly is that?"

"It means that the net electro force acting on the time traveler must be zero. That's the primary function of the time machine. It shields the subject from all electro-e and electro-g force components."

"So somehow it creates a free-fall environment for the subject?" asked the captain.

"No, an object can be in free fall yet still be under the influence of an electro-g field. The time machine actually nullifies the electro force field."

"Incredible," said Sargon.

"Anything else, mister?" said the captain.

"Only the details of the actual mechanics of a time transfer. The time machine must define the hemispherical space to be transmitted by enclosing it within a dome made of—"

"Hemispherical?" said Ensign Chandrasekhar. "Why hemispherical? I would have imagined it to be spherical, you know, because of symmetry requirements."

"That's a good question. I don't really understand Apocason's explanation of that point. Something about at each end of the time tunnel there is originally a spherical space but that the two spaces have opposite temporal polarities. When you transmit, the spherical space on the other end flips its vector rotational component such that one half of each space cancels its opposite number and the other halves reinforce one another. Whatever the reason, the result is that the shape of the actual volume of space transmitted is a hemisphere and not a sphere. The contents of identical size hemispherical volumes at each end of the time tunnel simply exchange places both in time and space."

"Things are looking better for the credibility of the kids' story," said the doc.

"Why is that?" asked Major Dale.

"Because the time machine they described was hemispherical in shape."

Chapter 9
The Solar Patrol

I'll have to admit that they seemed mostly considerate and polite, except for the sergeant and that Major Sargon," said Sarah.

"Sargon probably graduated from the Sleinad Evad School of Social Graces," said Alex, seemingly transfixed on the performance of his yo-yo in the base's artificial gravity field.

"Yeah," said Tom. "Those two could be brothers."

"I don't believe Major Sargon and Sleinad Evad are related," said Dave, "but as the former is about to enter the infirmary along with Captain Krater and Lieutenant Maser, you could ask him."

"No thanks," said Tom. "Uh, Dave, how about you forget we had this conversation."

"As you wish," said Dave, as the hatch opened to allow the three officers to enter.

"It is time to discuss your future," said the captain, addressing the teens.

"Cool," said Tom.

"Neat," said Alex.

The captain gave the doctor a quizzical look.

"I believe those are twentieth century colloquialisms," said the doc.

"Yes, of course," said the captain. He returned his attention to the three teens. "Please take a seat."

Tom and Alex gave each other a quick glance, somehow knowing that the other was tempted to say, "Where should I take it?" but had thought better of the idea.

"As was mentioned during the interro . . . debriefings, we see two possibilities with regards to your future. One is for you to be placed in a foster home, most likely somewhere on Earth. The other is to be inducted into the Solar Patrol."

"Neat," said Tom.

"Cool," said Alex. "We vote for joining up."

"Do we get a ray gun?" asked Tom, motioning towards the weapon housed in the captain's right holster.

"Yes, once you successfully complete your weapons training."

"I thought we were too young to join?" said Alex.

"We're making an exception in your cases. But before you make a decision you may wish to know more about what you may be getting yourself into."

"We wouldn't have to shoot anyone, would we?" said Sarah. "My family doesn't believe in guns."

"Don't believe in guns? What by the moon of Venus is that supposed to mean?" said Sargon, who then gave Captain Krater a questioning look.

The captain merely gave the XO a shrug, then turned to the girl. "Miss Gould, do you believe that people have a right to defend themselves?"

"Well—yes. But guns are yucky—and dangerous."

"I'm not sure about the 'yucky' part, but I do agree that guns are dangerous. That's why you will receive extensive training in their use. It may ease your concerns to know that ray guns have a paralyze mode. Should the need arise to use your weapon, you might have available the option to stun your opponent instead of killing or vaporizing them." The captain paused. "Well, on second thought, I guess killing and vaporizing are pretty much the same thing. The paralyze mode isn't effective for all life forms. For example, about the only way to handle a Mickey is the way Mr. Cobalt did on Epimetheus."

"Boy, I wish I could have seen that," said Alex, looking at his friend.

"Besides, we always try to avoid using force if a situation can be resolved by peaceful means." The captain glanced at his executive officer. "That is, most of us do.

The Solar Patrol was created to keep the peace among members of the Solar Alliance and to suppress piracy."

"You mean there are pirates around?" said Tom.

"Only in space, assuming I understand your question."

"Space pirates," said Alex, more to himself than to anyone in particular. "This keeps getting better and better."

"Ah, yes— As I was saying, it is our duty to protect the sovereignty and liberties of all the nations, free associations and confederations of the Solar Alliance, including those in other star systems."

"You can travel to the stars?" said Sarah.

"Yes, of course. How else, could we protect extra-solar settlements? Those extra-solar systems include the Delta-II system from which the two *Dino sapiens* in our crew hail from. I understand you've already met Kass."

"Yes," said Sarah. "Is it dangerous?"

"You mean 'is *she* dangerous?' Any member of this crew is dangerous when the need arises. Of course, the last person to address Kass as an 'it' had his head bitten off."

Sarah let out a gasp.

"Cool," said Tom.

"Neat," said Alex.

The captain smiled. "I'm kidding. Ah, where was I?

Enlistment in the Solar Patrol is voluntary. You may announce your resignation by giving ninety Terran days notice in writing, although the resignation will not be effective if you are serving aboard a patrol ship until a suitable port of call is reached. Otherwise you may serve until mandatory retirement age."

"What is that?" said Tom.

"Ninety-eight Terran years."

"Ninety-eight! You're kidding?" said Alex.

"There has been some disgruntlement about that, so there's a pending motion before the High Command to raise it."

"Huh, huh," said Tom.

"Presently we are at war with the Draconian Guard under the control and leadership of Sleinad Evad, may he burn in the sulfur pits of Io. As you have probably already surmised, we had believed hostilities to be pretty much over and Sleinad Evad dead along with two of his key henchmen, that is, until he turned up on Epimetheus.

Should you elect to enlist in the patrol—we tend to refer to the Solar Patrol as 'the patrol'—you will be inducted with the rank of cadet apprentice. This is a temporary rank that was created for you, since you are under the standard age for enlistment. In the past new inductees always entered the patrol with the rank of cadet. In other words, cadets will be senior to you."

Tom whispered to Alex, "Nothing like being low man on the totem pole."

"Kind of like being demoted to the seventh grade," said Alex.

"The Solar Patrol is a military organization which means that we observe military etiquette and operate under strict military discipline. Breach of such etiquette and discipline will be reprimanded. Since initially you will not be undergoing the normal training program for cadets, you will be allowed some leeway until it is deemed that you have acquired sufficient familiarity with how the patrol functions. The training will be continuous and demanding. As matter of fact, a patrol-man never completes his training.

Assuming that all three of you enlist, you will be part of the same training unit. Such a unit is called a *pod*." The captain noted the reaction from the teens when he said "pod." "By coincidence, training pods are always made up of three cadets. For the foreseeable future, you will serve as part of the crew of the *Antares* so that is where your training will take place."

"Cool," said Alex.

"Neat," said Tom.

Sarah raised her hand.

"Are there women in the Solar Patrol?"

"Yes, although normally women patrolmen do not serve on starcruiser class ships such as the *Antares*. However, we recognize that it will be awkward for you to be the only female human aboard the *Antares*. Therefore, Major Cynthia Dale has been assigned to our crew. You'll soon have the opportunity to meet her." The captain leaned close to Sarah. "She'll assist you with anything, ah, that is, learning about activities—well, she'll assist you with anything that's . . ."

"I think I understand," said a blushing Sarah.

The captain straightened. "Good. Are there any further questions?"

All three teens gave their heads a negative shake.

"In that case, we'll leave you to talk it over among yourselves. If you do happen to come up with additional questions just ask Artemis. When you're ready with your decision let Artemis know."

"Heck," said Tom, "I'm in."

"Me too," said Alex.

The boys looked at Sarah.

"I'd like some time to think about it."

"Are you sure about this?" said Sarah.

"Of course," said Tom. "What else would we do here in the future? This way we can see the wonders of the universe. Think about that. Besides, we owe these people our lives, and look at all the trouble they've gone through to accommodate us. They've even changed the rules and created a special rank so we can enlist."

"Do you want to go to a foster home?" said Alex. "You won't know anyone there. You may never see us again."

"I know. It's just that I've never imagined myself in the military. My family doesn't even believe in guns."

"Like Major Sargon, I have no idea what that's supposed to mean," said Alex. "Look, Sarah. These people have a very noble mission, to preserve the peace. Remember what it says in the Bible? Blessed are the peacemakers."

"I can't believe I'm listening to an agnostic quote the Bible," said the girl.

"Hey, just because I don't believe in it doesn't mean I haven't read it."

"Come on, Sarah. It's your chance to be part of a grand adventure," said Tom.

"Do you want me to come with you?" said the girl.

"Uh, well, yes." Tom's voice stammered a bit.

"Me too," said Alex, but Sarah was only looking at Tom.

"Suppose I fail the training?" said the girl.

"You're a smart girl. How tough can it be?" said Alex. "Besides, they'll no doubt modify things for us since we'll be the first thirteen-year old cadets they've ever had."

"I'm not worried about the learning part of the training. It's the physical part that concerns me. You know, like shooting guns and things. I mean, you're boys, not to mention scouts, so you're used to that kind of thing."

"We'll get you through it," said Tom. "My father was a marine in the Second World War. He told me that when he enlisted he never thought that he would make it, and he couldn't imagine anything worse than being kicked out. He said that fear of failure kept him going."

"What Tom is trying to say . . . ," began Alex. He hesitated a moment, before continuing. "Heck, I have no idea what Tom is trying to say."

"But it might be really dangerous," said Sarah. "I can't help thinking about what they showed me when I was in the room with all the officers. All those pods . . . Did you see it too?"

Both boys gave a nod.

"They don't even know what they are, where they come from, or, for that matter, what comes out of them. And the one we found in the apartment— It was so much bigger."

"Yeah, I'll admit," said Alex, "seeing those pods was kind of creepy. But what was really strange was seeing the name on that guy's space helmet. It was spelled a little strangely like everything else around here but I'm pretty sure the name was Cobalt. I guess he was this Commander guy."

"It sure as heck wasn't me," said Tom.

While Alex practiced with his yo-yo and Tom sparred with Neutronium, Sarah sat on her bunk studying the deck, obviously deep in thought. Finally, the girl stood and walked over to where Tom was teasing the cat. She began to absently stroke Neutronium's back, the cat returning the favor by rubbing its side against the girl's hand. Sarah looked up to make eye contact with Tom. "Okay, I'll do it. I'll enlist with you."

In the adjacent compartment, Major Sargon let out a groan and gave his head a disgusted shake. Lieutenant Maser laughed. "That's twenty-five credits you owe me, major."

"This is Spaceman Second Class Aristedes," said Lieutenant Maser. "He'll perform your in-processing."

The three teens, seated about the table in the room where the interrogations were held, didn't know what in-processing was, but figured they would soon find out.

"As members of the patrol you will be administered an oath," said Aristedes, "and receive a neurodic implant."

"A what?" said Alex.

The spaceman looked at the doctor.

"A neurodic implant," said Maser, "also known as a neurode. All patrolmen have them. It's a small device that's inserted at the base of the brain stem. Among other functions, it allows for short range telepathic communication between patrolmen and provides the host enhanced analytical capabilities such as being able to mentally perform complex arithmetic calculations."

"Neat," said Tom.

"Cool," said Alex.

"Will it hurt?" asked Sarah.

Maser laughed. "No. You'll be anesthetized when I do the installation. After that you'll never even notice it's there, except for the enhancement to your thought processes when you so desire to activate it and the telepathic communication you receive from other patrolmen. There are some other benefits to having it. For instance, it blocks your olfactory senses from responding to strong odors, like those of a Mickey. Naturally, it will require some training and getting used to until you can take advantage of all its features."

"This won't allow you to read our minds or control us or anything like that, will it?" asked Alex.

"No. You're probably thinking of a mindbender."

"A mindbender," said Sarah. "I remember Mr. Evad saying something about a mindbender when I overheard—"

"Eavesdropped," said Alex.

"Overheard!" said Sarah. "—when I overheard him talking with Mr. Serpens."

"Yes," said Maser. "The alien you knew as Jack Paine had been implanted with such a device. Mindbenders are illegal among all members of the Solar Alliance. They have been used by the Draconian Guard to turn innocent people into agents of the guard. The presence of a neurodic implant in a person blocks the mindbender's function. In other words, the neurode would have to be removed or neutralized before the mindbinder would be effective."

When the teens didn't seem to have any further questions about neurodic implants, the spaceman spoke up.

"We'll need to enter some information into patrol records before you're sworn in. We'll start with you, Miss Gould. State your full name please."

"Sarah Rebecca Gould," said Sarah Rebecca Gould.

"Species?"

"Huh?" said Sarah.

"Human. That's obvious. Sex?"

Sarah blushed. "No! I mean I never—that is, I'm—" She could hear the boys snickering behind her.

"Female, of course," said the spaceman.

Sarah gave the boys an angry glance. Alex immediately lost his grin and nudged Tom who was still trying to stifle his snicker but was being careful not to look at Sarah.

"Harrumph. Let us continue," said Mr. Aristedes. "Let's see, we already have your height, weight, place and date of birth, so next is— Terran frame of reference age at time of induction? Let's see, when did you enter the time machine?"

"Halloween, that is, October 31, 1959."

"That would make you thirteen plus 391 which gives 404 years of age." Aristedes smiled. "I'd like to see how the archives computer is going to handle that one. Next of kin?"

Sarah started to list the members of her family but stopped. She reached up and brushed away a tear that had formed at the corner of her eye.

The spaceman and doctor exchanged glances before the spaceman continued. "I guess we should enter *none* for that. Religious or philosophical conviction?"

Sarah swallowed. "My father is Jewish and my mother's a Baptist, but lately we've been attending the Methodist church, so I guess you should enter Methodist."

"We don't have Methodist as a selection, but we have several Jewish categories."

"How about Christian?" said the girl.

"Would that be Roman Catholic, Eastern Orthodox Catholic, Byzantine Catholic, Neo Christian, Reform Christian, American Heritage Christian . . . ?"

"How about just basic Christian?"

"Okay, I'll check the general Christian heading. We already have your genetic and physiological data filed, so you're all done."

"That's it?" said Sarah. "What about things like my race or—"

"Race?" said the spaceman. "I don't understand. You mean like athletics?"

"Never mind," said Sarah

"What's the reason for wanting to know our religious belief?" asked Tom.

"Burial rites."

"Pretty cool, huh?" said Tom. The grey uniform he was wearing seemed to fit perfectly.

"Yeah," said Alex who had also donned his new uniform. "I especially like the boots. Ensign Chandrasekhar said that should we go weightless they'll instantly magnetize so we don't go floating off all over the place. Say, wasn't that a weird shower?"

"Yeah. I never had a shower before that didn't use any water and only took five seconds. I can still feel my skin tingling."

"I wonder what's keeping Sarah?" said Alex.

"Shall I fetch her?" asked Dave.

"Nah," said Alex. "My father says that girls always take forever to get ready."

The hatch to the infirmary opened, but no one entered.

"There is Miss Gould," said the robot. Both boys shifted their position slightly to be better able to see across the infirmary through the open hatchway, but still there was no one in sight.

"Sarah, is that you?" said Alex.

A voice came from the outside corridor. "Yes."

"Is something wrong?"

"N-o-o-o."

"Then come in."

The girl appeared before the hatchway and then hesitantly entered the cabin, the hatch dropping in place behind her. Except for the insignia, her uniform was standard issue for human female patrolmen. The girl stood there, her hands clasped over the front of her short skirt as if to ensure that it wouldn't be lifted by a sudden gust of wind, not that there was much chance of that on a moon base. Both boys also stood there, with their mouths open.

"Are you sure this is the correct uniform?" Sarah asked the robot.

"Yes. Regulation all the way," said Dave. "Is there a problem?"

"Why is the skirt so short?"

"I don't know the answer to that," said the robot. "My guess would be tradition."

"You look like one of those girls in *Space Patrol*," said Tom, referring to a TV show that had been popular in the early 1950s. The boy still seemed unable to close his mouth even after he had finished speaking.

"Tom," said Alex.

"What?" said Tom, wrenching his gaze away from Sarah.

"Close your mouth," said Alex.

"Huh?" said Tom, as he closed his mouth.

The hatch opened again and into the cabin stepped Captain Krater followed by a stunning young woman attired in a uniform nearly identical to that worn by Sarah. At the sight of the blonde officer, the mouths of both boys opened and Alex mumbled something that sounded like "Hubba-hubba."

"Major Dale," said the captain. "These are our new recruits, soon to be sworn in as cadet apprentices. Sarah Gould, Thomas Cobalt, and Alex Banyon." The woman gave each of the teens a smile as they were introduced. "Recruits this is Major Cynthia Dale. Along with you, she will be joining the crew of the *Antares*."

Sarah was already feeling more comfortable having noticed that the major didn't seem at all self-conscious in her uniform.

The hatchway again opened allowing the remainder of the ship's officer corps to enter. Along with Major Dale, Major Sargon, Lieutenant Tanner, Lieutenant Maser, and Ensign Chandrasekhar formed a line abreast with the captain. Tom couldn't help notice the glances quickly exchanged between Sargon and the woman major. The two then looked straight ahead, as if determined to avoid further eye contact.

"Recruits will come to attention," said the captain. Tom and Alex immediately snapped to attention. Sarah hesitated a moment to study what the two boys had done and then tried her best to impersonate them.

"Patrolmen attention," barked the captain, and the line of officers, as if of a single mind, fell to attention with a simultaneous click of the heels of each officer's boots.

"I shall now administer to you the oath of the Solar Patrol. Raise your left hand." The two boys instinctively raised their right hands while Sarah, perhaps because not being a boy scout she had never taken an oath before, did as instructed. "Left hand." said the captain. The boys switched hands. "And repeat the words as they highlight before you." A set of words magically materialized before the teens, floating in space.

"Sir," said Alex. "I can't read this. A lot of the letters are strange."

"I believe it's a phonetic alphabet," said Tom.

"Hmm," said the captain. "That's right. English was still written in the old Roman alphabet back in the twentieth century. Artemis, please switch the oath to the Roman alphabet."

To the astonishment of the three teens, the text immediately

changed to all familiar letters. Then as each word in sequence brightened, the three teens recited the oath.

"I swear to protect the sovereignty and liberties of the citizens and
members of all established states, free associations, and constitutional
confederacies of the Solar Alliance, to maintain the peace and protect
free trade and commerce in all space under jurisdiction of the Solar
Patrol, to faithfully carry out all obligations and duties of a patrolman,
and to obey the lawful orders of my superior officers. To these ends I
renounce all other loyalties and associations that may conflict with this
oath. This I solemnly swear by all that I hold sacred."

When the words of the oath had vanished, the captain instructed
the three to lower their hands. "You are now members of the Solar
Patrol with the rank of cadet apprentice. One of your first assignments
as a member of the patrol will be to memorize the oath and take it
to heart. In coming years, as you perform your duties as a guardian
of freedom, I further admonish you to reflect upon the words of the
Roman poet Juvenal. 'Quis custodiet ipsos custodes.'"

"Captain, what does that mean?" said Tom

"Who will guard the guards?" said the captain. "Who will guard
the guards?"

Chapter 10
The Darwinian

To Tom it seemed not a lifeless machine, but a living creature, so powerful that it could break the bonds of gravity and soar into the cosmos beyond.

"Holy cow," said Alex. "It's so cool looking, and we're going to be riding in it."

"It's—beautiful," said Sarah.

The boys flinched at Sarah's appraisal of the *Antares*.

Tom's thoughts returned to the first and only prior time he had seen the *Antares*. Then he had been on the moon Epimetheus, the breath of life being slowly sucked out of his body, so his earlier recollection of the ship had been less than lucid. Now it stood before him, resting on the landing pad outside the transparent plasma dome of Iapetus Base. Since the ship's hull was featureless except for tails fins and wings, Tom found it difficult to judge the size of the *Antares* as well as that of the other two ships that stood beside it.

Cadet Isaac Gates seemed amused by the reaction of his three charges. They stood next to the elevator shaft that had transported them to the moon's surface.

"I brought you here because I figured that nothing beats seeing the ship for real."

The three cadet apprentices nodded in agreement.

"Next to the *Antares* is the *Agincourt*. She's a dreadnaught class ship so her mass displacement is approximately three times that of the *Antares*." The wingless spaceship indicated by Gates was similar in shape to the *Antares*, but squatter in appearance, with four tails fins versus the three sported by the *Antares*.

"The third ship is the frigate *Python*." The cadet indicated a ship that appeared to be more of a match for the *Antares* in size. In place of tail fins, the stern of the *Python's* main hull was cradled inside a circle of six smaller cylinders. Unlike the double-ended engines that graced the ends of the tail fins of the other two ships, the upper part of each of the six peripheral units ended in a pointed nosecone, similar in shape to that of the nose of the main hull of all three ships. "A frigate is a general-purpose vessel," explained the cadet. "It's more lightly armed than that of a similar sized combat vessel such as the *Antares*. Its main function is logistical, that is, the transport of supplies and personnel."

"How big is it compared to the *Antares*?" asked Tom.

"It displaces more mass," said Gates, "but not by much."

"How are we going to get to the *Antares*," asked Sarah. "Since it's outside the dome won't we need to put on spacesuits?"

"No," said the cadet. "See those vertical shafts running along the side of each ship?" The three cadet apprentices studied the cylindrical shaft that extended from the surface of the landing pad to a spot about two-thirds up the hull of the *Antares*. "Those are the service tubes. They function like the elevator we just exited. Before a launch, a ship's service tube is retracted. To get to the ship, we'll first return to a lower level of the base. From there we'll pass through an underground tunnel to the tube's lower airlock. Once inside the tube, we take an elevator to the ship's airlock. Is that clear?"

"No," came three replies.

"Rookies," mumbled the cadet to himself. "The underground entrance to the service tube is outside the base's electro field. The tunnel and service tube are both pressurized so you won't need to be suited to get to the ship. Of course, once you enter the underground tunnel through the base airlock, you'll no longer be subject to the base's higher gravitational field."

As before, the cadet's comments were met by three clueless stares. Cadet Gates scratched the side of his head before continuing. He pointed at the large, ovoid shaped object perched on top of a pole far above them. "See that?" The three cadet apprentices nodded. "That's the collector node for the electrogen. The remainder of the system is underground. One part consists of a large ring that encircles the lowest level of the base. Between the ring and the collector node exists a hemispherical electro field, a dome if you will. The electrogen creates within that dome an electro field equivalent to a third of Earth's gravity. That's sufficient for avoiding the annoyance of attempting to perform everyday tasks under Iapetus' natural gravity which is only about two percent of Earth's. To give you some idea how little gravity that is, if I dropped an object from waist height, it would take about three seconds to hit the ground.

"Cool," said Tom.

"Neat," said Alex.

Gates arched his eyebrows at the two boys before giving Sarah a questioning look.

"Don't mind them," said Sarah. "They're weird."

"I understand," said the cadet, not understanding. "Anyway, the boundary of the electro field above the moon's surface coincides with that of the transparent plasma dome. That's why we can survive here on the surface of the moon without spacesuits."

"So, it's the plasma dome and not the pseudo-gravity that keeps the air from escaping into space?" asked Alex.

"That's correct. The cold plasma field that makes up the dome is strong enough to prevent air molecules from penetrating it as well as people. If you tried to walk through the dome's boundary, it would stop you. It's sort of like attempting to pass through a wall of a resilient, transparent, elastic substance. It has some give to it, but you can't penetrate it. Just as the plasma dome keeps the air in, it also serves as a barrier to micro-meteoroids and harmful cosmic radiation. It's reasonably transparent to other radiation such as visible light."

"Cool," said Alex.

"Neat," said Sarah.

"Wait a minute," said Tom. "When we were on Epimetheus, I could have sworn I heard Evad's ship start up. Wouldn't it have had to be inside the plasma dome for me to hear it?"

"Something as massive as a spaceship can penetrate the plasma field," said Gates. "The *Antares*, for instance, could have landed right where we're standing. In that case its nose would then not only be outside the plasma dome but also outside the electro field. It would be similar to someone standing in a pool of water that only came up to his waist. Like the part of a person's body below the waterline displacing an equal volume of water, the part of the ship inside the dome would displace some of the air. For you to hear its engines, at least part of Sleinad Evad's ship must have been located within the base's field boundary."

"If a person can't pass through the field boundary," asked Sarah, "how can we leave it to get to the ship?"

"See that structure over there?" The cadet pointed to a small building with a door similar to that found in one of the base's compartments. The building appeared to be bisected by the plasma dome, that is, half of it was inside the dome and half outside. "That's an airlock through which you could exit the dome. When inside such an airlock, you can pass through the field boundary. It's a strange sensation though for as you pass through the field boundary the gravitational pull will differ on different parts of your body. The same thing occurs in the case where a field boundary penetrates the interior of a spaceship. I hope that was clear."

"No," said the three teens.

"You'll get to experience it yourselves when we exit the base through the underground airlock to get to the ship. When you pass through that airlock, you'll feel your weight change because you'll be leaving the base's gravitational field."

"Cool," said Alex.

"Neat," said Tom.

"Will it hurt?" asked Sarah.

"I have received an information bulletin from HQ," said Captain Krater addressing the three officers seated with him about the circular table. "The unclassified parts of it are for immediate release to all patrolmen. The remainder is classified top secret under codename trinity. Is that understood?"

Major Sargon, Major Dale and Lieutenant Maser all said, "Yes, sir."

"After we review this new information, I suggest we summarize what we know in regards to trinity material in an attempt to build a plausible hypothesis that makes sense of it all. Major," the captain indicated the blonde female officer, "I am about to reveal to you additional information classified under codename trinity that, as far as the personnel on this ship goes, only Major Sargon, Lieutenant Maser, and myself are aware of. Outside of us, only the C.I.C. and any others he has decided to take into his confidence have access to this information. Should you find yourself in command of the *Antares*, you will then have the privilege of deciding if any other members of the *Antares'* crew will be allowed access. Is that understood?"

"Yes, sir," said the major.

"Very well, let's start with the creature known as Jack Paine. This is a report from the science division of the academy." The captain handed each of the other officers a small thin slip of plastic. "This part of the release is for general distribution and is therefore unclassified. To summarize its contents, the alien known as Jack Paine appears to be a member of the dominant species of a planet in the Dorian system. The species are known as Darwinians and are classified as extraterrestrial sapient animal."

"Sir," said the doctor, "I've never heard of the Dorian system, nor of an extraterrestrial called a Darwinian."

"Neither have I," said Sargon.

"Nor I," said the other major.

"That makes four of us," said the captain. "As to why this is the first time we're being informed about this, that will become clear when I get to the classified part.

The second planet from the system's primary star was named Dorian and is thus the system's namesake. It is this planet that is home to the Darwinians. Due to the high eccentricity of its orbit combined with the extreme tilt of its axis of rotation and the exceptionally large tidal forces exerted by its only moon, the planet's surface conditions undergo extreme changes throughout the Dorian year. As you will note in the report that year is equivalent to 3.2 Earth years. In order to rapidly adapt to the changing environmental extremes, many of the higher life forms, including the most sapient advanced, that is, the Darwinians, have evolved an ability to consciously change their genetic makeup. A Darwinian's survivability is further enhanced by its ability to absorb the genetic material of a host species. It can pattern its own genetic makeup on that of the host. It is deemed likely that it can also absorb the host's memory. The memory assimilation is interesting in that it allows a Darwinian to even further improve its own chances for survival by taking advantage of the learned experiences of its host. It is conjectured that there exist limitations to this ability. If so such limitations are presently not known."

"That's incredible," said the doctor. Sargon gave a nod of agreement.

"It gets even more incredible. Darwinians hatch from eggs that resemble, to some extent, large terrestrial seed pods. Yes, I said 'pods.' When laid, the pods are about the size of a typical chicken egg, but they rapidly grow to be about a foot in length, after which the fetus may lay dormant inside its pod for years. We have no idea what the upper limit may be for its dormancy. To complete the birth process, at some point *activation* occurs when the fetus inside the pod first receives nutrients through an umbilical like tube, after which the pod will start to grow again along with its inhabitant. The size of the creature at the time of its hatching will vary depending on the local environment. The maximum size a pod can reach under optimal conditions is unknown."

"And I take it," said the woman officer, "that these pods fit the description of those the Commander found aboard Evad's flagship at the Quadrant Five engagement?"

"That's correct."

Lieutenant Maser let out a whistle. "There were hundreds of those things on that ship. Good thing the ship was destroyed."

"And when two of our new cadet apprentices were shown the recording of the Commander's discovery, they recognized them to be smaller versions of what they had found in Evad's compartment," added the captain. "The transcript you hold contains several conjectures of a Darwinian's adaptability. For instance, consider a Darwinian that has adapted to a wet, warm environment and is herbivorous. Its environment then undergoes a rapid change to one that is cold, arid, and barren of food sources. Most known species of animals would perish under such an extreme change of conditions. However, if the Darwinian can kill an animal that is adapted to the new environment, including even another Darwinian, it may yet survive. To do so, it will synthesize the genetic information of its prey along with its victim's memory, should the victim be sentient. Over a span of time that can range anywhere from a day or two to upwards to four weeks, depending on the amount of morphological and physiological modification required, the Darwinian will change its form and physiology to successfully adapt to the new environment.

"Amazing," said the doctor. "And will its new form match that of the animal whose genetic information it absorbed."

"According to this report, yes."

"By what means does it obtain the genetic data and memory of its prey?" asked Sargon.

"It has an internal tubular structure, termed a *proboscis*, that exits through the oral orifice of the creature. The structure resembles a tentacle with a sharp tip. The tip in turn is surrounded by a number of smaller flexible tentacles. It is propelled by a strong ejector muscle that allows the tip of the proboscis to penetrate the prey's hide. Normally the Darwinian attempts to strike the head of its prey, or whatever might pass for a head in being the location of the brain. If successful, it then literally sucks out the victim's brains. Although over time the rest of its body will morph to resemble that of its prey, the morphology of the proboscis remains unchanged. That's one means of identifying these things. A simple body scan will reveal the presence of the proboscis."

"Where would this proboscis be located in our friend *Jack*?" asked Sargon.

"In *Jack's* case," said the doctor, "our scan shows it to be the tongue. These things are unbelievable. The organ's outer appearance is that of a tongue. It's only the scan that shows it to be otherwise."

The captain continued. "It is hypothesized that one of the environmental variables that influences a Darwinian's adaptation is the strength of the local gravitational field. Because of Dorian's high gravity, the size of a mature pod on that planet is smaller than it would be if grown on Earth. That explains the large size of the pod found in Evad's apartment."

"You keep using words like conjecture and theorize. Is none of this actually verified?" asked Sargon.

"That is to some extent addressed in the confidential part of the transmittal."

"In other words, all of this is someone's guess as to what this Jack Paine thing is actually capable of?"

"Yes, by my understanding."

"Can we take a moment here to engage in some speculation," asked the doctor.

"Go ahead, Doc."

"It's seems obvious that the Darwinian we now have incarcerated on the *Antares* came out of that pod the kids found in Evad's apartment. Let's consider then the following scenario. Evad and Serpens implant a mindbender in the newly hatched Darwinian to ensure their control of it. They then kidnap the human Jack Paine and let the Darwinian feed on Paine's body and assimilate his memory. Then they make it look like Paine died in some sort of vehicular accident, if I correctly understood what the cadets told us. That would possibly cover up any damage done to the body by the Darwinian. The Darwinian then begins to morph into the shape of Paine. The changes we now observe in the Darwinian's form are probably being driven by the fact that it's now in a lesser gravitational field than that in which it was reared, that is, the Earth's."

"That all seems plausible to me," said the captain.

"But why have we never heard of these creatures?" asked Major Dale. "Such a species could potentially pose a grave threat to the security of the Solar Alliance. You would think a study of their natural history would be part of every patrolman's training."

"I agree, but we'll come to that," said the captain. "By the way, from this point on, all information is classified under codeword trinity. The species was discovered over eighty years ago. According to this, only a single expedition of record has ever visited Dorian. You're no doubt correct, major, in asserting that these things could pose a threat to the Solar Alliance. In spite of their lack of technology, the Darwinians managed to kill every member of that expedition save one. Fortunately, there was a survivor, otherwise we would not have had this report. The system was placed off limits to colonization and commercial exploitation, the fear of course being that if these things ever got seeded into other systems and were able to breed . . ."

"And we now know of at least one such incident," said Major Dale.

"Yes. We can only wonder if Evad has more of these creatures at hand," said the captain. "But to finish answering your question, major, the reason that none of us were ever informed of the existence of these beings is that all records of their existence had been erased from patrol databases as well as all other known Alliance databases. Fortunately, the description of the pod and Darwinian we submitted to the academy happened to jog the memory of a senior staffer in the science division. He had kept a hardcopy of the original report in his personal library."

"Huh? A hardcopy?" said the ship physician. "You mean like a—a book?"

"Yes."

"Why by the moon of Venus would he do such a thing?"

"I have no idea," said the captain. "Lucky for us, whatever might have been his reason, that he did."

"Sounds like someone purposely erased the databases," ventured the blonde major.

"No doubt," said the captain.

"Now that you mention databases," said Sargon, "I take it that we now have access to the Commander's complete records so that we can ascertain the relationship between him and the boy?"

"I was coming to that, major. HQ reports that their records relating to the Commander are no better than ours; that is, they only have the Commander's DNA along with photographs of him. So apparently sabotage has occurred there also. It looks like the patrol has been infiltrated by enemy agents."

"Impossible," exclaimed Major Dale.

"What other explanation can there be?" asked the captain.

"I can understand the Draconian Guard wanting to remove all knowledge of the existence of the Darwinians," said Major Dale, "but what would be their purpose in deleting information related to the Commander?"

"No idea."

"What's going to happen to our Darwinian?" asked the lieutenant.

Before answering, the captain mentally checked the time. "It's scheduled to be transferred from the *Antares* to the base lab as we speak. From there it will be transported to Earth and science division for further study."

"Is it still alive?" asked the female major.

"Yes," said the lieutenant. "Of course, it's sedated and confined."

"Can you be sure of that?" said Sargon. "I mean about being sedated. Seeing how it can change its physiology, could it not possibly counteract the effects of the sedative?"

"Lieutenant?" said the captain.

Lieutenant Maser was looking decidedly uncomfortable when the base alarm sounded.

"Wow," said Tom. "This is really neat."

Having exited the ship elevator, the three teens and Gates stood in the control room of the *Antares*. Gadget filled consoles and futuristic looking chairs lined the curved bulkhead. The scene reminded the boy of some of the control rooms of spaceships he had seen in various science fiction films and TV shows.

"The control room is always manned when the ship is in space," said the cadet. "There's no need for that now since we're docked. Besides, most of the crew is on shore leave."

"Could we see outside," asked Alex, "you know, like turning on that cosmos thing or whatever."

The cadet nodded. "Cleo, three-sixty external view please."

As had happened in the sickbay the previous night, the compartment darkened and the ceiling and bulkheads vanished. All three teens let out a yelp of surprise for it seemed as if the deck had dropped out from beneath them leaving them suspended high above the landing pad. Around and above was the black void of space, the most noticeable feature of which was the serene orb of Saturn and its incredible rings. Fortunately, the lights of the controls on the panels and chairs as well as the glow of the elevator from which they had recently exited were still visible, providing the teens a means of retaining their bearings.

Sensing the discomfort of his charges, the cadet ordered the ship computer to restore the deck to view. Below them, the surface of Iapetus was instantly replaced by the dark shine of a metal floor on which were reflected the lights of the room's instrument panels as well as the distant stars.

Off to his right Tom noticed the faintly luminous outline of the electro dome of Iapetus Base. At the top of a high pole at the dome's apex was the electrogen collector. Off in another direction, he could see the *Agincourt* and beyond that the *Python*.

Once onboard the *Antares*, the teens had found access from one deck to another was by means of a central elevator that ran the length of the ship's inhabitable core. Like the larger base elevators, its outward appearance was that of a transparent curved wall. To transfer from one deck to another, one simply walked through the 'wall' and then either spoke or thought of a destination. The passenger was immediately zipped to the desired deck by means of a levitation mechanism. Since the three teens had not yet received their neurodic implants, they didn't have the ability to select a destination by imagining it.

When in operation, the color of the elevator's shell changed from a light blue glow to a dull red, warning a prospective passenger to wait and not bump into a plasma wall that could no longer be passed through. An additional safety feature of the design was that the elevator would not operate if an object broke the wall's boundary. If Tom and Alex had had their way, they would have no doubt spent hours playing with the elevator and learning every secret of its design. In case of the elevator being out of commission, ladders provided a more primitive means of transfer from one deck to another when the ship was not in free fall. Two ladders, placed opposite of each other, hugged the outer bulkhead of the ship. The circular openings in each deck through which the ladders passed were closed by hatches.

Earlier on, when Tom and his friends had entered the base underground airlock on their way to the *Antares*, they felt their weight fall from about a third of their normal Earth weight to that of but a couple of pounds due to the weak natural gravitational pull of Iapetus. Fortunately, the soles of their boots automatically sensed the difference in the gravitational field strength and compensated by providing their wearers additional traction. The sudden change in weight caused the two boys to experience a queasy sensation in their stomachs and for a moment they had the urge to vomit. Sarah, on the other hand, appeared to be unfazed by the experience.

As they passed through the service tunnel on their way to the *Antares*, Gates warned the three to always keep one foot in contact with the tunnel's floor. He told them that any attempt to perform a jump inside the tunnel or ship could result in serious injury as they would most likely end up crashing into the overhead. Naturally, the suggestion caused some conflict in the minds of both boys as each stoically resisted the temptation to test the warning. Sarah, on the other hand, was entirely focused on ensuring that she had one foot in contact with the deck at all times as instructed.

Gates continued with his explanation of the different stations in the control room.

"This is the captain's station," he said indicating a chair that was elevated above the rest of the deck. "Next to it is the exec's station."

"That would be Major Sargon?" asked Tom.

"Correct. During general quarters, while the captain's station is in the control room, the executive officer's station is in engineering on the aft deck."

"Why is that?" asked Alex.

"Should the control room be knocked out, the exec would assume command from engineering."

Tom thought he saw Sarah give a shudder at the thought of the compartment they were standing in being obliterated during a battle in space.

"Normally, the senior officer present in the control room occupies the captain's station," said Gates. "Directly in front of the captain's station is where the pilot sits, and next to him is the astrogation station. Then communications and finally fire control, which completes the designated control room stations."

"Do you have many fires?" asked Sarah.

"Fires?' Gates looked puzzled.

"You said that was fire control." The girl pointed toward the last chair Gates had indicated.

Gates smiled. "That's fire control as in weapons."

"Oh," muttered the embarrassed girl

Alex pointed to an open, rectangular compartment attached to the nearest section of the bulkhead. "What is that by the wall."

"That's an emergency locker, and we like to refer to it as the bulkhead and not a wall." A score of devices were attached to the back of the open locker. "It contains weapons, medical supplies, auxiliary communications devices, and tools that might be required in an emergency. You'll note an identical locker on the opposing section of the bulkhead."

"What kind of weapon is this?" asked Alex, leaning forward to better examine the contents of the locker up close. He indicated an exotic looking gadget whose shape and size were similar to that of a ray pistol.

"Leave that be, cadet," said Gates. At the warning, Alex immediately straightened up. "That's a tool, not a weapon. It's an arc cutter.

It emits an adjustable plasma beam that will cut through just about anything except a neutronium doped alloy. Unlike the weapons, it has a manual safety lock, this switch here." The cadet indicated a small red lever flush with the side of the power tool.

"What's a safety lock?" asked Sarah. It seemed that anything associated with words like *safe* or *dangerous* got her undivided attention.

Gates unholstered his sidearm and attempted to hand it to the girl. Sarah backed off as if she feared touching the weapon would burn her. Gates smiled and handed the gun to Alex. "Shoot me," he instructed.

"What?" said Alex.

"I said shoot me, cadet. That's an order."

"Okay," said the boy, sounding hesitant. He cautiously raised the weapon and pointed it at Gates.

"Where should I shoot you?" stammered the boy.

"How about in the chest?" laughed Gates. "That's usually a good target."

Alex slowly squeezed the trigger, being tempted to close his eyes as he did so. Nothing happened. He increased the pressure on the trigger. Still nothing. He squeezed the trigger with as much strength as he could muster. Zilch.

"You see," said Gates, retrieving his weapon. "Because of the safety lock it won't fire. However, once you receive your neurodic implant and have mastered its use, you will be able to issue the weapon a mental command to override the lock and arm the gun. The safety lock prevents an enemy from using our own firearms against us."

"So, the lock is controlled by your mind?" asked Tom.

"That's correct."

"I think you're lucky that Alex doesn't have his neurodic implant yet," said Tom.

Gates laughed. "Well, even if he had it and had mastered its use, by default the gun is set to emit a harmless target beam, but it would have been embarrassing."

That's when the ship's alarm went off.

In a compartment two decks below the control room, Spaceman Second Class Reeves Aristedes checked the time. He was awaiting the arrival of a detachment of patrolmen from the base. Their task was to transfer to the base lab the body that lay unmoving on the table next to where the spaceman sat. The body was still dressed in the clothes it had worn when Evad had zapped it in Sullivans Woods.

Aristedes had just finished processing the information release on Darwinians. "Amazing," he thought to himself as he got to his feet to better study the sedated creature stretched out before him. While he had been reading the information that had floated before him regarding the alien life form, he had reflected on the wisdom of securing the subject with wrist and ankle clamps along with the metal band that encircled the being's torso.

"Mister Aristedes," came the voice over the intercom. "This is Iapetus Base Control. The detail assigned to take custody of the alien detainee in your charge have entered the connector tunnel. The release password is 'delphi sixty-two.'"

"Delphi sixty-two," repeated Aristedes. "Roger."

"Well, you Omicronian Trog-Turbler," said the spaceman, addressing the body on the slab, "we'll certainly be glad to get your ugly corpse off this ship." As he said it he noticed that the Darwinian's mouth was slightly open and one of the creature's fingers was twitching.

Aristedes drew his ray gun and leaned over the silent body, his face hovering close to the one that to some extent still resembled Jack Paine's.

"Wasn't its mouth closed?" were Aristedes' last thoughts as the creature's eyes flicked open. With a quickness that prevented any effective defense, the alien's proboscis shot through the opening of its mouth. With the sound of breaking bone, it penetrated the patrolman's

529

skull. Aristedes died instantly. For several seconds the alien savored the sensation of the kill, its deadly tentacle exploring the cranium of the deceased spaceman before it was withdrawn. As Aristedes' body slumped to the deck, the tentacle extended and then moved down to one of the wrist clamps. By feel alone, the flexible appendages at the end of the proboscis expertly manipulated the clamp's locking mechanism causing it to spring open. The Darwinian quickly repeated the maneuver with the other wrist clamp and then the torso clamp. Sitting up, it was an easy matter for it to release the ankle restraints.

Springing from the table as it retracted its proboscis, the alien retrieved the dead spaceman's weapon and then moved towards the compartment's hatch which obligingly sprang open. The moment he stepped through the hatchway and into the corridor beyond, the ship's alarm went off.

"What is that?" said Sarah.

"It's a red alert," said Gates. "There's a serious problem aboard the ship."

As if anticipating the question, the voice of the ship computer filled the control room. "Code red alert. There has been an unauthorized exit from the detainment compartment. There is no acknowledgement from Mr. Aristedes. His life signs are null."

"By Io's hell, it sounds like our detainee has escaped," said Gates, "and we're the only ones on board."

"What should we do?" asked Tom.

Instead of immediately answering, Gates reached over and detached a ray gun from the emergency locker. As he held it in his hand, the gun emitted a faint sound as if a gear was turning, and a green light on one side of the weapon briefly blinked. Tom suspected that the cadet was using his mind to arm the weapon.

"I've overridden the safety lock," said the cadet. "To fire, squeeze the trigger. It's set on paralyze for a human target. I would imagine that would incapacitate this creature since according to the bulletin its metabolism closely mimics that of a human. Here." He attempted to hand the weapon to Sarah. She took a step back, obviously not keen about the idea of having a weapon.

Gates thought better of the idea and so turned to Alex. "You've handled firearms, right?"

"You bet," said the boy, taking the ray gun.

The cadet repeated the same procedure with a second handgun from the locker and passed it on to Tom as the alarm continued to sound.

"Okay, here's the plan," said Gates. "Until we get specific orders to the contrary, we follow the standing directive. That's for me to do whatever I think best. We're on the uppermost deck of the ship so I propose we start a sweep to aft. But it's imperative that we don't leave the control room unmanned. You," he pointed at Tom, "will stay here and guard the control room. You two come with me." He then turned back to Tom. "If you see the elevator turn red, be ready to blast anything that comes out of it. Understand?"

"Yes, sir," said Tom.

"You two stick close to me, especially you." He gave Sarah a nod. Then Gates stepped through the transparent wall of the elevator. After a moment's hesitation, Alex and Sarah followed him. Sarah cast a worried glance back at Tom as she entered the elevator. The elevator's wall brightened for a moment and Tom found himself alone in the control room of the Solar Patrol starcruiser *Antares*.

The scene that surrounded the boy was surreal for the three-sixty external view that Gates had requested was still active. It was as if Tom and the fixtures of the control room were on a circular platform that floated above the surface of Iapetus with the starry firmament around and above him and the moon base off to one side. Beyond the *Antares* stood the *Agincourt* and beyond that the *Python*.

Tom took a couple of steps back from the glowing cylindrical elevator shaft so as to give himself a better chance to react should the alien pop out of it. With each step there was a quiet click as the soles of his boots contacted the deck and latched onto it with their magnetic-like hold. He looked about him. When the room had been lit with its normal internal lighting, it had been easy to locate the various hand-holds that were located on the deck, bulkhead and overhead to assist in mobility at times of weightlessness. To Tom's untrained eyes, they were now more difficult to see.

The boy examined the ray gun he held. "Cool," he thought to him-self. It felt weirdly light due to the weak pull of the moon's gravity. He spun it around his finger which wasn't difficult to do as the gun's mass hadn't changed. "Nice balance," thought the boy. Then, without con-sidering the consequences of his action in the lesser gravity of Iapetus, he tossed it into the air. His intention had been to do a half spin and catch it behind his back as it came back down like he had done count-less times with his toy cap guns four centuries earlier when he had been under Earth's familiar gravitational pull.

The weapon immediately soared straight up, hit the overhead and bounced off at an angle. Before Tom could determine where the gun had ended up, the emergency ladder hatch to his left popped open and out scrambled a grotesque facsimile of Jack Paine.

At first, startled by the other's unexpected presence, both fig-ures froze. Then Tom jumped back a step, his second mistake. As his boots broke contact with the deck, as had happened with his ray gun, he found himself soaring through the air on a collision course with the overhead. *Jack* aimed the gun he carried at the moving boy, but when he squeezed the trigger nothing happened. "It's the safety lock," thought Tom as he crashed into the ceiling and let out a yelp of pain. Instinctively before the collision he had thrust out his hands in an attempt to grab something. He succeeded in latching onto one of the overhead handholds, thus preventing his body from bouncing off the overhead and returning, who knew where, to the deck below.

Had Tom been more experienced in low gravity maneuvering, the next thing he would have done is coil his body around and lock onto the overhead with his magnetized boots, thus effectively using it as a surrogate deck to maneuver on, but the idea never occurred to the boy.

The Darwinian, upon realizing that his weapon wouldn't fire, used it as a missile as he hurled it at the boy clinging to the overhead. Tom saw it coming and using the muscles of the arm with which he gripped the handhold, easily jerked his body out of the way. From the fact that the alien had not been able to fire its weapon, the boy realized that the gun that Gates had given him was the only one in the room that was operational. But where was it?

The Darwinian attempted to step onto the deck from the open hatch. In the excitement of the moment, it failed to compensate for the low gravity. Unlike those worn by the boy, its shoes were not designed to grip the deck. The result was that it propelled itself into the air. At that point Tom released his grip, having decided to get back to the deck and attempt to retrieve his ray gun. Once more his lack of experience worked to his disadvantage as instead of giving himself a gentle push to send his body in the direction he wanted to go, he instead floated to the deck at a speed that seemed agonizingly slow. In the meantime, the Darwinian had collided with the overhead. Then, showing more skill than the boy, it immediately pushed off using just enough force so that its trajectory now intersected with the boy's path of descent.

Tom saw the alien heading towards him and, there being nothing in reach to push off against, could only brace himself for the collision. *Jack's* body crashed into the boy's and the Darwinian grabbed onto Tom with both hands. They bounced off the deck, the angle of their ricochet taking them into the back of a chair. The alien's face was within striking distance of the boy's and, considering that Tom had yet to be fully briefed on *Jack's* real nature including the lethal weapon it possessed in its proboscis, by all odds it should have been the end of the boy. The alien opened its mouth and ejected its deadly tentacle at Tom's head.

But the creature had not reckoned with Tom's almost supernatural fast reflexes. The boy was aiming a haymaker at his antagonist's face when as he saw something ungodly come shooting out of its open mouth. Instead of landing the blow, the boy grabbed the proboscis, stopping it before it could drill into his skull. For an instance both antagonists looked at each other with an expression of utter surprise, and then the boy, focusing all his strength into the arm holding the proboscis, gave the snakelike appendage a hard yank. The alien let out a roar of mixed pain and outrage and released its hold on the boy. At the same moment as he released his grip on the proboscis, Tom landed a blow with his fisted other hand squarely on the side of *Jack's* head, causing the creature to emit another howl of rage.

As fast as he could, Tom did a backwards crab walk across the deck. As he scurried towards the nearest bulkhead, he scanned the compartment for the missing weapon while at the same time keeping an eye on his antagonist. *Jack* was in close pursuit. By grabbing first one deck fixture and then another, it propelled itself across the control room in the manner of a climber scurrying up the face of a cliff. Just as the back of Tom's head collided with one of the emergency lockers, *Jack* was on him. Tom threw out his left hand in an attempt to straight arm the alien. He reached behind him with the other hand and felt it close upon the familiar shape of a pistol handle. He pulled the object off its supports and thrust it at the alien's face. It was an arc cutter. Once his hand had closed about the tool's handle, instinct took over. As the Darwinian opened its mouth to deliver another strike, Tom flipped the tool's safety and squeezed the trigger. Before the tentacle could smash through Tom's skull, a deadly spear of plasma sliced into *Jack's* face. The creature let out a piercing shriek of rage and stumbled backwards as it grabbed its mutilated face with both hands. Tom pushed forward, his improvised weapon held before him with his finger still depressing the trigger. Before his antagonist could recover, Tom swept the tool's beam from left to right. In slow motion *Jack's* head separated from its body. It took all of five seconds for the decapitated body and falling head to hit the deck.

Chapter 11
The Dream

When Gates, Sarah and Alex stepped from the elevator into the control room, they found Tom holding the arc cutter in one hand and the Darwinian's head by its hair in his other, in a manner reminiscent of Cellini's statue of Perseus with the head of the Medusa. Tom was giving the head a quizzical look. The Darwinian's deadly tentacle protruded from its mouth like some grotesque tongue, and its open eyes stared unseeing at the firmament above. Upon spying the decapitated head, Sarah turned away, overcome by a sudden urge to regurgitate.

Gates lowered his ray gun. "Cadet Gates to Iapetus Base. Stand down from condition red." Immediately the alarm ceased. He then told Cleo, the ship computer, to broadcast a view of the *Antares* control room to all points.

Throughout the compartments of Iapetus Base and the docked ships standing outside, there materialized three-dimensional scenes showing Tom holding the severed head of the Darwinian. A cheer erupted from the base personnel and the ships' crews.

"I'll be a Polluxian Snerg Blat," said Major Sargon. Along with the other officers of the *Antares*, he had just entered the connector tunnel that led to the ship.

"Cadet Gates, this is Captain Krater. What is your situation?" Images of the captain and the other officers of the *Antares* materialized before the far bulkhead.

"The alien is deader than an Antarean mustard slime. It looks as if Cadet Cobalt killed it with an arc cutter." Gates glanced at Tom, and Tom gave a nod. "Sir, we found Aristedes' body in the detainment compartment. The creature no doubt killed him and then made its way to the control room by one of the emergency ladders. I left Cadet Cobalt behind to secure the control room while I took the other two cadets with me to prevent it using the elevator to get to the upper decks. It's my fault that—"

"I believe you did the right thing, cadet, except why didn't you arm Cadet Cobalt?"

"But I did, sir. I also armed Cadet Banyon." Alex held up the ray gun he was carrying to show it to the captain, having ascertained that the captain had a view of the control room similar to the one he had of the captain and the other officers in the connector tunnel."

Before the captain could respond, several other patrolmen with drawn ray guns entered the control room from the illuminated elevator shaft.

"I can't believe I missed the whole thing again," said Alex, as he continued to explore the small two-man quarters that he would share with Tom aboard the *Antares*.

"Believe me," said Tom, trying to figure out how to strap himself into his bunk when under weightless conditions, "you wouldn't have wanted to be there."

"So, what else did the captain have to say?"

"He didn't seem too pleased when I told him about fooling around and losing the ray gun Gates had given me."

"Yeah, I can't believe you didn't think about what would happen when you tossed it in the air under Iapetus' gravity."

"Oh, and you would have?"

"Of course." said Alex. "What else did he say?"

"He said I was lucky to be alive."

"And——?"

"That was about it."

"I bet Major Sargon had a few things to say, none of them pleasant."

"No. That was strange. He just sat there looking at me. I was half expecting him to take up where the captain left off in chewing me out, but he didn't. He didn't say a word."

"So, what kind of look was he giving you, like one of loathing or something?"

"No," said Tom, having managed to get his body inside the zero-acceleration bedding. "He was just giving me a really strange look, that's all."

"So, describe the look," said Alex, "and I think your head goes at the other end."

"I don't know. I almost think it was, I know this sounds crazy, but kind of like one of respect or something, and I don't see why it matters which end my head is at."

"Yeah, that's strange for sure. You must have misread him."

"I'm sure I did."

"What else did the captain say?"

"That was it except, right as I was leaving, he said I needed to slow down and leave some guardsmen for the rest of them."

"That sounds like a compliment."

"Yeah—maybe, or maybe he was being sarcastic. I don't know."

"So, then you went and saw the doc? What did he do?"

"He just wanted to be sure I was okay—you know, not physically but mentally."

"Are you okay?"

"I guess. But if I have nightmares tonight, feel free to wake me."

"If you start screaming in your sleep, I'll just call Cleo and have her take care of it."

"How do you think Sarah's handling it?" said Tom.

"I think she's already regretting enlisting. On the positive side, now that Jack's dead, for the second time, she definitely won't have him to worry about."

"It sounds to me like the real Jack died back on Earth in the twentieth century," said Tom. "Whatever it was I killed certainly wasn't Jack."

"Makes sense to me. By the way, I believe the captain had a point there."

"About what?" said Tom.

"About your habit of sending aliens to their happy hunting grounds. That's four you've killed, all within forty-eight hours of arriving in the twenty-fourth century. Like the captain said, leave some for the rest of us."

"Come in, major."

Major Sargon entered the commanding officer's cabin aboard the *Antares*. The captain was sitting behind a small rectangular table that doubled as a desk, staring at glowing text floating before his eyes.

"Take a seat major," said the captain.

"I suppose that is the letter of condolence to the family of Mister Aristedes?" asked the major.

"Yes." The answer was barely audible. "I was just rereading it one more time." The captain switched his attention to his visitor. "This is the first one of these I've had to write in nearly three years."

"I'm sure it must be difficult, sir."

"You'll probably discover that for yourself before long."

"I don't understand."

"You'll no doubt soon have a command of your own," said the captain. "I recently finished your annual fitness report. In it I recommended you for promotion and an independent command."

Major Sargon opened his mouth and started to say something, but then closed it.

The captain broke into a grin. "Surprised, major?"

"Yes—yes, sir. Considering . . . Yes, I'm surprised."

"Were you about to say something along the lines of considering all the times you've questioned my decisions?"

"Sir? When have I questioned your decisions?"

"Like a good subordinate, you've never openly questioned them in front of the rest of the crew, but I know at times you've not been in full agreement with some of my orders."

"Yes, sir. That's true. By the way, I would like to admit that I may have been wrong about Cadet Cobalt. After how he handled that Darwinian . . . Well, it now seems credible that he did kill those Mickies on Epimetheus, although the part about activating the guardian with a lucky toss of a yo-yo seems pretty farfetched."

"According to the doc, Cadet Cobalt's right hand was broken at the time he was dispatching the Mickies?"

"I didn't know that," said Sargon. "Then again, if he had been focusing on his assignment while in the control room instead of playing with the weapon he was given—he was lucky that arc welder was there."

"That's certainly true," said the captain. "But I can imagine the Commander doing something equally foolish when he was that age."

"Yes, sir."

"Tell me, Major. Any change of opinion regarding our other two new recruits?"

"I find the evidence of Cadet Banyon's genetic tampering disturbing."

"Yes," said the captain. "I'm afraid we're in agreement there. And I take it you haven't changed your mind about Cadet Gould?"

Sargon simply gave his head a disgusted shake.

"Well, time will tell," said the captain, as he returned his attention to the letter he had drafted. After a moment he said, "Cleo, please transmit."

"Yes, captain," came a female voice. The hovering text vanished.

"Are the applicants to fill Mr. Aristedes' billet here?"

"Yes, sir," said Major Sargon, "but that's applicant, not applicants."

"Only one?"

"Yes, sir. I suspect that is Major Manning's doing."

"As base commander I take it he's none too happy to have been excluded from access to codeword trinity material?"

"No doubt," said Sargon. "He claims that he's short handed and that the applicant is the only patrolman he can spare. Not only that, the applicant is a cadet, not a spaceman second class."

"By the clouds of Venus, we'll be overrun with cadets. Well, get him in here."

"Her, sir."

"What?"

"He's a she. Here's her service record." Sargon handed the captain a thin piece of plastic. "You may want to take a minute to scan that before the interview."

After a few moments, the captain grunted, "Major Manning appears to be sending us the crud at the bottom of a fuel tank."

"That was my impression, sir."

"Very well, get her in here."

The hatch to the cabin popped open and a young, most attractive brunette stepped into the cabin. She gave the captain a salute. "Cadet Sameera Bindra, reporting as ordered, sir."

The captain returned the salute. "Have a seat, cadet."

As she took a seat, the cadet caste a glance in the direction of Major Sargon and gave a hard swallow, an action that didn't escape the notice of either officer.

"I am Captain Krater, the commander of the *Antares*, and this is my executive officer, Major Sargon."

"Yes, sir."

"Cadet, it's not necessary to sit at attention," said the captain.

"Yes, sir." Cadet Bindra attempted to relax but unsuccessfully.

"According to your service record you joined the patrol the day you turned eighteen, and now you are one Terran month shy of turning twenty-one."

"Yes, sir."

"That's almost three years as a cadet."

"Yes, sir."

"I've never heard of anyone remaining a cadet that long," sneered Sargon. "That must be a patrol record."

Cadet Bindra gave a noticeable jerk at the major's comment but offered no verbal response.

"According to this," said the captain, referring to the cadet's service record, "the only thing holding you back from promotion to spaceman second class is your commanding officer's recommendation."

"Yes, sir."

"I find it strange that Major Manning has not entered his reasons for failing to recommend you for promotion. Any idea what those reasons might be?"

"No, sir."

"You're telling us you have no idea why Major Manning won't recommend you for promotion?" said the major.

"Yes, sir. At least, I'm not certain, sir."

"Care to hazard a guess?"

"I— It may be that at times I have voiced some—doubts about the way Major Manning exercises his command. Perhaps those doubts have come to the base commander's attention."

"Cadet," said the major, "are you telling us that you, a lowly cadet, think you know how to run a Solar Patrol base better than its commanding officer?"

"No, sir."

"Then please explain why you saw fit to criticize the major."

"I—my error, sir."

"Do you expect us to believe that?" said Sargon.

"Yes, sir."

"Do I make you nervous?" said Sargon.

"Yes, sir."

"Does the captain make you nervous?"

"No, sir."

"Have you ever approached Major Manning as to why he has withheld his recommendation?" asked the captain.

"Yes, sir."

"And?"

Cadet Bindra took a deep breath. "He said . . . He said I was a misfit and that as long as I remained under his command he would never promote me."

"I must say I'm beginning to see the reason for Major Manning's judgment," said Sargon.

"Cadet, was the reason you volunteered for transfer to the *Antares* to get out from Major Manning's command?"

"I didn't volunteer, sir."

"Did Major Manning order you to request the transfer?" said the captain.

"Yes, sir."

"Then you don't wish to transfer?"

"Oh, no, sir. I would love—uh, be honored to serve aboard the *Antares*. The idea of requesting this assignment never entered my mind since I understood that women patrolmen didn't serve aboard starcruisers."

"I smell a dead Mickey," said the major. "Was there ever an announcement made by base command for volunteers to transfer to the *Antares*?"

"No, sir."

"So how exactly did you come to request a transfer?"

"Major Manning called me to his office and ordered me to. I thought that was a little strange since, as I mentioned, I understood that such assignments were contrary to regulations."

"Aside from having to serve under Major Manning, have you been happy with your assignments at Iapetus Base?" said the captain.

"Yes—that is, I was at first, but I've always wanted deep space duty."

"I take it you've had no deep space experience other than aboard the Academy training vessel *Corbett* and your transfer trip to Iapetus Base?" asked the major.

"Yes, sir."

"Did Major Manning tell you that we were really seeking a spaceman second class?" said the captain.

"No, sir."

The captain glanced at the cadet's service record again. As he did so, Sargon asked, "Cadet, is your hairstyle regulation?"

"I believe so, sir," said Cadet Bindra. The executive officer was obviously referring to the length of the cadet's braided ponytail that fell down her back almost to her waist. "At least, you're the first one to bring to my attention the possibility that it may not be."

"Should you ever get a chance to serve aboard a starship, the ship's executive officer will no doubt require you to shorten it," said Sargon.

"Cadet, do you have any questions?" said the captain.

"Sir, may I ask what became of the crew member you're seeking a replacement for?"

"He was killed?"

"When sir?"

"About three hours ago, one deck below us. Care to know the details?"

"Yes, sir."

"You've received the training bulletin on the Darwinian alien life form?"

"Yes, sir."

"A Darwinian penetrated his skull with its proboscis and scrambled his brains," said the captain.

Cadet Bindra took a hard swallow.

"Still want to sign up?" said Sargon.

The cadet fixed the major with her eyes. "Yes sir." She then turned to the captain. "Sir, may I ask another question?"

"Go ahead," said the captain.

"When was the regulation about women serving on starcruisers changed, or did I misunderstand?"

"It hasn't been changed. The *Antares* has been granted an exemption. Why is presently classified," said the captain. "Any other questions?"

"No, sir."

"Major?"

"No further questions, sir."

"Cadet, have you anything else to say?" asked the captain.

"No, sir."

"Please wait in the corridor. We'll let you know of our decision shortly. You're dismissed."

The cadet stood. "Yes, sir. Thank you for taking the time to—uh, see me, and I wish you and your crew spaceman's luck on your next mission." The woman patrolman turned and exited the cabin.

When the hatch had closed, the major swiveled his chair so as to face the captain. "I suggest we see if there are any patrol ships docked at Huygens City. If so, we could forward a request to their skippers for a spaceman second class transfer. Of course, obtaining a replacement isn't that important since we're comfortably above critical manning level."

"Major, if you ignore Major Manning's evaluation, in all other areas of assessment Cadet Bindra's record is most commendable."

"Captain, you can't be serious?"

"Suppose Cadet Bindra were a man? Would you view the situation differently?"

"No, sir—well, actually I haven't considered that scenario," said Sargon. "But that's not material. A cadet does not criticize her commanding officer."

"Cleo, send Cadet Bindra back in," said the captain.

The hatch immediately popped open and the cadet reentered the cabin, again snapping to attention and giving the captain a salute.

"Cadet," said Captain Krater, "you realize that it's traditional to salute a captain only upon initial arrival aboard his ship and is considered a courtesy."

"Yes, sir." The cadet looked most uneasy.

"Understand that although we're short one spaceman second class, that's not a manning problem, especially since we presently have five cadets onboard instead of the standard complement of two."

"Yes, sir, I understand," said the cadet.

"Major," said Captain Krater, "where do you intend for Cadet Bindra to bunk?"

Both the cadet and the major gave a start at the captain's words, the major quickly recovering from his surprise.

"I shall have Major Dale relocate to an officer's cabin and bunk Cadet Bindra with Cadet Apprentice Gould."

"Cadet," said the captain, "you had best look to getting your gear on board as liftoff is at eighteen-ten hours."

"Yes, sir. Thank you, sir. Eh, sir?"

"Yes, cadet."

"Did you say cadet apprentice?"

"Yes, it's a temporary rank, unique to three members of the crew of this ship. And to dispel any concerns you may have, your cabin mate is a human female."

Cadet Bindra looked relieved.

"She's thirteen years old."

Cadet Bindra looked startled.

"Such information is confidential and will not be shared with anyone off board the Antares."

"I understand, sir."

"Although you are now a member of the crew of the *Antares*, you may consider yourself excused from attending the service for Mister Aristedes. You stand dismissed, cadet."

"Yes, sir." Cadet Bindra turned to leave. "And thank you major——"

"Get out of here," growled Sargon.

"Yes, sir." Cadet Bindra scrambled out of the cabin. Just before the hatchway closed the captain and major heard a feminine shriek of elation.

"Well, major," grinned the captain, "any criticism of my decision?"

The major returned the captain's grin with a disgruntled look. "No, sir. Once we let the first human female onboard, what do a dozen or so more matter?"

"Are you sure it won't hurt?" asked Sarah.

Lieutenant Maser gave a sigh along with a shake of his head as he started to lean over the girl who was lying face down on one of the operating tables in the base infirmary. "You know, Miss Gould, some things in life are worth a little pain." Sarah raised her head so fast it almost collided with the doctor's.

"But you said——"

Maser placed a hand on the back of the girl's head and pushed her back down onto the table. "I assure you, you won't feel a thing. I was just making a point about life." He poked the back of the girl's neck with the instrument he held in his other hand.

"Ouch," was Sarah's only comment before she passed out.

"I always wondered about this thing called pain," said Dave, handing the doc a seamless scalpel in exchange for the anesthetic probe.

"Since you are incapable of experiencing either pleasure or pain, I'm not sure there's any way to explain it to you." With a single adept move of the scalpel, Maser opened the back of the girl's neck.

"Okay, I think I've seen enough," said Tom, backing up to take a seat alongside Neutronium on another operating table so that the robot blocked his view of the operation.

"Same here," seconded Alex, joining his friend.

"Implant," said Maser, handing the scalpel to Dave.

In no time at all the physician has finished with Sarah and it was Tom's turn.

Tom's last thought before losing consciousness was that the doc had been right. He hadn't felt a thing.

He awoke to find himself weightless. He was standing inside a narrow corridor that was grotesquely distorted and filled with assorted debris that looked to be the result of an explosion. Somehow, he knew he was inside a spaceship. Although upon initial inspection the corridor appeared to be blocked by a tangle of twisted beams and warped bulkheads, further examination revealed a means of egress past the blockage large enough for him to possibly squeeze through if he removed his helmet and gear. Helmet? Yes, he was wearing a helmet, a space helmet. As if by instinct, before he reached up to unlock the helmet's collar seal, he holstered the ray pistol he had been holding in his right hand. With a click, the seal was broken. The thought struck him that removing his helmet might not be the best of plans? Would he be wearing one if the atmosphere were breathable? But he had barely thought the thought when he lifted the helmet from his shoulders. He was still breathing, but the air was rancid, filled with the odor of smoke and melting electrics. He gave a cough as he unbuckled the belt to which were attached a pair of holstered sidearms and several small instruments. Holding it before him, he released it. The belt and its attachments at first seemed to hover in midair, then slowly moved away from him towards the opening in the debris. He next unbuckled the oxygen tanks from his back along with the attached respirator, heat radiator, waste recycler, and auxiliary gadgetry. It took but his imagining it for the soles of his boots to release their grip upon the metallic deck. He slowly pushed off, skillfully launching himself forward.

Grabbing the weapons belt on his way, he thrust it ahead of him, then with effort, began to twist, push and pull his body through the narrow opening.

An alarm sounded—a warning to abandon ship. Someone must have activated the ship's self-destruct, the alarm indicating the start of a three hundred second countdown. Should he go back? Did he have time to escape? He rejected the idea as with another push he cleared the constricting passageway. With a clank his boots contacted the deck and he was again standing upright. He refastened the belt around his waist, drew the pistol from the right holster, and set off down the corridor with the quick gallop all spacemen use to rapidly move through a ship when weightless, one foot always squarely in contact with the deck before the next broke contact. There was a hatch dead ahead. It opened automatically as he reached it, allowing him to maintain his speed as he burst into the compartment beyond.

The scene that greeted him caused him come to a halt. The compartment was huge, bigger than any he had ever beheld inside a spaceship. It had obviously been specially constructed by the removal of several interior bulkheads. Occupying the majority of the space inside the chamber was a dome, perhaps thirty feet across. It displayed a single, curved, triangular opening through which two men dressed in spacesuits had just entered. Although their backs were to him, the brief glance he was afforded before the portal closed showed the spacesuit of one of the men to be of a blue so dark as to be easily mistaken for black, while that of the other was of a dark metallic grey.

That left five adversaries, all in the process of turning to give him a look of surprise that no doubt matched his own. The one standing behind a panel of instruments to one side of the dome's closed portal wore a spacesuit, except for its red coloration, identical to those worn by the two men who had disappeared inside the dome.

The other four antagonists in the compartment reached for their holstered weapons as the compartment's lighting began to flicker and dim. With astonishing quickness, he shifted to a firing stance and lined up the virtual crosshairs of the front sight of his weapon with the chest of the man farthest to his left. As if by instinct, his mind focused on the gun sight rather than the target. His body froze as well as his breathing, except for his finger squeezing the trigger. There was the pop of the ray bolt being released by the weapon and the body of his first adversary jerked and went limp. A quick shift of the arm holding his gun brought its sight in line with the next man who was in the process of raising his own pistol into a firing position. He paused to ensure that the gun sight was properly aligned and his body was suitably posed. It was a pause that most other men would have thought to be dangerously prolonged. Another squeeze and the second man stiffened. As he shifted his stance slightly towards the third man, the sound of a hostile shot erupted and a bolt passed harmlessly to his left. Before the man could get off a second shot, he too collapsed like the first two, having been hit squarely in the chest. The fourth adversary let go with two hastily aimed shots, one missing widely and the other creasing the fabric of his left sleeve. The man began to move sideways while taking aim for another shot. He smoothly adjusted for the man's movement and stunned him with a bolt before the man could get off a third burst. Four for four in less than three seconds. Through it all, he had been able to steel his mind to ignore the distraction caused by the flickering lights as well as the adrenaline pulsing through his body. His adversaries had obviously been less successful in doing so. As taught, he had not rushed his firing and had correctly calculated that standing his ground was the better option than attempting to fire on the move. After all, one has no chance of ducking a bolt travelling at light speed. The academy's shooting instructor would have been proud of his star pupil.

The sound of his final bolt had no sooner echoed through the chamber than there was a deafening crack and the lights went out. There came a second loud bang. His nostrils smelled ozone.

Ignoring the confusion of sound and darkness, he began to move, fearful that his one remaining antagonist, the man by the control panel, was already drawing a bead on his present position with a ray weapon. With a mental command he released the magnetic hold of his boots with the deck and pushed off, propelling himself toward the overhead. Surprisingly, his remaining antagonist hadn't opened fire. Although engulfed in blackness, he was still able to stop his weightless flight through the compartment by grasping one of the overhead's projecting handgrips with which the bulkheads, overheads and decks of all ships were studded to allow for ease of maneuver in a weightless situation. The neurode connected to his mind had already started to adjust his vision to infrared when the chamber's lights clicked on. He immediately released a bolt in the general direction of the control panel, not taking the opportunity to line up his target. Just before he squeezed the trigger, the shocked realization dawned on him that his opponent was simply standing his ground, grinning. The bolt from his gun ricocheted in midair as if it had encountered some invisible shield, and struck his pistol, the impact sending a spasm of pain up his right arm and the weapon spinning from his grasp. He immediately lost all feeling in his right hand and wrist.

The man's grin morphed into a twisted smile. "Well, commander, this is a surprise. I'll have the pleasure of reporting your death to Maximum Leader." His antagonist began to leisurely reach for a holstered weapon.

He wasted no time in drawing and aiming his other sidearm with his uninjured hand. Upon spying the new weapon, his opponent's expression changed from one of gloating triumph to alarm, for the weapon the man now faced was not a ray pistol but an antique gunpowder firearm. He squeezed the trigger. There was a loud bang. The head of his enemy snapped back, a mixture of brains and bone exiting from the rear of the skull.

He holstered the firearm, and did a quick survey of his surroundings in an attempt to locate his missing ray pistol, but to no avail. The warming alarm continued to sound, reminding him that the seconds were counting down. Giving up the search for the ray gun, he pushed off the overhead and ended up at the instrument panel. His adversary's lifeless body hovered nearby, the blood leaking from the bullet hole in the head condensing into small, floating spheres.

How much time was left? How had his opponent planned to escape the doomed ship? The man had mentioned reporting to Evad, so he must have had a means in mind. An explosion would soon tear the vessel into a thousand fragments.

He began to methodically study the instrument panel before him. He had seen two men inside the dome before it had closed, one in a spacesuit that was known to be uniquely worn by Evad. Perhaps inside the dome was some sort of shelter that would be impervious to the pending explosion? But if so, why hadn't the man by the control panel also entered?

How to open the dome? He continued to focus on the panel and its controls. Messages were flashing on the panel. *Primary contact lost. Reset. Target undergoing reactivation. Alternate target destination acquired with 95/95 probability/confidence.* He saw a button labeled *Chamber Access* and pushed it. There was a sound. The triangular portal in the dome reappeared. Pistol drawn, he peered inside the curved enclosure. The two men who had previously entered had vanished. In the brief glimpse inside he had been given earlier, he could have sworn that the chamber had been empty. Now it was filled with floating clods of earth and shards of shrubs and other foliage. It must be some sort of matter transmitter was his first thought. From somewhere deep inside his mind a voice was shouting, "No, you fool."

The alarm pitch changed. Fifteen seconds until detonation. A new message flashed on the panel.

Target acquisition: 00:15 UTC, December 7, 1942.

Warning: Relative velocity vector outside safe tolerance limit.

Warning: Transmission risk factor 84.2%.

More by instinct than design, with the forefinger of his good hand he punched a control labeled *Activate* on the panel. The lights began to flicker and dim, and a countdown of two seconds flashed on the panel. He shoved off the control board and just cleared the dome's wall as the opening snapped closed behind him. Then everything went black. It was as if the universe had collapsed upon him.

Tom's eyes opened and at the same time he jerked to a sitting position. He could feel rivulets of sweat on his forehead. He was sitting upright on the operating table of the base infirmary. Alex was on another table across from him, with Sarah and Lieutenant Maser standing beside him. The three had expressions of surprise.

"Tom, what is it?" said Sarah.

Tom blinked at her. "I—I had a dream."

"Wow, it must have been some dream," said Alex. "You should see yourself."

"What do you mean you had a dream?" asked the lieutenant, his tone one of disbelief.

"I had a dream." Tom swallowed. "At least I think it was a dream. I mean, I don't remember ever having a dream like that. It was too—too real."

"No one dreams under anesthesia." The lieutenant sounded concerned. "It's not possible."

Chapter 12
Countdown and Liftoff

"And that's the last thing I can remember. I felt just like I did when I was in the time machine." Tom shifted his gaze in turn to each of the other occupants of the captain's cabin of the *Antares*. Whereas Majors Dale and Sargon and the doc were intently studying the boy, the captain's eyes were fixed on the far bulkhead, the man being obviously deep in thought.

"Do you think that neurode thing you put in me is broken or something?" asked Tom.

The question appeared to embarrass Lieutenant Maser. "It's most unlikely. I've never heard of one failing—"

"In millions of man-hours of experience," said Sargon, "there's never been one case of a neurode malfunctioning. Hence, such a thing occurring is next to impossible." The man shifted forward in his seat so as to bring his face closer to the boy's. "It is highly probable, however, that in this case the problem might be with the host."

"The three neurodes all passed the standard set of diagnostic tests before they were implanted," said the doc. "Dave and I both checked and signed off on the test results. All were positive, as was Cadet Cobalt's post-operation examination." The doc spread his hands palms up. "I have no explanation."

"Except that the subject here might be madder than a Bollixian

554

snarf," growled Sargon.

Major Dale gave her fellow major a scowl. "Perhaps we should replace Cadet Cobalt's neurode with a new one."

Maser shook his head. "The base's facilities are equipped for initial installation, not replacement, nor would I have any idea how to go about it if we had the proper equipment. It may require the resources of a class A medical facility to replace one, although to my knowledge it's never been done. Never needed to be done."

Captain Krater turned to face the boy. "Perhaps Cadet Cobalt might have a suggestion to make regarding what happened."

"Well . . ." What the heck was he supposed to say, if these people couldn't come up with anything? After all, he wasn't from around here. "Maybe the—neurode—was sending my mind some sort of message?"

"Neurodes only respond to queries from the host's mind. They cannot initiate a 'thought,'" said Sargon.

"That may be, but I'm telling you it was more than a dream, more real than any dream I've ever had before. I can remember the smells, the sensations, the sounds, everything about it. It was as if I was actually living it."

"Okay," said the captain. "Let's assume, for the sake of argument, that what Tom—Cadet Cobalt 'dreamed' was actually the memory of a real event."

"You can't be serious, sir?" asked Sargon.

"You're insinuating I'm making a joke, major?"

"No, sir. Of course not." Sargon glanced at Major Dale who shot him a grin.

"Is there anything in Cadet Cobalt's story that is incompatible with what could have transpired aboard Evad's flagship, the *Hydrus*, at Quadrant Five?" asked the captain.

"Not that I can see," said Major Dale. The doc nodded in agreement, followed by Sargon after some hesitation.

"May I ask a question?" said Tom.

"Go ahead, cadet."

"Why did my first shot—I mean the first shot of the person I was dreaming about—at the man in the red spacesuit not work?"

"He was obviously protected by a stasis field," explained the captain. "It's a transparent force field, impervious to penetration by ray bolts from the outside. However, bolts fired by someone inside the field have no problem passing through it. In principle, it's similar to the plasma dome that surrounds Iapetus Base."

"But why didn't the field stop the bullet from the other gun I—he fired?"

"Because objects of sufficient mass but low enough velocity such as a bullet, or a man for that matter, can pass through the field with no problem. A similar type of field is projected about the *Antares* when it reaches phase two velocity to supplement the neutronium hull as additional protection from radiation and particle abrasion."

"I have no idea what it was you just said," said Tom.

The captain smiled. "You will soon enough. Your cadet training commences tomorrow. Any other questions?"

"Yes. I notice that like that man in my dream you carry two pistols."

"That's right, and for the same reason. One of them is a primitive gunpowder firearm. Anything else?"

"Do you have any idea who the man in the dream might have been?"

"It was most likely the Commander," said Captain Krater.

"You mean the man that I supposedly look like?"

"Yes. Commander Thomas Jefferson Cobalt. We thought he was killed at the Battle of Quadrant Five—at least until now."

"And who were the other men in the room?"

"From the description of their spacesuits, the two that entered the time machine were Evad and Admiral Serpens. The one by the control panel would have been Admiral Sobek since you described his suit as being identical to Evad's but red in color. From the testimony of surviving guardsmen, all three members of the Draconian Guard high command at the Battle of Quadrant Five were aboard Evad's flagship, the *Hydrus*. The others were no doubt Draconian guardsmen."

Sargon spoke up. "And until now, no one had told you about the Quadrant Five engagement?"

"Yes, sir."

"So, someone did tell you about Quadrant Five?"

"No, sir."

"But you just said they did."

"No, sir. I was agreeing to your statement that 'no one told me anything about Quadrant Five.' I mean I had heard the name before, but I didn't know anything about it."

"You take over, major. I have no idea if he's answering yes or no to my question."

"And you never heard of Admiral Sobek?" said the woman officer.

"Yes, sir—er, ma'am."

Cynthia Dale gave Major Sargon a questioning look.

"Don't look at me. I have no idea if that was a yes or no. If you think he's difficult, wait until you try to get a straight answer out of the other one, Cadet Banyon."

"No, ma'am," said Tom. "I never heard of Admiral Sobek. I don't think I could even spell Sobek."

Major Dale gave the boy a smile. "And you're sure the date you saw flashed on the control panel was December 7, 1942?"

"Yes, ma'am."

"Does that date mean anything to you?"

"No, ma'am. It was before I was born. I don't know if this is important, but I believe that date is exactly one year after the Japanese attacked Pearl Harbor and started the Second World War. Well, actually, it was when America got into the war, as the war really started a couple of years—"

"Spare us the history lesson, cadet," growled Sargon.

"Yes, sir."

"Tom." Tom noticed that the captain had addressed him by his first name. "Did it seem like you were seeing the person in the dream as a bystander or did it seem like you were that person?"

"If I understand what you're asking, it was like I was that person. I have no idea what the person looked like. He never looked in a mirror or anything. It was like I was seeing everything through his eyes, and sometimes, like I was seeing it through his mind. That part of it kind of came and went. Sometimes I would be thinking like it was my thoughts and other times like it was someone else's thoughts. I'm not sure I can really explain it very well."

"Doctor," said the captain, "do you have any comment?"

"Sorry, sir. I have no explanation. We have of course been monitoring Cadet Cobalt's physical and psychological profiles throughout this interro—debriefing, and there's no indication of willful deception on his part."

"Huh?" said Tom.

"He means you've apparently been telling the truth," enlightened Sargon.

"Oh," said Tom. "Hey, of course I've been telling the truth. I'm a Boy Scout."

"Not any more. You're a cadet apprentice in the Solar Patrol."

"As to recommendations," said Lieutenant Maser, "as he doesn't appear to have been traumatized by the experience, I don't feel that any sort of medication is warranted." He addressed the boy. "Just let us know if the dream reoccurs, or if you have any similar experiences."

"Sure thing," said Tom.

"If there are no more questions," the captain silently polled the others in the room, "you're excused, cadet."

The four officers sat about a table in the compartment on Iapetus Base in which the interrogations of the twentieth century teens had previously been conducted. Captain Krater addressed the others—Majors

Sargon and Dale and Lieutenant Maser. "We'll get started as soon as Major Manning arrives."

"Manning?" blurted Sargon. "I thought we were going to discuss codeword trinity material."

"That's right, Major," said the captain. "A little over an hour ago we received orders from Patrol HQ to provide the base commander access to codeword trinity material. Major Dale has already briefed the major."

Sargon's scowl was interrupted by a double beep from the closed compartment's hatch, an indication that someone on the other side had just completed a clearance scan in order to gain entrance to the compartment. The hatch immediately slid open to reveal a patrol officer whose chiseled features, although handsome, carried an air of confidence, perhaps a little over confident, with a wisp of arrogance. The man's clean-shaven countenance broke into a triumphant grin, as he strode into the room. With the possible exception of the unusual cut of his blond hair, reminiscent of what was known in 1950s America as a "flattop," Major Manning appeared to be every measure the ideal of a Solar Patrol officer.

"Major," said the captain, "I believe you know everyone here."

"Yes, captain," replied the major. Stopping next to the one empty chair in the room, he nodded to Major Dale. "Major," said the major.

"Major," said Major Dale, returning Major Manning's greeting.

"Lieutenant," said the Major.

"Major," replied the lieutenant.

"And last, but certainly not least," chuckled Major Manning, "Major."

"Major," grunted Sargon. "When are you going to get a regulation haircut?"

"Base commander privilege," grinned the other male major, who then proceeded to take the empty seat.

"Gentlemen," said the captain, appearing somewhat relieved to have gotten through the introductions, "I've asked Major Dale to prepare a briefing on the codeword trinity material. She's been working from the transcripts of the interrogations, the results of Doc's examinations of the subjects, and all related data we have since received from HQ. Go ahead, major."

Major Dale placed a thin plastic sheet before each of the other officers seated around the small table in the captain's quarters of the *Antares*.

"You have before you a list of the issues I've attempted to address," said the blonde major. The other officers all glanced at the plastic sheets that lay on the table before them. "Please realize that my speculations are based on the results of the tests that Lieutenant Maser conducted on cadets Cobalt, Gould and Banyon, and on their testimonies during the recently conducted interro—er, debriefings.

We start with an attempted reconstruction of the final events aboard the Draconian flagship *Hydrus* during the Quadrant Five engagement."

"Those last minutes before she exploded?" asked the captain.

"Yes, sir. According to the testimony of the survivors from the crew of the *Hydrus*, the three members of the Draconian Guard high command, Evad, Serpens, and Sobek, were most likely still onboard the enemy flagship at the time the patrol boarding party breached the hull. That is consistent with the other known facts of the engagement. It had previously been believed that all three Draconian commanders had perished in the explosion that destroyed the *Hydrus* since they were not among the survivors captured by the patrol. Instead, it now appears that at least two of them managed to escape to the twentieth century by means of a time machine located onboard the flagship."

"Was the *Hydrus* large enough to have housed a time machine?" asked the doctor.

"Yes, if the design of its interior spaces had been suitably altered, and assuming our guess as to the probable size of such a machine is accurate based on an investigation of the wreckage found at the Epimetheus base. The *Hydrus* was, after all, a dreadnaught class ship. Also, by diverting all power from its reaction generators, the ship could provide enough to transmit two humans from the Quadrant Five engagement to twentieth century Earth, at least according to the analysis performed by the academy's physics department based on Apocason's theory. This also fits with events described by Cadet Cobalt in his dream."

"We are seriously considering a boy's dream as evidence?" Major Manning's tone was a cross between mockery and cynicism.

"We are excluding nothing," responded the female major.

"Two people?" said the captain.

"Yes. That's what the academy's analysis concludes but understand that the estimated carrying capacity of the time transfer includes a significant degree of uncertainty."

The captain nodded.

"I have reconstructed a possible chronology of events aboard the *Hydrus* from the time the patrol boarding party led by Commander Cobalt entered the critically damaged ship to the time of the ship's destruction. Approximately two minutes after entry, the boarding party discovered that a self-destruct countdown had been activated for the ship. At that point Commander Cobalt ordered the rest of the boarding party to evacuate. The Commander stayed behind and began to make his way to the ship's control room. It was in the ship's main logistics locker that he made his final transmission. That was, of course, the scene with the storage racks filled with the mysterious pods. It is not long after this point that the boy's dream supposedly starts with the self-destruct alarm sounding. Approximately five minutes later a power surge was detected in the *Hydrus'* reaction generators, followed by a lull of approximately thirty seconds, then a second power surge of equal magnitude, and finally the explosion that destroyed the ship. The explosion obviously eliminated all evidence of the time machine. Evad had no doubt timed the ship's automated destruction to activate shortly after he had safety escaped. It was the most fortuitous of circumstances for Evad that everything optimized at that particular time to allow him to timeport to the twentieth century. I find no contradictions between this scenario and the events of Cadet Cobalt's dream." Major Dale cast a hard look at Manning. "Assuming the dream was an accurate account of the events aboard the *Hydrus*, then it follows that Evad and Admiral Serpens were timeported by the first power surge, the Commander by the second. If the second time transfer was successful, the Commander would have been timeported to December 7, 1942."

"Any idea where?" asked the captain.

"Following Apocason's theory, it would have been where the receiver was located, mostly likely East Pencreek."

"If both timeports were to East Pencreek," said the captain, would the Commander have encountered Evad and Serpens in the twentieth century?"

"I would hazard from Cadet Cobalt's description that, although the Commander would have arrived at the same place, he probably arrived there at a different time from Evad and Serpens. That's just speculation on my part, of course."

"And only Evad knows the truth of that speculation," said the captain.

"Cadet Cobalt mentioned the display of a risk factor value on the control panel right before the Commander may have timeported. That was coupled with a velocity vector. I can only assume that the conditions for the second transport were less than ideal, that is, the velocity mismatch between the years 2347 and 1942 presented a high risk. If he did transport, it's possible that the Commander perished at the other end of the time tunnel. There was certainly nothing in the testimony from the three teens that indicates his presence in East Pencreek in 1959."

"If the commander had survived the transfer," said Sargon,

"assuming of course that the cadet's dream was an accurate account of real events, he certainly would have found a way to neutralize Evad and Serpens."

"Unless they killed him," said Maser.

"Well, it's all idle speculation, as it was just a dream," said Sargon.

"No, it was more than that," said Major Dale. "I polled the crew and no one recalls providing Cadet Cobalt any information regarding Quadrant Five. So how do you explain the details from his account?"

"I can't," said Sargon. "Are you suggesting that somehow Cadet Cobalt is some reincarnation of the Commander and therefore shares the Commander's memory, but at a subconscious level that only emerges through dreams? I'm with Major Manning on this one." Manning was beaming.

"I'm not suggesting anything," said Major Dale. "I'm just relaying the facts of the case."

"A strange reincarnation at that," said the captain, "as the subject was reincarnated in the past and not the future."

"By Venus' moon," said the doc. "Something just occurred to me."

"Yes, lieutenant," said Captain Krater.

"When I picked up the neurodes for the three cadets from the medical supply locker, the corpsman told me that they were part of a new shipment that had recently arrived aboard the *Python*. Along with the new shipment came orders to destroy the base's present inventory."

"That's odd," said Major Dale.

"It's more than that," said Maser. "As we all know, the quality control on neurodes has a history of infallibility. Why then would HQ order a supply of them destroyed?"

"What are you getting at?" asked Sargon.

"Suppose that dream had been programmed into the replacement neurodes?"

"What would be the motive, and who would have done it? Besides, the other two cadets didn't have any dreams."

Maser said, "I don't know."

"The entire supply could have been programmed identically," suggested the captain. "They could have been programmed to activate the dream only if implanted into Cadet Cobalt."

"Yes, that seems feasible," said Maser.

"As to whom might have done it and why it was done, I have no idea."

"It's almost as if someone knew what really happened in those final minutes aboard the *Hydrus*, and it was by this means that they let us know," said Major Dale.

"I'm not sure that the message was meant for us," said the captain. "Perhaps it was meant only for Cadet Cobalt." The captain leaned forward, folding his hands together on the table. "I've transmitted Cadet Cobalt's description of his dream to the C.I.C. Perhaps HQ can throw some light on the matter. Let's continue with your report, major."

"Yes, sir." The major checked her notes. "So far, HQ has been unable to confirm whether Serpens, back in the twentieth century, completed his mission of murdering the members of the Cobalt family."

"How would they go about confirming such a thing?" asked Major Manning.

"Though a check of historical records. Of course, the continuity of such records became problematical with the breakup of the United States of America. The use of two mindbenders was mentioned in the interrogation transcripts. One obviously was implanted in the Darwinian. The second was mentioned as being implanted in a 'kid.' If so, the recipient was not one of our three cadets."

"Seems like a waste of a mindbender," said Sargon.

"Moving on to the next item. Assuming that Apocason's explanation for time travel is correct, there must have been a receiver located in—," the major hesitated while she consulted her notes, "—Sullivans Woods in 1959. How did it get there? According to Apocason, it could not have been transported back to 1959 from a later time. It must have been created in 1959 or earlier."

"We certainly have evidence that infers that in the late Cretaceous period there was an advanced starfaring civilization in this part of the galaxy." said the captain. "How else does one explain the similarities in morphology and physiology among the life forms of some of the near-by star systems, especially in the proliferation of humanoid forms?"

"Add to that," said the doctor, "the origin of *Dino sapiens*. There is no fossil record on their home planet older than about sixty-eight million years. The earliest fossils there show forms almost identical, if not identical, to fossil species on the Earth at about the same time. The most reasonable explanation is that some advanced civilization transported a large sampling of fauna and flora from Earth to the Delta-II system at that time. Any culture capable of performing such a feat could most likely have mastered time travel. Therein, I hazard, lies the explanation for the existence of the receiver."

"Could such a device have survived for almost seventy million years?" said the captain.

Sargon gave his head a nod. "Considering their obvious advanced technology, I would think that would have been a trivial problem for its inventors to solve."

"Any other comments, before we move on to the results of the medical examinations?" said Major Dale.

"Yes," said the captain. "As I recall, back in 1959 we left Admiral Serpens, perhaps the Commander, a cyber-cat, and possibly a local human implanted with a mindbender and therefore under the control of Serpens. Do you concur?"

"Yes," said the major.

"The fact that the receiver was in Sullivans Woods explains why Evad and Serpens were living in East Pencreek," said the captain, "but why not just move the receiver to some place more convenient for transfer back to the present?"

"If I understand the physics correctly," said Major Dale, "in order to solve the equations of time travel to eliminate the momentum transfer roadblock, the operators on the future end of the time tunnel must know the exact location of the receiver in the past. Otherwise, the number of possible solutions becomes infinite."

"That appears reasonable," said the doc. "I suppose there's no way for one to 'cover up one's footprints,' so to speak, by bringing the receiver with them when they transport to the future?"

"I believe that would not be possible according to Apocason," said Sargon.

When no other comments were offered, Major Dale continued. "Okay, on to the examination results. Let's start with the easy one, the scratches on the back of Cadet Gould's neck, one of which had imbedded in it a piece of sheath from a cyber-cat claw. According to Sarah's account of that night in Sullivans Woods, she was attacked from behind. She felt something like claws sinking into the back of her neck. Apparently, the culprit was our mystery cyber-cat. And how did a cyber-cat get to the twentieth century? Most likely the same way Evad did, by time travel. But who sent it there and why? I believe this is a key piece of information. Had Sarah not been attacked, she would never have entered the temporal field, nor would have the two boys, and possibly neither would have the Darwinian. In which case, only Evad would have time-ported to Epimetheus."

"Are you suggesting that the whole thing was a setup?" asked Sargon.

"Yes."

"By whom?"

"I don't know."

"Obviously not by Sleinad Evad."

"Yes, obviously not by Sleinad Evad."

"This whole story is crazier than a Bollixian snarf," said Major Manning. "There's no way any sane person would come up with such a complicated plan and believe it would actually work."

"Not if its originator already knew what was going to happen," said Major Dale. "That is to say, not if the plan's originator had also been from the future. If so, and if Apocason is correct in that one cannot change the past—"

"I believe what you were getting at is, if time travel is a reality then all bets are off," said Sargon, "in which case we could spend hours creating possible scenarios. I say we move on."

"Agreed," said the captain.

"Next, we have the question of..."

"One moment," interrupted Manning. "I have to bring up an obvious flaw in the story these three kids would have us believe. Surely Evad and Serpens would have conducted a scan of the clearing when they entered it. These kids had no technology to jam it. So, someone please explain that." Manning sat back in his chair, crossed his arms over his chest, and gave his fellow officers a look of triumph.

In a tone of a wise elder patiently explaining the most obvious of facts to an ignorant child, Sargon said, "Because like someone else I know, those two smug morons were no doubt arrogant and overconfident. Why bother with a scan when there appeared to be no earthly reason for it?"

Major Dale could not help cracking a sliver of a grin at Sargon's retort as the captain and lieutenant tried their best to stifle similar reactions. Major Manning's smug look of arrogance and overconfidence was replaced by a hostile stare directed at the other male major.

Major Dale cleared her throat. "Let us continue. Next, we have the question of the relationship between Tom and Commander Cobalt. Unfortunately, since with the exceptions of photographs and his DNA profile, all other records of the Commander have mysteriously vanished. There appears to be no way to resolve this one. That leaves us with the two most probable explanations; that is, either they are one in the same person, or are identical twins."

"And is it true," said Sargon, "that there's also no record of the Commander's family?"

"Yes," said Dale.

"The Commander's early life is a blank," said the captain. "With the possible exception of the C.I.C., I probably knew him better than anyone. I can't recall him ever mentioning a family."

"This is maddening," said Sargon. "It's as if someone has purposely destroyed all evidence that would help us resolve this mystery. It's almost as if the Commander himself had been in on the conspiracy."

"Did the academy have an estimate for the year that Sleinad Evad and Serpens arrived in the past?" said the captain.

"So far they have been unable to make such an estimate," answered the blonde major, "but they continue to work on the problem."

"Okay, please continue, major."

"Hold on," said the base commander. "From what I recall from the kids' testimony, this Darwinian thing targeted the girl in the clearing. Someone please explain to me why it would do that?"

Sargon gave out a sigh before answering. "From HQ's report about these Darwinians, apparently, they retain some of the memories and personality of their host. The Darwinian in the clearing sucked out the brains of this Jack Paine guy, which of course explains the resemblance between the two. According to the cadets' testimony, Paine had some kind of the vendetta against the female cadet, and therefore, so did the Darwinian."

"Her name is Sarah," interjected Major Dale.

Major Sargon ignored Dale's remark. "I believe that's the explanation you were looking for."

The base commander shook his head. "All these explanations appear awfully contrived to me."

The captain looked at Major Dale. "Please continue, major."

"While the evidence supports cadets Gould and Cobalt being born in 1946, because of the presence of a genetic tag in his DNA, it is most likely that Cadet Banyon is from our century. So how then did he end up also being born in 1946?"

"I recall from his testimony that he was adopted?" said the captain.

"Yes," said Sargon. "He testified that the Banyons were not his biological parents. While there is no evidence to support his birth in 1946, there is evidence that he was born in our century. If so, while still a baby, he must have been timeported to the twentieth century."

"Not another timeport," said the captain. "First, we have Sleinad Evad and Serpens, although when they landed in the twentieth century is unknown, then possibly the Commander to 1942, then we have a cyber-cat, and now yet another human, this time apparently back to 1946."

"Mind boggling, isn't it?" chuckled the doctor.

"Anything else, major?"

"No, I don't believe so?"

"You have omitted one important piece of information?" said the doctor.

"Oh? And what is that?"

"The significance of the extra text at the end of the C.I.C.'s dispatch. The office of the C.I.C. denies having added it."

"What text?" said Major Dale.

"Sorry, we neglected to inform you of that," said the captain. "The transmission from the C.I.C. that conveyed the codeword trinity orders contained additional text following his signature. It read, 'Hail Ragnar, hail Einar.'"

"But there's never any text after the signature on a classified transmission," said the woman. "It must have been an error."

"That's what I at first maintained," said Sargon.

"Major," said the doctor, "what makes this fact so intriguing is not so much the appearance of additional text in the message, but the fact that the text mentions 'Ragnar' and 'Einar.'"

"Why is that?" said Major Dale.

"Because Cadets Cobalt and Banyon have been observed to address each other as Ragnar and Einar."

Major Manning let out a loud groan.

"Is my bunkmate really a thirteen-year-old girl?" asked Cadet Bindra. Her personal storage locker levitated behind her.

"Apparently," answered Cadet Gates, as he entered the airlock of the *Antares*, followed by the female cadet who in turn was followed by her storage locker.

"Apparently? What's that supposed to mean?"

Gates stopped, turned to his companion, and gave his head a shake. "Wait until you hear the rest. Of course, you've already been briefed that anything relating to the *Antares*, including any information regarding its crew is classified, and is not to leave this ship."

"Yes," said the female cadet, who had also stopped, as had her storage locker.

"The other two cadet apprentices are apparently thirteen years old, but boys."

"But why?"

"Probably because they were born that way," laughed Isaac Gates.

"You know what I mean. Why has the patrol enlisted thirteen-year-olds?"

"Perhaps because they may not really be thirteen years old."

"Huh?"

"Scuttlebutt has it that they may have been born in the twentieth century."

"What do you take me for, a Ceterian snidge snuckle?"

"I'm not even going to try to explain it. I'm not sure anyone can." The patrolman turned and resumed moving through the ship, followed by the female cadet and her locker. "You'll no doubt be briefed on the situation soon enough."

The two cadets had entered the central elevator shaft. There was a faint flash of light and a moment later they stepped out onto the higher deck where Bindra's cabin was located. As the female cadet was exiting the elevator Tom and Alex passed by. The boys gave the attractive female cadet a smile before hurrying on their way. Alex turned to Tom. "Must be Sarah's roommate."

It's difficult to say which startled Bindra more, the appearance of young teens dressed in patrol uniforms, or the uncanny resemblance of one of them to what the legendary Commander must have looked like at that age. Sameera Bindra, her attention fixed on the two boys, walked into a bulkhead.

Sameera was still massaging her injured nose when she entered the cabin. There to greet her stood a young girl dressed in a uniform similar to hers.

"Hello," said Sameera. "You must be Sarah."

"Yes, ma'am," said Sarah, looking uncertain. "Should I salute you?"

"No," laughed Sameera. "You only salute officers and only when you first report for duty, and even then, it's a courtesy and not regulations." Sameera held out her hand. "I'm Sameera, Cadet Sameera Bindra, your bunkmate."

"I'm Sarah Gould," said Sarah, shaking hands.

Sameera's storage locker had settled onto the deck behind her. The top panel popped opened in preparation for the cadet to start unpacking her personal items.

"So," said Sameera, reaching into the locker to retrieve a container of toiletries, "how exactly did you come to enlist in the Solar Patrol?"

"It was that or be put in a foster home."

"Oh." The older female cadet was caught off guard. "I'm so sorry. Did you recently lose your parents?"

"I guess you could say that, although they've been gone for over three centuries."

Tom glanced about the control room of the *Antares*. Each reclined seat in the compartment contained a human crew member. The exceptions were the specially designed seats, or what passed for seats, occupied by the ship's cat, Neutronium, and the two *Dino sapiens*, Kass and Trax. Except for the glow of various devices on the control panels and the shine of the stars, the room was bathed in darkness as it was set to the surround view of the exterior as it had been earlier that day when the new recruits had first toured it.

Cadet Bindra, now sporting a shortened ponytail, glanced over at Sarah in the seat immediately to her left and gave the girl a reassuring smile. Sarah returned the smile with a look of abject terror, as if she were trapped in a car on the world's tallest roller coaster, right before the first, death-defying plunge. In contrast to Sarah, the expression on Alex's face was one of unrestrained anticipation. He kept mumbling to himself, "Oh, boy, oh, boy, oh, boy."

Captain Krater gave Major Sargon a nod. The major's voice rang through the control room. "Iapetus Base. This is patrol starcruiser *Antares* standing by to raise ship."

An answering voice came over the control room intercom. "Roger, *Antares*. You are cleared for liftoff. Spaceman's luck."

"Engineering status," said Sargon.

"Engineering alpha," came a voice over the intercom.

"Communications status."

"Communications alpha," replied Spaceman Khitel, seated by the communications console.

"Bio-systems status."

"Bio-systems alpha," said Lieutenant Maser.

"Guidance and control status."

Starman McDonald answered, "Guidance and control alpha."

"Let's make sure the tubes are clean," said the executive officer. "Thrusters at five-point-zero gees for a one hundred second burn, followed by a step down to zero-point-eight gees standard cruising."

"Roger that," said the pilot. "Power systems locked in at five-point-zero gees for a one hundred second burn, followed by a step down to zero-point-eight gees standard cruising."

In keeping with a tradition now centuries old, Sargon issued his next order. "Astrogator, commence countdown."

"Five, four, three . . ."

Tom glanced at Sargon. For a moment in the darkened room the boy could have sworn that the officer's eyes showed a faint green glow, reminiscent of Evad's in the clearing of Sullivans Woods on that fateful night. What could that mean? The boy turned his attention back to the heavens directly overhead. Never before had the stars appeared so distinct, so bright, and so terrifying. He took a hard swallow.

". . . two, one, liftoff!"

Starman McDonald threw a switch on his control panel.

The starcruiser's mighty engines ripped to life, the sudden acceleration slamming the crew into their seats. The *Antares* surged upward, heading for deep space.

Third Interlude
1942 – East Pencreek, Pennsylvania

The strange artifact rested on the dining room table alongside a finished wooden box. The woman stared at the object as if hypnotized by it while her husband, seated to her right, slowly passed his hand over it. The man seated across from the couple continued to chatter excitedly.

"That's why I made a copy of all the documents, in case the originals ever got damaged or lost."

"Yes, that was no doubt a good idea," said the husband as he lifted his hand from the object. He gave his head a shake of disbelief. "Nikola Tesla . . ." The man was unable to disguise the reverence in his voice. He leaned back in his chair and gave his head another shake.

The woman turned to their visitor. "George, what do you think it is?"

The visitor gave a low laugh. "I couldn't even begin to guess. If Tesla doesn't know, what man would?"

"Do you think Tesla was serious when he said it might be the work of some alien civilization from outer space?"

"Yes, I believe he was, although of late I'm not sure if some days he's all there. The past few years have been very challenging for him."

"Well, we certainly appreciate you stopping by on your way to Pittsburgh and taking us into your confidence," said the husband.

"You're sure this isn't some sort of government secret; that you won't get into trouble for showing it to us?"

George laughed. "According to Tesla, the government doesn't know it exists. They can't make it against the law to tell folks about something that they themselves don't know about, now can they?"

The grandfather clock that sat in the corner of the dining room chimed. "Matt, look at the time," said the wife. "Shouldn't you be getting George back to the station so he doesn't miss his train."

"Yes, you're right," said her husband. He stood up and as he did, so did the visitor who proceeded to pick up the strange spherical object and place it on a folded towel that lay inside the box, the towel serving as a cradle for the artifact. He then closed the box's lid and locked it in place by flipping a simple brass latch.

As the two men donned their winter coats, Matt said, "Are you sure you want to leave the copies of the documents here?"

"Yes," said George. "Like I said, I was originally planning to turn both the originals and the copies over to the professor in Pittsburgh, but on the way here I had second thoughts. Should something ever happen to the originals, I at least know that copies still exist." With a noticeable effort, he picked up the box. "Thanks again Jane for dinner. As always it was excellent."

Jane Ferguson laid a hand on George's shoulder and gave him a peck on the cheek. "Now you are going to stop again on your way back to New York and this time stay the night."

"Only if you cook me another great meal," the man laughed as he followed Matt Ferguson to the front door. "Bye, Jane," he called back as he exited the house.

Upon reaching the automobile parked at the street's curb, Matt opened the rear door for his friend and George carefully placed the box on the back seat. No sooner had he done so when Jane poked her head out of the front door of the house and called, "Matt. Jake Morrison's on the phone."

"I'd better take this," said Matt. "It shouldn't take more than a couple of minutes, but there's no point in you waiting out here in the cold. Why don't you come back inside?"

George nodded and followed his friend into the house, leaving the box with its precious cargo unguarded on the back seat of the car. Neither George nor Matt Ferguson had taken any notice of the stranger who was coming up the sidewalk, approaching Matt's parked automobile.

It was the young man's last day of freedom, for on the morrow he was slated to be inducted into the U.S. Army. As he passed the automobile, he happened to glance through the car's back window. There, on the back seat, he spotted the wooden box. The young man stopped. He glanced about him, first at the house, then up and down the street, and finally again at the unguarded box. He didn't spend any time in analyzing the situation or in pondering the wrongfulness of his pending action. It was an impulse. He had never before contemplated stealing anything of consequence, nor had he ever been charged with so much as a misdemeanor. Perhaps it was the fact that he would be entering the army on the following day and then, most likely, going off to war that provoked his action. Whatever the reason, without another moment's hesitation, he opened the automobile's rear door, reached in, and lifted out the box. As he hefted the container to get a better grip on it, he gasped to no one in particular, "Heavy." Shifting the box slightly so he could balance it under his left arm, he used his right hand to close the car door. Switching again to both hands to hold the box, he walked around the vehicle and headed towards the woods on the far side of the road. As he walked, he kept glancing about him to ensure that no one had witnessed the theft.

Perhaps it was the sound of the car door closing that caused Jane Ferguson to peer out the front window of her home. She caught a glimpse of the wooden box that the young man carried before he turned his back towards her.

"George, Matt," she shouted. "I think someone has stolen the box!"

"What?" said her husband, holding the telephone.

"There's a young man out front. I think he took the box. He's heading towards the woods."

"Jake, I'll get back to you. Got to go," said Matt, dropping the phone and rushing after his friend George as the latter bolted out the front door.

On hearing the commotion, the young man gave a quick glance behind him. Two men were emerging from the house. The young man broke into a sprint and disappeared into the woodland.

George paused long enough to check the back seat of the automobile. "He's got it, alright." He stepped into the street but had to pull up to let a couple of automobiles pass. Having lost valuable seconds, both men rapidly crossed the street and entered the woods at the spot where they had seen the thief disappear.

"Jane's no doubt calling the police," puffed Matt, sounding winded from a combination of excitement and unfamiliar exertion. "But it will be dark soon . . ."

Not far into the woods the young man stopped next to the trunk of a large tree and listened for the sounds of pursuit. He could hear the two men making their way through the brush some distance off to his left. The man grinned to himself. "They're headed in the wrong direction. They must have assumed I kept going straight once I entered the woods. Let's see what we have here while there's still enough light." The man knelt to place the box on the ground, undid the latch and raised the lid. "What the . . . ?" He lifted the object in order to examine it more closely. "It's warm. Whatever it is, it must be valuable. No doubt they'll call the police. I better find a place to ditch this in case I'm caught, then it will be their word against mine, assuming they can even identify me." Leaving the box behind, he proceeded to move deeper into the woods, scanning the ever-darkening surroundings for a hiding place while keeping his ears peeled for sounds of pursuit. Several minutes of frantic searching proved unsuccessful until at last he spotted a dark opening in the ground. "Some sort of burrow," he thought, "perhaps that of a raccoon or skunk. Doesn't look like it's been used recently." Kneeling, he placed the object on the ground, then using his hands, he proceeded to enlarge the burrow's opening. After several minutes of work, he was finally able to shove the object deep into the burrow, out of view, after which he covered the opening with dirt and leaves. "Let's see them find it now."

The police officer studied the scribbling on his notepad. "And you say you have no idea what this thing is, but that it's warm to the touch and glows in the dark?"

"That's right, officer," said George, leaning back on the couch in the Ferguson living room. "That's why I was transporting it to the engineering department at the Carnegie Institute. Of course, there's no sense trying to put a dollar value on something like that."

"Well, shouldn't be too hard to identify if it turns up. I don't know what my fellow officers will make of this report. They'll probably think I've gone daft or something." The policeman smiled while shaking his head.

"It's too bad you didn't get a better look at that fellow," the officer continued. "From the little we have, there are just too many people that could fit your description. You understand?"

"Yes, certainly," said Matt Ferguson.

"Bill, would you care for another cup of coffee?" said Jane.

"No thanks," said the policeman. "I guess I've got everything that I need, a lot of good it will probably do us." He stood as he slid the notepad into his shirt pocket. "We'll resume searching the woods again tomorrow, although I don't hold out much hope we'll find anything." He cast George a sympathetic glance. "I'm sorry, sir. I realize . . ."

"No apologies, officer," said George, also standing. "I'm sure you and your men have done your best. Matt and Jane are gracious enough to put me up here for a couple of days. Should anything turn up in that time this is where you can reach me. After that, let Matt know if something should come up and he'll get in touch with me."

"Sure thing," said the police officer taking the jacket that Matt had fetched for him and proceeding to put it on. "Say, when are you two going to get around to starting a family?" He gave Matt and Jane a big grin.

"I'm not too sure now's the best time," said Jane, "you know, with the war and all."

"Well, that's probably a good point." The policeman stepped to the door and opened it, taking in the woods across the street as he did so. He turned and faced his friend Matt. "Say, any idea why it's called Sullivans Woods?"

"Sorry," said Matt. "No idea."

Part IV
1995 – East Pencreek, Pennsylvania

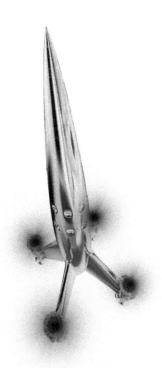

Chapter 1
Carol Haydn

"And that's how Sarah, Alex and I came to join the Solar Patrol," said the young man as he used his fork to spear the last piece of apple pie on his dessert plate.

"Well, you certainly convinced me that you are who you say you are," said Jerry.

"That's great, Jer," said the young man, beaming.

"I think Dad's being sarcastic," said the older son, Kevin.

"Oh." The young man features changed to reflect disappointment.

"Kevin, could you give Phil a nudge?" said Anne. "I'm afraid that second helping of apple pie might have made him a little sleepy."

"More likely it was Buck Rogers' story," said Kevin.

"Kevin Haydn!" said his mother. "You apologize to Tom."

"Sorry, sir," said the boy as he poked the chief of police with his elbow. Phil snorted and then opened his eyes.

"That's okay," said the young man. "I can on occasion be rather long winded. Perhaps I should be the one apologizing."

"It was a very—nice story," said Anne.

"Oh, yes," said Mrs. Gould. "I enjoyed it, especially the parts about my Sarah. I hope you've written other stories. I understand there's a good market these days for science fiction."

The young man let out a barely audible groan, lowered his head, and grasped the top of it with his hands.

"I believe you," said Brett, "only I wish there was more action in it, you know, like spaceship battles and ray gun fights and stuff."

The young man lifted his head and gave the youngster a nod. "Don't worry, there's a lot more action coming up, but because of the time we'll have to leave the telling of that part for another day."

"Speaking of another day, how long are you planning to be in town?" asked Jerry.

"I leave tomorrow morning after the completion of my mission."

"And this secret mission of yours that you can't tell us about?" said Jerry.

"I should think from what I told you that the purpose of my being here would be obvious."

"I thought you just came back for old time's sake," smirked Jerry.

"No, I came back to complete a mission. Being able to visit with my family has been an added benefit of my assignment."

"Okay, but I'm still not clear on why you're here."

The young man looked at Brett who was shaking with anticipation as if he desperately wanted to say something but had reservations about speaking up.

"Would you like to explain to your father why I'm here?" said the young man.

Brett beamed. "It's obvious Dad. Tom's here to stop that scoundrel Serpens from killing us." He looked at the young man. "Isn't that right?"

"Right as a unilateral snicker doog," said the young man, returning the boy's smile.

"Are you going to disintegrate him with your ray gun?" asked Brett.

"Wait a minute," said Jerry. "Serpens was the guidance counselor when I was in school. He hasn't been around for thirty years. What does . . . ?"

"No, he's still here," said Brett. "He's Kevin's physics teacher, remember?"

"Right again, Brett," said the young man.

"He's Mr. Rastaban?" said Kevin.

"Yes, if you were paying closer attention like your brother, you would have realized that. And I have to apprehend him or else when he fails to hear from Sleinad Evad, he'll kill you and your family and Katty's whole family too."

"That's absurd," said Jerry. "First off, Carol and Brett are both adopted. They don't have any Cobalt blood." At her husband's mention of their daughter Carol, Brett's twin sister, Anne took on a pained expression. Four weeks earlier Carol had been hit by an automobile while walking to school. The accident had left her in a comatose condition.

"That may not matter to Serpens," replied the young man. "After all, he's a syndroid. He could care less, and even if he did, he probably wouldn't want to leave any witnesses behind."

"What in the heck is a syndoid?" said Jerry.

"Gee, Dad, didn't you—," Brett started to say, but shut up when his father scowled at him.

"Syndroid," corrected the young man. "It's a designed human with bionic enhancements. Only seven of them were ever . . ." Upon seeing the stares from his audience, with the exception of Brett, the young man though better of continuing. "Ah, never mind. Suffice it to say that Serpens and Rastaban are no doubt one and the same person."

"Whatever," said Jerry. "So just how are you planning to apprehend Kevin's physics teacher and on what authority?"

"By the authority invested in me by the Solar Patrol. As to how I'm going to apprehend him, hopefully I can paralyze him and take him back with me to stand trial."

"Take him back? Where?" said Jerry.

"Back to the twenty-fourth century, of course."

"In a time machine, no doubt?"

"Well, how else would one travel to the future? Duh!"

Anne and Aunt Nan exchanged concerned looks before Anne

spoke up. "It's getting late. We should be leaving for the nursing home to see Carol before visiting hours end."

"Do I have to go?" said Brett.

"No," said Anne. "You and Kevin can stay home since you no doubt have homework to do and Kevin needs to study for his exams."

"And I should be hitting the road as it's getting late," said Phil, sounding almost relieved to have an excuse to leave. "Thank you all for the great dinner." Standing up, he glanced at the young man. "Good story, son. Uh, sorry I drifted off at the . . ."

"No problem," said the young man, also standing and offering the police officer his hand. "And again, I apologize for that gun thing."

"Yes, well, I probably should spend a little more time staying in shape."

Jerry also stood. "I'll see you to the door, Phil."

When they reached the front porch, Jerry turned to his friend.

"What are you going to do about him?"

"Jerry, what can I do?" said Phil.

"Can't you take him into custody?"

"On what charge? I don't think two counts of overactive imagination and one count of impersonating someone who disappeared thirty-six years ago is going to impress the judge."

"How about assaulting an officer? Remember when he took your gun away?"

The police chief examined the back of this hand. The fork marks were no longer visible. "I think we had better drop that one. Did I have just cause in reaching for my gun? I'd hate to have to argue that with an attorney."

"Okay, but you heard him say he was going to apprehend Kevin's physics teacher. What are you going to do about that?"

"Get serious, Jerry. For all I know that was part of that tall tale he told. Until he actually does something that constitutes breaking the law, my hands are tied. But I feel you have a right to be concerned. I'll have the office run a background check on this guy to see if we get any matches with some escapee from a lunatic asylum of something, and I'll put an around the clock stakeout on Aunt Nan's house. While he's in town, I'll make sure we keep a tail on him so we'll be able to arrest him should he try anything."

"Thanks, Phil. That makes me feel better. I certainly appreciate you coming over."

"And I appreciate dinner," said Phil. "It was a great meal as usual, and an interesting afternoon, that's for sure, even if I did doze off before the end of the story. Whoever he is, he certainly pricked my curiosity."

The two men shook hands and then Phil turned to leave, but hesitated.

"You know, just to ensure I have enough manpower, I think I'll give Brad Jones a call and see if he can't lend me a couple of his deputies."

"Sounds like a good idea," said Jerry.

"Brad should find this really interesting since he was in the story." Phil gave a laugh and continued on down the walk. "Have a good night."

"You too, Phil." Jerry turned to go back in the house and almost stepped on Tiger. The cat gave him one of those arrogant looks as if to say 'I dare you' and then let out a meow.

Upon entering Carol's room at the nursing home, the two men remained standing while the women took seats. As was always her custom, Anne sat next to the bed, holding her unconscious daughter's hand while she and the other two women made occasional small talk. Finally, Aunt Nan sensed her 'son' was getting antsy at the enforced inactivity and motioned for the young man to join her in the hall.

"She's been that way ever since the automobile accident," said Aunt Nan. "There hasn't been the least sign of improvement."

"There's always hope," said the young man.

The woman forced a smile. "I suppose in the future they can cure such things."

"Most likely."

"So, can you cure Carol?"

"Perhaps if I had the appropriate medication—then again, I'm not a doctor."

"You somehow knew Carol was in a coma before you came back, but you didn't think to bring with you something that could cure her?"

"Even if I had, there's the question of the impact on the future that changing the past would have."

"Yes, I remember you mentioning that at the dinner table this afternoon." The elderly woman gave a sigh. "I also remember reading a story about that kind of thing. It was about these people who traveled in a time machine to the age of the dinosaurs to hunt a—I believe it was a Tyrannosaur rex. They were only allowed to shoot one that would have otherwise died from natural causes not long afterwards. Something went wrong and a man accidentally stepped on an insect and killed it and thereby changed the future." Aunt Nan gave the young man a look of embarrassment. "I believe it's the only science fiction story I've ever read."

"That's the point exactly. But if Apocason is right, then it's a moot point."

"But you are now in what is your past. I would think that the very act of coming back here would change the future."

"Not according to Apocason. Whatever actions a time traveler takes while in his past is exactly what has already occurred. Nature always works so as to avoid paradoxes."

"Then there is no free will?"

"That's a good question. If I understand Apocason's principle correctly, there is still free will because the past has already occurred. Hence nothing will ever happen in the past that will lead to a future paradox."

"I don't follow."

"I'm not sure I do either," said the young man with a laugh.

Aunt Nan was silent for a moment, obviously attempting to analyze the ramifications of what the young man had told her.

"From what you said, according to this principle, if you had brought back a cure for Carol's coma, you could have done so without impacting the future."

The young man stared at the woman before answering. "Suppose I did something here that changes the future and then returned to the future, how would I know if I had changed it?"

"Suppose you returned to an earlier time in the future, a time that you had already experienced. Wouldn't you then be able to know if anything had changed?"

"An excellent point, Mom. Maybe you should have been a philosopher."

"You're not answering the question."

"I'm not sure I can. There's another idea of an infinite number of parallel universes that are continually being created at each moment in time to handle any eventually."

"I'm sensing a reluctance to answer my questions," said Aunt Nan.

"I'm sensing I'm being blamed for not being able to bring Carol out of her coma," said the young man.

"No, I'm not trying to accuse you of anything. It's just that . . ."

"I understand. You'll just have to believe me when I say I don't have the answers." The young man stepped forward and took the elderly woman in his arms, giving her a hug. "One should never give up hope."

She returned the hug. "You're right. I had always hoped that one day you would come back to me and you have." She looked up at the man who claimed to be her son. "If only you could stay longer."

"I have to leave tomorrow."

"Why?" The woman released her hold and took a step back.

"Duty."

Rebecca Gould entered the hall, followed by Anne, who like her mother was dabbing her eyes with a tissue. "I believe we're ready to go," said Rebecca.

They had reached the nursing home's exit when the young man said, "Oops, I believe I left my backpack in the room. I'll be right back."

"I don't believe this," said Jerry as he watched the young man hurry down the hallway in the direction of Carol's room. "The guy says he's traveled here all the way from some future century yet he can't even remember his backpack."

Entering the room, the man walked up to the side of the bed where the comatose girl lay. He reached into one of the pockets of his trousers and pulled out a small metallic object, about the size of a quarter.

"God forgive me for what I'm about to do," he said, keeping his voice low. A sharp point popped out of the object. The man thrust the point into one of the girl's closed eyelids. He held it there for a second then withdrew it. No mark appeared on the skin where the point had pierced it.

The man returned the object to his pocket, picked up his backpack and left the room.

Chapter 2
The Prophecy

Jerry and the young man were walking behind the three women as they made their way up the front walk of the Haydn home. As the women were crossing the front porch, the young man stopped. "Jerry, can I have a word with you—in private?"

Jerry also stopped, surprised that the young man had addressed him as "Jerry" instead of "Jer." "I guess so."

For a moment, the young man stared at the large tree trunk that rested across the front yard next to where they stood. "I can cut that up for you, if you'd like."

"Huh? You wanted to talk to me in private to ask me that?"

"No. I just wanted to draw your attention to it again before I get to the real issue."

"Which is —?"

"Look, I know you don't believe anything I've said, that you think I'm a phony, and no doubt have some diabolical scheme to harm Mom—your aunt in some way. I can certainly understand why you would see things that way. But I have some things to tell you, and it's really important that you remember them."

"I'm tired of putting up with this game of yours, whatever it is. Give it a rest."

"I can't, Jerry. Don't you get it? We're at war. You and your family are in it, whether you want to be or not."

"You mean that absurd assertion of yours that my son's physics teacher is going to murder us?"

"Yes. Now ask yourself, if there's even the faintest possibility that I may be telling the truth, why not at least hear me out?"

For reply, Jerry fixed the young man with an icy stare, and then to the young man's surprise, said, "Okay. Shoot."

"First off, don't worry about Carol. She'll be fine. She'll be coming out of the coma soon."

"Really? What makes you think so? The neurologist doesn't seem so optimistic."

"Call it a hunch, an educated hunch."

"Okay, mister space cadet, how soon?"

"Sorry, I can't tell you that."

"Then how do you know she'll be recovering?"

"I can't tell you that either."

"Oh, I keep forgetting. You're from the future, so of course you would know such things. So maybe you could give me a tip on this year's World Series?"

"This is no time for jests. As I mentioned this afternoon, I have no idea who wins this year's World Series. I couldn't even tell you who won last year's series, or who the teams were. But getting back to what I must tell you, first off, you probably don't want to tell other people about my return from the future. And caution your family not to mention it."

"Us, tell? Why people would think we were nuts, so no worries there, except maybe for Brett, but I'm going to have a talk with him. And I can't see Phil mentioning it."

"Great. Okay, the second thing is a date. August 15, 2002. You got that? August 15, 2002."

"Yeah, August 15, 2002. What happens then?"

"You'll be meeting another visitor from the twenty-fourth century."

"Huh? Okay, I'll bite. Who is coming to visit? You again?"

"Just remember the date. That's all I can tell you. Don't mention this to your family until it's close to that date. And it would be best that you not tell this person who shows up from the future about my visit."

"Why's that?"

"Sorry I can't answer that either. But it's also important that, as that date nears, you explain to the rest of your family the importance of not telling the person who arrives from the future about my visit."

"The rest of my family? Does that include Aunt Nan and Anne's mom?"

There was a noticeable delay before the young man answered. "Yes." There was something in the way he said the word "yes" that gave Jerry pause. For the first time since hearing the young man's claim that he was Jerry's long, lost cousin, the possibility that the young man was indeed Tom registered an air of credibility with Jerry.

"Are Aunt Nan and Rebecca still going to be—here in 2002?"

"I can't really say one way or the other."

"But you know the answer, right?"

The young man took a deep breath. "There are only three things you need to remember. The date August 15, 2002, not telling your family to expect another visitor from the future until right before that date, and that no one should mention to the person from the future about my visit."

When Jerry failed to respond, the young man continued. "I will also tell you this about the future. On August 15, 2002, you will be convinced that I've been telling the truth."

"Huh, huh," said Jerry. "Well, since we're having this chat, there are a couple of things you said this afternoon that sparked my curiosity that I would like to ask you about."

The young man gave Jerry a look of surprise. "Really?"

"Don't read too much into it. I know you're an imposter. But let's, for the sake of argument, pretend for a moment that you are—" The young man sensed from the other's hesitation that uttering the next word was most difficult for him. "—Tom."

"I'll be glad to answer any questions, Jerry, as long as they don't compromise my mission or reveal information about the future best left unknown."

"Okay. About Tom and this commander guy supposedly being the same person. You never said what the resolution of that was."

"An excellent question. I'm surprised no one else thought to ask that."

"As I recall no one asked you anything probably because, like me, they don't believe you," sneered Jerry. "Anyway, quit stalling. I asked you a question."

"To which I don't have an answer."

"Hah," taunted Jerry. "Another copout, not that I didn't expect it."

"It's not a copout. The issue was never resolved. I have no idea how the Commander and I came to have the same DNA. Sorry, but that's the way it is. Did you have another question?"

"Yeah, one more. I recall you saying the United States would no longer exist in the twenty-fourth century. I find that difficult to believe. So maybe it would help your credibility if you would at least explain to me how that came to be? I mean, what country would ever be strong enough to destroy America?"

"Like most great empires, it destroyed itself—it fell from within," said the young man.

"Huh-huh. Can you be more specific as to just what is going to destroy this country?"

"Daytime television."

"What? Cut me a break."

The young man grinned. "Sorry, I couldn't resist, although there is some truth in that answer. After all, what society can flourish when half its members are intent in turning themselves into vegetables?"

"So, you're not going to answer the question?"

"I'll give you the short answer, if you wish."

"Shoot."

"Let me paraphrase a statement attributed to Ben Franklin. Those who trade essential liberty for the promise of security will end up with neither liberty nor security."

Jerry hesitated before responding, obviously taking time to mull over in his mind the young man's answer. "Yeah, maybe old Ben was on to something there."

After the dinner dishes had been cleared away and some refreshments prepared, Jerry suggested that Anne take some pictures. Anne couldn't help noticing that something had changed between her husband and the young man. For example, the young man no longer addressed her husband as "Jer." Jerry, in turn, no longer seemed to treat the young man with distain.

Anne took some photos of the young man with Aunt Nan, then one of him with her mother, and finally one of the visitor and Brett. Next her mother took a photo of Anne with the young man.

Much to Brett's disappointment, instead of elaborating more on events of the twenty-fourth century, the young man insisted on spending the remainder of the visit browsing through family photo albums and hearing about the lives of his hosts. In marked contrast to that afternoon, the evening passed pleasantly. When Aunt Nan and the young man had finally taken their leave, a wave of relief swept over Anne. She considered it nothing less than a miracle, since their return from the nursing home, that Jerry had never once erupted in a fit of anger.

Chapter 3
Brad Jones

Diane Jones had finished checking the newspaper's TV listings. She looked up to find her husband sitting across from her in the living room. He was just sitting there, slouched in an easy chair, staring at the bookcase.

"Brad? Is everything all right?"

Her husband gave his head a small shake. "Oh, fine." He continued to intensely study the bookcase.

"A penny for your thoughts."

"Huh?" Her husband broke his concentration on the bookcase.

"I said, 'a penny for your thoughts.' You seem like you are miles away."

"I was thinking."

"About what?"

"This morning I found you looking at our old eighth grade memory book, and then you mentioned Tom Cobalt. What was that all about?"

"It was really weird. I didn't want to trouble you about it."

"Go ahead. Trouble me."

"OK. Remember when I was sunbathing out front this morning?"

Her husband gave her a nod.

"I had about dozed off and when I awoke, I was startled to find a man standing next to me."

"Someone came into our yard?"

"Yes."

"Who was he?"

"I don't know. I've never seen him before. But what was really strange was that he had picked up a section of the Sunday paper and was reading it."

"Yeah, that's odd. Why?"

"He said he was checking the date."

"What?"

"Yes. He was checking the date. And when I asked him why, it was—well, it wasn't like he was trying to figure out what day of the month it was but, so help me, I think he was looking for the year."

"Come on."

"Okay, I was probably imagining that. But, anyway, we got to talking."

"How old was this guy?"

"I'd say early twenties."

"So, you were out there in your swim suit flirting with a twenty-year old?" Brad smiled as he made the accusation.

"Well, he was darn good looking. But let me get to the really weird part. This guy looks to be in his early twenties, right? He says he's never heard of the Righteous Brothers or the Beatles or Michael Jackson, but when an Elvis tune comes on the radio, he recognizes it. He knows it's Elvis."

"So? He's probably cultured or something. Listens to Beethoven and stuff like that instead of pop music."

"There's more. I mean the guy is just walking around, no car apparently, with a backpack. He mentions the high school, only he calls it the new high school. Why would he say that? The high school was built before he was even born."

"I don't know."

"I'm not sure I can even recall all the other weird stuff that came up in our conversation. For example, he knows my maiden name, and I can't recall having ever met him before."

"So how did he know your maiden name?"

"I don't know. I asked him but, from what I remember, he changed the subject. Then he asked me if the Cobalts still lived on Oak Lane." At the mention of the Cobalts, Brad sat up.

"So, I mentioned Sam's funeral, and then he told me that he was related to the Cobalts."

"What's his relation?"

"I don't know. He never told me."

"A fine investigator you'd make. That's why I'm the sheriff in the family."

"And then he mentioned Caroline Cobalt, only he called her Katty."

"He what?"

"He called her Katty."

"Why would he call her that? The only person who ever called Caroline Katty was her brother Tom."

"Yes, those were exactly my thoughts. Anyway, then he left, and that's when I came inside and looked in the yearbook."

"Did you get his name?"

"Only his first name. He said it was Tom."

Brad felt a spasm surge through his brain. It wasn't painful, but it was uncomfortable. Sweat appeared on his forehead and on the palms of his hands.

Before he could ask another question, the telephone rang. Diane answered it.

"Honey, it's for you. It's Phil Bartley."

Brad picked up the receiver. "Phil?"

"Brad, something's come up. I was wondering if I could get some help from your department over the next day or so?"

"Shouldn't be any problem. What's going on?"

"This is going to sound really weird."

"Shoot. My wife already told me something pretty weird. Bet you can't top her story."

"Okay, here it goes. I get a call from Jerry Haydn early this afternoon . . ."

It was a good five minutes before Brad got off the phone with Phil. During the call Brad said little, spending most of the time listening. Diane sat there and watched her husband, her curiosity mounting by the minute. Finally, the call was finished.

"Well?" she said.

"Phil wants me to lend him some of my boys over the next day or so."

"Why?"

"Apparently your mysterious stranger from this morning showed up at the Haydn's house this afternoon along with Jerry's Aunt Nan."

"And . . . ?"

"It seems this guy claims he's Tom Cobalt."

"Okay, he said his name was Tom and that he was related to the Cobalts. So?"

"You don't understand. This guy claims he's actually Tom who disappeared in 1959."

Anne was setting the bedside alarm clock when Jerry came out of the bathroom and climbed onto the bed, settling in beside her.

"Some day, huh?" he said.

"So, what do you think?"

"You first."

"I don't know," said Anne. "One moment I'm thinking that he must really be who he says he is, and then the rational side of my mind screams 'no way.'" When Jerry didn't say anything, she continued. "Just now I had a really disturbing thought."

"What's that?"

"You remember what he told us about those horrible aliens, the ones he called Darwinians?"

"Yeah?"

"Well, suppose it's all true, that is, that he really is from the future . . ."

"Go on," said Jerry.

"But suppose he's not Tom. Suppose he's one of those Darwinian things made up to look like Tom." Anne waited for her husband to say something, but he only gave her a blank stare.

"I mean, how would we know? It wouldn't even have to look exactly like Tom, only resemble him. After all, the last we saw Tom was over thirty years ago and then he was only thirteen."

"Come on, Anne," said Jerry. "If my cousin's returning from the dead after over thirty years is preposterous, then some alien impersonating him is even more so."

"But——"

"And why go to all this trouble? What would be the motive?"

"Well, if he really is Tom, what's his motive?"

"As I recall, it's supposedly to keep Kevin's physics teacher, who apparently is also from the future and was our guidance counselor when we were in junior high, from killing us in a couple of years."

"I don't see how that is any less preposterous than my idea."

"Okay, suppose he is an alien instead of Tom. Why would he tell us about these Darwinian guys then?"

Anne gave her head a shake. "AHHHHHHH! I don't want to think about it any more. I just want to go to sleep."

"Good idea. Let's try to get some sleep."

Jerry leaned over and turned off the lamp on the bedside table.

"Good night, dear," he said.

"Good night. I love you."

"I love you," said Jerry.

For a few minutes they both lay there, neither one being able to steer their thoughts away from the day's events. It was Anne who first spoke up.

"Did I notice a change in your attitude towards him after we got back from the nursing home?"

Jerry sat up and turned the bedside lamp on. "Yeah," he said. "I'm no longer so cocksure he's an imposter."

"Why's that?"

"He told me not to tell you what I'm about to tell you until a few years from now, but here it goes."

"What?"

"He said that in 2002 we're going to get another visitor from the future."

"2002? That's seven years from now. He's coming back in seven years?"

"I'm not sure if it will be him. He wouldn't say who it was that would show up, but he gave an exact date. August 15, 2002. He also said that I wasn't to tell my family until right before that date."

"Okay, that's one promise you failed to honor."

"Hey, I don't recall promising him that I wouldn't tell you."

"Great," said Anne. "Now I'll be living in suspense for seven years. But why have you changed your mind about him?"

"I didn't say I changed my mind, I just said I'm not as certain as I used to be that he's an imposter."

"And why is that?"

Jerry shifted his position on the bed so as to face his wife. "When he asked me not to tell anyone about another visitor from the future, I asked him if that included your mom and Aunt Nan."

"And?"

"He said yes. But what bothered me was the way he hesitated before answering."

"I don't follow."

"Don't you see? If he really is who is says he is, if he really is from the future, it's not only probably true that we're going to have another visitor from the future, but that he knows whether your mom and Aunt Nan will still be alive in 2002." Anne looked uncomfortable. "Say your mom passes away between now and 2002 . . ."

Anne's eyes began to moisten. "I believe I understand."

"It was the way he said that one word, 'yes.' It was as if he knew it was a lie but realized that he may have been trapped into revealing something he'd prefer we didn't know."

Anne nodded. "Any other reasons?"

"Not really." Jerry took his wife's hand in his and gave it a gentle squeeze. "This is ridiculous. I mean there are so many holes in his story that it's obviously all nonsense."

"Such as?"

"Well—," said Jerry. "Hey, don't think I wasn't following all that double talk he was giving us. Okay, take the part about there having to be some kind of receiver here in 1995 for him to arrive from the future. He said that the receiver had to already be here, but it's so sophisticated that no one in this day and age could build it. So there. Where did the receiver come from?"

"That's a good point. But when he told us about it, he admitted that he didn't know how the receiver got here. To me, that makes his story more credible."

"No, it doesn't. That's a copout."

"Yes, it probably was. Okay, let's drop it. We could spend all night on this kind of thing and you have to go to work in the morning."

Jerry leaned over and gave his wife a kiss, then scrunched around and turned out the beside light.

Less than a minute had passed before Anne broke the silence. "Honey?"

"Yes."

"To his credit, he certainly did seem to know a lot about what went on back in 1959. You know, like all the people we knew back then and all that was happening."

"Too bad Diane and Brad Jones weren't here today. I believe they were in the same class with Tom and your sister and Alex. They might know how much he said was true."

"Maybe we should tell them about what happened," suggested Anne.

"Are you—they'd think we were nuts." Even with the light off and not being able to see his wife's expression, Jerry sensed his reaction had been too strong. "I'm sorry, I didn't mean—"

"No, you're right."

"Now that I think of it, I wouldn't be surprised if we get a call from Brad."

"Why?"

"Phil said he'd put Tom—eh, you-know-who under surveillance. Just to ensure he wasn't up to anything, you know, to protect Aunt Nan."

"Yes, that's no doubt a good idea."

"Anyway, Phil said he'd talk to Brad about getting some of his deputies to help out, so no doubt he already knows something of what went on today."

"Well, as I was saying, he seemed very familiar with people and events back then. And his characterization of my sister, I know I was only eleven when she disappeared, but as best as I can recall, it was dead on."

"Gee, you're saying that your sister was really that big of a pain-in-the-neck?"

"Very funny. I couldn't have asked for a more wonderful sister. But getting back to my point, if he wasn't there, then he must have learned all those details from someone who was."

"But from whom?" asked Jerry. "Who knew Tom well enough back then who's still around other than present company? Let's see, there's Aunt Nan, Brad and Diane, and Tom's sister."

"I don't know. Eh, honey, there's something else I wanted to ask you."

"Shoot."

"Would you mind if I had copies made of those photos he gave Mom?"

"You mean the ones that are supposedly of your sister?"

"Yes."

"No, go ahead."

"Thanks. I just wanted to make sure it wouldn't upset you. I mean, I accept that none of it is probably true—"

"No, like I said, go ahead. Besides you and your mom seem to feel that they're a good likeness of what your sister would have looked like a couple of years older than when you last saw her. You just have to wonder how he did it."

"You mean how he could have had those photos made, assuming he's a fraud?"

"Yeah. Even assuming he is who he says he is, it just doesn't make any sense."

"What doesn't?" asked Anne.

"Why your sister never got a nose job."

Anne hit her husband with a pillow.

"Wayne Franklin."

"Huh, what?" Jerry was just drifting off when Anne spoke up.

"Wayne Franklin."

"Wayne who?"

"We were wondering who might have provided him with all the details about what happened back in 1959."

"What time is it?" groaned Jerry.

"Honey, whatever happened to the Franklins?"

"The Franklins? Oh, you mean that family that lived in town back when we were growing up. I don't know. I can't even remember what their son Wayne looked like. I think they moved away or something not long after Tom disappeared."

"We should ask Aunt Nan. She might know. After all he was one of

Tom's best friends, that is, according to what we heard this afternoon."

"Brad might be a better person to ask."

"Yes. Great idea. So, if Diane or Brad call tomorrow, we'll ask them about Wayne. Okay?"

"Yeah, sure. Can we get some sleep now?"

"Yes, sorry."

"Good night."

"Good night. I love you."

"Ditto."

"Thanks for taking the time to talk."

"Sure thing."

"Jerry?"

Jerry sat up in bed and turned the light on. "What?" As soon as he said it, he realized he had sounded angry. Anne looked at her husband, the blanket pulled up so that it covered her nose.

"Do you think I'm pretty?"

"You know I do. Need you ask?"

"Look at me."

Jerry looked at his wife.

"Sarah was pretty, no, she was beautiful. I remember her as being beautiful. She was beautiful, and her nose was part of what made her so attractive."

Jerry gave a sigh. "Honey, I love you. Remember me telling you the first time I told you I loved you that if I ever changed my mind I would let you know?"

"Yes."

"Well, I've never changed my mind, and I can't see me ever doing so. So, pray tell me then why are we talking about your sister?"

"I didn't appreciate that crack you made about Sarah's nose."

Jerry collapsed back into bed. "Anne, believe me when I say I have no idea what this conversation is about."

"It's about his credibility."

Jerry rolled over on his side to face his wife who was peering at him, her nose still hidden by the blanket. "I'm sorry, but I'm not following you."

"Look at me."

"I am. You have beautiful eyes."

"Okay, now imagine me with a larger nose. Do you still find me beautiful?"

"Of course."

"No, you answered too fast. I don't think you took the time to imagine it. Please focus."

Jerry closed his eyes and concentrated. Opening them, he said, "Yes, you would still be beautiful. I'm sure of it. But I don't understand where this is going."

Anne pulled down the blanket and rolled over on her side, her face close to Jerry's. "From what I remember, my sister really liked Tom, just like he said this afternoon."

"Hey, what girl wouldn't like Tom? After all, consider how good looking I am. We share the same gene pool you know."

Anne smiled. "I think it was more than infatuation. I think that Sarah really liked Tom, and from what we heard today I think that Tom may have felt the same way about her."

"Anne, that was over thirty years ago. They were only thirteen years old, and I still don't know what it is you're driving at."

"I'm not sure. It's just that I really wish it was all true, that Sarah isn't dead and if it's all true, I would like to know how it all turns out. There are just so many loose ends. Like Aunt Nan seeing the young woman that looked like Sarah back in 1946. What was that all about?"

"It was probably a coincidence. My aunt saw someone who resembled the girl in the photos. After all, Aunt Nan had only met Sarah briefly and it was all so long ago."

"But it was the photographs that jarred Aunt Nan's memory, the photos of an older Sarah."

"Like I said, coincidence."

"What about the uniform Aunt Nan remembered the woman wearing? As I recall she said it had an insignia on it."

"Anne, I don't have any answers, and you would be just as beautiful with a larger nose. Now can we please get some sleep?"

"Yes, you're right. Thanks for taking the time to talk."

Jerry rolled over and turned out the light.

"The cat."

"Huh? What cat?" said Jerry.

"The one that Aunt Nan said she saw back in 1946 with the woman who looked like Sarah. She said the cat resembled Tiger. And the woman was carrying a baby. Wasn't Alex adopted?"

Jerry sat up in bed again and turned on the light. "Yeah, I believe that's right. Alex was adopted. As matter of fact I remember hearing that he was left as a newborn on the Banyon's front step, just like in some bad melodrama. I think most people who heard that story thought it was just made up."

"You don't think the baby might have been Alex?"

"I'm not sure. It's probably just another coincidence. Then again when you have so many coincidences piling up one on top of another, you have to wonder if they are really coincidences."

"But the woman said her baby's name was Tom, not Alex."

Jerry was staring at the far bedroom wall, his mind running at full throttle. "That wouldn't be relevant if the Banyons didn't know what the baby's real name was. They named him Alex." He turned to his wife. "Anne, you might want to go down to the courthouse tomorrow and see if you can find Alex's birth certificate. You know, check his date of birth."

Anne gave her husband a nod.

"And why do cats that resemble Aunt Nan's cat keep popping up everywhere?" he said.

"Alex's cat was named Tiger," said Anne, "so if the cat stayed with the baby, the Banyons probably adopted him too."

"And why did Aunt Nan name her cat Tiger?" asked Jerry.

"Coincidence?"

Jerry groaned. "Not another coincidence. I hate cats."

A meow came from the floor next to the bed. There sat Aunt Nan's cat Tiger.

"What the——" said Jerry. "How did he get in here?"

"Probably through Lady's dog door," said Anne. "Here, kitty, kitty." Tiger jumped up on the bed. Anne began to rub him behind the ears, her action being answered by loud purring.

"Must you?" said Jerry. "You know how I hate cats, especially this one."

"But he's such a sweetie and he's good company for your aunt, especially with Uncle Sam gone. Should we call Aunt Nan to let her know her cat's here?"

"It's probably way too late. If he's still here in the morning, I'll drop him off at Aunt Nan's on the way to work, even though it might mean another session with you-know-who."

Anne ruffled the cat's fur. "I sure wish you could talk. Are you Alex's old cat?"

"Anne, you know that's absurd. Cat's don't live that long."

"But remember him telling us about cyber-cats. Maybe Tiger's a cyber-cat from the future." Anne put her nose close to the cat's as she continued to ruffle its fur. "Are you a cyber-cat?"

"Rowow," said Tiger.

"Honey, what's the matter?" Diane twisted onto her side and turned the bedside lamp on. Brad was sitting up in bed. She glanced at the alarm clock. "It's two-thirty in the morning," she said.

"I had a nightmare."

"A nightmare?" Diane gave her husband a look of surprise. "Well, that's not like you. All these years and I can't ever remember you telling me about a nightmare."

Brad turned and looked directly at his wife. The expression on her husband's face shocked Diane.

"You don't understand," he said. "It wasn't an ordinary nightmare."

Diane sat up and put a hand on her husband's shoulder.

"What do you mean?"

"When I was a kid I had a couple of terrible nightmares. They were really awful. It was like someone was inside of my mind trying to take control of it. Like the one tonight, they were accompanied by a really bad headache."

"You never told me that?"

"I know. I believe I only had two, maybe three of them, and I've never had one since. That is until now. When I was having them, I thought that maybe I was going insane or something. But I never told anyone about them, not even my parents. I never told anyone about them until now."

Diane took her husband's hand. "Any idea what might have caused it?"

"I have a hunch. You remember talking about Tom Cobalt tonight?"

"Yes."

"When I had these nightmares as a kid, it was right around the time that Tom, Alex and Sarah disappeared."

"I see. Well, it seems likely that's what caused the nightmare to come back, this young man showing up and claiming to be Tom Cobalt. It reminded your subconscious of what happened back in 1959. The shock of the disappearance of your friends is probably what triggered them in the first place."

"No, I don't think that's it."

"How so?"

"Because as best I can recall, the nightmares started occurring a couple of nights before they disappeared."

Brad took a gulp of water to make swallowing the acetaminophen tablets easier.

"Is there anything I can do for you?" asked his wife.

"No," said Brad. "You go back to bed. I'll be okay. I'll probably stay up until these take hold."

"Okay," said Diane. "I love you."

"And I love you," said Brad.

Diane studied her husband for a moment, before leaving the kitchen and returning to their bedroom.

Brad walked into the living room, taking a seat on the sofa. He moved his right hand to his forehead and held it there. Then he closed his eyes. His body gave an involuntary jerk. He lowered his hand and opened his eyes. Reaching over, he picked up the phone and dialed a number. When the person on the other end of the line answered, Brad said a single word into the receiver. "Admiral."

Putting down the phone when the conversation had ended, Brad Jones rose from the sofa and walked to the door that led to the basement. He opened the door and descended the basement stairs, finally stopping before a workbench. Getting on his hands and knees, he reached underneath the bench's lowest shelf. After a few moments of searching, he pulled out a corroded metal tool box covered with dust. The box's lid was secured by a padlock. Brad dialed in a combination. The padlock snapped open. Removing the lock, he opened the tool box. Inside was an item wrapped in a rag. Picking up the covered item, he stood up and placed it on the workbench. After removing the rag, he grasped the object by its handle. Holding it up before his eyes, he examined the ray gun.

From outside one of the basement windows, an unseen pair of inhuman eyes followed Brad's every move.

Chapter 4
SHOWDOWN

The feel of something pressing on the mattress stirred her awake. Nancy Cobalt blinked, opened her eyes and beheld the young man who claimed to be her son sitting on the side of her bed.

"Good morning, Mom." He smiled.

The old woman stretched as she returned his greeting. "Goodness, how late were we up last night?"

"Until around four in the morning, I believe."

"What time is it?"

"About eight. I don't have long before I have to be off."

"Yes, I know." The woman sat up in bed, suddenly finding herself unable to look at the young man. She reached over and grabbed a robe that had been draped over the back of a chair by the side of the bed opposite from that on which the young man sat, and donned the garment over her nightgown. "I can make you a quick breakfast, or at least some coffee."

"Mom, you know I never drank coffee. Still don't. But some orange juice and toast would be great."

"Okay." The woman slipped out from beneath the sheet and blanket and stood up. As she came around the foot of the bed the young man also rose.

"Tommy, there's something I've been meaning to ask you."

"Shoot," said the young man.

"Your eyes."

"Oh, you want to know why they're no longer brown?"

"Yes."

"These are replacement eyes."

"Replacement eyes?"

"Yes. My eyes were damaged as a result of a delta-containment explosion. The medical officer didn't have any brown replacement eyes available, so he installed these."

"Installed?"

"Yeah. I just never got around to having the color changed." The young man took a moment to study the elderly woman's expression.

"Mom, I realize you still have your doubts, not that I blame you. Obviously, what I told you and the rest of the family yesterday seems totally unbelievable."

The woman began to protest. "No, Tommy. I—"

"Mom, it's important to me that you know in your heart that I'm your son. So, please, ask me anything you wish, any questions you feel might put to rest any doubts you may harbor."

Nancy Cobalt closed her eyes momentarily and let out a sigh. "Very well." She stared at the far wall, obviously deep in thought, before turning her face towards the young man. "What did I give you the night that you disappeared?"

The young man spent a moment pondering the question before saying, "I take it you mean something more material than a hug and a kiss?"

"Yes, something more material."

The man's face lit up. "Yes, of course. It was a medallion—a St. Christopher's medal. I'm sorry to say I lost it."

"Tommy, Tommy." Nancy put her arms around the neck of the young man and began to sob. "It's okay. It was only an old medallion." The man returned the woman's embrace, gently patting her back.

As she released her embrace she again looked into the young man's eyes. There was something about those eyes, those eyes of a wrong color. "And do you remember what was written on the back of the medal?" It was the sudden change in his pupils that caught the elderly woman's attention.

"Uh—no. I'm sorry Mom. I lost it so long ago . . ."

Although the woman tried to hide her reaction, the young man sensed that he had given the wrong answer.

As she watched him pick up the cup of orange juice she had placed on the kitchen table her attention was drawn to the tawny orange feline that now seemed always to take its place at the young man's feet.

"Why does Tiger never leave your side?"

The young man put down the cup and smiled. "Well, for a couple of reasons. First, this is Alex's old cat."

"But how can that be?"

"Remember me telling you about a cat named Neutronium? Like Neutronium, Tiger's a cyber-cat. Cyber-cats live a lot longer than normal cats, that is, if they don't get killed in the line of duty. Then again like normal cats, cyber-cats have nine lives so they're tough to get rid of."

"But that would mean that Tiger's from the future?"

"Yes."

"So that's how you knew his name?"

"Not exactly. Being a cyber-cat, he can communicate with me over a short range by telepathy. We both have neurodic implants."

"He speaks English to you?"

"Yep. Well, that's not quite accurate, just like my saying that I speak feline to him. Of course, when I was growing up, neither Alex nor I nor anyone else had any idea that Tiger was a cyber-cat from the future."

"If Tiger's from the future does he know what's going to happen?"

"To some extent. He tells me some things, like the fact that Brad

613

Jones is waiting for me in the alley, but he doesn't tell me everything he knows. He has his orders."

"Why would Brad Jones be waiting for you in the alley?"

"To kill me."

"What?"

"To kill me. Or at least that's what Tiger tells me. And now that I mention that, I might also tell you that Tiger has left my side since I've arrived. Like last night, while we stayed up talking, he was over spying on Brad."

"But why, and why would Brad want to kill you?"

"He's an enemy agent."

"Tommy, that's ridiculous. You've known Brad since—"

"Oh, he wasn't always an enemy agent." The young man took another gulp of orange juice. "According to Tiger, Serpens doped Brad with a mindbender, probably a couple of days before I disappeared."

"A what?"

"A mindbender. It's a device that's inserted in the back of the neck, right below the brain stem, similar to where a neurode is implanted. I believe I mentioned them yesterday."

"I'm sorry, Tommy, but I have a tough time remembering it all. This isn't making any sense to me."

"The mindbender he implanted in Brad allows Serpens to control Brad's actions. The recipient of the device has no idea that his mind has been doped. Whenever they desire, the people who inserted the device can take control of the mindbender's host and will him to follow their instructions. Otherwise, when not being actively controlled, the host will behave normally. Once the mindbender was implanted in him, Brad became an involuntary agent of the Draconian Guard. Tiger thinks he intends to kill me this morning and thereby prevent me from completing my mission."

"That's horrible. But if he's waiting for you in the alley, all you have to do is leave by the front door. He'll never see you."

"Didn't you notice the police car parked out front across the street?"

"What?"

"They'd just call Brad when they saw me leave by the front door. Anyway, I need to confront Brad."

"But suppose he kills you?"

"Mom, that's not likely to happen. For one thing, I have the element of surprise on my side. Brad doesn't know that I know that he's an enemy agent and that I know he's waiting for me."

Nancy sat down across the table from the young man. His seeming confidence had not dispelled her concern.

"Mom, it will be okay."

Nancy stared at Tiger who returned her stare and then licked his chops. "If Tiger's from the future, who sent him here?"

"I don't know. He won't tell me certain things, like that for instance. For all I know I could have sent him and ordered him not to tell me that I did it. No doubt there's a good reason why he can't tell me."

Nancy slowing moved her hands over the table top, obviously deep in thought. The young man stayed silent, observing the older woman while he took a bite of toast and began to chew it. "Tommy? Remember me mentioning that strange thing that happened one evening before you were born?"

"Where you met the woman who looked like Sarah, only older?"

"Yes. There was a tabby cat with her. An orange tabby I believe."

"I asked Tiger about that, but he wouldn't tell me anything. I suspect that that cat might have been him." The young man gave the cat a glance, but all he got in return was the usual noncommittal feline stare.

"Will he be going back to the future with you?"

"No, Tiger says he's staying here. Not only because he was ordered too, but because he wants to. He'll no doubt be with you for the rest of your days. But I sure would like to take him back with me. Imagine what he could tell us if we could convince him to talk. But then again, it's probably dangerous to know the future. I mean, if you knew the future you might wish to change it. Would trying to change it be an act of total futility as Apocason maintains?" The young man looked past the old woman, looked at the clock on the kitchen wall. "Time. It's probably the ultimate mystery of the universe. Understand time and you've caught a glimpse into the mind of God."

Nancy gave her cat a nod. "Well, I think Tiger is a very wise kitty. And I'd love for him to stay here. He'll always remind me of my son, and these few precious hours we've had together." Then she returned her attention to the young man. "Is there some reason why Sarah or Alex didn't come back with you?"

"Yes, but I won't go into that?"

"They're still alive, in the future I mean, aren't they?"

For reply, the young man simply smiled as he shrugged his shoulders.

"Oh, right. I guess you can't tell me that." Nancy decided not to pursue the subject any further since the young man seemed so reluctant at providing any details. She decided to move on to a different question.

"You said that there must be some sort of—thing—device here to allow you to travel here from the future."

"You mean a receiver?"

"Yes," said the woman. "Did you ever find it?"

"Yes. It was buried in Sullivans Woods."

"Really. How did it get there?"

"I don't know. But it explains why East Pencreek is such an important place, at least for time traveling from the twenty-fourth century. Before I return to the future, I'm going to move it."

"Why?"

"It's just something I have to do. The future demands it. Sorry, but I can't tell you more than that."

"Where are you going to take it?"

"I can't tell you that, either."

"I think I understand." Nancy gave a laugh, a laugh that seemed tinged with a bit of hysteria. "No, of course, I don't understand."

The young man smiled and then returned his attention to the contents of the cup he was holding. For a moment he stared at it, as if deep in thought.

"How I used to love hearing you play the piano," said Nancy. "I wish I had recordings of your playing. You were so talented."

"Being in the patrol, I haven't had time to keep up with it. Haven't played in years."

"I find that surprising. You loved it so."

The man took a final sip of orange juice and then rose. "I really need to be going."

"Why can't you stay? Your family is here. This is your home."

"Mom, try to understand. I am no longer a child of the twentieth century. I belong in the twenty-fourth. I must return after I've completed my mission. The window of opportunity is narrow. If I stay here too long, I'll miss it."

Nancy arose from her chair. "Tommy, I wish you all the happiness in the world. No, make that all the happiness in the universe. It sounds like this world is now far too small a place for you."

The man threw the backpack over one shoulder.

"Will I ever see you again?" asked Nancy.

"I can't answer that question."

"Yes, I figured as much. But you do know the answer, don't you?"

Instead of answering, he put his arms around the woman. "I love you. I will always remember you and love you." And then, after a pause, he whispered, "Please forgive me."

From the way he said it, the woman gathered that he was not asking forgiveness for what had happened back in 1959, but for what he had done in the past twenty-four hours.

"There is nothing to forgive," she said. "Your visit will always re-mind me of my son. For that, I am forever grateful."

They held the embrace for what seemed all too short a time, then the man relaxed his arms and kissed the woman on her forehead. She nodded and began to wipe the tears from her eyes as she collapsed back into the chair. She put her hands together before her face and broke down.

The man reached into his backpack and withdrew the ray gun. Holding the weapon in one hand, he gave the woman a forced smile then turned towards the back door. "Come on Tiger," he said to the cat. "We have work to do."

He opened the door and the cat scurried through it. "Good bye—Mom."

Nancy Cobalt looked up. "I'm not sure what it means," she sobbed, "but spaceman's luck."

This time the man's smile wasn't forced. "That's the best kind luck in the universe." He turned and closed the door behind him.

Nancy Cobalt remained seated, staring at but not seeing the back-door. Her sobs were so forceful, that her body actually shook with each one. In a voice that seemed to be elsewhere, she whispered, "Who are you?"

Jerry leaned over and gave his wife a peck on the back of her neck as he was putting on his sports coat. "One more week and the kids will be on summer vacation and you can sleep in."

"Jealous?" said Anne.

"No, just thankful that only one of us has to work." Jerry picked up a bag lunch from the kitchen counter. "You will call Aunt Nan to make sure she's okay?"

"Yes. And I'll let you know if I find out anything new about you-know-who."

"Hopefully we've seen the last of him," said Jerry as he headed towards the front door, with Lady Macbeth trailing behind.

As he made his way down the front walk, he heard a phone ring-ing inside the house. Jerry stopped and turned around. Perhaps it was Aunt Nan calling. As he waited, he happened to glance at the downed tree trunk that lay across the front yard. There was something odd . . . There was a segment about half a foot in width that stuck out from the rest of the trunk as if a surgeon had made two precise cross cuts about midway down the trunk and then rolled the cut piece a few inches to one side. Dropping his lunch bag, Jerry briskly walked over to exam-ine the cut piece more closely. Indeed, it looked as if it had been cut by a giant scalpel so flat and smooth were the surfaces. Even more strange was the fact that there was no sign of saw dust. Jerry leaned over, placed a hand on the trunk next to the protruding segment and gave a push. Another slice of tree trunk about the same size as the protruding segment rolled forward. Again, there was no sign of sawdust and no indication of how such a precise cut had been made. Jerry took a step to the left and gave another push and another piece separated from the rest of the tree.

"How?" Jerry asked himself. The whole trunk has been cut up but there was no sawdust. Jerry straightened and was about to call Anne when he recalled that the young man had told him that he could cut up the trunk for him, and last evening he had mentioned it again.

Anne swung open the front screen door.

"Jerry! The nursing home is on the phone. Carol's awake! They say she's conscious."

Jerry looked at his wife and then at the sliced-up tree trunk and then at the clear azure sky. Never before had life seemed so wonderful.

"Okay, I'll call work and tell them I won't be in today. Then we'll call your mom and Aunt Nan and give them the news." Jerry was pac-ing back and forth in the living room as he reeled off the words. Anne was watching her husband as she used a tissue to dab another tear from her cheek. "We'll stop by Brett's school on the way and pick him up first, and then your mom and finally Aunt Nan. Kevin's got exams this morning but his school is on the way to the nursing home from your mom's so we'll stop there and leave word for the office to give him the news. No, we'll call the high school now."

Anne gave each of Jerry's comments a nod.

"Did they give you any details as to how she was doing or any idea as to what might have happened?"

"No," said Anne. "They just said that the day nurse noticed that she was awake. They also said she spoke to the nurse. They certainly sounded like everything seemed okay. A doctor should be on his way to examine her. I'm sure they'll have more details when we get there."

"Yeah. No doubt. Okay, where was I?"

"You were going to call the office first."

"Right." Jerry reached for the phone and then froze.

"What's the matter?" said Anne.

Jerry stared at his wife. "He said she'd be coming out of the coma."

"What? Who?"

"Tom."

Outside the back entrance to the Cobalt home, a young man confronted an angry cat sitting on its haunches, glaring at him.

"Don't give me that kind of look. What was I supposed to do?"

"Rowow."

"Yeah, and if you had been me, I suppose you would have spilled the beans? Come on."

The two proceeded down the back pathway. As the young man rounded the tall hedge that marked the end of the Cobalt property and stepped into the alley he came to a sudden stop. Brad Jones was standing directly in front of him, a ray gun aimed at the young man's head at point blank range. The young man still held his weapon in his right hand but would have no time to raise it to fire before Brad pulled the trigger.

"Brad? Is that you?" said the young man. "Long time, no see—like about four centuries."

"Cut the crap, Tom" said Brad. "You shouldn't have come back, but that will be the last mistake you ever make."

"Gee, that doesn't sound like the old Brad I knew. Are you sure you have the right guy?"

"Nice try, but you are Tom. Okay, after all these years, you've changed somewhat. But I'm sure it's you. Dead sure, in your case." A smirk crossed the sheriff's face as he squeezed the trigger. The smirk disappeared when instead of a zap, the gun's charge canister ejected and landed on the gravel alley pavement with a plop. Tiger, sitting at the young man's feet, let out a triumphant meow. Brad first gave the charge canister lying on the ground a perplexed look, then the cat, and finally his disarmed weapon.

"What...?" he began to say.

"What's the matter, Brad?" said the young man, raising his weapon. "Cat got your gun?"

In the split second remaining to him, Brad looked directly into the barrel his adversary's ray gun. "Alex's cat!" was his last thought before the bolt from the ray gun struck him.

Brad went limp, the weapon slipped from his hand, and his body collapsed onto the gravel roadway.

"That was easy," said the young man, addressing the cat. "Thanks for the warning and, of course, neutralizing his weapon."

The young man stuffed his ray gun into his backpack, then took a few steps forward to retrieve the weapon of his adversary which he also stuffed into the backpack. From the backpack, he then took a silver object about the size and shape of a small bullet. Kneeling next to the unconscious sheriff, he flipped the body over and placed the silver object on the back of the man's neck. He began to move it in small circles. "That feels like the spot." The young man gave the instrument a firm squeeze, causing it to briefly vibrate. Standing, he returned the object to his backpack. "There you go Brad, old buddy, good as new, or as old might be more accurate in this case. No more nasty nightmares for you."

He turned to the cat. "Are you coming along to watch the fireworks or staying here?"

Tiger gave out a loud meow and proceeded to trot alongside the spaceman as the latter exited the alley, leaving behind a motionless Brad.

Mr. Rastaban, no first name, Kevin Haydn's physics teacher, was seated on a stool behind the instructor's lab table at the front of the classroom. To all appearances he appeared to be watching the students of his first period physics class laboriously work on the final exam, as if to ensure that none of them attempted any funny business while taking the test. In reality, the man's thoughts were elsewhere, on what now was taking place outside the Cobalt residence. The man's body gave an involuntary twitch.

"The signal," he thought. "I've lost the signal. He's failed!"

Mr. Rastaban hesitated but a moment before reaching down to a briefcase that rested on the floor next to him. He grasped its handle and lifted the briefcase, sitting it on the table in front of him. He gave the class another quick scan, then snapped open the briefcase. The height of the lab table combined with the position of the open briefcase ensured that none of the students could see what lay within. Reaching inside, the teacher lifted the padding that covered the ray gun. One glance ensured Mr. Rastaban that the ray gun was fully armed and functional.

The sign on the side of the school's entrance read, "All visitors must report to the main office." With the backpack still slung over his left shoulder, the young man opened one of the double doors and entered the high school with every intention of ignoring the sign. The evening before he had had Jerry's son, Kevin, describe to him the floor plan of the school building along with the location of the physics classroom. The route was etched into the patrolman's memory. Entering the main hallway, the young man observed that it was deserted. He reached into his backpack with his right hand and withdrew his weapon. He turned to stare at a fire alarm on the far wall from where he stood, next to the school's main office. He walked over to the alarm. As he reached it, the office door opened and a matronly looking woman stepped into the hall. She gave the young man a look of surprise, but didn't notice the weapon he was holding.

"May I help you?" she grumbled.

For answer, the man first flashed the woman a grin, then broke the fire alarm's glass with the butt of the gun handle. The clanging sound that immediately shattered the calm of the school building was deafening.

The woman's mouth fell open. She started to say something, but instead turned and scurried back into the office. The young man proceeded down the hallway to his left in the direction of the physics classroom. Students and teachers were already pouring out of the classrooms, quickly filling the hallway.

The man backed up against the nearest wall, carefully scanning the crowd as it flowed past, his senses focused on identifying Rastaban, alias Serpens. No more than a couple of minutes elapsed before the last of the students disappeared down the hallway on their way to the exit. In the pandemonium of the moment, no one had taken particular notice of the tall young man, nor of the strange object held at his side.

As expected, no one fitting Serpen's or, for that matter, Rastaban's description had appeared among the fleeing crowd. The man's hand slid along the side of his gun, his mind taking in the tactile feedback of his fingers. The weapon was ready and so was its owner.

The young man began to cautiously inch his way along the wall he had been standing next to, working his way to where the corridor turned at a right angle. As he passed a door marked "Women Faculty Rest Room," it opened and out stepped Diane Jones. The man spun around, his gun aimed directly at the woman's head, but on seeing Diane, he smiled and gave her a salute with the ray gun. The teacher stood as if frozen, a look of bewilderment on her face. "What?" Or at least that's what he thought she had said, as it was difficult to hear clearly over the ringing of the fire alarm. He turned and resumed his slow progress down the hallway as Diane scurried off in the opposite direction, obviously heading for the nearest exit.

Reaching the intersection, he dropped to his knees and positioned his gun on the floor so the barrel pointed around the corner, aiming down the new hallway. In his mind appeared a three-dimensional view of the new hallway, almost as if he himself was peering around the corner or more accurately, as if he had a third eye that was located on the weapon's gun sight. According to Kevin's description of the floor plan, the entrance to the physics classroom was the second door on the left. There was no one in sight. A soft click was followed by the coloration and appearance of the scene in the man's mind immediately changing. The young man had shifted the weapon's view to that of an infrared sensor, but no indication of another human being appeared. It was a wild shot, reasoned the man, but if his opponent was in the vicinity, he would no doubt have tuned his weapon to jam any infrared detection, just as the young man had adjusted his. Another soft click and the scene returned to normal.

The young man next carefully repositioned the weapon next to him and reached into his backpack. Retrieving a small metallic sphere about the size of a tennis ball, he quietly placed it on the floor and gave it a squeeze. Six thin appendages emerged from the bottom of the sphere raising it above the floor. The sphere began to move forward like some misshapen beetle, the six appendages functioning as legs. It made no noise as it turned the corner and proceeded down the hall, heading straight for the door of the physics classroom. When it reached the door, it hesitated for a moment, then turned and started to move on. Through the open doorway of the next classroom burst a man with a drawn ray gun. He threw himself on the floor and with his first shot exploded the cyber bug, filling the hall with smoke. Before the smoke thoroughly obscured his vision, the man got off a second shot that produced a hole through the wall, roughly three inches across, directly above where the young man knelt as well as a similar hole in the far wall that marked the path of the weapon's bolt.

The young man was on his feet. He slid across the floor into the smoke-filled hallway and released in rapid succession four bolts in the direction where Serpens had last been, two down the hallway which shattered the wall at its far end and two angled off to the right, cutting two slices out of the next corner's walls. He leaped to his feet and dove back behind the damaged wall to his former location. Several new holes appeared at various elevations in the wall against which he rested as well as in the far wall across the passageway. Added to the smoke from the young man's reconnaissance "bug" was the smoke from the wooden wall studs that had been set afire by the bolts from the ray guns. The odors of burning wood and ozone filled the air.

A voice filtered through the damaged school building, barely audible above the wail of the fire alarm. "Is that you, Tom?"

"You might say so, you deranged freak."

"Welcome back. I hadn't expected you so soon," said Serpens. "Actually, I hadn't expected you at all."

"I suppose that you wouldn't tell me if anyone besides Evad and you used the time machine to escape from Quadrant Five?"

There was a significant pause before Serpens answered. "Of course not."

"And I also take it there's no point in offering you the chance to surrender?"

"That's a laugh. I was going to make you the same offer. But I'll

625

tell you what. Instead of wrecking the whole place trying to kill each other, why don't we meet in the hallway, man-to-syndroid so to speak. We'll both holster our weapons and face off, like in one of those old western showdowns. Then we'll—"

A staccato of zaps echoed through the building as the young man let go several shots in the direction he judged the voice to be coming from. The patrolman had set the maximum range of his bursts to about thirty yards, a distance he calculated would preclude injury to any innocent bystanders outside the school. He wondered if Serpens was using the same precaution with his shots. Most likely not. As he got off the last of his shots he leaped to his feet and dashed down the hall in the direction of the main entrance. Another fusillade of shots riddled the walls behind him. He skidded to a stop and let go several more bolts, this time by his judgment to the left and right of the previous target location. The zaps were coming so rapidly now that it sounded as if a machine gun was going off in the building. There was a loud crash as a large section of ceiling gave way and the better part of several, second floor classrooms ended up on the first floor. The noise of the fire alarm ceased.

As he rounded the corner and the high school came into view, Jerry hit the van's breaks. "What the—" The sidewalk along the street was filled with students, teachers and staff members.

"What's going on?" said Anne.

"Darn if I know," said Jerry.

"Hey, there's Kevin," shouted Brett.

Jerry pulled the van up to the sidewalk near where Brett had spotted Kevin and parked. He jumped out along with his wife, youngest son, mother-in-law and aunt. Jerry hurried over to where Kevin was standing and grabbed him by the shoulder to get his attention.

"What's going on?" he said.

Kevin jerked around. "Dad? I don't know. There was a fire alarm and then . . ."

A loud crash came from the school building. Wisps of smoke were beginning to appear at several places above the building's roof, or more accurately, rising through a number of large holes that now perforated it. "What are you doing here?" Then the teen noticed the rest of his family coming up behind his father.

"It's your sister, Carol," said Jerry, having to raise his voice to make himself heard above all the commotion about him. "The nursing home called his morning. She's conscious."

"What? That's incredible," shouted Kevin.

"We were on our way to see her when—" There was another loud crash from the building causing Jerry to look in that direction. "I have a feeling that our mysterious visitor from yesterday is behind this."

"Yeah, no doubt," said Kevin. "He said he was going to go after Mr. Rastaban. I don't remember seeing him out here anywhere."

From a distance came the wail of an approaching fire engine.

Inside the building, the only means each antagonist had of determining the location of his opponent was the direction from which the bolts from the other's weapon appeared to be emanating from. The young man fired off several more shots aimed at where he guessed Serpens might be. A fusillade of return fire poked new holes in the nearby walls. The spaceman deduced they had originated some distance to the left of where he had placed his shots. Concluding that he had again failed to hit his foe, the young man decided to move to the basement, not only to avoid the smoke created by the burning fires but also the ceiling collapses caused by the failure of walls perforated with multiple holes from the bolts of the ray guns. Not knowing the location of a basement stairway, the young man fashioned a shortcut. With his weapon set on beam, he began to trace a large circle on the floor directly in front of him. As the circle was completed it gave way and crashed to the basement floor below. Sticking the gun in his belt, the young man easily swung himself through the hole and dropped to the lower level.

"Tom, you still alive?"

The young man remained silent as he retrieved his gun. He guessed that his antagonist was also now on the basement level.

"I might warn you that this building is heated by natural gas. It'll no doubt go up any moment now."

For answer, the young man unleashed a barrage of bolts in the direction from which he judged the voice had originated. The resulting explosion knocked the patrolman off his feet.

Many of the onlookers let out a scream as the sound of the gas explosion erupted across the school yard. Most threw themselves on the ground. The building shuttered as billows of smoke and dust were ejected in every direction along with an occasional piece of airborne debris and shattered glass.

Jerry, lying flat on his stomach, raised his head and looked about. "Anne, Aunt Nan, Mom, Brett, Kevin, you all okay?"

He stumbled back to his feet mentally noting the chorus of affirmatives that greeted his ears. Kevin rose beside him. Jerry walked over and helped Rebecca to her feet and then his aunt as Anne and Brett joined him. Not far from them a student was asking a teacher, "Mr. Kirkland, does this mean that finals are cancelled?"

"That crazy—," began Jerry, but then he noticed the look of concern on Aunt Nan's face.

"Do you think he was in there?" she said.

"Yeah, no doubt," said Jerry. "And probably Kevin's physics teacher too."

A single figure moved through the rubble strewn battlefield, his face blackened and clothing dirtied. The young man still clutched the ray gun in his right hand. Both the smoke and the fragments of the school's walls that still stood hid him from the view of the spectators lining the street that bordered the school property. He scrambled up a pile of rubble and then through a gap in an interior wall, stepping into a still relatively intact basement hallway. To his right a pair of shoes along with trouser covered legs emerged from under another pile of rubble. Nearby lay a ray gun. The patrolman walked over to the unmoving figure and knelt next to it. He began to clear away some of the pieces of ceiling from about where he reasoned the half-buried body's head would be. The face of the syndroid Serpens came into view.

The young man reached down and placed his fingers on the man's neck, checking for a pulse. "Well, admiral, we'll see if things are as they seem this time."

With effort, Serpens opened his eyes. "Cobalt . . ." The eyes of the dying man opened wider, expressing surprise and shock. "You!" he gasped. "Traitor—" The eyes flashed green and then went blank.

The young man removed his fingers from Serpens' neck. Standing, he walked over to where his deceased foe's pistol lay, picked it up, and stuffed it into his backpack. He aimed his weapon at the body. A bright red beam shot from the barrel. The young man slowly passed the beam along the body, turning the now dead flesh and its artificial parts into a voluminous plume of ashes, dust, and smoke that twisted, rose and diffused, mixing with the rising smoke from the numerous fires that burned throughout the now ruined shell of a school building. The odor of the burning flesh caused the young man to crease his nose. He released the trigger only when the last recognizable trace of the syndroid had vanished.

As the firemen and school administrators huddled together trying to decide on the best plan to safely clear the school property and return the students to their homes, Jerry turned to his oldest son.

"You might as well come with us to the nursing home to see Carol."

"Yeah," said Kevin, taking a last look at the smoldering wreckage that less than a quarter of an hour before had been a school building. "Gee, I wonder what they'll do about our exams?"

"You're lucky," said Brett. "Why couldn't it have been my school that got blown up?"

"Brett Haydn," said his mother. "What a terrible thing to wish for. Who knows how many people might have gotten hurt today?"

A pleasant meow caused everyone to look down. "Tiger!" said Aunt Nan. She stooped and gave the feline a scratch behind the ears.

"Well, at least the cat wasn't dumb enough to follow Flash Gordon into the school," said Jerry. "Okay, let's be off to see Carol."

As the rest of his family started towards the van, Jerry noticed that his aunt and the cat were still standing next to the sidewalk looking at what remained of the school building. Jerry walked over behind the elderly woman and placed his hand on her shoulder.

"I have to know that he's okay," she said without looking at her nephew.

Jerry studied the worried expression on his aunt's face while trying to decide how best to respond to her concern.

"We may have to wait until the news tonight to see if any bodies were found."

Aunt Nan turned towards her nephew. "You no doubt find it difficult to empathize with my concern for him when he probably just blew up the school, possibly endangering the lives of many innocent people."

Jerry gave a shallow nod.

"If what he said was true, that is, that Kevin's physics teacher was going to murder all of us in the near future, then—well, I don't know, perhaps he saw it as the only way to save us. Hopefully, everyone evacuated the school okay."

"We had best get going," said Jerry. "After all, Carol's waiting."

Aunt Nan nodded and turned towards the van where the other members of the family were already seated, except for Kevin who was holding a door open for his great aunt. As she walked to the car, she said, more to herself than to anyone in particular, "He was so like Tommy."

Jerry was about to ask his aunt what she meant but changed his mind.

As Aunt Nan was seating herself inside the van, Kevin pointed down the street and shouted, "Look!"

About a hundred yards in the distance stood a lone figure. He was at the edge of the school properly where the street they were on intersected the one that bordered Sullivans Woods. The figure gave a wave and then turned and hurried across the road to disappear into the woodland.

"Goodbye," whispered Aunt Nan.

Jerry mumbled something that might have been "good riddance," and then climbed into the driver's seat. As he started the engine, Anne said, "Do you think we'll ever see him again?"

"It wouldn't surprise me," said Jerry. "He seems to be one hard son-of-a—gun to kill."

Jerry headed the van down the street towards the woods since it was the shortest route to the nursing home. Right after he made the turn at the corner he swerved the vehicle to the right and came to a stop at the spot where they had seen the figure enter into the woods.

"Why are we stopping?" said Anne.

Jerry gave his wife a funny look, and then without saying anything opened and door and stepped out of the vehicle with the cat jumping out after him. The rest of his family remained seated for a moment, then they all followed suit. They stood at the edge of the woodland, staring into the trees, at first no one saying a word.

Finally, Kevin spoke up. "Well, are we going to go in and try to find him?"

"No," said Jerry. "We should be getting on to see Carol. It was just a hunch, that's all."

As soon as he had said it there came a whirling sound from deep in the woods.

"What's that strange noise?" asked Rebecca Gould.

"It sounds like a saucer," beamed Brett, "a flying saucer."

He wasn't sure why he did it, but Jerry tilted his head back so as to look above the tree line. The sound's pitch rose and then vanished. As it did, Jerry could have sworn he saw something, more a shimmer of air than an actual object, shoot up into the sky and disappear. Tiger let out a loud meow which caused Jerry to glance down at the cat. The feline's eyes were focused on the spot where Jerry had seen the apparition.

"Did you see that?" said Jerry. "Did any of you see that?"

"See what?" said Kevin.

The others gave Jerry inquisitive looks.

"I thought I saw something—well, something rise out of the woods and disappear into the sky."

Anne shook her head. "What did it look like?"

"I'm not sure."

"Was it a flying saucer?" said Brett.

"I'm not sure what it was or, for that matter, if I wasn't imagining things."

"We should be getting on to see Carol," said Rebecca, repeating her son-in-law's earlier proposal.

"Yes," said Jerry, "let's get going."

As the others piled back into the van, Jerry turned and took one more glance at the empty sky. "Spaceman's luck," he said.

"Rowow," said Tiger.

Epilogue
January 7, 1943 – New York City

When he had been a boy he had yearned for the future. And now, as death was relentlessly tightening its grip on his fading mortality, the old man pondered with regret what might have been. If only... If only...

He sat alone in his room, his sanctuary, and soon to be his coffin. The aged figure, whose skin stretched features already resembled that of a skull, stared without focusing on the meager surroundings. The greatest technical mind of the century, the man who had brought such wealth and blessings to humanity, now faced oblivion, and faced it without a single witness to his passing. Maybe this was the ultimate tragedy, the ultimate insult--to die without the company of another human being.

His room was perched high, thirty-three stories high, in the skyscraper forest of the busiest city in the world. Although the unnumbered thousands of living, breathing humanity carried on their lives all about him, he was as isolated as if he had been marooned on a planet orbiting the farthest star in the heavens. He would pass into the endless void without the chance to exchange a single word with another of his species. The greatest of minds would flicker and fade and be gone with no more notice than a dying spark from a fire or a roach smashed underfoot. Ashes to ashes, dust to dust.

The unexpected noise startled him. It had sounded like someone had knocked on the door to his hotel room. The gaunt figure turned his head to glance at the clock across the chamber. It was some time past 10 pm. No one would be knocking at this hour.

There is was again. Yes, it was definitely the sound of a fist striking the door. It was Death. Who else would be seeking entrance to his home at this hour? Had he locked the door? He didn't know. And then the absurdity of his thought hit him. What was a locked door to Death? For a moment, the anguish had vanished, and his mouth attempted to form a grin.

The door knob began to turn. Obviously, the door was unlocked. The knob turned slowly as if the intruder was attempting to attract as little attention as possible. The knob ceased moving and the door slowly swung inward.

The appearance of the figure standing in the doorway resembled in no way what the old man had imagined Death to look like. Instead of a damp, dark robe with hood that hid a grinning skull within, the figure before him was dressed casually in rather common-looking shirt and slacks, and was wearing an open, brown leather jacket that appeared as if it had seen action in the Great War. The visitor's head was adorned with an equally dilapidated fedora hat. He was tall, with a young, clean shaven but scarred face that held an expression of purpose and determination, but tempered with—was it empathy?

"Mr. Tesla, I presume?"

"Yes." was the old man's quaking response. "Do I know you? Who are you?"

Before saying another word, the stranger entered the room, closing the door behind him. He moved quickly, stopping before the seated old man. "No, you do not know me. We have never met."

"Are you Death?" asked the old man.

The question seemed to surprise the stranger, but not because it was so unexpected, but as if the old man had unveiled a secret the visitor was hoping to hide. For a brief moment, the two figures simply stared at each other, silent. Finally, the stranger resumed speaking.

"Yes, in a manner of speaking, but also your resurrection."

"I don't understand."

"I am about to kill your body, but at the same time I will save your mind. I was told that you do not have long to live anyway. You will probably not survive until tomorrow."

The old man forced a grin. "My young man, you are mad. Don't play games with me. If you've come here to rob me, please do so and leave me to die in peace."

The stranger knelt down on one knee before the old man. "I want you to understand that in doing what I am about to do I am following orders. I myself don't fully understand what it is all about."

"You are mad. Following orders? What is this nonsense? Someone's told you to kill me. Do you have any idea why?"

"No, but…"

"Someone orders you to kill a person and you just do it without asking any questions?"

"It's not possible for me to ask questions," said the visitor. "Trust me. I would not be doing this if I didn't have complete confidence that it was the right thing to do."

"Do you know who I am?" asked the old man.

"Yes. You are Nikola Tesla, probably the greatest mind of this century."

"You know who I am and yet you insist in going through with this. Why, in the name of God, why?

"All I know is that if I kill you instead of allowing you a natural death, you will still live, at least apparently your mind will. And some day it will be reborn, in a new body."

"Ha! You've been reading too many of those pulps, resurrecting the dead and all. I suppose I will be coming back as some sort of Frankenstein monster. This is sheer lunacy and you, my young scoundrel, if you actually believe any of this, are then some sort of lunatic. Is that what you are? A lunatic?"

The stranger ignored the questions. "I am to show you something that I was told would give you hope, that would better allow you to accept what is about to happen." The man reached into a pocket inside his jacket and pulled out a rolled-up piece of paper in the shape of a small scroll. He unwound the paper and held it out so the old man could read it. The paper contained a series of strange, alien characters.

As the old man's eyes focused on the characters, he gave out a gasp. "What...?" He stared at his visitor for a moment, then in a shaking voice accompanied by a shaking hand that attempted to point at the paper, he muttered, "It's the writing, the writing that was on the artifact. How? What does it mean?"

"I'm sorry," was the reply. "I don't know. My orders were simply to show it to you."

"You show me this and you tell me you don't know anything about it. I'm dying. How does this give me hope? Not knowing just makes dying all that more bitter."

The visitor released his hold on one end of the paper, and reaching out with his free hand, grasped the old man's hand that was pointing at the paper, and gently returned it to the old man's lap. "Only your body is dying. Your mind will not die. It will survive. That I promise." With that, he put away the paper. As he did so, the old man took on the expression of a child who had just been offered a cone of his favorite ice cream and then had it snatched away. From his jacket pocket, the stranger now produced a purple strap, about an inch in width and a couple feet in length. "This won't hurt," he said as he wrapped the mysterious flexible strap about the old man's head in the manner of a head band."

"What...?" the old man tried to say.

"You'll just drift off into a wonderful sleep. When you awake, all will be well. You will be in a new body, in a new world, in a new time."

"I don't understand."

"Again, neither do I," was the reply.

"Just following orders, huh?" said the old man.

"Yes," smiled the stranger. "Just following orders."

"And you trust the people who gave you the orders?"

"Yes."

"You swear to that, that you truly believe that what you are doing is the right thing?"

"Yes. I swear on my mother's grave."

At that the old man forced a weak grin. "You're going to kill me and you're swearing on a grave."

"Oh, yes, I see." The visitor also grinned. "I cross my heart and swear..., no wait, that's not very good either."

"Never mind. You may be a raving madman but at least you seem to be an honest madman. Go ahead, do what you think you have to do. You're no doubt right. I'm dying and this way it will be painless." The great inventor paused. "It will be painless will it not?"

"I believe so." The visitor's face wore an unsure expression.

"Great, so you don't know."

"Sorry," the visitor shrugged. "I'm just guessing that it won't hurt. Anything you'd like to say before I—you know."

The old man started to weep. "Thank you. Thank you for not letting me die alone."

"You're welcome." The visitor smiled. He reached forward and touched the strap on the old man's head.

The old man closed his eyes, forcing tears to glide down his cheeks. Then, in a last effort before losing consciousness, he opened them again. "Tell me, please. What is your name?"

"Tom," said Tom.

CPSIA information can be obtained
at www.ICGtesting.com
Printed in the USA
FFHW022116150319